D1611719

Science Fiction
A to Z

Science Fiction
A to Z

A DICTIONARY OF THE
GREAT S.F. THEMES

COLLECTED BY

Isaac Asimov
Martin H. Greenberg
Charles G. Waugh

*With an Introduction
by Isaac Asimov*

HOUGHTON MIFFLIN COMPANY BOSTON

1982

Library of Congress Cataloging in Publication Data
Main entry under title:

Science fiction A to Z.

1. Science fiction, American. 2. Science fiction,
English. I. Asimov, Isaac, date. II. Greenberg,
Martin Harry. III. Waugh, Charles.
PS648.S3S27   823'.0876'08   82-893
ISBN 0-395-31285-X   AACR2

Printed in the United States of America

V 10 9 8 7 6 5 4 3 2 1

The editors wish to thank the following for permission to reprint the stories listed:

Tom Godwin, "Too Soon to Die," © 1957 by Mercury Press, Inc. From *The
Magazine of Fantasy and Science Fiction*. Reprinted by permission of the author
and his agents, the Scott Meredith Literary Agency, Inc., 845 Third Ave., New
York, NY 10022.
Roger Zelazny, "A Museum Piece," © 1963 by Ziff-Davis Publishing Company.
Reprinted by permission of the author.
Alan Dean Foster, "Why Johnny Can't Speed," © 1971 by Alan Dean Foster;
first appeared in *Galaxy Magazine;* reprinted by permission of the author and his
agent, Virginia Kidd.
L. J. Stecher, Jr., "Man in a Quandary," © 1958 by Galaxy Publishing Corpora-
tion. Reprinted by permission of the author.

Contents

P

Q

R

S

T

Time Travel

Trains

U

UFOs

Utopias

V

Visions

W

Westerns

Women

X

Xenobiology

Y

Z

Dictionaries

ISAAC ASIMOV

What is a dictionary of science fiction?

Well (for I always try to begin at the beginning), what is a dictionary? The word comes from the Latin "dictio" meaning "a word," and that gives us all the hint we need. A dictionary is, essentially, a list of words with their meanings and with indication of their pronunciations, derivations, uses, synonyms, antonyms, and whatever else the compiler feels might be of interest.

(There's a perfectly good expression of Anglo-Saxon derivation for a dictionary — "wordbook" — but the prejudice in favor of words of classical derivation, where scholarly matters are in question, is insuperable. If you are a classicist, but feel that Latin is only half good, the Greek word for "word" is "lexis" and that gives us "lexicon.")

Generally, the words in a dictionary are listed in alphabetical order, not because there is some unbreakable cosmic law to that effect, but because there is no other way of making certain that any particular word can be found with reasonable ease. If you don't believe it, try to think of one.

You might, for instance, list all the known chemicals, and choose not to use the names in alphabetical order. Instead, you might list them by chemical formula in accordance with some system involving the numbers of atoms of different kinds and their arrangement within the molecule.

This precise situation comes up in connection with the use of the multi-volume *Handbook of Organic Chemistry,* usually known by the name of the original compiler — Beilstein. In my graduate school days I had to make use of it, and that meant I had to attend a series of lectures on the system Beilstein used to list the compounds in order. It took me several weeks to grow familiar with it, but once I did, I could find any compound I wanted after no more than half an hour's browsing. (How I wished alphabetical order were possible, after very little of this.)

One of my cherished memories in this respect is the time I came across my professor of organic chemistry (with whom I was on bad terms) in the chemistry library. He was leafing aimlessly through Beilstein. Curious, I asked (for I have always been riddled with curiosity about anything that wasn't my business), "What compound are you looking up, Professor E.?"

He told me, abstractedly, and I noiselessly vanished, spent a few minutes of concentrated search, then walked back to him with a book open to the correct page and presented it to him. He had been searching *in the wrong volume.* I don't think that bit of wise-guy behavior on my part did my final mark any good, but I think I would have been content to flunk, rather than miss that opportunity of getting a bit of my own back.

Dictionaries (no, I haven't forgotten) come in all varieties. They can try to be inclusive, even all-inclusive, listing every word ever used or heard, including dialectal forms, nonce words, slang, and so on. The ideal cannot ever be attained because living languages change day by day, with new words and new usages constantly arising. Thus, dictionaries fall out-of-date immediately upon publication; indeed, before publication.

Dictionaries that do try to include everything of any importance are "unabridged," like the sainted *Webster's Second Edition,* which I possess in onionskin.

Then, of course, you have dictionaries that limit themselves in one way or another, including only those words that the average student is likely to be interested in, for instance. This produces a volume which is more manageable and yet will fail you only a tiny percentage of the time.

There are dictionaries of special groups of words, too. You can, of course, have a "dictionary of science," in which words will be listed that are of particular interest to scientists. In such a dictionary, definitions can be given in greater detail and assume a greater basic scientific knowledge than in an ordinary dictionary.

You can have dictionaries that are confined to special portions of science, or of scholarship generally. If the portion in question is a particularly small splinter and the list of words is comparatively short, the result can be termed a "glossary," from the Latin word "glossa," referring to "a hard word that needs explanation."

Thus, the American Institute of Physics has put out a booklet entitled, *Glossary of Terms Frequently Used in Relativistic Astrophysics,* and next to it on my reference shelf are two similar booklets, one for cosmology and one for quasi-stellar radio sources (quasars).

I don't know if there are dictionaries or glossaries aimed at architects, coin-collectors, gardeners, and so on, but I would be the least surprised person in the world if there were.

Well, then, what is a "dictionary of science fiction"?

It could be a *Glossary of Terms Frequently Used in Science Fiction Stories* and, in fact, I have often thought such a book would be useful. In the first place, science fiction writers frequently use scientific terms not generally found in ordinary reference books, and the younger readers might find it useful to know what a "galaxy" or a "pulsar" or a "laser beam" might be without having to gather it from the story.

Secondly, and even more important, there are terms that are science-fictionish rather than scientific, and those you might not find at all in scientific dictionaries. What is an "android" and how does it differ from a "robot"? What is "hyperspace" and how does it differ from "subspace"? What is "subetheric communication"?

If one were to prepare such a dictionary, one might even seize the opportunity to include words not ordinarily used in science fiction stories, but that would nevertheless be useful to the art. For instance, it is frequently useful in science fiction stories to refer to "faster-than-light velocities." That is clear and straightforward, but a trifle gauche. We do not speak of "faster-than-sound velocities," we speak of "supersonic velocities." Therefore, by analogy we should speak of "superluminal velocities."

Again, an authoritative dictionary would step on such vile locutions as "Mercutian" and "Venutian," which originated in faulty analogy to "Martian," and make use of derivations from the proper Latin: "Mercurian" and "Venerian." If the latter is too suggestive of unpleasantness, then the classical alternative of "Aphrodisian" might be offered. And if that is too suggestive also, then how about "Cytheran"?

Again, a word might be included that I recently invented — "gynoid." This is a robot that resembles a woman, by analogy with "android," which is a robot that resembles a man.

However, the book you are now holding is not such a dictionary.

The book you are holding is a dictionary of science fiction themes in the sense that it lists, in alphabetical order, fifty words which could each easily inspire a science fiction writer to write a story.

Say to a science fiction writer, "Why don't you write a story about computers?" and he will say "Why not?"

Say, on the other hand, "Write a story about cement," and he will say "Cement? Why cement?"

So, "computer" is a good word for this dictionary of themes and "cement" isn't.

We have a special way of defining the fifty words we have chosen. We do it by choosing a very good science fiction story that happens to deal with the topic, just to show how the word might inspire a tale. Since we have fifty themes, we have fifty excellent science fiction stories.

We hope you enjoy every one of them.

Science Fiction
A to Z

A

a/li/en worlds — alien refers to something that is not one's own, something *unfamiliar*. In science fiction, alien worlds are the setting for many, if not most, stories and novels. These worlds may be planets in our solar system, in known galaxies, or in currently uncharted areas of our universe. There have been many anthologies of stories about the exploration of alien worlds, including *Flight Into Space* (Frederick Fell, 1950); *Possible Worlds of Science Fiction* (Vanguard Press, 1951); *To The Stars* (Hawthorn Books, 1971); and *Explorers of Space* (Thomas Nelson, 1975).

Too Soon to Die

TOM GODWIN

The Constellation, *bound for Athena with eight thousand colonists aboard, had not expected attack from the Gerns. There had been no indication when it left Earth that the cold war with the Gern Empire would suddenly flare into violence, and the world of Athena was a Terran discovery, four hundred light-years from the outer boundary of the Gern Empire.*

The two Gern cruisers appeared without warning and attacked with silent, vicious efficiency, demolishing the Constellation's *stern and rendering her driveless and powerless. Her single obsolete blaster fired once in futile defense and was instantly destroyed, together with the forward control room.*

Within seconds the Constellation *was helpless and leaderless, her air regen-*

*erators lifeless. Gerns boarded her and a Gern officer delivered the ultimatum
in quick, brittle words:*

*"A state of war now exists between the Gern Empire and Earth. This section
of space, together with the planet Athena, is claimed as part of the Gern
Empire.*

*"This ship has invaded Gern territory and fired upon a Gern cruiser, but we
are willing to extend a leniency not required by the circumstances. Terran
technicians and skilled workers in certain specific fields can be of use to us in
the factories we shall build on Athena. The others will not be needed and there
is not room on the cruisers to take them.*

*"You will be divided into two groups, the Acceptables and the Rejects. The
Rejects will be taken by the cruisers to an Earth-type planet near here and left,
together with ample supplies. The cruisers will then take the Acceptables on to
Athena.*

*"This division will split families but there will be no resistance to it. At the
first instance of rebellion the offer will be withdrawn and the cruisers will go
on their way again."*

*There was no choice for the colonists. The air was already growing stale and
within twenty hours they would start smothering to death. The division was
made.*

*Six hours later the Rejects, four thousand of them, stood in a bleak, rocky
valley, a 1.5 gravity dragging at them like a heavy burden, and watched the
cruisers roar away into the gray sky. A moaning wind sent the alkali dust
swirling in cold, bitter clouds, and things like gigantic black wolves could
already be seen gathering in the distance.*

*They realized fully, then, what had happened. They were on Ragnarok, the
hell-world, and their abandonment there was intended to be a death sentence
for all of them.*

The bright blue star dimmed and dawn touched the sky, bringing with it a
coldness that frosted the steel of the rifle in John Prentiss's hands and formed
beads of ice on his gray mustache. There was a stirring in the area behind
him as the weary Rejects in his group prepared to face the new day. A child
whimpered from the cold. There had not been time the evening before to
gather enough wood —

"Prowlers!"

The warning cry came from an outer guard as the enormous wolflike black
shadows materialized out of the dark dawn, their white fangs gleaming in
their devils' faces as they ripped through the outer guard line. Prentiss's rifle
licked out thin tongues of flame as he added his fire to that of the inner
guards. The prowlers came on, breaking through, but four of them went
down and the others swerved by the fire so that they struck only the outer
edge of the area where the Rejects were grouped.

At that distance they blended into the dark ground so that he could not find them in the sights of his rifle. He could only watch helplessly in the dawn's dim light and see a dark-haired woman caught in their path, trying to run with a child in her arms and already knowing it was too late. For a moment her white face was turned in hopeless appeal to the others. Then she fell, deliberately, going to the ground with her child beneath her so that her body would protect it from the prowlers. A man was running toward her, slow in the high gravity, an axe in his hands and his cursing a raging, impotent snarl.

The prowlers passed over her, pausing for an instant as they slashed the life from her, and raced on again. They vanished into the outer darkness, the farther guards firing futilely. Then there was silence but for the distant, hysterical sobbing of a woman.

It had happened within seconds; the fifth prowler attack that night and by far the mildest . . .

Full dawn had come by the time John Prentiss replaced the two guards killed by the last attack and made the rounds of the other guards. He came back by the place where the prowlers had killed the woman, walking wearily against the pull of gravity. She lay with her dark hair tumbled and stained with blood, her white face turned up to the reddening sky, and he saw her clearly.

It was Irene.

He stopped, gripping the rifle hard, not feeling the rear sight as it cut into his hand.

Irene . . . He had not known she was on Ragnarok. His one consolation had been the thought that she and Billy were safe among the Acceptables . . .

There was the sound of footsteps and a bold-faced girl in a red skirt stopped beside him, her glance going over him curiously.

"The little boy," he asked, "do you know if he's all right?"

"The prowlers cut up his face but he'll be all right," she said. "I came back after his clothes."

"Are you going to look after him?"

"Someone had to." She shrugged her shoulders. "I guess I was soft enough to elect myself for the job. Why — was his mother a friend of yours?"

"She was my daughter," he said. "I didn't know she was on Ragnarok till just now."

"Oh." The bold, brassy look was gone from her face for a moment, like a mask that had slipped. "I'm sorry. And I'll take care of Billy."

The first objection to his assumption of leadership occurred an hour later. The prowlers had withdrawn with the coming of full daylight and wood had been carried from the trees to renew the fires. Mary, one of the volunteer cooks, was asking two men to carry water when he approached. The smaller man picked up one of the clumsy containers, hastily improvised from canvas, and started for the creek, but the thick-chested man did not move.

"People are hungry and cold and sick," Mary said. "Aren't you going to help?"

The man continued to squat by the fire, his hands extended to its warmth. "Name somebody else," he said.

"But — "

Mary looked at Prentiss in uncertainty and he went to the thick-chested man, knowing there would be violence and welcoming it as something to help drive away the vision of Irene's pale, cold face under the red sky.

"She asked you to get her some water," he said. "Get it."

The man got quickly to his feet and swung to face him challengingly, his heavy shoulders hunched.

"You overlook one little point," he said. "No one has appointed you the head cheese around here. Now, there's the container you want filled, old timer, and there — " he made a small motion with one hand " — is the creek. Do you know what to do?"

"Yes," Prentiss said. "I know what to do."

He brought the butt of the rifle smashing up. It struck the man under the chin and there was a sharp cracking sound as his jawbone snapped. He slumped to the ground, his eyes glazing and his broken jaw askew.

"Now, go ahead and name someone else," Prentiss said to Mary . . .

He found that the prowlers had killed seventy of his group during the night. One hundred more had died from the Hell Fever that seemed to follow quickly behind exposure on Ragnarok and killed within an hour.

He went to the group that had arrived on the second cruiser to urge them to combine with his own group in their forthcoming move into the woods, where there would be ample fuel for the fires and some protection from the wind.

He found a leader in the second group, as he had known he would. It was a characteristic of human nature that leaders should appear in times of emergency.

His name was Lake, a man with cold blue eyes under pale brows and a smile as bleak as moonlight on an arctic glacier, and he agreed that they should move into the woods at once. "We'll have to combine," he said. "The prowlers raised hell here last night and I don't want that to happen again."

When the brief discussion of plans was finished and Prentiss was ready to go, Lake said, "It might be of help if we knew more about Ragnarok, besides its name." He quoted dryly, " '*the last day of gods and men.*' "

"I was with the Dunbar Expedition that discovered Ragnarok," Prentiss said. "We didn't stay to study it very long — there wasn't any reason to. Six men died and we marked it on the chart as uninhabitable. The Gerns knew it — when they left us here they were giving us death."

"Yes." Lake looked out across the camp, at the dead and the dying and the snow whipping from the frosty hills. "But it's too soon to die," he said.

The dead were buried in shallow graves and men set to work building crude shelters among the trees. Inventory was taken of the promised "ample supplies," which were no more than the few personal possessions that each Reject had been permitted to take along. There was very little food, and an inventory of the firearms and ammunition showed the total there to be discouragingly small.

There were a few species of herbivores on Ragnarok, the woods-goats in particular, but they would have to learn how to make and use bows and arrows as soon as possible.

An overcast darkened the sky and at noon black storm clouds came driving in from the west. Efforts were intensified to complete the move before the storm broke. Lake's group established itself beside his and by late afternoon they were ready.

The rain came at dark, a roaring downpour. The wind rose to a velocity that made the trees lean, and hammered and ripped at the hastily built shelters. Many of them were destroyed. The rain continued, growing colder and driven in almost horizontal sheets by the wind. One by one, the fires went out.

The rain turned to snow at midnight. Prentiss walked through it wearily, forcing himself on. He was no longer young — he was fifty — and he had had little rest.

He had known, of course, that successful leadership would involve more effort and sacrifice on his part than on the part of those he led. He had thought that what little he knew of Ragnarok might help the others to survive. So he had taken charge, tolerating no dispute to his claim as leader. It was, he supposed, some old instinct that forbids the individual to stand calmly aside and let the group die.

The snow stopped an hour later and the wind died to a frigid moaning. The clouds thinned, broke apart, and the giant star looked down upon the land with its cold, blue light. The prowlers came then, in sudden, ferocious attack.

Twenty got through, past the slaughtered south guards, and charged into the interior of the camp. As they did so, the call went up the guard lines: "Emergency guards — *close in!*"

Above the triumphant, demoniac yammering of the prowlers came the screams of women, the thinner cries of children, and the shouting and cursing of men as they tried to fight the prowlers with knives and clubs. Then the emergency guards — every third man from the east and west guard lines — came plunging through the snow, firing as they came.

The prowlers launched themselves away from their victims and toward the guards, leaving a woman to stagger aimlessly, blood spurting from a severed artery and splashing dark in the starlight on the white snow.

The air was filled with the cracking of gunfire and the deep, savage snarling of the prowlers. Ten of them got through, leaving four dead guards behind them. The other ten lay where they had fallen and the emergency guards turned to hurry back to their stations, reloading as they went.

The wounded woman was lying in the snow and a first-aid man knelt over her. He straightened, shaking his head, and joined the others as they searched for the injured among the prowlers' victims.

They found no injured, only the dead. The prowlers killed with grim efficiency.

"John — "

Chiara, in charge of the shelters in that section of the camp, hurried toward him, his dark eyes worried under ice-coated brows.

"The wood is soaked," he said. "It's going to take some time to get the fires going again. There are babies and small children who lost their mothers when the prowlers attacked. They're already cold and wet — they'll freeze to death before we can get the fires going."

Prentiss looked at the ten prowlers lying in the snow and motioned toward them. "They're warm. Take out their guts."

"What — " Then Chiara's eyes lighted with comprehension and he hurried away without further question.

He went on, to make the rounds of the guard stations. When he returned he saw that his order had been obeyed.

The prowlers lay in the snow as before, their fangs bared and their devils' faces twisted in their dying snarls. But snug and warm inside them, children slept.

There were three hundred dead when the wan sun lifted to shine down on the white, frozen land; two hundred from Hell Fever and one hundred from prowler attacks.

Lake reported approximately the same number of dead and said, "Our guards were too far apart."

"We'll have to move everyone in closer together," Prentiss agreed. "And we're going to have to have a stockade wall around the camp."

All were moved to the center of the camp area that day and work was started on building a log wall around the camp. When the prowlers came that night, they found a ring of guards and fires which kept most of them out.

Men moved heavily at their jobs as the days went by. Of all the forces on Ragnarok, the gravity was the worst. Even at night there was no surcease from it. Men fell into an exhausted sleep in which there was no real rest and from which they awoke tired and aching.

Each morning there would be some who did not awaken at all, though their hearts had been sound enough for living on Earth or Athena.

But overworked muscles strengthened and men moved with a little less laborious effort. The stockade wall was completed on the twentieth day and the camp was prowler-proof. The prowlers changed their tactics then and began lying in wait for the daytime hunting parties.

The days became weeks, and the giant blue star that was the other component of Ragnarok's binary grew swiftly in size as it preceded the yellow sun earlier each morning. The season was spring; when summer came the blue star would be a sun as hot as the yellow sun and Ragnarok would be between them. The yellow sun would burn the land by day and the blue one would sear it by the night that would not be night. Then would come the brief fall, followed by the long, frozen winter when the yellow sun would shine pale and cold, far to the south, and the blue sun would be a star again, two hundred and fifty million miles away and invisible behind the cold yellow sun.

The cemetery was thirty graves long by thirty wide and more were added each day. To all the fact became grimly obvious: they were swiftly dying out and they had yet to face Ragnarok at its worst.

The old survival instincts asserted themselves and there were marriages among the younger ones. Among the first to marry was Julia, the girl who had volunteered to take care of Billy.

She stopped to talk to Prentiss one evening. She had changed in the past weeks. She still wore the red skirt, faded and patched, but her face was tired and thoughtful and no longer bold.

"Is it true, John," she asked, "that only a few of us might be able to have children here and that most of us who try to have children in this gravity will die for it?"

"It's true," he said. "But you knew that when you married."

"Yes . . . I knew it." There was a little silence, then, "All my life I've had fun and done as I pleased. The human race didn't need me and we both knew it. But now — none of us can be apart from the others or be afraid of anything. If we're selfish and afraid there will come a time when the last of us will die and there will be nothing on Ragnarok to show we were ever here.

"I don't want it to end like that for us. I want there to be children, to live on after we're gone. So I'm going to try to have children. I'm not afraid and I won't be."

When he did not reply she said, almost self-consciously, "Coming from me that all sounds silly, doesn't it?"

"It sounds wise and splendid, Julia," he said, "and it's what I thought you were going to say."

Full spring came and the vegetation burst into leaf and bud and bloom quickly, for its growth instincts knew in their mindless ways how short was the time to grow and reproduce before the brown death of summer came. The prowlers were suddenly gone one day, to follow the spring north, and for a week men could work outside without protection.

Then the new peril appeared, the one they had not expected: the unicorns.

The stockade wall was a blue-black rectangle behind them and the blue star burned with the brilliance of a dozen moons, lighting the woods in blue shadow and azure light. Prentiss and the hunter walked a little in front of the two riflemen, winding to keep in the starlit glades.

"It was on the other side of the next grove of trees," the hunter said in a low voice. "Fred was dressing out the second woods-goat while I came in with the first one. He shouldn't have been over fifteen minutes behind me — and it's been over an hour."

They rounded the grove of trees. At first it seemed there was nothing before them but the empty, grassy glade. Then they saw it lying on the ground no more than twenty feet in front of them.

It was — it had been — a man. He was broken and stamped into hideous shapelessness.

For a moment there was dead silence, then the hunter whispered, *"What did that?"*

The answer came in the pounding of cloven hooves. A formless shadow beside the trees materialized into a monstrous charging bulk: a thing like a gray boar, eight feet tall at the shoulders with the starlight glinting along the curving, vicious length of its single horn.

"Unicorn!" Prentiss said, and jerked up his rifle.

The rifles cracked in a snarling volley. The unicorn squealed in fury and struck the hunter, catching him on its horn and hurling him thirty feet. One of the riflemen went down under the unicorn's hooves, his cry ending almost as soon as it began.

The unicorn ripped the sod in deep furrows as it whirled back to Prentiss and the remaining rifleman, not turning in the manner of four-footed beasts of Earth but rearing and spinning on its hind feet. It towered above them as it whirled, the tip of its horn fifteen feet above the ground and its front hooves swinging around like great clubs.

Prentiss shot again, his sights on what he hoped would be a vital spot, and the rifleman shot an instant later. The shots went true. The momentum of the unicorn's swing brought it on around, then it collapsed, falling to the ground with jarring heaviness.

"We got it!" the rifleman said. "We — "

It half scrambled to its feet and made a noise; a call that went out through the night like the blast of a mighty trumpet. Then it dropped back to the ground, to die while its call was still echoing from the nearer hills.

From the east came an answering trumpet blast, a trumpeting that was sounded again from the south and from the north. Then there came a low and muffled drumming, like the pounding of thousands of hooves.

The rifleman's face was blue-white in the starlight. "The others are coming — we'll have to run for it!"

He turned and began to run toward the distant bulk of the stockade.

"No!" Prentiss commanded, quick and harsh. "Not the stockade!"

The rifleman kept running, seeming not to hear him in his panic. He commanded again, "Not the stockade — you'll lead the unicorns into it!"

Again the rifleman seemed not to hear him.

The unicorns were coming into sight, converging in from the east and south and north, the sound of their hooves swelling to a thunder that filled the night. The rifleman would reach the stockade only a little ahead of them and they would go through the wall as though it had been made of paper. For a little while the area inside the stockade would be filled with the squealing of swirling, charging unicorns and the screams of the dying. It would be over very quickly and there would be no one left alive on Ragnarok.

There was only one thing for him to do.

He dropped to one knee so his aim would be steady and the sights caught the running man's back. He pressed the trigger and the rifle cracked viciously as it bucked against his shoulder.

The man spun and fell hard against the ground. He raised himself a little and looked back, his face white and accusing and unbelieving.

. . . *"You shot me!"*

Then he fell forward again and lay without moving.

Prentiss turned back to face the unicorns and to look at the trees in the nearby grove. He saw what he already knew: they were young trees and too small to offer any escape for him. There was no place to run, no place to hide.

There was nothing he could do but wait; nothing he could do but stand in the blue starlight and watch the devil's herd pound toward him and think, in the last moments of his life, how swiftly and unexpectedly death could come to a man.

The unicorns held the Rejects prisoners in their stockade the rest of the night and all the next day. Lake had seen the shooting of the rifleman and had watched the unicorn herd kill John Prentiss and then trample the dead rifleman. He ordered a series of fires built around the inside of the stockade walls, quickly, for the unicorns were already moving on toward them.

The fires were started and green wood was thrown on to make them smoulder and smoke for as long as possible. Then the unicorns were just outside and every person in the stockade went into the concealment of the shelters.

Lake had already given his last order: There would be absolute quiet until and if the unicorns left; a quiet that would be enforced with fist or club whenever necessary.

The unicorns were still outside when morning came. The fires could not be refueled; the sight of a man moving within the stockade would bring the entire herd crashing through the walls. The hours dragged by, the smoke from the dying fires dwindling to thin streamers. The unicorns grew increasingly bolder and suspicious, crowding closer to the walls and peering through the openings between the logs.

The sun was setting when one of the unicorns trumpeted; a sound different from that of the call to battle. The others threw up their heads to listen, then they turned and drifted away. Within minutes the entire herd was gone out of sight through the woods, toward the north.

"That was close," Barber said, coming over to where Lake stood by the south wall. "It's hard to make two thousand people stay quiet hour after hour. Especially the children — they didn't understand."

"We'll have to leave," Lake said.

"Leave?" Barber asked. "We can make this stockade strong enough to hold out unicorns."

"Look to the south," Lake told him.

Barber did so and saw what Lake had already seen; a broad, low cloud of dust moving slowly toward them.

"Another herd of unicorns," Lake said. "John didn't know they migrated — the Dunbar Expedition wasn't here long enough to learn that. There will be herd after herd coming through and no time for us to strengthen the walls. We'll have to leave tonight."

Preparations were made for the departure; preparations that consisted mainly of providing each person with as much in the way of food and supplies as he or she could carry. In the 1.5 gravity of Ragnarok, that was not much.

They left when the blue star rose. They filed out through the northern gate and the rear guard closed it behind them. There was almost no conversation, and some of them turned to take a last look at what had been the only home they had ever known on Ragnarok. Then they faced forward again to the northwest, where the foothills of the plateau might offer them sanctuary.

Lake stopped to look back to the south when they had climbed the first low ridge. The cloud of dust was much nearer and it was coming straight toward the stockade.

They found their sanctuary on the second day; a limestone ridge honeycombed with caves. Men were sent back at once to carry the food and supplies to the new home.

When they returned with the first load they reported that the second herd of unicorns had broken down the walls and ripped the interior of the stockade into wreckage. He sent them back twice more to bring everything, down to the last piece of bent metal or torn cloth. They would find uses for all of it in the future.

The blue star became a small sun and the yellow sun blazed hotter. The last of the unicorns disappeared to the north and there were suddenly very few woods-goats to be found. The final all-out hunt was made.

Preserving the meat was no problem — it was cut in strips and dried in the sun. But the hunters returned on the tenth day with an amount of meat far insufficient to last until fall brought the woods-goats back from the north.

Lake instituted rationing much stricter than before and bleakly contemplated the specter of famine that hovered over his charges.

Early summer came, to wither and curl the leaves of trees, and there were twelve hundred of them. The weeks dragged by and summer solstice arrived. The heat reached its fiercest height then and there was no escape from it, not even in the caves. There was no night; the blue sun rose in the east as the yellow sun set in the west. There was no life of any kind to be seen; nothing moved across the burned land but the swirling dust devils.

The death rate increased rapidly, especially among the children. The small supply of canned and dehydrated milk, fruit, and vegetables was reserved exclusively for them but it was far too little.

Each day thin and hollow-eyed mothers would come to him to plead with him to save their children. "It would take so little to save him — please — before it's too late — "

But the time was yet so long until fall would bring relief from the famine that he could only answer with a grim and final, "No."

And watch the last flickering hope fade from their eyes and watch them turn away, to go and sit beside their dying children.

There were six hundred and forty-three of them when the food theft was discovered. The thief was a man named Bemmon, one of the men who had been entrusted with storing the food supplies. His cache was found buried beside his pallet: dried meat, cans of milk, little plastic bags of dehydrated fruits and vegetables.

Lake summoned the four subleaders — Craig, Barber, Schroeder, Anders — and sent two of them to get Bemmon. Confronted by the evidence and by the grim quintet, Bemmon blustered briefly then broke and admitted his guilt.

"I won't ever do it again," he promised, wiping at his sweating face. "I swear I won't."

"I know you won't," Lake said. He spoke to Craig: "You and Barber take him to the lookout point."

"What — " Bemmon's protest was cut off as Craig and Barber took him by the arms and walked him swiftly away.

Lake turned to Anders. "Get a rope," he ordered.

Anders paled a little. "A — rope?"

"A rope. Do you object?"

"No," Anders said, a little weakly. "No — I don't object."

The lookout point was an out-jutting spur of the ridge, six hundred feet from the caves and in full view of them. A lone tree stood there, its dead limbs thrusting like white arms through the brown foliage of the limbs that still lived. Craig and Barber waited under the tree, Bemmon between them. The lowering sun shone hot and bright on his face as he squinted back toward the caves at the approach of Lake and the other two.

He twisted to look at Barber. "What is it — what are you going to do?" There was the tremor of fear in his voice. "What are you going to do to me?"

Barber did not answer and Bemmon turned back to Lake. He saw the rope in Anders's hand for the first time and his face went white with comprehension.

"No!"

He threw himself back with a violence that almost tore him loose from the grip of Craig and Barber. "No — no!"

Schroeder stepped forward to help hold him and Lake took the rope from Anders. He fashioned a noose in it while Bemmon struggled and made panting, animal sounds, his eyes fixed in horrified fascination on the rope.

When the noose was finished Lake threw the free end of the rope over the white limb above Bemmon. He released the noose and Barber caught it, to draw it snug around Bemmon's neck.

Bemmon stopped struggling then and sagged weakly. For a moment it appeared that he would faint. Then he worked his mouth soundlessly until words came: "You won't — you can't — really hang me?"

Lake spoke to him: "We're going to hang you. We trusted you and what you stole would have saved the lives of ten children. You've heard the children cry because they were so hungry. You've watched them become too weak to cry or care any more and you've watched them die.

"Your crime is the murder of ten children and the betrayal of our trust in you. If you have anything to say, say it now while you can."

"You can't — I have a right to live!" The words came quick and ragged with hysteria and he twisted to appeal to the ones who held him. "I have a right to live — you won't let him murder me."

Only Craig answered him, with a smile that was like the thin snarl of a wolf: "Two of the children who died were mine."

Lake nodded to Craig and Schroeder, not waiting any longer. They stepped back to seize the free end of the rope and Bemmon screamed at what was coming, tearing loose from the grip of Barber.

Then his scream was abruptly cut off as he was jerked into the air. There was a cracking sound and he kicked spasmodically, his head setting grotesquely to one side.

Craig and Schroeder and Barber watched him with hard, expressionless faces, but Anders turned quickly away, to be suddenly and violently sick.

"He was the first to betray us," Lake said. "Snub the rope and let him swing there. If there are any others like him, they'll know what to expect."

The blue sun rose as they went back to the caves. Behind them Bemmon swung and twirled aimlessly on the end of the rope. Two long, pale shadows swung and twirled with him; a yellow one to the west and a blue one to the east.

They numbered four hundred when the first rain came, the rain that meant the end of summer. The yellow sun moved southward and the blue sun shrank steadily. Grass grew again and the woods-goats returned. For a while there was meat in plenty and green herbs to prevent the diet deficiencies. Then the unicorns came, to make hunting dangerous, and behind them the prowlers to make hunting with bows and arrows almost impossible. But the supply of cartridges was at the vanishing point and the bowmen learned, through necessity, how to use their bows with increasing skill and deadliness.

They were prepared as best they could be when winter came. Wood had been gathered in great quantities and the caves had been fitted with crude doors and a ventilation system.

Men were put in charge of the food supplies. Lake took inventory at the beginning and held checkup inventories at irregular and unannounced intervals. He found no shortages. He had expected none — Bemmon had long since been buried, but the rope still hung from the dead limb, the noose swinging and turning in the wind.

A Ragnarok calendar was made and the corresponding Earth dates marked on it. By a coincidence, Christmas fell near the middle of the winter. There was still the same rationing of food on Christmas Day, but little brown trees were cut for the children and decorated with such ornaments as could be made from the materials at hand.

There were toys under the trees, toys that had been patiently whittled from wood or made from scraps of cloth and prowler skins while the children slept. They were crude and humble toys, but the pale, thin faces of the children were bright with delight when they beheld them. The magic of an Earth Christmas was recaptured for a few fleeting hours that day.

That night a child was born to the girl named Julia, on a pallet of dried grass and prowler skins. She asked for her baby before she died and they let her have it.

"I wasn't afraid, was I?" she asked. "But I wish it wasn't so dark — I wish I could see my baby before I go . . . "

They took the baby from her arms when she was gone and removed from it the enveloping blanket that had concealed from her that it was stillborn and pathetically deformed.

*

There were three hundred and fifty of them when the first violent storms of spring came. By then eighteen children had been born. Twelve were stillborn, four were deformed and lived only a little while, but two were like any normal babies on Earth. There was one difference: the 1.5 gravity of Ragnarok did not seem to affect the Ragnarok-born children as it had the ones born on Earth.

There were deaths from Hell Fever again, but two little boys and a girl contracted it and survived; the first proof that Hell Fever was not always and invariably fatal.

That summer there was not the famine of the first summer. There was sufficient meat and dried herbs; a diet rough and plain but adequate for those who had become accustomed to it.

Lake had taken a wife that spring and his son was born that following winter. It altered his philosophy and he began thinking of the future, not in terms of years to come but in terms of generations to come.

There was a man named West who had held degrees in philosophy on Earth, and he said to Lake one night, as they sat together by the fire: "Have you noticed the way the children listen to the stories of what used to be on Earth, what might have been on Athena, and what would be if only we could find a way to escape from Ragnarok?"

"I've noticed," he said.

"These stories already contain the goal for the future generations," West went on. "Someday, somehow, they will go to Athena, to kill the Gerns there and free the Terran slaves and reclaim Athena as their own."

He had listened to them talk of the interstellar flight to Athena as they sat by their fires and worked at making bows and arrows. Without the dream of someday leaving Ragnarok there would be nothing before them but the vision of generation after generation living and dying on a world that could never give them more than existence.

The dream was needed. But it, alone, was not enough. How long, on Earth, had it been from the Neolithic age to advanced civilization — how long from the time men were ready to leave their caves until they were ready to go to the stars?

Twelve thousand years.

There were men and women among the Rejects who had been specialists in various fields. There were a few books that had survived the trampling of the unicorns, and the unicorn hides possessed an inner skin that would make a parchment for writing upon with ink made from the black lance-tree bark.

The knowledge contained in the books and the learning of the Rejects still living should be preserved for the future generations. With the advantage of that learning perhaps they really could, someday, somehow, escape from their prison and reclaim Athena.

"We'll have to have a school," he said, and told West of what he had been thinking.

West nodded in agreement. "We should get started with the school and the writings as soon as possible. Especially the writings. Some of the textbooks will require more time to write than Ragnarok will give the authors."

A school for the children was started the next day and the writing of the textbooks begun. Two of the textbooks would be small but of such importance that it was decided to make four copies of each: Craig's *Interior Features of a Gern Cruiser* and Schroeder's *Operation of Gern Blasters.*

Spring came and the school and writings were interrupted until hot summer arrived; then they were resumed. There was another cessation of school and writing during the fall and they were resumed when winter came.

Year followed year, each much like the one that had preceded it but for the rapid aging of the Old Ones, as Lake and the others called themselves, and the growing up of the Young Ones. Five years passed and no woman among the Old Ones could any longer have children, but there had been eight normal, healthy children born. Twelve years passed and there were twenty of the Old Ones left, ninety Young Ones, ten Ragnarok-born children of the Old Ones, and two Ragnarok-born children of the Young Ones.

West died in the winter of the fifteenth year and Lake was the last of the Old Ones. White-haired and aged far beyond his years, he was still leader of the group that had shrunk to ninety. He knew, before spring arrived, that he would not be able to accompany the younger ones on the hunts. He could do little but sit by his fire and feel the gravity dragging at his heart, warning him the end was near.

It was time he chose his successor.

He had hoped to live to see his son take his place, but Jim was only thirteen. There was a scar-faced, silent boy of twenty among the Young Ones, not the oldest among them but the one who seemed to be the most thoughtful and stubbornly determined: John Prentiss's grandson, Bill Humbolt.

A violent storm was roaring outside the caves the night he told the others he wanted Bill Humbolt to be his successor. There were no objections and, with few words and without ceremony, he terminated his fifteen years of leadership.

He left the others, his son among them, and went back to the place where he slept. His fire was low, down to dying embers, but he was too tired to build it up again. He lay down on his pallet and saw, with neither surprise nor fear, that his time was much nearer than he had thought — it was already at hand.

He let the lassitude enclose him, not fighting it. He had done the best he could for the others and now the weary journey was ended.

The thought dissolved into the memory of the day fifteen years before. The roaring of the storm became the thunder of the Gern cruisers as they disappeared into the gray sky. Four thousand Rejects stood in the cold wind and watched them go, the children not yet understanding that they had been condemned to die. Somehow, his own son was among them —

He tried feebly to rise. There was work to do — a lot of work . . .

Bill Humbolt thought of the plan early that spring and considered it during the coming months.

For him the dream of someday leaving Ragnarok and taking Athena from the Gerns was a goal toward which they must fight with unswerving determination. He could remember a little of Earth and he could remember the excitement and high hopes as the *Constellation* embarked for Athena. Quite clearly he remembered the day the Gerns left them on Ragnarok, the wind moaning down the barren valley, his father gone and his mother trying not to cry. Above all other memories was the one of the cold, dark dawn when his mother had held him and shielded him while the prowlers tore the life from her. She could have escaped them, alone . . .

He would remember what the Gerns had done and hate them till the day he died. But to future generations the slow, uneventful progression of centuries might bring a false sense of security; might turn the stories of what the Gerns had done to the Rejects and the warnings of the Old Ones into legends and then into half-believed myths.

The Gerns would have to be lured to Ragnarok before that could happen.

He set the plan in action as soon as the spring hunting ended. Among the Young Ones was a man who had been fascinated by the study of electronics and had read all the material available on the subject and he went to him to ask him the question: "George, could you build a transmitter — one that would send a signal to Athena?"

George laid down the arrow he had been straightening. "A transmitter?"

"I know it would have to be a normal-space transmitter — you couldn't possibly rig up a hyperspace transmitter," he said. "That would be enough — just a dot-dash transmitter."

"It would take two hundred years for the signal to get to Athena," George said. "And forty days for a Gern cruiser to come to Ragnarok through hyperspace."

"I know."

"So you want our showdown with the Gerns to come no later than two hundred years from now?" George asked.

"You're as old as I am," he said. "You still remember the Gerns and what they did, don't you?"

"I'm older than you," George said. "I was nine when they left us here. They kept my father and mother and my sister was only three. I tried to keep her warm by holding her but I couldn't. The Hell Fever got her that first night. Yes . . . I remember the Gerns and what they did."

"The generations to come won't have the memories that we have. Someday the Gerns will come to Ragnarok, even if only by chance and a thousand years from now, and our people might by then have forgotten what the Gerns did to us and would do to them. But if they know the Gerns will be here two hundred years from now they won't have time to forget."

"You're not supposed to sit in a cave and build an interstellar transmitter," George said. "But it doesn't take much power with the right circuit. There's wire and various electronic gadgets here. There's metal that can be heated and shaped into a water-driven generator. It *might* be done . . . "

George completed the transmitter and generator five years later. It was set in operation and George observed its output as registered by the various meters, several of which he had made himself.

"Weak, but it will reach the Gern monitor station on Athena," he said. "It's ready to send — what do you want to say?"

"Make it something short," Humbolt told him. "Make it 'Ragnarok calling.' That will be enough to bring a Gern cruiser."

George poised his finger over the transmitting key. "This will set something in motion that will end two hundred years from now with either the Gerns or us going under. These signals can never be recalled."

"I think the Gerns will be the ones to go under," he said. "Send the signal."

"I think the same thing," George said. "I hope we're right. It's something we'll never know."

He began depressing the key.

A boy was given the job of sending the signals, and the call went out twice daily toward distant Athena until winter froze the creek and stopped the waterwheel that powered the generator.

Humbolt sent out prospecting expeditions that year and in following years to search for metallic ores. The Dunbar Expedition had reported Ragnarok to be virtually devoid of minerals, but he held to the hope that they might find enough metals to make weapons with which to meet the Gerns. Perhaps — fantastic hope though it was — even enough to plan the building of a small rocket ship with a hyperspace shuttle.

But no ores were found, other than iron ore of such low grade as to be useless. Neither did Ragnarok possess any fiber-bearing plants from which thread and cloth could be made.

At the end of ten years he was forced to accept the fact that Ragnarok did not and would never offer men more than the bare necessities of life. There would be no weapons or spaceship built in the future; there were no metals with which to build them. Ragnarok was a prison devoid of all means of escape but one: the possibility of luring the jailer to the cell door and over-powering him.

The sound had been made ten years before and was being made every year, that would bring the jailer to investigate, with his weapons and with his keys.

He was forty-five and the last of the Young Ones when he awoke one night to find himself burning with the Hell Fever. He waited quietly. There was no reason to call to the others. They could do nothing for him and he had already done all he could for them. Now they must carry on, forty-nine men, women, and children, and know that their last living link with the past was gone; that they were truly on their own.

They represented the lowest ebb in numbers of human life on Ragnarok, but they were all Ragnarok-born and their number would increase. For a while, perhaps, the immediate problems of survival would overshadow every-thing else. But the books would keep and there would always be some who would study them. They would grow in numbers as the generations went by and the lapse would be short-lived; the time for the coming of the Gerns, when measured in terms of generations, was already near.

Forces were in motion that would bring the seventh generation the trial of combat and the opportunity for freedom. But they, themselves, would have to achieve their own destiny.

He refused to let doubt touch his mind as to what that destiny would be. The men of Ragnarok were only furclad hunters who crouched in caves, but the time would come when they would walk as conquerers before beaten and humbled Gerns.

It was fifty years from the sending of the first signal and there were eighty-four of them . . .

Dave West stopped under a tree, his bow and padded arrow in his hands, and repressed a sigh of weariness as he scanned the clearing before him. He was fifteen and it was his third day of the intensive training that began for each boy when he reached that age; the hunter-and-hunted game in which his father, at the moment, was a prowler he was stalking and which was in turn stalking him. It was a very important game but the sun was hot and it seemed to him his father was unduly demanding —

He heard, too late, the whisper of running feet behind him. He whirled, bringing up the bow with the arrow notched in the string, and fell sprawling backward over a root he had not seen.

His father's body struck him and he was knocked blind and helpless under a rain of hard, openhanded blows. His efforts to resist were in vain and it seemed to him the lesson would never end.

When his father was finished he sat up dizzily and wiped the blood from his nose. His father squatted before him, his muscles rippling as he rocked on the balls of his feet and regarded him with thoughtful speculation.

"Didn't I tell you that prowlers will circle a hunter and attack him from the rear?" he asked.

"Yes, but I'd still have got you with the arrow if it hadn't been for that root," he defended himself.

His father reached out with a blow that caught him alongside the head and knocked him rolling in a blaze of white light.

"What did I tell you about watching your step?" he asked.

Dave sat up and gingerly held his hand to his ear. "To pay attention so I won't ever trip over anything. Next time I will."

He got to his feet to retrieve the arrow he had dropped, moving more quickly than before and with his desire to stop and rest forgotten.

His nose was still bleeding and all the other places still hurt, but it never occurred to him to feel the slightest resentment toward his father. His father was doing what all fathers did with their sons: teaching him how to survive. Soon he would have to hunt real prowlers and unicorns and they didn't give careless hunters a second chance — they killed them.

He wiped the blood from his nose again and looked at his father. "I'm ready," he said. "This time I'm going to make a dead prowler out of you."

It was one hundred years from the sending of the first signal and there were two hundred and ninety-four of them . . .

"You can kill prowlers and unicorns," Leader John Lake said, "but killing Gerns is harder to do."

The group of boys he addressed had recently and successfully gone through their first hunting season. They had proven they could face anything that walked on Ragnarok. Duane Craig answered with the confidence of youth, "An arrow will go through a Gern."

"If you get the chance to shoot it. But what do you think the Gern would be doing? Suppose the Gerns came today — what would you do?"

Duane Craig's answer came without hesitation: "Fight."

"An arrow won't go through a steel cruiser. One of their turret blasters could kill every human being on Ragnarok in one sweep."

"Then what should we do?" Duane asked.

"That's what you're going to learn next," he said. "You've learned how to kill prowlers and unicorns. Now you'll learn how to kill bigger game — Gerns. They'll be here in a hundred years for certain — a great many of your grandchildren will be alive yet when they come.

"But if you don't learn how to kill Gerns now you may never have any grandchildren. All of you know why — the Gerns might come tomorrow."

It was one hundred and twenty-five years from the sending of the first signal and there were five hundred and fifty-eight of them . . .

Bunker led the way into the starlit night just outside the mouth of the cave, his twelve pupils following him. They seated themselves beside him, ranging in age from a fourteen-year-old boy down to a girl of six, and waited for him to speak.

He pointed to the sky, where the group of stars called the Athena constellation blazed high in the east.

"There, at the tip of the Athena arrowhead, is Athena," he said. "But it's on beyond that star you see, so far that we can't see Athena's sun at all, so far that it takes light two hundred years to reach us from there.

"It will still be another seventy-five years before our first signal gets to Athena and the Gerns learn we are here. Why is it, then, that you and all the other groups of children have to study reading and writing and have to learn about all sorts of things you can't eat or wear, like history and physics and the way to fire a Gern blaster?"

The hand of every child went up. He selected eight-year-old Fred Humbolt. "Tell us, Freddy."

"Because we don't know when the Gerns will come," Freddy said. "In hyperspace their cruisers can travel a light-year every five days. One of their cruisers might pass by only forty or fifty light-years away and drop into normal space for some reason and pick up our signal. Then they would be here in only eight or nine days. So we have to know all about them and how to fight them because there aren't very many of us."

The little girl said, "The Gerns will come to kill part of us and make slaves out of the rest, like they did with the others a long time ago. They're awful mean and awful smart and we have to be smarter than they are."

The oldest boy, Steve Lake, was still watching the constellation of Athena.

"I hope they come," he said. "I hope they come just as soon as I'm old enough to kill them."

"How would a Gern cruiser look if it came at night?" Freddy asked. "Would it come from toward Athena?"

"It probably would," Bunker answered. "You would look toward Athena and you would see its rocket blast as it came down, like a bright trail of fire — "

A bright trail of fire burst suddenly into being, coming from the constellation of Athena and lighting up the woods and their startled faces as it arced down toward them.

"It's them!" a treble voice exclaimed, and there was a quick flurry of movement among the children.

Then the light vanished, leaving a faint glow where it had been.

"Only a meteor," Bunker said as he turned to the children.

He saw with deep satisfaction that none of them had run and that the older boys had shoved the smaller children behind them and were standing in a resolute little line, rocks in their hands with which to ward off the Gerns.

*

It was one hundred and fifty years from the sending of the first signal and there were twelve hundred and eighty of them . . .

Frank Schroeder opened the book to a fresh parchment page and dipped the pen in the clay bottle of lance-tree ink. What he would write would be only the observations of an old man who had recently transferred leadership to someone younger, but they were things he knew to be true, and he wanted those who lived in the years to come to read them and remember them.

He began to write:

We have adapted, as the Old Ones in the beginning believed we would do. We move as easily in the 1.5 gravity of Ragnarok as our ancestors did in the gravity of Earth. The Hell Fever has become unknown to us and the prowlers and unicorns are beginning to fear us.

We have survived; the generations that the Gerns presumed would never be born. We must never forget the characteristics that insured that survival: courage to fight, and die if necessary, and an unswerving loyalty of every individual to the group.

Fifty years from now the Gerns will come. There will be no one to help. Those on Athena are slaves and it is probable that Earth has been enslaved by now.

We will stand or fall, alone. But if we of today could know that those who meet the Gerns will still have the courage and the loyalty to one another that made our survival possible, then we would know that the Gerns are already defeated . . .

It was one hundred and seventy-five years from the sending of the first signal and there were two thousand and six hundred of them . . .

Julia Humbolt sat high on the hillside above the town, the book open in her lap and her short spear close to her right hand. Far below her the massive stockade wall, built to keep out unicorns, was a square surrounding the thick-walled houses. Wide canopies of logs and brush spread over the roofs to keep out the summer heat as much as possible. They were nice houses, she thought, much nicer to live in than the cave where she had been born.

Her own baby would be born in one of them in only seven months. And if it was a boy, he might be leader when the Gerns came!

She already knew what they would name him: John, after John Prentiss, the first of the great and wise Old Ones . . .

A twig snapped to her left. She reached instinctively for her spear as she jerked her head toward the sound.

It was a unicorn, just within the trees thirty feet away.

It abandoned its stealth at her movement and burst out of the trees in a squealing, pounding lunge. She came to her feet in one quick movement, the book falling unnoticed to the ground, and appraised the situation to determine what she must do to stay alive.

In her swift, calm appraisal she found but one thing to do: stand her ground and make use of the fact that a human could jump to one side more quickly than a four-footed beast in headlong charge. It was coming with its head lowered to impale her, and for a fraction of a second, if she could jump aside quickly enough and at exactly the right moment, the vulnerable spot behind its jaw would be within reach of her spear.

She felt the sod firm under her moccasined feet as she shifted her weight a little, her eyes on the lowered head of the unicorn and the spear held ready. The ground trembled under the pounding of its hooves and the black horn was suddenly an arm's length from her stomach.

She jumped aside then, swinging as she jumped, and thrust the spear with all her strength into the unicorn's neck.

The thrust was hard and true and the spear went deep into the flesh. She released it and flung herself back to dodge the flying hooves. The force of the unicorn's lunge took it past her, then its legs collapsed under it and its massive body crashed to the ground. It kicked once and then lay still.

She went to it and retrieved the spear, feeling a stirring of pride as she walked past her bulky victim. Eighteen-year-old boys had been known to kill unicorns with spears, but never before had an eighteen-year-old girl tried to do it. The son she carried would be proud of her when he —

She saw the book and gasped in horror, all else forgotten. The unicorn had struck it with one of its hooves and it lay knocked to one side, battered and torn.

She ran to it and picked it up, to smooth the torn leaves as best she could. It had been a very important book: one of the old books, printed on real paper, that told them things they would need to know when the Gerns came. Now, her carelessness had resulted in such damage to it that page after page was unreadable.

She would be punished for it, of course. She would have to go to the town hall and stand up where everybody could see her, while the chief of the council told her how she had been trusted to take good care of the book and how she had betrayed their trust in her. It would all be true and she would not be able to look anyone in the eyes as she stood there.

She was a traitor; she was a — a *Bemmon!*

She started slowly back down the hill toward town, not seeing the unicorn as she walked past it, the bloody spear trailing disconsolately behind her and her head hanging in shame.

It was two hundred years from the sending of the first signal and there were five thousand of them . . .

John Humbolt stood on the wide stockade wall and looked to the southeast, to the distant valley where the Gern cruisers had set down so long ago.

It was a bleak and barren scene to him, despite all the years he had known it. Winter was coming again; the gray afternoon sky was spitting flakes of snow and an icy wind was moaning down from the north. Always, on Ragnarok, either winter was coming or the burned death of summer. They had adapted to their environment, but Ragnarok was a prison that had no key; a harsh and barren prison in which all the distant years of the future held only the never-changing monotony of mere existence.

But the imprisonment should end soon. Restlessness and impatience stirred in him at the thought. He was of the generation that the Old Ones had planned would meet and overpower the Gerns. He was twenty-five years old and he had studied since he was six for that meeting. He could draw diagrams of the interior of a Gern cruiser, placing the compartments and corridors exactly where the old drawings showed them to be. He and many of the others could speak Gern, though probably with an accent since they had had only the written lessons. And all of them had spent many hours practicing with wooden models of the Gern hand blasters.

They were as prepared as they could ever be, and during the past year the anticipation of the coming of the Gerns had become a fever of desire among them all. It was hard to compel themselves to go patiently about their routine duties when any day or night the cruiser might come that would carry them to the stars; tall and black and incredibly deadly, and theirs if they could take it.

The Gerns would come, to look upon the men of Ragnarok with contempt. They would not fear the men of Ragnarok, thinking they were superior to them, and their belief in their superiority would bring their defeat —

A sound came above the moan of the wind, a roaring that raised in pitch and swelled in volume as it came nearer. He listened, watching the gray sky, and his heart hammered with exultation. As he watched it broke through the clouds, riding its rockets of flame.

The cruiser had come!

It settled to the ground, so near the stockade that it loomed high and menacing above the town with its blaster turrets looking down into it. It was beautiful in its menace — it was like some great and savage prowler that might be tamed and used to kill the other prowlers.

He turned and dropped the ten feet to the ground inside the stockade, landing lightly. The warning signal was being sounded from the center of the town; a unicorn horn that gave out the call they had used in the practice alarms. But this time it was real, this time there might never be an All Clear sounded. Already the women and children would be hurrying along the tunnels that led to the safety of the woods beyond the town. The Gerns might use their turret blasters to destroy the town and all in it before the day was over. There was no way of knowing what might happen before it ended, but whatever it was, it would be the action they had all been wanting.

He ran to where the others would be gathering, hearing the horn ring wild and savage and triumphant as it announced the end of two centuries of waiting.

*

"So we came two hundred light-years to find *this!*"

Commander Gantho indicated the viewscreen with a pudgy white hand — heavy in the gravity of Ragnarok — where the bearded savages could be seen among their pole and mud hovels.

Occasionally one of them would glance toward the cruiser with something like mild curiosity, and Subcommander Narth frowned with a combination of perplexity and resentment. These descendants of the Rejects had obviously degenerated into utter primitives, and primitives always reacted to the presence of a cruiser with a high degree of awe and fear. These merely ignored it.

"They behave like mindless animals," he said to the commander. *"They* couldn't have sent those signals."

"The transmitter was built two hundred years ago, before they degenerated," the commander said. "It must have been fitted with some means for automatic operation that required no further attention. Obviously, those specimens down there represent retrogression to the point where they have no knowledge whatever of the past."

"I suppose the medical students will want some of them for study since it had been assumed survival was impossible here," Narth remarked absently, his eyes on the viewscreen. "But the reason for sending the signals — I wonder what that could have been?"

The commander shrugged. "To ask us for assistance, no doubt." He glanced at the chronometer and his manner became brisk. "It's almost mealtime. Send out a detachment to bring some of them in for observation. They seem to be strong enough — if their intelligence isn't too abysmally low we can use them on Athena for simple manual labor."

"I'll go myself," Narth said. "I know a little Terran and it should be mildly entertaining to take a closer look at them."

"Take your detachment straight toward the stockade wall, not down it to the gate," the commander ordered. "I'll have one of the turret blasters destroy that section of the wall just before you get to it. The best way to get eager cooperation from primitives is to impress them with the futility of resistance."

The blaster beam lashed down from one of the cruiser's turrets and disintegrated three hundred feet of stockade wall into a billow of dust. Narth and his twelve men marched through the breach, their weapons in their hands. The thought occurred to him that they must appear to the natives as strange and terrible gods, striding through the dust created by their own genius for destruction.

But when he and his men emerged from the cloud of dust the natives were watching them with the same mild curiosity as before. He felt the gall of sharp irritation. He was a Gern and bearded savages did not ignore Gerns.

As if to add to his irritation, several of the watching men turned away and went back into the houses, not as men who sought concealment but as men who saw nothing of sufficient interest to keep them outside in the cold wind any longer.

He scowled in frustration.

He ordered his men to a halt when they were some distance from the first house and they stood in a line, their weapons held on the four natives who stood under the canopy of the house before them. He beckoned to the natives, a gesture too imperative for them to fail to understand, and ordered commandingly in Terran, "Come here!"

One of the natives yawned and went back in the house. The other three continued to watch with the same infuriating lack of interest.

"What's the matter?" The voice of the commander spoke from the communicator that hung from his neck.

"There are three natives by the house in front of me," Narth said. "You can't see them from the ship because of the canopy. I ordered them to come here, but apparently they no longer understand Terran."

"Then give them some action they can understand — drag them out by the heels. I can't wait all day for you to bring back a few specimens."

"Very well," Narth said. "It won't take long."

He and his men approached the natives again, Narth marveling at the ease with which they moved in the dragging gravity. They were splendidly muscled, not bulkily but in the way a Gern *theno* cat was muscled. If only their intelligence was not too low, Ragnarok would become the source of an endless supply of the strongest, most docile slaves the Gern Empire had ever possessed. The discard of the Rejects two hundred years before had produced a wholly unexpected reward —

The thought vanished like a punctured bubble as his approach brought him near enough to see them at close range. He had expected their eyes to be like the eyes of some near-mindless beast, dull and vacant. Instead, they were sharp with intelligence and waiting purpose.

Warning touched him like a cold finger and he would have ordered his men to halt again, but the brown-bearded native in the center spoke first, not in Terran but in Gern and to all of them: "Look up on the roof — and keep walking!"

Narth looked, and saw that thirteen bowmen had suddenly appeared along the edge of the roof, invisible to the ship because of the canopy. Thirteen broad-headed arrows were aimed at their throats and thirteen coldly intent pairs of eyes were watching them for the first move to lift a weapon.

Trapped!

They had walked into the simplest kind of trap, set for them by dull-witted savages. In his surge of surprise and anger he did not wonder how they had learned to speak Gern. The important thing was that they had tricked him and his men into a position that was not at all in keeping with his dignity as a Gern officer.

They would not live long enough to regret it, of course. He opened his mouth, to speak the quick words into the communicator that would bring the blaster beam lashing down and transform the house and the natives into disassociated atoms —

"Don't!"

The warning came from the brown-bearded one again. "Your next action was obvious before you thought of it," he said. "An arrow will go through you at the first word. We have nothing whatever to lose by killing you."

Narth looked again at the arrow aimed at his throat. The flint head of it looked broad enough and sharp enough to decapitate him, and the bowman seemed to be holding the taut bowstring in a dangerously careless manner.

His anger dwindled a little. It was true the natives had nothing to lose by killing him. He, on the other hand, had a lot to lose — his life. And their victory would be short-lived. It was inconceivable that such an absurd situation could last for long —

"A little faster," the native ordered. "Under the canopy here — move!"

They obediently quickened their pace and the bowmen on the roof dipped their arrows to follow their progress.

John Humbolt surveyed the line of Gerns, holding the Gern officer's communicator in one hand, the microphone muffled.

The red-bearded giant, Charley Craig, shook his head as though in wonder. "It was as easy as trapping a herd of woods-goats," he said.

"Young ones," the blond-bearded Norman Lake amended. His pale gray eyes went down the line of Gerns and back again. "And almost as dangerous."

To Humbolt the appearance of the Gerns was entirely different from what he had expected. They moved heavily and awkwardly, their bellies and faces were soft, and the officer before him was trying to conceal a high degree of uncertainty with bluster.

"The longer you hold us, the more painful and severe your punishment will be," he threatened. "Your trickery has gained you nothing."

"Trickery?" Humbolt asked. "All we did was go about our usual activities. Of course, when you destroyed a section of the wall that required months of hard labor to build and then invaded our town with drawn weapons we could only classify you as hostile intruders. As for punishment: your degree of punishment will depend upon how well you cooperate."

"Our punishment?" The Gern glared, his face purpling. *"Our* punishment? You ignorant fool — you insane, megalomaniac savage!"

Humbolt turned to Charley Craig. "Have we let him talk long enough for you to mimic his voice?" he asked.

"Long enough," Charley said.

"Mimic?" Question momentarily crossed the Gern's face, to be replaced by the rage. "I warn you for the last time: your death will be painful enough at best. Return that communicator at once!"

He reached for the communicator as he spoke. Humbolt flicked out his hand and there was the sharp snapping of finger bones. The Gern gasped, his face whitening, and the fury drained out of him as he held his broken hand.

Humbolt turned to Charley again and handed him the communicator. Charley slipped it around his neck and let his flaming beard conceal the microphone.

"Let's hope my accent won't be too conspicuous," he said as he pressed the call button.

The response came almost immediately from the ship. "Narth — what are you doing? Where are the natives you were sent after?"

Charley's beard parted in a smile at the words and Humbolt felt a sense of relief. What might have been a serious obstacle did not exist. Apparently Gern communicators were designed for serviceability rather than faithful tonal reproduction: the voice that came from the communicator was very metallic.

Charley answered in a voice that was almost a perfect imitation of that of the Gern officer: "We have thirteen captives and we're taking them to the ship now."

"He's referring to you Gerns, of course," Humbolt said to the officer. "Now, each of you Gerns will walk hand in hand with one of us. This may give your commander the idea you're leading us to the ship, which is all right. It may give one of you Gerns the idea to try to reach for his blaster. Don't try it. Our reflexes are far faster than yours and you would never touch it. Make no attempt to signal the ship or warn the others in any way. You will all thirteen be killed with your own blasters the moment we're discovered."

He saw nothing on the faces of the Gerns that resembled defiance. He said crisply to his own men, "Let's go."

They went as a group of thirteen pairs, the Gerns walking obediently a little in front of the humans and with the bone-crushing grip of the humans bringing winces of pain from them. The speaker in Charley's communicator made a surprised sound at their appearance and demanded, "What's the meaning of this? Why are you leading the natives? And why don't you have your blasters in your hands?"

"Our captives are very docile," Charley said, "and we can get them into the ship more easily if we lead them. Only one of them can speak Terran at all and he is very stupid."

The Terran-speaking officer reddened at the reference to himself but made no other move to show his resentment.

The airlock slid open when they reached the bottom of the boarding ramp and six armed Gerns stepped out, shackles in their hands.

"Orders of the commander, sir," the officer in charge of them said to the Gern officer beside Humbolt, looking down at him. "The natives will be chained together before taking them to the examination chamber. They will — "

He saw, belatedly, the strained expressions on the faces of the Gerns below him. He snapped a command as he jerked at the blaster he carried: "The natives — *kill them!*"

Humbolt shot him with the blaster of the officer beside him before he could fire. The other five went down a moment later, but not before one of them had killed Chiara.

The commander would have seen it all in his viewscreen. They had seconds left in which to carry out their plan.

"Into the ship!" he said. "Leave the Gerns."

They ran, the airlocks beginning to slide shut as they did so. They crowded through before the locks closed completely, leaving thirteen Gerns suddenly locked outside their own ship.

Alarm bells were ringing shrilly inside the ship and from the multiple-compartment shafts came the sounds of elevators dropping with reinforcements. They ran past the elevator shafts without pausing, to split forces as they had long ago planned; five men going with Charley to try to fight their way to the drive room and five going with Humbolt in the attempt to take the control room.

Humbolt found the manway ladder and they began to climb. There was one factor much in their favor; the Gerns would waste some time looking for them near the bottom of the elevator shafts.

They came to the control room level and ran down the short corridor. They turned left into the one that had the control room at its end and into the fire of six waiting Gerns.

For three seconds the corridor was an inferno of blaster beams that cracked and hissed as they met and crossed, throwing little chips of metal from the walls. When it was over one man remained standing beside Humbolt: the blond and nerveless Lake.

Thomsen and Barber and Leandro were dead and Jimmy West was bracing himself against the wall, a blaster hole in his chest and his legs giving way under him. He tried to smile and tried to say something: "We showed — showed — " He slid to the floor, the sentence unfinished.

They ran on, leaping the bodies of the Gerns. The control room door swung open a crack as they neared it, then was knocked wide open as Humbolt shot the Gern who had intended to take a cautious look outside.

They went through the door, to engage in the last brief battle. There were two officers in addition to the one who wore a commander's uniform, and the three of them swung up their blasters in the way that seemed so curiously slow to the men of Ragnarok. They killed the two officers before either could fire, and the commander's blaster was knocked across the room as Lake's hurled blaster smashed him across the knuckles.

Humbolt closed the door behind him and Lake recovered his blaster. The commander stared at them, astonishment and apprehension on his pale, fat face.

"What — how did you get past the guards?" he asked in heavily accented Terran, rubbing his bruised knuckles. Then he seemed to regain some of his courage and his tone became ominous with threat. "More guards will be here within a minute. Lay down your weapons and — "

"Don't talk until you're asked a question," Lake said.

"Lay down your weapons and surrender to me and I'll let you go free — "

Lake slapped him across the mouth with a backhanded blow that snapped his head back on his shoulders and split his lip.

"I said, don't talk. And above all, never lie to us like that."

The commander spat out a tooth and held his hand to his bleeding mouth. He did not speak again.

Humbolt located the communicator that would connect him with Charley. There was a rustling sound coming from it as though Charley were breathing heavily.

"Charley?" he asked.

"Here," the voice of Charley answered. "We made it to the drive room — three of us. How about you?"

"Lake and I have the control room. Cut their drives, just in case something should go wrong up here. I'll let you know as soon as the ship is ours."

He turned to the commander. "First, I want to know how the war is going."

"I — " The commander looked uncertainly at Lake.

"Just tell the truth," Lake said. "Whether you think we'll like it or not."

"We have all the planets but Earth itself," the commander said. "We'll have that soon."

"And the Terrans on Athena?"

"They're still — working for us."

"Now," Humbolt said, "you will order your men to return to their sleeping quarters. All of them. They will leave their blasters in the corridors outside and they will not resist the men who will come to take charge of the ship."

The commander made a last effort toward defiance: "And if I refuse?"

Lake answered, smiling at him with the smile of his that was no more than a quick showing of white teeth and with the savage eagerness in his pale eyes.

"If you refuse I'll start with your fingers and break every bone to your shoulders. If that isn't enough, I'll start with your toes and go to your hips."

The commander hesitated, sweat filming his face as he looked at them. Then he reached out to switch on the all-stations communicator and say into it, "Attention, all personnel: You will return to your quarters at once, leaving your weapons in the corridors outside. You are ordered to make no resistance when the natives come . . . "

There was a silence when the commander had finished. Humbolt and Lake looked at each other, bearded and clad in prowler skins but standing at last in the control room of the ship that was theirs; in a ship that could take them to Athena, to Earth, to the end of the galaxy.

The commander, watching them, could not conceal his last vindictive anticipation.

"You have the cruiser," he said, "but what can you do with it?"

"I'll tell you what we can do with it," Humbolt said kindly. "We've planned it for two hundred years. We have the cruiser and sixty days from now we'll have Athena. That will be only the beginning and you Gerns are going to help us do it."

It was not, Narth thought, the kind of homecoming he and the others had expected. Ragnarok lay a hundred and eighty-five light-years behind them and Athena was only three ship's days ahead of them. It had been only forty-nine days since he had gone out to bring back some of the natives for observation in the examination chamber and for appraisal of their worth as slaves. In those forty-nine days the men of Ragnarok had forced the Gerns to teach them how to operate the cruiser, learning with amazing speed.

"You have to learn fast on Ragnarok," the one called Charley had remarked. "Those who are slow in learning don't live long enough to produce any slow-learning children."

In retrospect, it seemed to Narth that the first two days had been an insane nightmare of bearded monsters who asked endless questions about the ship and calmly, deliberately, broke the bones of anyone who refused to answer or gave an answer that was not true. By the end of the second day they had learned that passive resistance was painful and futile, and two of them had learned that active resistance was fatal.

So they had ceased resisting in any manner, but it was only a temporary submission for strategic reasons. The savages had gained the upper hand by means of deceit and ruthlessness; they had been lucky in their trickery and had become masters of the cruiser but they were still savages from a mud and log village. They had dared to defy Gerns and when their luck ran out they would pay the penalty.

He clenched his hands at the thought. It was something to look forward to, the day when these savages would be taken back to Ragnarok and an example made of them in the center of the village, while their wives and their children and all the savages left behind watched and learned what it meant to defy the Gerns . . .

The red-bearded Charley was smiling at him from the copilot's chair.

"It's not much use to resent what happened," he said. "You Gerns made two big mistakes and this is the result."

Narth quickly forced his face into an expression of civil interest. "We made two big mistakes?" he asked.

It was very seldom that he held a conversation with any of the Ragnarok men. Humbolt would occasionally exchange a few words not relevant to the savages' plans, but only Charley ever exhibited any desire to engage in idle conversation with the Gerns. It seemed to amuse him to observe their reactions. Galling as it was, it was more comfortable than the cold menace that was so characteristic of the others. Especially the one called Lake. Lake had never threatened him in any way but there was an appalling aura of dangerousness about him that made threats unnecessary. It had been Lake who had avenged the death of the Ragnarok boy whom two Gerns had stabbed to death with long knives stolen from the galley. Lake had cornered them and then, without touching his weapons, he had proceeded to disembowel them with their own knives. He had stood and smiled down at them as they writhed and moaned and finally died . . .

"First, you Gerns underestimated us," Charley said. "You thought we were as primitive as we looked. Actually, we let our beards grow for the past year to help you think that. You were stupid enough to take it for granted we were stupid.

"Then you were afraid to do anything while there was yet time. You, yourself, were afraid to warn the ship. The commander was afraid to resist and hoped the men at the different stations would do something. The men at the different stations hoped that someone else would do something.

"Hope is a good thing but — " Charley smiled at him again " — you have to fight together and not be afraid of getting hurt."

Humbolt strode into the control room.

"We'll make the test now," he said to Charley.

He went to the board and seated himself, then punched the BATTLE STATIONS button. "You" — he looked at Narth — "strap yourself in for high-acceleration maneuvers."

Narth did so and asked, "High acceleration?"

"We want to make some tests with this cruiser so we'll know what we can do with the two we'll get at Athena. And there *are* two more cruisers at Athena — you didn't lie about it, did you?"

He asked the question in the tone that had so often presaged painful violence for Gerns who had lied, and Narth hastily assured him, "No — there are two cruisers there, as we told you. But what — when you get them — "

He stopped, wondering if he could tactfully ask Humbolt what he thought he could do with them.

"We'll take the three cruisers back to Ragnarok," Humbolt said. "We'll pick up the rest of the Ragnarok men who are neither too old nor too young and go on to Earth. I'll show you, in a minute, why we expect no trouble breaking through your lines around Earth. These Ragnarok men will be given training in the handling of both Gern and Terran ships and then we will destroy all the Gern ships around Earth that refuse to surrender."

Narth restrained a smile, some of his depression leaving him. It was a plan so fantastic it was amusing; it would be the last ambitious attempt the savages would ever make.

"As you know," Humbolt said, "the largest ship's blasters are good for only a relatively short range due to the dispersion. A space battle consists of firing your long-range projectiles and trying to dodge the projectiles of the enemy. The acceleration limitator makes certain that the projectile evader mechanism doesn't cause such a sudden change of direction or such a degree of acceleration that the crew will be injured or killed.

"We from Ragnarok are accustomed to a 1.5 gravity. We can withstand much higher degrees of acceleration than Gerns or men from Earth. Now, we're going to make some preliminary tests. We've had the acceleration limitator disconnected."

"Disconnected?" Narth heard the frantic note in his own cry. "Don't — you'll kill us all!"

"No," Humbolt said. "We won't go any farther right now than to make you unconscious."

"But it — "

Humbolt touched the acceleration control and Narth was shoved deep in the seat, his breath cut off as his diaphragm sagged. The cruiser swung in a curve and Narth was slammed sideways, the straps cutting into his flesh and his vision blurring. He thought Humbolt was watching him; he could not see to tell for sure.

"Now," he heard Humbolt say, his voice dim and distant, "we'll see how many G's you can take."

An instant later something smashed at him like a physical force and consciousness vanished.

"You didn't give us a chance to come anywhere near our own acceleration limit," Humbolt said to him after he had regained consciousness. "But you can see now that the Gern ships around Earth can never hope to out-maneuver us nor hope to hit us."

Narth saw, and what he saw was unpleasant to behold. The Ragnarok savages possessed a physical abnormality that would enable them to do as they planned. Earth and Athena would be lost and a corner of the Gern Empire thrust back.

But the Gerns were a race of conquerors who ruled across a thousand light-years of space. The existence of the Empire was proof of their superiority. While the savages strutted on Earth and Athena, boasting of their prowess, the Empire would be laying plans and preparing for their annihilation.

When the time was right the Gerns would strike, and when it was over the fate of Earth and Athena would be a grim example to all other subject worlds of the utter futility of defying Gern domination.

He looked at Humbolt, feeling the hatred and anticipation twist his face.

"We'll go on to engage the Gern home fleet without any waste of time," Humbolt said. "Then we'll destroy your Empire, world by world."

It seemed to Narth that the full and terrible implications were slow in coming to him.

"Destroy the Empire — *now?*"

"Were you foolish enough to think we would stop with the freeing of Earth and Athena? When a race has been condemned to die and manages, somehow, to survive, it learns a lesson well: it must never again let the other race be in a position to destroy it. So we're not going to give you time to do that. You yourselves sowed the seeds on Ragnarok two hundred and twenty years ago when you condemned us to die. Now, the time has come to reap the harvest.

"You understand, don't you?" Humbolt smiled at him in the mirthless way that Ragnarok men smiled at Gerns, and his voice was almost gentle. "You are a menace which we must remove."

Narth did not answer. There was no answer he could make. He sat without moving, the triumphant anticipation draining away from him. He had not thought they would dare challenge the Gern Empire — not so soon, before it was prepared to defeat them . . .

You yourselves sowed the seeds.

They would remember an incident that had happened two centuries before and they would shatter the Empire into dust, coldly, ruthlessly, without mercy.

The time has come to reap the harvest.

Only an incident in the Empire's history, unimportant, almost unrecorded, and the harvest would be destruction by the descendants of the unwanted, terror and death at the hands of the children of the condemned.

You are a menace which we must remove.

He wet his lips, feeling the weakness of a cold and bitter sickness inside him.

"But it's too soon to die . . . "

art — the activity of creating works like paintings, sculpture, music, and poetry. Works of art can tell us a great deal about the nature of any society, although as a *process,* artistic creation is not fully understood. The future of the arts in our age of electronic media is often hotly debated. There are two outstanding science fiction anthologies whose stories address possible artistic futures — *New Dreams This Morning* (Ballantine Books, 1966); and *The Arts and Beyond* (Doubleday, 1977).

A Museum Piece

ROGER ZELAZNY

Forced to admit that his art was going unnoticed in a frivolous world, Jay Smith decided to get out of that world. The four dollars and ninety-eight cents he spent for a mail-order course entitled *Yoga — The Path to Freedom* did not, however, help to free him. Rather, it served to accentuate his humanity, in that it reduced his ability to purchase food by four dollars and ninety-eight cents.

Seated in a padmasana, Smith contemplated little but the fact that his naval drew slightly closer to his backbone with each day that passed. While nirvana is a reasonably esthetic concept, suicide assuredly is not, particularly if you haven't the stomach for it. So he dismissed the fatalistic notion quite reasonably.

"How simply one could take one's own life in ideal surroundings!" he sighed (tossing his golden locks which, for obvious reasons, had achieved classically impressive lengths). "The fat stoic in his bath, fanned by slave girls and sipping his wine, as a faithful Greek leech opens his veins, eyes downcast! One delicate Circassian," he sighed again, *"there* perhaps, plucking upon a lyre as he dictates his funeral oration — the latter to be read by a faithful countryman, eyes all a-blink. How easily *he* might do it! But the fallen artist — nay! Born yesterday and scorned today he goes, like the elephant to his graveyard, alone and secret!"

He rose to his full height of six feet one and a half inches, and swung to face the mirror. Regarding his skin, pallid as marble, and his straight nose, broad forehead, and wide-spaced eyes, he decided that if one could not live by creating art, then one might do worse than turn the thing the other way about, so to speak.

He flexed those thews which had earned him half tuition as a halfback for the four years in which he had stoked the stithy of his soul to the forging of a movement all his own: two-dimensional painted sculpture.

"Viewed in the round," one crabbed critic had noted, "Mr. Smith's offerings are either frescoes without walls or vertical lines. The Etruscans excelled in the former form because they knew where it belonged; kindergartens inculcate a mastery of the latter in all five-year-olds."

Cleverness! Mere cleverness! Bah! He was sick of those Johnsons who laid down the law at someone else's dinner table!

He noted with satisfaction that his month-long ascetic regime had reduced his weight by thirty pounds to a mere two twenty-five. He decided that he could pass as a Beaten Gladiator, post-Hellenic.

"It is settled," he pronounced. "I'll *be* art."

Later that afternoon a lone figure entered the Museum of Art, a bundle beneath his arm.

Spiritually haggard (although clean-shaven to the armpits), Smith loitered about the Greek Period until it was emptied of all but himself and marble.

He selected a dark corner and unwrapped his pedestal. He secreted the various personal items necessary for a showcase existence, including most of his clothing, in its hollow bottom.

"Good-bye, world," he renounced, "you should treat your artists better," and mounted the pedestal.

His food money had not been completely wasted, for the techniques he had mastered for four ninety-eight while on the Path to Freedom had given him a muscular control such as allowed him perfect, motionless statuity whenever the wispy, middle-aged woman followed by forty-four children under age nine, left her chartered bus at the curb and passed through the Greek Period, as she did every Tuesday and Thursday between 9:35 and 9:40 in the morning. Fortunately, he had selected a seated posture.

Before the week passed he had also timed the watchman's movements to an alternate *tick* of the huge clock in the adjacent gallery (a delicate eighteenth-century timepiece, all of gold leaf, enamel, and small angels who chased one another in circles). He should have hated being reported stolen during the first week of his career, with nothing to face then but the prospect of second-rate galleries or an uneasy role in the cheerless private collections of cheerless and private collectors. Therefore, he moved judiciously when raiding staples from the stores in the downstairs lunch room, and strove to work out a sympathetic bond with the racing angels. The directors had never seen fit to secure the refrigerator or pantry from depredations by the exhibits, and he applauded their lack of imagination. He nibbled at boiled ham and pumpernickel (light), and munched ice cream bars by the dozen. After a month he was forced to take calisthenics (heavy) in the Bronze Age.

"Oh, lost!" he reflected amidst the Neos, surveying the kingdom he had once staked out as his own. He wept over the statue of Achilles Fallen as though it were his own. It was.

As in a mirror, he regarded himself in a handy collage of bolts and nutshells. "If you had not sold out," he accused, "if *you* had hung on a little longer — like these, the simplest of Art's creatures . . . But no! It could not be!

"Could it?" he addressed a particularly symmetrical mobile overhead. *"Could* it?"

"Perhaps," came an answer from somewhere, which sent him flying back to his pedestal.

But little came of it. The watchman had been taking guilty delight in a buxom Rubens on the other side of the building and had not overheard the colloquy. Smith decided that the reply signified his accidental nearing of Dharana. He returned to the Path, redoubling his efforts toward negation and looking Beaten.

In the days that followed he heard occasional chuckling and whispering, which he at first dismissed as the chortlings of the children of Mara and Maya, intent upon his distraction. Later, he was less certain, but by then he had decided upon a classical attitude of passive inquisitiveness.

And one spring day, as green and golden as a poem by Dylan Thomas, a girl entered the Greek Period and looked about, furtively. He found it difficult to maintain his marbly placidity, for lo! she began to disrobe!

And a square parcel on the floor, in a plain wrapper. It could only mean . . .

Competition!

He coughed politely, softly, classically . . .

She jerked to an amazing attention, reminding him of a women's underwear ad having to do with Thermopylae. Her hair was the correct color for the undertaking — that palest shade of Parian manageable — and her gray eyes glittered with the icy-orbed intentness of Athena.

She surveyed the room minutely, guiltily, attractively . . .

"Surely stone is not susceptible to virus infections," she decided. " 'Tis but ˙ my guilty conscience that cleared its throat. Conscience, thus do I cast thee off!"

And she proceeded to become Hecuba Lamenting, diagonally across from the Beaten Gladiator and, fortunately, not facing in his direction. She handled it pretty well, too, he grudgingly admitted. Soon she achieved an esthetic immobility. After a professional appraisal he decided that Athens was indeed mother of all the arts; she simply could not have carried it as Renaissance nor Romanesque. This made him feel rather good.

When the great doors finally swung shut and the alarms had been set she heaved a sigh and sprang to the floor.

"Not yet," he cautioned, "the watchman will pass through in ninety-three seconds."

She had presence of mind sufficient to stifle her scream, a delicate hand with which to do it, and eighty-seven seconds in which to become Hecuba Lamenting once more. This she did, and he admired her delicate hand and her presence of mind for the next eighty-seven seconds.

The watchman came, was nigh, was gone, flashlight and beard bobbing in musty will-o'-the-wispfulness through the gloom.

"Goodness!" she expelled her breath. "I had thought I was alone!"

"And correctly so," he replied. " 'Naked and alone we came into exile . . . Among bright stars on this most weary unbright cinder, lost! . . . O lost — ' "

"Thomas Wolfe," she stated.

"Yes," he sulked. "Let's go have supper."

"Supper?" she inquired, arching her eyebrows. "Where? I had brought some K rations, which I purchased at an army surplus store — "

"Obviously," he retorted, "you have a short-timer's attitude. I believe that chicken figured prominently on the menu for today. Follow me!"

They made their way through the T'ang Dynasty to the stairs.

"Others might find it chilly in here after hours," he began, "but I daresay you have thoroughly mastered the techniques of breath control?"

"Indeed," she replied, "my fiancé was no mere Zen faddist. He followed the more rugged path of Lhasa. Once, he wrote a modern version of the *Ramayana,* full of topical allusions and advice to modern society."

"And what did modern society think of it?"

"Alas! Modern society never saw it. My parents bought him a one-way ticket to Rome, first class, and several hundred dollars' worth of travelers' checks. He has been gone ever since. That is why I have retired from the world."

"I take it your parents did not approve of Art?"

"No, and I believe they must have threatened him also."

He nodded.

"Such is the way of society with genius. I, too, in my small way, have worked for its betterment and received but scorn for my labors."

"Really?"

"Yes. If we stop in the Modern Period on the way back, you can see my Achilles Fallen."

A very dry chuckle halted them.

"Who is there?" he inquired, cautiously.

No reply. They stood in the Glory of Rome, and the stone senators were still.

"*Someone* laughed," she observed.

"We are not alone," he stated, shrugging. "There've been other indications of such, but whoever they are, they're as talkative as Trappists — which is good.

"Remember, thou art but stone," he called gaily, and they continued on to the cafeteria.

One night they sat together at dinner in the Modern Period.

"Had you a name, in life?" he asked.

"Gloria," she whispered. "And yours?"

"Smith, Jay."

"What prompted you to become a statue, Smith — if it is not too bold of me to ask?"

"Not at all," he smiled, invisibly. "Some are born to obscurity and others only achieve it through diligent effort. I am one of the latter. Being an artistic failure, and broke, I decided to become my own monument. It's warm in here, and there's food below. The environment is congenial, and I'll never be found out because no one ever looks at anything standing around museums."

"No one?"

"Not a soul, as you must have noticed. Children come here against their wills, young people come to flirt with one another, and when one develops sufficient sensibility to look at anything," he lectured bitterly, "he is either myopic or subject to hallucinations. In the former case he would not notice, in the latter he would not talk. The parade passes."

"Then what good are museums?"

"My dear girl! That the former affianced of a true artist should speak in such a manner indicates that your relationship was but brief — "

"Really!" she interrupted. "The proper word is 'companionship.' "

"Very well," he amended, " 'companionship.' But museums mirror the past, which is dead, and the present, which never notices, and transmit the race's cultural heritage to the future, which is not yet born. In this, they are near to being temples of religion."

"I never thought of it that way," she mused. "Rather a beautiful thought, too. You should really be a teacher."

"It doesn't pay well enough, but the thought consoles me. Come, let us raid the icebox again."

They nibbled their final ice cream bars and discussed Achilles Fallen, seated beneath the great mobile which resembled a starved octopus. He told her of his other great projects and of the nasty reviewers, crabbed and bloodless, who lurked in Sunday editions and hated life. She, in turn, told him of her parents, who knew Art and also knew why she shouldn't like him, and of her parents' vast fortunes, equally distributed in timber, real estate, and petroleum. He, in turn, patted her arm and she, in turn, blinked heavily and smiled Hellenically.

"You know," he said, finally, "as I sat upon my pedestal, day after day, I often thought to myself: Perhaps I should return and make one more effort to pierce the cataract in the eye of the public — perhaps if I were secure and at ease in all things material — perhaps, if I could find the proper woman — but nay! There is no such a one!"

"Continue! Pray continue!" cried she. "I, too, have, over the past days, thought that, perhaps, another artist could remove the sting. Perhaps the poison of loneliness could be drawn by a creator of beauty — If we — "

At this point a small and ugly man in a toga cleared his throat.

"It is as I feared," he announced.

Lean, wrinkled, and grubby was he; a man of ulcerous bowel and much spleen. He pointed an accusing finger.

"It is as I feared," he repeated.

"Wh-who are you?" asked Gloria.

"Cassius," he replied, "Cassius Fitzmullen — art critic, retired, for the *Dalton Times.* You are planning to defect."

"And what concern is it of yours if we leave?" asked Smith, flexing his Beaten Gladiator halfback muscles.

Cassius shook his head.

"Concern? It would threaten a way of life for you to leave now. If you go, you will doubtless become an artist or a teacher of art — and sooner or later, by word or by gesture, by sign or by unconscious indication, you will communicate what you have suspected all along. I have listened to your conversations over the past weeks. You know, for certain now, that this is where all art critics finally come, to spend their remaining days mocking the things they have hated. It accounts for the increase of Roman senators in recent years."

"I have often suspected it, but never was certain."

"The suspicion is enough. It is lethal. You must be judged."

He clapped his hands.

"Judgment!" he called.

Other ancient Romans entered slowly, a procession of bent candles. They encircled the two lovers. Smelling of dust and yellow newsprint and bile and time, the old reviewers hovered.

"They wish to return to humanity," announced Cassius. "They wish to leave and take their knowledge with them."

"We would not tell," said Gloria, tearfully.

"It is too late," replied one dark figure. "You are already entered in the Catalogue. See here!" He produced a copy and read: " 'Number 28, Hecuba Lamenting. Number 32, The Beaten Gladiator.' No! It is too late. There would be an investigation."

"Judgment!" repeated Cassius.

Slowly, the senators turned their thumbs down.

"You *cannot* leave."

Smith chuckled and seized Cassius's tunic in a powerful sculptor's grip.

"Little man," he said, "how do you propose stopping us? One scream by Gloria would bring the watchman, who would sound an alarm. One blow by me would render you unconscious for a week."

"We shut off the guard's hearing aid as he slept," smiled Cassius. "Critics are not without imagination, I assure you. Release me, or you will suffer."

Smith tightened his grip.

"Try *anything.*"

"Judgment," smiled Cassius.

"He is modern," said one.

"Therefore, his tastes are catholic," said another.

"To the lions with the Christians!" announced a third, clapping his hands.

And Smith sprang back in panic at what he thought he saw moving in the shadows. Cassius pulled free.

"You cannot do this!" cried Gloria, covering her face. "We are from the Greek Period!"

"When in Greece, do as the Romans do," chuckled Cassius.

The odor of cats came to their nostrils.

"How could you — here . . . ? A lion . . . ?" asked Smith.

"A form of hypnosis privy to the profession," observed Cassius. "We keep the beast paralyzed most of the time. Have you not wondered why there has never been a theft from this museum? Oh, it has been tried, all right! We protect our interests."

The lean, albino lion which generally slept beside the main entrance padded slowly from the shadows and growled — once, and loudly.

Smith pushed Gloria behind him as the cat began its stalking. He glanced toward the Forum, which proved to be vacant. A sound, like the flapping of wings by a flock of leather pigeons, diminished in the distance.

"We are alone," noted Gloria.

"Run," ordered Smith, "and I'll try to delay him. Get out, if you can."

"And desert you? Never, my dear! Together! Now, and always!"

"Gloria!"

"Jay Smith!"

At that moment the beast conceived the notion to launch into a spring, which it promptly did.

"Good-bye, my lovely."

"Farewell. One kiss before dying, pray."

The lion was high in the air, uttering healthy coughs, eyes greenly aglow.

"Very well."

They embraced.

Moon hacked in the shape of cat, that palest of beasts hung overhead — hung high, hung menacingly, hung long . . .

It began to writhe and claw about wildly in that middle space between floor and ceiling for which architecture possesses no specific noun.

"Mm! Another kiss?"

"Why not? Life is sweet."

A minute ran by on noiseless feet; another pursued it.

"I say, what's holding up that lion?"

"I am," answered the mobile. "You humans aren't the only ones to seek umbrage amidst the relics of your dead past."

The voice was thin, fragile, like that of a particularly busy Aeolian Harp.

"I do not wish to seem inquisitive," said Smith, "but who are you?"

"I am an alien life form," it tinkled back, digesting the lion. "My ship suffered an accident on the way to Arcturus. I soon discovered that my appearance was against me on your planet, except in the museums, where I am greatly admired. Being a member of a rather delicate and, if I do say it, somewhat narcissistic race — " He paused to belch daintily, and continued, " — I rather enjoy it here — 'among bright stars on this most weary unbright cinder [belch], lost.' "

"I see," said Smith. "Thanks for eating the lion."

"Don't mention it — but it wasn't *wholly* advisable. You see, I'm going to have to divide now. Can the other me go with you?"

"Of course. You saved our lives, and we're going to need something to hang in the living room, when we have one."

"Good."

He divided, in a flurry of hemidemisemiquavers, and dropped to the floor beside them.

"Good-bye, me," he called upward.

"Good-bye," from above.

They walked proudly from the Modern, through the Greek, and past the Roman Period, with much hauteur and a wholly quiet dignity. Beaten Gladiator, Hecuba Lamenting, and Xenos ex Machina no longer, they lifted the sleeping watchman's key and walked out the door, down the stairs, and into the night, on youthful legs and drop-lines.

au/tos — self-propelled land vehicles which carry passengers and are normally powered by an internal combustion engine. Autos have changed the nature of life in most societies, allowing people to live great distances from their place of work for the first time in history, and permitting young people considerable freedom from parental supervision. The future of the auto is now in doubt because of the world energy crisis. More stories about the auto and its future can be found in *Car Sinister* (Avon Books, 1979).

Why Johnny Can't Speed

ALAN DEAN FOSTER

DEAR MR. AND MRS. MERWIN:

IT IS MY PAINFUL DUTY TO HAVE TO INFORM YOU THAT YOUR SON, ROBERT L. MERWIN, WAS KILLED IN COMMUTER ACTION ON THE SOUTHBOUND SAN DIEGO FREEWAY IN THE VICINITY OF THE SECOND IRVINE RANCH TURN-OFF, ORANGE COUNTY.

FROM WHAT OUR EVALUATORS HAVE BEEN ABLE TO RECONSTRUCT, YOUNG ROBERT APPARENTLY DISPUTED A LANE CHANGE WITH A BLACK GM CADDY MARAUDER. NO VIOLATION OF THE NORTH AMERICAN TRAFFIC CODE HAS COME TO MY NOTICE, BUT I WILL KEEP YOU INFORMED SHOULD ANY SUCH COME TO LIGHT. NORMAL INVESTIGATIONS ARE PROCEEDING. THE OTHER VEHICLE INVOLVED IS KNOWN TO ORANGE COUNTY POLICE. ITS OWNER WAS QUESTIONED BUT NOT DETAINED. DETAILS AND PARTICU-LARS ARE ENCLOSED. PLEASE ACCEPT MY PERSONAL CONDOLENCES.

> YOURS SINCERELY,
> GEORGE WILSON ANGEL
> CHIEF, SOUTHERN CALIFORNIA DIVISION
> CALIFORNIA DISTRICT HIGHWAY PATROL
> ENCL: I RPT. ACCID.
> I RPT. CORONER

Frank Merwin refolded the letter, replaced it in its envelope and laid it on the flange of the lamp stand, near the radio. He held his wife a little more tightly. Her sobbing had become less than hysterical, now that the terrible initial shock had somewhat worn. He managed to keep his own emotions pretty well in check, but then he had driven the Los Angeles area for some twenty years and was correspondingly toughened. When he finally spoke again there was as much bitterness in his voice as sorrow.

"Geez, Myrt, oh, geez."

He eased her down onto the big white couch, walked to the center of the room and paused there, hands clenching and unclenching, clasped behind his back. The woven patterns in the floor absorbed his attention.

"Goddamn it, Myrtle, I told him! I *told* him! 'Look, son, if you insist on driving all the way to Diego by yourself, at least take the Pontiac! Have some sense,' I told him! I don't know what's with the kids these days, hon. You'd think he'd listen to me just this once, wouldn't you? Me, who once drove all the way from Indianapolis to L.A. and was challenged only twice on the way — only *twice,* Myrt, but no, he hadda be a big shot! 'Listen Dad. This is something I've got to work out for myself. With my own car,' he tells me! I knew he'd have trouble in that VW. And I often told him so, too.

"But no, all he could think of to say was, 'Pops, the worst that can happen is I've gotta outmaneuver some other can, right? You've seen the way that bug corners, haven't you, huh? And if I get into a tough scrape, any other VW on the road is bound by oath to support me — in most actions anyway.'

"Whatta you tell a kid like that, Myrt? How do you get through to him?" His face registered utter bafflement. His wife's crying had slowed to a trickle. She was dabbing at her eyes with one of his old handkerchiefs.

"I don't know either, dear. I still don't understand why he had to drive down there. Why couldn't he have taken the Trans, Frank? Why?"

"Oh, you know why. What would his *friends* have said? 'Here's Bobby Merwin, too scared to drive his own rod,' and that sort of crud." His sarcasm was getting edgier. "Still felt he had to prove himself a man, the idiot! He'd already soloed on the freeways — why did he feel the need to try a cross-county expedition? But damn it, if he had to display his guts, why couldn't he have done so in the big car? Not even a professionally customized VW can mount much stuff.

"And on top of everything else, you'd think he'd have had the sense to shy off that kind of an argument. He had Driver's Training! Who ever heard of a VW disputing position with a Cad — a Marauder, no less! Where were his 'friends,' huh? I warned him about the light stretches between here and Diego, where flow is light, help is more than a hornblast away and some psycho can surprise you from behind an on-ramp!"

He paused to catch his breath, walked back to the lamp stand and picked up the letter. Familiar with the contents, he glanced at it only briefly this time. He offered it to his wife but she declined, so he returned it to the stand.

"You know what I have to do now, I suppose?"

She nodded, sniffling.

"Bob was taking that gift to a friend in Diego. I'm bound to see that it's delivered."

She looked up at him without much hope. She knew Frank.

"I don't suppose — "

He shook his head. His expression was gentle but firm.

"No, hon. I'm taking it down myself. I refuse to ship it and I certainly won't ride the Trans. Not after all these years. No, I'm going down the same way Bob went, by the same route. I'll have the J.J. tuned first, though."

She looked around dully, plucking fitfully at the delicate covering of the couch.

"I suppose you'll at least take it in to — "

"Hector? Certainly. In spite of what he charges he's damn well worth the money. Best mechanic around. I enjoy doing business with him. Know I'm getting my credit's worth, at least. We couldn't have me going somewhere else — now could we? Wouldn't want him to get the idea we're prejudiced or something. I've been going to him for, oh, five years. Almost forgotten what he is — "

"Going all the way down to Diego, eh, Mr. Merwin?" said the wiry *chicano*. He was trying to rub some of the grease off his hands. The filthy rag he was using already appeared incapable of taking on any more of the tacky, blue-black gunk.

"Yeah. So you'll understand, Hector, when I say the J.J.'s got to be in tiptop shape."

"*Ciertamente!* You want to open her up, please?"

Frank nodded and moved over to where the J.J. rested, just inside the rolled-up armor grille entrance to the big garage. He slid into the deep pile of the driver's bucket, flipped the three keys on the combination ignition, and then jabbed the hood release switch. As soon as the hood started up he climbed out, leaving the keys in the ON position. Hector was already bent over the car's power plant, staring intently into the works.

"Well, Mr. Merwin, from what I can see your engine at least is in excellent condition, yes, excellent! You want me to fill 'er up?"

Frank nodded wordlessly. He wasn't at all surprised at the mechanic's rapid inspection of the engine. After all, the J.J. had been given the best of professional care and the benefits of his own considerable work since he'd purchased her. Hector did not look up as he set about releasing the protective panels over the right-side .70 caliber.

"If I may ask, how do you plan to go?"

Frank had the big Meerschaum out and was tamping tobacco into it.

"Hmm. I'll go down Burbank to the San Diego Freeway and get on there. It'd be a little faster to get on the Ventura, but on a trip of this length that little bit of time saved would be negligible and I don't see the point in fighting the interchange."

Hector nodded approvingly. "Quite wise. You know, Mr. Merwin, you've got two pretty bad stretches on this trip. Very iffy. I read — about your son. I sorrow. The *jornada de la muerte* comes eventually to all of us."

Frank paused in lighting the pipe. "Couldn't be helped," he said tightly. "Bob didn't realize what was — what he was getting into, that's all. I blame myself, too, but what could I do? He was eighteen and by law there wasn't anything I could do to hold him back. He simply took on more than he could handle."

One of Hector's grease monks had wheeled over a bulky ammo cart. The mechanic waved the assistant off and proceeded about the loading himself. Frank appreciated the gesture.

"A Cad, wasn't it?"

"It was." He was leaning over the mechanic's shoulder, better to follow the loading process. Never could tell what you might have to do for yourself on the road. "What are you giving me? Explosive or armor-piercing?"

"Mixed." Hector slammed down the box-load cover to the heavy gun. It clicked shut, locked. He moved away to get a small, curved ladder, wheeled it back. At the top he began checking over the custom roof turret. "Both, alternating sequence. True, it's more expensive, but after all your son's car was destroyed by a Marauder. A black one?"

"Yes, that's right," said Frank, only mildly surprised. "How'd you find out?"

"Oh, among the trade the word gets passed along. I know of this particular vehicle, I believe. Owner does a lot of his own work, I understand. That's tough to tangle with, Mr. Merwin. Might you be thinking of — "

Frank shrugged, looked the other way. "Never know who you'll bump into on the roads these days, Hector. I've never been one to run from a dogfight."

"I did not mean to imply that you would. We all know your driver's combat record, Mr. Merwin. There are not all that many aces living in the Valley."

He gestured meaningfully at the side of the car. Eleven silhouettes were imprinted there. Four mediums, four compacts — crazy people. Gutsy, but crazy. Two sports cars — kids — a Jag and a Vet, as he recalled. He smiled in reminiscence. Speed wasn't *everything.* And one large gold stamping. He ran his hand over the impressions fondly. That big gold one, he'd gotten that baby on the legendary drive out from Indianapolis, back in 'eighty-three — no, 'eighty-two. The Imperial had been rough and, face it, he'd been lucky as hell, too young to know better. Ricochet shots were always against the odds, but hell, anyone could shoot at *tires!* So he'd thought twenty-odd years ago. Now he knew better — didn't he?

He wondered if Bob had tried something equally insane.

"Yes, well, you watch yourself, Mr. Merwin. A Marauder is bad news straight from the factory. Properly customized, it could mount enough stuff to take on a Greyhound busnought."

"Don't worry about me, Hector. I can take care of myself." He was checking the nylon sheathing on the rear tires. "Besides, the J.J. mounts a few surprises of her own!"

It was already warm outside, even at five in the morning. The weather bureau had forecast a high of 101° for downtown L.A. He'd miss most of that, but even with air-control and climate-conditioning things could get hot. He turned on the climate-cool as he backed the blue sedan out of the garage, put it in drive, and rolled toward the Burbank artery.

It was still too early for the real rush hour and he had little company on the feeder route as he moved past Van Nuys Boulevard toward the Sepulveda on-ramp. A Rambler at the light was slow in getting away at the change of signal. He blasted the horn once and the frantic driver of the vehicle marked heavily as neutral made haste to get out of his way. Theoretically all cars on the surface streets were equal. But some were more equal than others.

The Sepulveda on-ramp was an excellent one for entering the system for reasons other than merely being an easier way to pass through the Ventura interchange. Instead of sloping upward as most on-ramps did, it allowed the driver to descend a high hill. This enabled older cars to pick up a lot of valuable acceleration easily and also provided the driver with an aerial overview of the traffic pattern below.

He passed the commuter carpark at the Kester Trans station. It was just beginning to fill as the more passive commuters parked their personal vehicles in favor of the public Trans. He felt a surge of contempt, the usual reaction of the independent motorist to milk-footed drivers willfully abandoning their vehicular freedom for the crowding and crumpling of the mass-transit systems. What sort of person did it take, he wondered for the umpteenth time, to trade away his birthright for simple sardine-can safety? The country was definitely losing its backbone. He shook his head woefully as his practiced eye gauged the pattern shifting beneath him.

Mass Trans had required and still required a lot of money. One way in which the governments involved (meaning those of most industrial, developed nations) went about obtaining the necessary amounts was to cut back the expensive motorized forces needed to regulate the far-flung freeway systems. As the cutbacks increased, it gradually became accepted custom among the remaining overworked patrols to allow drivers to settle their own disputes. This custom was finalized by the Supreme Court's handing down of the famous *Brier* v. *Matthews and the State of Texas* decision of '79, in which it was ruled that all attempts to regulate interstate, nonstop highway systems were in direct violation of the First Amendment.

Any motorist who didn't feel up to potential arguments was provided with a safe, quiet alternative means of transportation in the new Mass Trans systems, most of which ran down the center and sides of the familiar freeway routes, high above the frantic traffic. Benefits were immediate. Less pollution from even the fine turbine-steam-electric engines of the private autos, an end to many downtown parking problems in the big cities —•and more. For the first time since their inception the freeways, even at rush hour, became negotiable at speeds close to those envisioned by their builders. And psychiatrists began to advise driving as excellent therapy for persons afflicted with violent or even homicidal instincts.

There were a few — un-American dirty commie pinko symps, no doubt — who decried the resultant proliferation of "argumentative" devices among high-powered autos. Some laughable folk even talked of an "arms race" among automakers. German cars made their biggest incursions into foreign markets in decades. Armor plating, bulletproof glassalloy, certain weaponry — how else did those nuts expect a decent man to Drive with Confidence?

He gunned the engine and the supercharged sedan roared down the on-ramp, gathering unnecessary but impressive momentum as it went. Frank had always believed in an aggressive entrance. *Let 'em know where you stand right away or they'll ride all over you.* The tactic was hardly needed in this instance — there were only two other cars in his entrance pattern, both in the far two lanes.

He switched slowly until he was behind them, looking into rear and side view mirror carefully for fast-approaching others. The lanes behind were clear and he had no trouble attaining the fourth lane of the five. Safer here. Plenty of room for feisty types to pass on either side and he could still maintain a decent speed without competing with dragsters. He pushed the J.J. up to an easy seventy-five miles per and settled back for the long drive.

He spotted only two wrecks as he sped smoothly through the Sepulveda pass — about normal for this early in the day. The helicrane crew were probably in the process of changing shifts, so these wrecks would lie a bit longer than at other, busier times of day.

His first view of action came as he approached the busy Wilshire on-ramps. Two compacts squared off awkwardly. The slow lane was occupied by a four-door Toyota. A Honda coupe, puffing mightily to build speed up the on-grade, came off the ramp at a bad position. It required one or the other to slow for a successful entrance and the sedan, having superior position, understandably refused to be the one. Instead of taking the quiet course, the Honda maintained its original approach speed and fired an unannounced broadside from its small — .25 cal., Frank judged — window-mounted swivel gun. The sedan swerved crazily for a moment as its driver, startled, lost control for a few seconds. Then it straightened out and regained its former attitude. Frank and the cars behind him slowed to give the combatants plenty of lane space in which to operate.

The armor glass was taking the attack and the sedan began to return fire — about equal, standard factory equipment, he guessed. They were already reaching the end of the entrance lane. Desperately, refusing to concede the match, the coupe cut sharply at the nose of the sedan. The sedan's owner swerved easily into the second lane and then cut tightly back. At this angle his starboard gun bore directly on the coupe. A loud bang heralded a shattered tire. With a short, almost slow-motion bump, the coupe hit the guard rail and flipped over out of sight. In his rearview mirror Frank could just make out the first few wisps of smoke as he shot past the spot.

Now that the fight was over, Frank floored the accelerator again, throwing the victorious driver a fast salute. It was returned gracefully. Considering his limited stuff, the fellow had done very well. He'd handled that figure C with ease, but the maneuver would have been useless against a larger car. Frank's own, for example. Still, compact drivers were a special breed and often made up for their lack of power, engine and fire in sheer guts. He still watched "Don Railman and his Supersub" religiously on the early Sunday Tele, even though the ratings were down badly from last season. He'd also never forget that time when a "Weekly Caripper's Telemanual" with old Ev Kelly had done a special on a hand-tooled Mighty Mite, low bore, cut down, with the Webcor antitank gun cleverly concealed in the front trunk. No, it paid not to take the compacts, even the subs, too lightly.

He passed the Santa Monica interchange without trouble. In fact, the only thing resembling a confrontation he had on the whole L.A. portion of the drive occurred a few minutes later as he swept past the Los Angeles Sub-International Airport rampings.

A new Vet, all shiny and gold, blasted up behind him. It stayed there, tailgating. That in itself was a fighting provocation. He could see the driver clearly — a young girl, probably in her late teens. About Bob's age, he thought tightly. No doubt Daddy dear had bought the bomb for her. She honked at him sharply, insistently. He ignored her. She could pass him to either side with ease. Instead she fired a low burst of tracers across his rear deck. When he resolutely continued to ignore her she pouted, then pulled alongside. Giggling, she drew him an obscene gesture which even his not-so-archaic mind could identify. He jerked hard on the wheel, then back. Her haughty expression disappeared instantly, to be replaced by one of fright. When she saw it was merely a feint on his part, she smiled again, although much less arrogantly, and shot ahead at a good hundred miles per.

Stupid kid better watch her manners, never live to make 20,000 miles. Maybe he should have given her a lesson, burnt off a tire, perhaps. Oh, well. He had a long way to drive. Let someone else play teacher.

He became quiet and watchful as he left Santa Ana and entered the Irvine area. There was little commuter traffic here and only a few harmless beachers this early in the day. He saw only one car in the Cad's class and that was an old yellow Thunderhood. Wasn't sure whether or not to be disappointed or relieved as he pulled into the San Clemente rest stop for breakfast. He could have eaten at home but preferred to slip out without waking Myrtle. He'd have a couple of eggs, some toast and jam, and enjoy a view of the Pacific along with his coffee, despite the low clouds which had been rolling in for the last twenty minutes. He hoped it wouldn't rain, even though rain would cut the heat. Weather was one reason he always avoided the safer but longer desert routes. Thundershowers inland were forecast and even the best tactical driver could be outmatched in a heavy downpour. He preferred to be in a situation where his talents could operate without complications wished on him by nature.

A few warm drops, fat and heavy, hit him as he left the diner. It had grown much darker and the humidity was fierce. Still, Irvine was behind him now. Best to make speed down to Diego and get home before dark.

He had only the well-policed Camp Pendleton lanes ahead and then the near-deserted Oceanside-to-La-Jolla run before he'd hit any real traffic again. Contrary to early predictions, the California population had spread inland instead of along the largely state-owned coast. If he'd had sense to buy that hundred acres near Mojave before the airport had gone in there . . .

On the left he could see the old Presidential Palace shining on its solitary hill. He waved nostalgically, then speeded up slightly as he approached the Pendleton cutoff.

The drizzle remained so light he didn't even bother with wipers. Pendleton was passed quickly and he had no reason to stop in Oceanside. Soon he was cruising among rolling, downy hills, mellow in the diffused sunlight. A few cattle were the only living creatures in evidence, along with a few big crows circling lazily overhead in the moist air. Once a cycle pack roared noisily past, long twenties damp with dew. Two tricycles headed up the front and rear of the pack, but the ugly snouts of their recoilless rifles were covered against a possible downpour. They took no notice of him, rumbling past at a solid ninety-five miles an hour. He had no wish to tangle with a gang, not in this empty territory. A good driver could knock out three or four of the big Harley-Davidsons and Yamahas easily enough, but the highly maneuverable bikes could swarm over anything smaller than a bus or trailer with ease, magnifying the effect of their light weaponry.

Maybe he could buy some land out here. He gazed absently at the green-and-gold hills, devoid of housing tracts and supermarkets. Not another Mojave, maybe, but still . . .

A sharp honking snapped his attention reflexively to his mirrors. He recognized the license of the big black coupe almost at the instant he identified the make and model. You're south of your territory, fella, he thought grimly. His hands clenched tightly on the wheel as he slid over one lane.

The Cad pulled up beside him, preparatory to passing. He judged the moment precisely, then tripped a switch on his center console. The portside flame thrower erupted in a jet of orange flame. The Cad jerked like a singed kitten. Instantly Frank cut over to the far lane, putting as much distance as possible between him and the big car, staying slightly ahead of the other.

A long dark streak showed clearly on the coupe's front, a deep gash in the tire material. The Cad would have trouble if it tried any sharp moves in his direction now and Frank saw no problem in holding his present position. Now he could duck at the first off-ramp if need arose. He activated the roof turret, an expensive option, but one which had proven its worth time and again. Myrtle had opted for the big grenade launcher, but Frank and the GM salesman had convinced her that while showiness might be fine for impressing the neighbors, on the road it was performance that counted. The twin fifties in the turret commenced hammering away at the Cad, nicking big chips of armorglass and battle sheathing from its front.

Frank was feeling confident until a violent explosion rocked him nastily and forced him to throw emergency power to the steering. Frightened, he glanced over his shoulder. Thank God for the automatic sprinklers! The rear of the car above the left wheel was completely gone, as was most of the rear deck. Twisted, blackened metal and torn insulation smoked and groaned. A look at the Cad confirmed his worst fears and sent more sweat pouring down his shirt collar. No wonder this Marauder had acquired such a reputation! In place of the standard, heavy Cad machine guns, a Mark IV rocket launcher protruded from the rear trunk! Fortunately the shot had hit at a bad angle or he'd be missing a wheel and his ability to maneuver would have been drastically, perhaps fatally, reduced. He did an S just in time. Another rocket shrieked past his bumper.

The turret fifties were doing their job, but it was slow, too slow! Another rocket strike would finish him and now the Cad had its big guns going, too. He wished to hell he was in the cab of a big United Truckers tractor-trailer, high above the concrete, with another driver and a gunner on the twin 60mm's. A crack appeared in his rear window as the Cad's guns concentrated their fire. He turned and twisted, accelerated and slowed, not daring to give his opponent another clear shot with those Mark IVs.

Chance time, Frank, baby. Remember Salt Lake City!

He cut hard left. The Cad cut right to get behind him. At the proper (yes, yes!) second he dropped an emergency switch.

The rear back-up lights dropped off the J.J. At the same time a violent *crrumpp!* threw him forward so hard he could feel the cross-harness bite into his chest. Fighting desperately for control and cursing all the way, he slammed into the resilient center divider with a jolt that rattled his teeth, two wheels spinning crazily off the pavement, then cut all the way back across the five lanes. Fighting a busted something all the way, he managed to wrestle the battered sedan to a tired halt on the gravel shoulder.

Panting heavily, he undid the safety harness, staggered out of the car, bracing himself against the metal sides. Behind him, a quarter mile or so down the empty road, a thick plume of roiling black smoke billowed up from a pile of twisted metal, plastics, and ceramics, all intertwined with bright orange flame. The big bad black Cad was quite finished. He took one step in its direction, then stopped, dizzied by the effort. No driver could survive that inferno. In his eagerness to get behind the sedan, the Cad's driver had shot over at least one, possibly both of the proximity mines Frank had released from where his back-up lights had been. Maybe revenge was an outdated commodity today, but he still felt exhilarated. And Myrtle might complain initially but he knew damn well she'd be pleased inside.

He became aware of something wet trickling down his cheek, more than could have come from the sporadically dripping sky. His hand told him a piece of his left ear was missing. The blood was staining his good driving blouse. Absently he dabbed at the nick with a handkerchief. His rear glass must have gone at the last possible minute. A look confirmed it, showing two neat holes and a third questionable one in his rear window. Umm. He'd had closer calls before — and this one was worth it. At least there'd be one license plate to lay on Bob's grave.

He sighed. Better stop off in Carlsbad and get that ear taken care of. Damnation, if only that boy had paid some attention in Driver's Ed. Eighteen years old and he'd never learned what his old man had known for years.

Be Safe. Drive Offensively.

B

bi/on/ic per/sons — people who have had substantial parts of their bodies replaced by specially engineered devices like artificial organs and mechanical limbs. Such individuals are sometimes called "cyborgs." Even something as small as a pacemaker implanted in the heart can be considered a bionic device. The term was made famous by the television series "The Bionic Man" and "The Bionic Woman." Bionic persons have long been featured in science fiction, and stories about them can be found in *Human-Machines* (Vintage Books, 1975).

Man in a Quandary

L. J. STECHER, JR.

Dear Miss Dix VI:

I have a problem. In spite of rumors to the contrary, my parents were properly married and were perfectly normal people at the time I was born. And so was I — normal, I mean. But that all contributed to the creation of my problem.

I do not know if you can help me resolve it, but you have helped so many others that I am willing to try you. I enjoin you not to answer this letter·in your column; write me privately, please.

You know all about me, of course. Who doesn't? But most of what you know about me is bound to be almost entirely wrong. So I will have to clarify my background before I present my problem.

Know, then, that I am Alfred the Magnificent. It surprises you, I imagine, that I would be writing a letter to Miss Dix VI. After all, in spite of the tax rate, I am one of the richest — I will say it! — one of the richest *men* in the world.

Every word of that last statement is true. My parents were enormously wealthy, but I have accumulated even more of the world's goods than they ever did. And if they had not been loaded with loot, I would not be here now to be writing this letter to you.

Please excuse any lack of smoothness in the style and execution of this letter. I'm doing this all myself. Usually I dictate to a secretary — a live secretary — but you understand that that would not be advisable for a letter of this kind, I'm sure.

So. My background. I was born in 2352 and, having passed my infantile I.Q. test with flying colors, was admitted to the Harvard Crèche for Superior Children at the usual age of three months.

The name of Alfred Vanderform naturally had been entered on the rolls much earlier. Ten years earlier, in point of fact. My parents had been fortunate enough to be selected to have three children, and I was to be their first. They chose to begin with a son. They had known that they would be chosen and that I would be a superior child, and had taken the wise precaution of signing me up for Harvard Crèche as soon as the planners had finished drawing up their preliminary charts.

In spite of what you may have heard, there was absolutely no chance of falsifying the initial I.Q. examination; in those days, at least. I was a physically normal, mentally superior child. My progress at the crèche was entirely satisfactory. I was an ordinarily above-average genius in every way.

At age six, I left the crèche for my sabbatical year at home with my parents, and it was there that my first disaster occurred.

My mother and father moved into the same house while I was there, which was the custom then (and may still be, for all I know) in order to provide a proper homelike atmosphere for me. Through some carelessness in original planning, this was also the year that had been selected for the birth of their second child, which was to be a girl. Both parents were to be the same for all three of their children. Under usual circumstances, they would have paid enough attention to me so that the disaster would never have been allowed to take place, but plans for their second child must have made them a trifle careless.

At any rate, in spite of my early age, an embolism somehow developed and major damage to my heart resulted. It was here that the great wealth of my parents proved invaluable.

Prognosis was entirely unfavorable for me. The routine procedure for a three-offspring couple would have been to cancel the unsuccessful quota and reissue it for immediate production. However, it was too late to arrange for twins in their second quota and my parents decided to attempt to salvage me.

An artificial heart was prepared and substituted for the original. It had a built-in atomic battery which would require renovation no oftener than every twenty years. Voluntary control was provided through connection with certain muscles in my neck, and I soon learned to operate it at least as efficiently as a normal heart with the normal involuntary controls.

The mechanism was considerably bigger than the natural organ, but the salvage operation was a complete success. The bulge between my shoulder blades for the battery and the one in front of my chest for the pump were not excessively unsightly. I entered the Princeton Second Stage Crèche for Greatly Superior Children on time, being accepted without objection in spite of my pseudo deformity.

It cannot be proved that any special emolument was offered to or accepted by the crèche managers in order to secure my acceptance. My personal belief is that nobody had to cough up.

Three years at Princeton passed relatively uneventfully for me. In spite of the best efforts and assurances of the crèche psychologists, there was naturally a certain lack of initial acceptance of me by some of my crèche mates. However, they soon became accustomed to my fore-and-aft bulges, and since I had greater endurance than they, with voluntary control over my artificial heart, I eventually gained acceptance and even a considerable measure of leadership — insofar as leadership by an individual is possible in a crèche.

Shortly after the beginning of my fourth year at the Princeton Crèche, the second great personal disaster struck.

Somehow or other — the cause has not been determined to this day — my artificial heart went on the blink. I did not quite die immediately, but the prognosis was once again entirely unfavorable. Considerable damage had somehow eventuated to my lungs, my liver, and my kidneys. I was a mess.

By this time, my parents had made such a huge investment in me, and my progress reports had been so uniformly excellent, that in spite of all the advice from the doctors, they determined to attempt salvage again.

A complete repackaging job was decided upon. Blood was to be received, aerated, purified, and pumped back to the arterial system through a single mechanism which would weigh only about thirty-five pounds. Of course, this made portability an important factor. Remember that I was only ten years old. I could probably have carried such a weight around on my back, but I could never have engaged in the proper development of my whole body and thus could never have been accepted back again by Princeton.

It was therefore determined to put the machinery into a sort of cart, which I would tow around behind me. Wheels were quickly rejected as being entirely unsatisfactory. They would excessively inhibit jumping, climbing, and many other boyish activities.

The manufacturers finally decided to provide the cart with a pair of legs.

This necessitated additional machinery and added about twenty-five pounds to the weight of the finished product. They solved the problem of how I would handle the thing with great ingenuity by making the primary control involuntary. They provided a connection with my spinal cord so that the posterior pair of legs, unless I consciously ordered otherwise, always followed in the footsteps of the anterior pair. If I ran, they ran. If I jumped, they jumped.

In order to make the connection to my body, the manufacturers removed my coccyx and plugged in at and around the end of my spinal column. In other words, I had a very long and rather flexible tail, at the end of which was a smoothly streamlined flesh-colored box that followed me around on its own two legs.

A human has certain normally atrophied muscles for control of his usually nonexistent tail. Through surgery and training, those muscles became my voluntary controllers for my tail and the cart. That is, I could go around waggin' my tail while draggin' my wagon.

Pardon me, Miss Dix VI. That just slipped out.

Well, the thing actually worked. You should have seen me in a high-hurdle race — me running along and jumping over the hurdles, with that contraption galloping along right behind me, clearing every hurdle I cleared. I kept enough slack in my tail so I wouldn't get pulled up short, and then just forgot about it.

Going off a diving board was a little bit different. I learned to do things like that with my back legs under voluntary control.

Speaking of diving boards, maybe you wonder how I could swim while towing a trailer. No trouble at all. I would just put my tail between my legs and have my cart grab me around the waist with a kind of body scissors. The cart's flexible air sac was on its top when it was in normal position, so this held it away from my body, where it would not get squeezed. I would take in just enough air so that it was neutrally buoyant, and with its streamlined shape, it didn't slow me down enough to notice.

I usually "breathed" — or took in my air — through the intakes of the cart, and they stayed under water, but there was an air connection through my tail up to the lung cavity anyway, allowing me to talk. So I just breathed through my mouth in the old-fashioned way.

Backing up was rather a problem, with my posterior legs leading the way, and dancing was nearly impossible until I got the idea of having my trailer climb up out of the way onto my shoulders while I danced. That got me by Princeton's requirements, but I must confess that I was never very much in demand as a dancing partner.

At any rate, that system got me through to my sixth and last year at Princeton. I sometimes believe that I may be considered to be what is occasionally called an "accident-prone." I seem to have had more than my share of tough luck. During my last year at Princeton, I got my throat cut.

It was an accident, of course. No Princeton man would ever dream of doing away with someone he had taken a dislike to quite so crudely. Or messily.

By voluntary control of my heart, I slowed the action down to the point where I managed to keep from bleeding to death, but my larynx was destroyed beyond repair. That was when I got my Voder installation. It fitted neatly where my lungs used to be, and because it used the same resonant cavities, I soon learned to imitate my own voice well enough so that nobody could tell the difference, "before" or "after."

Actually, it was a minor accident, but I thought I'd mention it because of what the news media sometimes call my "inhuman voice." It even enables me to sing, something I never was much good at before that accident. Also, I could imitate a banjo and sing at the same time, a talent that made me popular at picnics.

That was the last real accident I had for quite a while. I got through my second (and last) home sabbatical, my Upper School, my First College, and my Second College. I was chosen for, and got through, Advanced College with highest honors. Counting sabbaticals, that took a total of twenty-nine years, plus the last of my time at Princeton. And then, an eager youth of forty-two, I was on my own — ready to make my way in the world.

I was smart to avoid the government service that catches so many of us so-called super-geniuses. It's very satisfying work and all that, I suppose, but there's no money in it, and I was rich enough to want to get richer.

The cart containing my organs didn't get in my way too much. With my athletic days behind me, I taught it to come to heel instead of striding along behind me. It was less efficient, but it was a lot less conspicuous. I had a second involuntary control system built in so it would stay at heel without conscious thought on my part, once I put it there.

In my office, I would have it curl up at my feet like a sleeping dog. People told me it was hardly noticeable — even people who didn't work for me. It certainly didn't bother me or hold me back. I started to make money as though I had my own printing press, and managed to hang on to most of it.

In spite of what the doom-criers say, as long as there is an element of freedom in this country — and I think there always will be — there will be ways, and I mean legal ways, of coming into large hunks of cash. Within ten years, I was not only Big Rich, I was one of the most important people in the world. A Policy Maker. A Power.

It was about that time that I drank the bottle of acid.

Nobody was trying to poison me. I wasn't trying to kill myself, either. Not even subconsciously. I was just thirsty. All I can say is I did a first-rate job with what was left of my insides.

Well, they salvaged me again, and what I ended up with was a pair of carts, one trotting along beside each heel. The leash for the second one was plugged into me in front instead of in the back, naturally, but with my clothes on, nobody could tell, just by looking, that they were attached to me at all.

The doctors offered to get me by without the second trailer. They figured they could prepare predigested food and introduce it into my blood stream through the mechanism of my original wagon. I refused to let them; I had gotten too used to eating.

So whatever I ate was ground up and pumped into my new trailer — or should it be "preceder"? There it would be processed and the nutriments passed into my blood stream as required. I couldn't overeat if I tried. It was all automatic, not even hooked into my nervous system. Unusable products were compressed and neatly packaged for disposal at any convenient time. In cellophane. There was, of course, interconnection inside of me between the two carts.

I'm told I started quite a fad for walking dogs in pairs. It didn't affect me at all. I never got very good at voluntary control of my second trailer, but by that time my habit patterns were such that I hardly noticed it.

Oh, yes — about swimming. I still enjoyed swimming and I worked it out this way: Wagon number two replaced number one in straddling me, and wagon number one hung on to number two. It slowed me down, but it still let me swim. I quit diving. I couldn't spare the time to figure out how to manage it.

That took care of the next five years. I kept on getting richer. I was a happy man. Then came the crowning blow. What was left of me developed cancer.

It attacked my brain, among other things. And it was inoperable. It looked as if I had only a couple of years before deterioration of my mental powers set in, and then it would be the scrap heap for me.

But I didn't give up. By that time, I had gotten used to the parts-replacement program. And I was very rich. So I told them to get busy and build me an artificial brain as good as my own.

They didn't have time to make a neat package job this time. They took over three big buildings in the center of town and filled them with electronics. You should see the cable conduits connecting those buildings! Then they bought the Broadway Power Plant and used most of its output. They ran in new water mains to provide the coolant.

They used most of my money, and it took all of my influence to speed things up, but they got the job done in time.

It won't do you any good to ask me how they transferred my memories and my personality to that mass of tubes and wires and tapes and transistors. I don't know. They tell me that it was the easiest part of the job, and I know that they did it perfectly. My brain power and my personality came through unchanged. I used them to get rich again in mighty short order. I had to, to pay my water and power bills.

I came out of it "Alfred the Magnificent" and still I'm just as human as you are, even if a lot of people — a few billions of them, I guess — won't believe it. Granted, there isn't much of the Original Me left, but there's an old saying that Glands Make the Man. Underneath it all, I'm the same Alfred Vanderform, the same old ordinary super-genius that I have always been.

I have almost finished with the background material, Miss Dix VI, and am nearly ready to present you my problem. I am now approaching the age of sixty — and have therefore reached the time of Selection for Fatherhood. I have, in fact, been fortunate enough to be one of the few selected to father three children.

If you have chanced to hear rumors that money changed hands in getting me selected, let me tell you that they are entirely true. The only thing wrong about the rumors is that none of them has named a big enough amount — not nearly big enough. It isn't that I don't qualify by any honest evaluation. I do. But there has been a good deal of prejudice against me as a Father, and even some skepticism about my capability. But that doesn't matter; what does is that I *have* been selected.

What is more, a single superior female was chosen to be mother of all three of my children. By what is not at all a coincidence, this woman happens to be my private secretary. She is, I may add, very beautiful.

I am just old-fashioned enough to want my children to have all of the advantages that I had myself, including parents who are fully married, in the same way that my own mother and father were. Legal ceremony — religious service — everything!

So I have asked the chosen mother of my children-to-be to marry me, and Gloria — that's her name — has been gracious enough to accept. We are to be married week after next.

Now, Miss Dix VI, we come to my problem. How can I tell if Gloria is in love with me, or is just marrying me for my money?

> Perplexed,
> Alfred Vanderform
> (The Magnificent)

C

chil/dren — persons between infancy and puberty; the offspring of human beings. Some science fiction stories and novels are especially written for children, and children frequently play an important role in these works, as spectators, heroes/heroines, or as villains. *Children of Wonder* (Simon and Schuster, 1953), *Tomorrow's Children* (Doubleday, 1966), and *The Other Side of Tomorrow* (Random House, 1973) are three science fiction anthologies about children of the future.

The Cabbage Patch

THEODORE R. COGSWELL

Aunt Hester sent me to bed early that night. I lay quietly in the old four-poster, listening to the night sounds and the soft sleepy hisses as the narns who lived in the old fern tree underneath my window bedded themselves down in their holes. I was supposed to settle down too, but the tight, excited feeling inside my chest wouldn't go away. I pulled the soft down pillow over my head and tried to make everything black. I wanted to go to sleep right away so I could wake up in time to see the birth-fairy when she came down with my new sister.

Priscilla Winters said babies came from the cabbage patch but I knew better. She brought a cabbage to school one day to prove it, and that night when we were supposed to be asleep she opened it up and showed me a baby inside. It was squishy and white like all soon-babies are before they make the change, but I knew it wasn't a real baby because it didn't have any teeth. We made a birthing-box out of a jar and gave it some flies to eat but it wouldn't eat them, it just kept crawling around and waving its feelers as if it didn't like it there. When we woke up the next morning it had turned brown and was all dead.

The narns in the fern tree had stopped their whispering, but I still couldn't get to sleep. The little moon had chased the big one up over the horizon so far that its light was shining through the window right into my eyes. I got up and shut the blinds but even having the room dark again didn't help. I kept seeing pictures of the birth-fairy fluttering down like a beautiful butterfly, and then, after she'd put the babies safe in their birthing-box, flying off again with the year-father soaring after her on his fine new wings.

I wanted to see his wings but Mother wouldn't let me. For two months now she had kept him shut up in his room and she wouldn't even let me speak to him through the door. I wanted to say good-bye to him because, even if he was only a year-father, he'd been nice to me. I was never supposed to be with him unless Mother or Aunt Hester were around, but sometimes I'd slip into the kitchen when they were away and we'd talk about things. I liked being with him best when he was baking preska because he'd give me bits of the dough and let me make funny things out of them.

Once Aunt Hester caught me alone with him and her face got all hard and twisted and she was going to call the patrol and have him beaten, but Mother came in just then. She sent the year-father to his room and then took me into the parlor. I knew that she was getting ready for one of her heart-to-heart talks but there wasn't anything I could do about it, so I just sat there and listened. Mother's talks always got so wound in on themselves that when she was through I usually couldn't figure out what all the fuss had been about.

First she asked me if I'd felt anything funny when I was alone with the year-father. I asked her what she meant by "funny" and she sort of stuttered and her face got all red. Finally she asked me a funny question about my stinger and I said no. Then she started to tell me a story about the wasps and the meem but she didn't get very far with that either. She wanted to but she got all flustered and her tongue wouldn't work. Aunt Hester said nonsense, that I was still a little girl and next year would be soon enough. Mother said she wished she could be sure, then she made me promise that if ever my stinger felt funny when I was around a year-father, I'd run and tell her about it right away because if I didn't, something terrible might happen.

My pillow got all hot so I went and sat in my chair. The more I thought about the year-father, the more I wanted to go and see his new wings. Finally I went over to the door and listened. I could hear Mother and Aunt Hester talking in the front of the house so I tiptoed down the back stairs. When I got to the landing I stopped and felt around with my foot until I found the part of the next stair that was right against the railing. That's a bad stair because if you step in the middle of it without thinking, it gives a loud squeak that you can hear all over the house.

The year-father's room is right next to the kitchen. I gave a little scratch on the door so he would know who it was and not be frightened. I stood there in the dark waiting for him to open up but he didn't so I went inside and felt for him in his nest. He wasn't there.

First I thought maybe I should go back up and get in bed because Aunt Hester said that if she ever again caught me up at night when I was supposed to be sleeping, she'd give me a licking that I'd never forget. But then I started to think of what would happen to the year-father if he'd gone outside and the patrol caught him wandering around alone at night, and I decided that I'd better tell Mother right away, even if I did get a walloping afterward.

Then I thought that first I'd better look in the kitchen for him. It was dark in there too, so I shut the hall door and lit the lamp on the kitchen table. The stone floor was awfully cold on my feet and I began to wish that I'd remembered to put on my slippers before I came downstairs. Once my eyes got used to the light I looked all around, but the year-father wasn't there either. I was about to blow out the lamp and go and tell Mother when I heard a funny sound coming from the nursery.

I know it sounds funny to have a nursery in the kitchen, but since soon-babies have to be locked away in a dark place until it's time for them to make the change, Mother said we might as well use the old pantry instead of going to all the trouble of blacking out one of the rooms upstairs.

The big, thick door that Mother had put on was shut but she'd forgotten to take the key away so I went over and opened it a crack. I was real scared because at birthing time nobody is allowed to go in the nursery, not even Aunt Hester. Once the little ones are in the birthing-box, Mother locks the door and doesn't ever open it up again until after they've changed into real people like us.

At Priscilla's house they've got an honest-to-goodness nursery. There's a little window on the door that they uncover after the first month. It's awful dark inside but if you look real hard you can see the soon-babies crawling around inside. Priscilla let me look in once when her mother was downtown. They had big ugly mouths and teeth.

The sound came again so I opened the door. It was so dark inside that I couldn't see a thing so I went back and got the lamp. The noise seemed to be coming from the birthing-box so I went over and looked in. The year-father was hunched up in the bottom of it. He didn't have any wings.

He blinked up at me in the lantern light. He'd been crying and his face was all swollen. He motioned to me to go away but I couldn't. I'd never seen a father without his clothes on before and I kept staring and staring.

I knew that I should run and get Mother but somehow I couldn't move. Something terrible was happening to the year-father. His stomach was all swollen up and angry red, and every once in a while it would knot up and twist as if there were something inside that didn't like it there. When that would happen he'd roll his head back and bite down on his lower lip real hard. He seemed to want to yell but he'd choke it back until nothing came out but a little whimper.

There was a nasty half-healed place on his stomach that looked as if he'd fallen on a sharp stick and hurt himself real bad. He kept pushing his hands against it as if he was trying to hold back something that was inside trying to get out.

I heard Mother's voice calling from the kitchen and then Aunt Hester's voice saying something real sharp but I couldn't look up or answer. Blood was trickling out through the year-father's locked fingers. Suddenly he emptied out in a raw scream and fell back so limp that it looked as if all his bones were gone. His hands dropped away and from inside his stomach something tore at the half-healed place until it split and opened like a big mouth. Then I could see the something. I knew it for what it was and I felt sick and scared in a different sort of way. It inched its way out and wiggled around kind of lost-like, until it finally lost its balance and fell to the bottom of the box. It didn't move for a minute and I thought maybe it was dead, but then the feelers around its mouth began to reach out as if they were trying to find something. And then all of a sudden it started a fast wabbly crawl as if it knew just where it was going. I saw teeth as it found the year-father and nuzzled up to him. It was hungry.

Aunt Hester slammed and locked the pantry door. Then she made me a glass of hot milk and sent me up to bed. Mother came in to my room a little later and stood by my bed, looking down at me to see if I was asleep. I pretended I was because I didn't want to talk to her, and she finally left. I wanted to cry but I couldn't because if I did she'd hear me and come back up again. I pulled the pillow down over my face real tight until I could hardly breathe and there were little red flashes of light in the back of my eyes and a humming, hive sound in my head. I knew what my stinger was for and I didn't want to think about it.

When I did get to sleep I didn't dream about the year-father, I dreamed about the wasps and the meem.

cit/ies — places where a substantial number of human beings live. Cities are closely associated with the development of irrigation, which made farming possible. Today, a large proportion of the world's population lives in and around cities. The process of moving from the countryside to cities is called urbanization. Spectacular cities — some technological wonders, other menacing places — occur frequently in science fiction. Future cities have provided the theme for at least four anthologies — *Cities of Wonder* (Doubleday, 1966); *Future City* (Trident Press, 1973); *Hot and Cold Running Cities* (Holt, Rinehart and Winston, 1974); and *The City: 2000*A.D. (Fawcett Crest, 1976).

A Touch of Grapefruit

RICHARD MATHESON

THESIS SUBMITTED AS PARTIAL REQUIREMENT
FOR MASTER OF ARTS DEGREE

The phenomenon known in scientific circles as the Los Angeles Movement came to light in the year 2002 when Dr. Albert Grimsby, A.B., B.S., A.M., Ph.D., professor of physics at the California Institute of Technology, made an unusual discovery.

"I have made an unusual discovery," said Dr. Grimsby.
"What is that?" asked Dr. Maxwell.
"Los Angeles is alive."
Dr. Maxwell blinked.
"I beg your pardon," he said.
"I can understand your incredulity," said Dr. Grimsby. "Nevertheless . . . "
He drew Dr. Maxwell to the laboratory bench.
"Look into this microscope," he said, "under which I have isolated a piece of Los Angeles."
Dr. Maxwell looked. He raised his head, a look of astonishment on his face.
"It moves," he said.

This was first published under the title *The Creeping Terror*.

Having made this strange discovery, Dr. Grimsby, oddly enough, saw fit to promulgate it only in the smallest degree. It appeared as a one-paragraph item in the *Science News Letter* of June 2, 2002, under the heading: CAL-TECH PHYSICIST FINDS SIGNS OF LIFE IN L.A.

Perhaps due to unfortunate phrasing, perhaps to normal lack of interest, the item aroused neither attention nor comment. This unfortunate negligence proved ever after a plague to the man originally responsible for it. In later years it became known as "Grimsby's Blunder."

Thus was introduced to a then unresponsive nation a phenomenon that was to become in the following years a most shocking threat to that nation's very existence.

Of late, researchers have discovered that knowledge concerning the Los Angeles Movement predates Dr. Grimsby's find by years. Indeed, hints of this frightening crisis are to be found in works published as much as fifteen years prior to the ill-fated "Cal-Tech Disclosure."

Concerning Los Angeles, the distinguished journalist John Gunther wrote: "What distinguishes it is . . . its octopuslike growth."[1]

Yet another reference to Los Angeles mentions that: "In its amoebalike growth it has spread in all directions . . ."[2]

Thus can be seen primitive approaches to the phenomenon that are as perceptive as they are unaware. Although there is no present evidence to indicate that any person during that early period actually knew of the fantastic process, there can hardly be any doubt that many *sensed* it, if only imperfectly.

Active speculation regarding freakish nature behavior began in July and August of 2002. During a period of approximately forty-seven days, the states of Arizona and Utah in their entirety and great portions of New Mexico and lower Colorado were inundated by rains that frequently bettered the five-inch mark.

Such water-fall in previously arid sections aroused great agitation and discussion. First theories placed responsibility for this uncommon rainfall on previous southwestern atomic tests.[3] Government disclaiming of this possibility seemed to increase rather than eliminate mass credulity of this later disproved supposition.

Other "precipitation postulations" — as they were then known in investigative parlance — can be safely relegated to the category of "crackpotia."[4] These include theories that excess commercial airflights were upsetting the

1. John Gunther, *Inside U.S.A.,* p. 44.
2. Henry G. Alsberg ed., *The American Guide,* p. 1200.
3. Symmes Chadwick, "Will We Drown the World?" *Southwestern Review 4* (Summer 2002): 698 ff.
4. Guillaume Gaulte, "Les Théories de l'Eau de Ciel Sont Cuckoo," *Jaune Journale,* August 2002.

natural balance of the clouds, that deranged Indian rainmakers had unwittingly come upon some lethal condensation factor and were applying it beyond all sanity, that strange frost from outer space was seeding Earth's overhead and causing this inordinate precipitation.

And, as seems an inevitable concomitant to all alien deportment in nature, hypotheses were propounded that this heavy rainfall presaged Deluge II. It is clearly recorded that several minor religious groups began hasty construction of "salvation arks." One of these arks can still be seen on the outskirts of the small town of Dry Rot, New Mexico, built on a small hill, "still waiting for the flood."[5]

Then came that memorable day when the name of farmer Cyrus Mills became a household word.

"Tarnation!" said Farmer Mills.
He gaped in rustic amazement at the object he had come across in his corn field. He approached it cautiously. He prodded it with a sausage finger.
"Tarnation," he repeated, less volubly.
Jason Gullwhistle of the *United States Experimental Farm Station No. 3,* Nebraska, drove his station wagon out to Farmer Mills's farm in answer to an urgent phone call. Farmer Mills took Mr. Gullwhistle out to the object.
"That's odd," said Jason Gullwhistle. "It looks like an orange tree."
Close investigation revealed the truth of this remark. It was indeed an orange tree.
"Incredible," said Jason Gullwhistle. "An orange tree in the middle of a Nebraska corn field. I never."
Later they returned to the house for a lemonade and there found Mrs. Mills in halter and shorts, wearing sunglasses and an old chewed-up fur jacket she had exhumed from her crumbling hope chest.
"Think I'll drive into Hollywood," said Mrs. Mills, sixty-five if she was a day.

By nightfall every wire service had embraced the item, every paper of any prominence whatever had featured it as a humorous insertion on page one.

Within a week, however, the humor had vanished as reports came pouring in from every corner of the state of Nebraska, as well as portions of Iowa, Kansas and Colorado: reports of citrus trees discovered in corn and wheat fields as well as more alarming reports relative to eccentric behavior in the rural populace.

Addiction to the wearing of scanty apparel became noticeable, an inexplicable rise in the sales of frozen orange juice manifested itself, and oddly similar letters were received by dozens of chambers of commerce: letters which heatedly demanded the immediate construction of motor speedways, supermarkets, tennis courts, drive-in theaters and drive-in restaurants, and which complained of smog.

5. Harry L. Schuler, "Not Long for This World," *South Orange Literary Review 40* (September 2002): 214.

But it was not until a marked increase in daily temperatures and an equally marked increase of unfathomable citrus tree growth began to imperil the corn and wheat crop that serious action was taken. Local farm groups organized spraying operations but to little or no avail. Orange, lemon, and grapefruit trees continued to flourish in geometric proliferation and a nation, at long last, became alarmed.

A seminar of the country's top scientists met in Ragweed, Nebraska, the geographical center of this multiplying plague, to discuss possibilities.

"Dynamic tremors in the alluvial substrata," said Dr. Kenneth Loam of the University of Denver.

"Mass chemical disorder in soil composition," said Spencer Smith of the Dupont Laboratories.

"Momentous gene mutation in the corn seed," said Professor Jeremy Brass of Kansas College.

"Violent contraction of the atmospheric dome," said Professor Lawson Hinkson of M.I.T.

"Displacement of orbit," said Roger Cosmos of the Hayden Planetarium.

"I'm scared," said a little man from Purdue.

What positive results emerged from this body of speculative genius is yet to be appraised. History records that a closer labeling of the cause of this unusual behavior in nature and man occurred in early October of 2002 when Associate Professor David Silver, a young research physicist at the University of Missouri, published in *The Scientific American* an article entitled "The Collecting of Evidences."

In this brilliant essay, Professor Silver first voiced the opinion that all the apparently disconnected occurrences were, in actuality, superficial revelations of one underlying phenomenon. To the moment of this article, scant attention had been paid to the erratic behavior of people in the affected areas. Professor Silver attributed this behavior to the same cause which had effected the alien growth of citrus trees.

The final deductive link was forged, oddly enough, in a Sunday supplement of the now defunct Hearst newspaper syndicate.[6] The author of this piece, a professional article-writer, in doing research for an article stumbled across the paragraph recounting Dr. Grimsby's discovery. Seeing in this a most salable feature, he wrote an article combining the theses of Dr. Grimsby and Professor Silver and emerging with his own amateur concept which, strange to say, was absolutely correct. (This fact was later obscured in the severe litigation that arose when Professors Grimsby and Silver brought suit against the author for not consulting them before writing the article.)

Thus did it finally become known that Los Angeles, like some gigantic fungus, was overgrowing the land.

6. H. Braham, "Is Los Angeles Alive?" *Los Angeles Sunday Examiner,* October 29, 2002.

A period of gestation followed, during which various publications in the country slowly built up the import of the Los Angeles Movement until it became a national byword. It was during this period that a fertile-minded columnist dubbed Los Angeles "Ellie, the meandering metropolis," a title later reduced merely to "Ellie" — a term which became as common to the American mind as "ham and eggs" or "World War II."

Now began a cycle of data collection and an attempt by various of the prominent sciences to analyze the Los Angeles Movement with a regard to arresting its strange pilgrimage which had now spread into parts of South Dakota, Missouri, Arkansas, and as far as the sovereign state of Texas. (To the mass convulsion this caused in the Lone Star State a separate paper might be devoted.)

REPUBLICANS DEMAND FULL INVESTIGATION

Claim L.A. Movement Subversive Camouflage

After a hasty dispatch of agents to all points in the infected area, the American Medical Association promulgated throughout the nation a list of symptoms by which all inhabitants might be forewarned of the approaching terror.

SYMPTOMS OF "ELLIEITIS"[7]

1. An unnatural craving for any of the citrus fruits, whether in solid or liquid form.
2. Partial or complete loss of geographical distinction. (I.e., a person in Kansas City might speak of driving down to San Diego for the weekend.)
3. An unnatural desire to possess a motor vehicle.
4. An unnatural appetite for motion pictures and motion picture previews. (Including a subsidiary symptom, not all-inclusive but nevertheless a distinct menace. This is the insatiable hunger of young girls to become movie stars.)
5. A taste for weird apparel. (Including fur jackets, shorts, halters, slacks, sandals, blue jeans, and bathing suits — all usually of excessive color.)

This list, unfortunately, proved most inadequate for its avowed purpose. It did not mention, for one thing, the adverse effect of excess sunlight on residents of the northern states. With the expected approach of winter being forestalled indefinitely, numerous unfortunates, unable to adjust to this alteration, became neurotic and often lost their senses completely.

The story of Matchbox, North Dakota, a small town in the northernmost part of that state, is typical of accounts which flourished throughout the late fall and winter of 2002.

7. *Ellieitis: Its Symptoms,* A.M.A. pamphlet, Fall 2002.

The citizens of this ill-fated town went berserk to a man waiting for the snow and, eventually running amuck, burned their village to the ground.

The pamphlet also failed to mention the psychological phenomenon known later as "Beach Seeking,"[8] a delusion under which masses of people, wearing bathing suits and carrying towels and blankets, wandered helplessly across the plains and prairies searching for the Pacific Ocean.

In October, the Los Angeles Movement (the process was given this more staid title in late September by Professor Augustus Wrench in a paper sent to the National Council of American Scientists) picked up momentum and, in a space of ten days, had engulfed Arkansas, Missouri, and Minnesota and was creeping rapidly into the borderlands of Illinois, Wisconsin, Tennessee, Mississippi, and Louisiana. Smog drifted across the nation.

Up to this point, citizens on the East Coast had been interested in the phenomenon but not overly perturbed since distance from the diseased territory had lent detachment. Now, however, as the Los Angeles city limits stalked closer and closer to them, the coastal region became alarmed.

Legislative activity in Washington was virtually terminated as congressmen were inundated with letters of protest and demand. A special committee, heretofore burdened by general public apathy in the East, now became enlarged by the added membership of several distinguished congressmen, and a costly probe into the problem ensued.

It was this committee that, during the course of its televised hearings, unearthed a secret group known as the L.A. Firsters.

This insidious organization seemed to have sprung almost spontaneously from the general chaos of the Los Angeles envelopment. General credence was given for a short time that it was another symptom of "Ellieitis." Intense interrogation, however, revealed the existence of L.A. Firster cells in East Coast cities that could not possibly have been subject to the dread virus at that point.

This revelation struck terror into the heart of a nation. The presence of such calculated subversion in this moment of trial almost unnerved the national will. For it was not merely an organization loosely joined by emotional binds. This faction possessed a carefully wrought hierarchy of men and women which was plotting the overthrow of the national government. Nationwide distribution of literature had begun almost with the advent of the Los Angeles Movement. This literature, with the cunning of insurgent casuistry, painted a roseate picture of the future of — The United States of Los Angeles!

8. Fritz Felix DerKatt, "Das Beachen Seeken," *Einzweidrei,* November 2002.

PEOPLE ARISE![9]

People arise! Cast off the shackles of reaction! What sense is there in opposing the march of PROGRESS! It is inevitable! — and you the people of this glorious land — a land dearly bought with *your* blood and *your* tears — should realize that *Nature herself* supports the L.A. FIRSTERS!

How? — you ask. How does Nature support this glorious adventure? The question is simple enough to answer.

NATURE HAS SUPPORTED THE L.A. FIRSTER MOVEMENT FOR THE BETTERMENT OF YOU! AND *YOU!*

Here are a few facts:

In those states that have been blessed

1. Rheumatism has dropped 52%
2. Pneumonia has dropped 61%
3. Frostbite has *vanished*
4. Incidence of the COMMON COLD has dropped *73%!*

Is this bad news? Are these the changes brought about by anti-PROGRESS? NO!!!

Wherever Los Angeles has gone, the deserts have fled, adding millions of new fertile acres to our beloved land. Where once there was only sand and cactus and *bleached bones,* are now plants and trees and FLOWERS!

This pamphlet closed with a couplet that aroused a nation to fury:

Sing out O land, with flag unfurled!
Los Angeles! Tomorrow's World!

The exposure of the L.A. Firsters caused a tide of reaction to sweep the country. Rage became the keynote of this counterrevolution; rage at the subtlety with which the L.A. Firsters had distorted truth in their literature; rage at their arrogant assumption that the country would inevitably fall to Los Angeles.

Slogans of "Down with the L.A. Lovers!" and "Send Them Back Where They Came From!" rang throughout the land. A measure was forced through Congress and presidential signature outlawing the group and making membership in it the offense of treason. Rabid groups attached a rider to this measure which would have enforced the outlawry, seizure, and destruction of all tennis- and beach-supply manufacturing. Here, however, the N.A.M. stepped in to the scene and, through the judicious use of various pressure means, defeated the attempt.

Despite this quick retaliation, the L.A. Firsters continued underground and at least one fatality of its persistent agitation was the state of Missouri.

In some manner as yet undisclosed, the L.A. Firsters gained control of the state legislature and jockeyed through an amendment to the constitution of

9. *The Los Angeles Manifesto,* L.A. Firster Press, Winter 2002.

Missouri which was hastily ratified and made the Show-Me State the first
area in the country to legally make itself a part of Los Angeles County.

UTTER McKINLEY OPENS
FIVE NEW PARLORS
IN THE SOUTHWEST

In the succeeding months there emerged a notable upsurge in the production of automobiles, particularly those of the convertible variety. In those
states affected by the Los Angeles Movement, every citizen apparently had
acquired that symptom of "Ellieitis" known as *automania.* The car industry
entered accordingly upon a period of peak production, its factories turning
out automobiles twenty-four hours a day, seven days a week.

In conjunction with this increase in automotive fabrication, there began a
near maniacal splurge in the building of drive-in restaurants and theaters.
These sprang up with mushroomlike celerity through the western and midwestern United States, their planning going beyond all feasibility. Typical of
these thoughtless projects was the endeavor to hollow out a mountain and
convert it to a drive-in theater.[10]

As the month of December approached, the Los Angeles Movement engulfed Illinois, Wisconsin, Mississippi, half of Tennessee, and was lapping at
the shores of Indiana, Kentucky, and Alabama. (No mention will be made
of the profound effect this movement had on racial segregation in the South,
this subject demanding a complete investigation in itself.)

It was about this time that a wave of religious passion obsessed the nation.
As is the nature of the human mind suffering catastrophe, millions turned to
religion. Various cults had in this calamity grist for their metaphysical mills.

Typical of these were the San Bernardino Vine Worshipers, who claimed
Los Angeles to be the reincarnation of their deity Ochsalia — The Vine
Divine. The San Diego Sons of the Weed claimed in turn that Los Angeles
was a sister embodiment to their deity, which they claimed had been creeping
for three decades prior to the Los Angeles Movement.

Unfortunately for all concerned, a small fascistic clique began to usurp
control of many of these otherwise harmless cults, emphasizing dominance
through "power and energy." As a result, these religious bodies too often
degenerated into mere fronts for political cells which plotted the overthrow
of the government for purposes of self-aggrandizement. (Secret documents
discovered in later years revealed the intention of one perfidious brotherhood
of converting the Pentagon Building to an indoor race track.)

During a period beginning in September and extending for years, there also
ensued a studied expansion of the motion-picture industry. Various of the
major producers opened branch studios throughout the country (for example

10. L. Savage, "A Report on the Grand Teton Drive-In," *Fortune,* January 2003.

M.G.M. built one in Terre Haute, Paramount in Cincinnati, and Twentieth-Century Fox in Tulsa). The Screen Writer's Guild initiated branch offices in every large city and the term "Hollywood" became even more of a misnomer than it had previously been.

Motion-picture output more than quadrupled as theaters of all description were hastily erected everywhere west of the Mississippi, sometimes wall to wall for blocks.[11] These buildings were rarely well-constructed and often collapsed within weeks of their "grand openings."

Yet, in spite of the incredible number of theaters, motion pictures exceeded them in quantity (if not quality). It was in compensation for this economically dangerous situation that the studios inaugurated the expedient practice of burning films in order to maintain the stability of the price floor. This aroused great antipathy among the smaller studios that did not produce enough films to burn any.

Another liability involved in the production of motion pictures was the geometric increase in difficulties raised by small but voluble pressure groups.

One typical coterie was the Anti-Horse League of Dallas which put up strenuous opposition to the utilization of horses in films. This, plus the increasing incidence of car owning which had made horse breeding unprofitable, made the production of Western films (as they had been known) an impossible chore. Thus was it that the so-called Western gravitated rapidly toward the "drawing room" drama.

SECTION OF A TYPICAL SCREENPLAY[12]

Tex D'Urberville comes riding into Doomtown on the Colorado, his Jaguar raising a cloud of dust in the sleepy western town. He parks in front of the Golden Sovereign Saloon and steps out. He is a tall, rangy cowhand, impeccably attired in waistcoat and fawn-skin trousers with a ten-gallon hat, boots, and pearl-gray spats. A heavy sixgun is belted at his waist. He carries a gold-topped Malacca cane.

He enters the saloon and every man there scatters from the room, leaving only Tex and a scowling hulk of a man at the other end of the bar. This is Dirty Ned Updyke, local ruffian and gunman.

TEX *(Removing his white gloves and, pretending he does not see Dirty Ned, addressing the bartender):* Pour me a whisky and seltzer will you, Roger, there's a good fellow.

ROGER: Yes sir.

Dirty Ned scowls over his apéritif but does not dare to reach for his Webley Automatic which is concealed in a holster beneath his tweed jacket.

Now Tex D'Urberville allows his icy blue eyes to move slowly about the room until they rest on the craven features of Dirty Ned.

TEX: So . . . you're the beastly cad what shot my brother.

11. "Gulls Creek Gets Its Forty-Eighth Theater," *The Arkansas Post-Journal,* March 12, 2003.
12. Maxwell Brande, "Altercation at Deadwood Spa," Epigram Studios, April, 2003.

Instantly they draw their cane swords and, approaching, salute each other grimly.

An additional result not to be overlooked was the effect of increased film production on politics. The need for high-salaried workers such as writers, actors, directors, and plumbers was intense and this mass of *nouveau riche,* having come upon good times so relatively abruptly, acquired a definite guilt neurosis which resulted in their intensive participation in the so-called liberal and progressive groups. This swelling of radical activity did much to alter the course of American political history. (This subject being another which requires separate inquiry for a proper evaluation of its many and varied ramifications.)

Two other factors of this period which may be mentioned briefly are the increase in divorce due to the relaxation of divorce laws in every state affected by the Los Angeles Movement, and the slow but eventually complete bans placed upon tennis and beach supplies by a rabid but powerful group within the N.A.M. This ban led inexorably to a brief span of time which paralleled the so-called Prohibition period of the 1920s. During this infamous period, thrill seekers attended the many bootleg tennis courts throughout the country, which sprang up wherever perverse public demand made them profitable ventures for unscrupulous men.

In the first days of January of 2003 the Los Angeles Movement reached almost to the Atlantic shoreline. Panic spread through New England and the southern coastal region. The country and, ultimately, Washington reverberated with cries of *"Stop Los Angeles!"* and all processes of government ground to a virtual halt in the ensuing chaos. Law enforcement atrophied, crime waves spilled across the nation and conditions became so grave that even the outlawed L.A. Firsters held revival meetings in the streets.

On February 11, 2003, the Los Angeles Movement forded the Hudson River and invaded Manhattan Island. Flame-throwing tanks proved futile against the invincible flux. Within a week the subways were closed and car purchases had trebled.

By March 2003, the only unaltered states in the union were Maine, Vermont, New Hampshire, and Massachusetts. This was later explained by the lethargic adaptation of the fungi to the rocky New England soil and to the immediate inclement weather.

These northern states, cornered and helpless, resorted to extraordinary measures in a hopeless bid to ward off the awful encrustation. Several of them legalized the mercy killing of any person discovered to have acquired the taint of "Ellieitis." Newspaper reports of shootings, stabbings, poisonings, and strangulations became so common in those days of "The Last-Ditch Defense" that newspapers inaugurated a daily section of their contents to such reports.

> Boston, Mass. April 13, AP — Last rites were held today for Mr. Abner Scrounge, who was shot after being found in his garage attempting to remove the top of his Rolls Royce with a can opener.

The history of the gallant battle of Boston to retain its essential dignity would, alone, make up a large work. The story of how the intrepid citizens of this venerable city refused to surrender their rights, choosing mass suicide rather than submission, is a tale of enduring courage and majestic struggle against insurmountable odds.

What happened after the movement was contained within the boundaries of the United States (a name soon discarded) is data for another paper. A brief mention, however, may be made of the immense social endeavor which became known as the "Bacon and Waffles" movement, which sought to guarantee $250 per month for every person in Los Angeles over forty years of age.

With this incentive before the people, state legislatures were helpless before an avalanche of public demand and, within three years, the entire nation was a part of Los Angeles. The government seat was in Beverly Hills and ambassadors had been hastened to all foreign countries within a short period of time.

Ten years later, the North American continent fell and Los Angeles was creeping rapidly down the Isthmus of Panama.

Then came that ill-fated day in 2014.

> On the island of Pingo Pongo, Maona, daughter of Chief Luana, approached her father.
> "Omu la golu si mongo," she said.
> (Anyone for tennis?)
> Whereupon her father, having read the papers, speared her on the spot and ran screaming from the hut.

com/put/ers — immobile robots that compute, "think" logically, and corre-
late information provided them by human beings. We are currently living at
the dawn of the computer age, and these devices will certainly play a large
role in our lives in the coming decades. Computers are standard background
elements in many science fiction stories and also figure prominently in some,
either as dangerous to humankind or, less often, as a trusted "friend." Many
robot anthologies also contain stories about computers, including *Science
Fiction Thinking Machines* (Vanguard Press, 1953). An interesting specialized anthology is *Computers, Computers, Computers: In Fiction and in Verse*
(Elsevier/Nelson, 1977).

Answer

FREDRIC BROWN

Dwar Ev ceremoniously soldered the final connection with gold. The eyes of
a dozen television cameras watched him and the sub-ether bore throughout
the universe a dozen pictures of what he was doing.

He straightened and nodded to Dwar Reyn, then moved to a position
beside the switch that would complete the contact when he threw it. The
switch that would connect, all at once, all of the monster computing machines of all the populated planets in the universe — ninety-six billion planets
— into the supercircuit that would connect them all into one supercalculator,
one cybernetics machine that would combine all the knowledge of all the
galaxies.

Dwar Reyn spoke briefly to the watching and listening trillions. Then after
a moment's silence he said, "Now, Dwar Ev."

Dwar Ev threw the switch. There was a mighty hum, the surge of power
from ninety-six billion planets. Lights flashed and quieted along the miles-
long panel.

Dwar Ev stepped back and drew a deep breath. "The honor of asking the
first question is yours, Dwar Reyn."

"Thank you," said Dwar Reyn. "It shall be a question which no single
cybernetics machine has been able to answer."

He turned to face the machine. "Is there a God?"

The mighty voice answered without hesitation, without the clicking of a single relay.

"Yes, *now* there is a God."

Sudden fear flashed on the face of Dwar Ev. He leaped to grab the switch.

A bolt of lightning from the cloudless sky struck him down and fused the switch shut.

D

di/no/saurs — extinct reptiles of the Mesozoic era. Although usually pictured as huge, dinosaurs actually existed in all sizes. They are encountered in science fiction in time-travel stories, with people traveling back to hunt or study them. These "prehistoric" settings have provided some of the most interesting stories in science fiction. *The Science Fictional Dinosaur* (Avon Books, 1982) and *Dawn of Time* (Elsevier/Nelson, 1979) contain science fiction stories featuring these amazing creatures.

A Gun for Dinosaur

L. SPRAGUE DE CAMP

No, Mr. Seligman, I won't take you hunting late-Mesozoic dinosaur.

Why not? How much d'you weigh? A hundred and thirty? Let's see, that's under ten stone, which is my lower limit.

I'll take you to any period in the Cenozoic. I'll get you a shot at an entelodont or a titanothere or a uintathere. They've all got fine heads.

I'll even stretch a point and take you to the Pleistocene, where you can try for one of the mammoths or the mastodon.

I'll take you back to the Triassic where you can shoot one of the smaller ancestral dinosaur.

But I will not — will jolly well not — take you to the Jurassic or Cretaceous. You're just too small.

No offense, of course.

What's your weight got to do with it?

Look here, old boy, what did you think you were going to shoot them with? You hadn't thought, eh?

Well, sit there a minute . . . Here you are, my own private gun for that work, a Continental .600. Does look like a shotgun, doesn't it? But it's rifled, as you can see by looking through the barrels. Shoots a pair of .600 nitro express cartridges the size of bananas; weighs fourteen and a half pounds and has a muzzle energy of over seven thousand foot-pounds. Costs fourteen hundred and fifty dollars. Lot of money for a gun, what?

I have some spares I rent to the sahibs. Designed for knocking down elephant. Not just wounding them, knocking them base-over-apex. That's why they don't make guns like this in America, though I suppose they will if hunting parties keep going back in time through Prochaska's machine.

I've been guiding hunting parties for twenty years. Guided 'em in Africa until the game gave out there except on the preserves. That just about ended the world's real big-game hunting.

My point is, all that time I've never known a man your size who could handle the six-nought-nought. It knocks 'em over. Even when they stay on their feet, they get so scared of the bloody cannon after a few shots that they flinch. Can't hit an elephant at spitting range. And they find the gun too heavy to drag around rough Mesozoic country. Wears 'em out.

It's true, lots of people have killed elephant with lighter guns: the .500, .475, and .465 doubles, for instance, or even .375 magnum repeaters. The difference is that with a .375 you have to hit something vital, preferably the heart, and can't depend on simple shock-power.

An elephant weighs — let's see — four to six tons. You're planning to shoot reptiles weighing two or three times as much as an elephant and with much greater tenacity of life. That's why the syndicate decided to take no more people dinosaur-hunting unless they could handle the .600. We learned the hard way, as you Americans say. There were some unfortunate incidents . . .

I'll tell you, Mr. Seligman. It's after seventeen hundred. Time I closed the office. Why don't we stop at the bar on our way out while I tell you the story?

It was about the Raja's and my fifth safari. The Raja? Oh, he's the Aiyar half of Rivers & Aiyar. I call him the Raja because he's the hereditary monarch of Janpur. Means nothing nowadays, of course. Knew him in India and ran into him in New York running the Indian tourist agency. That dark chap in the photograph on my office wall, the one with his foot on the dead saber-tooth.

Well, the Raja was fed up with handing out brochures about the Taj Mahal and wanted to do a bit of hunting again. I was at loose ends when we heard of Professor Prochaska's time machine at Washington University.

Where is the Raja? Out on safari in the early Oligocene, after titanothere, while I run the office. We take turn about now, but the first few times we went out together.

Anyhow, we caught the next plane to St. Louis. To our mortification, we found we weren't the first.

Lord, no! There were other hunting guides and no end of scientists, each with his own idea of the right use for the machine.

We scraped off the historians and archeologists right at the start.

Seems the bloody machine won't work for periods more recent than 100,000 years ago. From there, up to about a billion years.

Why? Oh, I'm no four-dimensional thinker, but as I understand it, if people could go back to a more recent time, their actions would affect our own history, which would be a paradox or contradiction of facts. Can't have that in a well-run universe. But before 100,000 B.C., more or less, the actions of the expeditions are lost in the stream of time before human history begins. At that, once a stretch of past time has been used, say the month of January, one million B.C., you can't use that stretch over again by sending another party into it. Paradoxes again.

But the professor isn't worried; with a billion years to exploit, he won't soon run out of eras.

Another limitation of the machine is the matter of size. For technical reasons, Prochaska had to build the transition chamber just big enough to hold four men with their personal gear, plus the chamber-wallah. Larger parties have to be sent through in relays. That means, you see, it's not practical to take jeeps, boats, aircraft, or other powered vehicles.

On the other hand, since you're going to periods without human beings, there's no whistling up a hundred native bearers to trot along with your gear on their heads. So we usually take a train of asses — burros, they call them here. Most periods have enough natural forage to get you where you want to go.

As I say, everybody had his own idea for using the machine. The scientists looked down their noses at us hunters and said it would be a crime to waste the machine's time pandering to our sadistic amusements.

We brought up another angle. The machine cost a cool thirty million. I understand this came from the Rockefeller Board and such people, but that only accounted for the original cost, not the cost of operation. And the thing uses fantastic amounts of power. Most of the scientists' projects, while worthy as worthy could be, were run on a shoestring, financially speaking.

Now we guides catered to people with money, a species with which America seems overstocked. No offense, old boy. Most of these could afford a substantial fee for passing through the machine to the past. Thus we could help finance the operation of the machine for scientific purposes, provided we got a fair share of its time.

Won't go into the details, but in the end the guides formed a syndicate of eight members, one member being the partnership of Rivers & Aiyar, to apportion the machine's time.

We had rush business from the start. Our wives — the Raja's and mine — raised bloody hell with us. They'd hoped when the big game gave out they'd never have to share us with lions and things again, but you know how women are. Can't realize hunting's not really dangerous if you keep your head and take precautions.

On the fifth expedition, we had two sahibs to wet-nurse: both Americans in their thirties, both physically sound, and both solvent. Otherwise they were as different as can be.

Courtney James was what you chaps call a playboy: a rich young man from New York who'd always had his own way and didn't see why that agreeable condition shouldn't continue. A big bloke, almost as big as I am; handsome in a florid way, but beginning to run to fat. He was on his fourth wife, and when he showed up at the office with a blonde with "model" written all over her, I assumed this was the fourth Mrs. James.

"Miss Bartram," she corrected me, with an embarrassed giggle.

"She's not my wife," James explained. "My wife is in Mexico, I think, getting a divorce. But Bunny here would like to go along — "

"Sorry," I said, "we don't take ladies. At least not to the late Mesozoic."

This wasn't strictly true, but I felt we were running enough risks, going after a little-known fauna, without dragging in people's domestic entanglements. Nothing against sex, you understand. Marvelous institution and all that, but not where it interferes with my living.

"Oh, nonsense," said James. "If she wants to go, she'll go. She skis and flies my airplane, so why shouldn't she — "

"Against the firm's policy."

"She can keep out of the way when we run up against the dangerous ones."

"No, sorry."

"Damn it," said he, getting red. "After all, I'm paying you a goodly sum and I'm entitled to take who I please."

"You can't hire me to do anything against my best judgment," I said. "If that's how you feel, get another guide."

"All right, I will. And I'll tell all my friends you're a goddamn — " Well, he said a lot of things I won't repeat. It ended with my telling him to get out of the office or I'd throw him out.

I was sitting in the office thinking sadly of all that lovely money James would have paid me if I hadn't been so stiff-necked, when in came my other lamb, one August Holtzinger. This was a little slim pale chap with glasses, polite and formal where the other had been breezily self-confident to the point of obnoxiousness.

Holtzinger sat on the edge of his chair and said: "Uh — Mr. Rivers, I don't want you to think I'm here under false pretenses. I'm really not much of an outdoorsman and I'll probably be scared to death when I see a real dinosaur. But I'm determined to hang a dinosaur head over my fireplace or die in the attempt."

"Most of us are frightened at first," I soothed him, and little by little I got the story out of him.

While James had always been wallowing in money, Holtzinger was a local product who'd only lately come into the real thing. He'd had a little business here in St. Louis and just about made ends meet when an uncle cashed in his chips somewhere and left little Augie the pile.

He'd never been married but had a fiancée. He was building a big house, and when it was finished, they'd be married and move into it. And one furnishing he demanded was a ceratopsian head over the fireplace. Those are the ones with the big horned heads with a parrot-beak and frill over the neck, you know. You have to think twice about collecting them, because if you put a seven-foot triceratops head into a small living room, there's apt to be no room left for anything else.

We were talking about this when in came a girl, a small girl in her twenties, quite ordinary-looking, and crying.

"Augie!" she wept. "You can't! You mustn't! You'll be killed!" She grabbed him round and said to me: "Mr. Rivers, you mustn't take him! He's all I've got! He'll never stand the hardships!"

"My dear young lady," I said, "I should hate to cause you distress, but it's up to Mr. Holtzinger to decide whether he wishes to retain my services."

"It's no use, Claire," said Holtzinger. "I'm going, though I'll probably hate every minute of it."

"What's that, old boy?" I asked. "If you hate it, why go? Did you lose a bet or something?"

"No," said Holtzinger. "It's this way. Uh — I'm a completely undistinguished kind of guy. I'm not brilliant or big or strong or handsome. I'm just an ordinary Midwestern small businessman. You never even notice me at Rotary luncheons, I fit in so perfectly. But that doesn't say I'm satisfied. I've always hankered to go to far places and do big things. I'd like to be a glamorous, adventurous sort of guy. Like you, Mr. Rivers."

"Oh, come," I protested. "Professional hunting may seem glamorous to you, but to me it's just a living."

He shook his head. "Nope. You know what I mean. Well, now I've got this legacy, I could settle down to play bridge and golf the rest of my life and try to act like I wasn't bored. But I'm determined to do something big for once. Since there's no more real big-game hunting, I'm gonna shoot a dinosaur and hang his head over my mantel. I'll never be happy otherwise."

Well, Holtzinger and his girl, whose last name was Roche, argued, but he wouldn't give in. She made me swear to take the best care of her Augie and departed, sniffling.

When Holtzinger had left, who should come in but my vile-tempered friend Courtney James. He apologized for insulting me, though you could hardly say he groveled.

"I don't actually have a bad temper," he said, "except when people won't cooperate with me. Then I sometimes get mad. But so long as they're cooperative, I'm not hard to get along with."

I knew that by "cooperate" he meant to do whatever Courtney James wanted, but I didn't press the point. "How about Miss Bartram?" I asked.

"We had a row," he said. "I'm through with women. So if there's no hard feelings, let's go on from where we left off."

"Absolutely," I agreed, business being business.

The Raja and I decided to make it a joint safari to eighty-five million years ago: the early upper Cretaceous, or the middle Cretaceous, as some American geologists call it. It's about the best period for dinosaur in Missouri. You'll find some individual species a little larger in the late upper Cretaceous, but the period we were going to gives a wider variety.

Now, as to our equipment, the Raja and I each had a Continental .600 like the one I showed you and a few smaller guns. At this time, we hadn't worked up much capital and had no spare .600s to rent.

August Holtzinger said he would rent a gun, as he expected this to be his only safari and there was no point in spending over a thousand dollars for a gun he'd shoot only a few times. But since we had no spare .600s, his choice was between buying one of those and renting one of our smaller pieces.

We drove into the country to let him try the .600. We set up a target. Holtzinger heaved up the gun as if it weighed a ton and let fly. He missed completely and the kick knocked him flat on his back with his legs in the air.

He got up, looking paler than ever, and handed me back the gun, saying: "Uh — I think I'd better try something smaller."

When his shoulder stopped being sore, I tried him out on the smaller rifles. He took a fancy to my Winchester 70, chambered for the .375 magnum cartridge. It's an excellent all-round gun —

What's it like? A conventional magazine rifle with a Mauser-type bolt action. It's perfect for the big cats and bears, but a little light for elephant and very definitely light for dinosaur. I should never have given in, but I was in a hurry and it might have taken months to get him a new .600. They're made to order, you know, and James was getting impatient. James already had a gun, a Holland & Holland .500 double express. With 5700 foot-pounds of muzzle energy, it's almost in a class with the .600.

Both sahibs had done a bit of shooting, so I didn't worry about their accuracy. Shooting dinosaur is not a matter of extreme accuracy but of sound judgment and smooth coordination so you shan't catch twigs in the mechanism of your gun, or fall into holes, or climb a small tree the dinosaur can pluck you out of, or blow your guide's head off.

People used to hunting mammals sometimes try to shoot a dinosaur in the brain. That's the silliest thing you can do, because dinosaur haven't got any. To be exact, they have a little lump of tissue about the size of a tennis ball on the front end of their spines, and how are you going to hit that when it's imbedded in a moving six-foot skull?

The only safe rule with dinosaur is — always try for a heart shot. They have big hearts, over a hundred pounds in the largest species, and a couple of .600 slugs through the heart will kill them just as dead as a smaller beast. The problem is to get the slugs through that mountain of muscle and armor around it.

Well, we appeared at Prochaska's laboratory one rainy morning: James and Holtzinger, the Raja and I, our herder Beauregard Black, three helpers, a cook, and twelve jacks. Burros, that is.

The transition chamber is a little cubbyhole the size of a small lift. My routine is for the men with the guns to go first in case a hungry theropod might be standing in front of the machine when it arrives. So the two sahibs, the Raja, and I crowded into the chamber with our guns and packs. The operator squeezed in after us, closed the door, and fiddled with his dials. He set the thing for April twenty-fourth, eighty-five million B.C., and pressed the red button.

The lights went out, leaving the chamber lit by a little battery-operated lamp. James and Holtzinger looked pretty green, but that may have been the dim lighting. The Raja and I had been through all this before, so the vibration and vertigo didn't bother us.

I could see the little black hands of the dials spinning round, some slowly and some so fast they were a blur. Then they slowed down and stopped. The operator looked at his ground-level gauge and turned a handwheel that raised the chamber so it wouldn't materialize underground. Then he pressed another button and the door slid open.

No matter how often I do it, I get a frightful thrill out of stepping into a bygone era. The operator had raised the chamber a foot above ground level, so I jumped down, my gun ready. The others came after. We looked back at the chamber, a big shiny cube hanging in midair a foot off the ground, with this little lift-door in front.

"Right-ho," I told the chamber-wallah, and he closed the door. The chamber disappeared and we looked around. The scene hadn't changed from my last expedition to this era, which had ended, in Cretaceous time, five days before this one began. There weren't any dinosaur in sight, nothing but lizards.

In this period, the chamber materializes on top of a rocky rise from which you can see in all directions as far as the haze will let you.

To the west, you see the arm of the Kansas Sea that reaches across Missouri and the big swamp around the bayhead where the sauropods live.

It used to be thought the sauropods became extinct before the Cretaceous, but that's not so. They were more limited in range because swamps and lagoons didn't cover so much of the world, but there were plenty of them if you knew where to look.

To the north is a low range that the Raja named the Janpur Hills, after the little Indian kingdom his forebears had ruled. To the east, the land slopes up to a plateau, good for ceratopsians, while to the south is flat country with more sauropod swamps and lots of ornithopods: duckbills and iguanadonts.

The finest thing about the Cretaceous is the climate: balmy, like the South Sea Islands, with little seasonal change, but not so muggy as most Jurassic climates. We happened to be there in spring, with dwarf magnolias in bloom all over, but the air feels like spring almost any time of year.

A thing about this landscape is that it combines a fairly high rainfall with an open type of vegetation-cover. That is, the grasses hadn't yet evolved to the point of forming solid carpets over all open ground, so the ground is thick with laurel, sassafras, and other shrubs, with bare ground between. There are big thickets of palmettos and ferns. The trees around the hill are mostly cycads, standing singly and in copses. Most people call them palms, though my scientific friends tell me they're not true palms.

Down toward the Kansas Sea are more cycads and willows, while the uplands are covered with screw pine and ginkos.

Now I'm no bloody poet — the Raja writes the stuff, not me — but I can appreciate a beautiful scene. One of the helpers had come through the machine with two of the jacks and was pegging them out, and I was looking through the haze and sniffing the air, when a gun went off behind me — *bang! bang!*

I turned round and there was Courtney James with his .500 and an ornithomime legging it for cover fifty yards away. The ornithomimes are medium-sized running dinosaurs, slender things with long necks and legs, like a cross between a lizard and an ostrich. This kind is about seven feet tall and weighs as much as a man. The beggar had wandered out of the nearest copse and James gave him both barrels. Missed.

I was a bit upset, as trigger-happy sahibs are as much a menace as those who get panicky and freeze or bolt. I yelled, "Damn it, you idiot, I thought you weren't to shoot without word from me!"

"And who the hell are you to tell me when I'll shoot my own gun?" he demanded.

We had a rare old row until Holtzinger and the Raja got us calmed down.

I explained: "Look here, Mr. James, I've got reasons. If you shoot off all your ammunition before the trip's over, your gun won't be available in a pinch and it's the only one of its caliber. Second, if you empty both barrels at an unimportant target, what would happen if a big theropod charged before you could reload? Finally, it's not sporting to shoot everything in sight.

I'll shoot for meat, or for trophies, or to defend myself, but not just to hear the gun go off. If more people had exercised moderation in killing, there'd still be decent sport in our own era. Understand?"

"Yeah, I guess so," he said. Mercurial sort of bloke.

The rest of the party came through the machine and we pitched our camp a safe distance from the materializing place. Our first task was to get fresh meat. For a twenty-one-day safari like this, we calculate our food requirements closely so we can make out on tinned stuff and concentrates if we must, but we count on killing at least one piece of meat. When that's butchered, we go on a short tour, stopping at four or five camping places to hunt and arriving back at base a few days before the chamber is due to appear.

Holtzinger, as I said, wanted a ceratopsian head, any kind. James insisted on just one head: a tyrannosaur. Then everybody'd think he'd shot the most dangerous game of all time.

Fact is, the tyrannosaur's overrated. He's more a carrion-eater than an active predator, though he'll snap you up if he gets the chance. He's less dangerous than some of the other theropods — the flesh-eaters — such as the big saurophagus of the Jurassic, or even the smaller gorgosaurus from the period we were in. But everybody's read about the tyrant lizard and he does have the biggest head of the theropods.

The one in our period isn't the rex, which is later and a little bigger and more specialized. It's the trionyches with the forelimbs not reduced to quite such little vestiges, though they're too small for anything but picking the brute's teeth after a meal.

When camp was pitched, we still had the afternoon, so the Raja and I took our sahibs on their first hunt. We already had a map of the local terrain from previous trips.

The Raja and I have worked out a system for dinosaur hunting. We split into two groups of two men and walk parallel from twenty to forty yards apart. Each group consists of one sahib in front and one guide following and telling the sahib where to go.

We tell the sahibs we put them in front so they shall have first shot, which is true, but another reason is they're always tripping and falling with their guns cocked, and if the guide were in front, he'd get shot.

The reason for two groups is that if a dinosaur starts for one, the other gets a good heart shot from the side.

As we walked, there was the usual rustle of lizards scuttling out of the way: little fellows, quick as a flash and colored like all the jewels in Tiffany's, and big gray ones that hiss and plod off. There were tortoises and a few little snakes. Birds with beaks full of teeth flapped off squawking. And always that marvelous mild Cretaceous air. Makes a chap want to take his clothes off and dance with vine leaves in his hair, if you know what I mean. Not that I'd ever do such a thing, you understand.

Our sahibs soon found that Mesozoic country is cut up into millions of nullahs — gullies, you'd call them. Walking is one long scramble, up and down, up and down.

We'd been scrambling for an hour and the sahibs were soaked with sweat and had their tongues hanging out, when the Raja whistled. He'd spotted a group of bonehead feeding on cycad shoots.

These are the troödonts, small ornithopods about the size of men with a bulge on top of their heads that makes them look quite intelligent. Means nothing, because the bulge is solid bone and the brain is as small as in other dinosaur, hence the name. The males butt each other with these heads in fighting over the females. They would drop down to all fours, munch a shoot, then stand up and look around. They're warier than most dinosaur because they're the favorite food of the big theropods.

People sometimes assume that because dinosaur are so stupid, their senses must be dim, but it's not so. Some, like the sauropods, are pretty dim-sensed, but most have good smell and eyesight and fair hearing. Their weakness is that, having no minds, they have no memories; hence, out of sight, out of mind. When a big theropod comes slavering after you, your best defense is to hide in a nullah or behind a bush, and if he can neither see nor smell you, he'll just forget all about you and wander off.

We sneaked up behind a patch of palmetto downwind from the bonehead. I whispered to James: "You've had a shot already today. Hold your fire until Holtzinger shoots and then shoot only if he misses or if the beast is getting away wounded."

"Uh-huh," said James and we separated, he with the Raja and Holtzinger with me. This got to be our regular arrangement. James and I got on each other's nerves, but the Raja, once you forget that Oriental-potentate rot, is a friendly, sentimental sort of bloke nobody can help liking.

Well, we crawled round the palmetto patch on opposite sides and Holtzinger got up to shoot. You daren't shoot a heavy-caliber rifle prone. There's not enough give and the kick can break your shoulder.

Holtzinger sighted round the last few fronds of palmetto. I saw his barrel wobbling and weaving and then off went James's gun, both barrels again. The biggest bonehead went down, rolling and thrashing, and the others ran on their hind legs in great leaps, their heads jerking and their tails sticking up behind.

"Put your gun on safety," I said to Holtzinger, who'd started forward. By the time we got to the bonehead, James was standing over it, breaking open his gun and blowing out the barrels. He looked as smug as if he'd inherited another million and he was asking the Raja to take his picture with his foot on the game. His first shot had been excellent, right through the heart. His second had missed because the first knocked the beast down. James couldn't resist that second shot even when there was nothing to shoot at.

I said: "I thought you were to give Holtzinger first shot."

"Hell, I waited," he said, "and he took so long, I thought something must have gone wrong. If we stood around long enough, they'd see us or smell us."

There was something in what he said, but his way of saying it got me angry. I said: "If that sort of thing happens just once more, we'll leave you in camp the next time we go out."

"Now, gentlemen," said the Raja. "After all, Reggie, these aren't experienced hunters."

"What now?" asked Holtzinger. "Haul the beast back ourselves or send out the men?"

"I think we can sling him under the pole," I said. "He weighs under two hundred." The pole was a telescoping aluminum carrying pole I had in my pack, with yokes on the ends with sponge-rubber padding. I brought it along because in such eras you can't always count on finding saplings strong enough for proper poles on the spot.

The Raja and I cleaned our bonehead, to lighten him, and tied him to the pole. The flies began to light on the offal by thousands. Scientists say they're not true flies in the modern sense, but they look and act like them. There's one conspicuous kind of carrion fly, a big four-winged insect with a distinctive deep note as it flies.

The rest of the afternoon, we sweated under that pole. We took turns about, one pair carrying the beast while the other two carried the guns. The lizards scuttled out of the way and the flies buzzed round the carcass.

When we got to camp, it was nearly sunset. We felt as if we could eat the whole bonehead at one meal. The boys had the camp running smoothly, so we sat down for our tot of whiskey feeling like lords of creation while the cook broiled bonehead steaks.

Holtzinger said: "Uh — if I kill a ceratopsian, how do we get his head back?"

I explained: "If the ground permits, we lash it to the patented aluminum roller-frame and sled it in."

"How much does a head like that weigh?" he asked.

"Depends on the age and the species," I told him. "The biggest weigh over a ton, but most run between five hundred and a thousand pounds."

"And all the ground's rough like today?"

"Most of it. You see, it's the combination of the open vegetation-cover and the high rainfall. Erosion is frightfully rapid."

"And who hauls the head on its little sled?"

"Everybody with a hand. A big head would need every ounce of muscle in this party and even then we might not succeed. On such a job, there's no place for side."

"Oh," said Holtzinger. I could see him wondering whether a ceratopsian head would be worth the effort.

The next couple of days, we trekked round the neighborhood. Nothing worth shooting; only a herd of fifty-odd ornithomimes that went bounding off like a lot of bloody ballet dancers. Otherwise there were only the usual lizards and pterosaurs and birds and insects. There's a big lace-winged fly that bites dinosaurs, so you can imagine its beak makes nothing of a human skin. One made Holtzinger leap into the air when it bit through his shirt. James joshed him about it, saying: "What's all the fuss over one little bug?"

The second night, during the Raja's watch, James gave a yell that brought us all out of our tents with rifles. All that had happened was that a dinosaur tick had crawled in with him and started drilling into his armpit. Since it's as big as your thumb even when it hasn't fed, he was understandably startled. Luckily he got it before it had taken its pint of blood. He'd pulled Holtzinger's leg pretty hard about the fly bite, so now Holtzinger repeated: "What's all the fuss over one little bug, buddy?"

James squashed the tick underfoot and grunted. He didn't like being twitted with his own words.

We packed up and started on our circuit. We meant to take them first to the borders of the sauropod swamp, more to see the wildlife than to collect anything.

From where the transition chamber materializes, the sauropod swamp looks like a couple of hours' walk, but it's an all-day scramble. The first part is easy, as it's down hill and the brush isn't heavy. But as you get near the swamp, the cycads and willows grow so thickly, you have to worm your way among them.

There was a sandy ridge on the border of the swamp that I led the party to, for it's pretty bare of vegetation and affords a fine view. When we got to the ridge, the sun was about to go down. A couple of crocs slipped off into the water. The sahibs were so exhausted, being soft yet, that they flopped down in the sand as if dead.

The haze is thick round the swamp, so the sun was deep red and distorted by the atmospheric layers — pinched in at various levels. There was a high layer of clouds reflecting the red and gold, too, so altogether it was something for the Raja to write one of his poems about. Only your modern poet prefers to write about a rainy day in a garbage dump. A few little pterosaurs were wheeling overhead like bats, only they don't flutter like bats. They swoop and soar after the big night-flying insects.

Beauregard Black collected firewood and lit a fire. We'd started on our steaks, and that pagoda-shaped sun was just slipping below the horizon, and something back in the trees was making a noise like a rusty hinge, when a sauropod breathed out in the water. If Mother Earth were to sigh over the misdeeds of her children, it would sound just about like that.

The sahibs jumped up, waving and shouting: "Where is he? Where is he?"

I said, "That black spot in the water, just to the left and this side of that point."

They yammered while the sauropod filled its lungs and disappeared. "Is that all?" yelped James. "Won't we see any more of him?"

Holtzinger said: "I read they never come out of the water because they're too heavy."

"No," I explained. "They can walk perfectly well and often do, for egg-laying and moving from one swamp to another. But most of the time they spend in the water, like hippopotamuses. They eat eight hundred pounds of soft swamp plants a day, all with those little heads. So they wander about the bottoms of lakes and swamps, chomping away, and stick their heads up to breathe every quarter hour or so. It's getting dark, so this fellow will soon come out and lie down in the shallows to sleep."

"Can we shoot one?" demanded James.

"I wouldn't," said I.

"Why not?"

I said: "There's no point in it and it's not sporting. First, they're even harder to hit in the brain than other dinosaurs because of the way they sway their heads about on those long necks and their hearts are too deeply buried in tissue to reach unless you're awfully lucky. Then, if you kill one in the water, he sinks and can't be recovered. If you kill one on land, the only trophy is that little head. You can't bring the whole beast back because he weighs thirty tons or more. We don't need thirty tons of meat."

Holtzinger said: "That museum in New York got one."

"Yes," I agreed. "The American Museum of Natural History sent a party of forty-eight to the early Cretaceous, with a fifty-caliber machine gun. They assembled the gun on the edge of a swamp, killed a sauropod — and spent two solid months skinning it and hacking the carcass apart and dragging it to the time machine. I know the chap in charge of that project and he still has nightmares in which he smells decomposing dinosaur. They also had to kill a dozen big theropods who were attracted by the stench and refused to be frightened off, so they had *them* lying round and rotting, too. And the theropods ate three men of the party despite the big gun."

Next morning, we were finishing breakfast when one of the helpers called: "Look, Mr. Rivers! Up there!"

He pointed along the shoreline. There were six big duckbills feeding in the shallows. They were the kind called parasaurolophus, with a crest consisting of a long spike of bone sticking out the back of their heads, like the horn of an oryx, and a web of skin connecting this with the back of their neck.

"Keep your voices down," I said. The duckbills, like the other ornitho-pods, are wary beasts because they have no armor or weapons against the theropods. Duckbill feed on the margins of lakes and swamps, and when a gorgosaur rushes out of the trees, they plunge into deep water and swim off.

Then when a phobosuchus, the supercrocodile, goes for them in the water, they flee to the land. A hectic sort of life, what?

Holtzinger said: "Uh — Reggie, I've been thinking over what you said about ceratopsian heads. If I could get one of those yonder, I'd be satisfied. It would look big enough in my house, wouldn't it?"

"I'm sure of it, old boy," I said. "Now look here. I could take you on a detour to come out on the shore near there, but we should have to plow through half a mile of muck and brush, up to our knees in water, and they'd hear us coming. Or we can creep up to the north end of this sand spit, from which it's four or five hundred yards — a long shot, but not impossible. Think you could do it?"

"With my 'scope sight and a sitting position — yes, I'll try it."

"You stay here," I said to James. "This is Augie's head and I don't want any argument over your having fired first."

James grunted while Holtzinger clamped his 'scope to his rifle. We crouched our way up the spit, keeping the sand ridge between us and the duckbills. When we got to the end where there was no more cover, we crept along on hands and knees, moving slowly. If you move slowly directly toward or away from a dinosaur, it probably won't notice you.

The duckbills continued to grub about on all fours, every few seconds rising to look round. Holtzinger eased himself into the sitting position, cocked his piece, and aimed through the 'scope. And then —

Bang! bang! went a big rifle back at the camp.

Holtzinger jumped. The duckbills jerked up their heads and leaped for the deep water, splashing like mad. Holtzinger fired once and missed. I took a shot at the last duckbill before it disappeared. I missed, too: the .600 isn't designed for long ranges.

Holtzinger and I started back toward the camp, for it had struck us that our party might be in theropod trouble and need reinforcements.

What happened was that a big sauropod, probably the one we'd heard the night before, had wandered down past the camp under water, feeding as it went. Now the water shoaled about a hundred yards offshore from our spit, halfway over to the edge of the swamp on the other side. The sauropod had ambled up the slope until its body was almost all out of water, weaving its head from side to side and looking for anything green to gobble. This kind looks like the well-known brontosaurus, but a little bigger. Scientists argue whether it ought to be included in the genus camarasaurus or a separate genus with an even longer name.

When I came in sight of the camp, the sauropod was turning round to go back the way it had come, making horrid groans. It disappeared into deep water, all but its head and ten or twenty feet of neck, which wove about for some time before they vanished into the haze.

When we came up to the camp, James was arguing with the Raja. Holtzinger burst out: "You bastard! That's the second time you've spoiled my shots!" Strong language for little August.

"Don't be a fool," said James. "I couldn't let him wander into camp and stamp everything flat."

"There was no danger of that," objected the Raja politely. "You can see the water is deep offshore. It is just that our trigger-happy Mr. James cannot see any animal without shooting."

I said: "If it did get close, all you needed to do was throw a stick of firewood at it. They're perfectly harmless." This wasn't strictly true. When the Comte de Lautrec ran after one for a close shot, the sauropod looked back at him, gave a flick of its tail, and took off the Comte's head as neatly as if he'd been axed in the Tower.

"How was I to know?" yelled James, getting purple. "You're all against me. What the hell are we on this goddamn trip for except to shoot things? You call yourselves hunters, but I'm the only one who's hit anything!"

I got pretty wrothy and said he was just an excitable young skite with more money than brains, whom I should never have brought along.

"If that's how you feel," he said, "give me a burro and some food and I'll go back to the base by myself. I won't pollute your air with my loathsome presence!"

"Don't be a bigger ass than you can help," I snapped. "That's quite impossible."

"Then I'll go all alone!" He grabbed his knapsack, thrust a couple of tins of beans and an opener into it, and started off with his rifle.

Beauregard Black spoke up: "Mr. Rivers, we cain't let him go off like that by hisself. He'll get lost and starve or be et by a theropod."

"I'll fetch him back," said the Raja and started after the runaway. He caught up as James was disappearing into the cycads. We could see them arguing and waving their hands, but couldn't make out what they said. After a while, they started back with arms around each other's necks like old school pals. I simply don't know how the Raja does it.

This shows the trouble we get into if we make mistakes in planning such a do. Having once got back into the past, we had to make the best of our bargain. We always must, you see.

I don't want to give the impression Courtney James was only a pain in the rump. He had his good points. He got over these rows quickly and next day would be as cheerful as ever. He was helpful with the general work of the camp — when he felt like it, at any rate. He sang well and had an endless fund of dirty stories to keep us amused.

We stayed two more days at that camp. We saw crocodile, the small kind, and plenty of sauropod — as many as five at once — but no more duckbill. Nor any of those fifty-foot supercrocodiles.

So, on the first of May, we broke camp and headed north toward the

Janpur Hills. My sahibs were beginning to harden up and were getting impatient. We'd been in the Cretaceous a week and no trophies.

I won't go into details of the next leg. Nothing in the way of a trophy, save a glimpse of a gorgosaur out of range and some tracks indicating a whopping big iguanodont, twenty-five or thirty feet high. We pitched camp at the base of the hills.

We'd finished off the bonehead, so the first thing was to shoot fresh meat. With an eye on trophies, too, of course. We got ready the morning of the third.

I told James: "See here, old boy, no more of your tricks. The Raja will tell you when to shoot."

"Uh-huh, I get you," he said, meek as Moses. Never could tell how the chap would act.

We marched off, the four of us, into the foothills. We were looking for bonehead, but we'd take an ornithomime. There was also a good chance of getting Holtzinger his ceratopsian. We'd seen a couple on the way up, but mere calves without decent horns.

It was hot and sticky and we were soon panting and sweating like horses. We'd hiked and scrambled all morning without seeing a thing except lizards, when I picked up the smell of carrion. I stopped the party and sniffed. We were in an open glade cut up by these little dry nullahs. The nullahs ran together into a couple of deeper gorges that cut through a slight depression choked with a denser growth, cycad and screw pine. When I listened, I heard the thrum of carrion flies.

"This way," I said. "Something ought to be dead — ah, here it is!"

And there it was: the remains of a huge ceratopsian lying in a little hollow on the edge of the copse. Must have weighed six or eight tons alive; a three-horned variety, perhaps the penultimate species of *Triceratops*. It was hard to tell because most of the hide on the upper surface had been ripped off and many bones had been pulled loose and lay scattered about.

Holtzinger said: "Oh, hell! Why couldn't I have gotten to him before he died? That would have been a darn fine head." Associating with us rough types had made little August profane, you'll observe.

I said, "On your toes, chaps. A theropod's been at this carcass and is probably nearby."

"How d'you know?" James challenged, with the sweat running off his round red face. He spoke in what was for him a low voice, because a nearby theropod is a sobering thought even to the flightiest.

I sniffed again and thought I could detect the distinctive rank odor of theropod. But I couldn't be sure because the stench of the carcass was so strong. My sahibs were turning green at the sight and smell of the cadaver.

I told James: "It's seldom even the biggest theropod will attack a full-grown ceratopsian. Those horns are too much for them. But they love a dead or dying one. They'll hang round a dead ceratopsian for weeks, gorging and then sleeping their meals off for days at a time. They usually take cover in the heat of the day anyhow, because they can't stand much direct hot sunlight. You'll find them lying in copses like this or in hollows, anywhere there's shade."

"What'll we do?" asked Holtzinger.

"We'll make our first cast through this copse, in two pairs as usual. Whatever you do, don't get impulsive or panicky." I looked at Courtney James, but he looked right back and then merely checked his gun.

"Should I still carry this broken?" he wanted to know.

"No; close it, but keep the safety on till you're ready to shoot," I said. It's risky carrying a double closed like that, especially in brush, but with a theropod nearby, it would have been a greater risk to carry it open and perhaps catch a twig in it when one tried to close it.

"We'll keep closer than usual, to be in sight of each other," I said. "Start off at that angle, Raja. Go slowly and stop to listen between steps."

We pushed through the edge of the copse, leaving the carcass but not its stink behind us. For a few feet, we couldn't see a thing. It opened out as we got in under the trees, which shaded out some of the brush. The sun slanted down through the trees. I could hear nothing but the hum of insects and the scuttle of lizards and the squawks of toothed birds in a treetop. I thought I could be sure of the theropod smell, but told myself that might be imagination. The theropod might be any of several species, large or small, and the beast itself might be anywhere within a half-mile radius.

"Go on," I whispered to Holtzinger, for I could hear James and the Raja pushing ahead on my right and see the palm fronds and ferns lashing about as they disturbed them. I suppose they were trying to move quietly, but to me they sounded like an earthquake in a crockery shop.

"A little closer," I called, and presently they appeared slanting in toward me.

We dropped in to a gully filled with ferns and clambered up the other side, then found our way blocked by a big clump of palmetto.

"You go round that side; we'll go round this," I said, and we started off, stopping to listen and smell. Our positions were exactly the same as on that first day when James killed the bonehead.

I judge we'd gone two thirds of the way round our half of the palmetto when I heard a noise ahead on our left. Holtzinger heard it and pushed off his safety. I put my thumb on mine and stepped to one side to have a clear field.

The clatter grew louder. I raised my gun to aim at about the height a big theropod's heart would be at the distance it would appear to us out of the greenery. There was a movement in the foliage — and a six-foot-high bonehead stepped into view, walking solemnly across our front from left to right, jerking its head with each step like a giant pigeon.

I heard Holtzinger let out a breath and had to keep myself from laughing. Holtzinger said. "Uh — "

"Quiet," I whispered. "The theropod might still — "

That was as far as I got when that damned gun of James's went off, *bang! bang!* I had a glimpse of the bonehead knocked arsy-varsy with its tail and hind legs flying.

"Got him!" yelled James, and I heard him run forward.

"My God, if he hasn't done it again!" I groaned. Then there was a great swishing, not made by the dying bonehead, and a wild yell from James. Something heaved up and out of the shrubbery and I saw the head of the biggest of the local flesh-eaters, tyrannosaurus trionyches himself.

The scientists can insist that rex is bigger than trionyches, but I'll swear this tyrannosaur was bigger than any rex ever hatched. It must have stood twenty feet high and been fifty feet long. I could see its big bright eye and six-inch teeth and the big dewlap that hangs down from its chin to its chest.

The second of the nullahs that cut through the copse ran athwart our path on the far side of the palmetto clump. Perhaps six feet deep. The tyrannosaur had been living in this, sleeping off its last meal. Where its back stuck up above ground level, the ferns on the edge of the nullah masked it. James had fired both barrels over the theropod's head and woke it up. Then James, to compound his folly, ran forward without reloading. Another twenty feet and he'd have stepped on the tyrannosaur's back.

James understandably stopped when this thing popped up in front of him. He remembered his gun was empty and he'd left the Raja too far behind to get a clear shot.

James kept his nerve at first. He broke open his gun, took two rounds from his belt and plugged them into the barrels. But in his haste to snap the gun shut, he caught his right hand between the barrels and the action — the fleshy part between his thumb and palm. It was a painful pinch and so startled James that he dropped his gun. That made him go to pieces and he bolted.

His timing couldn't have been worse. The Raja was running up with his gun at high port, ready to snap it to his shoulder the instant he got a clear view of the tyrannosaur. When he saw James running headlong toward him, it made him hesitate, as he didn't want to shoot James. The latter plunged ahead and, before the Raja could jump aside, blundered into him and sent them both sprawling among the ferns. The tyrannosaur collected what little wits it had and crashed after to snap them up.

And how about Holtzinger and me on the other side of the palmettos? Well, the instant James yelled and the tyrannosaur's head appeared, Holtzinger darted forward like a rabbit. I'd brought my gun up for a shot at the tyrannosaur's head, in hope of getting at least an eye, but before I could find it in my sights, the head was out of sight behind the palmettos. Perhaps I should have shot at where I thought it was, but all my experience is against wild shots.

When I looked back in front of me, Holtzinger had already disappeared round the curve of the palmetto clump. I'm pretty heavily built, as you can see, but I started after him with a good turn of speed, when I heard his rifle and the click of the bolt between shots: *bang* — click-click — *bang* — click-click, like that.

He'd come up on the tyrannosaur's quarter as the brute started to stoop for James and the Raja. With his muzzle twenty feet from the tyrannosaur's hide, he began pumping .375s into the beast's body. He got off three shots when the tyrannosaur gave a tremendous booming grunt and wheeled round to see what was stinging it. The jaws came open and the head swung round and down again.

Holtzinger got off one more shot and tried to leap to one side. He was standing on a narrow place between the palmetto clump and the nullah. So he fell into the nullah. The tyrannosaur continued its lunge and caught him, either as he was falling or after he struck bottom. The jaws went chomp and up came the head with poor Holtzinger in them, screaming like a doomed soul.

I came up just then and aimed at the brute's face. Then I realized its jaws were full of my friend and I'd be shooting him. As the head went up, like the business end of a big power shovel, I fired a shot at the heart. But the tyrannosaur was already turning away and I suspect the ball just glanced along the ribs.

The beast took a couple of steps away when I gave it the other barrel in the back. It staggered on its next step but kept on. Another step and it was nearly out of sight among the trees, when the Raja fired twice. The stout fellow had untangled himself from James, got up, picked up his gun, and let the tyrannosaur have it.

The double wallop knocked the brute over with a tremendous smash. It fell into a dwarf magnolia and I saw one of its hindlegs waving in the midst of a shower of incongruously pretty pink-and-white petals.

Can you imagine the leg of a bird of prey enlarged and thickened until it's as big around as the leg of an elephant?

But the tyrannosaur got up again and blundered off without even dropping its victim. The last I saw of it was Holtzinger's legs dangling out one side of its jaws (by now he'd stopped screaming) and its big tail banging against the tree trunks as it swung from side to side.

The Raja and I reloaded and ran after the brute for all we were worth. I tripped and fell once, but jumped up again and didn't notice my skinned elbow till later. When we burst out of the copse, the tyrannosaur was already at the far end of the glade. I took a quick shot, but probably missed, and it was out of sight before I could fire another.

We ran on, following the tracks and spatters of blood, until we had to stop from exhaustion. Their movements look slow and ponderous, but with those tremendous legs, they don't have to step very fast to work up considerable speed.

When we'd finished gasping and mopping our foreheads, we tried to track the tyrannosaur, on the theory that it might be dying and we should come up to it. But the spoor faded out and left us at a loss. We circled round hoping to pick it up, but no luck.

Hours later, we gave up and went back to the glade, feeling very dismal.

Courtney James was sitting with his back against a tree, holding his rifle and Holtzinger's. His right hand was swollen and blue where he'd pinched it, but still usable.

His first words were: "Where the hell have you been? You shouldn't have gone off and left me; another of those things might have come along. Isn't it bad enough to lose one hunter through your stupidity without risking another one?"

I'd been preparing a pretty warm wigging for James, but his attack so astonished me, I could only bleat: "*We* lost — ?"

"Sure," he said. "You put us in front of you, so if anybody gets eaten, it's us. You send a guy up against these animals undergunned. You — "

"You stinking little swine," I began and went on from there. I learned later he'd spent his time working out an elaborate theory according to which this disaster was all our fault — Holtzinger's, the Raja's, and mine. Nothing about James's firing out of turn or panicking or Holtzinger's saving his worthless life. Oh, dear, no. It was the Raja's fault for not jumping out of his way, et cetera.

Well, I've led a rough life and can express myself quite eloquently. The Raja tried to keep up with me, but ran out of English and was reduced to cursing James in Hindustani.

I could see by the purple color on James's face that I was getting home. If I'd stopped to think, I should have known better than to revile a man with a gun. Presently James put down Holtzinger's rifle and raised his own, saying, "Nobody calls me things like that and gets away with it. I'll just say the tyrannosaur ate you, too."

The Raja and I were standing with our guns broken open, under our arms, so it would take a good part of a second to snap them shut and bring them up to fire. Moreover, you don't shoot a .600 holding it loosely in your hands, not if you know what's good for you. Next thing, James was setting the butt of his .500 against his shoulder, with the barrels pointed at my face. Looked like a pair of blooming vehicular tunnels.

The Raja saw what was happening before I did. As the beggar brought his gun up, he stepped forward with a tremendous kick. Used to play football as a young chap, you see. He knocked the .500 up and it went off so the bullet missed my head by an inch and the explosion jolly well near broke my eardrums.

The butt had been punted away from James's shoulder when the gun went off, so it came back like a kick of a horse. It spun him half around.

The Raja dropped his own gun, grabbed the barrels, and twisted it out of James's hands, nearly breaking the bloke's trigger finger. He meant to hit James with the butt, but I rapped James across the head with my own barrels, then bowled him over and began punching the stuffing out of him. He was a good-sized lad, but with my sixteen stone, he had no chance.

When his face was properly discolored, I stopped. We turned him over, took a strap out of his knapsack and tied his wrists behind him. We agreed there was no safety for us unless we kept him under guard every minute until we got him back to our time. Once a man has tried to kill you, don't give him another opportunity. Of course he might never try again, but why risk it?

We marched James back to camp and told the crew what we were up against. James cursed everybody and dared us to kill him.

"You'd better, you sons of bitches, or I'll kill you some day," he said. "Why don't you? Because you know somebody'd give you away, don't you? Ha-ha!"

The rest of that safari was dismal. We spent three days combing the country for that tyrannosaur. No luck. It might have been lying in any of those nullahs, dead or convalescing, and we should never see it unless we blundered on top of it. But we felt it wouldn't have been cricket not to make a good try at recovering Holtzinger's remains, if any.

After we got back to our main camp, it rained. When it wasn't raining, we collected small reptiles and things for our scientific friends. When the transition chamber materialized, we fell over one another getting into it.

The Raja and I had discussed the question of legal proceedings by or against Courtney James. We decided there was no precedent for punishing crimes committed eighty-five million years before, which would presumably be outlawed by the statute of limitations. We therefore untied him and pushed him into the chamber after all the others but us had gone through.

When we came out in the present, we handed him his gun — empty — and his other effects. As we expected, he walked off without a word, his arms full of gear. At that point, Holtzinger's girl, Claire Roche, rushed up crying: "Where is he? Where's August?"

I won't go over the painful scene except to say it was distressing in spite of the Raja's skill at that sort of thing.

We took our men and beasts down to the old laboratory building that

Washington University has fitted up as a serai for expeditions to the past. We paid everybody off and found we were nearly broke. The advance payments from Holtzinger and James didn't cover our expenses and we should have damned little chance of collecting the rest of our fees from James or from Holtzinger's estate.

And speaking of James, d'you know what that blighter was doing all this time? He went home, got more ammunition, and came back to the university. He hunted up Professor Prochaska and asked him: "Professor, I'd like you to send me back to the Cretaceous for a quick trip. If you can work me into your schedule right now, you can just about name your own price. I'll offer five thousand to begin with. I want to go to April twenty-third, eighty-five million B.C."

Prochaska answered: "Vot do you vant to go back again so soon so badly for?"

"I lost my wallet in the Cretaceous," said James. "I figure if I go back to the day before I arrived in that era on my last trip, I'll watch myself when I arrived on that trip and follow myself till I see myself lose the wallet."

"Five thousand is a lot for a vallet."

"It's got some things in it I can't replace. Suppose you let me worry about whether it's worth my while."

"Vell," said Prochaska, thinking, "the party that vas supposed to go out this morning has phoned that they vould be late, so maybe I can vork you in. I have alvays vondered vot vould happen vhen the same man occupied the same time tvice."

So James wrote out a check and Prochaska took him to the chamber and saw him off. James's idea, it seems, was to sit behind a bush a few yards from where the transition chamber would appear and pot the Raja and me as we emerged.

Hours later, we'd changed into our street clothes and phoned our wives to come and get us. We were standing on Forsythe Boulevard waiting for them when there was a loud crack, like an explosion or a close-by clap of thunder, and a flash of light not fifty feet from us. The shock-wave staggered us and broke windows in quite a number of buildings.

We ran toward the place and got there just as a policeman and several citizens came up. On the boulevard, just off the curb, lay a human body. At least it had been that, but it looked as if every bone in it had been pulverized and every blood vessel burst. The clothes it had been wearing were shredded, but I recognized an H. & H. .500 double-barreled express rifle. The wood was scorched and the metal pitted, but it was Courtney James's gun. No doubt whatever.

Skipping the investigations and the milling about, what had happened was this: Nobody had shot us as we emerged on the twenty-fourth and that, of course, couldn't be changed. For that matter, the instant James started to do anything that would make a visible change in the world of eighty-five million B.C., the spacetime forces would snap him forward to the present to prevent a paradox.

Now that this is better understood, the professor won't send anybody to a period less than five hundred years *prior* to the time that some time traveler has already explored, because it would be too easy to do some act, like chopping down a tree or losing some durable artifact, that would affect the later world. Over long periods, he tells me, such changes average out and are lost in the stream of time.

We had a bloody rough time after that, with the bad publicity and all, though we did collect a fee from James's estate. The disaster hadn't been entirely James's fault. I shouldn't have taken him when I knew what a spoiled, unstable sort he was. And if Holtzinger could have used a heavy gun, he'd probably have knocked the tyrannosaur down, even if he didn't kill it, and so given the rest of us a chance to finish it.

So that's why I won't take you to that period to hunt. There are plenty of other eras, and if you think them over, I'm sure you'll find —

Good Lord, look at the time! Must run, old boy; my wife'll skin me. Good night!

dis/as/ters — natural or human-caused events that involve great devastation and loss of life. There are many kinds of disasters, including floods, fires, explosions, airplane accidents, and storms of various types. Science fiction disasters generally involve the destruction of the universe, our solar system, the earth, or human civilization, but some stories revolve around efforts to prevent such cataclysms. Twenty science fictional disasters are found in *Catastrophes!* (Fawcett Crest, 1981).

A Pail of Air

FRITZ LEIBER

Pa had sent me out to get an extra pail of air. I'd just about scooped it full and most of the warmth had leaked from my fingers when I saw the thing.

You know, at first I thought it was a young lady. Yes, a beautiful young lady's face all glowing in the dark and looking at me from the fifth floor of the opposite apartment, which hereabouts is the floor just above the white blanket of frozen air. I'd never seen a live young lady before, except in the old magazines — Sis is just a kid and Ma is pretty sick and miserable — and it gave me such a start that I dropped the pail. Who wouldn't, knowing everyone on Earth was dead except Pa and Ma and Sis and you?

Even at that, I don't suppose I should have been surprised. We all see things now and then. Ma has some pretty bad ones, to judge from the way she bugs her eyes at nothing and just screams and screams and huddles back against the blankets hanging around the Nest. Pa says it is natural we should react like that sometimes.

When I'd recovered the pail and could look again at the opposite apartment, I got an idea of what Ma might be feeling at those times, for I saw it wasn't a young lady at all but simply a light — a tiny light that moved stealthily from window to window, just as if one of the cruel little stars had come down out of the airless sky to investigate why Earth had gone away from the sun, and maybe to hunt down something to torment or terrify, now that Earth didn't have the sun's protection.

I tell you, the thought of it gave me the creeps. I just stood there shaking, and almost froze my feet and did frost my helmet so solid on the inside that I couldn't have seen the light even if it had come out of one of the windows to get me. Then I had the wit to go back inside.

Pretty soon I was feeling my familiar way through the thirty or so blankets and rugs Pa has got hung around to slow down the escape of air from the Nest, and I wasn't quite so scared. I began to hear the tick-ticking of the clocks in the Nest and knew I was getting back into air, because there's no sound outside in the vacuum, of course. But my mind was still crawly and uneasy as I pushed through the last blankets — Pa's got them faced with aluminum foil to hold in the heat — and came into the Nest.

Let me tell you about the Nest. It's low and snug, just room for the four of us and our things. The floor is covered with thick woolly rugs. Three of the sides are blankets, and the blankets roofing it touch Pa's head. He tells me it's inside a much bigger room, but I've never seen the real walls or ceiling.

Against one of the blanket-walls is a big set of shelves, with tools and books and other stuff, and on top of it a whole row of clocks. Pa's very fussy about keeping them wound. He says we must never forget time, and without a sun or moon, that would be easy to do.

The fourth wall has blankets all over except around the fireplace, in which there is a fire that must never go out. It keeps us from freezing and does a lot more besides. One of us must always watch it. Some of the clocks are alarm and we can use them to remind us. In the early days there was only Ma to take turns with Pa — I think of that when she gets difficult — but now there's me to help, and Sis too.

It's Pa who is the chief guardian of the fire, though. I always think of him that way: a tall man sitting cross-legged, frowning anxiously at the fire, his lined face golden in its light, and every so often carefully placing on it a piece of coal from the big heap beside it. Pa tells me there used to be guardians of the fire sometimes in the very old days — vestal virgins, he calls them — although there was unfrozen air all around then and you didn't really need one.

He was sitting just that way now, though he got up quick to take the pail from me and bawl me out for loitering — he'd spotted my frozen helmet right off. That roused Ma and she joined in picking on me. She's always trying to get the load off her feelings, Pa explains. He shut her up pretty fast. Sis let off a couple of silly squeals too.

Yet it's that glimmery white stuff in the pail that keeps us alive. It slowly melts and vanishes and refreshes the Nest and feeds the fire. The blankets keep it from escaping too fast. Pa'd like to seal the whole place, but he can't — building's too earthquake-twisted, and besides he has to leave the chimney open for smoke.

Pa says air is tiny molecules that fly away like a flash if there isn't something to stop them. We have to watch sharp not to let the air run low. Pa always keeps a big reserve supply of it in buckets behind the first blankets, along with extra coal and cans of food and other things, such as pails of snow to melt for water. We have to go way down to the bottom floor for that stuff, which is a mean trip, and get it through a door to outside.

You see, when the earth got cold, all the water in the air froze first and made a blanket ten feet thick or so everywhere, and then down on top of that dropped the crystals of frozen air, making another white blanket sixty or seventy feet thick maybe.

Of course, all the parts of the air didn't freeze and snow down at the same time.

First to drop out was the carbon dioxide — when you're shoveling for water, you have to make sure you don't go too high and get any of that stuff mixed in, for it would put you to sleep, maybe for good, and make the fire go out. Next there's the nitrogen, which doesn't count one way or the other, though it's the biggest part of the blanket. On top of that and easy to get at, which is lucky for us, there's the oxygen that keeps us alive. Pa says we live better than kings ever did, breathing pure oxygen, but we're used to it and don't notice. Finally, at the very top, there's a slick of liquid helium, which is funny stuff. All of these gases in neat separate layers. Like a pussy caffay, Pa laughingly says, whatever that is.

I was busting to tell them all about what I'd seen, and so as soon as I'd ducked out of my helmet and while I was still climbing out of my suit, I cut loose. Right away Ma got nervous and began making eyes at the entry-slit in the blankets and wringing her hands together — the hand where she'd lost three fingers from frostbite inside the good one, as usual. I could tell that Pa was annoyed at me scaring her and wanted to explain it all away quickly, yet could see I wasn't fooling.

"And you watched this light for some time, son?" he asked when I finished.

I hadn't said anything about first thinking it was a young lady's face. Somehow that part embarrassed me.

"Long enough for it to pass five windows and go to the next floor."

"And it didn't look like stray electricity or crawling liquid or starlight focused by a growing crystal, or anything like that?"

He wasn't just making up those ideas. Odd things happen in a world that's about as cold as can be, and just when you think matter would be frozen dead, it takes on a strange new life. A slimy stuff comes crawling toward the Nest, just like an animal snuffing for heat — that's the liquid helium. And once, when I was little, a bolt of lightning — not even Pa could figure where it came from — hit the nearby steeple and crawled up and down it for weeks, until the glow finally died.

"Not like anything I ever saw," I told him.

He stood for a moment frowning. Then, "I'll go out with you, and you show it to me," he said.

Ma raised a howl at the idea of being left alone, and Sis joined in, too, but Pa quieted them. We started climbing into our outside clothes — mine had been warming by the fire. Pa made them. They have plastic headpieces that were once big double-duty transparent food cans, but they keep heat and air in and can replace the air for a little while, long enough for our trips for water and coal and food and so on.

Ma started moaning again, "I've always known there was something outside there, waiting to get us. I've felt it for years — something that's part of the cold and hates all warmth and wants to destroy the Nest. It's been watching us all this time, and now it's coming after us. It'll get you and then come for me. Don't go, Harry!"

Pa had everything on but his helmet. He knelt by the fireplace and reached in and shook the long metal rod that goes up the chimney and knocks off the ice that keeps trying to clog it. Once a week he goes up on the roof to check if it's working all right. That's our worst trip and Pa won't let me make it alone.

"Sis," Pa said quietly, "come watch the fire. Keep an eye on the air, too. If it gets low or doesn't seem to be boiling fast enough, fetch another bucket from behind the blanket. But mind your hands. Use the cloth to pick up the bucket."

Sis quit helping Ma be frightened and came over and did as she was told. Ma quieted down pretty suddenly, though her eyes were still kind of wild as she watched Pa fix on his helmet tight and pick up a pail and the two of us go out.

Pa led the way and I took hold of his belt. It's a funny thing, but when Pa's along I always want to hold on to him. Habit, I guess, and then there's no denying that this time I was a bit scared.

You see, it's this way. We know that everything is dead out there. Pa heard the last radio voices fade away years ago, and had seen some of the last folks die who weren't as lucky or well-protected as us. So we knew that if there was something groping around out there, it couldn't be anything human or friendly.

Besides that, there's a feeling that comes with it always being night, *cold* night. Pa says there used to be some of that feeling even in the old days, but then every morning the sun would come and chase it away. I have to take his word for that, not ever remembering the sun as being anything more than a big star. You see, I hadn't been born when the dark star snatched us away from the sun, and by now it's dragged us out beyond the orbit of the planet Pluto, Pa says, and taking us farther out all the time.

I found myself wondering whether there mightn't be something on the dark star that wanted us, and if that was why it had captured Earth. Just then we came to the end of the corridor and I followed Pa out on the balcony.

I don't know what the city looked like in the old days, but now it's beautiful. The starlight lets you see it pretty well — there's quite a bit of light in those steady points speckling the blackness above. (Pa says the stars used to twinkle once, but that was because there was air.) We are on a hill and the shimmery plain drops away from us and then flattens out, cut up into neat squares by the troughs that used to be streets. I sometimes make my mashed potatoes look like it, before I pour on the gravy.

Some taller buildings push up out of the feathery plain, topped by rounded caps of air crystals, like the fur hood Ma wears, only whiter. On these buildings you can see the darker squares of windows, underlined by white dashes of air crystals. Some of them are on a slant, for many of the buildings are pretty badly twisted by the quakes and all the rest that happened when the dark star captured Earth.

Here and there a few icicles hang, water icicles from the first days of the cold, other icicles of frozen air that melted on the roofs and dripped and froze again. Sometimes one of those icicles will catch the light of a star and send it to you so brightly you think the star has swooped into the city. That was one of the things Pa had been thinking of when I told him about the light, but I had thought of it myself first and known it wasn't so.

He touched his helmet to mine so we could talk easier and he asked me to point out the windows to him. But there wasn't any light moving around inside them now, or anywhere else. To my surprise, Pa didn't bawl me out and tell me I'd been seeing things. He looked all around quite a while after filling his pail, and just as we were going inside he whipped around without warning, as if to take some peeping thing off guard.

I could feel it, too. The old peace was gone. There was something lurking out there, watching, waiting, getting ready.

Inside, he said to me, touching helmets, "If you see something like that again, son, don't tell the others. Your Ma's sort of nervous these days and we owe her all the feeling of safety we can give her. Once — it was when your sister was born — I was ready to give up and die, but your mother kept me trying. Another time she kept the fire going a whole week all by herself when I was sick. Nursed me and took care of the two of you, too.

"You know that game we sometimes play, sitting in a square in the Nest, tossing a ball around? Courage is like a ball, son. A person can hold it only so long, and then he's got to toss it to someone else. When it's tossed your way, you've got to catch it and hold it tight — and hope there'll be someone else to toss it to when you get tired of being brave."

His talking to me that way made me feel grown-up and good. But it didn't wipe away the thing outside from the back of my mind — or the fact that Pa took it seriously.

It's hard to hide your feelings about such a thing. When we got back in the Nest and took off our outside clothes, Pa laughed about it all and told them it was nothing and kidded me for having such an imagination, but his words fell flat. He didn't convince Ma and Sis any more than he did me. It looked for a minute like we were all fumbling the courage-ball. Something had to be done, and almost before I knew what I was going to say, I heard myself asking Pa to tell us about the old days, and how it all happened.

He sometimes doesn't mind telling that story, and Sis and I sure like to listen to it, and he got my idea. So we were all settled around the fire in a wink, and Ma pushed up some cans to thaw for supper, and Pa began. Before he did, though, I noticed him casually get a hammer from the shelf and lay it down beside him.

It was the same old story as always — I think I could recite the main thread of it in my sleep — though Pa always puts in a new detail or two and keeps improving it in spots.

He told us how Earth had been swinging around the sun ever so steady and warm, and the people on it fixing to make money and wars and have a good time and get power and treat each other right or wrong, when without warning there comes charging out of space this dead star, this burned-out sun, and upsets everything.

You know, I find it hard to believe in the way those people felt, any more than I can believe in the swarming number of them. Imagine people getting ready for the horrible sort of war they were cooking up. Wanting it, even, or at least wishing it were over so as to end their nervousness. As if all folks didn't have to hang together and pool every bit of warmth just to keep alive. And how can they have hoped to end danger, any more than we can hope to end the cold?

Sometimes I think Pa exaggerates and makes things out too black. He's cross with us once in a while and was probably cross with all those folks. Still, some of the things I read in the old magazines sound pretty wild. He may be right.

The dark star, as Pa went on telling it, rushed in pretty fast and there wasn't much time to get ready. At the beginning they tried to keep it a secret from most people, but then the truth came out, what with the earthquakes and floods — imagine, oceans of *unfrozen* water! — and people seeing stars blotted out by something on a clear night. First off they thought it would hit the sun, and then they thought it would hit the earth. There was even the start of a rush to get to a place called China, because people thought the star would hit on the other side. But then they found it wasn't going to hit either side, but was going to come very close to Earth.

Most of the other planets were on the other side of the sun and didn't get involved. The sun and the newcomer fought over Earth for a little while — pulling it this way and that, like two dogs growling over a bone, Pa described it this time — and then the newcomer won and carried us off. The sun got a consolation prize, though. At the last minute he managed to hold on to the moon.

That was the time of the monster earthquakes and floods, twenty times worse than anything before. It was also the time of the Big Jerk, as Pa calls it, when all Earth got yanked suddenly, just as Pa has done to me once or twice, grabbing me by the collar to do it, when I've been sitting too far from the fire.

You see, the dark star was going through space faster than the sun, and in the opposite direction, and it had to wrench the world considerably in order to take it away.

The Big Jerk didn't last long. It was over as soon as Earth was settled down in its new orbit around the dark star. But it was pretty terrible while it lasted. Pa says that all sorts of cliffs and buildings toppled, oceans slopped over, swamps and sandy deserts gave great sliding surges that buried nearby lands. Earth was almost jerked out of its atmosphere blanket and the air got so thin in spots that people keeled over and fainted — though of course, at the same time they were getting knocked down by the Big Jerk and maybe their bones broke or skulls cracked.

We've often asked Pa how people acted during that time, whether they were scared or brave or crazy or stunned, or all four, but he's sort of leery of the subject, and he was again tonight. He says he was mostly too busy to notice.

You see, Pa and some scientist friends of his had figured out part of what was going to happen — they'd known we'd get captured and our air would freeze — and they'd been working like mad to fix up a place with airtight walls and doors, and insulation against the cold, and big supplies of food and fuel and water and bottled air. But the place got smashed in the last earthquakes and all Pa's friends were killed then and in the Big Jerk. So he had to start over and throw the Nest together quick without any advantages, just using any stuff he could lay his hands on.

I guess he's telling pretty much the truth when he says he didn't have any time to keep an eye on how other folks behaved, either then or in the Big Freeze that followed — followed very quick, you know, both because the dark star was pulling us away very fast and because Earth's rotation had been slowed in the tug-of-war, so that the nights were ten old nights long.

Still, I've got an idea of some of the things that happened from the frozen folk I've seen, a few of them in other rooms in our building, others clustered around the furnaces in the basements where we go for coal.

In one of the rooms, an old man sits stiff in a chair, with an arm and a leg in splints. In another, a man and woman are huddled together in a bed with heaps of covers over them. You can just see their heads peeking out, close together. And in another a beautiful young lady is sitting with a pile of wraps huddled around her, looking hopefully toward the door, as if waiting for someone who never came back with warmth and food. They're all still and stiff as statues, of course, but just like life.

Pa showed them to me once in quick winks of his flashlight, when he still had a fair supply of batteries and could afford to waste a little light. They scared me pretty bad and made my heart pound, especially the young lady.

Now, with Pa telling his story for the umpteenth time to take our minds off another scare, I got to thinking of the frozen folk again. All of a sudden I got an idea that scared me worse than anything yet. You see, I'd just remembered the face I'd thought I'd seen in the window. I'd forgotten about that on account of trying to hide it from the others.

What, I asked myself, if the frozen folk were coming to life? What if they were like the liquid helium that got a new lease on life and started crawling toward the heat just when you thought its molecules ought to freeze solid forever? Or like the electricity that moves endlessly when it's just about as cold as that? What if the ever-growing cold, with the temperature creeping down the last few degrees to the last zero, had mysteriously wakened the frozen folk to life — not warm-blooded life, but something icy and horrible?

That was a worse idea than the one about something coming down from the dark star to get us.

Or maybe, I thought, both ideas might be true. Something coming down from the dark star and making the frozen folk move, using them to do its work. That would fit with both things I'd seen — the beautiful young lady and the moving, starlike light.

The frozen folk with minds from the dark star behind their unwinking eyes, creeping, crawling, snuffing their way, following the heat to the Nest.

I tell you, that thought gave me a very bad turn and I wanted very badly to tell the others my fears, but I remembered what Pa had said and clenched my teeth and didn't speak.

We were all sitting very still. Even the fire was burning silently. There was just the sound of Pa's voice and the clocks.

And then, from beyond the blankets, I thought I heard a tiny noise. My skin tightened all over me.

Pa was telling about the early years in the Nest and had come to the place where he philosophizes.

"So I asked myself then," he said, "what's the use of going on? What's the use of dragging it out for a few years? Why prolong a doomed existence of hard work and cold and loneliness? The human race is done. The earth is done. Why not give up, I asked myself — and all of a sudden I got the answer."

Again I heard the noise, louder this time, a kind of uncertain, shuffling tread, coming closer. I couldn't breathe.

"Life's always been a business of working hard and fighting the cold," Pa was saying. "The earth's always been a lonely place, millions of miles from the next planet. And no matter how long the human race might have lived, the end would have come some night. Those things don't matter. What matters is that life is good. It has a lovely texture, like some rich cloth or fur, or the petals of flowers — you've seen pictures of those, but I can't describe how they feel — or the fire's glow. It makes everything else worthwhile. And that's as true for the last man as the first."

And still the steps kept shuffling closer. It seemed to me that the inmost blanket trembled and bulged a little. Just as if they were burned into my imagination, I kept seeing those peering, frozen eyes.

"So right then and there," Pa went on, and now I could tell that he heard the steps, too, and was talking loud so we maybe wouldn't hear them, "right then and there I told myself that I was going on as if we had all eternity ahead of us. I'd have children and teach them all I could. I'd get them to read books. I'd plan for the future, try to enlarge and seal the Nest. I'd do what I could to keep everything beautiful and growing. I'd keep alive my feeling of wonder even at the cold and the dark and the distant stars."

But then the blanket actually did move and lift. And there was a bright light somewhere behind it. Pa's voice stopped, his eyes turned to the widening slit, and his hand went out until it touched and gripped the handle of the hammer beside him.

In through the blanket stepped the beautiful young lady. She stood there looking at us the strangest way, and she carried something bright and un- winking in her hand. And two other faces peered over her shoulders — men's faces, white and staring.

Well, my heart couldn't have been stopped for more than four or five beats before I realized she was wearing a suit and helmet like Pa's homemade ones, only fancier, and that the men were, too — and that the frozen folk certainly wouldn't be wearing those. Also, I noticed that the bright thing in her hand was just a kind of flashlight.

The silence kept on while I swallowed hard a couple of times, and after that there was all sorts of jabbering and commotion.

They were simply people, you see. We hadn't been the only ones to survive; we'd just thought so, for natural enough reasons. These three people had survived, and quite a few others with them. And when we found out *how* they'd survived, Pa let out the biggest whoop of joy.

They were from Los Alamos and they were getting their heat and power from atomic energy. Just using the uranium and plutonium intended for bombs, they had enough to go on for thousands of years. They had a regular little airtight city, with airlocks and all. They even generated electric light and grew plants and animals by it. (At this Pa let out a second whoop, waking Ma from her faint.)

But if we were flabbergasted at them, they were double-flabbergasted at us.

One of the men kept saying, "But it's impossible, I tell you. You can't maintain an air supply without hermetic sealing. It's simply impossible."

That was after he had got his helmet off and was using our air. Meanwhile, the young lady kept looking around at us as if we were saints, and telling us we'd done something amazing, and suddenly she broke down and cried.

They'd been scouting around for survivors, but they never expected to find any in a place like this. They had rocket ships at Los Alamos and plenty of chemical fuel. As for liquid oxygen, all you had to do was go out and shovel the air blanket at the top level. So after they'd got things going smoothly at Los Alamos, which had taken years, they'd decided to make some trips to likely places where there might be other survivors. No good trying long-distance radio signals, of course, since there was no atmosphere to carry them around the curve of Earth.

Well, they'd found other colonies at Argonne and Brookhaven and way around the world at Harwell and Tanna Tuva. And now they'd been giving our city a look, not really expecting to find anything. But they had an instrument that noticed the faintest heat waves and it had told them there was something warm down here, so they'd landed to investigate. Of course we hadn't heard them land, since there was no air to carry the sound, and they'd had to investigate around quite a while before finding us. Their instruments had given them a wrong steer and they'd wasted some time in the building across the street.

By now, all five adults were talking like sixty. Pa was demonstrating to the men how he worked the fire and got rid of the ice in the chimney and all that. Ma had perked up wonderfully and was showing the young lady her cooking and sewing stuff, and even asking about how the women dressed at Los Alamos. The strangers marveled at everything and praised it to the skies. I could tell from the way they wrinkled their noses that they found the Nest a bit smelly, but they never mentioned that at all and just asked bushels of questions.

In fact, there was so much talking and excitement that Pa forgot about things, and it wasn't until they were all getting groggy that he looked and found the air had all boiled away in the pail. He got another bucket of air quick from behind the blankets. Of course that started them all laughing and jabbering again. The newcomers even got a little drunk. They weren't used to so much oxygen.

Funny thing, though — I didn't do much talking at all and Sis hung on to Ma all the time and hid her face when anybody looked at her. I felt pretty uncomfortable and disturbed myself, even about the young lady. Glimpsing her outside there, I'd had all sorts of mushy thoughts, but now I was just embarrassed and scared of her, even though she tried to be nice as anything to me.

I sort of wished they'd all quit crowding the Nest and let us be alone and get our feelings straightened out.

And when the newcomers began to talk about our all going to Los Alamos, as if that were taken for granted, I could see that something of the same feeling struck Pa and Ma, too. Pa got very silent all of a sudden and Ma kept telling the young lady, "But I wouldn't know how to act there and I haven't any clothes."

The strangers were puzzled like anything at first, but then they got the idea. As Pa kept saying, "It just doesn't seem right to let this fire go out."

Well, the strangers are gone, but they're coming back. It hasn't been decided yet just what will happen. Maybe the Nest will be kept up as what one of the strangers called a "survival school." Or maybe we will join the pioneers who are going to try to establish a new colony at the uranium mines at Great Slave Lake or in the Congo.

Of course, now that the strangers are gone, I've been thinking a lot about Los Alamos and those other tremendous colonies. I have a hankering to see them for myself.

You ask me, Pa wants to see them, too. He's been getting pretty thoughtful, watching Ma and Sis perk up.

"It's different, now that we know others are alive," he explains to me. "Your mother doesn't feel so hopeless any more. Neither do I, for that matter, not having to carry the whole responsibility for keeping the human race going, so to speak. It scares a person."

I looked around at the blanket walls and the fire and the pails of air boiling away and Ma and Sis sleeping in the warmth and the flickering light.

"It's not going to be easy to leave the Nest," I said, wanting to cry, kind of. "It's so small and there's just the four of us. I get scared at the idea of big places and a lot of strangers."

He nodded and put another piece of coal on the fire. Then he looked at the little pile and grinned suddenly and put a couple of handfuls on, just as if it was one of our birthdays or Christmas.

"You'll quickly get over that feeling, son," he said. "The trouble with the world was that it kept getting smaller and smaller, till it ended with just the Nest. Now it'll be good to have a real huge world again, the way it was in the beginning."

I guess he's right. You think the beautiful young lady will wait for me till I grow up? I'll be twenty in only ten years.

E

ESP, or extrasensory perception — the ability to communicate beyond the range of normal senses like seeing and hearing. Scientists are divided on the actual existence of ESP, and the subject remains unresolved and controversial. Many of the stories of extrasensory perception are in the realm of fantasy and the supernatural, but these "gifts" do occur in science fiction, especially in stories about *mutants,* humans or other beings who have been changed by radioactivity or other means. ESP stories can be found in *14 Great Tales of ESP* (Fawcett Gold Medal, 1969).

The Odor of Thought

ROBERT SHECKLEY

Leroy Cleevy's real trouble started when he was taking Mailship 243 through the uncolonized Seergon Cluster. Before this, he had had the usual problems of an interstellar mailman: an old ship, scored tubes, and faulty astrogation. But now, while he was taking line-of-direction readings, he noticed that his ship was growing uncomfortably warm.

He sighed unhappily, switched on the refrigeration, and contacted the postmaster at Base. He was at the extreme limit of radio contact, and the postmaster's voice floated in on a sea of static.

"More trouble, Cleevy?" the postmaster asked, in the ominous tones of a man who writes schedules and believes in them.

"Oh, I don't know," Cleevy said brightly. "Aside from the tubes and astrogation and wiring, everything's fine except for the insulation and refrigeration."

"It's a damned shame," the postmaster said, suddenly sympathetic. "I know how you feel."

Cleevy switched the refrigeration to FULL, wiped perspiration from his eyes, and decided that the postmaster only *thought* he knew how he felt.

"Haven't I asked the government for new ships over and over again?" The postmaster laughed ruefully. "They seem to feel that I can get the mail through in any old crate."

At the moment Cleevy wasn't interested in the postmaster's troubles. Even with the refrigeration laboring at FULL, the ship was overheating.

"Hang on a moment," he said. He went to the rear of the ship, where the heat seemed to be emanating from, and found that three of his tanks were filled not with fuel, but with a bubbling white-hot slag. The fourth tank was rapidly undergoing the same change.

Cleevy stared for a moment, turned, and sprinted to the radio.

"No more fuel," he said. "Catalytic reactions, I think. I told you we needed new tanks. I'm putting down on the first oxygen planet I can find."

He pulled down the *Emergency Manual* and looked up the Seergon Cluster. There were no colonies in the group, but the oxygen worlds had been charted for future reference. What was on them, aside from oxygen, no one knew. Cleevy expected to find out, if his ship stayed together long enough.

"I'll try 3-M-22!" he shouted over the mounting static.

"Take good care of the mail," the postmaster howled back. "I'm sending a ship right out."

Cleevy told him what he could do with the mail, all twenty pounds of it. But the postmaster had signed off by then.

Cleevy made a good landing on 3-M-22, exceptionally good, taking into consideration that his instruments were too hot to touch, his tubes were warped by heat, and the mail sack strapped to his back hampered his movements. Mailship 243 sailed in like a swan. Twenty feet above the planet's surface it gave up and dropped like a stone.

Cleevy held on to consciousness, although he was certain every bone in his body was broken. The sides of the ship were turning a dull red when he stumbled through the escape hatch, the mail sack still firmly strapped to his back.

He staggered 100 yards, eyes closed. Then the ship exploded and knocked him flat on his face. He stood up, took two more steps, and passed out completely.

When he recovered consciousness, he was lying on a little hillside, face down in tall grass. He was in a beautiful state of shock. He felt that he was detached from his body, a pure intellect floating in the air. All worries, emotions, fears remained with his body; *he* was free.

He looked around and saw that a small animal was passing near him. It was about the size of a squirrel, but with dull green fur.

As it came close, he saw that it had no eyes or ears.

This didn't surprise him. On the contrary, it seemed quite fitting. Why in hell *should* a squirrel have eyes or ears? Squirrels were better off not seeing the pain and torture of the world, not hearing the anguished screams of . . .

Another animal approached, and this one was the size and shape of a timber wolf, but also colored green. Parallel evolution? It didn't matter in the total scheme of things, he decided. This one, too, was eyeless and earless. But it had a magnificent set of teeth.

Cleevy watched with only faint interest. What does a pure intellect care for wolves and squirrels, eyeless or otherwise? He observed that the squirrel had frozen not more than five feet from the wolf. The wolf approached slowly. Then, not three feet away, he seemed to lose the scent. He shook his head and turned a slow circle. When he moved forward again, he wasn't going in the right direction.

The blind hunt the blind, Cleevy told himself, and it seemed a deep and eternal truth. As he watched, the squirrel quivered; the wolf whirled, pounced, and devoured it in three gulps.

What large teeth wolves have, Cleevy thought. Instantly the eyeless wolf whirled and faced him.

Now he's going to eat me, Cleevy thought. It amused him to realize that he was the first human to be eaten on this planet.

The wolf was snarling in his face when Cleevy passed out again.

It was evening when he recovered. Long shadows had formed over the land, and the sun was low in the sky. Cleevy sat up and flexed his arms and legs experimentally. Nothing was broken.

He got on one knee, groggy, but in possession of his senses. What had happened? He remembered the crash as though it were a thousand years ago. The ship had burned, he had walked away and fainted. After that he had met a wolf and a squirrel.

He climbed unsteadily to his feet and looked around. He must have dreamed that last part. If there had been a wolf, he would have been killed.

Glancing down at his feet, he saw the squirrel's green tail and, a little farther away, its head.

He tried desperately to think. So there *had* been a wolf, and a hungry one. If he expected to survive until the rescue ship came, he had to find out exactly what had happened, and why.

Neither animal had eyes or ears. How did they track each other? Smell? If so, why did the wolf have so much trouble finding the squirrel?

He heard a low growl and turned. There, not fifty feet away, was something that looked like a panther. A yellow-brown, eyeless, earless panther.

Damned menagerie, Cleevy thought, and crouched down in the tall grass. This planet was rushing him along too fast. He needed time to think. How did these animals operate? Instead of sight, did they have a sense of location?

The panther began to move away.

Cleevy breathed a little easier. Perhaps, if he stayed out of sight, the panther . . .

As soon as he thought the word "panther," the beast turned in his direction.

What have I done? Cleevy asked himself, burrowing deeper into the grass. He can't smell me or see me or hear me. All I did was decide to stay out of his way . . .

Head high, the panther began to pace toward him.

That did it. Without eyes or ears, there was only one way the beast could have detected him.

It had to be telepathic!

To test his theory, he thought the word "panther," identifying it automatically with the animal that was approaching him. The panther roared furiously and shortened the distance between them.

In a fraction of a second, Cleevy understood a lot of things. The wolf had been tracking the squirrel by telepathy. The squirrel had frozen — perhaps it had even stopped thinking! The wolf had been thrown off the scent — until the squirrel wasn't able to keep from thinking any longer.

In that case, why hadn't the wolf attacked him while he was unconscious? Perhaps he had stopped thinking — or at least, stopped thinking on a wavelength that the wolf could receive. Probably there was more to it than that.

Right now, his problem was the *panther.*

The beast roared again. It was only thirty feet away and closing the distance rapidly.

All he had to do, Cleevy thought, was not to think of — was to think of something else. In that way, perhaps the — well, perhaps it would lose the scent. He started to think about all the girls he had ever known, in painstaking detail.

The panther stopped and pawed the ground doubtfully.

Cleevy went on thinking; about girls, and ships, and planets, and girls, and ships, and everything but panthers . . .

The panther advanced another five feet.

Damn it, he thought, how do you *not* think of something? You think furiously about stones and rocks and people and places and things, but your mind always returns to — but you ignore that and concentrate on your sainted grandmother, your drunken old father, the bruises on your right leg. (Count them. Eight. Count them again. Still eight.) And now you glance up, casually, seeing, but not really recognizing the — anyhow, it's still advancing.

Cleevy found that trying *not* to think of something is like trying to stop an avalanche with your bare hands. He realized that the human mind couldn't be inhibited so directly and consciously as all that. It takes time and practice.

He had about fifteen feet left in which to learn how not to think of a . . .

Well, there are also card games to think about, and parties, and dogs, cats, horses, mice, sheep, wolves (move away!), and bruises, battleships, caves, lairs, dens, cubs (watch out), *p-paramounts,* and tantamounts and gadabouts and roundabouts and roustabouts and ins-and-outs (about eight feet), meals, food, fire, fox, fur, pigs, pokes, prams, and p-p-p-p- . . .

The panther was about five feet away now and crouching for the spring. Cleevy couldn't hold back the thought any longer. Then, in a burst of inspiration, he thought:

Pantheress!

The panther, still crouching, faced him doubtfully.

Cleevy concentrated on the idea of a pantheress. *He* was a pantheress, and what did this panther mean by frightening her that way? He thought about his (her, damn it!) cubs, a warm cave, the pleasure of tracking down squirrels . . .

The panther advanced slowly and rubbed against Cleevy. Cleevy thought desperately, What fine weather we've been having, and what a fine panther this chap really is, so big, so strong, and with such enormous teeth.

The panther purred!

Cleevy lay down and curled an imaginary tail around him and decided he was going to sleep. The panther stood by indecisively. He seemed to feel that something was wrong. He growled once, deep in his throat, then turned and loped away.

The sun had just set, and the entire land was a deep blue. Cleevy found that he was shaking uncontrollably, and on the verge of hysterical laughter. If the panther had stayed another moment . . .

He controlled himself with an effort. It was time for some serious thinking.

Probably every animal had its characteristic thought-smell. A squirrel emitted one kind, a wolf another, and a human still another. The all-important question was, could he be traced only when he thought of some animal? Or could his thought patterns, like an odor, be detected even when he was not thinking of anything in particular?

Apparently, the panther had scented him only when he thought specifically of it. But that could be due to unfamiliarity. His alien thought-smell might have confused the panther — this time.

He'd just have to wait and see. The panther probably wasn't stupid. It was just the first time that trick had been played on him.

Any trick will work — once.

Cleevy lay back and stared at the sky. He was too tired to move, and his bruised body ached. What would happen now, at night? Did the beasts continue to hunt? Or was there a truce of some sort? He didn't give a damn.

To hell with squirrels, wolves, panthers, lions, tigers, and reindeer.

He slept.

The next morning, he was surprised to find himself still alive. So far, so good. It might be a good day after all. Cheerfully he walked to his ship.

All that was left of Mailship 243 was a pile of twisted metal strewn across the scorched earth. Cleevy found a bar of metal, hefted it, and slid it into his belt below the mail sack. It wasn't much of a weapon, but it gave him a certain confidence.

The ship was a total loss. He left and began to look for food. In the surrounding countryside there were several fruit-bearing shrubs. He sampled one warily and found it tart, but not unpleasant. He gorged himself on fruit and washed it down with water from a nearby stream.

He hadn't seen any animals so far. Of course, for all he knew, they could be closing in on him now.

He avoided the thought and started looking for a place to hide. His best bet was to stay out of sight until the rescue ship came. He tramped over the gentle rolling hills, looking for a cliff, a tree, a cave. But the amiable landscape presented nothing larger than a six-foot shrub.

By afternoon he was tired and irritated, and scanning the skies anxiously. Why wasn't the ship here? It should take no longer than a day or two, he estimated, for a fast emergency ship to reach him.

If the postmaster was looking on the right planet.

There was a movement in the sky. He looked up, his heart racing furiously. There was something there!

It was a bird. It sailed slowly over him, balancing easily on its gigantic wings. It dipped once, then flew on.

It looked amazingly like a vulture.

He continued walking. In another moment, he found himself face to face with four blind wolves.

That took care of one question. He *could* be traced by his characteristic thought-smell. Evidently the beasts of this planet had decided he wasn't too alien to eat.

The wolves moved cautiously toward him. Cleevy tried the trick he had used the other day. Lifting the metal bar out of his belt, he thought of himself as a female wolf searching for her cubs. Won't one of you gentlemen help me find them? They were here only a few minutes ago. One was green, one was spotted, and the other . . .

Perhaps these wolves didn't have spotted cubs. One of them leaped at

Cleevy. Cleevy struck him in midair with his bar, and the wolf staggered back.

Shoulder to shoulder, the four closed in.

Desperately, Cleevy tried to think himself out of existence. No use. The wolves kept on coming.

Cleevy thought of a panther. *He* was a panther, a big one, and he was looking forward to a meal of wolf.

That stopped them. They switched their tails anxiously, but held their ground.

Cleevy growled, pawed the earth, and stalked forward. The wolves retreated, but one started to slip in back of him.

He moved sideways, trying to keep from being circled. It seemed that they really didn't believe him. Perhaps he didn't make a good panther. They had stopped retreating. One was in back of him, and the others stood firm, their tongues lolling out on their wet, open jaws. Cleevy growled ferociously and swung his club. A wolf darted back, but the one behind him sprang, landed on the mail sack, and knocked him over.

As they piled on, Cleevy had another inspiration. He imagined himself to be a snake, very fast, deadly, with poison fangs that could take a wolf's life in an instant.

They were off him at once. Cleevy hissed and arched his boneless neck. The wolves howled angrily, but showed no inclination to attack.

Then Cleevy made a mistake. He knew that he should stand firm and brazen it out. But his body had its own ideas. Involuntarily he turned and sprinted away.

The wolves loped after him, and glancing up, Cleevy could see the vultures gathering for the remains. He controlled himself and tried to become a snake again, but the wolves kept coming.

The vultures overhead gave him an idea. As a spaceman, he knew what the land looked like from the air. Cleevy decided to become a bird. He imagined himself soaring, balanced easily on an updraft, looking down on the green, rolling land.

The wolves were confused. They ran in circles and leaped into the air. Cleevy continued soaring, higher and higher, backing away slowly as he did so.

Finally he was out of sight of the wolves, and it was evening. He was exhausted. He had lived through another day. But evidently his gambits were good only once. What was he going to do tomorrow, if the rescue ship didn't come?

After it grew dark, he lay awake for a long time, watching the sky. But all he saw were stars. And all he heard was the occasional growl of a wolf, or the roar of a panther dreaming of his breakfast.

*

Morning came too soon. Cleevy awoke still tired and unrefreshed. He lay back and waited for something to happen.

Where was the rescue ship? They had had plenty of time, he decided. Why weren't they here? If they waited too long, the panther . . .

He shouldn't have thought it. In answer, he heard a roar on his right.

He stood up and moved away from the sound. He decided he'd be better off facing the wolves . . .

He shouldn't have thought that either, because now the roar of the panther was joined by the howl of a wolf pack.

Cleevy met them simultaneously. A green-yellow panther stepped daintily out of the underbrush in front of him. On the other side, he could make out the shapes of several wolves. For a moment, he thought they might fight it out. If the wolves jumped the panther, he could get away . . .

But they were interested only in him. Why should they fight each other, he realized, when he was around, broadcasting his fears and helplessness for all to hear?

The panther moved toward him. The wolves stayed back, evidently content to take the remains. Cleevy tried the bird routine, but the panther, after hesitating a moment, kept on coming.

Cheevy backed toward the wolves, wishing he had something to climb. What he needed was a cliff, or even a decent-sized tree . . .

But there were shrubs! With inventiveness born of desperation, Cleevy became a six-foot shrub. He didn't really know how a shrub would think, but he did his best.

He was blossoming now. And one of his roots felt a little wobbly — the result of that last storm. Still, he was a pretty good shrub, taking everything into consideration.

Out of the corner of his branches, he saw the wolves stop moving. The panther circled him, sniffed, and cocked his head to one side.

Really now, he thought, who would want to take a bite out of a shrub? You might have thought I was something else, but actually, I'm just a shrub. You wouldn't want a mouthful of leaves, would you? And you might break a tooth on my branches. Who ever heard of panthers eating shrubs? And I *am* a shrub. Ask my mother. She was a shrub, too. We've all been shrubs, ever since the Carboniferous Age.

The panther showed no signs of attacking. But he showed no signs of leaving, either. Cleevy wondered if he could keep it up. What should he think about next? The beauties of spring? A nest of robins in his hair?

A little bird landed on his shoulder.

Isn't that nice, Cleevy thought. He thinks I'm a shrub, too. He's going to build a nest in my branches. That's perfectly lovely. All the other shrubs will be jealous of me.

The bird tapped lightly at Cleevy's neck.

Easy, Cleevy thought. Wouldn't want to kill the tree that feeds you . . .

The bird tapped again, experimentally. Then, setting its webbed feet firmly, proceeded to tap at Cleevy's neck with the speed of a pneumatic hammer.

A damned woodpecker, Cleevy thought, trying to stay shrublike. He noticed that the panther was suddenly restive. But after the bird had punctured his neck for the fifteenth time, Cleevy couldn't help himself. He picked up the bird and threw it at the panther.

The panther snapped, but not in time. Outraged, the bird flew around Cleevy's head, scouting. Then it streaked away for the quieter shrubs.

Instantly, Cleevy became a shrub again, but that game was over. The panther cuffed at him. Cleevy tried to run, stumbled over a wolf, and fell. With the panther growling in his ear, he knew that he was a corpse already.

The panther hesitated.

Cleevy now became a corpse to his melting fingertips. He had been dead for days, weeks. His blood had long since drained away. His flesh stank. All that was left was rot and decay. No sane animal would touch him, no matter how hungry it was.

The panther seemed to agree. He backed away. The wolves howled hungrily, but they, too, were in retreat.

Cleevy advanced his putrefaction several days. He concentrated on how horribly indigestible he was, how genuinely unsavory. And there was conviction in back of his thought. He honestly didn't believe he would make a good meal for anyone.

The panther continued to move away, followed by the wolves. He was saved! He could go on being a corpse for the rest of his life, if necessary . . .

And then he smelled *truly* rotten flesh. Looking around, he saw that an enormous bird had landed beside him.

On Earth, it would have been called a vulture.

Cleevy could have cried at that moment. Wouldn't anything work? The vulture waddled toward him, and Cleevy jumped to his feet and kicked it away. If he had to be eaten, it wasn't going to be by a vulture.

The panther came back like a lightning bolt, and there seemed to be anger and frustration on that blank, furry face. Cleevy raised his metal bar, wishing he had a tree to climb, a gun to shoot, or even a torch to wave . . .

A torch!

He knew at once that he had found the answer. He blazed in the panther's face, and the panther backed away, squealing. Quickly Cleevy began to burn in all directions, devouring the dry grass, setting fire to the shrubs.

The panther and the wolves darted away.

Now it was his turn! He should have remembered that all animals have a deep, instinctive dread of fire. By God, he was going to be the greatest fire that ever hit this place!

A light breeze came up and fanned him across the rolling land. Squirrels fled from the underbrush and streaked away from him. Families of birds took flight, and panthers, wolves, and other animals ran side by side, all thought of food driven from their minds, wishing only to escape from the fire — to escape from him!

Dimly, Cleevy realized that he had now become truly telepathic himself. Eyes closed, he could see on all sides of him and sense what was going on. As a roaring fire he advanced, sweeping everything before him. And he could *feel* the fear in their minds as they raced away.

It was fitting. Hadn't man always been the master because of his adaptability, his superior intelligence? The same results obtained here, too. Proudly he jumped a narrow stream three miles away, ignited a clump of bushes, flamed, spurted . . .

And then he felt the first drop of water.

He burned on, but the one drop became five, then fifteen, then five hundred. He was drenched, and his fuel, the grass and shrubs, were soon dripping with water.

He was being put out.

It just wasn't fair, Cleevy thought. By rights he should have won. He had met this planet on its own terms and beaten it — only to have an act of nature ruin everything.

Cautiously, the animals were starting to return.

The water poured down. The last of Cleevy's flames went out. Cleevy sighed, and fainted.

". . . a damned fine job. You held on to your mail, and that's the mark of a good postman. Perhaps we can arrange a medal."

Cleevy opened his eyes. The postmaster was standing over him, beaming proudly. He was lying on a bunk, and overhead he could see curving metal walls.

He was on the rescue ship.

"What happened?" he croaked.

"We got you just in time," the postmaster said. "You'd better not move yet. We were almost too late."

Cleevy felt the ship lift and knew that they were leaving the surface of 3-M-22. He staggered to the port and looked at the green land below him.

"It was close," the postmaster said, standing beside Cleevy and looking down. "We got the ship's sprinkler system going just in time. You were standing in the center of the damnedest grass fire I've ever seen." Looking down at the unscarred green land, the postmaster seemed to have a moment of doubt. He looked again, and his expression reminded Cleevy of the panther he had tricked.

"Say — how come you weren't burned?"

ex/tra/ter/res/tri/als — creatures who live elsewhere than on the earth. None have been discovered so far, although they are widely believed by scientists and a majority of the general public to exist somewhere in the universe. Usually called "aliens" in science fiction, they come in all shapes, sizes, and compositions, and can be friendly, dangerous, or just plain uninterested. Human beings who do not live on Earth can also be considered extraterrestrials. A good collection of stories about these creatures is *Aliens!* (Pocket Books, 1980).

The Last Monster

POUL ANDERSON

The sun woke him.

He stirred uneasily, feeling the long shafts of light slant over the land. The muted gossip of birds became a rush of noise and a small wind blew till the leaves chattered at him. Wake up, wake up, wake up, Rugo, there is a new day on the hills and you can't lie sleeping, wake up!

The light reached under his eyelids, roiling the darkness of dreams. He mumbled and curled into a tighter knot, drawing sleep back around him like a cloak, sinking toward the dark and the unknowingness with his mother's face before him.

She laughed down the long ways of night, calling and calling, and he tried to follow her, but the sun wouldn't let him.

Mother, he whimpered. Mother, please come back, Mother.

She had gone and left him, once very long ago. He had been little then and the cave had been big and gloomy and cold, and there were flutterings and watchings in the shadows of it and he had been frightened. She had said she was going after food, and had kissed him and gone off down the steep moonlit valley. And there she must have met the Strangers, because she never came back. And he had cried for a long time and called her name, but she didn't return.

That had been so long ago that he couldn't number the years. But now that

This was first published under the title *Terminal Quest*.

he was getting old, she must have remembered him and been sorry she left, for lately she often came back at night.

The dew was cold on his skin. He felt the stiffness in him, the ache of muscle and bone and dulling nerve, and forced himself to move. If he stirred all at once, stretching himself and not letting his throat rasp with the pain of it, he could work the damp and the cold and the earth out, he could open his eyes and look at the new day.

It was going to be hot. Rugo's vision wasn't so good any more; the sun was only a blur of fire low on the shadowy horizon, and the mist that streamed through the dales turned it ruddy. But he knew that before midday it would be hot.

He got up, slowly climbing to all four feet, pulling himself erect with the help of a low branch. Hunger was a dull ache in him. He looked emptily around at the thicket, a copse of scrub halfway up the hillside. There were the bushes and the trees, a hard summer green that would be like metal later in the day. There were the dead leaves rustling soggily underfoot, still wet with the dew that steamed away in white vapors. There were birds piping up the sun, but nowhere food, nowhere anything to eat.

Mother, he thought, you said you would bring back something to eat.

He shook his big scaly head, clearing out the fog of dreams. Today he would have to go down into the valley. He had eaten the last berries on the hillside, he had waited here for days with weakness creeping from his belly through his bones, and now he would have to go down to the Strangers.

He went slowly out of the thicket and started down the hillside. The grass rustled under his feet, the earth quivered a little beneath his great weight. The hill slanted up to the sky and down to the misty dales, and he was alone with the morning.

Only grass and the small flowers grew here. Once the hills had been tall with forest; he recalled cool shadowy depths and the windy roar of the treetops, small suns spattered on the ground and the drunken sweetness of resin smell in summer and the blaze of broken light from a million winter crystals. But the Strangers had cut down the woods and now there were only rotting stumps and his blurred remembering. His alone, for the men who had hewed down the forest were dead and their sons never knew — and when he was gone, who would care? Who would be left to care?

He came to a brook that rushed down the hillside, rising from a spring higher up and flowing to join the Thunder River. The water was cold and clean and he drank heavily, slopping it into him with both hands and wriggling his tail with the refreshment of it. This much remained to him, at least, though the source was dwindling now that the watershed was gone. But he would be dead before the brook was dry, so it didn't matter too much.

He waded over it. The cold water set his lame foot to tingling and needling. Beyond it he found the old logging trail and went down that. He walked slowly, not being eager to do that which he must, and tried to make a plan.

The Strangers had given him food now and then, out of charity or in return for work. Once he had labored almost a year for a man, who had given him a place to sleep and as much as he wanted to eat — a good man to work for, not full of the hurry which seemed to be in his race, with a quiet voice and gentle eyes. But then the man had taken a woman, and she was afraid of Rugo, so he had had to leave.

A couple of times, too, men from Earth itself had come to talk to him. They had asked him many questions about his people. How had they lived, what was their word for this and that, did he remember any of their dances or music? But he couldn't tell them much, for his folk had been hunted before he was born, he had seen a flying-thing spear his father with flame and later his mother had gone to look for food and not come back. The men from Earth had, in fact, told him more than he could give them, told him about cities and books and gods which his people had had, and if he had wanted to learn these things from the Strangers they could have told him more. They, too, had paid him something, and he had eaten well for a while.

I am old now, thought Rugo, and not very strong. I never was strong, beside the powers they have. One of us could drive fifty of them before him — but one of them, seated at the wheel of a thing of metal and fire, could reap a thousand of us. And I frighten their women and children and animals. So it will be hard to find work, and I may have to beg a little bread for no more return than going away. And the grain that they will feed me grew in the soil of this world; it is strong with the bones of my father and fat with the flesh of my mother. But one must eat.

When he came down into the valley, the mists had lifted in ragged streamers and already he could feel the heat of the sun. The trail led onto a road, and he turned north toward the human settlements. Nobody was in sight yet, and it was quiet. His footfalls rang loud on the pavement; it was hard under his soles and the impact of walking jarred up into his legs like small sharp needles. He looked around him, trying to ignore the hurting.

They had cut down the trees and harrowed the land and sowed grain of Earth, until now the valley lay open to the sky. The brassy sun of summer and the mordant winds of winter rode over the deep glens he remembered, and the only trees were in neat orchards bearing alien fruit. It was as if these Strangers were afraid of the dark, as if they were so frightened by shadows and half-lights and rustling unseen distances that they had to clear it all away, one sweep of fire and thunder and then the bright inflexible steel of their world rising above the dusty plains.

Only fear could make beings so vicious, even as fear had driven Rugo's folk to rush, huge and scaled and black, out of the mountains, to smash houses and burn grain fields and wreck machines, even as fear had brought an answer from the Strangers which heaped stinking bodies in the tumbled ruins of the cities he had never seen. Only the Strangers were more powerful, and their fears had won.

He heard the machine coming behind him, roaring and pounding down the road with a whistle of cloven air flapping in its wake, and remembered in a sudden gulping that it was forbidden to walk in the middle of the road. He scrambled to one side, but it was the wrong one, the side they drove on, and the truck screamed around him on smoking tires and ground to a halt on the shoulder.

A Stranger climbed out, and he was almost dancing with fury. His curses poured forth so fast that Rugo couldn't follow them. He caught a few words: "Damned weird thing . . . Coulda killed me . . . Oughta be shot . . . Have the law on yuh . . ."

Rugo stood watching. He had twice the height of the skinny pink shape that jittered and railed before him, and some four times the bulk, and though he was old, one sweep of his hand would stave in the skull and spatter the brains on the hot hard concrete. Only all the power of the Strangers was behind the creature, fire and ruin and flying steel, and he was the last of his folk and sometimes his mother came at night to see him. So he stood quietly, hoping the man would get tired and go away.

A booted foot slammed against his shin, and he cried out with the pain of it and lifted one arm the way he had done as a child when the bombs were falling and metal rained around him.

The man sprang back. "Don't yuh try it," he said quickly. "Don't do nothing. They'll hunt yuh down if yuh touch me."

"Go," said Rugo, twisting his tongue and throat to the foreign syllables which he knew better than the dimly recalled language of his people. "Please go."

"Yuh're on'y here while yuh behave yuhrself. Keep yuhr place, see. Nasty devil! Watch yuhrself." The man got back into the truck and started it. The spinning tires threw gravel back at Rugo.

He stood watching the machine, his hands hanging empty at his sides, until it was beyond his aging sight. Then he started walking again, careful to stay on the correct edge of the road.

Presently a farm appeared over a ridge. It lay a little way in from the highway, a neat white house sitting primly among trees, with its big outbuildings clustered behind it and the broad yellowing grainfields beyond. The sun was well into the sky now, mist and dew had burned away, the wind had fallen asleep. It was still and hot. Rugo's feet throbbed with the hardness of the road.

He stood at the entrance, wondering if he should go in or not. It was a rich place, they'd have machines and no use for his labor. When he passed by here before, the man had told him shortly to be on his way. But they could perhaps spare a piece of bread and a jug of water, just to be rid of him or maybe to keep him alive. He knew he was one of the neighborhood sights, the last native. Visitors often climbed up his hill to see him and toss a few coins at his feet and take pictures while he gathered them.

He puzzled out the name on the mailbox. Elias Whately. He'd try his luck with Elias Whately.

As he came up the driveway a dog bounded forth and started barking, high shrill notes that hurt his ears. The animal danced around and snapped with a rage that was half panic. None of the beasts from Earth could stand the sight and smell of him; they knew he was not of their world and a primitive terror rose in them. He remembered the pain when teeth nipped his rheumatic legs. Once he had killed a dog that bit him, a single unthinking swipe of his tail, and the owner had fired a shotgun at him. His scales had turned most of the charge, but some was still lodged deep in his flesh and bit him again when the days were cold.

"Please," he said to the dog. His bass rumbled in the warm, still air and the barking grew more frantic. "Please, I will not harm, please do not bite."

"O-oh!"

The woman in the front yard let out a little scream and ran before him, up the steps and through the door to slam it in his face. Rugo sighed, feeling suddenly tired. She was afraid. They were all afraid. They had called his folk trolls, which were something evil in their old myths. He remembered that his grandfather, before he died in a shelterless winter, had called them torrogs, which he said were pale bony things that ate the dead, and Rugo smiled with a wryness that was sour in his mouth.

But little use in trying here. He turned to go.

"You!"

He turned back to face the tall man who stood in the door. The man held a rifle, and his long face was clamped tight. Behind him peeked a red-headed boy, maybe thirteen years old, a cub with the same narrow eyes as his father.

"What's the idea of coming in here?" asked the man. His voice was like the grating of iron.

"Please, sir," said Rugo, "I am hungry. I thought if I could do some work, or if you had any scraps — "

"So now it's begging, eh?" demanded Whately. "Don't you know that's against the law? You could be put in jail. By heaven, you ought to be! Public nuisance, that's all you are."

"I only wanted work," said Rugo.

"So you come in and frighten my wife? You know there's nothing here for a savage to do. Can you run a tractor? Can you repair a generator? Can you even eat without slobbering it on the ground?" Whately spat. "You're a squatter on somebody else's land, and you know it. If I owned that property you'd be out on your worthless butt so fast you wouldn't know which end was up.

"Be glad you're alive! When I think of what you murdering slimy monsters did — Forty years! Forty years, crammed in stinking spaceships, cutting themselves off from Earth and all the human race, dying without seeing ground, fighting every foot of all the light-years, to get to Tau Ceti — and then you said the Earthmen couldn't stay! Then you came and burned their homes and butchered women and children! The planet's well rid of you, all the scum of you, and it's a wonder somebody doesn't take a gun and clear off the last of the garbage." He half lifted his weapon.

It was no use explaining, thought Rugo. Maybe there really had been a misunderstanding, as his grandfather had claimed, maybe the old counselors had thought the first explorers were only asking if more like them could come and had not expected settlers when they gave permission — or maybe, realizing that the Strangers would be too strong, they had decided to break their word and fight to hold their planet.

But what use now? The Strangers had won the war, with guns and bombs and a plague virus that went like a scythe through the natives; they had hunted the few immunes down like animals, and now he was the last of his kind in all the world and it was too late to explain.

"Sic 'im, Shep!" cried the boy. "Sic 'im! Go get 'im!"

The dog barked in closer, rushing and retreating, trying to work its cowardice into rage.

"Shut up, Sam," said Whately to his son. Then to Rugo, "Get!"

"I will leave," said Rugo. He tried to stop the trembling that shuddered in him, the nerve-wrenching fear of what the gun could spit. He was not afraid to die, he thought sickly, he would welcome the darkness when it came — but his life was so deep-seated, he would live and live and live while the slugs tore into him. He might take hours to die.

"I will be on my way, sir," he said.

"No, you won't," snapped Whately. "I won't have you going down to the village and scaring little kids there. Back where you came from!"

"But, sir — please — "

"Get!" The gun pointed at him, he looked down the muzzle and turned and went out the gate. Whately waved him to the left, back down the road.

The dog charged in and sank its teeth in an ankle where the scales had fallen away. He screamed with the pain of it and began to run, slowly and heavily, weaving in his course. The boy Sam laughed and followed him.

"Nyaah, nyaah, nyaah, ugly ol' troll, crawl back down in yuhr dirty ol' hole!"

*

After a while there were other children, come from the neighboring farms in that timeless blur of running and raw lungs and thudding heart and howling, thundering noise. They followed him, and their dogs barked, and the flung stones rattled off his sides with little swords where they struck.

"Nyaah, nyaah, nyaah, ugly ol' troll, crawl back down in yuhr dirty ol' hole!"

"Please," he whispered. "Please."

When he came to the old trail he hardly saw it. The road danced in a blinding glimmer of heat and dust, the world was tipping and whirling about him, and the clamor in his ears drowned out their shrilling. They danced around him, sure of their immunity, sure of the pain and the weakness and the loneliness that whimpered in his throat, and the dogs yammered and rushed in and nipped his tail and his swollen legs.

Presently he couldn't go on. The hillside was too steep, there was no will left to drive his muscles. He sat down, pulling in knees and tail, hiding his head in his arms, hardly aware in the hot, roaring, whirling blindness that they stoned him and pummeled him and screamed at him.

Sadly he thought to himself, Night and rain and the west wind crying in high trees, a cool wet softness of grass and the wavering little fire, the grave eyes of my father and the dear lost face of my mother — Out of the night and the rainy wind and the forest they hewed down, out of the years and the blurring memories and the shadowland of dreams, come to me, mother, come to me and take me in your arms and carry me home.

After a while they grew tired of it and went away, some turning back and some wandering higher up into the hills after berries. Rugo sat unmoving, buried in himself, letting a measure of strength and the awareness of his pain seep back.

He burned and pulsed, jagged bolts shot through his nerves, his throat was too dry for swallowing and the hunger was like a wild animal deep in his belly. And overhead the sun swam in a haze of heat, pouring it down over him, filling the air with an incandescence of arid light.

After still a longer time, he opened his eyes. The lids felt raw and sandy, vision wavered as if the heat-shimmer had entered his brain. There was a man who stood watching him.

Rugo shrank back, lifting a hand before his face. But the man stood quietly, puffing away on a battered old pipe. He was shabbily dressed and there was a rolled bundle on his shoulders.

"Had a pretty rough session there, didn't you, old-timer?" he asked. His voice was soft. "Here." He bent a lanky frame over the crouching native. "Here, you need a drink."

Rugo lifted the canteen to his lips and gulped till it was empty. The man looked him over. "You're not too banged up," he decided. "Just cuts and abrasions; you trolls always were a tough breed. I'll give you some aneurine, though."

He fished a tube of yellow salve out of one pocket and smeared it on the wounds. The hurt eased, faded to a warm tingle, and Rugo sighed.

"You are very kind, sir," he said unsurely.

"Nah. I wanted to see you, anyway. How you feel now? Better?"

Rugo nodded, slowly, trying to stop the shivers which still ran in him. "I am well, sir," he said.

"Don't 'sir' me. Too many people'd laugh themselves sick to hear it. What was your trouble, anyway?"

"I — I wanted food, sir — pardon me. I w-wanted food. But they — he — told me to go back. Then the dogs came, and the young ones — "

"Kids can be pretty gruesome little monsters at times, all right. Can you walk, old fella? I'd like to find some shade."

Rugo pulled himself to his feet. It was easier than he had thought it would be. "Please, if you will be so kind, I know a place with trees — "

The man swore, softly and imaginatively. "So that's what they've done. Not content with blotting out a whole race, they have to take the guts from the last one left. Look, you, I'm Manuel Jones, and you'll speak to me as one free bum to another or not at all. Now let's find your trees."

They went up the trail without speaking much, though the man whistled a dirty song to himself, and crossed the brook and came to the thicket. When Rugo lay down in the light-speckled shade it was as if he had been born again. He sighed and let his body relax, flowing into the ground, drawing of its old strength.

The human started a fire and opened some cans in his pack and threw their contents into a small kettle. Rugo watched hungrily, hoping he would give him a little, ashamed and angry with himself for the way his stomach rumbled. Manuel Jones squatted under a tree, shoved his hat off his forehead, and got his pipe going afresh.

Blue eyes in a weatherbeaten face watched Rugo with steadiness and no hate nor fear. "I've been looking forward to seeing you," he said. "I wanted to meet the last member of a race which could build the Temple of Otheii."

"What is that?" asked Rugo.

"You don't *know*?"

"No, sir — I mean, pardon me, no, Mr. Jones — "

"Manuel. And don't you forget it."

"No, I was born while the Strangers were hunting the last of us — Manuel. We were always fleeing. I was only a few years old when my mother was killed. I met the last other Gunnur — member of my race — when I was only about twenty. That was almost two hundred years ago. Since then I have been the last."

"God," whispered Manuel. "God, what a race of free-wheeling devils we are!"

"You were stronger," said Rugo. "And anyway it is very long ago now. Those who did it are dead. Some humans have been good to me. One of them saved my life; he got the others to let me live. And some of the rest have been kind."

"Funny sort of kindness, I'd say." Manuel shrugged. "But as you put it, Rugo, it's too late now."

He drew heavily on his pipe. "Still, you had a great civilization. It wasn't technically minded like ours, it wasn't human or fully understandable to humans, but it had its own greatness. Oh, it was a bloody crime to slaughter you, and we'll have to answer for it some day."

"I am old," said Rugo. "I am too old to hate."

"But not too old to be lonesome, eh?" Manuel's smile was lopsided. He fell into silence, puffing blue clouds into the blaze of air.

Presently he went on, thoughtfully, "Of course, one can understand the humans. They were the poor and the disinherited of our land-hungry Earth, they came forty years over empty space with all their hopes, giving their lives to the ships so their children might land — and then your council forbade it. They *couldn't* return, and man never was too nice about his methods when need drove him. They were lonely and scared, and your hulking horrible appearance made it worse. So they fought. But they needn't have been so thorough about it. That was sheer hellishness."

"It does not matter," said Rugo. "It was long ago."

They sat for a while in silence, huddled under the shade against the white flame of sunlight, until the food was ready.

"Ah." Manuel reached gratefully for his eating utensils. "It's not too good, beans and stuff, and I haven't an extra plate. Mind just reaching into the kettle?"

"I — I — It is not needful," mumbled Rugo, suddenly shy again.

"The devil it isn't! Help yourself, old-timer, plenty for all."

The smell of food filled Rugo's nostrils, he could feel his mouth going wet and his stomach screaming at him. And the Stranger really seemed to mean it. Slowly, he dipped his hands into the vessel and brought them out full and ate with the ungraceful manners of his people.

Afterward they lay back, stretching and sighing and letting the faint breeze blow over them. There hadn't been much for one of Rugo's size, but he had emptied the kettle and was more full than he had been for longer than he could well recall.

"I am afraid this meal used all your supplies," he said clumsily.

"No matter," yawned Manuel. "I was damn sick of beans anyway. Meant to lift a chicken tonight."

"You are not from these parts," said Rugo. There was a thawing within him. Here was someone who seemed to expect nothing more than friendship. You could lie in the shade beside him and watch a lone shred of cloud drift over the hot blue sky and let every nerve and muscle go easy. You felt the fullness of your stomach, and you lolled on the grass, and idle words went from one to another, and that was all there was and it was enough.

"You are not a plain tramp," he added thoughtfully.

"Maybe not," said Manuel. "I taught school a good many years ago, in Cetusport. Got into a bit of trouble and had to hit the road and liked it well enough not to settle down anywhere since. Hobo, hunter, traveler to any place that sounds interesting — it's a big world and there's enough in it for a lifetime. I want to get to know this New Terra planet, Rugo. Not that I mean to write a book or any such nonsense. I just want to know it."

He sat up on one elbow. "That's why I came to see you," he said. "You're part of the old world, the last part of it except for empty ruins and a few torn pages in museums. But I have a notion that your race will always haunt us, that no matter how long man is here something of you will enter into him." There was a half-mystical look on his lean face. He was not the dusty tramp now but something else which Rugo could not recognize.

"The planet was yours before we came," he said, "and it shaped you and you shaped it; and now the landscape which was yours will become part of us, and it'll change us in its own slow and subtle ways. I think that whenever a man camps out alone on New Terra, in the big hills where you hear the night talking up in the trees, I think he'll always remember something. There'll always be a shadow just beyond his fire, a voice in the wind and in the rivers, something in the soil that will enter the bread he eats and the water he drinks, and that will be the lost race which was yours."

"It may be so," said Rugo unsurely. "But we are all gone now. Nothing of ours is left."

"Some day," said Manuel, "the last man is going to face your loneliness. We won't last forever either. Sooner or later age or enemies or our own stupidity or the darkening of the universe will come for us. I hope that the last man can endure life as bravely as you did."

"I was not brave," said Rugo. "I was often afraid. They hurt me, sometimes, and I ran."

"Brave in the way that counts," said Manuel.

They talked for a while longer, and then the human rose. "I've got to go, Rugo," he said. "If I'm going to stay here for a while, I'll have to go down to the village and get a job of some sort. May I come up again tomorrow and see you?"

Rugo got up with him and wrapped the dignity of a host about his nakedness. "I would be honored," he said gravely.

He stood watching the man go until he was lost to sight down the curve of the trail. Then he sighed a little. Manuel was good, yes, he was the first one in a hundred years who had not hated or feared him, or been overly polite and apologetic, but had simply traded words as one free being to another.

What had he said? "One free bum to another." Yes, Manuel was a good bum.

He would bring food tomorrow, Rugo knew, and this time there would be more said, the comradeship would be wholly easy and the eyes wholly frank. It pained him that he could offer nothing in return.

But wait, maybe he could. The farther hills were thick with berries, some must still be there even this late in the season. Birds and animals and humans couldn't have taken them all, and he knew how to look. Yes, he could bring back a great many berries that would go well with a meal.

It was a long trip, and his sinews protested at the thought. He grunted and set out, slowly. The sun was wheeling horizonward, but it would be a few hours yet till dark.

He went over the crest of the hill and down the other side. It was hot and quiet, the air shimmered around him, leaves hung limp on the few remaining trees. The summer-dried grass rustled harshly under his feet; rocks rolled aside and skittered down the long slope with a faint click. Beyond, the range stretched into a blue haze of distance. It was lonely up here, but he was used to that and liked it.

Berries — yes, a lot of them clustered around Thunder Falls, where there was always coolness and damp. To be sure, the other pickers knew that as well as he, but they didn't know all the little spots, the slanting rocks and the wet crannies and the sheltering overgrowths of brush. He could bring home enough for a good meal.

He wound down the hillside and up the next. More trees grew here. He was glad of the shade and moved a little faster. Maybe he should pull out of this district altogether. Maybe he would do better in a less thickly settled region, where there might be more people like Manuel. He needed humans, he was too old now to live off the country, but they might be easier to get along with on the frontier.

They weren't such a bad race, the Strangers. They had made war with all the fury that was in them, had wiped out a threat with unnecessary savagery; they still fought and cheated and oppressed each other; they were silly and cruel and they cut down the forests and dug up the earth and turned the rivers dry. But among them were a few like Manuel, and he wondered if his own people had boasted more of that sort than the Strangers did.

Presently he came out on the slope of the highest hill in the region and started climbing it toward Thunder Falls. He could hear the distant roaring of a cataract, half lost in the pounding of his own blood as he fought his aging body slowly up the rocky slant, and in the dance of sunlight he stopped to breathe and tell himself that not far ahead were shadow and mist and a coolness of rushing waters. And when he was ready to come back, the night would be there to walk home with him.

The shouting falls drowned out the voices of the children, nor had he looked for them since he knew they were forbidden to visit this danger spot without adults along. When he topped the stony ridge and stood looking down into the gorge, he saw them just below and his heart stumbled in sickness.

The whole troop was there, with red-haired Sam Whately leading them in a berry hunt up and down the cragged rocks and along the pebbled beach. Rugo stood on the bluff above them, peering down through the fine cold spray and trying to tell his panting body to turn and run before they saw him. Then it was too late; they had spotted his dark form and were crowding closer, scrambling up the bluff with a wicked rain of laughter.

"Looka that!" He heard Sam's voice faintly through the roar and crash of the falls. "Looky who's here! Ol' Blackie!"

A stone cracked against his ribs. He half turned to go, knowing dully that he could not outrun them. Then he remembered that he had come to gather berries for Manuel Jones, who had called him brave, and a thought came.

He called out in a bass that trembled through the rocks, "Do not do that!"

"Yaah, listen what he says, ha-ha-ha!"

"Leave me alone," cried Rugo, "or I will tell your parents that you were here."

They stopped then, almost up to him, and for a moment only the yapping dogs spoke. Then Sam sneered at him. "Aw, who'd lissen to yuh, ol' troll?"

"I think they will believe me," said Rugo. "But if you do not believe it, try and find out."

They hovered for a moment, unsure, staring at each other. Then Sam said, "Okay, ol' tattletale, okay. But you let us be, see?"

"I will do that," said Rugo, and the hard-held breath puffed out of him in a great sigh. He realized how painfully his heart had been fluttering, and weakness was watery in his legs.

They went sullenly back to their berry gathering, and Rugo scrambled down the bluff and took the opposite direction.

They called off the dogs, too, and soon he was out of sight of them.

The gorge walls rose high and steep on either side of the falls. Here the river ran fast, green and boiling white, cold and loud as it sprang over the edge in a veil of rainbowed mist. Its noise filled the air, rang between the crags and hooted in the water-hollowed caves. The vibrations of the toppling stream shivered unceasingly through the ground. It was cool and wet here, and there was always a wind blowing down the length of the ravine. The fall wasn't high, only about twenty feet, but the river thundered down it with brawling violence and below the cataract it was deep and fast and full of rocks and whirlpools.

Plants were scattered between the stones, small bushes and a few slender trees. Rugo found some big tsuga leaves and twisted them together into a good-sized bag as his mother had taught him, and started hunting. The berries grew on low, round-leafed bushes that clustered under rocks and taller plants, wherever they could find shelter, and it was something of an art to locate them easily. Rugo had had many decades of practice.

It was peaceful work. He felt his heart and lungs slowing; content and restfulness stole over him. So had he gone with his mother, often and often in the time that was clearer to him than all the blurred years between, and it was as if she walked beside him now and showed him where to look and smiled when he turned over a bush and found the little blue spheres. He was gathering food for his friend, and that was good.

After some time, he grew aware that a couple of the children had left the main group and were following him, a small boy and girl tagging at a discreet distance and saying nothing. He turned and stared at them, wondering if they meant to attack him after all, and they looked shyly away.

"You sure find a lot of them, Mister Troll," said the boy at last, timidly.

"They grow here," grunted Rugo with unease.

"I'm sorry they was so mean to you," said the girl. "Me and Tommy wasn't there or we wouldn't of let them."

Rugo couldn't remember if they had been with the pack that morning or not. It didn't matter. They were only being friendly in the hope he would show them where to find the berries.

Still, no few of the Stranger cubs had liked him in the past, those who were too old to be frightened into screaming fits by his appearance and too young to be drilled into prejudice, and he had been fond of them in turn. And whatever the reason of these two, they were speaking nicely.

"My dad said the other day he thought he could get you to do some work for him," said the boy. "He'd pay you good."

"Who is your father?" asked Rugo uncertainly.

"He's Mr. Jim Stackman."

Yes, Stackman had never been anything but pleasant, in the somewhat strained and awkward manner of humans. They felt guilty for what their grandparents had done, as if that could change matters. But it was something. Most humans were pretty decent; their main fault was the way they stood, by when others of their race did evil, stood by and said nothing and felt embarrassed.

"Mr. Whately won't let me go down there," said Rugo.

"Oh, him!" said the boy with elaborate scorn. "My dad'll take care of old Sourpuss Whately."

"I don't like Sam Whately neither," said the girl. "He's mean, like his old man."

"Why do you do as he says, then?" asked Rugo.

The boy looked uncomfortable. "He's bigger'n the rest of us," he muttered.

Yes, that was the way of humans, and it wasn't really their fault that the Manuel Joneses were so few among them. They suffered more for it than anyone else, probably.

"Here is a nice berry bush," said Rugo. "You can pick it if you want to."

He sat down on a mossy bank, watching them eat, thinking that maybe things had changed today. Maybe he wouldn't need to move away after all.

The girl came and sat down beside him. "Can you tell me a story, Mister Troll?" she asked.

"H'm?" Rugo was startled out of his reverie.

"My daddy says an old-timer like you must know lots of things," she said.

Why, yes, thought Rugo, he did know a good deal, but it wasn't the sort of tale you could give children. They didn't know hunger and loneliness and shuddering winter cold, weakness and pain and the slow grinding out of hope, and he didn't want them ever to know it. But, well, he could remember a few things besides. His father had told him stories of what had once been, and —

Your race will always haunt us, no matter how long man is here something of you will enter into him . . . There'll always be a shadow just beyond the fire, a voice in the wind and in the rivers, something in the soil that will enter the bread he eats and the water he drinks, and that will be the lost race which was yours.

"Why, yes," he said slowly. "I think so."

The boy came and sat beside the girl, and they watched him with large eyes. He leaned back against the bank and fumbled around in his mind.

"A long time ago," he said, "before people had come to New Terra, there were trolls like me living here. We built houses and farms, and we had our songs and our stories just like you do. So I can tell you a little bit about that, and maybe some day when you are grown up and have children of your own you can tell them."

"Sure," said the boy.

"Well," said Rugo, "there was once a troll king named Utorri who lived in the Western Dales, not far from the sea. He lived in a big castle with towers reaching up so they nearly scraped the stars, and the wind was always blowing around the towers and ringing the bells. Even when the trolls were asleep they could hear the shivering of the bells. And it was a rich castle, whose doors always stood open to any wayfarers, and each night there was a feast where all the great trolls met and music sounded and the heroes told of their wanderings — "

"Hey, look!"

The children's heads turned, and Rugo's annoyed glance followed theirs. The sun was low now, its rays were long and slanting and touched the hair of Sam Whately with fire where he stood. He had climbed up on the highest crag above the falls and balanced swaying on the narrow perch, laughing. The laughter drifted down through the boom of waters, faint and clear in the evening.

"Gee, he shouldn't," said the little girl.

"I'm the king of the mountain!"

"Young fool," grumbled Rugo.

"I'm the king of the mountain!"

"Sam, come down — " The child's voice was almost lost in thunder.

He laughed again and crouched, feeling with his hands along the rough stone for a way back. Rugo stiffened, remembering how slippery the rocks were and how the river hungered.

The boy started down, and lost his hold and toppled.

Rugo had a glimpse of the red head as it rose over the foaming green. Then it was gone, snuffed like a torch as the river sucked it under.

Rugo started to his feet, yelling, remembering that even now he had the strength of many humans and that a man had called him brave. Some dim corner of his mind told him to wait, to stop and think, and he ran to the shore with the frantic knowledge that if he did consider the matter wisely he would never go in.

The water was cold around him, it sank fangs of cold into his body and he cried out with the pain.

Sam's head appeared briefly at the foot of the cataract, whirling downstream. Rugo's feet lost bottom and he struck out, feeling the current grab him and yank him from shore.

Swimming, whipping downstream, he shook the water from his eyes and gasped and looked wildly around. Yes, there came Sam, a little above him, swimming with mindless reflex.

The slight body crashed against his shoulder. Almost, the river had its way, then he got a clutch on the arm and his legs and tail and free hand were working.

They whirled on down the stream and he was deaf and blind and the strength was spilling from him like blood from an open wound.

There was a rock ahead. Dimly he saw it through the cruel blaze of sunlight, a broad flat stone rearing above a foam of water. He flailed, striving for it, sobbing the wind into his empty lungs, and they hit with a shock that exploded in his bones.

Wildly he grabbed at the smooth surface, groping for a handhold. One arm lifted Sam Whately's feebly stirring body out, fairly tossed it on top of the rock, and then the river had him again.

The boy hadn't breathed too much water, thought Rugo in his darkening brain. He could lie there till a flying-thing from the village picked him up.

Only — why did I save him? Why did I save him? He stoned me, and now I'll never be able to give Manuel those berries. I'll never finish the story of King Utorri and his heroes.

The water was cool and green around him as he sank. He wondered if his mother would come for him.

A few miles farther down, the river flows broad and quiet between gentle banks. Trees grow there, and the last sunlight streams through their leaves to glisten on the surface. This is down in the valley, where the homes of man are built.

F

---

films — motion pictures that are normally shown in theaters. Movies are very popular with all age groups and cover a wide spectrum of subjects. Science fiction films are among the most popular, and pictures like "Close Encounters of the Third Kind" (1977), "Star Wars" (1977), and "The Empire Strikes Back" (1980) have broken box office records in many cities. Science fiction is now firmly entrenched as a regular product of Hollywood studios. An anthology which collects science fiction stories that were made into films is *They Came from Outer Space* (Doubleday, 1981).

History Lesson

ARTHUR C. CLARKE

No one could remember when the tribe had begun its long journey. The land of great rolling plains that had been its first home was now no more than a half-forgotten dream.

For many years Shann and his people had been fleeing through a country of low hills and sparkling lakes, and now the mountains lay ahead. This summer they must cross them to the southern lands. There was little time to lose. The white terror that had come down from the poles, grinding continents to dust and freezing the very air before it, was less than a day's march behind.

Shann wondered if the glaciers could climb the mountains ahead, and within his heart he dared to kindle a little flame of hope. This might prove a barrier against which even the remorseless ice would batter in vain. In the southern lands of which the legends spoke his people might find refuge at last.

It took weeks to discover a pass through which the tribe and the animals could travel. When midsummer came, they had camped in a lonely valley where the air was thin and the stars shone with a brilliance no one had ever seen before.

The summer was waning when Shann took his two sons and went ahead to explore the way. For three days they climbed, and for three nights slept as best they could on the freezing rocks. And on the fourth morning there was nothing ahead but a gentle rise to a cairn of gray stones built by other travelers centuries ago.

Shann felt himself trembling, and not with cold, as they walked toward the little pyramid of stones. His sons had fallen behind. No one spoke, for too much was at stake. In a little while they would know if all their hopes had been betrayed.

To east and west, the wall of mountains curved away as if embracing the land beneath. Below lay endless miles of undulating plain, with a great river swinging across it in tremendous loops. It was a fertile land: one in which the tribe could raise crops knowing that there would be no need to flee before the harvest came.

Then Shann lifted his eyes to the south and saw the doom of all his hopes. For there at the edge of the world glimmered that deadly light he had seen so often to the north — the glint of ice below the horizon.

There was no way forward. Through all the years of flight, the glaciers from the south had been advancing to meet them. Soon they would be crushed beneath the moving walls of ice . . .

Southern glaciers did not reach the mountains until a generation later. In that last summer the sons of Shann carried the sacred treasures of the tribe to the lonely cairn overlooking the plain. The ice that had once gleamed below the horizon was now almost at their feet. By spring it would be splintering against the mountain walls.

No one understood the treasures now. They were from a past too distant for the understanding of any man alive. Their origins were lost in the mists that surrounded the Golden Age, and how they had come at last into the possession of this wandering tribe was a story that now would never be told. For it was the story of a civilization that had passed beyond recall.

Once, all these pitiful relics had been treasured for some good reason, and now they had become sacred though their meaning had long been lost. The print in the old books had faded centuries ago though much of the lettering was still visible — if there had been any to read it. But many generations had passed since anyone had had a use for a set of seven-figure logarithms, an atlas of the world, and the score of Sibelius's Seventh Symphony, printed, according to the flyleaf, by H. K. Chu and Sons, at the City of Pekin in the year 2371 A.D.

The old books were placed reverently in the little crypt that had been made to receive them. There followed a motley collection of fragments — gold and platinum coins, a broken telephoto lens, a watch, a cold-light lamp, a microphone, the cutter from an electric shaver, some midget radio tubes — the flotsam that had been left behind when the great tide of civilization had ebbed forever.

All these treasures were carefully stowed away in their resting place. Then came three more relics, the most sacred of all because the least understood.

The first was a strangely shaped piece of metal, showing the coloration of intense heat. It was, in its way, the most pathetic of all these symbols from the past, for it told of man's greatest achievement and of the future he might have known. The mahogany stand on which it was mounted bore a silver plate with the inscription:

Auxiliary Igniter from Starboard Jet
Spaceship "Morning Star"
Earth-Moon, A.D. 1985

Next followed another miracle of the ancient science — a sphere of transparent plastic with strangely shaped pieces of metal imbedded in it. At its center was a tiny capsule of synthetic radioelement, surrounded by the converting screens that shifted its radiation far down the spectrum. As long as the material remained active, the sphere would be a tiny radio transmitter, broadcasting power in all directions. Only a few of these spheres had ever been made. They had been designed as perpetual beacons to mark the orbits of the asteroids. But man had never reached the asteroids and the beacons had never been used.

Last of all was the flat, circular tin, wide in comparison with its depth. It was heavily sealed and rattled when shaken. The tribal lore predicted that disaster would follow if it were ever opened, and no one knew that it held one of the great works of art of nearly a thousand years before.

The work was finished. The two men rolled the stones back into place and slowly began to descend the mountainside. Even to the last, man had given some thought to the future and had tried to preserve something for posterity.

That winter the great waves of ice began their first assault on the mountains, attacking from north and south. The foothills were overwhelmed in the first onslaught, and the glaciers ground them into dust. But the mountains stood firm, and when the summer came the ice retreated for a while.

So, winter after winter, the battle continued, and the roar of the avalanches, the grinding of rock and the explosions of splintering ice filled the air with tumult. No war of man's had been fiercer than this, and even man's battles had not quite engulfed the globe as this had done.

At last the tidal waves of ice began to subside and to creep slowly down the flanks of the mountains they had never quite subdued. The valleys and passes were still firmly in their grip. It was a stalemate. The glaciers had met their match, but their defeat was too late to be of any use to Man.

So the centuries passed, and presently there happened something that must occur once at least in the history of every world in the universe, no matter how remote and lonely it may be.

The ship from Venus came five thousand years too late, but its crew knew nothing of this. While still many millions of miles away, the telescopes had seen the great shroud of ice that made Earth the most brilliant object in the sky next to the sun itself.

Here and there the dazzling sheet was marred by black specks that revealed the presence of almost buried mountains. That was all. The rolling oceans, the plains and forests, the deserts and lakes — all that had been the world of man was sealed beneath the ice, perhaps forever.

The ship closed in to Earth and established orbit less than a thousand miles away. For five days it circled the planet, while cameras recorded all that was left to see and a hundred instruments gathered information that would give the Venusian scientists many years of work.

An actual landing was not intended. There seemed little purpose in it. But on the sixth day the picture changed. A panoramic monitor, driven to the limit of its amplification, detected the dying radiation of the five-thousand-year-old beacon. Through all the centuries, it had been sending out its signals with ever-failing strength as its radioactive heart steadily weakened.

The monitor locked on the beacon frequency. In the control room, a bell clamored for attention. A little later, the Venusian ship broke free from its orbit and slanted down toward Earth, toward a range of mountains that still towered proudly above the ice, and to a cairn of gray stones that the years had scarcely touched . . .

The great disc of the sun blazed fiercely in a sky no longer veiled with mist, for the clouds that had once hidden Venus had now completely gone. Whatever force had caused the change in the sun's radiation had doomed one civilization, but had given birth to another. Less than five thousand years before, the half-savage people of Venus had seen the sun and stars for the first time. Just as the science of Earth had begun with astronomy, so had that of Venus, and on the warm, rich world that man had never seen progress had been incredibly rapid.

Perhaps the Venusians had been lucky. They never knew the Dark Age that held Man enchained for a thousand years. They missed the long detour into chemistry and mechanics but came at once to the more fundamental laws of radiation physics. In the time that man had taken to progress from the Pyramids to the rocket-propelled spaceship, the Venusians had passed from the discovery of agriculture to antigravity itself — the ultimate secret that Man had never learned.

The warm ocean that still bore most of the young planet's life rolled its breakers languidly against the sandy shore. So new was this continent that the very sands were coarse and gritty. There had not yet been time enough for the sea to wear them smooth.

The scientists lay half in the water, their beautiful reptilian bodies gleaming in the sunlight. The greatest minds of Venus had gathered on this shore from all the islands of the planet. What they were going to hear they did not yet know, except that it concerned the third world and the mysterious race that had peopled it before the coming of the ice.

The Historian was standing on the land, for the instruments he wished to use had no love of water. By his side was a large machine which attracted many curious glances from his colleagues. It was clearly concerned with optics, for a lens system projected from it toward a screen of white material a dozen yards away.

The Historian began to speak. Briefly he recapitulated what little had been discovered concerning the third planet and its people.

He mentioned the centuries of fruitless research that had failed to interpret a single word of the writings of Earth. The planet had been inhabited by a race of great technical ability. That, at least, was proved by the few pieces of machinery that had been found in the cairn upon the mountain.

"We do not know why so advanced a civilization came to an end," he observed. "Almost certainly, it had sufficient knowledge to survive an ice age. There must have been some factor of which we know nothing. Possibly disease or racial degeneration may have been responsible. It has even been suggested that the tribal conflicts endemic to our own species in prehistoric times may have continued on the third planet after the coming of technology.

"Some philosophers maintain that knowledge of machinery does not necessarily imply a high degree of civilization, and it is theoretically possible to have wars in a society possessing mechanical power, flight, and even radio. Such a conception is alien to our thoughts, but we must admit its possibility. It would certainly account for the downfall of the lost race.

"It has always been assumed that we should never know anything of the physical form of the creatures who lived on Planet Three. For centuries our artists have been depicting scenes from the history of the dead world, peopling it with all manner of fantastic beings. Most of these creations have resembled us more or less closely, though it has often been pointed out that because *we* are reptiles it does not follow that all intelligent life must necessarily be reptilian.

"We now know the answer to one of the most baffling problems of history. At last, after a hundred years of research, we have discovered the exact form and nature of the ruling life on the third planet."

There was a murmur of astonishment from the assembled scientists. Some were so taken aback that they disappeared for a while into the comfort of the ocean, as all Venusians were apt to do in moments of stress. The Historian waited until his colleagues re-emerged into the element they so disliked. He himself was quite comfortable, thanks to the tiny sprays that were continually playing over his body. With their help he could live on land for many hours before having to return to the ocean.

The excitement slowly subsided and the lecturer continued:

"One of the most puzzling of the objects found on Planet Three was a flat metal container holding a great length of transparent plastic material, perforated at the edges and wound tightly into a spool. This transparent tape at first seemed quite featureless, but an examination with the new subelectronic microscope has shown that this is not the case. Along the surface of the material, invisible to our eyes but perfectly clear under the correct radiation, are literally thousands of tiny pictures. It is believed that they were imprinted on the material by some chemical means, and have faded with the passage of time.

"These pictures apparently form a record of life as it was on the third planet at the height of its civilization. They are not independent. Consecutive pictures are almost identical, differing only in the detail of movement. The purpose of such a record is obvious. It is only necessary to project the scenes in rapid succession to give an illusion of continuous movement. We have made a machine to do this, and I have here an exact reproduction of the picture sequence.

"The scenes you are now going to witness take us back many thousands of years, to the great days of our sister planet. They show a complex civilization, many of whose activities we can only dimly understand. Life seems to have been very violent and energetic, and much that you will see is quite baffling.

"It is clear that the third planet was inhabited by a number of different species, none of them reptilian. That is a blow to our pride, but the conclusion is inescapable. The dominant type of life appears to have been a two-armed biped. It walked upright and covered its body with some flexible material, possibly for protection against the cold, since even before the Ice Age the planet was at a much lower temperature than our own world. But I will not try your patience any further. You will now see the record of which I have been speaking."

A brilliant light flashed from the projector. There was a gentle whirring, and on the screen appeared hundreds of strange beings moving rather jerkily to and fro. The picture expanded to embrace one of the creatures, and the scientists could see that the Historian's description had been correct.

The creature possessed two eyes, set rather close together, but the other facial adornments were a little obscure. There was a large orifice in the lower portion of the head that was continually opening and closing. Possibly it had something to do with the creature's breathing.

The scientists watched spellbound as the strange being became involved in a series of fantastic adventures. There was an incredibly violent conflict with another, slightly different creature. It seemed certain that they must both be killed, but when it was all over neither seemed any the worse.

Then came a furious drive over miles of country in a four-wheeled mechanical device that was capable of extraordinary feats of locomotion. The ride ended in a city packed with other vehicles moving in all directions at breathtaking speeds. No one was surprised to see two of the machines meet head-on with devastating results.

After that, events became even more complicated. It was now quite obvious that it would take many years of research to analyze and understand all that was happening. It was also clear that the record was a work of art, somewhat stylized, rather than an exact reproduction of life as it actually had been on the third planet.

Most of the scientists felt themselves completely dazed when the sequence of pictures came to an end. There was a final flurry of motion, in which the creature that had been the center of interest became involved in some tremendous but incomprehensible catastrophe. The picture contracted to a circle, centered on the creature's head.

The last scene of all was an expanded view of its face, obviously expressing some powerful emotion. But whether it was rage, grief, defiance, resignation, or some other feeling could not be guessed. The picture vanished. For a moment some lettering appeared on the screen, then it was all over.

For several minutes there was complete silence, save the lapping of the waves upon the sand. The scientists were too stunned to speak. The fleeting glimpse of Earth's civilization had had a shattering effect on their minds. Then little groups began to start talking together, first in whispers and then more and more loudly as the implications of what they had seen became clearer. Presently the Historian called for attention and addressed the meeting again.

"We are now planning," he said, "a vast program of research to extract all available knowledge from this record. Thousands of copies are being made for distribution to all workers. You will appreciate the problems involved. The psychologists in particular have an immense task confronting them.

"But I do not doubt that we shall succeed. In another generation, who can say what we may have learned of this wonderful race? Before we leave, let us look again at our remote cousins, whose wisdom may have surpassed our own but of whom so little has survived."

Once more the final picture flashed on the screen, motionless this time, for the projector had been stopped. With something like awe, the scientists gazed at the still figure from the past, while in turn the little biped stared back at them with its characteristic expression of arrogant bad temper.

For the rest of time it would symbolize the human race. The psychologists of Venus would analyze its actions and watch its every movement until they could reconstruct its mind. Thousands of books would be written about it. Intricate philosophies would be contrived to account for its behavior.

But all this labor, all this research, would be utterly in vain. Perhaps the proud and lonely figure on the screen was smiling sardonically at the scientists who were starting their age-long, fruitless quest.

Its secret would be safe as long as the universe endured, for no one now would ever read the lost language of Earth. Millions of times in the ages to come those last words would flash across the screen, and none could ever guess their meaning:

A WALT DISNEY PRODUCTION.

G

gov/er/nance sys/tems — ways of organizing groups (including societies) for purposes of giving direction and exercising control. These systems range from absolute or constitutional monarchies and dictatorships to representative democracy. Common governance systems in science fiction include feudal relationships, as well as those mentioned above. Possible future governance systems can be found in *Political Science Fiction* (Prentice-Hall, 1974) and *American Government Through Science Fiction* (Rand McNally, 1974).

The Troublemaker

CHRISTOPHER ANVIL

12/02/96 Probably the closest thing to hell on a commercial spaceship is to have the gravitor control run wild. Next on the list is what happens when there's a troublemaker in the crew.

Three years ago, we had the first experience. It looks as if we are now about to have the second.

The trouble started when Krotec, our cargo-control man, was killed by a freak meteor at the cut-loose point. We had just thrown the cargo section into hyperdrive and were swinging around to get an empty returned section from the recovery crew when the meteor hit. We all felt bad about Krotec's death. But there was nothing we could do except head back to the loading center as usual.

When we got back to the loading center, word came in that a replacement for Krotec was due on board at 2330.

The captain insists that each new man be greeted as he comes on board. Willis and I, respectively third and second in command, offered to do the greeting. Willis got the job.

Around 0130, Willis woke me up.

"Listen," he said, "that replacement hasn't showed up yet. The transport office says he started out in a little one-man taxi-boat two hours and twenty minutes ago. Do you suppose he's drunk?"

"I *hope* not."

A cargo-control man has to inspect and approve each cargo before it can be shipped. Because of this, a drunk cargo-control man can cause a long delay. Each delay cuts down the ship's competitive rating. And each cut in the rating means a cut in the bonus given to the officers and crew of the fastest ships.

"Listen," I said. "We're just loading grain, aren't we?"

"We are. Just a few hours more and we'll be full up. If we can get out of here by 0800, we've got a chance to beat *Nova* and get first place for a change. But we've got to get this cretin to start checking cargo before we can even think of leaving."

"How about the transport office? Do they know where this one-man taxi-boat is now?"

"All they can say is that a rough fix shows it's somewhere in B cargo area, and it's sending out an 'unoccupied' signal. That means our replacement has matched locks with some other boat or ship in our area, and left the one-man boat."

It took a few moments to absorb what this meant. Each ship takes its share of fast and slow cargoes. While we were loading grain and leaving tomorrow, other ships were taking on fragile goods that would keep them at the loading center for several days. On some of these ships, roaring parties were now going on. If our wandering cargo-control officer got into one of these parties, it would be no easy job to get him out.

"Well," I said, dressing quickly, "we can't very well start asking where he is."

"No," said Willis sourly. "There are those who would load him up with rum and hide him somewhere just to gain a few points on us."

"That means there's nothing else to do but get another taxi-boat and go hunt for him. One-man boats aren't used much, so we've got a chance."

A couple of hours later, this chance seemed to have gotten pretty thin. I had been staring into the glaring lights and shadows all over B cargo area, and Willis had been calling the transport office at intervals. The transport office insisted the one-man boat was still in B area. But if so, I hadn't seen it. An unpleasant possibility was just beginning to dawn on me when Willis appeared on the little screen, his face white and set.

"Don't bother looking for him any more. He's here."

The screen went blank. I went back to the ship, and saw that the boatlike bulk of the pressure loader had stopped pulsating. Willis was waiting in the control room as I went in.

"You know," he said, "that so-and-so was right here all the time? He was hooked onto the cargo section's lock, out of sight in the shadow of the ship. That means he has been alone in the cargo section for a long time, without our knowing it."

"I notice we aren't loading."

"No, we aren't loading. He came in here, and used the screen to get the chief inspector's office. He says there's 'danger of possible weevil infestation' in the cargo, and he's slapped a forty-eight-hour delay on the ship."

"That's ridiculous."

"Is it? Don't forget, the inspector here is a stickler for caution. Any cargo-control man who shows caution gets a pat on the head. And since Krotec got hit before we picked up the empty cargo section, that means we were without a regular cargo-control officer to check the cargo section."

"Yes," I said, "but the captain checked it himself." I was thinking that the captain is a fanatic for efficiency, a rigid teetotaler, an early-to-bed-early-to-rise man with iron habits and unvarying devotion to duty. It suddenly occurred to me that this would carry no weight whatever with the chief inspector. "Look," I said, "the captain has qualified as a cargo-control man. He's perfectly able to serve as one in a pinch."

Willis smiled. "Sure. But what I am talking about is how it will look on paper. The captain is not a *regular* cargo-control man. The inspector, not knowing the captain, will generously assume that the captain was out of practice and missed something. We will therefore be hung up here till the inspector goes through all his motions. *Nova* will beat us by light-years. But what I am thinking about most is what life on board the same ship as this self-seeking troublemaker is going to be like."

12/03/96 After about three hours' sleep, I woke up to find that the captain wanted to see me. Willis was on the way out as I went in. The captain listened intently as I told what little I knew of what had happened the night before. Then he leaned back with his eyes narrowed.

"Well," he said, "we want to be fair to this man. But I don't think we ought to lean over backward so far he can kick our feet out from under us. Suppose you go out there and study his record folder while I get him in here and study him."

I agreed, and in due time started back to the captain's compartment carrying the record folder of one L. Sneat in a portfolio. The captain's door opened up and our new cargo-control man backed out with a slightly glazed look, and both hands spread wide. He was talking in the low, earnest voice of the smooth wolf suddenly face-to-face with the girl's father and three tough brothers.

"Why should I, Captain?" he was saying. "It wouldn't make sense, would it? Honestly, I *mean* it. Who would do a thing like that? And to the people he has to live with, too?"

"Just bear in mind," came the captain's voice, "if you have several hundred dollars in the bank, you can write quite a few twenty-dollar checks, and nothing happens to you. But write just one check too many and all hell breaks loose."

"Captain, I just don't understand — "

"Then go think it over."

Our new replacement moved away protesting his innocence as I went in and shut the door. The captain was frowning slightly.

"Some people," he said, "are all tactics and no strategy. They are so busy elbowing their way to the head of the line that they never look to see where the line is going." He glanced at me and said, "What did you find out?"

"Our friend was born in '68 on an outpost world called Broke. He passed a company competitive exam, got good grades, and has been a cargo-control man a little less than four years. He has several commendations on his record and no black marks. Our ship is the eighth ship he has been cargo-control man on."

"In four years?"

"Yes, sir. Eight ships in four years."

"Let's see that folder."

I handed it to him.

It may have been imagination, but I thought I saw the captain's back hair rise up as he looked at the names of those ships. He growled, "Go get the latest rating and bonus list."

"Right here, sir."

The captain put it beside the record folder and glanced from one to the other.

Glancing over the captain's shoulder, I could see the names of the seven ships our new cargo-control man had been on before being assigned to ours. They were *Calliope, Derna, Hermes, Orion, Quicksure, Light Lady,* and *Bonanza.*

The lowest seven names on the rating and bonus lists were: *Calliope, Derna, Hermes, Orion, Quicksure, Light Lady,* and *Bonanza.*

Bonanza was in such bad shape that it had a bonus of minus 27.92. That is, the officers and men of *Bonanza* were paying back 27.92 cents out of every dollar they earned, as a fine for inefficiency.

The captain looked at this for a while, then sent for the records tape covering previous rating and bonus lists.

A quick glance at these lists showed us that the month before Sneat boarded *Bonanza,* that ship had a rating of 94.98 out of a possible 100.00.

One month later, *Bonanza*'s rating was 76.01.

The captain looked at the record folder again. He had much the same expression as a settler on a new planet who walks slowly past a tree, axe in hand, while he judges which way the tree will naturally fall, whether it is worth felling, and if so, where to sink the axe in first.

Then he looked up, smiled, and said we'd certainly have to work hard to make up for the delay. That was all he had to say for the moment.

12/04/96 Well, we're moving at last. No weevils were found. But Sneat produced some debris containing what could have been either pieces of bast-weevil wing-covers — or else bits of the brownish semitransparent insulation used on much of the wiring aboard ship. If it was from wiring, of course, it could have been carelessly dropped by anyone. Sneat has tried to get out of a head-on clash with the captain by claiming that this stuff was found, not inside the inner part of the cargo section, but in the outer inspection corridor. This corridor was thoroughly gone over by Gaites, one of our technicians, before the captain ever went into the cargo section itself. But since Gaites has a reputation for taking life easy, Sneat has succeeded in unloading part of the blame. Meanwhile, Sneat has on his record the inspector's commendation for extreme thoroughness.

12/07/96 Sneat seems to be weathering his unpopularity pretty well, all considered. For some reason, Gaites is now getting most of the blame for the delay.

12/08/96 Another facet of Sneat's character has come to light. The one officer on the ship with any social standing is Grunwald, the navigator. Grunwald's uncle is governor of New Venus. Grunwald likes chess. Sneat has now taken several tapes on chess out of the ship's library.

12/12/96 In the rec. room tonight were Grunwald and Sneat, playing chess. Afterward, Grunwald expansively pointed out certain fine points of the game. Sneat was all ears — an attentive student eager to learn from the master.

A peculiar thing has turned up lately. On most of our trips, there is a feeling on the ship of well-earned contentment. On this trip, however, there is an undercurrent of rankling dissatisfaction. The original delay and the charges and countercharges between Sneat and Gaites seem to have started it. But now that it *is* started, it apparently goes along by itself, one man speaking sharply to another, to produce a vicious circle that is gradually changing the emotional atmosphere of the ship.

What the captain plans to do about it isn't clear. I've remarked on it to him, but it may well be that he doesn't appreciate it. Around him personally, everything is as it was before.

12/15/96 Sneat now seems to be close friends with Grunwald. He is also getting to be friends with Meeres, the medic. Meeres is interested in psychology. Lately, Sneat has been busy with the psychology tapes. Soon he should be able to listen and ask questions intelligently, which should seem fine to Meeres.

12/18/96 If Sneat isn't playing chess with Grunwald, he is likely to be talking psychology with Meeres.

12/19/96 So as to keep Sneat from step-by-step turning the whole ship, with the exception of the captain and me, into an "I love Sneat" society, I've pointed out to Willis what is going on. Strange to say, Willis hadn't noticed it. Now that he does notice it, he is once more turning a cold eye on Sneat. The sorry part of this is that the ship is being split into factions.

12/20/96 Willis tells me that Sneat has been needling Ferralli, the drive technician, because Ferralli is overweight. The rest of the crew has also kidded Ferralli, but that was good-natured. Sneat's procedure is different. The other day he asked Ferralli, "Say, boy, are you expecting?" Ferralli smiled dutifully. After a few wisecracks, any other crewman would have let it go. But Sneat harps on the theme: "Say, is it going to be a boy or a girl?" "What are you going to call it?" Sneat has now given this mythical baby a name — "Oswald" — and the whole business is getting on Ferralli's nerves. This is the kind of joke other crewmen will drift into when they can't think of anything better to say, and it is only a matter of time till Ferralli lashes back. Very quickly we may get into a situation where everyone is jabbing everyone else's weak point, and then this ship will be quite a place to live.

12/21/96 I just had a talk with Ferralli. In the less than three weeks since this trip started he has changed from a happy-go-lucky crewman to a mass of bitterness. He says everywhere he turns, someone asks, "How's Oswald?" Everyone, that is, except Sneat. When the going gets rough, Sneat is likely to stop it, saying, "Ah, come on, fellows, break it up. He needs his strength." Ferralli says he knows Sneat starts it; but when Sneat gets the others to leave him alone, Ferralli actually finds himself feeling grateful. The thought goes through his head, "Sneat isn't such a bad guy, after all." I said I supposed this was exactly what Sneat wanted. Ferralli suddenly burst out, "If he doesn't leave me alone, I'll kill him!"

12/22/96 Now, too late, I see why Sneat singled out Ferralli to pick on. Nearly everyone is now afraid of Sneat's tongue. If this were a military ship, we would no doubt so cramp Sneat that his effect would be barely a tenth what it is now. But as it is, it's a civilian ship, with civilian restrictions, and on top of that the captain seems to be patiently waiting for something. What he is waiting for, I don't know. Meanwhile, there is a steadily increasing amount of bad feeling building up, which gives the impression of an open powder keg just waiting for a match. Sneat has begun calculatedly insulting Willis and me, so it seems obvious which way the force of the explosion is supposed to go. So far, Willis and I have had several clashes with Sneat, but he is clever with words and always wins. Lately I have caught myself wondering how Sneat would react if he found himself stuffed head first into the garbage disposal unit.

12/23/96 Willis suggested that I change shifts at dinner tonight so I could see for myself how Sneat operates during meals. The captain generally switches from shift to shift to check on the quality of the food, and as a rule takes his tray elsewhere at dinner so that if we lesser ranks want to indulge in horseplay, he won't cramp our style.

But tonight, to my surprise the captain stayed to eat with the rest of us.

We had hardly sat down, in a general atmosphere of dull brooding apathy, when Willis nudged me and I heard Sneat make a needling comment to Meeres, to the effect that Ferralli seemed to be "eating for two," didn't he?

I was just starting to wonder how anyone could possibly control that kind of needling when the captain's voice said coldly, "What was that, Sneat?"

For just an instant, Sneat looked jolted. Then he glanced up and said ironically, "Did you say something, Captain?"

In the same cold voice the captain said, "As you know, Sneat, you just made a comment about someone 'eating for two.' Explain it."

"Just part of a private conversation, Captain."

"You mean it doesn't have anything to do with anyone else here? Just you and Meeres?"

"Did I say that?"

The captain didn't say anything for a moment, and Sneat smiled very faintly. I glanced at the captain, feeling the same frustration I'd felt when arguing with Sneat myself. The captain, however, was looking at Sneat with an expression of intense concentration. Something seemed to rise up in the backs of his eyes as he said, in a very gentle voice, "Do you understand the laws on 'incitement to mutiny,' Sneat?"

A heavy silence settled in the room. Sneat looked jarred for the second time. So was I. It seemed to me that Sneat had skillfully avoided that pitfall.

Before Sneat could say anything, the captain said, looking directly at Sneat, "Why are you so afraid to explain that comment you just made to Meeres?"

"I've already explained to you, Captain, that that was part of a private conversation."

"I notice, Sneat, that you avoid the word 'sir' as if you were afraid of it. Just what is it you're afraid of?"

A faint puzzled expression crossed Sneat's face. He opened his mouth and shut it again. Then he stiffened angrily. It occurred to me that somehow the captain had thrown him off balance.

Again, before Sneat could say anything, the captain spoke.

"You know, Sneat, a private conversation is usually a conversation not many people know about. You don't carry out a private conversation in a loud voice, with other people around, do you?"

Sneat relaxed, and spoke in a drawling voice.

"Well, if you must know, Captain, and if you want to make Ferralli feel bad — go ahead and ask."

"Then you admit that what you said was intended to make Ferralli feel bad?"

"No, but your rubbing it in might make him feel bad. Probably has already, in fact. Why don't you drop it, Captain?"

By now, everybody was glancing tensely from Sneat to the captain. The captain was looking directly into Sneat's eyes as he spoke again.

"You know, you can start trouble, but you can't expect always to drop it and slip out from under, leaving other people to bear the burden."

Sneat started to speak, and the captain added, "There comes a time when the burden lands on *you.*"

Sneat sat very still, then casually shoved his chair back.

"You're the first captain I've ever met who tried to badger his crew. I don't think I care to finish this meal."

"People who needle others shouldn't be so sensitive. Just as a cargo-control man who causes a forty-eight hour delay shouldn't try to shift the blame to someone else."

This caused a general stir in the room. The captain made this comment just as Sneat started out, and added, "Naturally, if you have nothing to say in your own defense, you *should* go."

Sneat suddenly swung around and snapped, "That cargo section was filthy!"

Gaites was at the table, and stood up. "The devil it was! It was clean!"

Sneat cast a shrewd calculating glance at Gaites. "Everyone knows you're lazy."

"Yeah? Do you want a punch in the teeth?"

The captain said coldly, "Gaites has been on this ship for a long time, and we never had a delay or a complaint. You no sooner stepped on board than we had a forty-eight hour delay, for weevils that weren't there. Every previous trip we've taken has been pleasant. Since you've been here there's been nothing but trouble." The captain paused, then added, "Unfortunately, I am forbidden by regulations to reveal anything about the ship or ships you were assigned to before this one."

Sneat opened his mouth, then closed it again. A look of angry indignation crossed his face.

The captain waited politely, and then someone started to laugh. In a moment, everyone would have been laughing, because Sneat was neatly caught in his own traps. Everyone *would* have been laughing but the instant the first person laughed, Sneat glanced directly at him and said, "Shut up."

This produced another tense silence, and suddenly something in the air of the ship seemed to change.

A tall crewman stood up, and said slowly, "I was laughing, Sneat. Now, with all respect to the captain, I would like to make just one comment. If I may, sir?"

He glanced courteously at the captain.

"Go ahead," said the captain.

Sneat abruptly turned on his heel and started out of the room.

The tall crewman looked at our cargo-control man's retreating back and said clearly, "I am inviting you, Sneat, to tell me 'shut up' just once more, either now or later."

Sneat walked out without replying.

The tall crewman glanced around before sitting down. A set of hard approving glances answered him. Then he looked directly at the captain and said, "Thank you, *sir.*"

The captain smiled. "You're very welcome." He added, "Now, I would like to make a brief announcement." There was an immediate silence, and the captain said, "The base has granted us a Christmas present. We have been given permission to land and spend December 25 and 26 on the planet of New Cornwall."

There was a startled silence, then a roar of cheers. *Planetfall!* How the captain managed to wring that out of Base, I don't know. But all of a sudden we were the same old ship again. The mood and atmosphere that had been missing were back once more. Suddenly the crew began to sing, "For he's a jolly good fellow."

In the midst of all this renewed good will, with everyone feeling like his own self again, I happened to look at the door.

And there was Sneat, looking in.

He was still with us.

*

12/24/96 I asked the captain today if there was anything we could do to transfer Sneat, or in some way get him off the ship. I suggested that if he happened to stay behind on New Cornwall, that would be fine.

"You mean," said the captain smiling, "if he should by chance get cracked over the head and dumped up some secluded alley, just before we take off?"

"That's what I had in mind, sir."

"Hm-m-m. Well, we can reserve that as a last resort. But I don't think it will be necessary. Do you know much about New Cornwall?"

"No, sir. Of course, we've all been looking it up in the atlas. It's a planet now well into its first stage of industrialization, with a fast-growing population. I don't understand their government system."

"What don't you understand about their government?"

"According to the atlas it's a 'representative absolute monarchy.' There couldn't be such a thing."

"Well," said the captain, smiling, "wait a while. And don't be too hasty about tossing Sneat up an alley with a big bump on his head. Bear in mind how men have always dealt with troublesome creatures."

"What do you mean, sir?"

"Men bait rattraps with cheese and bacon."

I stared. "But how does this help us with Sneat?"

"Why does Sneat try to terrorize a whole ship? What does he like about this? I'll tell you my opinion: Sneat likes power."

12/26/96 Well, we came down to the planet in the tender, and yesterday was a wonderful Christmas.

To begin with, we no sooner landed than crowds of people welcomed us, and we were all given invitations to spend Christmas with individual families. While we were still overwhelmed from this, we got the additional shock of seeing local officials snap to attention, salute the captain, and call him "Your Highness." This seemed fairly ridiculous, but the captain took it calmly and pretty soon a white motorcar drove up, there was a blast of trumpets, and everyone fell on his face except the captain and the rest of us from *Starlight.* This incident left us feeling totally out of focus. But that is small price for having forty-eight hours' leave on a real planet. We were willing to overlook the strange local customs.

The next thing we knew, a flunky jumped off the back of the white car, grabbed a polished silver handle and hauled open the rear door. He flattened himself in the dust as a fresh crew of flunkies rushed to unroll a long purple rug about two and a half feet wide. This stretched from the rear door of the car to the captain. This bunch of flunkies then fell in the dust.

While we were staring at this, there stepped out of the car a tall man with a grim enduring look, dressed in several yards of white cloth trimmed in gold and silver, with flashing epaulettes, several rows of medals on each side of his chest, a purple sash, a sword, and a silver and gold baton in his hand.

This mass of flashing color strode up toward the captain, and they stared each other in the eye.

The captain seemed to have a faint smile as he said in a loud clear voice, "How stands the kingdom, Your Royal and Imperial Majesty?"

"It stands well, as you left it, Your Royal Highness."

Just in front of the car, one of the loyal subjects was getting this all down with some kind of camera on a tall tripod. He was doing this while lying flat on his stomach, and staring into a periscope arrangement with a couple of remote-control handles that aimed the camera.

I was beginning to wonder if this wasn't some kind of joke or carnival performance, when somebody nudged my arm. I realized it was Sneat. In a low voice, he said, "Look there."

I looked, and saw, about eighty feet away, an armored car with its gun aimed at us. There was another one nearby, and near that about thirty men carrying long guns and wearing over their left breast pockets an emblem like a silver gunsight.

I glanced around uneasily. "What is this, a trap?"

"No, no," said Sneat, in a low excited voice. "It's the king's guard. See that crown on their left shoulders?"

True enough, that did seem to be it. I looked hard at Sneat in curiosity. It was the first time I had seen him with that eager, excited look.

Well, in due time the formalities between the captain and the local king were all concluded, they bowed to each other, and the king turned around and started back to the car. The set of flunkies that handled the purple rug sprang into action and rolled it up behind the king as he neared the car. A new set staggered around carrying another rolled-up rug, which they set down in front of the captain. As fast as the first set rolled up the purple rug, the second set unrolled a light pink rug with a purple stripe down each side. Along this, the captain walked.

I glanced around as this procession headed for the car. First the king, then a bunch of flunkies rolling the rug up about two steps behind him, then a new bunch unrolling another rug, then the captain walking along about two steps behind them. All around me were men from *Starlight* with their jaws hanging open, eyes staring, and glancing back and forth from the car to the line of armed guards.

About this time, a third set of flunkies heaved the top off the rear of the royal car, and a fussy individual began rearranging the cushions. The king and the captain got in, all the rugs were rolled up, and the car set off to a blast of trumpets.

Sneat said in irritation, "That business with rugs was overdone."

I stared at him, trying to see his viewpoint. But now all the populace, which had been flat on their faces a minute ago, stood up. They seemed to think nothing of having spent all that time flat on the ground, but immediately took up the conversation where they had left off, so that in a few minutes we were each setting out in company with a different family.

Well, we had a morning of sightseeing, many of us went to church, and we all had a big Christmas dinner. The main topic of local conversation was the coming selection. I listened in silence as long as I could, but finally was overcome by curiosity.

"*Election?*" I asked.

"Oh no," said my host. "*Selection.* You see, His Majesty has worked at the job for a decade now. Naturally he's tired. Tomorrow a successor will select himself."

"Select *himself?*"

"Of course. The job is a tremendous burden, you know. It would hardly be fair to *force* it upon anyone."

"You mean, someone *volunteers* to be king?"

"Exactly."

"Well — What if a halfwit — "

"Such people are not qualified."

"All right. But if your kings are *absolute* monarchs, what's to prevent you from ending up under a dictator?"

Everyone laughed. "True," said my host, "in the bad old days back on Earth, such things happened. But here, modern science prevents it. *Our* kings think only of the good of their subjects."

"How does modern science manage that?"

"I'm sure I couldn't say."

"How do your kings 'select themselves'?"

"Why, we gather in the great arena. The first man to cross the line is king."

I stared. "A sort of race?"

"Oh no. Not a race. There is never a rush to step over the line. You'll see what I mean."

It developed that the tests we had been required to pass to become spacemen were stiff enough to qualify any of us to become king of New Cornwall if we wanted, and therefore we all ended up the next day with our hosts in a gigantic sports arena hung with silver and gold banners, and with a long straight purple line drawn down the length of the arena.

As we watched, a military band played a march, a line of horsemen in blue uniforms with silver breastplates and drawn swords rode in, and there was a blast of trumpets. The king came in followed by a herald with a big scroll, who walked out to a microphone set almost at the purple line, raised the scroll, and read:

Be it known that our illustrious king and emperor, desiring to lay down the heavy burden of his duty, hereby throws open to all you qualified and assembled — be you of native birth or whatever, so long as you be human — the right to ascend the throne.

With this right, be it well and clearly known, pass the command of all the armed forces of the planet New Cornwall and the absolute right to command of each citizen what you will, and to be obeyed.

Whosoever desires to achieve this absolute authority, and whosoever is willing to accept the heavy burden it entails, let him so signify by stepping forward across this line.

There followed a half-hour harangue to point out the nobility of taking up the burden and the need to give the present king, who had worked hard all this time, a well-earned rest.

At the end of this half-hour, Sneat stepped forward and crossed the line. Sneat is now king of New Cornwall.

12/27/96 This evening I was busy filling out the necessary forms to account for the disappearance of Sneat, when the captain walked in.

"Well," he said, "that was better than bashing him over the head, wasn't it?"

"Yes, sir," I said. "This really gets him out of the crew for good. A little rough on the planet, though."

"Oh, no. Sneat will make a good king." The captain spoke in the positive manner of one who knows by direct experience. He added, "After all, he hasn't any *choice* in that matter."

I shoved back the forms and turned around to face the captain. He was looking at me with his usual expression, which is a sort of quiet authority. A slight change of the lines around mouth and eyes can shift this expression to one of friendly warmth or arctic chill. It was now necessary to risk the chill.

"Sir," I said, "you realize that this ship is a mass of boiling curiosity?"

"It's good for them," said the captain, with a faint grin. "It will take their minds off their troubles."

"I can't think," I said, "of anyone I'd want to have over me as an absolute monarch. But if I *had* to choose someone for that position, the last person I'd pick would be Sneat."

"And yet," said the captain, "most people you might pick would kick and scream to get out of the job. Sneat *wants* it."

"Yes," I said. "As you remarked earlier, Sneat seems to love power. But does that mean he should *have* power? Human history is overburdened with men who loved power, got it, misused it, made their subjects miserable, and were finally overthrown by some new power-maniac. Then the new man went through the same process as the one before."

"True, but all that is systematized down on New Cornwall. The average king only lasts about eight to ten years. After that, he can't get rid of the power fast enough."

"Then there must be special conditions," I said.

The captain nodded. "There are special conditions. It would be interesting to know why it is that great genius will suddenly appear in one place and not in another place where conditions look just as favorable. New Cornwall, as you know, is not fully industrialized. But its citizens trade their products with worlds that are industrialized. Advanced electronics equipment is available on the planet, and of course it has to be kept in repair. Skilled repairmen make an excellent living. It is like this on other worlds, but it was on New Cornwall that the genius appeared."

I listened intently, and the captain went on. "This man became interested in the relationship between the electrical current used in manmade apparatus, and the impulse that passes along a nerve in the body of an animal. The result of his studies was a tiny device called a 'neurister'. A neurister, surgically inserted in the proper place, can receive from outside a signal especially keyed to it. The result of this signal is that the neurister stimulates a nerve nearby. And the result of this is that the person in whom the neurister has been inserted feels a sensation from that part of his body."

A chill traveled up and down my spine. "What kind of sensation?"

"Depending on the circumstances, a sense of uneasiness, a pressure, an itching, a burning, a feeling of pain, or — in the extreme — downright agony. From the king down through the dukes and earls to the lowest squire, the governing authorities on New Cornwall are all liberally supplied with neuristers."

The captain glanced at his watch and added, "About this time, I imagine, Sneat is stretched out on the operating table."

"Much as I dislike Sneat," I said, "I wouldn't have wished this on him."

"You didn't have to. He chose it himself."

"Who pulls the switch that sends the pain through him if he gets out of line?"

"Each of the nobles has, while he's in office, not only a set of neuristers, but what corresponds to a relay, located within his body cavity. Each of the loyal subjects, on the other hand, has within him a small device corresponding to a transmitter."

Suddenly it dawned on me. "You mean — If, say, some dark night there's a catastrophe like an earthquake or a flood — ?"

A faint grin crossed the captain's face, and he nodded. "Squires, knights, baronets, barons, viscounts, earls, marquis, dukes, princes, and king — everyone having any authority in the region — suddenly wakes up with a pain in the part of his anatomy that corresponds to the source of the trouble. The king, for instance, is likely to come to at 3:00 A.M. with a peculiar grinding pain in the upper part of the calf of his left leg, whereupon he will jump out of bed shouting, 'Quick! I think another typhoon just hit Bijitoa! Get the disaster crews ready!' The viscount of Bijitoa, whose whole body is now one living ache, will already be doing everything possible."

"But," I said, "if Sneat has absolute authority, tell me why couldn't he order the neuristers removed?"

"Yes, but here is the real work of genius. A special type of neurister-transmitter responds directly to a triggering impulse from the brain of the king or nobleman who has it. The activating impulse is the thought of evading duty."

"Then what happens?"

"Every neurister in the body is activated. It's like a slow dip in boiling oil.

"It has its compensations," said the captain. "He will have as much authority and respect as he could easily ask for. After the conventional term, a new selection will be held, the neuristers will be removed, and he'll have a bonus and a small but steady income. The people will respect him, and whenever he's on the planet he'll have full honors and the courtesy title of 'Your Highness'."

Suddenly I was alert. "They'll call him, 'Your Highness'?"

The captain nodded, then smiled and rolled back his sleeve. Above the wrist, his muscular arm was marked with a number of small fine scars. He said, "I know whereof I speak."

A moment later we had said goodnight, and he was gone.

I sat still, aware of the change that had taken place in the ship in the past few days. Once more everything seemed smooth, efficient, and good-natured.

There could be little doubt that the captain knew how to run things.

No wonder.

H

hy/per/space — a hypothetical area beyond space in which travel is accomplished much more quickly than in normal space. This concept is used to avoid Einstein's Theory of Relativity, which limits speed to 186,000 miles per second (the speed of light). Some writers have starships accelerate into hyperspace through the light barrier — as jets penetrate the sound barrier. Others have their ships porpoise beneath normal space, assuming either straight line short-cuts through a curved normal space or some sort of subspacial jet stream.

The Game of Rat and Dragon

CORDWAINER SMITH

THE TABLE

Pinlighting is a hell of a way to earn a living. Underhill was furious as he closed the door behind himself. It didn't make much sense to wear a uniform and look like a soldier if people didn't appreciate what you did.

He sat down in his chair, laid his head back in the headrest and pulled the helmet down over his forehead.

As he waited for the pin-set to warm up, he remembered the girl in the outer corridor. She had looked at it, then looked at him scornfully.

"Meow." That was all she had said. Yet it had cut him like a knife.

What did she think he was — a fool, a loafer, a uniformed nonentity?

Didn't she know that for every half-hour of pinlighting, he got a minimum of two months' recuperation in the hospital?

By now the set was warm. He felt the squares of space around him, sensed himself at the middle of an immense grid, a cubic grid, full of nothing. Out in that nothingness, he could sense the hollow, aching horror of space itself and could feel the terrible anxiety which his mind encountered whenever it met the faintest trace of inert dust.

As he relaxed, the comforting solidity of the sun, the clockwork of the familiar planets and the Moon rang in on him. Our own solar system was as charming and as simple as an ancient cuckoo clock filled with familiar ticking and with reassuring noises. The odd little moons of Mars swung around their planet like frantic mice, yet their regularity was itself an assurance that all was well. Far above the plane of the ecliptic, he could feel half a ton of dust more or less drifting outside the lanes of human travel.

Here there was nothing to fight, nothing to challenge the mind, to tear the living soul out of a body with its roots dripping in effluvium as tangible as blood.

Nothing ever moved in on the solar system. He could wear the pin-set forever and be nothing more than a sort of telepathic astronomer, a man who could feel the hot, warm protection of the sun throbbing and burning against his living mind.

Woodley came in.

"Same old ticking world," said Underhill. "Nothing to report. No wonder they didn't develop the pin-set until they began to planoform. Down here with the hot sun around us, it feels so good and so quiet. You can feel everything spinning and turning. It's nice and sharp and compact. It's sort of like sitting around home."

Woodley grunted. He was not much given to flights of fantasy.

Undeterred, Underhill went on, "It must have been pretty good to have been an Ancient Man. I wonder why they burned up their world with war. They didn't have to planoform. They didn't have to go out to earn their livings among the stars. They didn't have to dodge the Rats or play the Game. They couldn't have invented pinlighting because they didn't have any need of it, did they, Woodley?"

Woodley grunted, "Uh-huh." Woodley was twenty-six years old and due to retire in one more year. He already had a farm picked out. He had gotten through ten years of hard work pinlighting with the best of them. He had kept his sanity by not thinking very much about his job, meeting the strains of the task whenever he had to meet them and thinking nothing more about his duties until the next emergency arose.

Woodley never made a point of getting popular among the Partners. None of the Partners liked him very much. Some of them even resented him. He was suspected of thinking ugly thoughts of the Partners on occasion, but since none of the Partners ever thought a complaint in articulate form, the other pinlighters and the chiefs of the instrumentality left him alone.

Underhill was still full of the wonder of their job. Happily he babbled on, "What does happen to us when we planoform? Do you think it's sort of like dying? Did you ever see anybody who had his soul pulled out?"

"Pulling souls is just a way of talking about it," said Woodley. "After all these years, nobody knows whether we have souls or not."

"But I saw one once. I saw what Dogwood looked like when he came apart. There was something funny. It looked wet and sort of sticky as if it were bleeding and it went out of him — and you know what they did to Dogwood? They took him away, up in that part of the hospital where you and I never go — way up at the top part where the others are, where the others always have to go if they are alive after the Rats of the Up-and-Out have gotten them."

Woodley sat down and lit an ancient pipe. He was burning something called tobacco in it. It was a dirty sort of habit, but it made him look very dashing and adventurous.

"Look here, youngster. You don't have to worry about that stuff. Pinlighting is getting better all the time. The Partners are getting better. I've seen them pinlight two Rats forty-six million miles apart in one and a half milliseconds. As long as people had to try to work the pin-sets themselves, there was always the chance that with a minimum of four hundred milliseconds for the human mind to set a pinlight, we wouldn't light the Rats up fast enough to protect our planoforming ships. The Partners have changed all that. Once they get going, they're faster than Rats. And they always will be. I know it's not easy, letting a Partner share your mind — "

"It's not easy for them, either," said Underhill.

"Don't worry about them. They're not human. Let them take care of themselves. I've seen more pinlighters go crazy from monkeying around with Partners than I have ever seen caught by the Rats. How many do you actually know of them that got grabbed by Rats?"

Underhill looked down at his fingers, which shone green and purple in the vivid light thrown by the tuned-in pin-set, and counted ships. The thumb for the *Andromeda,* lost with crew and passengers, the index finger and the middle finger for release ships 43 and 56, found with their pin-sets burned out and every man, woman, and child on board dead or insane. The ring finger, the little finger, and the thumb of the other hand were the first three battleships to be lost to the Rats — lost as people realized that there was something out there *underneath space itself* which was alive, capricious, and malevolent.

Planoforming was sort of funny. It felt like —

Like nothing much.

Like the twinge of a mild electric shock.

Like the ache of a sore tooth bitten on for the first time.

Like a slightly painful flash of light against the eyes.

Yet in that time, a forty-thousand-ton ship lifting free above Earth disappeared somehow or other into two dimensions and appeared half a light-year or fifty light-years off.

At one moment, he would be sitting in the Fighting Room, the pin-set ready and the familiar solar system ticking around inside his head. For a second or a year (he could never tell how long it really was, subjectively), the funny little flash went through him and then he was loose in the Up-and-Out, the terrible open spaces between the stars, where the stars themselves felt like pimples on his telepathic mind and the planets were too far away to be sensed or read.

Somewhere in this outer space, a gruesome death awaited, death and horror of a kind which Man had never encountered until he reached out for interstellar space itself. Apparently the light of the suns kept the Dragons away.

Dragons. That was what people called them. To ordinary people, there was nothing, nothing except the shiver of planoforming and the hammer blow of sudden death or the dark, spastic note of lunacy descending into their minds.

But to the telepaths, they were Dragons.

In the fraction of a second between the telepaths' awareness of a hostile something out in the black hollow nothingness of space and the impact of a ferocious, ruinous psychic blow against all living things within the ship, the telepaths had sensed entities something like the dragons of ancient human lore, beasts more clever than beasts, demons more tangible than demons, hungry vortices of aliveness and hate compounded by unknown means out of the thin, tenuous matter between the stars.

It took a surviving ship to bring back the news — a ship in which, by sheer chance, a telepath had a light-beam ready, turning it out at the innocent dust so that, within the panorama of his mind, the Dragon dissolved into nothing at all and the other passengers, themselves nontelepathic, went about their way not realizing that their own immediate deaths had been averted.

From then on, it was easy — almost.

Planoforming ships always carried telepaths. Telepaths had their sensitiveness enlarged to an immense range by the pin-sets, which were telepathic amplifiers adapted to the mammal mind. The pin-sets in turn were electronically geared into small dirigible light-bombs. Light did it.

Light broke up the Dragons, allowed the ships to reform three-dimensionally, skip, skip, skip, as they moved from star to star.

The odds suddenly moved down from a hundred to one against mankind to sixty to forty in mankind's favor.

This was not enough. The telepaths were trained to become ultrasensitive, trained to become aware of the Dragons in less than a millisecond.

But it was found that the Dragons could move a million miles in just under two milliseconds and that this was not enough for the human mind to activate the light-beams.

Attempts had been made to sheathe the ships in light at all times.

This defense wore out.

As mankind learned about the Dragons, so, too, apparently, the Dragons learned about mankind. Somehow they flattened their own bulk and came in on extremely flat trajectories very quickly.

Intense light was needed, light of sunlike intensity. This could be provided only by light-bombs. Pinlighting came into existence.

Pinlighting consisted of the detonation of ultravivid, miniature photo-nuclear bombs, which converted a few ounces of a magnesium isotope into pure visible radiance.

The odds kept coming down in mankind's favor, yet ships were being lost.

It became so bad that people didn't even want to find the ships because the rescuers knew what they would see. It was sad to bring back to Earth three hundred bodies ready for burial and two hundred or three hundred lunatics, damaged beyond repair, to be wakened, and fed, and cleaned, and put to sleep, wakened and fed again until their lives were ended.

Telepaths tried to reach into the minds of the psychotics who had been damaged by the Dragons, but they found nothing there beyond vivid spouting columns of fiery terror bursting from the primordial id itself, the volcanic source of life.

Then came the Partners.

Man and Partner could do together what Man could not do alone. Men had the intellect. Partners had the speed.

The Partners rode their tiny craft, no larger than footballs, outside the spaceships. They planoformed with the ships. They rode beside them in their six-pound craft, ready to attack.

The tiny ships of the Partners were swift. Each carried a dozen pinlights, bombs no bigger than thimbles.

The pinlighters threw the Partners — quite literally threw — by means of mind-to-firing relays directly at the Dragons.

What seemed to be dragons to the human mind appeared in the form of gigantic rats in the minds of the Partners.

Out in the pitiless nothingness of space, the Partners' minds responded to an instinct as old as life. The Partners attacked, striking with a speed faster than Man's, going from attack to attack until the Rats or themselves were destroyed. Almost all the time, it was the Partners who won.

With the safety of the interstellar skip, skip, skip of the ships, commerce increased immensely, the population of all the colonies went up, and the demand for trained Partners increased.

Underhill and Woodley were a part of the third generation of pinlighters and yet, to them, it seemed as though their craft had endured forever.

Gearing space into minds by means of the pin-set, adding the Partners to those minds, keying up the mind for the tension of a fight on which all depended — this was more than human synapses could stand for long. Underhill needed his two months' rest after half an hour of fighting. Woodley needed his retirement after ten years of service. They were young. They were good. But they had limitations.

So much depended on the choice of Partners, so much on the sheer luck of who drew whom.

THE SHUFFLE

Father Moontree and the little girl named West entered the room. They were the other two pinlighters. The human complement of the Fighting Room was now complete.

Father Moontree was a red-faced man of forty-five who had lived the peaceful life of a farmer until he reached his fortieth year. Only then, belatedly, did the authorities find he was telepathic and agree to let him late in life enter upon the career of pinlighter. He did well at it, but he was fantastically old for this kind of business.

Father Moontree looked at the glum Woodley and the musing Underhill. "How're the youngsters today? Ready for a good fight?"

"Father always wants a fight," giggled the little girl named West. She was such a little girl. Her giggle was high and childish. She looked like the last person in the world one would expect to find in the rough, sharp dueling of pinlighting.

Underhill had been amused one time when he found one of the most sluggish of the Partners coming away happy from contact with the mind of the girl named West.

Usually the Partners didn't care much about the human minds with which they were paired for the journey. The Partners seemed to take the attitude that human minds were complex and fouled up beyond belief, anyhow. No Partner ever questioned the superiority of the human mind, though very few of the Partners were much impressed by that superiority.

The Partners liked people. They were willing to fight with them. They were even willing to die for them. But when a Partner liked an individual the way, for example, that Captain Wow or the Lady May liked Underhill, the liking had nothing to do with intellect. It was a matter of temperament, of feel.

Underhill knew perfectly well that Captain Wow regarded his, Underhill's, brains as silly. What Captain Wow liked was Underhill's friendly emotional structure, the cheerfulness and glint of wicked amusement that shot through Underhill's unconscious thought patterns, and the gaiety with which Underhill faced danger. The words, the history books, the ideas, the science — Underhill could sense all that in his own mind, reflected back from Captain Wow's mind, as so much rubbish.

Miss West looked at Underhill. "I bet you've put stickum on the stones."

"I did not!"

Underhill felt his ears grow red with embarrassment. During his novitiate, he had tried to cheat in the lottery because he got particularly fond of a special Partner, a lovely young mother named Murr. It was so much easier to operate with Murr and she was so affectionate toward him that he forgot pinlighting was hard work and that he was not instructed to have a good time with his Partner. They were both designed and prepared to go in to deadly battle together.

One cheating had been enough. They had found him out and he had been laughed at for years.

Father Moontree picked up the imitation-leather cup and shook the stone dice which assigned them their Partners for the trip. By senior rights, he took first draw.

He grimaced. He had drawn a greedy old character, a tough old male whose mind was full of slobbering thoughts of food, veritable oceans full of half-spoiled fish. Father Moontree had once said that he burped cod-liver oil for weeks after drawing that particular glutton, so strongly had the telepathic image of fish impressed itself upon his mind. Yet the glutton was a glutton for danger as well as for fish. He had killed sixty-three Dragons, more than any other Partner in the service, and was quite literally worth his weight in gold.

The little girl West came next. She drew Captain Wow. When she saw who it was, she smiled.

"I *like* him," she said. "He's such fun to fight with. He feels so nice and cuddly in my mind."

"Cuddly, hell," said Woodley. "I've been in his mind, too. It's the most leering mind in this ship, bar none."

"Nasty man," said the little girl. She said it declaratively, without reproach.

Underhill, looking at her, shivered.

He didn't see how she could take Captain Wow so calmly. Captain Wow's mind *did* leer. When Captain Wow got excited in the middle of a battle, confused images of Dragons, deadly Rats, luscious beds, the smell of fish, and the shock of space all scrambled together in his mind as he and Captain Wow, their consciousness linked together through the pin-set, became a fantastic composite of human being and Persian cat.

That's the trouble with working with cats, thought Underhill. It's a pity that nothing else anywhere will serve as Partner. Cats were all right once you got in touch with them telepathically. They were smart enough to meet the needs of the fight, but their motives and desires were certainly different from those of humans.

They were companionable enough as long as you thought tangible images at them, but their minds just closed up and went to sleep when you recited Shakespeare or Colegrove, or if you tried to tell them what space was.

It was sort of funny realizing that the Partners who were so grim and mature out here in space were the same cute little animals that people had used as pets for thousands of years back on Earth. He had embarrassed himself more than once while on the ground by saluting perfectly ordinary nontelepathic cats because he had forgotten for the moment that they were not Partners.

He picked up the cup and shook out his stone dice.

He was lucky — he drew the Lady May.

The Lady May was the most thoughtful Partner he had ever met. In her, the finely bred pedigree mind of a Persian cat had reached one of its highest peaks of development. She was more complex than any human woman, but the complexity was all one of emotions, memory, hope, and discriminated experience — experience sorted through without benefit of words.

When he had first come into contact with her mind, he was astonished at its clarity. With her he remembered her kittenhood. He remembered every mating experience she had ever had. He saw in a half-recognizable gallery all the other pinlighters with whom she had been paired for the fight. And he saw himself, radiant, cheerful, and desirable.

He even thought he caught the edge of a longing —

A very flattering and yearning thought: What a pity he is not a cat.

Woodley picked up the last stone. He drew what he deserved — a sullen, scared old tomcat with none of the verve of Captain Wow. Woodley's Partner was the most animal of all the cats on the ship, a low, brutish type with a dull mind. Even telepathy had not refined his character. His ears were half chewed off from the first fights in which he had engaged.

He was a serviceable fighter, nothing more.

Woodley grunted.

Underhill glanced at him oddly. Didn't Woodley ever do anything but grunt?

Father Moontree looked at the other three. "You might as well get your

Partners now. I'll let the Scanner know we're ready to go into the Up-and-Out."

THE DEAL

Underhill spun the combination lock on the Lady May's cage. He woke her gently and took her into his arms. She humped her back luxuriously, stretched her claws, started to purr, thought better of it, and licked him on the wrist instead. He did not have the pin-set on, so their minds were closed to each other, but in the angle of her mustache and in the movement of her ears he caught some sense of the gratification she experienced in finding him as her Partner.

He talked to her in human speech, even though speech meant nothing to a cat when the pin-set was not on.

"It's a damn shame, sending a sweet little thing like you whirling around in the coldness of nothing to hunt for Rats that are bigger and deadlier than all of us put together. You didn't ask for this kind of fight, did you?"

For answer, she licked his hand, purred, tickled his cheek with her long fluffy tail, turned around and faced him, golden eyes shining.

For a moment, they stared at each other, man squatting, cat standing erect on her hind legs, front claws digging into his knee. Human eyes and cat eyes looked across an immensity which no words could meet, but which affection spanned in a single glance.

"Time to get in," he said.

She walked docilely to her spheroid carrier. She climbed in. He saw to it that her miniature pin-set rested firmly and comfortably against the base of her brain. He made sure that her claws were padded so that she could not tear herself in the excitement of battle.

Softly he said to her, "Ready?"

For answer, she preened her back as much as her harness would permit and purred softly within the confines of the frame that held her.

He slapped down the lid and watched the sealant ooze around the seam. For a few hours, she was welded into her projectile until a workman with a short cutting arc would remove her after she had done her duty.

He picked up the entire projectile and slipped it into the ejection tube. He closed the door of the tube, spun the lock, seated himself in his chair, and put his own pin-set on.

Once again he flung the switch.

He sat in a small room, *small, small, warm, warm,* the bodies of the other three people moving close around him, the tangible lights in the ceiling bright and heavy against his closed eyelids.

As the pin-set warmed, the room fell away. The other people ceased to be people and became small glowing heaps of fire, embers, dark red fire, with the consciousness of life burning like old red coals in a country fireplace.

As the pin-set warmed a little more, he felt Earth just below him, felt the ship slipping away, felt the turning moon as it swung on the far side of the world, felt the planets and the hot, clear goodness of the sun which kept the Dragons so far from mankind's native ground.

Finally, he reached complete awareness.

He was telepathically alive to a range of millions of miles. He felt the dust which he had noticed earlier high above the ecliptic. With a thrill of warmth and tenderness, he felt the consciousness of the Lady May pouring over into his own. Her consciousness was as gentle and clear and yet sharp to the taste of his mind as if it were scented oil. It felt relaxing and reassuring. He could sense her welcome of him. It was scarcely a thought, just a raw emotion of greeting.

At last they were one again.

In a tiny, remote corner of his mind, as tiny as the smallest toy he had ever seen in his childhood, he was still aware of the room and the ship, and of Father Moontree picking up a telephone and speaking to a Scanner captain in charge of the ship.

His telepathic mind caught the idea long before his ears could frame the words. The actual sound followed the idea the way that thunder on an ocean beach follows the lightning inward from far out over the seas.

"The Fighting Room is ready. Clear to planoform, sir."

THE PLAY

Underhill was always a little exasperated by the way that Lady May experienced things before he did.

He was braced for the quick vinegar thrill of planoforming, but he caught her report of it before his own nerves could register what happened.

Earth had fallen so far away that he groped for several milliseconds before he found the sun in the upper rear right-hand corner of his telepathic mind.

That was a good jump, he thought. This way we'll get there in four or five skips.

A few hundred miles outside the ship, the Lady May thought back at him, "O warm, O generous, O gigantic man! O brave, O friendly, O tender and huge Partner! O wonderful with you, with you so good, good, good, warm, warm, now to fight, now to go, good with you . . . "

He knew that she was not thinking words, that his mind took the clear amiable babble of her cat intellect and translated it into images which his own thinking could record and understand.

Neither one of them was absorbed in the game of mutual greetings. He reached out far beyond her range of perception to see if there was anything near the ship. It was funny how it was possible to do two things at once. He could scan space with his pin-set mind and yet at the same time catch a vagrant thought of hers, a lovely, affectionate thought about a son who had had a golden face and a chest covered with soft, incredibly downy white fur.

While he was still searching, he caught the warning from her.

We jump again!

And so they had. The ship had moved to a second planoform. The stars were different. The sun was immeasurably far behind. Even the nearest stars were barely in contact. This was good Dragon country, the open, nasty, hollow kind of space. He reached farther, faster, sensing and looking for danger, ready to fling the Lady May at danger wherever he found it.

Terror blazed up in his mind, so sharp, so clear, that it came through as a physical wrench.

The little girl named West had found something — something immense, long, black, sharp, greedy, horrific. She flung Captain Wow at it.

Underhill tried to keep his own mind clear. "Watch out!" he shouted telepathically at the others, trying to move the Lady May around.

At one corner of the battle, he felt the lustful rage of Captain Wow as the big Persian tomcat detonated lights while he approached the streak of dust which threatened the ship and the people within.

The lights scored near-misses.

The dust flattened itself, changing from the shape of a stingray into the shape of a spear.

Not three milliseconds had elapsed.

Father Moontree was talking human words and was saying in a voice that moved like cold molasses out of a heavy jar, "C-A-P-T-A-I-N." Underhill knew that the sentence was going to be "Captain, move fast!"

The battle would be fought and finished before Father Moontree got through talking.

Now, fractions of a millisecond later, the Lady May was directly in line. Here was where the skill and speed of the Partners came in. She could react faster than he. She could see the threat as an immense Rat coming directly at her.

She could fire the light-bombs with a discrimination which he might miss.

He was connected with her mind, but he could not follow it.

His consciousness absorbed the tearing wound inflicted by the alien enemy. It was like no wound on Earth — raw, crazy pain which started like a burn at his navel. He began to writhe in his chair.

Actually he had not yet had time to move a muscle when the Lady May struck back at their enemy.

Five evenly spaced photonuclear bombs blazed out across a hundred thousand miles.

The pain in his mind and body vanished.

He felt a moment of fierce, terrible, feral elation running through the mind of the Lady May as she finished her kill. It was always disappointing to the cats to find out that their enemies, whom they sensed as gigantic space Rats, disappeared at the moment of destruction.

Then he felt her hurt, the pain and the fear that swept over both of them as the battle, quicker than the movement of an eyelid, had come and gone. In the same instant, there came the sharp and acid twinge of planoform.

Once more the ship went skip.

He could hear Woodley thinking at him, "You don't have to bother much. This old son-of-a-gun and I will take over for a while."

Twice again the twinge, the skip.

He had no idea where he was until the lights of the Caledonia space board shone below.

With a weariness that lay almost beyond the limits of thought, he threw his mind back into rapport with the pin-set, fixing the Lady May's projectile gently and neatly in its launching tube.

She was half dead with fatigue, but he could feel the beat of her heart, could listen to her panting, and he grasped the grateful edge of a thanks reaching from her mind to his.

THE SCORE

They put him in the hospital at Caledonia.

The doctor was friendly but firm. "You actually got touched by that Dragon. That's as close a shave as I've ever seen. It's all so quick that it'll be a long time before we know what happened scientifically, but I suppose you'd be ready for the insane asylum now if the contact had lasted several tenths of a millisecond longer. What kind of cat did you have out in front of you?"

Underhill felt the words coming out of him slowly. Words were such a lot of trouble compared with the speed and the joy of thinking, fast and sharp and clear, mind to mind! But words were all that could reach ordinary people like this doctor.

His mouth moved heavily as he articulated words, "Don't call our Partners cats. The right thing to call them is Partners. They fight for us in a team. You ought to know we call them Partners, not cats. How is mine?"

"I don't know," said the doctor contritely. "We'll find out for you. Meanwhile, old man, you take it easy. There's nothing but rest that can help you. Can you make yourself sleep, or would you like us to give you some kind of sedative?"

"I can sleep," said Underhill. "I just want to know about the Lady May."

The nurse joined in. She was a little antagonistic. "Don't you want to know about the other people?"

"They're okay," said Underhill. "I knew that before I came in here."

He stretched his arms and sighed and grinned at them. He could see they were relaxing and were beginning to treat him as a person instead of a patient.

"I'm all right," he said. "Just let me know when I can go see my Partner."

A new thought struck him. He looked wildly at the doctor. "They didn't send hcr off with the ship, did they?"

"I'll find out right away," said the doctor. He gave Underhill a reassuring squeeze of the shoulder and left the room.

The nurse took a napkin off a goblet of chilled fruit juice.

Underhill tried to smile at her. There seemed to be something wrong with the girl. He wished she would go away. First she had started to be friendly and now she was distant again. It's a nuisance being telepathic, he thought. You keep trying to reach even when you are not making contact.

Suddenly she swung around on him.

"You pinlighters! You and your damn cats!"

Just as she stamped out, he burst into her mind. He saw himself a radiant hero, clad in his smooth suede uniform, the pin-set crown shining like ancient royal jewels around his head. He saw his own face, handsome and masculine, shining out of her mind. He saw himself very far away and he saw himself as she hated him.

She hated him in the secrecy of her own mind. She hated him because he was — she thought — proud, and strange, and rich, better and more beautiful than people like her.

He cut off the sight of her mind and, as he buried his face in the pillow, he caught an image of the Lady May.

"She *is* a cat," he thought. "That's *all* she is — a *cat!*"

But that was not how his mind saw her — quick beyond all dreams of speed, sharp, clever, unbelievably graceful, beautiful, wordless, and undemanding.

Where would he ever find a woman who could compare with her?

I

im/mor/tal/i/ty — life that does not end in death. Although human life spans have constantly increased through the centuries, recent studies seem to indicate that the rate of increase has slowed. However, medical engineering, just now entering widespread use, may change this trend. *Eternal* life remains a science fictional concept, one that has provided beautiful and entertaining stories, such as *The Immortals,* by James E. Gunn (Bantam Books, 1962).

Let's Be Frank

BRIAN W. ALDISS

Four years after pretty little Anne Boleyn was executed in the Tower of London, a child was born into the Gladwebb family — an unusual child.

That morning, four people stood waiting in the drafty antechamber to milady's bedroom, where the confinement was taking place — her mother, an aunt, a sister-in-law, and a page. The husband, young Sir Frank Gladwebb, was not present; he was out hunting. At length the midwife bustled out to the four in the antechamber and announced that the Almighty (who had recently become a Protestant) had seen fit to bless milady with a son.

"Why, then, do we not hear the child crying, woman?" milady's mother, Cynthia Chinfont St. Giles, demanded, striding in to the room to her daughter. There the reason for the child's silence became obvious: it was asleep.

It remained in the "sleep" for nineteen years.

Young Sir Frank was not a patient man; he suffered, in an ambitious age, from ambition, and anything which stood between him and his advancement got short shrift. Returning from the hunt to find his first-born comatose, he was not pleased. The situation, however, was remedied by the birth of a second son in the next year, and of three more children in the four years thereafter. All of these offspring were excessively normal, the boy taking holy orders and becoming eventually the abbot of St. Duckwirt, where simony supplemented an already generous income.

The sleeping child grew as it slept. It stirred in its sleep, sometimes it yawned, it accepted the bottle. Sir Frank kept it in an obscure room in the manor, appointing an old harridan called Nan to attend it. In moments of rage, or when he was in his cups, Sir Frank would swear to run a sword through the child; yet the words were idle, as those about him soon perceived. There was a strange bond between Sir Frank and the sleeping child. Though he visited it rarely, he never forgot it.

On the child's third birthday, he went up to see it. It lay in the center of a four-poster, its face calm. With an impulse of tenderness, Sir Frank picked it up, cradling it, limp and helpless, in his arms.

"It's a lovely lad, sire," Nan commented. And at that moment the sleeping child opened its eyes and appeared to focus them on its father. With a cry, Sir Frank staggered back dizzily, overwhelmed by an indescribable sensation. He sprawled on the bed, holding the child tightly to keep it from harm. When the giddy feeling had gone, he looked and found the child's eyes shut again, and so they remained for a long while.

The Tudor springs and winters passed, the sleeping child experiencing none of them. He grew to be a handsome young boy, and a manservant was engaged for him; still his eyes never opened, except on the rare occasions when his father — now engrossed in the affairs of court — came to see him. Because of the weakness which took him at these times, Sir Frank saw to it that they were few.

Good King Harry died, the succession passed to women and weaklings, Sir Frank came under the patronage of Robert Devereux, earl of Essex. And in the year of the coronation of Elizabeth, the sleeping child awoke.

Sir Frank, now a prosperous forty-one, had gone in to see his first-born for the first time in thirty months. On the four-poster lay a handsome, pale youth of nineteen, his straggling growth of beard the very shade of his father's more luxuriant crop. The manservant was out of the room.

Strangely perturbed, as if something inexpressible lay just below the surface of his thoughts, Sir Frank went over to the bed and rested his hands on the boy's shoulders. He seemed to stand on the brink of a precipice.

"Frank," he whispered — for the sleeping child had been given his own name — "Frank, why don't you wake up?"

In answer to the words, the youth's eyes opened. The usual wash of dizziness came and went like a flash; Sir Frank found himself looking up into his own eyes.

He found more than that.

He found he was a youth of nineteen whose soul had been submerged until now. He found he could sit up, stretch, run a hand marveling through his hair and exclaim, "By our Lady!" He found he could get up, look long at the green world beyond his window, and finally turn back to stare at himself.

And all the while "himself" had watched the performance with his own eyes. Shaking, father and son sat down together on the bed.

"What sorcery is this?" Sir Frank muttered.

But it was no sorcery, or not in the sense Sir Frank meant. He had merely acquired an additional body for his ego. It was not that he could be in either as he pleased; he was in both at the same time. When the son came finally to consciousness, it was to his father's consciousness.

Warily, experimenting that day and the next few days — when the whole household rejoiced at this awakening of the first-born — Sir Frank found that his new body could do all he could do: could ride, could fence, could make love to a kitchen wench: could indeed do these things better than the old body, which was beginning, just a little, to become less pliant under approaching middle age. His experience, his knowledge, all were resources equally at the command of either body. He was, in fact, two people.

A later generation could have explained the miracle to Sir Frank — though explaining in terms he would not have understood. Though he knew well enough the theory of family traits and likenesses, it would have been impossible then to make him comprehend the intricacy of a chromosome which carries inside it — not merely the stereotypes of parental hair or temperament — but the secret knowledge of how to breathe, how to work the muscles to move the bones, how to grow, how to remember, how to commence the processes of thought . . . all the infinite number of secret "how to's" that have to be passed on for life to stay above jelly level.

A freak chromosome in Sir Frank ensured he passed on, together with these usual secrets, the secret of his individual consciousness.

It was extraordinary to be in two places at once, doing two different things — extraordinary, but not confusing. He merely had two bodies which were as integrated as his two hands had been.

Frank II had a wonderful time; youth and experience, foresight and a fresh complexion, were united as never before. The combination was irresistible. The Virgin Queen, then in her late twenties, summoned him before her and sighed deeply. Then, catching Essex's eye, she put him out of reach of temptation by sending him off to serve the ambassador at the court of her brother-in-law, Philip.

Frank II liked Spain. Philip's capital was gayer, warmer, and more sanitary than London. It was intoxicating to enjoy the best of both courts. It proved also extremely remunerative: the shared consciousness of Franks I and II was by far the quickest communicational link between the two rival countries, and as such was worth money. Not that Frank revealed his secret to a soul, but he let it be known he had a fleet of capable spies who moved without risk of detection between England and Spain. Burly Lord Burleigh beamed upon him. So did the duke of Medina Sidonia.

So fascinating was it being two people at once that Frank I was slow to take any systematic survey of other lurking advantages. An unfortunate tumble from a horse, however, gave him leisure for meditation. Even then, he might have missed the vital point, were it not for something that happened in Madrid.

Frank III was born.

Frank II had passed on the renegade chromosome via a little Spanish courtesan. The child was called Sancha. There was no coma about him! As if to defy the extreme secrecy under which the birth took place, he wailed lustily from the start. And he had the shared consciousness of his father and grandfather.

It was an odd feeling indeed, opening this new annex to life and experiencing the world through all the child's weakness and helplessness. There were many frustrations for Frank I, but compensations too — not the least being closeted so intimately with the babe's delightful mother.

This birth made Frank realize one striking, blinding fact: as long as the chromosome reproduced itself in sufficient dominance, he was immortal! To him, in an unscientific age, the problem did not present itself quite like that; but he realized that here was a trait to be kept in the family.

It happened that Frank had married one of his daughters off to an architect called Tanyk. This union produced a baby daughter some two weeks after the secret birth of Frank III (they hardly thought of him as Sancha). Franks I and II arranged that III should come to England and marry Miss Tanyk just as soon as both were old enough; the vital chromosome ought to be latent in her and appear in her children.

Relations between England and Spain deteriorating, Frank II came home shortly with the boy Frank III acting as his page. The fruits of several other liaisons had to be left behind with their mothers; they had no shared consciousness, only ordinary good red English blood.

Frank II had been back in the aptly named mother country for only a few months when a lady of his acquaintance presented him with Frank IV. Frank IV was a girl, christened Berenice. The state of coma which had ensnared Frank II for so long did not afflict Berenice, or any other of his descendants.

Another tremendous adjustment in the shared consciousness had to be made. That also had its compensations; Frank was the first man ever really to appreciate the woman's point of view.

So the eventful years rolled on. Sir Frank's wife died; the Abbey of St. Duckwirt flourished; Frank II sailed over to Hispaniola; the Armada sailed against England and was repulsed. And in the next year, Frank III (Sancha), with his Spanish looks and English money, won the hand of Rosalynd Tanyk, as prearranged. When his father returned from the New World (with his English looks and Spanish money), it was in time to see in person his daughter, Berenice, alias Frank IV, also taken in wedlock.

By this year, Frank I was old and gray and retired in the country. While he was experiencing old age in that body, he was experiencing active middle age in his son's and the delights of matrimony in his grandson's and granddaughter's.

He awaited anxiously the issue of Frank III (Sancha)'s marriage to his cousin Rosalynd. There were offspring enough. One in 1590. Twins in 1591. Three lovely children — but, alas, ordinary mortals, without shared consciousness. Then, while watching an indifferent and bloody play called *Titus Andronicus*, two years later, Rosalynd came into labor, and was delivered at a tavern in Cheapside of Frank V.

In the succeeding years, she delivered Franks VI and VIII. Frank VII sprang from Berenice's (Frank IV's) union. So did Frank IX. The freak chromosome was getting into its stride.

Full of years, Sir Frank's body died. The diphtheria which carried him off caused him as much suffering as it would have done an ordinary man; dying was not eased by his unique gift. He slid out into the long darkness — but his consciousness continued unabated in eight other bodies.

It would be pleasant to follow the history of these Franks (who, of course, really bore different surnames and Christian names), but space forbids. Suffice it to say that there were vicissitudes — the old queen shut Frank II in the Tower, Frank VI had a dose of the clap, Frank IX ruined himself trying to grow asparagus, then newly discovered from Asia. Despite this, the shared consciousness spread; the five who shared it in this third generation prospered and produced children with the same ability.

The numbers grew. Twelve in the fourth generation, twenty-two in the fifth, fifty in the sixth, and in the seventh, by the time William and Mary came to the throne, one hundred and twenty-four.

These people, scattered all over the country, a few of them on the continent, were much like normal people. To outsiders, their relationship was not apparent; they certainly never revealed it; they never met. They became traders, captains of ships that traded with the Indies, soldiers, parliamentarians, agriculturalists; some plunged into, some avoided, the constitutional struggles that dogged most of the seventeenth century. But they were all

— male or female — Franks. They had the inexpressible benefit of their progenitor's one hundred and seventy-odd years' experience, and not only of his, but of all the other Franks. It was small wonder that, with few exceptions, whatever they did they prospered.

By the time George III came to the throne and rebellion broke out in the British colonies in America the tenth generation of Franks numbered 2,160.

The ambition of the original Frank had not died; it had grown subtler. It had become a wish to sample everything. The more bodily habitations there were with which to sample, the more tantalizing the idea seemed: for many experiences, belonging only to one brief era, are never repeated, and may be gone before they are perceived and tasted.

Such an era was the Edwardian decade from 1901 to 1911. It suited Frank's Elizabethan spirit, with its bounce and vulgarity and the London streets packed tight with horse vehicles. His manifestations prospered; by the outbreak of World War I they numbered over three and a half million.

The war, whose effect on the outlook and technology of the whole world was to be incalculable, had a terrific influence on the wide-spread shared consciousness of Frank. Many Franks of the sixteenth generation were killed in the muck of the trenches, he died not once but many times, developing an obsessive dread of war which never left him.

By the time the Americans entered the war, he was turning his many thoughts to politics.

It was not an easy job. Until now, he had concentrated on diversity in occupations, savoring them all. He rode the fiery horses of the Camargue; he played in the orchestras of La Scala, Milan; he farmed daffodils in the Scilly Isles; he built dikes along the Zuyder Zee; filmed with Réné Clair; preached in the Vienna cathedral; operated in Bart's; fished in the bilious Bay of Biscay; argued with the founder of the Bauhaus. Now he turned the members of his consciousness among the rising generation into official posts, compensating for the sameness and grayness of their jobs with the thought that the change was temporary.

His plans had not gone far enough before the Second World War broke out. His consciousness, spread over eleven million people, suffered from Plymouth and Guernsey to Siam and Hong Kong. It was too much. By the time the war ended, world domination had become his aim.

Frank's chromosome was now breeding as true as ever. Blood group, creed, color of skin — nothing was proof against it. The numbers with shared consciousness, procreating for all they were worth, trebled every generation.

Seventeenth generation: eleven million in 1940.

Eighteenth generation: thirty-three million in 1965.

Nineteenth generation: a hundred million in 1990.

Twentieth generation: three hundred million in 2015.

Frank was well placed to stand as a member of parliament, for all his alter egos could vote for him. He stood as several members, one of whom eventually became prime minister; but the intricacies of office proved a dismal job. There was, after all, a simpler and far more thorough way of ruling the country: by simple multiplication.

At this task, all the Franks set to with a will.

By the beginning of the twenty-first century, Great Britain consisted only of Franks. Like a great multiplicity of mirrors, they faced each other across counter and club; young or old, fat or thin, rich or poor, all shared one massive consciousness.

Many modifications in private and public life took place. Privacy ceasing to exist, all new houses were glass-built, curtains abolished, walls pulled down. Police went, the entire legal structure vanished overnight — a man does not litigate against himself. A parody of Parliament remained, to deal with foreign affairs, but party politics, elections, leaders in newspapers (even newspapers themselves) were scrapped.

Most of the arts went. One manifestation of Frank did not care to see another manifestation of Frank performing. TV, publishing, Tin Pan Alley, film studios . . . out like lights.

The surplus Franks, freed from all these dead enterprises and many more, went abroad to beget more Franks.

All these radical changes in the habits of the proverbially conservative British were noticed elsewhere, particularly by the Americans and Canadians. They sent observers over to report on the scene.

Before long, the same radical changes were sweeping Europe. Frank's chromosome conquered everywhere. Peace was guaranteed.

By the end of another century's ruthless intermarriage, Russia and Asia were engulfed as thoroughly as Europe, and by the same loving methods. Billions of people: one consciousness.

And then came Frank's first setback in all the centuries of his polydextrous existence. He turned his reproductive powers toward the Americas. He was repulsed.

From Argentina to Alaska, and all ports in between, the conqueror chromosome failed to conquer.

The massive, massed intellect set itself to work on the problem, soon arriving at the answer. Another chromosome had got there first. Evidence of the truth of this came when the drastic modifications in domestic and public life which had swept the rest of the world swept the linked continents of North and South America. There was a second shared consciousness.

By various deductions, Frank concluded that the long-dead Frank II's visit to Hispaniola had scattered some of the vital chromosome there. Not properly stable at that time, it had developed its own separate shared consciousness, which had spread through the Americas much as the Frank chromosome had spread round the rest of the world.

It was a difficult situation. The Franks and the Hispaniolas shared the globe without speaking to each other. After a decade of debate, the Franks took an obvious way out of the impasse: they built themselves a fleet of spaceships and headed into the solar system.

That, ladies, gentlemen, and neuters, is a brief account of the extraordinary race which recently landed on our planet, Venus, as they call it. I think we may congratulate ourselves that our method of perpetuating our species is so vastly different from theirs; nothing else could have saved us from that insidious form of conquest.

in/va/sion of earth — attacks on our planet by alien forces. These can either be direct, or secretive, as in the movie "Invasion of the Body Snatchers" (1955, remade in 1979). The invasion of earth is one of the great staple themes of science fiction. A representative group of stories can be found in *Invasion From Space* (Hawthorn, 1972).

The Easy Way Out

LEE CORREY

They came out of space armed and ready.

The alien ship skittered into Earth's atmosphere in an easterly direction and landed surreptitiously about midnight in the Rocky Mountains of North America. The Master had chosen the approach trajectory and landing area after a long survey in far orbit.

"*Whew!*" Ulmnarrgh breathed with relief as the ship's sensors reported no great hubbub created by the silent landing in the meadow among the high peaks. "I don't think we were detected. There were no probing emissions in the electromagnetic spectrum and no phasing of the gravito-inertial field."

"Keep your guard detectors up," the Master directed. "We'll wait for daylight. In the meantime, run out the screens and keep all defenses on the alert."

Harmarrght fidgeted. "By the Great Overlord!" he snapped under his breath to his mentor, the exobiologist Norvallk. "The old boy acts as though he's scared to death."

Turning an eye toward the youngster, Norvallk gently replied, "Don't cover up your nervousness with bravado. All of us remember how we felt on our first landing as a cadet. A certain amount of caution is always indicated, particularly in the face of the fact that the previous probe ship didn't come back from this world."

"The only logical reason for that is a technical malfunction," the youngster shot back.

The exobiologist shook his head sadly. "Logical answers don't always hold true in exploration. This planet's inhabited by communicating beings. If you're going to insist on using logic, calculate the conclusion you get when you take into account the loss of a ship on a planet whose inhabitants have an unknown level of technology. Mukch on that for a while!"

Harmarrght didn't. He had an immediate answer. "I've studied the history of our conquests for the Great Overlord, and nowhere on a thousand worlds has our high technology been equalled. *That,* sir, is an established fact! So now we crawl in here with pseudopods rolled up like a frightened orh. Why should we be so cautious when our technology makes conquest so simple?"

"You're here to learn why," Norvallk told him. "So shut up and observe. You've been trained; now you're about to be educated . . . " These young cubs just out of the Institute were always impetuous, he reminded himself. Such attitudes made excellent warriors for the Great Overlord, but when were the professional institutes going to learn to temper their indoctrination when training explorers?

The Master called for a confrontation in the control bay. This was a welcome relief to Norvallk who, as the chief exobiologist aboard, had nothing to do but sit and shiver until he could get out and have a look at things.

"Our position here, while secure at the moment, may be perilous," the Master pointed out to his crew. "I want to impress again on you the complete nature of the situation. You have all seen the reconnaissance images from the first orbiting probes that revealed the unmistakable sign of intelligent life: deliberate conversion of natural resources into more orderly features such as artificial waterways and geometrical groupings of artificial dwellings.

"It's unusual to find a planet inhabited by intelligent life. But this planet appears to be unique in that it seems to support more than one type of intelligent life.

"Communication is by means of electromagnetic radiation. There is no way of knowing at this time whether this is a naturally evolved trait, such as we found on Vagarragh Four, or the technically developed, artificial-extension-of-pressure-wave communication such as we have. Rastharrh, tell us what you have discovered."

The information theory expert was somewhat hesitant. "I don't quite know what to make of it. There's more than one coding group involved. I've even run onto a highly unusual code group consisting completely of periodic transmissions of a carrier, and this may be highly indicative of a life form here that communicates by electromagnetic means. It's difficult to conceive of any planetwide intelligent life form that uses more than one type of communication symbol code. Here, there are many. It leads me to believe that this planet may have evolved several high life forms, each communicating differently."

"Norvallk, is this possible?" the Master asked.

Norvallk shrugged. "Anything is possible when dealing with intelligent, communicating beings. The physical arrangement of the planet's land areas suggests that Rastharrh's hypothesis may be correct. I wouldn't discount it. We have got to have a first-hand look."

"And that's what we're going to get." The Master gave his orders.

There was barely enough time to accomplish anything before the sun rose. The planet had a very short rotational period.

It was not a bad-looking world, Norvallk decided as he surveyed the landing site. He pointed out several features to Harmarrght. "Frozen water over there on those high peaks. And note the abundant inverted life forms growing stationary on the hills. If they are at all like the ones on Chinarrghk, they have their brains in the ground and their energy receptors above ground. And probably immobile as well . . . "

"No problem to overcome them if they can't move," Harmarrght stated flatly.

"That depends upon their biological operation and natural defenses, youngster. They could exude poisonous gases when disturbed, for example."

"We can handle that."

"Once we know about it."

"There is no obvious reason why we can't take over this planet for the Great Overlord."

"There may be several reasons why we can't. It all depends on the native life forms, particularly with regard to their Intelligence Index, Adaptability Index, and, most important, Ferocity Index."

"Oh, come now! If they're incapable of defending themselves against our advanced technology, they don't stand a chance!"

Norvallk did not answer his protégé. Lecturing no longer was effective.

It was nearly midday by the time the ground party was organized to leave the ship. Norvallk led it, supported by Rastharrh, the morphologist Grahhgh, three well-trained and experienced recording specialists, the three warrior techs. The whole party was armed with both energy weapons and projectile hurlers. Harmarrght accompanied Norvallk as his direct assistant.

The ten aliens proceeded down the slope from the meadow into the valley. There was a stream on the valley floor and a chance of encountering advanced life forms.

"There are life forms everywhere!" Harmarrght remarked.

"And they take many shapes, but they don't bother us. We'll have to set automatic traps for those flying forms; they're much too fast," Norvallk observed.

They did not reach the stream until well after sunset, but the light shed by the world's natural satellite permitted the party to find its way and continue to record some data.

At sunrise, they found the grizzly bear.

"Let's take it back to the ship!" was Harmarrght's first excited comment.

"Not so fast!" Norvallk cautioned. "We watch first. Quietly. It's feeding. Look how it reaches down into the water and knocks those water-dwellers out onto the bank."

"By the Great Overlord! It's *fast!*"

"Let's see if the Master can find some counterpart from a known world." Norvallk instructed the data recorders to beam their images back to the ship. In a quick communication with the Master, Norvallk set up the search through the memory banks of the ship's computer. As he was waiting for the answer, he gave a little instruction to Harmarrght. "Notice the covering of organic filaments that may either be manipulators, sensors, or thermal insulation. And the grouping of sensory transducers around the food intake orifice."

"It carries no weapons," Harmarrght pointed out.

"It may not need them. But note the plurality of sharp artifacts on the end of each appendage. Are you willing to state unequivocally that they are not artificial?"

A message came from the ship. Zero read-out from the memory bank. Plus the Master's direct order, "Bring the life form in for study, preferably functioning."

With obvious relish, Harmarrght hefted his energy projector and started forward. Norvallk tried to stop him, but it was too late.

Very few native life forms will bother a feeding grizzly bear. *Ursus horribilis* is not only strong, but easily provoked. But Harmarrght didn't know this. He found out quickly.

He fired an energy bolt at what should have been an area of vital control in the bear's midsection with the intent to paralyze the beast. The shot singed white-tipped hair and burned a hole through the skin. It hurt the bear and drew its attention to the young alien.

"Cover him!" Norvallk yelled to his party. One of the warrior techs burst forward to get between Harmarrght and the bear.

The bear stopped fishing and let out a bellowing roar. This panicked the warrior tech, who fired a projectile toward the bear's head. Another of the warrior techs got into position. But the bear moved . . . fast.

The grizzly brought its huge forepaw down on the closest warrior alien. Armor and all, the warrior splattered.

The next swipe of the huge paw demolished Grahhgh, who had the misfortune to get within range. While trying to get to the second warrior, the bear stepped on Rastharrh, putting part of him out of commission. The bear rose on its hind legs to its full height of eight feet and started to swing again, aiming toward Harmarrght, but the second warrior fired an explosive bolt that caught the grizzly in the roof of the mouth and congealed its brain.

It took a little time for Norvallk to get things straightened out again. As the four transports came from the ship to pick up the dead and injured, he whirled on Harmarrght, managed to suppress his anger, and said sarcastically, "So. It had no weapons, eh? Evidence of a low technology, huh? I thought that you had studied bio-engineering . . . "

The young cadet could only remark, "Its Ferocity Index must be unreasonably high . . . "

Three more transports had to be sent from the ship to lift the grizzly's carcass. The party then resumed its course down the stream, minus three of its members. "Standing orders," Norvallk told them. "We take no further action against indigenous life forms except when attacked. We'll merely observe and record data. It seems that most of the other life forms have a very low Ferocity Index, but I am not going to take the chance of losing the rest of this party."

Harmarrght said nothing; he was now reasonably subdued.

Two sunrises later, the party discovered another silvertip grizzly. The aliens didn't repeat their first mistake; they stood well back and watched this bear carefully.

It was leisurely dining on the remains of a freshly killed white-tail deer at the edge of a small clearing alongside the stream. Apparently wanting a bit of variety in its diet, the bear had managed to find an easy mark in an unsuspecting young deer.

"I am beginning to suspect that the Ferocity Index of this life form is a little bit too high for comfort," Norvallk observed.

"But still nothing that we can't overcome with our existing weapons," Harmarrght added.

"There are many other things yet to consider," his mentor told him. "Observe and remember."

While they were watching the second grizzly dine, a report came in from the ship. "The dead beast has been given a preliminary examination. Its colloidal control network is very complex and contains a highly organized colloidal computer near its primary sensors. It has the capability of a very high Intelligence Index," the Master told them.

Norvallk hastily briefed the Master on their current find and added, "We see no signs of artifacts associated with the beast unless those sharp instruments on its appendages are tools."

"They aren't. They are natural."

"In that event, it isn't using tools. I don't know whether or not it's communicating right now. Too bad Rastharrh was injured; we could use him. A new life form has just arrived! It's smaller but covered with the same sort of organic filaments. Same configuration. It's going right up to the larger beast. We may be witnessing our first example of symbiosis on this world where the large beast does the hunting and shares the meal with a smaller communicating form."

The bear looked up from its meal and recognized the small bearlike form with its broad ribbon of light brown fur down each side. But the bear was still young and still hungry; it decided to put up a defense of its meal. It had yet to learn that there are few animals of any size willing to tangle with *Gulo luscus,* the wolverine.

The wolverine simply attacked the bear as though it did not know the meaning of fear. Its flashing teeth and slashing claws were smaller and less strong than the bear's, but sheer meanness was on its side. It ripped in to kill, giving no quarter. After the first encounter, in which the bear's huge paw missed in a roundhouse swing, the battle was very short and very one-sided.

The grizzly took the easy way out. It retreated, ambling off into the pine forest as rapidly as it could move.

Norvallk was shaken, but Harmarrght was now petrified. "Let me kill it!" the youngster urged.

"No. You may not be able to," Norvallk stayed him.

"It will be easy!" He hefted his energy projector and patted it.

"We tried that once. Three of us for one of them. And the Ferocity Index on this little animal is going to be very difficult to compute. It's high. Let's see what the Master's computer says." Norvallk fed all of the available data back to the ship.

The computer chewed up the available data regarding size, probable body mass, and other related factors of the two different animals, bear and wolverine; it then compared this with data from other worlds, considered the possibility of reducing the high Ferocity Index of the bear, found that it could not logically do so, discovered that it could not handle the Ferocity Index of the wolverine, and ended up in a stoppage. The wolverine's Ferocity Index was off-scale.

In the meantime, Norvallk and his group kept observing and reporting. "It's cleaning up what's left of the carcass, and it acts as though it hasn't eaten for days. It's simply glutting itself."

"Its Ferocity Index may diminish when its hunger drive is satiated," Harmarrght ventured to predict.

"In any case, it can't finish that carcass, and we'll be able to take it back to the ship for analysis."

"Ugh! I wonder." Harmarrght remarked, reeling from the odor that now wafted in their direction.

"It's fouling the remains of the carcass with musk!" Norvallk observed in amazement, and almost gagged.

The wolverine, being unable to finish, had simply protected what was left so he could return to complete the meal at a later date. It then sat up on its haunches, shaded its eyes with a forepaw, and looked around.

The alien party worked very hard at remaining unseen and unheard, although most of them were gasping as a result of the horrible smell.

"Did you say something about technology earlier?" Norvallk managed to ask his student between stifled coughs.

The wolverine found its direction again and ambled off.

"Do we follow?" Harmarrght asked. "Or do we stay here and suffocate?"

"Let's go! Keep it in sight, but *don't* let it detect you," Norvallk ordered his party. He had no desire to tangle with this little beast. But he had to find out more about it.

As they went along, Norvallk asked Harmarrght, "Do you still think that this world would be easy to conquer?"

"Well . . . Nothing so far that our weapons couldn't cope with. It might be expensive and it might take time, but we could do it . . . if what we've seen is any indication. They're tough, but we're just as tough and just as well armed."

"Wouldn't you say that this being has a reasonably high Ferocity Index?"

"Yes," Harmarrght admitted.

"Which means we would have to kill them all or subdue them. From the looks of them, we'd probably have to kill them. But suppose we don't get them all. Would you like to live here knowing that one of those things was on the loose?"

"If I'm armed and expecting it, why not?"

"What did you learn at the Institute?" Norvallk exploded. "Didn't they teach you anything about the economics of conquest and exploitation? Didn't they teach you how to evaluate the Indices?"

"Well, yes, but . . . "

"Did you ever stop to consider the difficulties of conquering a world whose inhabitants have a low Intelligence Index, low Adaptability Index, low Technical Index, but a high Ferocity Index? Under those circumstances, a takeover becomes a disaster if the natives fight to the death with no quarter given! *Successful* colonization requires that the native life not only be overcome, but also be retrained and made suitable to work under the direction of the colonizers. You can't spend all your time fighting. Now that you're on a new planet for the first time, maybe you'll realize that a planet is a big chunk of real estate. You *can't* wipe out every dangerous animal on it, but if they're too dangerous you *must* dispatch them lest they continue to breed and remain a constant threat. Under a situation like that, you have to withdraw from the planet and write it off."

"Retreat? But we've never had to do that! We've *never* written off a world!" Harmarrght objected.

"We'd have written off a dozen of them if we'd known then what we know now. Those worlds were very expensive acquisitions," Norvallk reminded him as they moved along, keeping the wolverine in sight but not permitting their conversation to betray their presence. "You were filled with propaganda about the glorious exploits of those who did the dirty work. It looks different when you've been on the scene. Or it should. What is your evaluation of this world thus far? Apply what you've been taught. You can even use logic if you want."

"Thus far, we've discovered two life forms with high Ferocity Indices," Harmarrght said by way of review and lead-in. "But they evidenced no obvious Communications Indices, moderate Intelligence Indices, and very low Technology Indices . . . "

"I'm not willing to concede that point yet," Norvallk put in, "but go on."

"Ergo, the dominant species might not have a high Ferocity Index, being dependent upon symbiosis with other species to acquire this factor. I make the presumption that the Ferocity Index would logically have to be lower in more intelligent, communicating beings than . . . "

"An assumption without adequate evidence," Norvallk pointed out.

"Well, on the other hand, the two forms already discovered might not be the dominant species on the planet. They might simply coexist with the dominant form."

"Suppose the dominant form has a higher Ferocity Index," Norvallk said.

"Oh, quite unlikely! We've *never* encountered anything before with the fantastic Ferocity Index that would be required!"

"Harmarrght, it's a big universe."

"Yes, but very few planets exist with the physical characteristics of this one. It seems to me that the Overlord might be unhappy with a recommendation to abandon it now that . . . "

"Which means that we must gather as much data as we can." Norvallk indicated the wolverine. "Watch! The animal is hunting something new."

By climbing a tree, the wolverine finished off a squirrel. Very shortly thereafter, a porcupine managed to get out of its way. The wolverine then proceeded to catch a rabbit and a chipmunk, but it befouled them and cached them instead of eating them.

"Well, we seem to have stumbled on the beast that probably has the highest Ferocity Index in this neighborhood," Norvallk commented, then stopped in his tracks as the wolverine emerged into a clearing.

"A dwelling!" Harmarrght exclaimed. "If it belongs to this beast, it indicates a much higher Intelligence Index than I expected for it. Look: smoke comes from a vent on the roof, indicating a mastery of the chemical combustion process which . . . "

"Don't assume that it belongs to the animal," Norvallk cut in, and pointed out the tools scattered here and there around the cabin and the plot of ground that was a garden. "It couldn't possibly handle tools of that size. It's demonstrably a hunter, and I wouldn't expect it to be a farmer, too." He snapped orders to his exploring party. Quietly, the various specialists ranged themselves in hiding around the clearing so that their recorders had a view of the cabin from several sides. The warriors were given strict orders not to use their weapons except in defense of the party.

The wolverine prowled around the cabin for some time. Norvallk waited patiently, but Harmarrght fidgeted nervously. "Let me go up and see what's inside that dwelling," he finally suggested.

"Not while I'm in charge of the party," Norvallk said. "This is an exploration crew, not a military group. I equate such bravery to stupidity at this point. I do not want to have to return your remains to the ship . . . providing that the animal left any remains or that we could get to you afterwards."

"But one bolt from this projector . . . "

"How many others might be inside that dwelling?" Norvallk posed the rhetorical question to his student.

There was a movement behind one of the windows. Then, as Norvallk came up on the alert, two human children dashed out of the cabin with yells of delight.

With great consternation, Norvallk watched these two new life forms run fearlessly up to the wolverine.

"Glutton! You're back!" one of them cried.

They dropped to the ground in front of the little animal and began to stroke its coat. The wolverine responded playfully, for it had known these children all its life. They had found it as a cub, half-frozen and starved, somehow separated from its mother. Although these children had raised it as a pet, it often reverted to feral state and disappeared into the hills for days. But it always came back. Hunting was difficult and dangerous; it was far easier to be fed on schedule by the children. And the humans were capable of giving it something very pleasurable and desirable: love.

Glutton, the wolverine, rolled on its back and permitted great indignities to be taken. One of the children ran into the house and returned with some meat in a dish — and was disappointed when the wolverine refused it. But Glutton did not befoul this meal as it had done with others it could not eat.

The young bipeds talked to it, played with it, and fondled it for some time. The aliens recorded every movement and sound. Norvallk was very busy trying to make things add up in his mind; he was quite unhappy with the conclusions he was reaching. Harmarrght merely watched in great confusion; he was having great difficulty rationalizing what his own logic told him with what he had been taught.

A larger biped appeared in the cabin door. "Boys! Lunch time! Come in now!"

They started to go, but the wolverine wanted more play and love. It growled and tried to nip at one boy's leg.

The human child turned around and cuffed the wolverine smartly, scolding it as he did so.

The wolverine shook its fur and followed the boys into the cabin.

Norvallk wasted no time regrouping his party and getting them back to the ship.

"You've done an excellent job under most hazardous conditions," the Master told Norvallk and the rest of the party. "Your data confirm the conclusion we've already reached here. Ulmnarrgh has received radiations from life forms that are orbiting this world as well as in transit to nearby planets. The varied inhabitants of this world are already out in space and expanding with explosive speed. I will be recommending rather drastic measures to the Overlord. In the meantime, we raise ship at once and try to get out of here without being destroyed."

As the ship boosted away under maximum drive, Norvallk sat reviewing the data with his student. "It should be perfectly obvious to you at this point that the standard methods of evaluating the Ferocity Index and integrating the various Indices are useless for this planet. Tell me, have you ever run an exercise with data like these?"

"Well . . . no," Harmarrght admitted. "But this is a very slim amount of data taken in restricted locality. I will admit that the planet is dangerous . . . "

"It's the most dangerous planet I know of."

"Well . . . yes. Even our most difficult conquests involved life forms with Ferocity Indices that we could at least measure. But the drastic measures the Master spoke of might certainly . . . "

"Forgive me for anticipating you," Norvallk broke in, "but those drastic recommendations are likely to involve the rerouting of ship lanes away from this vicinity and perhaps even the abandonment of nearby outposts."

"But we could certainly overcome . . . "

"Again, my apologies. Do you think we could fight the several life forms we saw on that planet without expending millions of warriors and a great deal of equipment? Remember the universal law of living organisms: the Law of Least Effort. This is a big galaxy, and there are more comfortable and less expensive parts of it in which to operate."

"I guess you're right," Harmarrght admitted. "There are easier things to do."

Back on the planet, the wolverine, although it didn't consciously know the Law of Least Effort, responded to it, too. It curled up on the rug in front of the fireplace and snoozed while beings with a higher Ferocity Index quietly ate their lunch around a table.

in/vis/i/bil/i/ty — the quality of not being visible to other living things. Modern science has not yet achieved invisibility, although efforts have reportedly been made. In science fiction, invisibility was made famous by H. G. Wells in his classic *The Invisible Man* (1897). More recent stories can be found in *Invisible Men* (Ballantine Books, 1960), though some of these stories are fantasy, not science fiction.

All Cats Are Gray

ANDRE NORTON

Steena of the Spaceways — that sounds just like a corny title for one of the Stellar-Vedo spreads. I ought to know, I've tried my hand at writing enough of them. Only this Steena was no glamorous babe. She was as colorless as a lunar planet — even the hair netted down to her skull had a sort of grayish cast, and I never saw her but once draped in anything but a shapeless and baggy gray spaceall.

Steena was strictly background stuff, and that is where she mostly spent her free hours — in the smelly, smoky, background corners of any stellar-port dive frequented by free spacers. If you really looked for her you could spot her — just sitting there listening to the talk — listening and remembering. She didn't open her mouth often. But when she did, spacers had learned to listen. And the lucky few who heard her rare spoken words — these will never forget Steena.

She drifted from port to port. Being an expert operator on the big calculators, she found jobs wherever she cared to stay for a time. And she came to be something like the masterminded machines she tended — smooth, gray, without much personality of their own.

But it was Steena who told Bub Nelson about the Jovan moon rites — and her warning saved Bub's life six months later. It was Steena who identified the piece of stone Keene Clark was passing around a table one night, rightly calling it unworked slitite. That started a rush which made ten fortunes overnight for men who were down to their last jets. And, last of all, she cracked the case of the *Empress of Mars*.

All the boys who had profited by her queer store of knowledge and her photographic memory tried at one time or another to balance the scales. But she wouldn't take so much as a cup of canal water at their expense, let alone the credits they tried to push on her. Bub Nelson was the only one who got around her refusal. It was he who brought her Bat.

About a year after the Jovan affair, he walked in to the Free Fall one night and dumped Bat down on her table. Bat looked at Steena and growled. She looked calmly back at him and nodded once. From then on they traveled together — the thin gray woman and the big gray tomcat. Bat learned to know the inside of more stellar bars than even most spacers visit in their lifetimes. He developed a liking for Vernal juice, drank it neat and quick, right out of the glass. And he was always at home on any table where Steena elected to drop him.

This is really the story of Steena, Bat, Cliff Moran, and the *Empress of Mars,* a story which is already a legend of the spaceways. And it's a damn good story, too. I ought to know, having framed the first version of it myself.

For I was there, right in the Rigel Royal, when it all began on the night that Cliff Moran blew in, looking lower than an antman's belly and twice as nasty. He'd had a spell of luck foul enough to twist a man into a slug snake, and we all knew that there was an attachment out for his ship. Cliff had fought his way up from the back courts of Venaport. Lose his ship and he'd slip back there — to rot. He was at the snarling stage that night when he picked out a table for himself and set out to drink away his troubles.

However, just as the first bottle arrived, so did a visitor. Steena came out of her corner, Bat curled around her shoulders stolewise, his favorite mode of travel. She crossed over and dropped down, without invitation, at Cliff's side. That shook him out of his sulks. Because Steena never chose company when she could be alone. If one of the man-stones on Ganymede had come stumping in, it wouldn't have made more of us look out of the corners of our eyes.

She stretched out one long-fingered hand, set aside the bottle he had ordered, and said only one thing. "It's about time for the *Empress of Mars* to appear."

Cliff scowled and bit his lip. He was tough, tough as jet lining — you have to be granite inside and out to struggle up from Venaport to a ship command. But we could guess what was running through his mind at that moment. The *Empress of Mars* was just about the biggest prize a spacer could aim for. But in the fifty years she had been following her queer derelict orbit through space, many men had tried to bring her in — and none had succeeded.

A pleasure ship carrying untold wealth, she had been mysteriously abandoned in space by passengers and crew, none of whom had ever been seen or heard of again. At intervals thereafter she had been sighted, even boarded. Those who ventured into her either vanished or returned swiftly without any believable explanation of what they had seen — wanting only to get away from her as quickly as possible. But the man who could bring her in — or even strip her clean in space — that man would win the jackpot.

"All right!" Cliff slammed his fist on the table. "I'll try even that!"

Steena looked at him, much as she must have looked at Bat that day Bub Nelson brought him to her, and nodded. That was all I saw. The rest of the story came to me in pieces, months later and in another port half the system away.

Cliff took off that night. He was afraid to risk waiting — with a writ out that could pull the ship from under him. And it wasn't until he was in space that he discovered his passengers — Steena and Bat. We'll never know what happened then. I'm betting Steena made no explanation at all. She wouldn't.

It was the first time she had decided to cash in on her own tip and she was there — that was all. Maybe that point weighed with Cliff, maybe he just didn't care. Anyway, the three were together when they sighted the *Empress* riding, her deadlights gleaming, a ghost ship in night space.

She must have been an eerie sight because her other lights were on too, in addition to the red warnings at her nose. She seemed alive, a Flying Dutchman of space. Cliff worked his ship skillfully alongside and had no trouble in snapping magnetic lines to her lock. Some minutes later the three of them passed into her. There was still air in her cabins and corridors, air that bore a faint corrupt taint which set Bat to sniffing greedily and could be picked up even by the less sensitive human nostrils.

Cliff headed straight for the control cabin, but Steena and Bat went prowling. Closed doors were a challenge to both of them and Steena opened each as she passed, taking a quick look at what lay within. The fifth door opened on a room which no woman could leave without further investigation.

I don't know what had been housed there when the *Empress* left port on her last lengthy cruise. Anyone really curious can check back on the old photo-reg cards. But there was a lavish display of silk trailing out of two travel kits on the floor, a dressing table crowded with crystal and jeweled containers, along with other lures for the female which drew Steena in. She was standing in front of the dressing table when she glanced into the mirror — glanced into it and froze.

Over her right shoulder she could see the spider-silk cover on the bed. Right in the middle of that sheer, gossamer expanse was a sparkling heap of gems, the dumped contents of some jewel case. Bat had jumped to the foot of the bed and flattened out as cats will, watching those gems, watching them and — something else!

Steena put out her hand blindly and caught up the nearest bottle. As she unstoppered it, she watched the mirrored bed. A gemmed bracelet rose from the pile, rose in the air and tinkled its siren song. It was as if an idle hand played . . . Bat spat almost noiselessly. But he did not retreat. Bat had not yet decided his course.

She put down the bottle. Then she did something which perhaps few of the men she had listened to through the years could have done. She moved without hurry or sign of disturbance on a tour about the room. And, although she approached the bed, she did not touch the jewels. She could not force herself to do that. It took her five minutes to play out her innocence and unconcern. Then it was Bat who decided the issue.

He leaped from the bed and escorted something to the door, remaining a careful distance behind. Then he mewed loudly twice. Steena followed him and opened the door wider.

Bat went straight on down the corridor, as intent as a hound on the warmest of scents. Steena strolled behind him, holding her pace to the unhurried gait of an explorer. What sped before them was invisible to her, but Bat was never baffled by it.

They must have gone into the control cabin almost on the heels of the unseen — if the unseen had heels, which there was good reason to doubt — for Bat crouched just within the doorway and refused to move on. Steena looked down the length of the instrument panels and officers' station seats to where Cliff Moran worked. Her boots made no sound on the heavy carpet, and he did not glance up but sat humming through set teeth, as he tested the tardy and reluctant responses to buttons which had not been pushed in years.

To human eyes they were alone in the cabin. But Bat still followed a moving something, which he had at last made up his mind to distrust and dislike. For now he took a step or two forward and spat — his loathing made plain by every raised hair along his spine. And in that same moment Steena saw a flicker — a flicker of vague outline against Cliff's hunched shoulders, as if the invisible one had crossed the space between them.

But why had it been revealed against Cliff and not against the back of one of the seats or against the panels, the walls of the corridor or the cover of the bed where it had reclined and played with its loot? What could Bat see?

The storehouse memory that had served Steena so well through the years clicked open a half-forgotten door. With one swift motion, she tore loose her spaceall and flung the baggy garment across the back of the nearest seat.

Bat was snarling now, emitting the throaty rising cry that was his hunting song. But he was edging back, back towards Steena's feet, shrinking from something he could not fight but which he faced defiantly. If he could draw it after him, past that dangling spaceall . . . He had to — it was their only chance!

"What the . . . " Cliff had come out of his seat and was staring at them.

What he saw must have been weird enough: Steena, bare-armed and bare-shouldered, her usually stiffly netted hair falling wildly down her back;

Steena watching empty space with narrowed eyes and set mouth, calculating a single wild chance. Bat, crouched on his belly, was retreating from thin air step by step and wailing like a demon.

"Toss me your blaster." Steena gave the order calmly — as if they were still at their table in the Rigel Royal.

And as quietly, Cliff obeyed. She caught the small weapon out of the air with a steady hand — caught and leveled it.

"Stay where you are!" she warned. "Back, Bat, bring it back."

With a last throat-splitting screech of rage and hate, Bat twisted to safety between her boots. She pressed with thumb and forefinger, firing at the spaceall. The material turned to powdery flakes of ash — except for certain bits which still flapped from the scorched seat — as if something had protected them from the force of the blast. Bat sprang straight up in the air with a screech that tore their ears.

"What . . . ?" began Cliff again.

Steena made a warning motion with her left hand. *"Wait!"*

She was still tense, still watching Bat. The cat dashed madly around the cabin twice, running crazily with white-ringed eyes and flecks of foam on his muzzle. Then he stopped abruptly in the doorway, stopped and looked back over his shoulder for a long, silent moment. He sniffed delicately.

Steena and Cliff could smell it too, now, a thick oily stench which was not the usual odor left by an exploding blaster shell.

Bat came back, treading daintily across the carpet, almost on the tips of his paws. He raised his head as he passed Steena, and then he went confidently beyond to sniff, to sniff and spit twice at the unburned strips of the spaceall. Having thus paid his respects to the late enemy, he sat down calmly and set to washing his fur with deliberation. Steena sighed once and dropped into the navigator's seat.

"Maybe now you'll tell me what in the hell's happened?" Cliff exploded as he took the blaster out of her hand.

"Gray," she said dazedly, "it must have been gray — or I couldn't have seen it like that. I'm color-blind, you see. I can see only shades of gray — my whole world is gray. Like Bat's — his world is gray, too — all gray. But he's been compensated, for he can see above and below our range of color vibrations, and apparently so can I!"

Her voice quavered, and she raised her chin with a new air Cliff had never seen before — a sort of proud acceptance. She pushed back her wandering hair, but she made no move to imprison it under the heavy net again.

"That is why I saw the thing when it crossed between us. Against your spaceall it was another shade of gray — an outline. So I put out mine and waited for it to show against that — it was our only chance, Cliff.

"It was curious at first, I think, and it knew we couldn't see it — which is why it waited to attack. But when Bat's actions gave it away, it moved.

So I waited to see that flicker against the spaceall, and then I let him have it. It's really very simple . . . "

Cliff laughed a bit shakily. "But what *was* this gray thing? I don't get it."

"I think it was what made the *Empress* a derelict. Something out of space, maybe, or from another world somewhere." She waved her hands. "It's invisible because it's a color beyond our range of sight. It must have stayed in here all these years. And it kills — it must — when its curiosity is satisfied." Swiftly she described the scene, the scene in the cabin, and the strange behavior of the gem pile which had betrayed the creature to her.

Cliff did not return his blaster to its holder. "Any more of them aboard, d'you think?" He didn't look pleased at the prospect.

Steena turned to Bat. He was paying particular attention to the space between two front toes in the process of a complete bath. "I don't think so. But Bat will tell us if there are. He can see them clearly, I believe."

But there weren't any more and two weeks later, Cliff, Steena, and Bat brought the *Empress* into the lunar quarantine station. And that is the end of Steena's story because, as we have been told, happy marriages need no chronicles. Steena had found someone who knew of her gray world and did not find it too hard to share with her — someone besides Bat. It turned out to be a real love match.

The last time I saw her, she was wrapped in a flame-red cloak from the looms of Rigel and wore a fortune in Jovan rubies blazing on her wrists. Cliff was flipping a three-figured credit bill to a waiter. And Bat had a row of Vernal juice glasses set up before him. Just a little family party out on the town.

J

ju/di/cial sys/tem — the way in which justice is administered. There have been several different judicial systems employed over the centuries, including monarchical courts, state courts of various types, and religious courts. In the American system the defendant is assumed to be innocent until proven guilty — the reverse is the case in most European countries. Courtroom settings have been successfully used in science fiction; for some examples, see *Criminal Justice Through Science Fiction* (New Viewpoints, 1977).

The Man from Earth

GORDON R. DICKSON

The Director of the crossroads world of Duhnbar had no other name, nor needed any; and his handsomeness and majesty were not necessarily according to the standards of the human race. But then, he had never heard of the human race.

He sat in his equivalent of a throne room day by day, while the representatives of a thousand passing races conducted their business below and before the dais on which his great throne chair sat. He enjoyed the feeling of life around him, so he permitted them to be there. He did not like to be directly involved in that life. Therefore none of them looked or spoke in his direction.

Before him, he saw their numbers spread out through a lofty hall. At the far end of the hall, above the lofty portal, was a balcony pierced through to the outside, so that it overlooked not only the hall but the armed guards on the wide steps that approached the building. On this balcony, more members of different races talked and stood.

Next to the Director's chair, on his left, was a shimmering mirrored surface suspended in midair, so that by turning his head only slightly he could see himself reflected at full length. Sometimes he looked and saw himself.

But at this moment, now, he looked outward. In his mind's eye, he looked beyond the throne room and the balcony and the steps without. He saw in his imagination all the planetwide city surrounding, and the five other worlds of this solar system that were the machine shops and granaries of this crown-world of Duhnbar. This world and system he . . . *ruled* is too mild a word. This world he owned, and wore like a ring on his finger.

All of it, seen in his mind's eye, had the dull tinge of familiarity and sameness.

He moved slightly the index one of his four-jointed fingers, of which he had three, with an opposed thumb on each hand. The male adult of his own race who currently filled a role something like that of chamberlain stepped forward from behind the throne chair. The Director did not look at the chamberlain, knowing he would be there. The Director's thin lips barely moved in his expressionless, pale green face.

"It has been some moments," he said. "Is there still nothing new?"

"Director of All," said the low voice of the chamberlain at his ear. "Since you last asked, there has been nothing on the six worlds which has not happened before. Only the landing here at the throne city of a single alien of a new race. He has passed into the city now, omitting to sacrifice at a Purple Shrine but otherwise behaving as all behave on your worlds."

"Is there anything new," said the Director, "about his failure to sacrifice?"

"The failure is a common one," said the chamberlain. "It has been many generations since anyone seriously worshipped at a Purple Shrine. The sacrifice is a mere custom of our port. Strangers not knowing of it invariably fail to light incense on the cube before the Purple."

The Director said nothing immediately. The chamberlain stood waiting. If he had been left to wait until he collapsed from fatigue or starvation, another would have taken his place.

"Is there a penalty for this?" said the Director at last.

"The penalty," said the chamberlain, "by ancient rule is death. But for hundreds of years it has been remitted on payment of a small fine."

The Director turned these words over in his mind.

"There is a value in old customs," he said after a while. "Old customs long fallen into disuse seem almost like something new when they are revived. Let the ancient penalty be re-established."

"For this transgressor," asked the chamberlain, "as well as all others after?"

The Director moved his index finger in silent assent and dismissal. The chamberlain stepped backward and spoke to the under-officers who were always waiting.

The Director, sated with looking out over the hall, turned his gaze slightly to his own seated image in the mirrored surface at his left. He saw there an individual a trifle over seven feet in height seated in a tall, carven chair with ornate armrests. Four-fingered hands lay upon the curved ends of the armrests. The arms, the legs, the body was covered in a slim, simple garment of sky blue. From the neck of the garment emerged a tall and narrow head with lean features, a straight, almost lipless mouth, narrow nose, and a greenish, hairless skull. The eyes were golden, enormous, and beautiful.

But neither the eyes nor the face showed any expression. The faces of the chamberlain and the guards and others of the race sometimes showed expressions. But the Director's face, never. He was several hundreds of years old and would live until some rare accident killed him or he became weary of life.

He had never known what it was to be sick. He had never known cold, hunger, or any discomfort. He had never known fear, hatred, loneliness, or love. He watched himself now in the mirror, for he posed an unending enigma to himself — an enigma that alone relieved the boredom of his existence. He did not attempt to investigate the enigma. He only savored it as a connoisseur might savor a fine wine.

The image in the mirror he gazed upon was the image of a being who could find no alternative but to consider himself as a god.

Will Mauston was broken-knuckled and wrinkled about the eyes. The knuckles he had broken on human and alien bones, fighting for what belonged to him. The wrinkles about the eyes had come from the frowning harshness of expression evolved from endless bargains driven. On the infrequent occasions that he got back to Earth to see his wife and two young children, the wrinkles almost disappeared . . . for a while. But Earth was overcrowded and the cost of living there was high. He always had to leave again, and the wrinkles always came back. He was twenty-six years old.

He had heard of Duhnbar through a race of interstellar traders called the Kjaka, heavy-bodied, lion-featured, and honest. He had assumed there must be such a world, as on Earth in the past there had been ancient cities like Samarkand under Tamerlane, where the great trade route crossed. He had searched and inquired and the Kjakas had told him. Duhnbar was the Samarkand of the stars. One mighty stream of trade flowed out from the highly developed worlds of the galaxy's center and met here with several peripheral routes among the outlying, scattered stars.

Will had come alone and he was the first from Earth to reach it. From this one trip, he could well make enough to retire and not have to leave his family on Earth again. The Kjakas were honest and had taught him the customs of the Duhnbar port. They had sent him to Khal Dohn, one of their own people on Duhnbar, who would act as Will's agent there. They had forgotten the small matter of the Purple Shrine. The custom was all but obsolete, the fine was nominal. They had talked of larger transactions and values.

Passing through the terminal building of the port, Will saw a cube of metal, a purple cloth hanging on the wall above it, and small purple slivers that fumed and reeked. He passed at a good distance. Experience had taught him not to involve himself with the religions and customs of people he did not know.

Riding across the city in an automated vehicle set for the address of his agent, Will passed a square in which there was what seemed to be a sort of forty-foot-high clothespole. What was hung on it, however, was not clothes, but bodies. The bodies were not all of the native race, and he was glad to leave it behind.

He reached the home of the Kjakan agent. It was a pleasant, two-story, four-sided structure surrounding an interior courtyard rich with vegetation unknown to Will. He and his host sat on an interior balcony of the second floor overlooking the courtyard, and talked. Khal Dohn ate a narcotic candy particular to his own race and saw that Will was supplied with a pure mixture of distilled water and ethyl alcohol — to which Will added a scotch flavor from one of the small vials he carried at his belt. Will had set up a balance of credit on several Kjakan worlds. Khal Dohn would buy for him on Duhnbar against that credit.

They were beginning a discussion of what was available on Duhnbar that would be best for Will to purchase, speaking in the stellar lingua franca, the trading language among the stars. Abruptly, they were interrupted by a voice from one of the walls, speaking in a tongue Will did not understand. Khal Dohn listened, answered, and turned his heavy, leonine face on Will.

"We must go downstairs," he said.

He led Will back down to the room which led to the street before his home. Waiting there were two of the native race in black, short robes, belted at the waist with silver belts. A black rod showed in a sort of silver pencil-case attached to the belt of each native.

As Will and Khal came down a curving ramp to them, the golden eyes of both natives fastened on Will with mild curiosity.

"Stranger and alien," said one of them in the trade tongue, "you are informed that you are under arrest."

Will looked at them and opened his mouth. But Khal Dohn was already speaking in the native tongue; and after a little while the natives bowed shortly and went out. Khal Dohn turned back to Will.

"Did you see in the terminal — " Khal Dohn described the Purple Shrine. Will nodded. "Did you go near it?"

"No," said Will. "I always steer clear of such things unless I know about them."

Khal Dohn stared at him for a long moment. Below the heavy, rather oriental fold of flesh, his eyes were sad, dark, and unreadable to Will.

"I don't understand," he said at last. "But you are my guest, and my duty is to protect you. We'd better go see an acquaintance of mine — one who has more influence here in the throne city than I do."

He led Will out to one of the automated vehicles. On their way to the home of the acquaintance he answered Will's questions by describing the custom of the Purple Shrine.

"I don't understand," the Kjaka said. "I should have been able to pay your fine to the police and settle it. But they had specific orders to arrest you and take you in."

"Why didn't they, then?" asked Will.

The dark eyes swung and met his own.

"You're my guest," said Khal Dohn. "I've taken on the responsibility of your surrender at the proper time, while they fulfill my request for the verification of the order to arrest you."

Outside the little vehicle, as they turned into the shadow of a taller building, a coolness seemed to gather about them and reach inside to darken and slow Will's spirits.

"Do you think it's something really important?" he said.

"No," answered Khal Dohn. "No. I'm sure it's all a mistake."

They stopped before a building very like the home of Khal Dohn. Khal led Will up a ramp to a room filled with oversized furniture. From one large chair rose a narrow-bodied, long-handed alien with six fingers to a hand. His face was narrow and horselike. He stood better than seven and a half feet, in jacket and trousers of a dark red color. A dagger hung at his belt.

"You are my guest as always, Khal Dohn!" he cried. His voice was strident and high-pitched. He spoke the trade tongue, but he pronounced the Kjakan name of Khal Dohn with a skill Will had not been able to master. "And welcome as the guest of my guest is — " he turned to Will, speaking to Khal — "what is its name — ?"

"*His* name," said Khal, "is Will Mau — " his Kjakan tongue failed at the English *st* sound — "Will Mauzzon."

"Welcome," said the tall alien. "I am Avoa. What is it?"

"Something I don't understand." Khal switched to the native tongue of Duhnbar and Will was left out of the conversation. They talked some little while.

"I will check," cried Avoa, finally, breaking back into the trade tongue. "Come tomorrow early, Khal Dohn. Bring it with you."

"Him," said Khal. "I will bring him."

"Of course. Of course. Come together. I'll have news for you then. It can be nothing serious."

Khal and Will left and came back to the balcony above the courtyard of Khal's home. They sat talking. The sunset of the planet spread across the western skyline of the throne city, its light staining the white ceiling above them with a wash of red.

"You're sure it's nothing to worry about?" Will asked the Kjaka.

"I'm sure." Khal Dohn fingered one of his narcotic candies in thick fingers. "They have a strict but fair legal code here. And if there is any misunderstanding, Avoa can resolve it. He has considerable influence. Shall we return to talk of business?"

So they talked as the interior lights came on. Later they ate their different meals together — Will's from supplies he had brought from his ship — and parted for the night.

It was a comfortable couch in a pleasant, open-balconied room giving on the courtyard below, that Khal assigned Will. But Will found sleep standing off some distance from him. He was a man of action, but here there was no action to be taken. He walked to the balcony and looked down into the courtyard.

Below, the strange plants were dim shapes in the light of a full moon too weak and pale to be the moon of Earth. He wondered how his wife and the two children were. He wondered if, across the light-years of distance, they were thinking of him at this moment, perhaps worrying about him.

He breathed the unfamiliar, tasteless night air and it seemed heavy in his lungs. At his belt was a container of barbiturates, four capsules of seconal. He had never found the need to take one before in all these years between the stars. He took one now, washing it down with the flat, distilled water they had left in this room for him.

He slept soundly after that, without dreams.

When he woke in the morning, he felt better. Khal Dohn seemed to him to be quite sensible and undisturbed. They rode over to the home of Avoa together, and Will took the opportunity he had neglected before to pump Khal about the city as they rode through it.

When they entered the room where they had met Avoa the day before, the tall alien was dressed in clothing of a lighter, harsher red but seemed the same in all other ways.

"Well," said Will to him, smiling, after they had greeted each other in the trade tongue. "What did you find out the situation is?"

Avoa stared back at him for a moment, then turned and began to speak rapidly to Khal in the native tongue. Khal answered. After a moment they both stopped and looked at Will without speaking.

"What's happened?" said Will. "What is it?"

"I'm sorry," said Khal slowly, in the trade tongue. "It seems that nothing can be done."

Will stared at him. The words he had heard made no sense.

"Nothing can be done?" he said. "About what? What do you mean?"

"I'm sorry," said Khal. "I mean, Avoa can do nothing."

"Nothing?" said Will.

Neither of the aliens answered. They continued to watch him. Suddenly, Avoa shifted his weight slightly on his long feet, and half turned toward the doorway of the room.

"I am sorry!" he cried sharply. "Very sorry. But it is a situation out of my control. I can do nothing."

"Why?" burst out Will. He turned on Khal. "What's wrong? You told me their legal system was fair. I didn't know about the shrine!"

"Yes," said Khal. "But this isn't a matter for their law. Their Director has given an order."

"Director?" The word buzzed as fatally and foolishly as a tropical mosquito in Will's ears. "The one on the throne? What's he got to do with it?"

"It was his command," said Avoa suddenly in his strident voice. "The ancient penalty was to be enforced. After he heard about your omission. From now on, newcomers will be warned. They are fair here."

"Fair!" the word broke from between Will's teeth. "What about me? Doesn't this Director know about me? What is he, anyway?"

Khal and Avoa looked at each other, then back at Will.

"These people here," said Khal slowly, "control trade for light-years in every direction. Not because of any virtue in themselves, but because of the accident of their position here among the stars. They know this — so they need something. A symbol, something to set up, to reassure themselves of their right position."

"In all else, they are reasonable," said Avoa.

"Their symbol," said Khal, "is the Director. They identify with him as being all-powerful, over things in the universe. His slightest whim is obeyed without hesitation. He could order them all to cut their own throats and they would do it, without thinking. But of course he will not. He is not in the least irresponsible. He is sane and of the highest intelligence. But the only law he knows is his own."

Cried Avoa, "He is all but impotent. Ordinarily he does nothing. We interest and amuse him, and he is bored, so he lets us trade here with impunity. But if he does act, there is no appeal. It is a risk we all take. You are not the only one."

"But I've got a wife — " Will broke off suddenly. He had shouted out without thinking in English. They were gazing back at him now without understanding. For a moment a watery film blurred them before his eyes.

The desert-dry wind of a despair blew through him, shriveling his hopes. What did they know of wives and children, or Earth? He saw their faces clearly now, both alien, one heavy and leonine, one patrician and equine. He thought of his wife again, and the children. Without his income they would be forced to emigrate. A remembrance of the bitter, crude, and barren livings on the frontier planets came to his mind like strangling smoke.

"Wait," he said, as Avoa turned to go. Will brought his voice down to a reasonable tone. "There must be someone I can appeal to. Khal Dohn." He turned to the Kjaka. "I'm your guest."

"You are my guest," said Khal. "But I can't protect you against this. It's like a natural, physical force — a great wind, an earthquake against which I would be helpless to protect any guest, or even myself."

He looked at Will with his dark, alien eyes, like the eyes of an intelligent beast.

"Pure chance — the chance of the Director hearing about you and the shrine when he did — " said Khal, "has selected you. All those who face the risk of trading among the stars know the chance of death. You must have figured the risk, as a good trader should."

"Not like this — " said Will between his teeth, but Avoa interrupted, turning to leave.

"I must go," he said. "I have appointments on the throne room balcony. Khal Dohn, give it anything that will make these last hours comfortable and my house will supply. You must surrender it before midday to the police."

"No!" Will called after the tall alien. "If nobody else can save me, then I want to see him!"

"Him?" said Khal. Avoa suddenly checked, and slowly turned back.

"The Director." Will looked at both of them. "I'll appeal to him."

Khal and Avoa looked at each other. There was a silence.

"No," said Avoa, finally. "It is never done. No one speaks to him." He seemed about to turn again.

"Wait." It was Khal who spoke this time. Avoa looked sharply at him. Khal met the taller alien's eyes. "Will Mauzzon is my guest."

"It is not *my* guest," said Avoa.

"*I* am your guest," said Khal, without emotion.

Avoa stared now at the shorter, heavier-bodied alien. Abruptly he said something sharply in the native tongue.

Khal did not answer. He stood looking at Avoa without moving.

"It is already dead," Avoa said at last slowly, in the trade tongue, glancing at Will, "and being dead can have no further effect upon the rest of us. You waste your credit with me."

Still Khal neither spoke nor moved. Avoa turned and went out.

"My guest," said Khal, sitting down heavily in one of the oversized chairs of the room, "you have little cause for hope."

After that he sat silent. Will paced the room. Occasionally he glanced at the chronometer on his wrist, adjusted to local time. It showed the equivalent of two and three-quarters hours to noon when the wall chimed and spoke in Avoa's voice.

"You have your audience," said Khal, rising. "I would still advise against hope." He looked with his heavy face and dark eyes at Will. "Worlds can't afford to war against worlds to protect their people, and there is no reason for the Director to change his mind."

He took Will in one of the small automated vehicles to the throne room. Inside the portal, at the steps leading up to the balcony, he left Will.

"I'll wait for you above," Khal said. "Good luck, my guest."

Will turned. At the far end of the room he saw the dais and the Director. He went toward it through the crowd, which at first had hardly noticed him but grew silent and parted before him as he proceeded, until he could hear in the great and echoing silence of the hall the sound of his own footsteps as he approached the dais, the seated figure, and the throne, behind which stood natives with the silver pencil-cases and black rods at their silver belts.

He came at last to the edge of the dais and stopped, looking up. Above him, the high greenish skull, the narrow mouth, the golden eyes leaned forward to look down at him; and he saw them profiled in the mirrored surface alongside. The profile was no more remote than the living face it mirrored.

Will opened his mouth to speak, but one of the natives behind the throne, wearing the chamberlain's silver badge, stepped forward as the finger of the Director gestured.

"Wait," said the chamberlain in the trade tongue. He turned and spoke behind him. Will waited, and the silence stretched out long in the hall. After a while there was movement and two natives appeared, one with a small chair, one with a tube-shaped container of liquid.

"Sit," said the chamberlain. "Drink. The Director has said it."

Will found himself seated and with the tube in his hand. An odor of alcohol diluted with water came to his nostrils, and for a moment a burst of wild laughter trembled inside him. Then he controlled it and sipped from the tube.

"What do you say?" said the chamberlain.

Will lifted his face to the unchanging face of the Director. Like the unreachable stare of an insect's eyes the great golden orbs regarded him.

"I haven't intentionally committed any crime," said Will.

"The Director," said the chamberlain, "knows this."

His voice was flat, uninflected. But he seemed to wait. The golden eyes of the throned figure seemed to wait, also watching. Irrationally, Will felt the first small flame of a hope flicker to life within him. His trader's instinct stirred. If they would listen, there must always be a chance.

"I came here on business," he said, "the same sort of business that brings so many. Certainly this world and the trading done on it are tied together. Without Duhnbar there could be no trading place here. And without the trading would Duhnbar and its other sister worlds still be the same?"

He paused, looking upward for some reaction.

"The Director," said the chamberlain, "is aware of this."

"Certainly, then," said Will, "if the traders here respect the laws and customs of Duhnbar, shouldn't Duhnbar respect the lives of those who come to trade?" He stared at the golden eyes hanging above him, but he could read no difference in them, no response. They seemed to wait still. He took a deep breath. "Death is — "

He stopped. The Director had moved on his throne. He leaned slowly forward until his face hung only a few feet above Will's. He spoke in the trade tongue, in a slow, deep, unexpectedly resonant voice.

"Death," he said, "is the final new experience."

He sat slowly back in his chair. The chamberlain spoke.

"You will go now," he said.

Will sat staring at him, the tube of alcohol and water still in his grasp.

"You will go," repeated the chamberlain. "You are free until midday and the moment of your arrest."

Will's head jerked up. He snapped to his feet from the chair.

"Are you all insane?" he shouted at the chamberlain. "You can't do this sort of thing without an excuse! My people take care of their own — "

He broke off at the sight of the chamberlain's unmoved face. He felt suddenly dizzy and nauseated at the pit of his stomach.

Said the chamberlain, "It is understandable that you do not want to die. You will go now or I will have you taken away."

Something broke inside Will. It was like the last effort of a man in a race who feels the running man beside him pulling away and tries, but cannot match the pace. Dazedly, dully, he turned. Blindly he walked the first few steps back toward the distant portal.

"*Wait.*"

The chamberlain's voice turned him around.

"Come back," said the chamberlain. "The Director will speak."

Numbly he came back. The Director leaned forward once more, until when Will halted their faces were only a few feet apart.

"You will not die," said the Director.

Will stared up at the alien face without understanding. The words rang and re-echoed like strange, incomprehensible sounds in his ears.

"You will live," said the Director. "And when I send for you, from time to time, you will come again and talk to me."

Will continued to stare. He felt the smooth, flexible tube of liquid in his right hand, and he felt it bulge between his fingers as his fingers contracted spasmodically. He opened his lips but no words worked their way past the tight muscles of his throat.

"It is interesting," said the deep and thrilling voice of the Director, as his great, golden eyes looked down at Will, "that you do not understand me. It is interesting to explain myself to you. You give me reasons why you should not die."

" — Reasons?" Between Will's dry lips, the little word slipped huskily out. Miraculously, out of the ashes of his despair, he felt the tiny warmth of a new hope.

"Reasons," said the Director. "You give me reasons. And there are no reasons. There is only me."

The hope flickered and stumbled in its reach for life.

"I will make you understand now," said the deep and measured voice of the Director. "It is I who am responsible for all things that happen here. It is my whim that moves them. There is nothing else."

The golden eyes looked into Will's.

"It was my whim," said the Director, "that the penalty of the shrine's neglect should be imposed once more. Since I had decided so, it was unavoidable that you should die. For when I decide, all things follow inexorably. There is no other way or thing."

Will stared, the muscles of his neck stiff as an iron brace.

"But then," said the deep voice beneath the glorious eyes, "as you were leaving another desire crossed my mind. That you might interest me again on future occasions."

He paused.

"Once more," he said, "all things followed. If you were to interest me in the future, you could not die. And so you are not to." His eyes held Will's. "And now you understand."

A faint thoughtfulness clouded his golden eyes.

"I have done something with you this day," he said almost to himself, "that I have never done before. It is quite new. I have made you know what you are, in respect to what I am. I have taken a creature not even of my own people and made it understand it has no life or death or reasons of its own, except those my desires desire."

He stopped speaking. But Will still stood, rooted.

"Do not be afraid," said the Director. "I killed you. But I have brought another creature who understands to life in your body. One who will walk this world of mine for many years before he dies."

A sudden brilliance like a sheet of summer lightning flared in Will's head, blinding him. He heard his own voice shouting, in a sound that was rage without meaning. He flung his right arm forward and up as his sight cleared, and saw the liquid in the tube he had held splash itself against the downward-gazing, expressionless face above him, and the container bounce harmlessly from the sky-blue robe below the face.

There was a soundless jerk through all the natives behind the throne. A soundless gasp as if the air had changed. Native hands had flown to the black rods. But there they hung.

The Director had not moved. The watered alcohol dripped slowly from his nose and chin. But his features were unchanged, his hands were still, no finger on either hand stirred.

He continued to gaze at Will. After a long second, Will turned. He was not quite sure what he had done, but something sullen and brave burned redly in him.

He began to walk up the long aisle through the crowd, toward the distant portal. In that whole hall he was the only thing moving. The thousand different traders followed him with their eyes, but otherwise none moved, and no one made a sound. From the crowd there was silence. From the balcony overlooking, and the steps beyond the entrance, there was silence.

Step by echoing step he walked the long length of the hall and passed through the towering archway into the bright day outside. He made it as far as halfway down the steps before, inside the hall, the Director's finger lifted, the message of that finger was flashed to the ranked guards outside, and the black rods shot him down with flame in the sunlight.

On the balcony above, overlooking those steps, Avoa stirred at last, turning his eyes from what was left of Will and looking down at Khal Dohn beside him.

"What was . . . " Avoa's voice fumbled and failed. He added, almost humbly, "I am sorry. I do not even know the proper pronoun."

"He," said Khal Dohn, still looking down at the steps.

"He. What did he call himself?" Avoa said. "You told me, but I do not remember. I should have listened, but I did not. What did you say — what was he?"

Khal Dohn lifted his heavy head and looked up at last.

"He was a man," said Khal Dohn.

K

knights — medieval soldiers, usually members of brotherhoods, who fought on behalf of monarchs. Knights are generally pictured mounted on horses, wearing heavy armor, and coming to the rescue of beautiful maidens in distress, but they really led grim lives. Knights are frequently encountered in fantasy, less often in science fiction.

Dream Damsel

EVAN HUNTER

I went first to the Lady Eloise, since I was her champion, and it was only fair and knightly that she should be the first to know.

There was a fair sky overhead that day, with scudding clouds beyond the bannered towers of Camelot, and below their stately ramparts the rich green curve of the earth bending to meet the eggshell blue of the sky. We sat in the stone courtyard while an attendant played the lute, plucking gently at the strings, and I did not bid him cease because music seemed somehow fitting for the sorrow of the occasion. The lady Eloise sat with her hands folded demurely in her lap, awaiting my pleasure. I raised my visored helmet and said, "Elly . . . "

She lifted incredibly long lashes, tilting her amber eyes to mine. The bodice of her gown rose and fell with her gentle breathing. "Yes, my Lord Larimar," she said.

"I've something on my mind," I told her, "and it behooves me to give tongue to it."

"Give it tongue, then," Eloise said. "Trippingly, I pray you."

I rose and began pacing the courtyard. I had recently jousted with Sir Mordred, and a few of my armor joints were loose, and I'm afraid I made a bit of noise as I paced. I lifted my voice above the noise and said, "As you know, I've been your champion for, lo, these many months."

"Yes, m'lord," she said.

"Many a dragon have I slain for you," I said. I gave heed to the lute music, and corrected it to, "For thee," waxing flowery to befit the occasion.

"That's true," Eloise said. "Most true, Larry."

"Yes." I nodded my head, and my helmet rattled. "And many an ogre have I sent to a dishonorable death, Elly, many a vile demon have I decapitated in thy name, wearing thy favor, charging forth to do battle upon my courageous steed, rushing over hill and dale, down valley, across stream . . ."

"Yes, m'lord," Eloise said.

"Yes. And all for thy love, Elly, all for thy undying love."

"Yes, Larry?" she said, puzzled.

"Arthur himself has seen fit to honor me for my undaunting courage, my unwavering valor. I carry now, among others, the Medal of the Sainted Slayer, the Croix de Tête de Dragon, and even . . ."

"Yes?" Eloise asked excitedly.

"Even," I said modestly, "the much coveted Clustered Blueberry Sprig."

"You are very brave," Eloise said, lowering her lashes, "and a most true knight, m'lord."

"Fie," I shouted over the music of the lute, "I come not to speak of bravery. For what is bravery?" I snapped my gauntleted fingers. "Bravery is naught!"

"Naught, m'lord?"

"Naught. I come because I must speak my mind, else I cannot live with honor or keep my peace with mine own self."

"Thine own self? Speak then, m'lord," Eloise said, "and trippingly, pray you."

"I desire," I said, "to call it quits."

"Sir?"

"Quits. Finis. *Pfttt.*"

"*Pfttt,* m'lord?"

"Pfttt, Elly."

"I see."

"It is not that I do not love thee, Elly," I said. "Perish the thought."

"Perish it," she said.

"For you are lovely and fair and true and constant and a rarity among women. And I am truly nothing when compared to thee."

"True," Eloise said, nodding her head. "That's true."

"So it is not that I do not love thee. It is that . . . "

I paused because my visor fell over my face.

"Yes?"

I lifted the visor. "It is that I love another better than thee."

"Oh."

"Yes."

"Guinivere?" she asked. "Has that wench . . . "

"Nay, not Guinivere, our beloved queen."

"Elaine then? Elaine the fair, Elaine the . . . "

"Nay, nor is it Elaine."

"Pray who then, pray?"

"The Lady Agatha."

"The Lady who?"

"Agatha."

"I know of no maiden named Agatha. Are you jesting with me, my Lord Larimar? Do you pull my maidenly leg?"

"Nay. There is an Agatha, Elly, and I do love her, and she doth love me, and we do intend to join our plights in holy matrimony."

"I see," Eloise said.

"'I have therefore petitioned Arthur to release me from my vows concerning thee, Eloise. I tell you this now because it would not be fair if I am to marry Agatha — which I fully intend doing — to maintain me as a champion when my heart would elsewhere be."

"I see," Eloise said again.

"Yes. I hope you understand, Elly. I hope we can still be friends."

"Of course," Eloise said, smiling weakly. "And I suppose you'll want your Alpha Beta Tau pin back."

"Keep it," I said magnanimously. And then, to show how magnanimous I really was, I reached into my tunic and said, "Ho, lute player! Here are a pair of dragon ears for thee, for thy fine music!"

The lute player dropped to the stones and kissed both my feet, and I smiled graciously.

I killed two small dragons that day, catching the second one with my mace before he'd even had a chance to breathe any fire upon me. I cut off their heads and slung them over my jeweled saddle and then rode back to the shining spires of Camelot. Launcelot and Guinivere were just leaving for their afternoon constitutional, so I waved at them and then took my gallant steed to the stables where I left him with my squire, a young boy named Gawain.

I wandered about a bit, watching Merlin playing pinochle with some unsuspecting knight trainees, and then stopping to pass the time of day with Galahad, a fellow I've never enjoyed talking to because his white armor and helmet are so blinding in the sun. Besides, he is a bit of a braggart, and I soon tired of his talk and went to eat a small lunch of roast pheasant, lamb, mutton, cheese, bread, wine, nuts, apples, and grapes, topping it off with one of Arthur's best cigars.

I went back to the stables after lunch to get my gallant steed, and then I rode in the jousting exercises, knocking Mordred for a row of beer barrels, and being in turn knocked head-over-teacups by Launcelot, whose ride with Guinivere seemed to have done him well.

I gathered myself together afterwards, and was leading my horse back to the stables when Arthur caught up with me.

"Larry!" he called, "Ho there, Larry! Wait up!"

I stopped and waited for Arthur to come alongside, and I said, "What's up, beloved King?"

"Just what I wanted to ask you, Larry," he said, blowing out a tremendous cloud of cigar smoke. "What *is* all this nonsense?"

"What nonsense, my liege?"

"About wanting to break your champion vows. Now, hell, Larry, that just isn't done, and you know it."

"It's the only honorable thing to do, Art," I said.

"Honor, shmonor," Arthur answered. "I'm thinking of the paperwork involved. These dispensations are a pain in the neck, Larry. After all, you should have thought of this when you took the vows. Any knight . . . "

"I'm sorry, Art," I said, "but it's the only way. I've given it a lot of thought, believe me."

"But I don't understand," Arthur said, blowing some more smoke at me. "What's wrong between you and Elly? Now, she's a damn fine kid, Larry, and I hope . . . "

"She *is* a damn fine kid," I agreed, "but it's all off between us."

"Why?"

"I've found another damsel."

"This Agatha? Now look, Larry, this is old Artie you're talking to, and not some kid still wet behind the ears. Now you know as well as I do that there's no Agatha in my court, so how . . . "

"I know that, Art. I never said she was in your court."

"But you call her the Lady Agatha!" Arthur said.

"I know."

"A foreign broad?" Arthur asked.

"No. A dream damsel."

"A *what?*"

"A dream damsel. I dream her."

"Now, what was that again, Larry?"

"I dream her. I dream the Lady Agatha."

"That's what I thought you . . . say, Larry, did Launcelot hurt you today during the joust? He plays rough, that fellow, and I've been meaning to . . . "

"No, he didn't hurt me at all. Few ribs, but nothing serious. I really do dream my lady, Art."

"You mean at night? When you're asleep?"

"Aye."

"You mean you just think her up?"

"Aye."

"Yes, you! Do you think her up?"

"That's what I'm trying to tell you."

"Then she isn't real?" Arthur asked.

"Oh, she's real all right. Not during the day, of course, but when I dream her up at night, she's real as can be."

"Foo," Arthur said. "This is all nonsense. Now you get back to Elly and tell her . . . "

"No, my liege," I said. "I intend to marry the Lady Agatha."

"But she's only a dream!" Arthur protested.

"Not *only* a dream, noble King. Much more than a dream to me. A woman of flesh and blood. A woman who loves me truly, and whom I do truly love."

"Fie," Arthur said. "You're being absurd. I'll send Merlin around to say a few incantations over you. You're probably bewitched."

"Nay, my lord, I'm not bewitched. I dream the Lady Agatha of my own accord. There's no enchantment whatever attached to it."

"No enchantment, eh? Perhaps you've been taking to the grape then, Larry? Perhaps the enchantment is all in a cup?"

"Nay, that neither. I tell you I dream her of my own accord."

Arthur puffed on his cigar again.

"How on earth do you do that?"

"It's really quite simple," I said. "I set me down on my couch, and I close my eyes, and I visualize a damsel with blonde hair and blue eyes, and lips like the blushing rose, and skin like Oriental ivory. Carmine nails, like pointed drops of blood, and an hourglass waist. A voice like the brush of velvet, flanks like a good horse in joust, a wit as sharp as any pike, a magic as potent as Merlin's. That is my Lady Agatha, Art. I visualize her and then I fall asleep, and she materializes."

"She . . . materializes," Arthur said, stroking his beard.

"Aye. And she loves me."

"You?" Arthur asked, examining me with scrutiny.

"Yes, me." I paused. "What's wrong with that?"

"Nothing, nothing," Arthur said hastily. "But tell me, Larry, how do you plan on marrying her? I mean, a dream, after all . . . "

"Look at it this way, Art," I said. "During the daytime, I go to work anyway. There's always another dragon to kill, or some giant to fell, and ogres by the dozen, Lord knows, not to mention other assorted monsters of various sizes and shapes, and maidens in distress, and sea serpents, and . . . oh, you know. You've been in the business much longer than I."

"So?"

"So what does a man need a wife for during the daytime? He'd never get to see her anyway. Do you follow me?"

"Yes," Arthur said, "but . . . "

"Therefore, I'll marry the Lady Agatha and see her at night, when most knights see their wives anyway. Why, I wouldn't be surprised if that's why they're called knights, Art."

"But how do you propose to marry her? Who will . . . "

"I shall dream a friar, and he shall marry us."

"I do believe you've been slaying too many dragons, my Lord Larimar," Arthur said. "After all, your dream girl — in all fairness — doesn't sound any lovelier than the fair Eloise."

I poked the king in the ribs and said, "Art, you're just getting old, that's all."

"Maybe so, boy," he reflected, "but I think I'll send Merlin around, anyway. Few incantations never hurt anyone."

"Art, please . . . "

"He's salaried," Arthur said, and so I conceded . . .

Merlin and Eloise came to me together, he looking very wise and very magical in his pointed hat and flowing robes; she looking very sad and very lovely, though not as lovely as my Lady Agatha.

"Tell me," Merlin said, "all about your dream damsel."

"What is there to tell?"

"Well, what does she look like?"

"She's blonde . . . "

"Um-huh, then we shall need some condor livers," Merlin said.

"And blue-eyed," I went on.

"Then we'll need a few dragon eggs, pastel-hued."

"And . . . oh, she's very lovely."

"I see," Merlin said wisely. "And do you love her?"

"I do indeed."

"And she you?" he asked, cocking an eyebrow.

"Verily."

"She truthfully loves thee?"

"Of course."

"She is lovely you say, and she loves — forgive me — *thee?*"

"Why, yes," I said.

"She loves . . . *thee?*"

"Three times already has she loved me, and still you do not hear? Turn up your hearing aid, wizard," I said.

"Forgive me," Merlin said, shaking his head. "I just . . . "

"She has told me upon many an occasion that I am just what she has been waiting for," I said. "Tall, manly, bold, courageous, and very handsome!"

"She said these things about *you?*" Merlin asked.

"Yes, of course."

"That you were the man she waited for? That you were . . . tall?"

"Yes."

"And . . . and manly?"

"Yes."

Merlin coughed, perhaps first realizing how tall and manly I really was. "And . . . and . . . " he coughed again " . . . handsome?"

"All those," I said.

Merlin continued coughing until I thought he would choke. "And all those she waited for, and all those she found in . . . ," he coughed again, " . . . *you?*"

"And why not, wizard?" I asked.

"You are truly bewitched, Lord Larimar," he said, "truly."

He pulled back the sleeve of his robe, and spread his fingers wide, and then he said, *"Alla-bah-roomuh-jig-bah-roo, zing, zatch, zootch!"*

I listened to the incantation and I yawned. But apparently Eloise was taking all this nonsense to heart because she stared at Merlin wide-eyed, looking lovely but not so lovely as my Lady Agatha, and then she looked at me, and her eyes got wider and wider and wider . . .

Oh, there was so much to do in preparation. My dispensation from Arthur came through the next week, and I went about busily making plans for my wedding to Agatha. I wanted to dream up something really special, something that would never be forgotten as long as England had a history. I wanted a big wedding, and so I had to plan beforehand so that I could dream it all up in one night, which was no easy task.

I wanted to dream up the entire court on white stallions, their shields blazing, their swords held high to catch the gleaming rays of the sun, the gallery packed with damsels in pink and white and the palest blue. I wanted to dream the banners of Camelot fluttering in green and yellow and orange over the towers, with a pale sky beyond, and a mild breeze blowing. I wanted to dream a friar who would be droll and yet serious, chucklingly fat, but piously religious.

And most of all, I wanted to dream the Lady Agatha in her wedding gown, a fine thing of lace and pearls, with a low bodice and a hip-hugging waist. All these things I wanted to dream, and they had to be planned beforehand. So what with slaying dragons and ogres and planning for the wedding, I was a fairly busy young knight, and I didn't get around to visiting Eloise again until the night before the wedding.

Her lady in waiting was most cordial.

"My mistress is asleep," she said.

"Asleep?" I glanced at my hour glass. "Why, it's only four minutes past six."

"She has been retiring early of late," the woman said.

"Poor child," I said, wagging my head. "Her heart is doubtless breaking. Ah well, c'est la guerre."

"C'est," the woman said.

"When she awakes on the morrow, tell her I am going to dream her a seat of honor at the wedding. Tell her. She will be pleased."

"Sir?"

"Just tell her. She'll understand."

"Yes, sir."

"Matter of fact," I said, "I'd better get to bed myself. Want to practice up. I've a lot to dream tomorrow night."

"Sir?"

"Never mind," I said. I reached into my tunic and said, "Here's a dragon's tooth for lending a kind ear."

I ripped the tooth from my hourglass fob and deposited it in her excitedly overwhelmed, shaking, grateful palm.

Then I went home and to bed to dream of my Lady Agatha.

I went first to the Lady Eloise on the morrow, since it was only fair and knightly that she should be the first to know. I did not raise my visor for I did not desire her to see my face.

"Elly," I said, "I've got something on my mind, and it behooves me to give tongue to it."

"Give it tongue, then," Eloise said. "Trippingly, pray you."

"It's all off," I told her. "The Lady Agatha and me. We're through. She called it quits."

"Quits?" Eloise said. "Finis? *Pfttt?*"

"Even so," I said.

"Really now," Eloise said, smiling.

"There's someone else, Elly. My Lady Agatha has someone else. Someone taller, manlier, handsomer. I know it's hard to believe. But there is someone else, someone who just came along . . . suddenly."

"How terrible for you," Eloise said happily.

"Yes. I can't understand it. He just popped up, just like that, right there beside her. I . . . I saw him, Elly, a big handsome knight on a white horse. Right there in my dream, I saw him."

"Did you really?" Eloise asked sadly, clapping her hands together.

"Yes," I said. "So she wants him, and not me. So I thought, if you'll still have me, Elly, if you'll still take me as your champion . . . "

"Well . . . "

" . . . and perhaps someday as your husband, then . . . "

Eloise stepped forward, and there was a twinkle in her eye when she lifted my visor.

"You're tall and manly and handsome enough for me, you goof," she said. I looked at her and suddenly remembered that she'd been doing an awful lot of sleeping lately, and I started to say, "Hey!"

But she wrapped her arms around my armor and kissed me soundly on the mouth, and all I could do was stare at her in wonder and murmur, "Eloise! I never dreamed!"

Eloise smiled secretly and said, "*I* did."

L

last man — or woman — in science fiction the last survivor, normally on Earth, after some sort of holocaust has devastated the planet. Usually the story or novel takes the form of a struggle to survive in the face of great odds; occasionally, the survivor is trying to hold out until he/she can be rescued by forces from off the planet. A superior example of the last-man story is *I Am Legend,* by Richard Matheson (paperback, 1954; Walker and Company, 1970).

The Underdweller

WILLIAM F. NOLAN

In the waiting, windless dark, Lewis Stillman pressed into the building-front shadows along Wilshire Boulevard. Breathing softly, the automatic poised and ready in his hand, he advanced with animal stealth toward Western Avenue, gliding over the night-cool concrete past ravaged clothing shops, drug- and ten-cent stores, their windows shattered, their doors ajar and swinging. The city of Los Angeles, painted in cold moonlight, was an immense graveyard; the tall, white, tombstone buildings thrust up from the silent pavement, shadow-carved and lonely. Overturned metal corpses of trucks, buses and automobiles littered the streets.

He paused under the wide marquee of the Fox Wiltern. Above his head, rows of splintered display bulbs gaped — sharp glass teeth in wooden jaws.

This was first published under the title *The Small World of Lewis Stillman.*

Lewis Stillman felt as though they might drop at any moment to pierce his body.

Four more blocks to cover. His destination: a small corner delicatessen four blocks south of Wilshire, on Western. Tonight he intended bypassing the larger stores like Safeway or Thriftimart, with their available supplies of exotic foods; a smaller grocery was far more likely to have what he needed. He was finding it more and more difficult to locate basic foodstuffs. In the big supermarkets only the more exotic and highly spiced canned and bottled goods remained — and he was sick of caviar and oysters!

Crossing Western, he had almost reached the far curb when he saw some of *them*. He dropped immediately to his knees behind the rusting bulk of an Oldsmobile. The rear door on his side was open, and he cautiously eased himself into the back seat of the deserted car. Releasing the safety catch on the automatic, he peered through the cracked window at six or seven of them, as they moved toward him along the street. God! Had he been seen? He couldn't be sure. Perhaps they were aware of his position! He should have remained on the open street where he'd have a running chance. Perhaps, if his aim were true, he could kill most of them; but even with its silencer the gun might be heard and more of them would come. He dared not fire until he was certain they had discovered him.

They came closer, their small dark bodies crowding the walk, six of them, chattering, leaping, cruel mouths open, eyes glittering under the moon. Closer. Their shrill pipings increased, rose in volume. Closer. Now he could make out their sharp teeth and matted hair. Only a few feet from the car . . . His hand was moist on the handle of the automatic; his heart thundered against his chest. Seconds away . . .

Now!

Lewis Stillman fell heavily back against the dusty seat cushion, the gun loose in his trembling hand. They had passed by; they had missed him. Their thin pipings diminished, grew faint with distance.

The tomb silence of late night settled around him.

The delicatessen proved a real windfall. The shelves were relatively un-touched and he had a wide choice of tinned goods. He found an empty cardboard box and hastily began to transfer the cans from the shelf nearest him.

A noise from behind — a padding, scraping sound.

Lewis Stillman whirled about, the automatic ready.

A huge mongrel dog faced him, growling deep in its throat, four legs braced for assault. The blunt ears were laid flat along the short-haired skull and a thin trickle of saliva seeped from the killing jaws. The beast's powerful chest-muscles were bunched for the spring when Stillman acted.

His gun, he knew, was useless; the shots would be heard. Therefore, with the full strength of his left arm he hurled a heavy can at the dog's head. The stunned animal staggered under the blow, legs buckling. Hurriedly, Stillman gathered his supplies and made his way back to the street.

How much longer can my luck hold? Lewis Stillman wondered, as he bolted the door. He placed the box of tinned goods on a wooden table and lit the tall lamp nearby. Its flickering orange glow illumined the narrow, low-ceilinged room.

Twice tonight, his mind told him, twice you've escaped them — and they could have seen you easily on both occasions if they had been watching for you. They don't know you're alive. But when they find out . . .

He forced his thoughts away from the scene in his mind, away from the horror; quickly he began to unload the box, placing the cans on a long shelf along the far side of the room.

He began to think of women, of a girl named Joan, and of how much he had loved her . . .

The world of Lewis Stillman was damp and lightless; it was narrow and its cold stone walls pressed in upon him as he moved. He had been walking for several hours; sometimes he would run, because he knew his leg muscles must be kept strong, but he was walking now, following the thin yellow beam of his hooded lantern. He was searching.

Tonight, he thought, I might find another like myself. Surely, *someone* is down here; I'll find someone if I keep searching. I *must* find someone!

But he knew he would not. He knew he would find only chill emptiness ahead of him in the long tunnels.

For three years he had been searching for another man or woman down here in this world under the city. For three years he had prowled the seven hundred miles of storm drains which threaded their way under the skin of Los Angeles like the veins in a giant's body — and he had found nothing. *Nothing.*

Even now, after all the days and nights of search, he could not really accept the fact that he was alone, that he was the last man alive in a city of seven million . . .

The beautiful woman stood silently above him. Her eyes burned softly in the darkness; her fine red lips were smiling. The foam-white gown she wore continually swirled and billowed around her motionless figure.

"Who are you?" he asked, his voice far off, unreal.

"Does it matter, Lewis?"

Her words, like four dropped stones in a quiet pool, stirred him, rippled down the length of his body.

"No," he said. "Nothing matters now except that we've found each other.

God, after all these lonely months and years of waiting! I thought I was the last, that I'd never live to see — "

"Hush, my darling." She leaned to kiss him. Her lips were moist and yielding. "I'm here now."

He reached up to touch her cheek, but already she was fading, blending into darkness. Crying out, he clawed desperately for her extended hand. But she was gone, and his fingers rested on a rough wall of damp concrete.

A swirl of milk-fog drifted away in slow rollings down the tunnel.

Rain. Days of rain. The drains had been designed to handle floods so Lewis Stillman was not particularly worried. He had built high, a good three feet above the tunnel floor and the water had never yet risen to this level. But he didn't like the sound of the rain down here: an orchestrated thunder through the tunnels, a trap-drumming amplified and continuous. And since he had been unable to make his daily runs he had been reading more than usual. Short stories by Welty, Gordimer, Aiken, Irwin Shaw, and Hemingway; poems by Frost, Lorca, Sandburg, Millay, Dylan Thomas. Strange, how unreal this present-day world seemed when he read their words. Unreality, however, was fleeting, and the moment he closed a book the loneliness and the fears pressed back. He hoped the rain would stop soon.

Dampness. Surrounding him, the cold walls and the chill and the dampness. The unending gurgle and drip of water, the hollow, tapping splash of the falling drops. Even in his cot, wrapped in thick blankets, the dampness seemed to permeate his body. Sounds . . . Thin screams, pipings, chatterings, reedy whisperings above his head. They were dragging something along the street, something they'd no doubt killed: an animal — a cat or a dog perhaps . . . Lewis Stillman shifted, pulling the blankets closer about his body. He kept his eyes tightly shut, listening to the sharp, scuffling sounds on the pavement and swore bitterly.

"Damn you," he said. "Damn all of you!"

Lewis Stillman was running, running down the long tunnels. Behind him a tide of midget shadows washed from wall to wall; high, keening cries, doubled and tripled by echoes, rang in his ears. Claws reached for him; he felt panting breath, like hot smoke, on the back of his neck; his lungs were bursting, his entire body aflame.

He looked down at his fast-pumping legs, doing their job with pistoned precision. He listened to the sharp slap of his heels against the floor of the tunnel — and he thought: I might die at any moment, but my *legs* will escape! They will run on down the endless drains and never be caught. They move so fast while my heavy, awkward upper body rocks and sways above them, slowing them down, tiring them — making them angry. How my legs must hate me! I must be clever and humor them, beg them to take me along to safety. How well they run, how sleek and fine!

Then he felt himself coming apart. His legs were detaching themselves from his upper body. He cried out in horror, flailing the air, beseeching them not to leave him behind. But the legs cruelly continued to unfasten themselves. In a cold surge of terror, Lewis Stillman felt himself tipping, falling toward the damp floor — while his legs raced on with a wild animal life of their own. He opened his mouth, high above those insane legs, and screamed.

Ending the nightmare.

He sat up stiffly in his cot, gasping, drenched in sweat. He drew in a long shuddering breath and reached for a cigarette, lighting it with a trembling hand.

The nightmares were getting worse. He realized that his mind was rebelling as he slept, spilling forth the bottled-up fears of the day during the night hours.

He thought once more about the beginning six years ago, about why he was still alive. The alien ships had struck Earth suddenly, without warning. Their attack had been thorough and deadly. In a matter of hours the aliens had accomplished their clever mission — and the men and women of Earth were destroyed. A few survived, he was certain. He had never seen any of them, but he was convinced they existed. Los Angeles was not the world, after all, and since he escaped so must have others around the globe. He'd been working alone in the drains when the aliens struck, finishing a special job for the construction company on B tunnel. He could still hear the weird sound of the mammoth ships and feel the intense heat of their passage.

Hunger had forced him out, and overnight he had become a curiosity. The last man alive. For three years he was not harmed. He worked with them, taught them many things, and tried to win their confidence. But, eventually, certain ones came to hate him, to be jealous of his relationship with the others. Luckily he had been able to escape to the drains. That was three years ago and now they had forgotten him.

His subsequent excursions to the upper level of the city had been made under cover of darkness — and he never ventured out unless his food supply dwindled. He had built his one-room structure directly to the side of an overhead grating — not close enough to risk their seeing it, but close enough for light to seep in during the sunlight hours. He missed the warm feel of open sun on his body almost as much as he missed human companionship, but he dare not risk himself above the drains by day.

When the rain ceased, he crouched beneath the street gratings to absorb as much as possible of the filtered sunlight. But the rays were weak and their small warmth only served to heighten his desire to feel direct sunlight upon his naked shoulders.

*

The dreams . . . always the dreams.

"Are you cold, Lewis?"

"Yes, yes, cold."

"Then go out, dearest. Into the sun."

"I can't. Can't go out."

"But Los Angeles is your world, Lewis! You are the last man in it. The last man in the world."

"Yes, but they own it all. Every street belongs to them, every building. They wouldn't let me come out. I'd die. They'd kill me."

"Go out, Lewis." The liquid dream-voice faded, faded. "Out into the sun, my darling. Don't be afraid."

That night he watched the moon through the street gratings for almost an hour. It was round and full, like a huge yellow floodlamp in the dark sky, and he thought, for the first time in years, of night baseball at Blues Stadium in Kansas City. He used to love watching the games with his father under the mammoth stadium lights when the field was like a pond, frosted with white illumination, and the players dream-spawned and unreal. Night baseball was always a magic game to him when he was a boy.

Sometimes he got insane thoughts. Sometimes, on a night like this, when the loneliness closed in like a crushing fist and he could no longer stand it, he would think of bringing one of them down with him, into the drains. One at a time, they might be handled. Then he'd remember their sharp savage eyes, their animal ferocity, and he would realize that the idea was impossible. If one of their kind disappeared, suddenly and without trace, others would certainly become suspicious, begin to search for him — and it would all be over.

Lewis Stillman settled back into his pillow; he closed his eyes and tried not to listen to the distant screams, pipings, and reedy cries filtering down from the street above his head.

Finally he slept.

He spent the afternoon with paper women. He lingered over the pages of some yellowed fashion magazines, looking at all the beautifully photographed models in their fine clothes. Slim and enchanting, these page-women, with their cool enticing eyes and perfect smiles, all grace and softness and glitter and swirled cloth. He touched their images with gentle fingers, stroking the tawny paper hair, as though, by some magic formula, he might imbue them with life. Yet, it was easy to imagine that these women had never *really* lived at all — that they were simply painted, in microscopic detail, by sly artists to give the illusion of photos.

He didn't like to think about these women and how they died.

*

"A toast to courage," smiled Lewis Stillman, raising his wine glass high. It sparkled deep crimson in the lamplit room. "To courage and to the man who truly possesses it!" He drained the glass and hastily refilled it from a tall bottle on the table beside his cot.

"Aren't you going to join me, Mr. H.?" he asked the seated figure slouched over the table, head on folded arms. "Or must I drink alone?"

The figure did not reply.

"Well, then — " He emptied the glass, set it down. "Oh, I know all about what one man is supposed to be able to do. Win out alone. Whip the damn world singlehanded. If a fish as big as a mountain and as mean as all sin is out there then this one man is supposed to go get him, isn't that it? Well, Papa H., what if the world is *full* of big fish? Can he win over them all? One man. Alone. Of course he can't. Nosir. Damn well right he can't!"

Stillman moved unsteadily to a shelf in one corner of the small wooden room and took down a slim book.

"Here she is, Mr. H. Your greatest. The one you wrote cleanest and best — *The Old Man and The Sea.* You showed how one man could fight the whole damn ocean." He paused, voice strained and rising. "Well, by God, show me, *now,* how to fight this ocean. My ocean is full of killer fish and I'm one man and I'm alone in it. I'm ready to listen."

The seated figure remained silent.

"Got you now, haven't I, Papa? No answer to this one, eh? Courage isn't enough. Man was not meant to live alone or fight alone — or drink alone. Even with courage he can only do so much alone, and then it's useless. Well, I say it's useless. I say the hell with your book and the hell with *you!*"

Lewis Stillman flung the book straight at the head of the motionless figure. The victim spilled back in the chair; his arms slipped off the table, hung swinging. They were lumpy and handless.

More and more, Lewis Stillman found his thoughts turning to the memory of his father and of long hikes through the moonlit Missouri countryside, of hunting trips and warm campfires, of the deep woods, rich and green in summer. He thought of his father's hopes for his future, and the words of that tall, gray-haired figure often came back to him.

"You'll be a fine doctor, Lewis. Study and work hard and you'll succeed. I know you will."

He remembered the long winter evenings of study at his father's great mahogany desk, pouring over medical books and journals, taking notes, sifting and resifting facts. He remembered one set of books in particular — Erickson's monumental three-volume text on surgery, richly bound and stamped in gold. He had always loved those books, above all others.

What had gone wrong along the way? Somehow, the dream had faded; the bright goal vanished and was lost. After a year of pre-med at the University of California he had given up medicine; he had become discouraged and quit college to take a laborer's job with a construction company. How ironic that this move should have saved his life! He'd wanted to work with his hands, to sweat and labor with the muscles of his body. He'd wanted to earn enough to marry Joan and then, later perhaps, he would have returned to finish his courses. It all seemed so far away now, his reason for quitting, for letting his father down.

Now, at this moment, an overwhelming desire gripped him, a desire to pour over Erickson's pages once again, to recreate, even for a brief moment, the comfort and happiness of his childhood.

He'd once seen a duplicate set on the second floor of Pickwick's book store in Hollywood, in their used book department, and now he knew he must go after them, bring the books back with him to the drains. It was a dangerous and foolish desire, but he knew he would obey it. Despite the risk of death, he would go after the books tonight. *Tonight.*

One corner of Lewis Stillman's room was reserved for weapons. His prize, a Thompson submachine gun, had been procured from the Los Angeles police arsenal. Supplementing the Thompson were two automatic rifles, a Luger, a Colt .45 and a .22 Hornet pistol, equipped with a silencer. He always kept the smallest gun in a spring-clip holster beneath his armpit, but it was not his habit to carry any of the larger weapons with him into the city. On this night, however, things were different.

The drains ended two miles short of Hollywood — which meant he would be forced to cover a long and particularly hazardous stretch of ground in order to reach the book store. He therefore decided to take along the .30 caliber Savage rifle in addition to the small hand weapon.

You're a fool, Lewis, he told himself as he slid the oiled Savage from its leather case, risking your life for a set of books. Are they *that* important? Yes, a part of him replied, they are that important. You want these books, then go *after* what you want. If fear keeps you from seeking that which you truly want, if fear holds you like a rat in the dark, then you are worse than a coward. You are a traitor, betraying yourself and the civilization you represent. If a man wants a thing and the thing is good he must go after it, no matter what the cost, or relinquish the right to be called a man. It is better to die with courage than to live with cowardice.

Ah, Papa Hemingway, breathed Stillman, smiling at his own thoughts. I see that you are back with me. I see that your words have rubbed off after all. Well then, all right — let us go after our fish, let us seek him out. Perhaps the ocean will be calm . . .

Slinging the heavy rifle over one shoulder, Lewis Stillman set off down the tunnels.

Running in the chill night wind. Grass, now pavement, now grass beneath his feet. Ducking into shadows, moving stealthily past shops and theaters, rushing under the cold high moon. Santa Monica Boulevard, then Highland, then Hollywood Boulevard, and finally — after an eternity of heartbeats — the book store.

The Pickwick.

Lewis Stillman, his rifle over one shoulder, the small automatic gleaming in his hand, edged silently into the store.

A paper battleground met his eyes.

In the filtered moonlight, a white blanket of broken-backed volumes spilled across the entire lower floor. Stillman shuddered; he could envision them, shrieking, scrabbling at the shelves, throwing books wildly across the room at one another. Screaming, ripping, destroying.

What of the other floors? *What of the medical section?*

He crossed to the stairs, spilled pages crackling like a fall of dry autumn leaves under his step, and sprinted up the first short flight to the mezzanine. Similar chaos!

He hurried up to the second floor, stumbling, terribly afraid of what he might find. Reaching the top, heart thudding, he squinted into the dimness.

The books were undisturbed. Apparently they had tired of their game before reaching these.

He slipped the rifle from his shoulder and placed it near the stairs. Dust lay thick all around him, powdering up and swirling as he moved down the narrow aisles; a damp, leathery mustiness lived in the air, an odor of mold and neglect.

Lewis Stillman paused before a dim hand-lettered sign: MEDICAL SEC-TION. It was just as he remembered it. Holstering the small automatic, he struck a match, shading the flame with a cupped hand as he moved it along the rows of faded titles. Carter . . . Davidson . . . Enright . . . *Erickson.* He drew in his breath sharply. All three volumes, their gold stamping dust-dulled but legible, stood in tall and perfect order on the shelf.

In the darkness, Lewis Stillman carefully removed each volume, blowing it free of dust. At last all three books were clean and solid in his hands.

Well, you've done it. You've reached the books and now they belong to you.

He smiled, thinking of the moment when he would be able to sit down at the table with his treasure, and linger again over the wondrous pages.

He found an empty carton at the rear of the store and placed the books inside. Returning to the stairs, he shouldered the rifle and began his descent to the lower floor.

So far, he told himself, my luck is still holding.

But as Lewis Stillman's foot touched the final stair, his luck ran out.

The entire lower floor was alive with them!

Rustling like a mass of great insects, gliding toward him, eyes gleaming in the half light, they converged upon the stairs. They'd been waiting for him.

Now, suddenly, the books no longer mattered. Now only his life mattered and nothing else. He moved back against the hard wood of the stair-rail, the carton of books sliding from his hands. They had stopped at the foot of the stairs; they were silent, looking up at him, the hate in their eyes.

If you can reach the street, Stillman told himself, then you've still got half a chance. That means you've got to get through them to the door. All right then, *move.*

Lewis Stillman squeezed the trigger of the automatic. Two of them fell under his bullets as Stillman rushed into their midst.

He felt sharp nails claw at his shirt, heard the cloth ripping away in their grasp. He kept firing the small automatic into them, and three more dropped under the hail of bullets, shrieking in pain and surprise. The others spilled back, screaming, from the door.

The pistol was empty. He tossed it away, swinging the heavy Savage free from his shoulder as he reached the street. The night air, crisp and cool in his lungs, gave him instant hope.

I can still make it, thought Stillman, as he leaped the curb and plunged across the pavement. If those shots weren't heard, then I've still got the edge. My legs are strong; I can outdistance them.

Luck, however, had failed him completely on this night. Near the intersection of Hollywood Boulevard and Highland, a fresh pack of them swarmed toward him over the street.

He dropped to one knee and fired into their ranks, the Savage jerking in his hands. They scattered to either side.

He began to run steadily down the middle of Hollywood Boulevard, using the butt of the heavy rifle like a battering ram as they came at him. As he neared Highland, three of them darted directly into his path. Stillman fired. One doubled over, lurching crazily into a jagged plate-glass storefront. Another clawed at him as he swept around the corner to Highland, but he managed to shake free.

The street ahead of him was clear. Now his superior leg-power would count heavily in his favor. Two miles. Could he make it before others cut him off?

Running, reloading, firing. Sweat soaking his shirt, rivering down his face, stinging his eyes. A mile covered. Halfway to the drains. They had fallen back behind his swift stride.

But more of them were coming, drawn by the rifle shots, pouring in from side streets, from stores and houses.

His heart jarred in his body, his breath was ragged. How many of them around him? A hundred? Two hundred? More coming. God!

He bit down on his lower lip until the salt taste of blood was on his tongue.

You can't make it, a voice inside him shouted, they'll have you in another block and you know it!

He fitted the rifle to his shoulder, adjusted his aim, and fired. The long rolling crack of the big weapon filled the night. Again and again he fired, the butt jerking into the flesh of his shoulder, the bitter smell of burnt powder in his nostrils.

It was no use. Too many of them. He could not clear a path.

Lewis Stillman knew that he was going to die.

The rifle was empty at last, the final bullet had been fired. He had no place to run because they were all around him, in a slowly closing circle.

He looked at the ring of small cruel faces and he thought: The aliens did their job perfectly; they stopped Earth before she could reach the age of the rocket, before she could threaten planets beyond her own moon. What an immensely clever plan it had been! To destroy every human being on Earth above the age of six — and then to leave as quickly as they had come, allowing our civilization to continue on a primitive level, knowing that Earth's back had been broken, that her survivors would revert to savagery as they grew into adulthood.

Lewis Stillman dropped the empty rifle at his feet and threw out his hands. "Listen," he pleaded, "I'm really one of you. You'll *all* be like me soon. Please, *listen* to me."

But the circle tightened relentlessly around Lewis Stillman. He was screaming when the children closed in.

lin/guis/tics — the structure of human speech and the study of language. Language is one of the most decisive means by which people define themselves, and linguistics is a growing, dynamic field of intellectual enterprise. In science fiction, authors have dealt with alien languages in fascinating ways — see for example *The Languages of Pao,* by Jack Vance (Avalon, 1957) and *Babel-17* by Samuel R. Delany (Ace Books, 1966; Gregg Press, 1976). An interesting nonfiction book on the subject is *Aliens and Linguists: Language Study and Science Fiction* (University of Georgia Press, 1980).

Top Secret

ERIC FRANK RUSSELL

Ashmore said, with irritating phlegmaticism, "The Zengs have everything to gain and nothing to lose by remaining friendly with us. I'm not worried about them."

"But I am," rasped General Railton. "I'm paid to worry. It's my job. If the Zeng empire launches a treacherous attack upon ours and gains some initial successes, who'll get the blame? Who'll be accused of military unpreparedness?" He tapped his two rows of medal ribbons. "I will!"

"Understanding your position, I cannot share your alarm," maintained Ashmore, refusing to budge. "The Zeng empire is less than half the size of ours. The Zengs are an amiable and cooperative form of life and we've been on excellent terms with them since the first day of contact."

"I'll grant you all that." General Railton tugged furiously at his large and luxuriant mustache while he examined the great star map that covered an entire wall. "But I have to consider things purely from the military viewpoint. It's my task to look to the future and expect the worst."

"Well, what's worrying you in particular?" Ashmore invited.

"Two things." Railton placed an authoritative finger on the star map. "Right here we hold a fairly new planet called Motan. You can see where it is — out in the wilds, far beyond our long-established frontiers. It's located in the middle of a close-packed group of solar systems, a stellar array that represents an important junction in space."

"I know all that."

"At Motan we've got a foothold of immense strategic value. We're in ambush on the crossroads, so to speak. Twenty thousand Terrans are there, complete with two spaceports and twenty-four light cruisers." He glanced at the other. "And what happens?"

Ashmore offered no comment.

"The Zengs," said Railton, making a personal grievance of it, "move in and take over two nearby planets in the same group."

"With our agreement," Ashmore reminded. "We did not need those two planets. The Zengs did want them. They put in a polite and correct request for permission to take over. Greenwood told them to help themselves."

"Greenwood," exploded Railton, "is someone I could describe in detail were it not for my oath of loyalty."

"Let it pass," suggested Ashmore, wearily. "If he blundered, he did so with the full approval of the World Council."

"The World Council," Railton snorted. "All they're interested in is exploration, discovery, trade. All they can think of is culture and cash. They're completely devoid of any sense of peril."

"Not being military officers," Ashmore pointed out, "they can hardly be expected to exist in a state of perpetual apprehension."

"Mine's not without cause." Railton had another go at uprooting his mustache. "The Zengs craftily position themselves adjacent to Motan." He swept spread fingers across the map in a wide arc. "And all over here are Zeng outposts mixed up with ours. No orderliness about it, no system. A mob, sir, a scattered mob."

"That's natural when two empires overlap," informed Ashmore. "And, after all, the mighty cosmos isn't a parade ground."

Ignoring that, Railton said pointedly, "Then a cipher book disappears."

"It was shipped back on the *Laura Lindsay*. She blew apart and was a total loss. You know that."

"I know only what they see fit to tell me. I don't know that the book was actually on the ship. If it was not, where is it? Who's got it? What's he doing with it?" He waited for comment that did not come, and finished, "So I had to move heaven and earth to get that cipher canceled and have copies of a new one sent out."

"Accidents happen," said Ashmore.

"Today," continued Railton, "I discover that Commander Hunter, on Motan, has been given the usual fat-headed emergency order. If war breaks out, he must fight a defensive action and hold the planet at all costs."

"What's wrong with that?"

Staring at him incredulously, Railton growled, "And him with twenty-four light cruisers. Not to mention two new battleships soon to follow."

"I don't quite understand."

"Wars," explained Railton, as one would to a child, "cannot be fought without armed ships. Ships cannot function usefully without instructions based on careful appraisal of tactical necessities. Somebody has to plan and give orders. The orders have to be received by those appointed to carry them out."

"So?"

"How can Zeng warships receive and obey orders if their planetary beam-stations have been destroyed?"

"You think that immediately war breaks out the forces on Motan should bomb every beam-station within reach?"

"Most certainly, man!" Railton looked pleased at long last. "The instant the Zengs attack we've got to retaliate against their beam-stations. That's tantamount to depriving them of their eyes and ears. Motan must be fully prepared to do its share. Commander Hunter's orders are out of date, behind the times, in fact plain stupid. The sooner they're rectified, the better."

"You're the boss," Ashmore reminded. "You've the authority to have them changed."

"That's exactly what I intend to do. I am sending Hunter appropriate instructions at once. And not by direct-beam either." He indicated the map again. "In this messy muddle there are fifty or more Zeng beam-stations lying on the straight line between here and there. How do we know how much stuff they're picking up and deciphering?"

"The only alternative is the tight-beam," Ashmore said. "And that takes ten times as long. It zigzags all over the star-field from one station to another."

"But it's a thousand times safer and surer," Railton retorted. "Motan's station has just been completed and now's the time to make use of the fact. I'll send new instructions by tight-beam, in straight language, and leave no room for misunderstanding."

He spent twenty minutes composing a suitable message, finally got it to his satisfaction. Ashmore read it, could suggest no improvements. In due course it flashed out to Centauri, the first staging-post across the galaxy.

> In event of hostile action in your sector the war must be fought to outstretch and rive all enemy's chief lines of communication.

"That," said Railton, "expresses it broadly enough to show Hunter what's wanted but still leave him with some initiative."

At Centauri the message was unscrambled, read off in clear, read into another beam of different frequency, and boosted to the next nearest station. There it was sorted out, read off in clear, repeated into another beam and squirted onward.

It went leftward, rightward, upward, downward, and was dutifully recited eighteen times by voices ranging from Terran-American deep-South-suh to

Bootean-Ansanite far-North-yezzah. But it got there just the same.

Yes, it got there.

Lounging behind his desk, Commander Hunter glanced idly at the Motan thirty-hour clock, gave a wide yawn, wondered for the hundredth time whether it was something in the alien atmosphere that gave him the gapes. A knock sounded on his office door.

"Come in!"

Tyler entered, red-nosed and sniffy as usual. He saluted, dumped a signal form on the desk. "Message from Terra, sir." He saluted again and marched out, sniffing as he went.

Picking it up, Hunter yawned again as he looked at it. Then his mouth clapped shut with an audible crack of jawbones. He sat bolt upright, eyes popping, and read it a second time.

Ex Terra Space Control. Tight-Beam, Straight. Top Secret. To Motan. An event of hospitality your section the foremost when forty-two ostriches arrive on any cheap line of communication.

Holding it in one hand he walked three times round the room, but it made no difference. The message still said what it said.

So he reseated himself, reached for the phone and bawled, "Maxwell? Is Maxwell there? Send him in at once!"

Maxwell appeared within a couple of minutes. He was a long, lean character who maintained an expression of chronic disillusionment. Sighing deeply, he sat down.

"What's it this time, Felix?"

"Now," said Hunter, in the manner of a dentist about to reach for the big one at the back, "you're this planet's chief equipment officer. What you don't know about stores, supplies, and equipment isn't worth knowing, eh?"

"I wouldn't go so far as to say that. I — "

"You know *everything* about equipment," insisted Hunter, "else you've no right being here and taking money for it. You're skinning the Terran taxpayers by false pretenses."

"Calm down, Felix," urged Maxwell. "I've enough troubles of my own." His questing eyes found the paper in the other's hand. "I take it that something's been requisitioned of which you don't approve. What is it?"

"Forty-two ostriches," informed Hunter.

Maxwell gave a violent jerk, fell off his chair, regained it and said, "Ha-ha! That's good. Best I've heard in years."

"You can see the joke all right?" asked Hunter, with artificial pleasantness. "You think it a winner?"

"Sure," enthused Maxwell. "It's really rich." He added another ha-ha by way of support.

"Then," said Hunter, a trifle viciously, "maybe you'll explain it to me; I'm too dumb to get it on my own." He leaned forward, arms akimbo. *"Why* do we require forty-two ostriches, eh? Tell me that!"

"Are you serious?" asked Maxwell, a little dazed.

For answer, Hunter shoved the signal form at him. Maxwell read it, stood up, sat down, read it again, turned it over and carefully examined the blank back.

"Well?" prompted Hunter.

"I've had nothing to do with this," assured Maxwell, hurriedly. He handed back the signal form as though anxious to be rid of it. "It's a Terran-authorized shipment made without demand from this end."

"My limited intelligence enabled me to deduce that much," said Hunter. "But as I have pointed out, you know all about equipment required for given conditions on any given world. All I want from you is information on why Motan needs forty-two ostriches — and what we're supposed to do with them when they come."

"I don't know," Maxwell admitted.

"You don't know?"

"No."

"That's a help." Hunter glowered at the signal. "A very big help."

"How about it being in code?" inquired Maxwell, desperate enough to fish around.

"It says here it's in straight."

"That could be an error."

"All right. We can soon check." Unlocking a big wall safe, Hunter extracted a brass-bound book and scrabbled through its pages. Then he gave it to Maxwell. "See if you can find a reference to ostriches or any reasonable resemblance thereto."

After five minutes Maxwell voiced a dismal no.

"Well," persisted Hunter, "have you sent a demand for forty-two of anything that might be misread as ostriches?"

"Not a thing." He meditated a bit, adding glumly, "I did order a one-pint blowtorch."

Taking a tight grip on the rim of the desk, Hunter said, "What's that got to do with it?"

"Nothing. I was just thinking. That's what I ordered. You ought to see what I got." He gestured toward the door. "It's right out there in the yard. I had it dragged there for your benefit."

"Let's have a look at it."

Hunter followed him outside and inspected the object of the other's discontent. It had a body slightly bigger than a garbage can, and a nozzle five inches in diameter by three feet in length. Though empty, it was as much as the two could manage to lift.

"What the deuce is it, anyway?" demanded Hunter, scowling.

"A one-pint blowtorch. The consignment note says so."

"Never seen anything like it. We'd better check the stores catalogue." Returning to the office, he dug the tome out of the safe, thumbed through it rapidly, found what he wanted somewhere among the middle pages.

19112. Blowtorch, butane, ½ pint capacity.

19112A. Blowtorch, butane, 1 pint capacity.

19112B. Blowtorch (tar-boiler pattern), kerosene, 15 gallons capacity.

19112B(a). Portable trolley for 19112B.

"You've got B in lieu of A," Hunter diagnosed.

"That's right. I order A and I get B."

"Without the trolley?"

"Correct."

"Some moron is doing his best." He returned the catalogue to the safe. "You'll have to ship it back. It's a fat lot of use to us without the trolley even if we do find the need to boil some tar."

"Oh, I don't know," Maxwell said. "We can handle it by sheer muscle when the two hundred left-legged men get here."

Hunter plonked himself in his chair and gave the other the hard eye. "Quit beating about the bush. What's on your mind?"

"The last ship," said Maxwell, moodily, "brought two hundred pairs of left-legged rubber thigh-boots."

"The next ship may bring two hundred pairs of right-legged ones to match up," said Hunter. "Plus forty-two ostriches. When that's done we'll be ready for anything. We can defy the cosmos." He suddenly went purple in the face, snatched up the phone and yelled, "Tyler! Tyler!"

When that worthy appeared he said, "Blow your nose and tight-beam this message: 'why forty-two ostriches?' "

It went out, scrambled and unscrambled and rescrambled, upward, downward, rightward, leftward, recited in Sirian-Kham lowlands accents and Terran-Scottish highlands accents and many more. But it got there just the same.

Yes, it got there.

General Raiiton glanced up from a thick wad of documents and rapped impatiently. "What is it?"

"Top secret message from Motan, sir."

Taking it, Railton looked it over.

We've fought two ostriches.

"Ashmore!" he yelled. "Pennington! Whittaker!"

They came on the run, lined up before his desk, assumed habitual expressions of innocence. He eyed them as though each was personally responsible for something dastardly.

"What," he demanded, "is the meaning of this?"

He tossed the signal form at Pennington, who gave it the glassy eye and passed it to Whittaker, who examined it fearfully and got rid of it on Ashmore. The latter scanned it, dumped it back on the desk. Nobody said anything.

"Well," said Railton, "isn't there a useful thought among the three of you?"

Picking up courage, Pennington ventured, "It must be in code, sir."

"It is clearly and plainly captioned as being in straight."

"That may be so, sir. But it doesn't make sense in straight."

"Do you think I'd have summoned you here if it did?" Railton let go a snort that quivered his mustaches. "Bring me the current code-book. We'll see if we can get to the bottom of this."

They fetched him the volume then in use, the sixth of Series B. He sought through it at length. So did they, each in turn. No ostriches.

"Try the earlier books," Railton ordered. "Some fool on Motan may have picked up an obsolete issue."

So they staggered in with a stack of thirty volumes and worked back to BA. No ostriches. After that, they commenced on AZ and laboriously headed toward AA.

Pennington, thumbing through AK, let go a yelp of triumph. "Here it is, sir. An ostrich is a food supply and rationing code-word located in the quartermaster section."

"What does it mean?" inquired Railton, raising expectant eyebrows.

"One gross of fresh eggs," said Pennington, in the manner of one who sweeps aside the veil of mystery.

"Ah!" said Railton, in tones of exaggerated satisfaction. "So at last we know where we stand, don't we? Everything has become clear. On Motan they've beaten off an attack by three hundred fresh eggs, eh?"

Pennington looked crushed.

"Fresh eggs," echoed Ashmore. "That may be a clue!"

"What sort of clue?" demanded Railton, turning attention his way.

"In olden times," explained Ashmore, "the word fresh meant impudent, bold, brazen. And an egg was a person. Also, a hoodlum or thug was known as a hard egg or a tough egg."

"If you're right, that means Motan has resisted a raid by three hundred impertinent crooks."

"Offhand, I just can't think of any more plausible solution," Ashmore confessed.

"It's not credible," decided Railton. "There are no pirates out that way. The only potential menace is the Zengs. If a new and previously unsuspected life-form has appeared out there, the message would have said so."

"Maybe they meant they've had trouble with Zengs," suggested Whittaker.

"I doubt it," Railton said. "In the first place, the Zengs would not be so dopey as to start a war by launching a futile attack with a force a mere three hundred strong. In the second place, if the culprits were Zengs the fact could have been stated. On the tight-beam system there's no need for Motan to be obscure."

"That's reasonable enough," Ashmore agreed.

Railton thought things over, said at last, "The message looks like a routine report. It doesn't call for aid or demand fast action. I think we'd better check back. Beam them asking which book they're quoting."

Out it went, up, down and around, via a mixture of voices.

Which code-book are you using?

Tyler sniffed, handed it over, saluted, sniffed again, and ambled out. Commander Hunter picked it up.

Which goad-hook are you using?

"Maxwell! Maxwell!" When the other arrived, he said, "There'll never be an end to this. What's a goad-hook?"

"I'd have to look it up in the catalogue."

"Meaning that you don't know?"

"There's about fifty kinds of hooks," informed Maxwell, defensively. "And for many of them there are technical names considerably different from space-navy names or even stores equipment names. A tension hook, for instance, is better known as a tightener."

"Then let's consult the book." Getting it from the safe, Hunter opened it on the desk while Maxwell positioned himself to look over the other's shoulder. "What'll it be listed under?" Hunter asked. "Goad-hooks or hooks, goad? G or H?"

"Might be either."

They sought through both. After checking item by item over half a dozen pages, Maxwell stabbed a finger at a middle column.

"There it is."

Hunter looked closer. "That's *guard hooks:* things for fixing wire fence to steel posts. Where's *goad*-hooks?"

"Don't seem to be any," Maxwell admitted. Sudden suspicion flooded his features and he went on, "Say, do you suppose this has anything to do with those ostriches?"

"Darned if I know. But it's highly probable."

"Then," announced Maxwell, "I know what a goad-hook is. And you won't find it in that catalogue."

Slamming the book shut, Hunter said wearily, "All right. Proceed to enlighten me."

"I saw a couple of them in use," informed Maxwell. "Years ago, in the movies."

"The movies?"

"Yes. They were showing an ostrich farm in South Africa. When the farmer wanted to extract a particular bird from the flock, he used a pole about eight to ten feet long. It had a sort of metal prod on one end and a wide hook at the other. He'd use the sharp end to poke other birds out of the way, then use the hook end to snake the bird he wanted around the bottom of its neck and drag it out."

"Oh," said Hunter, staring at him.

"It's a thing like bishops carry for lugging sinners into the path of right-eousness," Maxwell finished.

"Is it really?" said Hunter, blinking a couple of times. "Well, it checks up with that signal about the ostriches." He brooded a bit and went on, "But it implies that there is more than one kind of goad-hook. Also, that we are presumed to have one particular pattern in stores here. They want to know which one we've got. What are we going to tell them?"

"We haven't got any," Maxwell pointed out. "What do we need goad-hooks for?"

"Ostriches," said Hunter. "Forty-two of them."

Maxwell thought it over. "We've no goad-hooks, not one. But they think we have. What's the answer to that?"

"You tell me," Hunter invited.

"That first message warned us that the ostriches were coming on any cheap line of communication, obviously meaning a chartered tramp ship. So they won't get here for quite a time. Meanwhile, somebody has realized that we'll need goad-hooks to handle them and shipped a consignment by fast service-boat. Then he's discovered that he can't remember which pattern he's sent us. He can't fill out the necessary forms until he knows. He's asking you to give with the information."

"If that's so," commented Hunter, "some folk have a nerve to tight-beam such a request and mark it top secret."

"Back at Terran H.Q.," said Maxwell, "one is not shot at dawn for sabo-tage, treachery, assassination, or any other equally trifling misdeed. One is blindfolded and stood against the wall for not filling out forms, or for filling out the wrong ones, or for filling out the right ones with the wrong details."

"Nuts to that!" snapped Hunter, fed up. "I'm wasting no time getting a headquarters dope out of a jam. We're supposed to have a consignment of goad-hooks. We haven't got it. I'm going to say so — in plain language." He boosted his voice a few decibels. "Tyler! Tyler!"

Half an hour later the signal squirted out, brief and to the point, lacking only its original note of indignation.

No goad hyphen hooks. Motan.

*

Holding it near the light, Railton examined it right way up and upside down. His mustache jittered. His eyes squinted slightly. His complexion assumed a touch of magenta.

"Pennington!" he bellowed. "Saunders! Ashmore! Whittaker!"

Lining up, they looked at the signal form. They shifted edgily around, eyed each other, the floor, the ceiling, the walls. Finally they settled for the uninteresting scene outside the window.

Oh God how I hate mutton.

"Well?" prompted Railton, poking this beamed revelation around his desk. Nobody responded.

"First," Railton pointed out, "they're fighting it out with a pair of ostriches. Now they've developed an aversion to mutton. If there's a connection, I fail to see it. There's got to be an explanation somewhere. What is it?"

Nobody knew.

"We might as well invite the Zengs to accept everything as a gift," said Railton. "It'll save a lot of bloodshed."

Stung by that, Whittaker protested, "Motan is trying to tell us something, sir. They must have cause to express themselves the way they are doing."

"Perhaps they have good reason to think that the tight-beam is no longer tight. Maybe a Zeng interceptor station has opened right on one of the lines. So Motan is hinting that it's time to stop beaming in straight."

"They could have said so in code, clearly and unmistakably. There's no need to afflict us with all this mysterious stuff about ostriches and mutton."

Up spoke Saunders, upon whom the gift of tongues had descended. "Isn't it possible, sir, that ostrich flesh is referred to as mutton by those who eat it? Or that, perhaps, it bears close resemblance to mutton?"

"*Anything* is possible," shouted Railton, "including the likelihood that everyone on Motan is a few cents short in his mental cash." He fumed a bit, added acidly, "Let us assume that ostrich flesh is identical with mutton. Where does that get us?"

"It could be, sir," persisted Saunders, temporarily drunk with words, "that they've discovered a new and valuable source of food in the form of some large, birdlike creature which they call ostriches. Its flesh tastes like mutton. So they've signaled us a broad hint that they're less dependent upon supplementary supplies from here. Maybe in a pinch they can feed themselves for months or years. That, in turn, means the Zengs can't starve them into submission by blasting all supply ships to Motan. So — "

"Shut up!" Railton bawled, slightly frenzied. He snorted hard enough to make the signal form float off his desk. Then he reached for the phone. "Get me the zoological department . . . Yes, that's what I said." He waited a while and then growled into the mouthpiece, "Is ostrich flesh edible and, if so, what does it taste like?" Then he listened, slammed the phone down, and glowered at his audience. "Leather," he said.

"That doesn't necessarily apply to the Motan breed," Saunders pointed out. "You can't judge an alien species by — "

"For the last time, keep quiet!" He shifted his glare to Ashmore. "We can't go any further until we know which code they're using out there."

"It should be the current one, sir. They had strict orders to destroy each preceding copy."

"I know what it *should* be. But *is* it? We've asked them about this and they haven't replied. Ask them again, by *direct*-beam. I don't care if the Zengs do pick up the question and answer. They can't make use of the information. They've known for years that we use code as an elementary precaution."

"I'll have it beamed right away, sir."

"Do that. And let me have the reply the minute it arrives." Then, to the four of them, "Get out of my sight."

The signal shot straight to Motan without any juggling around.

Identify your code forthwith. Urgent.

Two days later the answer squirted back and got placed on Railton's desk pending his return from lunch. In due course he paraded along the corridor and into his office. His thoughts were actively occupied with the manpower crisis in the Sirian sector and nothing was further from his mind than the antics of Motan. Sitting at his desk, he glanced at the paper.

All it said was, BF.

He went straight up and came down hard.

"Ashmore!" he roared. "Pennington! Saunders! Whittaker!"

*

Ex Terra Space Control. Direct-Beam, Straight. To Motan. Commander Hunter recalled forthwith. Captain Maxwell succeeds with rank of commander as from date of receipt.

Putting on a broad grin of satisfaction, Hunter reached for the phone. "Send Maxwell here at once." When the other arrived, he announced, "A direct-beam recall has just come in. I'm going home."

"Oh," said Maxwell without enthusiasm. He looked more disillusioned than ever.

"I'm going back to H.Q. You know what that means."

"Yes," agreed Maxwell, a mite enviously. "A nice, soft job, better conditions, high pay, quicker promotion."

"Dead right. It is only proper that virtue should be rewarded." He eyed the other, holding back the rest of the news. "Well, aren't you happy about it?"

"No," said Maxwell flatly.

"Why not?"

"I've become hardened to you. Now I'll have to start all over again and adjust myself to some other nut."

"No you won't, chum. *You're* taking charge." He poked the signal form across the desk. "Congratulations, Commander!"

"Thanks," said Maxwell. "For nothing. Now I'll have to handle your grief. Ostriches. Forty-two of them."

At midnight Hunter stepped aboard the destroyer D10 and waved goodbye. He did it with all the gratified assurance of one who's going to get what's coming to him. The prospect lay many weeks away but was worth waiting for.

The ship snored into the night until its flame trail faded out to the left of Motan's fourth moon. High above the opposite horizon glowed the Zeng's two planets of Korima and Koroma, one blue, the other green. Maxwell eyed the shining firmament, felt the weight of new responsibility pressing hard upon his shoulders.

He spent the next two weeks checking back on his predecessor's correspondence, familiarizing himself with all the various problems of planetary governorship. At the end of that time he was still baffled and bothered.

"Tyler!" Then when the other came in, "Man, can't you stop perpetually snuffling? Send this message out at once."

Taking it, Tyler asked, "Tight- or straight-beam, sir?"

"Don't send it direct-beam. It had better go by tight. The subject is tagged top secret by H.Q. and we've got to accept their definition."

"Very well, sir." Giving an unusually loud sniff, Tyler departed and squirted the query to the first repeater station.

Why are we getting ostriches?

It never reached Railton or any other brass hat. It fell into the hands of a new Terran operator who'd become the victim of three successive technical gags. He had no intention whatsoever of being made a chump a fourth time. So he read it with eyebrows waggling.

When are we getting ostriches?

With no hesitation he destroyed the signal and smacked back at the smarty on Motan.

Will emus do?

In due course Maxwell got it, read it twice, walked around the room with it and found himself right back where he'd started.

Will amuse you.

*

For the thirtieth time in four months Maxwell went to meet a ship at the spaceport. So far there had arrived not a goad-hook, not a feather, not even a caged parrot.

It was a distasteful task because every time he asked a captain whether he'd brought the ostriches, he got a look that pronounced him definitely tetched in the head.

Anyway, this one was not a tramp boat. He recognized its type even before it sat down and cut power — a four-man Zeng scout. He also recognized the first Zeng to scramble down the ladder. It was Tormin, the chief military officer on Koroma.

"Ah, Mr. Maxwell," said Tormin, his yellow eyes worried. "I wish to see the commander at once."

"Hunter's gone home. I'm the commander now. What's your trouble?"

"Plenty," Tormin informed. "As you know, we placed ordinary settlers on Korima. But on the sister planet of Koroma we placed settlers and a large number of criminals. The criminals have broken out and seized arms. Civil war is raging on Koroma. We need help."

"Sorry, but I can't give it," said Maxwell. "We have strict orders that in no circumstances whatever may we interfere in Zeng affairs."

"I know, I know," Tormin gestured excitedly with long, skinny arms. "We do not ask for your ships and guns. We are only too willing to do our own dirty work. Besides, the matter is serious but not urgent. Even if the criminals conquer the planet they cannot escape from it. We have removed all ships to Korima."

"Then what do you want me to do?"

"Send a call for help. We can't do it — our beam-station is only half built."

"I am not permitted to make direct contact with the Zeng authorities," said Maxwell.

"You can tell your own H.Q. on Terra. They'll inform our ambassador there. He'll inform our nearest forces."

"That'll mean some delay."

"Right now there's no other way," urged Tormin. "Will you please oblige us? In the same circumstances we'd do as much for you."

"All right," agreed Maxwell, unable to resist this appeal. "The responsibility for getting action will rest with H.Q., anyway." Bolting to his office, he gave Tyler the message, adding, "Better send it tight-beam, just in case some

Zeng stickler for regulations picks it up and accuses us of poking our noses in."

Out it went, to and fro, up and down, in one tone or another, this accent or that.

Civil war is taking place among local Zengs. They are asking for assistance.

It got there a few minutes behind Hunter, who walked into Railton's office, reached the desk, came smartly to attention.

"Commander Hunter, sir, reporting from Motan."

"About time, too," snapped Railton, obviously in no mood to give with a couple of medals. "As commander of Motan you accepted full responsibility for the text of all messages beamed therefrom, did you not?"

"Yes, sir," agreed Hunter, sensing a queer coldness in his back hairs.

Jerking open a drawer, Railton extracted a bunch of signal forms, slapped them on the desk.

"This," he informed, mustache quivering, "is the appalling twaddle with which I have been afflicted since Motan's station came into operation. I can find only one explanation for all this incoherent rubbish about ostriches and mutton, that being that you're overdue for mental treatment. After all, it is not unknown for men on alien planets to go off the rails."

"Permit me to say, sir — " began Hunter.

"I don't permit you," shouted Railton. "Wait until I have finished. And don't flare your nostrils at me. I have replaced you with Maxwell. The proof of your imbecility will be the nature of the next signals from Motan."

"But, sir — "

"Shut up! I will let you see Maxwell's messages and compare them with your own irrational nonsense. If that doesn't convince — "

He ceased his tirade as Ashmore appeared and dumped a signal form on his desk.

"Urgent message from Motan, sir."

Railton snatched it up and read it while Ashmore watched and Hunter fidgeted uneasily.

Sibyl Ward is making faces among local Zengs. They are asking for her sister.

The resulting explosion will remain a space legend for all time.

love — affection for another person that can be expressed in various ways. Love is one of the most important emotions felt by human beings and has provided the basis for much of the great literature produced by the world's cultures. Love between men and women was secondary to plot and action in the great bulk of early science fiction, although this important dimension of life has received greater attention in more recent sf. Examples of science fiction love stories can be found in *Love 3000* (Elsevier/ Nelson, 1980).

One Love Have I

ROBERT F. YOUNG

It had been one of those rural suppers, which were being revived at the time. Philip had just arrived in the little academic village that evening and he had just finished unpacking his clothes and his books. There had been nothing more for him to do till morning when he was due to report at the university, and feeling restless, and feeling a little lonely too (as he'd admitted to Miranda later), he had left the boarding house with the intention of wandering about the village till he was tired enough to sleep. He had hardly gone two blocks, however, before he had come to the brightly lit community hall where the supper was in progress, and strangely intrigued, perhaps motivated by the stirring of some pleasant racial memory, he had paused before the entrance.

Through the wide-flung doors he had seen the long table in the middle of the floor, and the food-laden tables — each with a girl in blue behind it — lining the walls. He had seen the men and women passing the food tables, carrying trays, and he had heard the clatter of dishes and the reassuring sound of homely voices. He had noticed the sign above the entrance then, and the simplicity of it had touched him: 77c COMMUNITY SUPPER — SQUARE DANCE TO FOLLOW. It had touched him and filled him with a yearning he hadn't experienced since he was a boy, and he had climbed the wide steps that led to the open doors and stepped into the hall. It was a warm night in September and the curtains at the big windows were breathing in a gentle wind.

He saw her instantly. She was behind the ham sandwich table on the opposite side of the room, tall, dark-haired, her face a lovely flower above the blue petals of her collar. The moment he stepped through the doorway she became the cynosure of the scene, and everything else — tables, diners, walls, floor — became vague extraneous details which an artist adds to a picture to accentuate its central subject.

He was only dimly aware of the other people as he walked across the room. He was halfway to her table before she looked up and saw him. Their eyes touched then, her blue ones and his gray; touched and blended, achieved a moment apart from time. And he had fallen in love with her, and she with him, and it didn't matter what the Freudian psychologists said about that kind of love because the Freudian psychologists simply didn't know about that kind of love, about the way it was to walk into a room and see a girl and know instantly, without understanding how you knew — or caring even — that she, and she alone, was the girl for you, the girl you wanted and had always wanted, would want forever —

Forever and a day . . .

His hands were shaking again and he made them place a cigarette between his lips and then he made them light it. But when they had finished the task and the first pale exhalation of smoke was hovering in the little compartment, they were still shaking, and he held them tightly together on his lap and forced his eyes to look out the window of the monorail car at the passing countryside.

The land was a tired green, a September green. There was goldenrod on hillsides, and the tips of sumac leaves were just beginning to redden. The car swayed as the overhead rail curved around a hill and spanned a valley. It was a lovely valley but it wasn't a familiar one. However, Philip wasn't perturbed: the car was still too far from Cedarville for him to be seeing familiar places. He'd never been much for traveling and it would be some time yet before he could start looking for remembered hills and forests, valleys, roads, houses — houses sometimes stood for a hundred years. Not very often, maybe, but once in a while. It wasn't too much to ask.

He lay his head back on the pneumatic headrest and tried to relax. That was what the Deepfreeze Rehabilitation director had instructed him to do. "Relax. Keep your mind empty. Let things enter into your awareness gradually, and above all don't think of the past." Relax, Philip thought. Don't think of the past. The past is past, past, past . . .

The car swayed again and his head turned slightly. The monorail bordered a spaceport at this point, but he had never seen a spaceport before and for a moment he thought that the car was passing through a vast manmade desert. Then he saw the lofty metallic towers pointing proudly into the afternoon sky, and presently he realized that they weren't towers at all, but ships instead.

He stared at them, half frightened. They were one of the phenomena of the new era for which he was unprepared. There had been spaceships in his own era of course, but there hadn't been very many of them and they had been rather puny affairs, strictly limited to interplanetary travel. They bore no resemblance to the magnificent structures spread out before his eyes now.

The Sweike drive hadn't been discovered till the year of his trial, and he began to realize the effect it had had on space travel during the ensuing century. In a way it was not surprising. Certainly the stars were a greater incentive to man than the lifeless planets of the home system ever could have been.

Alpha Centauri, Sirius, Altair, Vega — one of the ships had gone as far as Arcturus, the Rehabilitation director had told him. It had returned scarcely six months ago after an absence of almost sixty-five years. Philip shook his head. It was data he could not accept, data too fantastic for him to accept. To him it belonged in a probability story, a story that you read with interest, then forgot the moment you laid it aside.

He had always considered himself modern. He had always kept abreast of his age and accepted change as a part of the destiny of man. Scientific progress had never dismayed him; rather, it had stimulated him, and in his chosen field of political philosophy he had been far ahead of his contemporaries, both in vision and in practical application. He had been, in fact, the epitome of modern civilized man —

One hundred years ago . . .

Wearily he turned his eyes from the window and regarded the gray walls of the compartment. He remembered his cigarette when it nipped his fingers, and he dropped it into the disposal tray. He picked up the magazine he had been trying to read some time before and tried to read it again, but his mind stumbled over unfamiliar words, over outrageous idioms, faltered before undreamed-of concepts. The magazine slipped from his fingers to the seat again and he let it lie there.

He felt like an old, old man, yet, in a subjective sense he wasn't old at all. Despite the fact that he had been born one hundred and twenty-seven years ago, he was really only twenty-seven. For the years in the Deepfreeze didn't count — a hundred-year term in suspended animation was nothing more than a wink in subjective time.

He lay his head back on the headrest again. Relax, he told himself. Don't think of the past. The past is past past past . . . Tentatively he closed his eyes. The moment he did so he knew it had been a mistake, but it was too late then, for the time stream already had eddied back more than a hundred years to a swiftly flowing September current . . .

It had been a glorious day for a picnic and they had discovered a quiet place on a hill above the village. There was a cool spring not far away, and above their heads an enormous oak spread its branches against a lazy autumn sky. Miranda had packed liverwurst sandwiches in little pink bags and she had made potato salad. She spread a linen tablecloth on the grass, and they ate facing each other, looking into each other's eyes. A light wind gamboled about them, left ephemeral footprints on the hillside.

The potato salad had been rather flat, but he had eaten two helpings so that she wouldn't suspect that he didn't like it; and he'd also eaten two of the liverwurst sandwiches, though he didn't care for liverwurst at all. After they finished eating they drank coffee, Miranda pouring it from the large picnic thermos into paper cups. She had been very careful not to spill a drop, but she had spilt a whole cup instead, on his shirtsleeve. She had been contrite and on the verge of tears, but he had only loved her all the more; because her awkwardness was as much a part of her as her dark brown hair, as her blue eyes, as her dimples and her smile. It softened the firm maturity of her young woman's body, lent her movements a schoolgirlish charm; put him at ease in the aura of her beauty. For it was reassuring to know that so resplendent a goddess as Miranda had human frailties just as lesser creatures did.

After the coffee they had reclined in the shade, and Miranda had recited "Afternoon on a Hill" and Philip had remembered some of Rupert Brooke's "The Old Vicarage, Grantchester." Miranda was in her final year at the university — she was twenty-one — and she was majoring in English literature. That had put them on common ground from the start, for Philip had loved literature since the moment he had opened *Huckleberry Finn* as a boy, and during the ensuing years he had never lost contact with it.

He had been affecting a pipe at the time (a pipe lent you a desperately needed dignity when you were only twenty-six and commencing your first semester of teaching), and Miranda had filled it for him, holding his lighter over the bowl while he puffed the tobacco into ruddy life . . . It had been such a splendid afternoon, such a glorious afternoon, filled with September wind and September sunshine, with soft words and quiet laughter. The sun was quite low when they prepared to leave, and Philip hadn't wanted to leave at all. Miranda had seemed reluctant too, folding the linen tablecloth slowly, being far more meticulous than she usually was when she folded things, and then picking up the bowl half filled with potato salad, intending to set it in the picnic basket. She didn't quite make the basket, however, for the bowl was large and clumsy and she was using only one hand. It escaped her fingers somehow, and overturned, and his lap was just beneath. That had been the last time he had ever worn his Madagascar slacks.

Her eyes had become so big and so round with dismay that he would have laughed if they had been anyone else's eyes besides Miranda's. You could never laugh at Miranda's eyes; they were too deep and too blue. He had only smiled instead, and said it didn't matter, and wiped his slacks with his handkerchief. Then he had seen her tears, and he had seen her standing there helplessly, tall and gawky, a child really, a lovely child who had become a woman a little too soon, and a beautiful woman too. And something within him had collapsed and a softness had spread all through him, and he had taken her into his arms and said, "Miranda, Miranda. Will you marry me, Miranda?"

The spaceport was far behind and the car was twisting through hills, humming on its overhead rail. It skimmed the treetops of a forest and passed high above a river. Looking down at the river bank, Philip saw his first familiar landmark.

It was nothing more than a pile of crumbled masonry now, overgrown with river weeds and sumac, but once, he knew, yesterday or a hundred years ago, it had been a public villa, and he had spent an afternoon on one of its sun-splashed patios, sipping cocktails and idly watching the white flurries of sails on the blue water below. And thinking of nothing, absolutely nothing —

Except Miranda.

Desperately he forced her out of his mind. It had been all right to think of her a century ago. It wasn't now. He couldn't think of her now because thinking of her tore him apart; because he had a reality to face and if he thought of her the way she had been a hundred years ago he wouldn't be able to face it — he wouldn't be able to search for her in the Cedarville cemetery and put flowers on her grave.

The Rehabilitation director had told him that in a way his sentence had been merciful, merciful by accident of course, and not design. It would have been far worse, the Rehabilitation director had said, for him to have been sentenced for only fifty years and then to have gone home, a man of twenty-seven, to a wife who had just passed seventy-two.

But it was naive to speak of mercy, even accidental mercy, in connection with the age of the Congressional Regime. An age that could condemn a man to suspended animation, tear him forcibly from the moment in time where he belonged, to be resurrected decades later in a moment in time where he did not belong — an age like that had no mercy, had no conception of the meaning of the word. Such an age was brutal, or more brutal, or less brutal; but it was never merciful.

And an age like the present one, while it had rediscovered mercy, was incapable of bestowing it upon a resurrected criminal. It could apologize to him for the cruelty of the preceding age, and it could remunerate him handsomely for the lost years, make him independent for life; but it could not give him back that moment in time that was uniquely his own, it could not bring back the soft smile and the unforgettable laughter of the woman he loved.

It could not obliterate a cemetery lot with a grave that had no right to be there, a grave that had not been there a subjective yesterday ago. It could not erase the words "Miranda Lorring, b. 2024, d. 20 — " or was it "21 — "? — he couldn't know of course, not yet, but he hoped she'd lived long and happily, and that she'd remarried and had children. She had been meant to have children. She had been too full of love not to have had them.

But if she had remarried, then her name wouldn't be Miranda Lorring. It would be Miranda something else, Miranda Green, perhaps, or Miranda Smith; and perhaps she had moved away from Cedarville, perhaps he was going home for nothing. No, not for nothing. He'd at least be able to trace her from Cedarville, trace her to wherever she'd gone to live, find her grave and cover it with forget-me-nots — forget-me-nots had been her favorite flower — and shed a tear on some quiet afternoon, her kiss of a hundred years ago a warm memory on his lips.

He got up in the gently swaying compartment and stepped over to the water cooler and dialed a drink. He had to do something, anything at all, to distract his mind. And the dial was so simple, so child-simple, requiring but the flick of his finger, and no thought, no attention. It could not interrupt the flow of his thoughts even briefly, and the cool taste of the water only gave the flow impetus, sent it churning through his mind, wildly, turning his knees weak, sending him staggering back to the seat, his grief a tight-packed lump swelling upward from his chest to his throat, and the memories, released, flowing freely now, catching him up and carrying him back to the light days, to the bright glorious days, back to his finest moment —

It had been a simple wedding. Miranda had worn blue and Philip had worn his academic dacrons. The Cedarville justice of the peace had performed the ceremony, being very brusque about it, saying the words as fast as he could and even holding out his hand for the fee the moment he had finished. But Philip had not minded. Nothing seemed ugly to him that day, not even the November rain that began to fall when they left the justice's house, not even the fact that he had been unable to obtain leave of absence from the university. The wedding took place on Friday night and that gave them Saturday and Sunday; but two days weren't enough for a trip, and they decided to spend their honeymoon in the little house Philip had bought on Maple Street.

It was an adorable house, Miranda said for the hundredth time when they paused before it in the rain. Philip thought so too. It was set well back from the street and there were two catalpa trees in the front yard, one on either side of the little walk. There was a tiny porch, latticed on each side, and a twentieth-century paneled door.

He had carried her over the threshold, breathing a little hard, for she was quite heavy, and set her down in the middle of the living room. All of his books were there, on built-in shelves on either side of the open fireplace, and Miranda's knickknacks covered the mantel. The new parlor suite matched the mauve-gray curtains.

She had been shy when he kissed her, and he hadn't known quite what to say. Being alone together in their own house involved an intimacy for which neither of them had been prepared, despite all the whispered phrases and stolen kisses, the looks passed in the university corridors, the afternoons shared, and the autumn evenings walking together along leaf-strewn streets. Finally she had said, "I'll make some coffee," and had gone into the kitchen. The first thing she had done was to drop the coffee canister, and there was the coffee, dark against the gleaming floor, and there was Miranda, her blue eyes misted, lovely in her blue dress, a goddess in the room, his goddess; and then a goddess in his arms, soft-lipped and pliant, then warm and suddenly tight-pressed against him, her arms about his neck and her dark hair soft against his face . . .

A village showed in the distance, between wooded hills. It was a deserted village and it had fallen into ruin, but there were remnants of remembered buildings still standing and Philip recognized it as a little town not far from Cedarville.

He had very few memories associated with it, so he experienced but little pain. He experienced fear instead, for he knew that very soon the car would be slowing, that shortly he would be stepping down to the rotting platform of the Cedarville station. And he knew that he would be seeing another deserted village, one with many memories, and he was afraid that he couldn't endure the sight of remembered streets choked with weeds, of beloved houses fallen into decay, of vacant staring windows that long ago had glowed with warmth and life.

The Rehabilitation director had explained about the deserted villages, the emptying cities, the approaching desuetude of Earth. Interstellar travel had given back the dream that interplanetary travel had taken away. Arid Venus and bleak Mars were uninhabitable, and the ice-choked outer planets weren't planets at all, but wheeling glaciers glinting malevolently in pale sunlight. Alpha Centauri 4 was something else, however, and Sirius 41 was a dream come true.

The Sweike drive had delivered man from the dilemma in which his proclivity to overproduce himself had involved him, and Earth was losing its population as fast as ships could be built to transport colonists to the stars.

There were colonies as far out as Vega and before long there would be one in the Arcturus system. Except for the crews who manned the ships, interstellar runs were a one-way proposition. People went out to distant suns and settled in spacious valleys, in virgin timberlands, at the feet of unexploited mountains. They did not return. And it was better that way, the Rehabilitation director had said, for a one way ticket resolved the otherwise irresolvable problem of the Lorentz transformation.

Philip looked out at the tumbled green hills through which the car was passing. It was late afternoon, and long shadows lay coolly in deep valleys. The sun was low in the sky, reddening, and around it cumulus clouds were becoming riotous with color. A wind wrinkled the foliage of new forests, bent the meadow grass on quiet hillsides.

He sighed. Earth was sufficient for him. The stars could give him nothing that he could not find here: a woodland to walk in, a stream to read by, a blue sky to soften his sorrow . . .

The tumbled hills gave way to fields, and the fields ushered in a vaguely familiar stand of cedars. He became aware that the car was slowing, and glancing up at the station screen he saw the nostalgic name spelled out in luminescent letters: CEDARVILLE. He got up numbly and pulled his slender valise from the overhead rack. His chest was tight and he could feel a throbbing in his temple.

Through the window he caught glimpses of outlying houses, of collapsed walls and sagging roofs, of moldering porches and overgrown yards. For a moment he thought that he couldn't go through with it, that he couldn't force himself to go through with it. Then he realized that the car had stopped, and he saw the compartment door slide open and the metallic steps leaf out. He descended the steps without thinking, down to the reinforced platform. His feet had hardly touched the ancient timbers before the car was in motion again, humming swiftly away on its overhead rail, losing itself in the haze of approaching evening.

He stood without moving for a long time. The utter silence that precedes evening in the country was all around him. In the west, the wake of the sun was deepening from orange to scarlet, and the first night shadows were creeping in from the east.

Presently he turned and started up the street that led to the center of the village. He walked slowly, avoiding the clumps of grass that had thrust up through the cracks and crevices in the old macadam, ducking beneath the low limbs of tangled maples. The first houses began to appear, standing forlornly in their jungles of yards. Philip looked at them and they looked back with their sunken staring eyes, and he looked quickly away.

When he reached the point where the street sloped down into the little valley where the village proper lay, he paused. The cemetery was on the opposite slope of the valley and to reach it he would have to pass Maple

Street, the community hall, the university, and half a hundred other remembered places. No matter how much he steeled himself, he would experience the tug of a thousand associations, relive a thousand cherished moments.

Suddenly his strength drained from him and he sat down on his upended valise. What is hell? he asked himself. Hell, he answered himself, is the status reserved for the individuals of a totalitarian state who voice truths contrary to the rigid credo of that state; who write books criticizing the self-appointed guardians of mass man's intellectual boundaries.

Hell is what remains to a man when everything he loves has been taken away . . .

It had been a modest book, rather thin, with an academic jacket done in quiet blue. It had been published during the fall of the same year he had married Miranda, and at first it had made no stir at all. The name of it had been *The New Sanhedrin*.

Then, during the winter, it had caught the collective eye of that subdivision of the Congressional State known as the Subversive Literature Investigative Body, and almost immediately accusations had begun to darken the front pages of newspapers and to resound on the newscasts. The SLIB had wasted no time. It set out to crucify Philip, the way the high priests of the Sanhedrin had set out to crucify Christ over two thousand years ago.

He had not believed they would go so far. In developing his analogy between the Congressional State and the Sanhedrin, demonstrating how both guarded their supreme power by eliminating everyone who deviated from the existent thought-world, he had anticipated publicity, perhaps even notoriety. He had never anticipated imprisonment, trial, and condemnation; he had never dreamed that a political crime could rate the supreme punishment of that new device of inhuman ingenuity which had supplanted the chair and the gas chamber and the gallows — the Suspended Animation Chambers, popularly known as the Deepfreeze.

He had underestimated the power of his own prose and he had underestimated the power of the group his prose had censured. He had forgotten that totalitarian governments are always on the lookout for scapegoats; someone to make an example of, a person with few funds and with no political influence, and preferably a person engaged in one of the professions which the mass of men have always resented. Specifically, an obscure political philosopher.

He had forgotten, but he had remembered. He had remembered on that bleak morning in April, when he heard the puppet judge intone the sentence — "One hundred years' suspended animation for subversive activities against the existent governing body, term to begin September 14, 2046 and to expire September 14, 2146. Gradient cell locks to be employed, so that any attempt by future governing authorities to alleviate said term shall result in the instant death of the prisoner . . . "

The months between April and September had fled like light. Miranda visited him every day, and the two of them tried to force the rest of their lives into fleeting seconds, into precious moments that kept slipping through their fingers. In May they celebrated Philip's birthday, and in July, Miranda's. The celebration in each case consisted of a "Happy Birthday, darling," and a kiss stolen behind the omnipresent guard's back.

And all the while he had seen the words in her eyes, the words she had wanted to say desperately and couldn't say, the words, "I'll wait for you, darling." And he knew that she would have waited if she only could have, that she would have waited gladly; but no woman could wait for you a hundred years, no matter how much she loved you, no matter how faithful she was.

He had seen the words in her eyes in the last moment, had seen them trembling on her lips; and he had known what not being able to say them had done to her. He had seen the pain in the soft lines of her childlike face, in the curve of her sensitive mouth, and he had felt it in her farewell kiss — the anguish, the despair, the hopelessness. And he had stood there woodenly before the elevator, between the guards, unable to cry because tears were inadequate, unable to smile because his lips were stiff, because his cheeks were stone, and his jaw granite.

She was the last thing he saw before the elevator door slid shut, and that was as it should have been. She was standing in front of the Deepfreeze window and behind her, behind the cruel interstices of wire mesh, the blue September sky showed, the exact hue of her eyes. That was the way he had remembered her during the descent to the underground units and along the clammy corridor to his refrigerated cell . . .

The days of dictatorships, whether they be collective or individual, are numbered. The budding dictatorship of Philip's day was no more than an ugly memory now. The Sweike drive had thwarted it, had prevented it from coming into flower. For man's frustrations faded when he found that he could reach the stars, and without frustrations to exploit, no dictatorship can survive.

But the harm small men do outlives them, Philip thought. And if that axiom had been true before the advent of the Deepfreeze, it was doubly true now. With the Deepfreeze man had attained Greek tragedy.

He lit a cigarette and the bright flame of his lighter brought the deepening shadows of the street into bold relief. With a shock he realized that night had fallen, and looking up between the tangled trees he saw the first star.

He stood up and started down the sloping street. As he progressed, more stars came out, bringing the ancient macadam into dim reality. A night wind came up and breathed in the trees, whispered in the wild timothy that had pre-empted tidy lawns, rattled rickety shutters.

He knew that seeing the house would only cause him pain, but it was a pain he had to endure, for homecoming would not be complete until he had stepped upon his own doorstep. So when he came to Maple Street he turned down the overgrown sidewalk, making his way slowly between giant hedges and riotous saplings. For a moment he thought he saw the flicker of a light far down the street, but he could not be sure.

He knew of course that there was very little chance that the house would still be standing — a hundred years is a long time for a house to live — that if it were still standing it would probably be changed beyond recognition, decayed beyond recognition.

And yet, it was still standing and it had not changed at all. It was just the same as it had been when he had left it over a hundred years ago, and there was a light shining in the living room window.

He stood very still in the shambles of the street. The house isn't real, he told himself. It can't be real. I won't believe that it's real until I touch it, until I feel its wood beneath my fingertips, its floor beneath my feet. He walked slowly up the little walk. The front lawn was neatly trimmed and there were two tiny catalpa trees standing in newly turned plots of ground. He mounted the steps to the latticed porch and the steps were solid beneath his feet and gave forth the sound of his footsteps.

He touched the print lock of the door with the tip of his ring finger and the door obediently opened. Diffidently he stepped over the threshold and the door swung gently to behind him.

There was a mauve-gray parlor suite in the living room and it matched the mauve-gray curtains on the windows. Pine knots were ruddy in the open fireplace and his books stood in stately rows on the flanking built-in shelves. Miranda's knickknacks covered the mantel.

His easy chair was drawn up before the fire and his slippers were waiting on the floor beside it. His favorite pipe reposed on a nearby end table and a canister of his favorite tobacco stood beside it. On the arm of the chair was a brand new copy of *The New Sanhedrin*.

He stood immobile just within the door, trying hard to breathe. Then he superimposed a rigid objectivity upon the subjective chaos of his thoughts, and forced himself to see the room as it really was and not as he wished it to be.

The lamp in the window was like the lamp Miranda had kept in the window a hundred years ago, but it wasn't the same lamp. It was a duplication. And the parlor suite was very much like the one that had been in the room a hundred years ago when he had carried Miranda over the threshold, and yet it wasn't quite the same, and neither were the curtains. There were differences in the material, in the design — slight differences, but apparent enough if you looked for them. And his easy chair — that was a duplication too, as were his slippers and his pipe; *The New Sanhedrin.*

The fireplace was the same, and yet not quite the same: the pattern of the bricks was different, the bricks themselves were different, the mantel was different. And the knickknacks on the mantel —

He choked back a sob as he walked over to examine them more closely, for they were not duplications. They were originals and time had been unkind to them. Some of them were broken and a patina of the years covered all of them. They were like children's toys found in an attic on a rainy day . . .

He bent over his books, and they were originals too. He pulled one from the shelf and opened it. The yellowed pages betrayed the passage of the years and he replaced it tenderly. Then he noticed the diary on the topmost shelf.

He took it down with trembling hands, opened and turned its pages. When he saw the familiar handwriting, he knew whose diary it was and suddenly his knees were weak and he could not stand, and he collapsed into the easy chair before the fire.

Numbly he turned the pages to the first entry. It was dated September 15, 2046 —

I walked down the steps, the stone slabs of steps that front the tomb in which men are buried alive, and I walked through the streets of the city.

I walked through the streets, the strange streets, past hordes of indifferent people. Gradually I became aware of the passing hours, the fleeting minutes, the swift-flying seconds; and each second became an unbearable pain, each minute a dull agony, each hour a crushing eternity . . .

I do not know how I came to the spaceport. Perhaps God directed my footsteps there. But the moment I saw the shimmering spires of the new ships pointing into the September sky, everything I had ever read concerning the Sweike drive coalesced blindingly in my mind, and I knew what I had to do.

A clock which is in motion moves slower than a stationary clock. The difference is imperceptible at ordinary velocities, but when the speed of light is approached, the difference is enormous.

The Sweike drive approaches the speed of light. It approaches the speed of light as closely as it can be approached, without both men and ship becoming pure energy.

A clock on a ship employing the Sweike drive would barely move at all —

Not daring to believe, he skipped a page —

September 18, 2046 — They tell me it will take two years! Two of my sweet, my precious years to become a space-line stewardess! But there's no other way, no other way at all, and my application is already in. I know they will accept it — with everyone clamoring for the stars the need for ship's personnel is —

His hands were shaking uncontrollably and the pages escaped from his fingers, days, months, years fluttering wildly by. He halted them finally —

June 3, 2072 (Sirius 41) — I have measured time by many moving clocks, and moving clocks are kind. But when planetfall arrives, stationary clocks take over, and stationary clocks are not kind. You wait in some forsaken port for the return run and you count each minute and resent its passage bitterly. For over the decades, the minutes add together into months and years and you are afraid that despite the moving clocks, you will be too old after all —

The pages escaped again and he stopped them at the final entry —

February 9, 2081 — Today I was officially notified that my application for the Arcturus run has been accepted! I have been in a kind of ecstatic trance ever since, dreaming and planning, because I *can* dream and plan now! Now I *know* that I shall see my beloved again, and I shall wear a white gardenia in my hair, and the perfume he likes the best, and I shall have our house rebuilt and everything in it restored — there'll be plenty of time if the sixty-five-year estimate is correct; and when my beloved is released I shall be there waiting to take him in my arms, and though I shall not be as young as he remembers me, I shall not be old either. And the lonely years between the stars shall not have been in vain —
  For I have only one love. I shall never have another.

The words blurred on the page and Philip let the diary slip from his fingers to the arm of the chair. "Miranda," he whispered.
  He stood up. "Miranda," he said.
  The house was silent. "Miranda!" he called. "Miranda!"
  There was no answer. He went from the living room to the bedroom. The bedroom was the way it had been a hundred years ago except that it was empty now. Empty of Miranda.
  He returned to the living room and went into the kitchen. The kitchen was the same too, but there was no Miranda in it. He switched on the light and stared at the porcelain sink, the chrome stove, the white cupboards, the gleaming utility table —
  There was a hand mirror lying on the table, and beside it was a crumpled gardenia. He picked up the gardenia and it was cool and soft in his hand. He held it to his nostrils and breathed its fresh scent. There was another scent mingled with it, a delicate fragrant scent. He recognized it immediately as Miranda's perfume.
  Suddenly he could not breathe, and he ran out of the house and into the darkness. He saw the light flickering at the end of the street then, and he walked toward it with unbelieving steps. The community hall grew slowly out of the darkness and the light became many lights, became bright windows.

From somewhere in the surrounding shadows he heard the humming of a portable generator.

When he climbed the steps a hundred years flew away. There was no 77c supper of course, and the hall showed unmistakable signs of age, despite the fact that it had been recently remodeled. But there was Miranda. Miranda standing by a lonely table. Miranda crying. A more mature Miranda, with lines showing on her face where no lines had showed before, but light lines, adorable lines . . .

He realized why she had not met him at the Deepfreeze. She had been afraid, afraid that the moving clocks had not moved slowly enough after all; and she must have decided to meet him at the house instead, for she knew he would come home. She must have heard the monorail car pull in, must have known he was on his way —

Suddenly he remembered the mirror and the crumpled gardenia.

Silly girl, lovely girl — His eyes misted and he felt the tears run down his cheeks. He stumbled into the room, and she came hesitantly forward to meet him, her face beautiful with the new years. A goddess in the room, a mature goddess, the awkwardness gone forever, the schoolgirlish charm left somewhere in the abysses between the stars; his goddess — and then a goddess in his arms, warm and suddenly tight-pressed against him, her dark hair soft against his face, her voice whispering in his ear, across the years, across the timeless infinities, "Welcome home, darling. Welcome home."

M

The Snowball Effect

KATHERINE MACLEAN

"All right," I said, "what *is* sociology good for?"

Wilton Caswell, Ph.D., was head of my sociology department, and right then he was mad enough to chew nails. On the office wall behind him were three or four framed documents in Latin that were supposed to be signs of great learning, but I didn't care at that moment if he papered the walls with his degrees. I had been appointed dean and president to see to it that the university made money. I had a job to do, and I meant to do it.

He bit off each word with great restraint: "Sociology is the study of social institutions, Mr. Halloway."

I tried to make him understand my position. "Look, it's the big-money men who are supposed to be contributing to the support of this college. To them, sociology sounds like socialism — nothing can sound worse than that

— and an institution is where they put Aunt Maggy when she began collecting Wheaties in a stamp album. We can't appeal to them that way. Come on now." I smiled condescendingly, knowing it would irritate him. "What are you doing that's worth anything?"

He glared at me, his white hair bristling and his nostrils dilated like a war-horse about to whinny. I can say one thing for them — these scientists and professors always keep themselves well under control. He had a book in his hand and I was expecting him to throw it, but he spoke instead.

"This department's analysis of institutional accretion, by the use of open system mathematics, has been recognized as an outstanding and valuable contribution to — "

The words were impressive, whatever they meant, but this still didn't sound like anything that would pull in money. I interrupted, "Valuable in what way?"

He sat down on the edge of his desk thoughtfully, apparently recovering from the shock of being asked to produce something solid for his position, and ran his eyes over the titles of the books that lined his office walls.

"Well, sociology has been valuable to business in initiating worker efficiency and group motivation studies, which they now use in management decisions. And, of course, since the depression, Washington has been using sociological studies of employment, labor, and standards of living as a basis for its general policies of — "

I stopped him with both raised hands. "Please, Professor Caswell! That would hardly be a recommendation. Washington, the New Deal, and the present administration are somewhat touchy subjects to the men I have to deal with. They consider its value debatable, if you know what I mean. If they got the idea that sociology professors are giving advice and guidance — No, we have to stick to brass tacks and leave Washington out of this. What, specifically, has the work of this specific department done that would make it as worthy to receive money as — say, a heart disease research fund?"

He began to tap the corner of his book absently on the desk, watching me. "Fundamental research doesn't show immediate effects, Mr. Halloway, but its value is recognized."

I smiled and took out my pipe. "All right, tell me about it. Maybe I'll recognize its value."

Dr. Caswell smiled back tightly. He knew his department was at stake. The other departments were popular with donors and pulled in gift money by scholarships and fellowships, and supported their professors and graduate students by research contracts with the government and industry. Caswell had to show a way to make his own department popular — or else. I couldn't fire him directly, of course, but there are ways of doing it indirectly.

He laid down his book and ran a hand over his ruffled hair.

"Institutions — organizations, that is — " his voice became more resonant; like most professors, when he had to explain something he instinctively slipped into his platform lecture mannerisms, and began to deliver an essay — "have certain tendencies built into the way they happen to have been organized, which cause them to expand or contract without reference to the needs they were founded to serve."

He was becoming flushed with the pleasure of explaining his subject. "All through the ages, it has been a matter of wonder and dismay to men that a simple organization — such as a church to worship in, or a delegation of weapons to a warrior class merely for defense against an outside enemy — will either grow insensately and extend its control until it is a tyranny over their whole lives, or, like other organizations set up to serve a vital need, will tend to repeatedly dwindle and vanish, and have to be painfully rebuilt.

"The reason can be traced to little quirks in the way they were organized, a matter of positive and negative power feedbacks. Such simple questions as, 'Is there a way a holder of authority in this organization can use the power available to him to increase his power?' provide the key. But it still could not be handled until the complex questions of interacting motives and long-range accumulations of minor effects could somehow be simplified and formulated. In working on the problem, I found that the mathematics of open system, as introduced to biology by Ludwig von Bertalanffy and George Kreezer, could be used as a base that would enable me to develop a specifically social mathematics, expressing the human factors of intermeshing authority and motives in simple formulas.

"By these formulations, it is possible to determine automatically the amount of growth and period of life of any organization. The UN, to choose an unfortunate example, is a shrinker-type organization. Its monetary support is not in the hands of those who personally benefit by its governmental activities, but, instead, in the hands of those who would personally lose by any extension and encroachment of its authority on their own. Yet by the use of formula analysis — "

"That's theory," I said. "How about proof?"

"My equations are already being used in the study of limited-size federal corporations. Washington — "

I held up my palm again. "Please, not that nasty word again. I mean, where else has it been put into operation? Just a simple demonstration, something to show that it works, that's all."

He looked away from me thoughtfully, picked up the book and began to tap it on the desk again. It had some unreadable title and his name on it in gold letters. I got the distinct impression again that he was repressing an urge to hit me with it.

He spoke quietly. "All right, I'll give you a demonstration. Are you willing to wait six months?"

"Certainly, if you can show me something at the end of that time."

Reminded of time, I glanced at my watch and stood up.

"Could we discuss this over lunch?" he asked.

"I wouldn't mind hearing more, but I'm having lunch with some executors of a millionaire's will. They have to be convinced that by 'furtherance of research into human ills,' he meant that the money should go to research fellowships for postgraduate biologists at the university, rather than to a medical foundation."

"I see you have your problems, too," Caswell said, conceding me nothing. He extended his hand with a chilly smile. "Well, good afternoon, Mr. Halloway. I'm glad we had this talk."

I shook hands and left him standing there, sure of his place in the progress of science and the respect of his colleagues, yet seething inside because I, the president and dean, had boorishly demanded that he produce something tangible.

I frankly didn't give a hoot if he blew his lid. My job isn't easy. For a crumb of favorable publicity and respect in the newspapers and an annual ceremony in a silly costume, I spend the rest of the year going hat in hand, asking politely for money at everyone's door, like a well-dressed panhandler, and trying to manage the university on the dribble I get. As far as I was concerned, a department had to support itself or be cut down to what student tuition pays for, which is a handful of overcrowded courses taught by an assistant lecturer. Caswell had to make it work or get out.

But the more I thought about it, the more I wanted to hear what he was going to do for a demonstration.

At lunch three days later, while we were waiting for our order, he opened a small notebook. "Ever hear of feedback effects?"

"Not enough to have it clear."

"You know the snowball effect, though."

"Sure, start a snowball rolling downhill and it grows."

"Well, now — " He wrote a short line of symbols on a blank page and turned the notebook around for me to inspect it. "Here's the formula for the snowball process. It's the basic general growth formula — covers everything."

It was a row of little symbols arranged like an algebra equation. One was a concentric spiral going up, like a cross-section of a snowball rolling in snow. That was a growth sign.

I hadn't expected to understand the equation, but it was almost as clear as a sentence. I was impressed and slightly intimidated by it. He had already explained enough so that I knew that, if he was right, here was the growth of the Catholic Church and the Roman Empire, the conquests of Alexander and the spread of the smoking habit and the change and rigidity of the unwritten law of styles.

"Is it really as simple as that?" I asked.

"You notice," he said, "that when it becomes too heavy for the cohesion strength of snow, it breaks apart. Now in human terms — "

The chops and mashed potatoes and peas arrived.

"Go on," I urged.

He was deep in the symbology of human motives and the equations of human behavior in groups. After running through a few different types of grower- and shrinker-type organizations, we came back to the snowball, and decided to run the test by making something grow.

"You add the motives," he said, "and the equation will translate them into organization."

"How about a good selfish reason for the ins to drag others into the group — some sort of bounty on new members, a cut of their membership fee?" I suggested uncertainly, feeling slightly foolish. "And maybe a reason why the members would lose if any of them resigned, and some indirect way they could use to force each other to stay in."

"The first is the chain letter principle," he nodded. "I've got that. The other . . . " He put the symbols through some mathematical manipulation so that a special grouping appeared in the middle of the equation. "That's it."

Since I seemed to have the right idea, I suggested some more, and he added some, and juggled them around in different patterns. We threw out a few that would have made the organization too complicated, and finally worked out an idyllically simple and deadly little organization setup where joining had all the temptation of buying sweepstakes tickets, going in deeper was as easy as hanging around a race track, and getting out was like trying to pull free from a Malayan thumb trap. We put our heads closer together and talked lower, picking the best place for the demonstration.

"Abington?"

"How about Watashaw? I have some student sociological surveys of it already. We can pick a suitable group from that."

"This demonstration has got to be convincing. We'd better pick a little group that no one in his right mind would expect to grow."

"There should be a suitable club — "

Picture Professor Caswell, head of the Department of Sociology, and with him the president of the university, leaning across the table toward each other, sipping coffee and talking in conspiratorial tones over something they were writing in a notebook.

That was us.

"Ladies," said the skinny female chairman of the Watashaw Sewing Circle. "Today we have guests." She signaled for us to rise, and we stood up, bowing to polite applause and smiles. "Professor Caswell, and Professor Smith." (My alias.) "They are making a survey of the methods and duties of the clubs of Watashaw."

We sat down to another ripple of applause and slightly wider smiles, and then the meeting of the Watashaw Sewing Circle began. In five minutes I began to feel sleepy.

There were only about thirty people there, and it was a small room, not the halls of Congress, but they discussed their business of collecting and repairing second-hand clothing for charity with the same endless boring parliamentary formality.

I pointed out to Caswell the member I thought would be the natural leader, a tall, well-built woman in a green suit, with conscious gestures and a resonant, penetrating voice, and then went into a half doze while Caswell stayed awake beside me and wrote in his notebook. After a while the resonant voice roused me to attention for a moment. It was the tall woman holding the floor over some collective dereliction of the club. She was being scathing.

I nudged Caswell and murmured, "Did you fix it so that a shover has a better chance of getting into office than a nonshover?"

"I think there's a way they could find for it," Caswell whispered back, and went to work on his equation again. "Yes, several ways to bias the elections."

"Good. Point them out tactfully to the one you select. Not as if she'd use such methods, but just as an example of the reason why only *she* can be trusted with initiating the change. Just mention all the personal advantages an unscrupulous person could have."

He nodded, keeping a straight and sober face as if we were exchanging admiring remarks about the techniques of clothes repairing, instead of conspiring.

After the meeting, Caswell drew the tall woman in the green suit aside and spoke to her confidentially, showing her the diagram of organization we had drawn up. I saw the responsive glitter in the woman's eyes and knew she was hooked.

We left the diagram of organization and our typed copy of the new bylaws with her and went off soberly, as befitted two social science experimenters. We didn't start laughing until our car passed the town limits and began the climb for University Heights.

If Caswell's equations meant anything at all, we had given that sewing circle more growth drives than the Roman Empire.

Four months later I had time out from a very busy schedule to wonder how the test was coming along. Passing Caswell's office, I put my head in. He looked up from a student research paper he was correcting.

"Caswell, about that sewing club business — I'm beginning to feel the suspense. Could I get an advance report on how it's coming?"

"I'm not following it. We're supposed to let it run the full six months."

"But I'm curious. Could I get in touch with that woman — what's her name?"

"Searles. Mrs. George Searles."

"Would that change the results?"

"Not in the slightest. If you want to graph the membership rise, it should be going up in a log curve, probably doubling every so often."

I grinned. "If it's not rising, you're fired."

He grinned back. "If it's not rising, you won't have to fire me — I'll burn my books and shoot myself."

I returned to my office and put in a call to Watashaw.

While I was waiting for the phone to be answered, I took a piece of graph paper and ruled it off into six sections, one for each month. After the phone had rung in the distance for a long time, a servant answered with a bored drawl, "Mrs. Searles's residence."

I picked up a red gummed star and licked it.

"Mrs. Searles, please."

"She's not in just now. Could I take a message?"

I placed the star at the thirty line in the beginning of the first section. Thirty members they'd started with.

"No, thanks. Could you tell me when she'll be back?"

"Not until dinner. She's at the meetin'."

"The sewing club?" I asked.

"No, *sir,* not that thing. There isn't any sewing club any more, not for a long time. She's at the Civic Welfare meeting."

Somehow I hadn't expected anything like that.

"Thank you," I said and hung up, and after a moment noticed I was holding a box of red gummed stars in my hand. I closed it and put it down on top of the graph of membership in the sewing circle. No more members . . .

Poor Caswell. The bet between us was ironclad. He wouldn't let me back down on it even if I wanted to. He'd probably quit before I put through the first slow move to fire him. His professional pride would be shattered, sunk without a trace. I remembered what he said about shooting himself. It had seemed funny to both of us at the time, but . . . What a mess *that* would make for the university.

I had to talk to Mrs. Searles. Perhaps there was some outside reason why the club had disbanded. Perhaps it had not just died.

I called back. "This is Professor Smith," I said, giving the alias I had used before. "I called a few minutes ago. When did you say Mrs. Searles will return?"

"About six-thirty or seven o'clock."

Five hours to wait.

And what if Caswell asked me what I had found out in the meantime? I didn't want to tell him anything until I had talked it over with that woman Searles first.

"Where is this Civic Welfare meeting?"

She told me.

Five minutes later I was in my car, heading for Watashaw, driving considerably faster than my usual speed and keeping a careful watch for highway patrol cars as the speedometer climbed.

The town meeting hall and theater was a big place, probably with lots of small rooms for different clubs. I went in through the center door and found myself in the huge central hall where some sort of rally was being held. A political-type rally — you know, cheers and chants, with bunting already down on the floor, people holding banners, and plenty of enthusiasm and excitement in the air. Someone was making a speech up on the platform. Most of the people there were women.

I wondered how the Civic Welfare League could dare hold its meeting at the same time as a political rally that could pull its members away. The group with Mrs. Searles was probably holding a shrunken and almost memberless meeting somewhere in an upper room.

There probably was a side door that would lead upstairs.

While I glanced around, a pretty girl usher put a printed bulletin in my hand, whispering, "Here's one of the new copies." As I attempted to hand it back, she retreated. "Oh, you can keep it. It's the new one. Everyone's supposed to have it. We've just printed up six thousand copies to make sure there'll be enough to last."

The tall woman on the platform had been making a driving, forceful speech about some plans for rebuilding Watashaw's slum section. It began to penetrate my mind dimly as I glanced down at the bulletin in my hands.

"Civic Welfare League of Watashaw. The United Organization of Church and Secular Charities." That's what it said. Below began the rules of membership.

I looked up. The speaker, with a clear, determined voice and conscious, forceful gestures, had entered the homestretch of her speech, an appeal to the civic pride of all citizens of Watashaw.

"With a bright and glorious future — potentially without poor and without uncared-for ill — potentially with no ugliness, no vistas which are not beautiful — the best people in the best-planned town in the country — the jewel of the United States."

She paused and then leaned forward intently, striking her clenched hand on the speaker's stand with each word for emphasis.

"All we need is more members. Now get out there and recruit!"

I finally recognized Mrs. Searles, as a sudden answering blast of sound half deafened me. The crowd was chanting at the top of its lungs: "Recruit, Recruit!"

Mrs. Searles stood still at the speaker's table and behind her, seated in a row of chairs, was a group that was probably the board of directors. It was mostly women, and the women began to look vaguely familiar, as if they could be members of the sewing circle.

I put my lips close to the ear of the pretty usher while I turned over the stiff printed bulletin on a hunch. "How long has the League been organized?" On the back of the bulletin was a constitution.

She was cheering with the crowd, her eyes sparkling. "I don't know," she answered between cheers. "I only joined two days ago. Isn't it wonderful?"

I went into the quiet outer air and got into my car with my skin prickling. Even as I drove away, I could hear them. They were singing some kind of organization song with the tune of "Marching Through Georgia."

Even at the single glance I had given it, the constitution looked exactly like the one we had given the Watashaw Sewing Circle.

All I told Caswell when I got back was that the sewing circle had changed its name and the membership seemed to be rising.

Next day, after calling Mrs. Searles, I placed some red stars on my graph for the first three months. They made a nice curve, rising more steeply as it reached the fourth month. They had picked up their first increase in membership simply by amalgamating with all the other types of charity organizations in Watashaw, changing the club name with each fusion, but keeping the same constitution — the constitution with the bright promise of advantages as long as there were always new members being brought in.

By the fifth month, the League had added a mutual baby-sitting service and had induced the local school board to add a nursery school to the town service, so as to free more women for League activity. But charity must have been completely organized by then, and expansion had to be in other directions.

Some real estate agents evidently had been drawn into the whirlpool early, along with their ideas. The slum improvement plans began to blossom and take on a tinge of real estate planning later in the month.

The first day of the sixth month, a big two-page spread appeared in the local paper of a mass meeting which had approved a full-fledged scheme for slum clearance of Watashaw's shack-town section, plus plans for rehousing, civic building, and rezoning. *And* good prospects for attracting some new industries to the town, industries which had already been contacted and seemed interested by the privileges offered.

And with all this, an arrangement for securing and distributing to the club members *alone* most of the profit that would come to the town in the form of a rise in the price of building sites and a boom in the building industry. The profit-distributing arrangement was the same one that had been built into the organization plan for the distribution of the small profits of membership fees and honorary promotions. It was becoming an openly profitable business. Membership was rising more rapidly now.

By the second week of the sixth month, news appeared in the local paper that the club had filed an application to incorporate itself as the Watashaw Mutual Trade and Civic Development Corporation, and all the local real estate promoters had finished joining en masse. The Mutual Trade part sounded to me as if the Chamber of Commerce was on the point of being pulled in with them, ideas, ambitions, and all.

I chuckled while reading the next page of the paper, on which a local politician was reported as having addressed the club with a long, flowery oration on their enterprise, charity, and civic spirit. He had been made an honorary member. If he allowed himself to be made a *full* member with its contractual obligations and its lures, if the politicians went into this, too . . .

I laughed, filing the newspaper with the other documents on the Watashaw test. These proofs would fascinate any businessman with the sense to see where his bread was buttered. A businessman is constantly dealing with organizations, including his own, and finding them either inert, cantankerous, or both. Caswell's formula could be a handle to grasp them with. Gratitude alone would bring money into the university in carload lots.

The end of the sixth month came. The test was over and the end reports were spectacular. Caswell's formulas were proven to the hilt.

After reading the last newspaper reports, I called him up.

"Perfect, Wilt, *perfect!* I can use this Watashaw thing to get you so many fellowships and scholarships and grants for your department that you'll think it's snowing money!"

He answered somewhat disinterestedly, "I've been busy working with students on their research papers and marking tests — not following the Watashaw business at all, I'm afraid. You say the demonstration went well and you're satisfied?"

He was definitely putting on a chill. We were friends now, but obviously he was still peeved whenever he was reminded that I had doubted that his theory could work. And he was using its success to rub my nose in the realization that I had been wrong. A man with a string of degrees after his name is just as human as anyone else. I had needled him pretty hard that first time.

"I'm satisfied," I acknowledged. "I was wrong. The formulas work beautifully. Come over and see my file of documents on it if you want a boost for your ego. Now let's see the formula for stopping it."

He sounded cheerful again. "I didn't complicate that organization with negatives. I wanted it to *grow*. It falls apart naturally when it stops growing for more than two months. It's like the great stock boom before an economic crash. Everyone in it is prosperous as long as the prices just keep going up and new buyers come into the market, but they all knew what would happen if it stopped growing. You remember, we built in as one of the incentives that the members know they are going to lose if membership stops growing. Why, if I tried to stop it now, they'd cut my throat."

I remembered the drive and frenzy of the crowd in the one early meeting I had seen. They probably would.

"No," he continued. "We'll just let it play out to the end of its tether and die of old age."

"When will that be?"

"It can't grow past the female population of the town. There are only so many women in Watashaw, and some of them don't like sewing."

The graph on the desk before me began to look sinister. Surely Caswell must have made some provision for —

"You underestimate their ingenuity," I said into the phone. "Since they wanted to expand they didn't stick to sewing. They went from general charity to social welfare schemes to something that's pretty close to an incorporated government. The name is now the Watashaw Mutual Trade and Civic Development Corporation, and they're filing an application to change it to Civic Property Pool and Social Dividend, membership contractual, open to all. That social dividend sounds like a technocrat climbed on the bandwagon, eh?"

While I spoke, I carefully added another red star to the curve above the thousand-member level, checking with the newspaper that still lay open on my desk. The curve was definitely some sort of log curve now, growing more rapidly with each increase.

"Leaving out practical limitations for a moment, where does the formula say it will stop?" I asked.

"When you run out of people to join it. But after all, there are only so many people in Watashaw. It's a pretty small town."

"They've opened a branch office in New York," I said carefully into the phone, a few weeks later.

With my pencil, very carefully, I extended the membership curve from where it was then.

After the next doubling, the curve went almost straight up and off the page.

Allowing for a lag of contagion from one nation to another, depending on how much their citizens intermingled, I gave the rest of the world about twelve years.

There was a long silence while Caswell probably drew the same graph in his own mind. Then he laughed weakly. "Well, you asked me for a demonstration."

That was as good an answer as any. We got together and had lunch in a bar, if you can call it lunch. The movement we started will expand by hook or by crook, by seduction or by bribery or by propaganda or by conquest, but it will expand. And maybe a total world government will be a fine thing — until it hits the end of its rope in twelve years or so.

What happens then, I don't know.

But I don't want anyone to pin that on me. From now on, if anyone asks me, I've never heard of Watashaw.

mat/ter trans/mit/ters — machines that transmit objects through space to another physical location much like radio waves. Explanations of such mechanisms usually suggest they operate by instantaneously decomposing things into atoms and transmitting them, much like radio waves, to a receiver which then quickly reconstructs them. However, such machines might also be hypothesized to work by punching temporary doorways through a higher-dimensional space. A closely related concept is "teleporting," an imaginary psychic ability to transmit oneself from one place to another by the simple use of will power.

The Santa Claus Problem

J. W. SCHUTZ

Being, like most men of science, of an enquiring mind, I have recently turned my attention to what I shall call, for reasons which will immediately become obvious, the Santa Claus Problem.

The parameters of the problem are well known. I repeat them here purely for reference. On the night of December 24 of each year, a personage, variously known as Father Christmas, Saint Nicholas, or Santa Claus, visits, by means of a flying device drawn by a team of reindeer, each household on Earth where there are children, descends through the chimney of the house and leaves presents in stockings (mainly in North America) or in shoes (principally in Europe) for the said children. In certain instances he is also said to take the time for last-minute decoration of a Christmas tree, but, since in the majority of cases the tree is predecorated, this factor may be ignored.

Before proceeding to its solution I have considered it advisable to establish the reality and indeed the pertinence of the problem itself. This turned out to be relatively simple, since for during more than fifteen hundred years countless millions of individuals have agreed that the phenomenon does occur and have described with astonishing consistency the flying device, with the appearance of a miniature sleigh, and its team of animals, as well as the' appearance, and even the costume, of Claus himself. There can be no doubt therefore that the problem is factually based.

Next I considered the total extent of the problem. The population of Earth is estimated at 4.2×10^9 individuals. The average family consists of 2 parents and 2.7 children. In order to remain on the conservative side in what follows, it must be assumed, then, that each visited household contains 5 persons and that there are thus $(4.2 \div 5) \times 10^9$ such households or 8.4×10^8. If we further neglect, in the interests of conservatism, those families among the Hottentots, the Maoris, Polynesians, etc., not visited by Claus (either because of their refusal to build fireplaces with chimneys or for other reasons) the number of visited households can reasonably be reduced by an order of magnitude, leaving us with 8.4×10^7 households.

The following step is of crucial importance and one which required many hours of painstaking and timeconsuming research: considering every dwelling on Earth with a fireplace connected to the roof by a chimney, what is the average distance between them?

In the residential sections of most cities, the distance is small — a matter of a few yards — but in rural areas, and considering the average distance between cities, the distance may attain several miles. I will not detail my methods in this article, but the enquiring reader may obtain a complete description of them from my thesis, published February 30, 1916 by the University Press of Doowahdiddy, Georgia. It turns out, however, that the average distance is approximately 104.957 yards. Again in order to remain on the conservative side, the fraction may be dropped and the distance set at 104 yards.

Now, multiplying 8.4×10^7 (the number of visited households) by 104 (the number of yards between them) we obtain 8.736×10^9 yards or 4.963×10^6 miles. This, then, is the average distance traveled by Claus and his team during the night of December 24.

I next considered the time available to cover this distance. It is not, as might at first be supposed, the period covering the hours of darkness at any single locality — that is to say between 10:00 P.M., and 4:00 A.M. — but, since the entire globe is under consideration, twenty-four hours plus two additional hours at the start of the journey and four more at its end, a total of thirty hours.

Dividing the distance covered by the time available we have a velocity of 4,936,000/30 or 164,533.33 miles per hour. This is not only many times greater than the speed of sound but indeed greater than the escape velocity from Earth itself. There can be no doubt therefore that Claus and his team are the fastest-moving living creatures on Earth if not in the entire universe.

An interesting sidelight on the problem reveals that Claus has only 1.286×10^{-3} second to descend each chimney, place presents in stockings, regain his vehicle, and reach the next visited household.

Assuming that the given parameters are accurate and that the above calculations have been carefully carried out, we may now move on to our conclusions.

There are three possibilities:

(1) Claus and his reindeer are a myth and the children's parents are responsible for the appearance of presents on Christmas morning.

(2) Being physically unable to accomplish his self-appointed task alone, Claus has recruited a vast number of helpers.

(3) Claus does indeed personally visit and leave presents at 8.4×10^7 households, but does so by means as yet undiscovered by science.

Let us examine these hypotheses one by one.

(1) The myth. There is some small amount of support for this hypothesis in the fact that for months before the fatal date the stores are jammed with harried adults buying a wide variety of semi-useful as well as totally useless presents including "educational" toys. There is also the occurrence of widespread cynicism among the older children. The myth possibility must be ruled out, however, not only on the basis of the facts set forth in paragraph three of this article, but also on the grounds that the shopping adults are in 98.753 percent of the time buying presents for each other, and on the far more important grounds that the children invariably receive presents which no sane parent would willingly purchase for them, such as various cutting tools, air rifles, candid cameras, and the like.

(2) The helpers theory. Here too there is a modicum of support for this hypothesis. It is widely believed, for example, that Claus has recruited the services of a large number of gnomes who spend their time during the year manufacturing the vast numbers of toys required, receiving, classifying, and tabulating correspondence from children, etc. While there may be some basis for this belief, this researcher has been completely unable to uncover any evidence that any of the gnomes accompany Claus on his annual voyage or make such voyages in his stead. If the gnomes exist, they cannot be numerous since their presence, even at the North Pole, would have been discovered before now. As for their making millions of individual voyages disguised as Claus himself, they would, if operating at normal subsonic speeds, be so numerous that they would surely by now have been admitted to membership in the United Nations and would be wooed by both the US and the USSR because of their highly strategic location and their one-night potential for espionage. The helpers theory too must then be ruled out.

Which brings us inevitably to the third possibility.

(3) Claus visits 8.4×10^7 households in a period of thirty hours but does so by as yet unknown means.

The support for the first part of this hypothesis is overwhelming. (*Viz.* paragraph 3 at the beginning of this paper and the giving of such presents as chemistry sets and little nurse outfits.) There are certain objections, however, to the physical means of accomplishing the objective, at least by means now known to science.

Consider first the velocity of the vehicle drawn by these admittedly remarkable reindeer. At 164,533 miles per hour the energy requirements would be astronomical. Since the fuel is tundra moss, notably low in caloric value, this single night's work would require the northern hemisphere's tundra to be totally stripped to a depth of three feet. As a corollary, several millimeters of reindeer excrement would be distributed over the whole surface of the globe. Nothing of the sort is known to occur. Similarly, with one household visited every 1.3 thousandths of a second at supersonic speeds, the night of December 24 would be made hideous with a continuous thunder of supersonic booms, making sleep on this traditionally peaceful night impossible.

Since the appearance once a year of Claus's presents in millions of households is an unquestioned fact and since it is logically incontrovertible that Claus and Claus alone is responsible, we must inevitably conclude that Claus exists and that he has done so for at least fifteen hundred years.

It seems equally clear — given the considerations concerning speed and energy consumption mentioned two paragraphs previous — that Claus must have at his disposal some other means of delivery than physically visiting each several home.

We are thus inexorably led to the following conclusions:

(a) That the entity variously known as Claus, Nicholas, etc., is an extraterrestrial as evidenced by his great age.

(b) That this entity possesses scientific abilities well beyond those of twentieth-century savants and that at least one of his devices is a matter transmitter.

In support of conclusion (b), I offer the following tentative hypothesis.

It is quite easily conceivable that Claus is capable of putting his vehicle into a circumpolar orbit, making one circuit every ninety-plus minutes. Indeed modern man is himself able to perform this feat. In the thirty hours available on the night of December 24 he would have time to make twenty orbits, covering every locality on the face of the globe. It is also easily within the realms of possibility that the Claus-entity possesses a computer capable of recording the locale of every one of eighty-odd million homes having children. Given, then, a matter transmitter, he makes his leisurely twenty orbits and, with the help of his in-flight computer, leaves behind him a blanket of millions of useless or actually dangerous toys, silently and instantaneously appearing on millions of hearths. I will go further. It is well known that Christmas toys are usually destroyed by their recipients no later than the beginning of summer vacations, at which time the last trace of them disappears. It is my contention that the Claus-entity makes a second trip at this time, recovers the wreckage of his gifts and recycles them in preparation for the following December.

It has been said, with justice, that once a thing is known to be possible, men will do it. Being firmly persuaded that a device equivalent to a matter transmitter is not only possible but that one actually exists, I am devoting my future scientific efforts to the construction of one. I will even go so far as to hint that I have several promising leads, papers concerning which I plan to publish through the University Press of Doowahdiddy some time within the next twelve months, and, hopefully, before December 24 of next year.

mu/sic — sound organized so as to draw a pleasing response from listeners. Music is one of mankind's oldest creations and pleasures and is also a multi-billion dollar industry annually. It is safe to say that music has brought people from different cultures closer together, at least in spirit. Science fiction stories about music can be found in the anthologies mentioned under *art,* and in *The Metallic Muse,* a collection of short stories by Lloyd Biggle, Jr. (Doubleday, 1972).

The Ship Who Sang

ANNE MCCAFFREY

She was born a thing and as such would be condemned if she failed to pass the encephalograph test required of all newborn babies. There was always the possibility that though the limbs were twisted, the mind was not, that though the ears would hear only dimly, the eyes see vaguely, the mind behind them was receptive and alert.

The electroencephalogram was entirely favorable, unexpectedly so, and the news was brought to the waiting, grieving parents. There was the final, harsh decision: to give their child euthanasia or permit it to become an encapsulated "brain," a guiding mechanism in any one of a number of curious professions. As such, their offspring would suffer no pain, live a comfortable existence in a metal shell for several centuries, performing unusual service to Central Worlds.

She lived and was given a name, Helva. For her first three vegetable months she waved her crabbed claws, kicked weakly with her clubbed feet, and enjoyed the usual routine of the infant. She was not alone for there were three other such children in the big city's special nursery. Soon they all were removed to Central Laboratory School where their delicate transformation began.

One of the babies died in the initial transferral, but of Helva's "class," seventeen thrived in the metal shells. Instead of kicking feet, Helva's neural responses started her wheels; instead of grabbing with hands, she manipulated mechanical extensions. As she matured, more and more neural synapses would be adjusted to operate other mechanisms that went into the maintenance and running of a space ship. For Helva was destined to be the "brain" half of a scout ship, partnered with a man or a woman, whichever she chose, as the mobile half. She would be among the elite of her kind. Her initial intelligence tests registered above normal and her adaptation index was unusually high. As long as her development within her shell lived up to expectations, and there were no side effects from the pituitary tinkering, Helva would live a rewarding, rich, and unusual life, a far cry from what she would have faced as an ordinary, "normal" being.

However, no diagram of her brain patterns, no early IQ tests recorded certain essential facts about Helva that Central must eventually learn. They would have to bide their official time and see, trusting that the massive doses of shell psychology would suffice her, too, as the necessary bulwark against her unusual confinement and the pressures of her profession. A ship run by a human brain could not run rogue or insane with the power and resources Central had to build into their scout ships. Brain ships were, of course, long past the experimental stages. Most babes survived the techniques of pituitary manipulation that kept their bodies small, eliminating the necessity of transfers from smaller to larger shells. And very, very few were lost when the final connection was made to the control panels of ship or industrial combine. Shell people resembled mature dwarfs in size whatever their natal deformities were, but the well-oriented brain would not have changed places with the most perfect body in the Universe.

So, for happy years, Helva scooted around in her shell with her classmates, playing such games as Stall, Power-Seek, studying her lessons in trajectory, propulsion techniques, computation, logistics, mental hygiene, basic alien psychology, philology, space history, law, traffic, codes: all the et ceteras that eventually became compounded into a reasoning, logical, informed citizen. Not so obvious to her, but of more importance to her teachers, Helva ingested the precepts of her conditioning as easily as she absorbed her nutrient fluid. She would one day be grateful to the patient drone of the subconscious-level instruction.

Helva's civilization was not without busy, do-good associations, exploring possible inhumanities to terrestrial as well as extraterrestrial citizens. One such group got all incensed over shelled "children" when Helva was just turning fourteen. When they were forced to, Central Worlds shrugged its shoulders, arranged a tour of the laboratory schools and set the tour off to a big start by showing the members case histories, complete with photographs. Very few committees ever looked past the first few photos. Most of their original objections about "shells" were overridden by the relief that these hideous (to them) bodies *were* mercifully concealed.

Helva's class was doing Fine Arts, a selective subject in her crowded program. She had activated one of her microscopic tools which she would later use for minute repairs to various parts of her control panel. Her subject was large — a copy of the *Last Supper* — and her canvas, small — the head of a tiny screw. She had tuned her sight to the proper degree. As she worked she absentmindedly crooned, producing a curious sound. Shell people used their own vocal cords and diaphragms but sound issued through microphones rather than mouths. Helva's hum then had a curious vibrancy, a warm, dulcet quality even in its aimless chromatic wanderings.

"Why, what a lovely voice you have," said one of the female visitors.

Helva "looked" up and caught a fascinating panorama of regular, dirty craters on a flaky pink surface. Her hum became a gurgle of surprise. She instinctively regulated her "sight" until the skin lost its cratered look and the pores assumed normal proportions.

"Yes, we have quite a few years of voice training, madam," remarked Helva calmly. "Vocal peculiarities often become excessively irritating during prolonged intrastellar distances and must be eliminated. I enjoyed my lessons."

Although this was the first time that Helva had seen unshelled people, she took this experience calmly. Any other reaction would have been reported instantly.

"I meant that you have a nice singing voice . . . dear," the lady amended.

"Thank you. Would you like to see my work?" Helva asked, politely. She instinctively sheered away from personal discussions but she filed the comment away for further meditation.

"Work?" asked the lady.

"I am currently reproducing the *Last Supper* on the head of a screw."

"Oh, I say," the lady twittered.

Helva turned her vision back to magnification and surveyed her copy critically.

"Of course, some of my color values do not match the old master's and the perspective is faulty, but I believe it to be a fair copy."

The lady's eyes, unmagnified, bugged out.

"Oh, I forget," and Helva's voice was really contrite. If she could have blushed, she would have. "You people don't have adjustable vision."

The monitor of this discourse grinned with pride and amusement as Helva's tone indicated pity for the unfortunate.

"Here, this will help," suggested Helva, substituting 'a magnifying device in one extension and holding it over the picture.

In a kind of shock, the ladies and gentlemen of the committee bent to observe the incredibly copied and brilliantly executed *Last Supper* on the head of a screw.

"Well," remarked one gentleman who had been forced to accompany his wife, "the good Lord can eat where angels fear to tread."

"Are you referring, sir," asked Helva politely, "to the Dark Age discussions of the number of angels who could stand on the head of a pin?"

"I had that in mind."

"If you substitute 'atom' for 'angel,' the problem is not insoluble, given the metallic content of the pin in question."

"Which you are programmed to compute?"

"Of course."

"Did they remember to program a sense of humor, as well, young lady?"

"We are directed to develop a sense of proportion, sir, which contributes the same effect."

The good man chortled appreciatively and decided the trip was worth his time.

If the investigation committee spent months digesting the thoughtful food served them at the laboratory school, they left Helva with a morsel as well.

"Singing" as applicable to herself required research. She had, of course, been exposed to and enjoyed a music appreciation course which had included the better known classical works such as *Tristan und Isolde, Candide, Oklahoma, Nozze di Figaro,* the Atomic Age singers, Eileen Farrell, Elvis Presley, and Geraldine Todd, as well as the curious rhythmic progressions of the Venusians, Capellan visual chromatics, and the sonic concerti of the Altairians. But "singing" for any shell person posed considerable technical difficulties to be overcome. Shell people were schooled to examine every aspect of a problem or situation before making a prognosis. Balanced properly between optimism and practicality, the nondefeatist attitude of the shell people led them to extricate themselves, their ships, and personnel from bizarre situations. Therefore, the problem that Helva couldn't open her mouth to sing, among other restrictions, did not bother her. She would work out a method, bypassing her limitations, whereby she could sing.

She approached the problem by investigating the methods of sound reproduction, human and instrumental, through the centuries. Her own sound production equipment was essentially more instrumental than vocal. Breath control and the proper enunciation of vowel sounds within the oral cavity appeared to require the most development and practice. Shell people did not, strictly speaking, breathe. For their purposes, oxygen and other gases were not drawn from the surrounding atmosphere through the medium of lungs, but sustained artificially by solution in their shells. After experimentation, Helva discovered that she could manipulate her diaphragmic unit to sustain tone. By relaxing the throat muscles and expanding the oral cavity well into the frontal sinuses, she could direct the vowel sounds into the most felicitous position for proper reproduction through her throat microphone. She compared the results with tape recordings of modern singers and was not unpleased, although her own tapes had a peculiar quality about them, not at all unharmonious, merely unique. Acquiring a repertoire from the laboratory library was no problem to one trained to perfect recall. She found herself able to sing any role and any song which struck her fancy. It would not have occurred to her that it was curious for a female to sing bass, baritone, tenor, alto, mezzo, soprano, and coloratura as she pleased. It was, to Helva, only a matter of the correct reproduction and diaphragmic control required by the music attempted.

If the authorities remarked on her curious avocation, they did so among themselves. Shell people were encouraged to develop a hobby so long as they maintained proficiency in their technical work.

On the anniversary of her sixteenth year in her shell, Helva was unconditionally graduated and installed in her ship, the XH-834. Her permanent titanium shell was recessed behind an even more indestructible barrier in the central shaft of the scout ship. The neural, audio, visual, and sensory connections were made and sealed. Her extendibles were diverted, connected, or augmented and the final, delicate-beyond-description brain taps were completed while Helva remained anesthetically unaware of the proceedings. When she awoke, she *was* the ship. Her brain and intelligence controlled every function from navigation to such loading as a scout ship of her class needed. She could take care of herself and her ambulatory half, in any situation already recorded in the annals of Central Worlds and in any situation its most fertile minds could imagine.

Her first actual flight, for she and her kind had made mock flights on dummy panels since she was eight, showed her complete mastery of the techniques of her profession. She was ready for her great adventures and the arrival of her mobile partner.

There were nine qualified scouts sitting around collecting base pay the day Helva was commissioned. There were several missions which demanded instant attention, but Helva had been of interest to several department heads in Central for some time and each man was determined to have her assigned to *his* section. Consequently no one had remembered to introduce Helva to the prospective partners. The ship always chose his or her own partner. Had there been another "brain" ship at the base at the moment, Helva would have been guided to make the first move. As it was, while Central wrangled among itself, Robert Tanner sneaked out of the pilots' barracks, out to the field, and over to Helva's slim metal hull.

"Hello, anyone at home?" Tanner wisecracked.

"Of course," replied Helva logically, activating her outside scanners. "Are you my partner?" she asked hopefully, as she recognized the Scout Service uniform.

"All you have to do is ask," he retorted hopefully.

"No one has come. I thought perhaps there were no partners available and I've had no directives from Central."

Even to herself Helva sounded a little self-pitying but the truth was she was lonely, sitting on the darkened field. Always she had had the company of other shells and, more recently, technicians by the score. The sudden solitude had lost its momentary charm and become oppressive.

"No directives from Central is scarcely a cause for regret, but there happen to be eight other guys biting their fingernails to the quick just waiting for an invitation to board you, you beautiful thing."

Tanner was inside the central cabin as he said this, running appreciative fingers over her panel and the scout's gravity-couch, poking his head into the cabins, the galley, the head, the pressured-storage compartments.

"Now, if you want to give Central a shove and do *us* a favor all in one, call up the barracks and let's have a ship-warming partner-picking party. Hmmmm?"

Helva chuckled to herself. He was so completely different from the occasional visitors or the various laboratory technicians she had encountered. He was so gay, so assured, and she was delighted by his suggestion of a partner-picking party. Certainly it was not against anything in her understanding of regulations.

"Cencom, this is XH-834. Connect me with Pilot Barracks."

"Visual?"

"Please."

A picture of lounging men in various attitudes of boredom came on her screen.

"This is XH-834. Would the unassigned scouts do me the favor of coming aboard?"

Eight figures galvanized into action, grabbing pieces of wearing apparel, disengaging tape mechanisms, disentangling themselves from bedsheets and towels.

Helva dissolved the connection while Tanner chuckled gleefully and settled down to await their arrival.

Helva was engulfed in an unshell-like flurry of anticipation. No actress on her opening night could have been more apprehensive, fearful, or breathless. Unlike the actress, she could throw no hysterics, china objets d'art, or greasepaint to relieve her tension. She could, of course, check her stores for edibles and drinks, which she did, serving Tanner from the virgin selection of her commissary.

Scouts were colloquially known as "brawns" as opposed to their ship "brains." They had to pass as rigorous a training program as the brains and only the top one percent of each contributory world's highest scholars were admitted to the Central Worlds Scout Training Program. Consequently the eight young men who came pounding up the gantry into Helva's hospitable lock were unusually fine-looking, intelligent, well-coordinated, and adjusted young men, looking forward to a slightly drunken evening, Helva permitting, and all quite willing to do each other dirt to get possession of her.

Such a human invasion left Helva mentally breathless, a luxury she thoroughly enjoyed for the brief time she felt she should permit it. She sorted out the young men. Tanner's opportunism amused but did not specifically attract her; the blond Nordsen seemed too simple; dark-haired Al-atpay had a kind of obstinacy for which she felt no compassion; Mir-Ahnin's bitterness hinted an inner darkness she did not wish to lighten although he made the biggest outward play for her attention. Hers was a curious courtship — this would be only the first of several marriages for her, for brawns retired after seventy-five years of service, or earlier if they were unlucky. Brains, their bodies safe from any deterioration, served two hundred years, and were then permitted to decide for themselves if they wished to continue. Helva had actually spoken to one shell person three hundred and twenty-two years old. She had been so awed by the contact she hadn't presumed to ask the personal questions she had wanted to.

Her choice did not stand out from the others until Tanner started to sing a scout ditty, recounting the misadventures of the bold, dense, painfully inept Billy Brawn. An attempt at harmony resulted in cacophony and Tanner wagged his arms wildly for silence.

"What we need is a roaring good lead tenor. Jennan, besides palming aces, can you sing?"

"Only sharp," Jennan replied with easy good humor.

"If a tenor is absolutely necessary, I'll attempt it," Helva volunteered.

"My good *woman,*" Tanner protested.

"Sound your 'A'," laughed Jennan.

Into the stunned silence that followed the rich, clear, high "A," Jennan remarked quietly, "Such an A, Caruso would have given the rest of his notes to sing."

It did not take them long to discover her full range.

"All Tanner asked for was one roaring good lead tenor," Jennan complained jokingly, "and our sweet mistress supplies us an entire repertory company. The boy who gets this ship will go far, far, far."

"To the Horsehead Nebula?" asked Nordsen, quoting an old Central saw.

"To the Horsehead Nebula and back, we shall make beautiful music," countered Helva, chuckling.

"Together," Jennan amended. "Only you'd better make the music and with my voice, I'd better listen."

"I rather imagined it would be I who listened," suggested Helva.

Jennan executed a stately bow with an intricate flourish of his crush-brimmed hat. He directed his bow toward the central control pillar where Helva *was.* Her own personal preference crystallized at that precise moment and for that particular reason: Jennan, alone of the men, had addressed his remarks directly at her physical presence, regardless of the fact that he knew she could pick up his image wherever he was in the ship and regardless of the fact that her body was behind massive metal walls. Throughout their partnership, Jennan never failed to turn his head in her direction no matter where he was in relation to her. In response to this personalization, Helva at that moment and from then on always spoke to Jennan only through her central mike, even though that was not always the most efficient method.

Helva didn't know that she fell in love with Jennan that evening. As she had never been exposed to love or affection, only the drier cousins, respect and admiration, she could scarcely have recognized her reaction to the warmth of his personality and consideration. As a shell person, she considered herself remote from emotions largely connected with physical desires.

"Well, Helva, it's been swell meeting you," said Tanner suddenly, as she and Jennan were arguing about the baroque quality of "Come All Ye Sons of Art." "See you in space some time, you lucky dog, Jennan. Thanks for the party, Helva."

"You don't have to go so soon?" pleaded Helva, realizing belatedly that she and Jennan had been excluding the others.

"Best man won," Tanner said, wryly. "Guess I'd better go get a tape on love ditties. May need 'em for the next ship, if there're any more at home like you."

Helva and Jennan watched them leave, both a little confused.

"Perhaps Tanner's jumping to conclusions?" Jennan asked.

Helva regarded him as he slouched against the console, facing her shell directly. His arms were crossed on his chest and the glass he held had been empty for some time. He was handsome, they all were; but his watchful eyes were unwary, his mouth assumed a smile easily, his voice (to which Helva was particularly drawn) was resonant, deep, and without unpleasant overtones or accent.

"Sleep on it, Helva. Call me in the morning if it's your opt."

She called him at breakfast, after she had checked her choice through Central. Jennan moved his things aboard, received their joint commission, had his personality and experience file locked into her reviewer, gave her the coordinates of their first mission and the XH-834 officially became the JH-834.

Their first mission was a dull but necessary crash priority (Medical got Helva), rushing a vaccine to a distant system plagued with a virulent spore disease. They had only to get to Spica as fast as possible.

After the initial, thrilling forward surge of her maximum speed, Helva realized her muscles were to be given less of a workout than her brawn on this tedious mission. But they did have plenty of time for exploring each other's personalities. Jennan, of course, knew what Helva was capable of as a ship and partner, just as she knew what she could expect from him. But these were only facts and Helva looked forward eagerly to learning that human side of her partner that could not be reduced to a series of symbols. Nor could the give and take of two personalities be learned from a book. It has to be experienced.

"My father was a scout, too, or is that programmed?" began Jennan their third day out.

"Naturally."

"Unfair, you know. You've got all my family history and I don't know one blamed thing about yours."

"I've never known either," Helva confided. "Until I read yours, it hadn't occurred to me I must have one, too, some place in Central's files."

Jennan snorted. "Shell psychology!"

Helva laughed. "Yes, and I'm even programmed against curiosity about it. You'd better be, too,"

Jennan ordered a drink, slouched into the gravity couch opposite her and put his feet on the bumpers, turning himself idly from side to side on the gimbals.

"Helva — a made-up name . . . "

"With a Scandinavian sound."

"You aren't blonde," Jennan said positively.

"Well, then, there're dark Swedes."

"And blonde Turks and this one's harem is limited to one."

"Your woman in purdah, yes, but you can comb the pleasure houses — " Helva found herself aghast at the edge to her carefully trained voice.

"You know," Jennan interrupted her, deep in some thought of his own, "my father gave me the impression he was a lot more married to his ship, Silvia, than to my mother. I know I used to think Silvia was my grandmother. She was a low number so she must have been a great-great-grandmother at least. I used to talk to her for hours."

"Her registry?" asked Helva, unwitting of the jealousy for everyone and anyone who had shared his hours.

"422. I think she's TS now. I ran into Tom Burgess once."

Jennan's father had died of a planetary disease, the vaccine for which his ship had used up in curing the local citizens.

"Tom said she'd got mighty tough and salty. You lose your sweetness and I'll come back and haunt you, girl," Jennan threatened.

Helva laughed. He startled her by stamping up to the control panel, touching it with light, tender fingers.

"I *wonder* what you look like," he said softly, wistfully.

Helva had been briefed about this natural curiosity of scouts. She didn't know anything about herself and neither of them ever would or could.

"Pick any form, shape, and shade and I'll be yours obliging," she countered as training suggested.

"Iron Maiden, I fancy blondes with long tresses," and Jennan pantomimed Lady Godiva-like tresses. "Since you're immolated in titanium, I'll call you Brunehilda, my dear," and he made his bow.

With a chortle, Helva launched into the appropriate aria just as Spica made contact.

"What'n'ell's that yelling about? Who are you? And unless you're Central Worlds Medical go away. We've got a plague with no visiting privileges."

"My ship is singing, we're the JH-834 of Worlds and we've got your vaccine. What are our landing coordinates?"

"Your *ship* is singing?"

"The greatest S.A.T.B. in organized space. Any requests?"

The JH-834 delivered the vaccine but no more arias and received immediate orders to proceed to Leviticus IV. By the time they got there, Jennan found a reputation awaiting him and was forced to defend the 834's virgin honor.

"I'll stop singing," murmured Helva contritely as she ordered up poultices for his third black eye in a week.

"You will not," Jennan said through gritted teeth. "If I have to blacken eyes from here to the Horsehead to keep the snicker out of the title, we'll be the ship who sings."

After the "ship who sings" tangled with a minor but vicious narcotic ring in the Lesser Magallenics, the title became definitely respectful. Central was aware of each episode and punched out a "special interest" key on JH-834's file. A first-rate team was shaking down well.

Jennan and Helva considered themselves a first-rate team, too, after their tidy arrest.

"Of all the vices in the universe, I *hate* drug addition," Jennan remarked as they headed back to Central Base. "People can go to hell quick enough without that kind of help."

"Is that why you volunteered for Scout Service? To redirect traffic?"

"I'll bet my official answer's on your review."

"In far too flowery wording. 'Carrying on the traditions of my family, which has been proud of four generations in Service,' if I may quote you your own words."

Jennan groaned. "I was *very* young when I wrote that and I certainly hadn't been through final training and once I was in final training, my pride wouldn't let me fail . . .

"As I mentioned, I used to visit Dad on board Silvia and I've a very good idea she might have had her eye on me as a replacement for my father because I had had massive doses of scout-oriented propaganda. It took. From the time I was seven, I was going to be a scout or else." He shrugged as if deprecating a youthful determination that had taken a great deal of mature application to bring to fruition.

"Ah, so? Scout Sahir Silan on the JS-422 penetrating into the Horsehead Nebula?"

Jennan chose to ignore her sarcasm. "With *you*, I may even get that far, but even with Silvia's nudging *I* never daydreamed myself *that* kind of glory in my wildest flights of fancy. I'll leave the whoppers to your agile brain, henceforth. I have in mind a smaller contribution to space history."

"So modest?"

"No. Practical. We also serve, et cetera." He placed a dramatic hand on his heart.

"Glory hound!" scoffed Helva.

"Look who's talking, my nebula-bound friend. At least I'm not greedy. There'll only be one hero like my dad at Parsaea, but I *would* like to be remembered for some kudos. Everyone does. Why else do or die?"

"Your father died on his way back from Parsaea, if I may point out a few cogent facts. So he could never have known he was a hero for damming the flood with his ship. Which kept the Parsaean colony from being abandoned. Which gave them a chance to discover the antiparalytic qualities of Parsaea. Which *he* never knew."

"*I* know," said Jennan softly.

Helva was immediately sorry for the tone of her rebuttal. She knew very well how deep Jennan's attachment to his father had been. On his review a note was made that he had rationalized his father's loss with the unexpected and welcome outcome of the Affair at Parsaea.

"Facts are not human, Helva. My father was and so am I. And *basically,* so are you. Check over your dial, 834. Amid all the wires attached to you is a heart, an underdeveloped human heart. Obviously!"

"I apologize, Jennan," she said contritely.

Jennan hesitated a moment, threw out his hands in acceptance and then tapped her shell affectionately.

"If they ever take us off the milk runs, we'll make a stab at the nebula, huh?"

As so frequently happened in the Scout Service, within the next hour they had orders to change course, not to the nebula, but to a recently colonized system with two habitable planets, one tropical, one glacial. The sun, named Ravel, had become unstable; the spectrum was that of a rapidly expanding shell, with absorption lines rapidly displacing toward violet. The augmented heat of the primary had already forced evacuation of the nearer world, Daphnis. The pattern of spectral emissions gave indication that the sun would sear Chloe as well. All ships in the vicinity were to report to Disaster Headquarters on Chloe to effect removal of the remaining colonists.

The JH-834 obediently presented itself and was sent to outlying areas on Chloe to pick up scattered settlers who did not appear to appreciate the urgency of the situation. Chloe, indeed, was enjoying the first temperatures above freezing since it had been flung out of its parent. Since many of the colonists were religious fanatics who had settled on rigorous Chloe to fit themselves for a life of pious reflection, Chloe's abrupt thaw was attributed to sources other than a rampaging sun.

Jennan had to spend so much time countering specious arguments that he and Helva were behind schedule on their way to the fourth and last settlement. Helva jumped over the high range of jagged peaks that surrounded and sheltered the valley from the former raging snows as well as the present heat. The violent sun with its flaring corona was just beginning to brighten the deep valley.

"They'd better grab their toothbrushes and hop aboard," Helva commented. "H.Q. says speed it up."

"All women," remarked Jennan in surprise as he walked down to meet them. "Unless the men on Chloe wear furred skirts."

"Charm 'em but pare the routine to the bare essentials. And turn on your two-way private."

Jennan advanced smiling, but his explanation was met with absolute incredulity and considerable doubt as to his authenticity. He groaned inwardly as the matriarch paraphrased previous explanations of the warming sun.

"Revered mother, there's been an overload on that prayer circuit and the sun is blowing itself up in one obliging burst. I'm here to take you to the spaceport at Rosary — "

"That Sodom?" the worthy woman glowered and shuddered disdainfully at his suggestion. "We thank you for your warning but we have no wish to leave our cloister for the rude world. We must go about our morning meditation which has been interrupted — "

"It'll be permanently interrupted when that sun starts broiling. You must come now," Jennan said firmly.

"Madame," said Helva, realizing that perhaps a female voice might carry more weight in this instance than Jennan's very masculine charm.

"Who spoke?" cried the nun, startled by the bodiless voice.

"I, Helva, the ship. Under my protection you and your sisters-in-faith may enter safely and be unprofaned by association with a male. I will guard you and take you safely to a place prepared for you."

The matriarch peered cautiously into the ship's open port.

"Since only Central Worlds is permitted the use of such ships, I acknowledge that you are not trifling with us, young man. However, we are in no danger here."

"The temperature at Rosary is now 99°," said Helva. "As soon as the sun's rays penetrate directly into this valley, it will also be 99°, and it is due to climb to approximately 180° today. I notice your buildings are made of wood with moss chinking. Dry moss. It should fire around noontime."

The sunlight was beginning to slant into the valley through the peaks and the fierce rays warmed the restless group behind the matriarch. Several opened the throats of their furry parkas.

"Jennan," said Helva privately to him, "our time is very short."

"I can't leave them, Helva. Some of those girls are barely out of their teens."

"Pretty, too. No wonder the matriarch doesn't want to get in."

"Helva."

"It will be the Lord's will," said the matriarch stoutly and turned her back squarely on rescue.

"To burn to death?" shouted Jennan as she threaded her way through her murmuring disciples.

"They want to be martyrs? Their opt, Jennan," said Helva dispassionately. "*We* must leave and that is no longer a matter of option."

"How can I leave, Helva?"

"Parsaea?" Helva flung tauntingly at him as he stepped forward to grab one of the women. "You can't drag them *all* aboard and we don't have time to fight it out. Get on board, Jennan, or I'll have you on report."

"They'll die," muttered Jennan dejectedly as he reluctantly turned to climb on board.

"You can risk only so much," Helva said sympathetically. "As it is we'll just have time to make a rendezvous. Lab reports a critical speed-up in spectral evolution."

Jennan was already in the airlock when one of the younger women, screaming, rushed to squeeze in the closing port. Her action set off the others and they stampeded through the narrow opening. Even crammed back to breast, there was not enough room inside. Jennan broke out spacesuits for the three who would have to remain with him in the airlock. He wasted valuable time explaining to the matriarch that she must put on the suit because the airlock had no independent oxygen or cooling units.

"We'll be caught," said Helva grimly to Jennan on their private connection. "We've lost eighteen minutes in this last-minute rush. I am now overloaded for maximum speed and I must attain maximum speed to outrun the heat wave."

"Can you lift? We're suited."

"Lift? Yes," she said, doing so. "Run? I stagger."

Jennan, bracing himself and the women, could feel her sluggishness as she blasted upward. Heartlessly, Helva applied thrust as long as she could, despite the fact that the gravitational force mashed her cabin passengers brutally and crushed two fatally. It was a question of saving as many as possible. The only one for whom she had any concern was Jennan and she was in desperate terror about his safety. Airless and uncooled, protected by only one layer of metal, not three, the airlock was not going to be safe for the four trapped there, despite their spacesuits. These were only the standard models, not built to withstand the excessive heat to which the ship would be subjected.

Helva ran as fast as she could but the incredible wave of heat from the explosive sun caught them halfway to cold safety.

She paid no heed to the cries, moans, pleas, and prayers in her cabin. She listened only to Jennan's tortured breathing, to the missing throb in his suit's purifying system and the sucking of the overloaded cooling unit. Helpless, she heard the hysterical screams of his three companions as they writhed in the awful heat. Vainly, Jennan tried to calm them, tried to explain they would soon be safe and cool if they could be still and endure the heat. Undisciplined by their terror and torment, they tried to strike out at him despite the close quarters. One flailing arm became entangled in the leads to his power pack and the damage was quickly done. A connection, weakened by heat and the dead weight of the arm, broke.

For all the power at her disposal, Helva was helpless. She watched as Jennan fought for his breath, as he turned his head beseechingly toward *her,* and died.

Only the iron conditioning of her training prevented Helva from swinging around and plunging back into the exploding sun. Numbly she made rendezvous with the refugee convoy. She obediently transferred her burned, heat-prostrated passengers to the assigned transport.

"I will retain the body of my scout and proceed to the nearest base for burial," she informed Central dully.

"You will be provided escort," was the reply.

"I have no need of escort," she demurred.

"Escort is provided, XH-834," she was told curtly.

The shock of hearing Jennan's initial severed from her call number cut off her half-formed protest. Stunned, she waited by the transport until her screens showed the arrival of two other slim brain ships. The cortege proceeded homeward at unfuneral speeds.

"834? The ship who sings?"

"I have no more songs."

"Your scout was Jennan?"

"I do not wish to communicate."

"I'm 422."

"Silvia?"

"Silvia died a long time ago. I'm 422. Currently MS," the ship rejoined curtly. "AH-640 is our other friend, but Henry's not listening in. Just as well — he wouldn't understand it if you wanted to turn rogue. But I'd stop *him* if he tried to delay you."

"Rogue?" the term snapped Helva out of her apathy.

"Sure. You're young. You've got power for years. Skip. Others have done it. 732 went rogue two years ago after she lost her scout on a mission to that white dwarf. Hasn't been seen since."

"I never heard about rogues," gasped Helva.

"As it's exactly the thing we're conditioned against, you sure wouldn't hear about it in school, my dear," 422 said.

"Break conditioning?" cried Helva, anguished, thinking of the white, white furious hot heart of the sun she had just left.

"For you I don't think it would be hard at the moment," 422 said quietly, her voice devoid of her earlier cynicism. "The stars are out there, winking."

"Alone?" cried Helva from her heart.

"Alone!" 422 confirmed bleakly.

Alone with all of space and time. Even the Horsehead Nebula would not be far enough away to daunt her. Alone with a hundred years to live with her memories and nothing . . . nothing more.

"Was Parsaea worth it?" she asked 422 softly.

"Parsaea?" 422 came back, surprised. "With his father? Yes. We were there, at Parsaea when we were needed. Just as you . . . and his son . . . were at Chloe. When you were needed. The crime is always not knowing where need is and not being there."

"But *I* need *him*. Who will supply *my* need?" said Helva bitterly . . .

"834," said 422 after a day's silent speeding. "Central wishes your report. A replacement awaits your opt at Regulus Base. Change course accordingly."

"A replacement?" That was certainly not what she needed . . . a reminder inadequately filling the void Jennan left. Why, her hull was barely cool of Chloe's heat. Atavistically, Helva wanted time to mourn Jennan.

"Oh, none of them are impossible if *you're* a good ship," 422 remarked philosophically. "And it is just what you need. The sooner the better."

"You told them I wouldn't go rogue, didn't you?" Helva said heavily.

"The moment passed you even as it passed me after Parsaea, and before that, after Glen Arhur, and Betelgeuse."

"We're conditioned to go on, aren't we? We *can't* go rogue. You were testing."

"Had to. Orders. Not even Psycho knows why a rogue occurs. Central's very worried, and so, daughter, are your sister ships. I asked to be your escort. I . . . don't want to lose you both."

In her emotional nadir, Helva could feel a flood of gratitude for Silvia's rough sympathy.

"We've all known this grief, Helva. It's no consolation but if we couldn't feel with our scouts, we'd only be machines wired for sound."

Helva looked at Jennan's still form stretched before her in its shroud and heard the echo of his rich voice in the quiet cabin.

"Silvia! I *couldn't* help him," she cried from her soul.

"Yes, dear. I know," 422 murmured gently and then was quiet.

The three ships sped on, wordless, to the great Central Worlds base at Regulus. Helva broke silence to acknowledge landing instructions and the officially tendered regrets.

The three ships set down simultaneously at the wooded edge where Regulus's gigantic blue trees stood sentinel over the sleeping dead in the small Service cemetery. The entire Base complement approached with measured step and formed an aisle from Helva to the burial ground. The honor detail, out of step, walked slowly into her cabin. Reverently they placed the body of her dead love on the wheeled bier, covered it honorably with the deep blue, star-splashed flag of the Service. She watched as it was driven slowly down the living aisle which closed in behind the bier in last escort.

Then, as the simple words of interment were spoken, as the atmosphere planes dipped wings in tribute over the open grave, Helva found voice for her lonely farewell.

Softly, barely audible at first, the strains of the ancient song of evening and requiem swelled to the final poignant measure until black space itself echoed back the sound of the song the ship sang.

mu/tants — in science fiction, human beings who differ from others because of alterations to their organisms. These changes are frequently the result of exposure to radioactivity, although some authors ascribe these changes to other causes. Mutants are one of the staple themes in science fiction, although they were more popular in the 1945–1960 period than today. Two good science fiction anthologies about mutants are *Science Fiction Adventures in Mutation* (Vanguard Press, 1956) and *Mutants* (Thomas Nelson, 1974).

No Harm Done

JACK SHARKEY

The boy was a good-looking youth, with shiny — if over-long — blond hair, and bright white teeth. But his eyes were cloudy with the emptiness that lay behind them, and the blue circles of their irises hinted at no more mental activity than do the opaque black dots on a rag doll. He sat with vacuous docility upon the small metal stool the guards had provided, and let his arms dangle limp as broken clothesline at his sides, not even crossing them in his lap. He had been led to the chair, told to sit, and left there. If he were not told to arise, he would remain there until the dissolution of his muscle cells following death by starvation caused him to topple from his low perch.

"Total schizophrenia," said Dr. Manton. "For all practical purposes, he is an ambulant — when instructed to move, of course — vegetable."

"How terrible," said Lisa, albeit perfunctorily. Lisa Nugent, for all her lovely twenty-seven years, was a trained psychologist, and rarely allowed emotion to take her mind from its well-ordered paths of analysis. To be unfeeling was heartless — But to become emotional about a patient was pointless.

"Yes, it's intolerable," nodded Dr. Jeff Manton, keeping his mind strictly on Lisa's scientific qualifications, and deliberately blocking out any other information sent to his brain by his alert senses. The warmth of her smile, the flash of sunlight in her auburn hair, the companionable lilt she could not keep out of her "on-duty" voice — All these were observed, noted, and filed for future reference. At the moment, nothing must go wrong with their capacity for observation of the patient. Emotion had a way of befuddling even the most dedicated minds.

"But why out here?" Lisa said suddenly, returning the conversation to a prior topic. "I should think conditions would be easier to control in the lab."

"Simply because," said Jeff, patting the small metal camera-like device on its rigid tripod, "I as yet have no experimental knowledge of the range of my machine. It may simply be absorbed by the plaster in the walls, back inside the sanatarium. Then again, it may penetrate, likely or not, even the steel beams of the building, with roentgenic ease. There are too many other people in the building, Li — Dr. Nugent. Until I can be certain just what effect the rays have upon a human brain, I dare not use it any place where there might be leakage, possible synaptic damage."

"I understand," said Lisa, nodding after a brief smile at his near-slip with her name. "You assume the earth will absorb any rays that pass beyond this boy's brain, and render them — if not harmless — at least beyond the contamination point with another human being."

"Precisely," said Jeff Manton, moving the tripod a short distance closer to the seated boy. "Now, I want you to assist me in watching him, and if you note in him any change — either in his expression or posture — tell me at once. Then we can turn off the machine and test him for results. For positive results, at any rate."

Lisa could not repress a slight tremor. The trouble with schizophrenia in its most advanced stage was the inability of contacting the patient. The boy, although readily capable of executing simple commands, could not be counted on to aid Dr. Manton or herself in even the most basic test of his mental abilities. If the machine made him any worse — there would hardly be a way for them to discover it. If better — then new hope was born for others similarly afflicted.

"Steady, now," said Jeff, turning the tiny knob at the side of the metal box a quarter turn. "Keep your eye on him. I'm going to turn it on."

Lisa felt the sweat prickling along her back as Jeff flicked the toggle switch atop the box. Her eyes began to burn, and she realized she wasn't even blinking as she locked her gaze upon the figure of the boy through whose brain was now coursing a ray of relatively unknown effect. Rabbits and rats and monkeys in the lab were one thing. This, now, was a human being. Whether the effect upon him would be similar to that of the ray upon test animals (scientifically driven crazy before exposure) remained to be seen.

"Anything?" muttered Jeff, sighting anxiously along the side of the box. "Anything at *all?*"

"He — No. He just sits there, Doctor. So far as I can see, there is no appreciable effect." She sighed resignedly. "He doesn't even flicker a muscle."

"Damn," said Jeff. He kept his finger lightly atop the sun-glinting toggle switch. "I'm going to give it one more minute before I give up. This thing *should* be vitalizing his brain by *now!*"

"But he's not even — " Lisa began, discouraged.

"Keep your eyes on *him,* damn it!" snapped Jeff, catching the turn of her head from the corner of his eye. "This *must* work! We daren't miss the least sign that it has!"

Man and woman stood side by side in the hot light of the afternoon sun, staring, staring at the immobile form of the patient, the patient whose disrupted mind they were attempting to reunite into an intelligent whole . . .

My name, he thought. Funny, I should know my own name. I've heard it often enough . . . It's . . . Is it — is it Garret? That sounds like it, but — I can't seem to recall . . .

He thought about the man who tended and took care of him. He had called him by name, hadn't he? And it was most certainly Garret. Yes, of course it was Garret . . . Or was it Curt?

His mind, like badly exposed film, refused to give him an accurate sensation from any of his senses. All he got for strenuous mental gymnastics was vague, blurry reception and muddled thought. And yet, there was a warm sensation that had never been in his mind before — Before what? Try as he might, he could not recall anything coherent before this moment in time. Just vague feelings of being alive, and simply growing up . . .

The warmth of the sun was beginning to penetrate. He could feel it, coursing down upon him, soaking into him, revitalizing him . . . But it was unlike this other warmth, this *penetrating* warmth, that tingled through his mind. With the awareness of the sunlight came a slow awareness of shades of light, then of color, then of figures. And, for the first time, he made a strong effort, and — and *looked.*

He saw the man and woman standing in the sunlight a few feet from himself, saw the harsh glitter of that sunlight upon the strange object on three legs that rested on the ground before them. He tried to speak to them, but something restrained him.

If I can move . . . If I can just move a little bit, he realized, they'll see me, and they'll know I'm alive and well and aware.

He tried. He tried desperately to move. His body felt rigid, imprisoned. Just a little frantic, he thought of blinking at them, of moving his eyes toward them for sharp definite focus, so that they would *know* . . .

Nothing happened.

I'm paralyzed! he thought for a terrifying moment. Then — No, I'm just not used to directing myself. I haven't the necessary coordination or experience, that must be it. Take it easy, now. Slow and easy. Don't panic.

He strained desperately, and felt just the slightest hint of movement. Had they seen? he wondered. He was certain he had moved. What was the *matter* with the two of them?!

He watched them there in the sunlight, this man and woman who stood so intensely still, the man's hand upon that metallic thing on three legs. Then he knew that that thing was the source of the warmth in his mind. It had brought him to awareness.

But what *good* is it! his mind screamed. To be alive and aware, and unable to let them know it! The coldly frantic feeling was growing within him, now, taking hold of his brain with the frightening fingers of raw panic.

"Look!" he cried out, then knew with crushing despair that the word had gone no farther than his brain. *Please,* he begged silently, *see me here, see that I am alive, that I am not what I was!*

Desperately, he strove to rise, felt the strange sensation of bondage that restrained his body, fought it . . . and won. It hurt. The sensation was unbearable. Yet he had moved. Perhaps only the quarter part of an inch, but he had moved. The woman — Had she seen?

Then he saw the man straighten up, heave his shoulders in a great sigh, and cut off the machine with a finger-flick. The tingling warmth died within his brain, and for an icy moment, he expected to plunge back to semicomatose nothingness. But, after a giddy scintilla of dizziness, his mind remained strong and intelligent and alive.

Ignoring the blaze of pain that racked his entire being, he tensed himself, pushed, with strangled cries bursting inside his brain at the self-torture, and made himself move another quarter of an inch.

Did they see? Did they? Did they know? Would they free his mind, and leave his body imprisoned to his innermost pleas for release?

No, he thought, giddy with joy. They . . .They're coming nearer! . . .

It's no use, Lisa," said Jeff, looking down upon the motionless figure on the stool. "The machine is a flop. Rabbits and lesser creatures, fine, but for the mind of man, no use at all."

"I'm sorry, Jeff," said Lisa, knowing that his calling her by her first name meant that work was done for that day. "Maybe, with some adjustments — "

"Yeah," he grunted bitterly, as two white-jacketed guards led the boy back to his cell, *"maybe!"*

"At least," said Lisa, taking him gently by the arm, "he's no worse off. The experiment just didn't work out, that's all. But there's no harm done, at any rate."

"Nope. I suppose you're right," Jeff said bitterly, reaching to lift the stool from its patch of sunlight. Then, with a brief surge of anger at the futility he felt, he lashed out with his foot and kicked the green parsleylike top clean off a carrot that jutted just a bit higher than its fellows in the garden bed behind the stool. "No harm done," he muttered angrily, and went back with Lisa toward the sanatarium.

While a silent, agony-filled voice behind him kept shrieking, over and over, *"My eyes! He kicked out my eyes! I'm blind! Help me! Help me!"*

N

There Will Come Soft Rains

RAY BRADBURY

The house was a good house and had been planned and built by the people who were to live in it, in the year 1980. The house was like many another house in that year; it fed and slept and entertained its inhabitants, and made a good life for them. The man and wife and their two children lived at ease there, and lived happily, even while the world trembled. All of the fine things of living, the warm things, music and poetry, books that talked, beds that warmed and made themselves, fires that built themselves in the fireplaces of evenings, were in this house, and living there was a contentment.

And then one day the world shook and there was an explosion followed by ten thousand explosions and red fire in the sky and a rain of ashes and radioactivity, and the happy time was over.

In the living room the voice-clock sang, *Ticktock, seven A.M. o'clock, time to get up!* as if it were afraid nobody would. The house lay empty. The clock talked on into the empty morning.

The kitchen stove sighed and ejected from its warm interior eight eggs, sunny-side up, twelve bacon slices, two coffees, and two cups of hot cocoa. *Seven-nine, breakfast time, seven-nine.*

Today is April 28, 1985, said a phonograph voice in the kitchen ceiling. "Today, remember, is Mr. Featherstone's birthday. Insurance, gas, light, and water bills are due."

Somewhere in the walls, relays clicked, memory tapes glided under electric eyes. Recorded voices moved beneath steel needles: *Eight-one, run, run, off to school, off to work, run, run, ticktock, eight-one o'clock!*

But no doors slammed, no carpets took the quick tread of rubber heels. Outside, it was raining. The voice of the weather box on the front door sang quietly: *Rain, rain, go away, rubbers, raincoats for today.* And the rain tapped on the roof.

At eight-thirty the eggs were shriveled. An aluminum wedge scraped them into the sink, where hot water whirled them down a metal throat which digested and flushed them away to the distant sea.

Nine-fifteen, sang the clock, *time to clean.*

Out of warrens in the wall, tiny mechanical mice darted. The rooms were acrawl with the small cleaning animals, all rubber and metal. They sucked up the hidden dust, and popped back in their burrows.

Ten o'clock. The sun came out from behind the rain. The house stood alone on a street where all the other houses were rubble and ashes. At night, the ruined town gave off a radioactive glow which could be seen for miles.

Ten-fifteen. The garden sprinkler filled the soft morning air with golden fountains. The water tinkled over the charred west side of the house where it had been scorched evenly free of its white paint. The entire face of the house was black, save for five places. Here, the silhouette, in paint, of a man mowing a lawn. Here, a woman bent to pick flowers. Still farther over, their images burned on wood in one titanic instant, a small boy, hands flung in the air — higher up, the image of a thrown ball — and opposite him a girl, her hands raised to catch a ball which never came down.

The five spots of paint — the man, the woman, the boy, the girl, the ball — remained. The rest was a thin layer of charcoal.

The gentle rain of the sprinkler filled the garden with falling light.

Until this day, how well the house had kept its peace. How carefully it had asked, "Who goes there?" and getting no reply from rains and lonely foxes and whining cats, it had shut up its windows and drawn the shades. If a sparrow brushed a window, the shade snapped up. The bird, startled, flew off! No, not even an evil bird must touch the house.

And inside, the house was like an altar with nine thousand robot attendants, big and small, servicing, attending, singing in choirs, even though the gods had gone away and the ritual was meaningless.

A dog whined, shivering, on the front porch.

The front door recognized the dog voice and opened. The dog padded in wearily, thinned to the bone, covered with sores. It tracked mud on the carpet. Behind it whirred the angry robot mice, angry at having to pick up mud and maple leaves, which, carried to the burrows, were dropped down cellar tubes into an incinerator which sat like an evil Baal in a dark corner.

The dog ran upstairs, hysterically yelping at each door. It pawed the kitchen door wildly.

Behind the door, the stove was making pancakes which filled the whole house with their odor.

The dog frothed, ran insanely, spun in a circle, biting its tail, and died.

It lay in the living room for an hour.

One o'clock.

Delicately sensing decay, the regiments of mice hummed out of the walls, soft as blown leaves, their electric eyes glowing.

One-fifteen.

The dog was gone.

The cellar incinerator glowed suddenly and a whirl of sparks leaped up the flue.

Two-thirty-five.

Bridge tables sprouted from the patio walls. Playing cards fluttered onto pads in a shower of pips. Martinis appeared on an oaken bench.

But the tables were silent, the cards untouched.

At four-thirty the tables folded back into the walls.

Five o'clock. The bathtubs filled with clear hot water. A safety razor dropped into a wall-mold, ready.

Six, seven, eight, nine o'clock.

Dinner made, ignored, and flushed away; dishes washed; and in the study, the tobacco stand produced a cigar, half an inch of gray ash on it, smoking, waiting. The hearth fire bloomed up all by itself, out of nothing.

Nine o'clock. The beds began to warm their hidden circuits, for the night was cool.

A gentle click in the study wall. A voice spoke from above the crackling fireplace: *Mrs. McClellan, what poem would you like to hear this evening?*

The house was silent.

The voice said, *Since you express no preference, I'll pick a poem at random.* Quiet music rose behind the voice. *Sara Teasdale. A favorite of yours, as I recall.*

> There will come soft rains and the smell of the ground,
> And swallows circling with their shimmering sound;

And frogs in the pools singing at night,
And wild plum-trees in tremulous white;

Robins will wear their feathery fire
Whistling their whims on a low fence-wire;

And not one will know of the war, not one
Will care at last when it is done.

Not one would mind, neither bird nor tree
If mankind perished utterly;

And Spring herself, when she woke at dawn,
Would scarcely know that we were gone.

The voice finished the poem. The empty chairs faced each other between the silent walls, and the music played.

At ten o'clock, the house began to die.

The wind blew. The bough of a falling tree smashed the kitchen window. Cleaning solvent, bottled, crashed on the stove.

Fire! screamed voices. *Fire!* Water pumps shot down water from the ceilings. But the solvent spread under the doors, making fire as it went, while other voices took up the alarm in chorus.

The windows broke with heat and the wind blew in to help the fire. Scurrying water rats, their copper wheels spinning, squeaked from the walls, squirted their water, ran for more.

Too late! Somewhere, a pump stopped. The ceiling sprays stopped raining. The reserve water supply, which had filled baths and washed dishes for many silent days, was gone.

The fire crackled upstairs, ate paintings, lay hungrily in the beds! It devoured every room.

The house was shuddering, oak bone on bone, the bared skeleton cringing from the heat, all the wires revealed as if a surgeon had torn the skin off to let the red veins quiver in scalded air. Voices screamed, *Help, help, fire, run!* Windows snapped open and shut, like mouths, undecided. *Fire, run!* the voices wailed a tragic nursery rhyme, and the silly Greek chorus faded as the sound-wires popped their sheathings. Ten dozen high, shrieking voices died, as emergency batteries melted.

In other parts of the house, in the last instant under the fire avalanche, other choruses could be heard announcing the time, the weather, appointment, diets; playing music, reading poetry in the fiery study, while doors opened and slammed and umbrellas appeared at the doors and put themselves away — a thousand things happening, like the interior of a clock shop at midnight, all clocks striking, a merry-go-round of squeaking, whispering, rushing, until all the film spools were burned and fell, and all the wires withered and the circuits cracked.

In the kitchen, an instant before the final collapse, the stove, hysterically hissing, could be seen making breakfasts at a psychopathic rate, ten dozen pancakes, six dozen loaves of toast.

The crash! The attic smashing kitchen down into cellar and subcellar. Deepfreeze, armchairs, film-tapes, beds, were thrown in a cluttered mound deep under.

Smoke and silence.

Dawn shone faintly in the east. In the ruins, one wall stood alone. Within the wall, a voice said, over and over again and again, even as the sun rose to shine upon the heaped rubble and steam: *Today is April 29, 1985. Today is April 29, 1985. Today is . . .*

O

oc/cu/pa/tion — the activity that an individual does to provide the basic necessities of life. The choice of an occupation is one of the most important decisions in a person's life. Most science fictional jobs are simply extrapolations from present occupations, but a few authors have created entirely new ones.

In the Jaws of Danger

PIERS ANTHONY

The Enen — for Dr. Dillingham preferred the acronym to "North Nebula humanoid species" — rushed in and chewed out a message-stick with machinelike dispatch. He handed it to Dillingham and stood by anxiously.

The dentist popped it into the hopper of the transcoder. "Emergency," the little speaker said. "Only you can handle this, Doctor!"

"You'll have to be more specific, Holmes," he said and watched the transcoder type this on to another stick. Since the Enens had no spoken language and he had not learned to decipher their tooth-dents, the transcoder was the vital link in communication.

The names he applied to the Enens were facetious. These galactics had no names in their own language, and they comprehended his humor in this regard no more than had his patients back on distant Earth. But at least they were industrious folk and very clever at physical science.

*

The Enen read the stick and put it between his teeth for a hurried footnote. It was amazing, Dillingham thought, how effectively they could flex their jaws for minute variations in depth and slant. Compared to this, the human jaw was a clumsy portcullis.

The message went back to the machine. "It's a big toothache that no one can cure. You must come."

"Oh, come now, Watson," Dillingham said, deeply flattered. "I've been training your dentists for six months now, and I must admit they're experienced and intelligent specialists. They know their maxillaries from their mandibulars. As a matter of fact, some of them are a good deal more adept than I, except in the specific area of metallic restorations. Surely — "

But the Enen grabbed the stick before any more could be imprinted by the machine's clattering jaws. "Doctor — this is an *alien*. It's the son of the high muckamuck of Gleep." The terms, of course, were the ones he had programmed to indicate any ruling dignitary of any other planet. He wondered whether he would be well advised to substitute more serious designations before someone caught on. Tomorrow, perhaps, he would see about it. "You, Doctor, are our only practicing exodontist."

Ah — now it was becoming clear. He was a stranger from a far planet — and a dentist. Ergo, he must know all about off-world dentition. The Enen's faith was touching. Well, if this was a job they could not handle, he could at least take a look at it. The "alien" could hardly have stranger dentition than the Enens themselves, and success might represent a handsome credit toward his eventual freedom. It would certainly be more challenging than drilling his afternoon class in Applications of Supercolloid.

"I'm pretty busy with that new group of trainees," he said. This was merely a dodge to elicit more information, since the Enens tended to omit important details. They did not do so intentionally; it was just that their notions of importance differed here and there from his own.

"The muckamuck has offered fifty pounds of frumpstiggle for this one service," the Enen replied.

Dillingham whistled, and the transcoder dutifully printed the translation. Frumpstiggle was neither money nor merchandise. He had never been able to pin down exactly what it *was*, but for convenience thought of it as worth its exact weight in gold: $35 per ounce, $560 per pound. The Enens did not employ money as such, but their avid barter for frumpstiggle seemed roughly equivalent. His commission on fifty pounds would amount to a handsome dividend and would bring his return to Earth that much closer.

"All right," he said. "Bring the patient in."

The Enen became agitated. "The high muckamuck's family can't leave the planet. You must go to Gleep."

He had half expected something of this sort. The Enens gallivanted from planet to planet and system to system with dismaying nonchalance. Dillingham had not yet become accustomed to the several ways in which they far excelled Earth technology, or to the abrupt manner of their transactions. One of their captains (strictly speaking, they didn't have officers, but this was a minor matter) had required dental help and simply stopped off at the nearest inhabited planet, skipping the normal formalities, and visited a local practitioner. Realizing that local technique was in some respects superior to that of the home planet, the captain had brought the practitioner along.

Thus Dillingham had found himself the property of the Enens — he who had never dreamed of anything other than conventional retirement in Florida. He was no intrepid spaceman, no seeker of fortune. He had been treated well enough, and certainly the Enens respected his abilities more than had his patients on Earth; but galactic intercourse was more unsettling than exciting for a man of his maturity.

I'll go and pack my bag," he said.

II

Gleep turned out to be a water world. The ship splashed down beside a floating waystation, and they were transferred to a tanklike amphibious vehicle. It rolled into the ocean and paddled along somewhat below the surface.

Dillingham had read somewhere that intelligent life could not evolve in water because of the inhibiting effect of the liquid medium upon the motion of specialized appendages. Certainly the fish of Earth had never amounted to much. How could primitive swimmers hope to engage in interstellar commerce?

Evidently that particular theory was wrong, elsewhere in the galaxy. Still, he wondered just how the Gleeps had circumvented the rapid-motion barrier. Did they live in domes *under* the ocean?

He hoped the patient would not prove to be too alien. Presumably it had teeth; but that might very well be the least of the problems. At any rate, he could draw on whatever knowledge the Enens had, and he had also made sure to bring a second transcoder keyed to Gleep. It was awkward to carry two machines, but too much could be lost in retranslation if he had to get the Gleep complaints relayed through the Enens.

A monstrous whale-shape loomed in the porthole. The thing spied the sub, advanced, and opened a cavernous maw. "Look out!" he yelled, wishing the driver had ears.

The Enen glanced indifferently at the message-stick and chomped a casual reply. "Everything is in order, Doctor."

"But a leviathan is about to engulf us!"

"Naturally. That's a Gleep."

Dillingham stared out the port, stunned. No wonder the citizens couldn't leave the planet! It was a matter of physics, not convention.

The vessel was already inside the colossal mouth, and the jaws were closing. "You mean — you mean this is the *patient?*" But he already had his answer. Damn those little details the Enens forgot to mention. A whale!

The mouth was shut now, and the headlight of the sub speared out to reveal encompassing mountains of flexing flesh. The treads touched land — probably the tongue — and took hold. A minute's climb brought them into a great domed air chamber.

They came to a halt beside what reminded him of the White Cliffs of Dover. The hatch sprang open, and the Enens piled out. None of them seemed concerned about the possibility that the creature might involuntarily swallow, so Dillingham put that thought as far from his mind as he was able. His skull seemed determined to hold it in, unfortunately.

"This is the tooth," the Enen's message said. The driver pointed to a solid marble boulder.

Dillingham contemplated it. The tooth stood about twelve feet high, counting only the distance it projected from the spongy gingival tissue. Much more would be below, of course.

"I see," he said. He could think of nothing more pertinent at the moment. He looked at the bag in his hand, which contained an assortment of needle-pointed probes, several ounces of instant amalgam, and sundry additional staples. In the sub was a portable drill with a heavy-duty needle attachment that could easily excavate a cavity a full inch deep.

Well, they *had* called it a "big toothache." He just hadn't been alert.

They brought forth a light extendible ladder and leaned it against the tooth. They set his drill and transcoders beside it. "Summon us when you're finished," their parting message said.

Dillingham felt automatically for the electronic signal in his pocket. By the time he drew breath to protest, the amphibian was gone.

He was alone in the mouth of a monster.

Well, he'd been in awkward situations before. He tried once again to close his mind to the horrors that lurked about him and ascended the ladder, holding his lantern aloft.

The occlusive surface was about ten feet in diameter. It was slightly concave and worn smooth. In the center was a dark trench about two feet wide and over a yard long. This was obviously the source of the irritation.

He walked over to it and looked down. A putrid stench sent him gasping back. Yes — this was the cavity. It seemed to range from a foot in depth at the edges to four feet in the center.

"That," he said aloud, "is a case of dental caries for the record book."

Unfortunately, he had no record book. All he possessed was a useless bag of implements and a smarting nose. But there was nothing for it but to explore the magnitude of the decay. It probably extended laterally within the pulp, so that the total infected area was considerably larger than that visible from above. He would have to check this directly.

He forced himself to breathe regularly, though his stomach danced in protest. He stepped down into the cavity.

The muck was ankle-deep and the miasma overpowering. He summoned the dregs of his willpower and squatted to poke into the bottom with one finger. Under the slime, the surface was like packed earth. He was probably still inches from the material of the tooth itself; these were merely layers of crushed and spoiling food.

He remembered long-ago jokes about eating apple compote, pronouncing the word with an internal "s." Compost. It was not a joke any more.

He located a dry area and scuffed it with one foot. Some dark flakes turned up, but no real impression had been made. He wound up and drove his toe into the wall as hard as he could.

There was a thunderous roar. He clapped his hands to his ears as the air pressure increased explosively. His footing slipped, and he fell into the reeking center section of the trench.

An avalanche of muck descended upon him. Overhead, hundreds of tons of flesh and bone and gristle crashed down imperiously, seeming ready to crush every particle of matter within its compass into further compost.

The jaws were closing.

Dillingham found himself face down in sickening garbage, his ears ringing from the atmospheric compression and his body quivering from the mechanical one. The lantern, miraculously, was undamaged and bright, and his own limbs were sound. He sat up, wiped some of the sludge from face and arms and grabbed for the slippery light.

He was trapped between clenched jaws — inside the cavity.

Frantically he activated the signal. After an interminable period while he waited in mortal fear of suffocation, the ponderous upper jaw lifted. He scrambled out, dripping.

The bag of implements was now a thin layer of color on the surface of the tooth. "Perfect occlusion," he murmured professionally, while shaking in violent reaction to the realization that his fall had narrowly saved him from the same fate.

The ladder was gone. Anxious to remove himself from the dangerous biting surface as quickly as possible, he prepared to jump but saw a gigantic mass of tentacles reaching for his portable drill near the base of the tooth. Each tentacle appeared to be thirty feet or more in length and as strong as a python's tail.

The biting surface no longer seemed so dangerous. Dillingham remained where he was and watched the drill being carried into the darkness of the mouth's center.

In a few more minutes the amphibian vehicle appeared. The Enen driver emerged, chewed a stick, presented it. Dillingham reached for the transcoder and discovered that it was the wrong one. All he had now was the useless Gleep interpreter.

Chagrined, he fiddled with it. At least he could set it to play back whatever the Gleep prince might have said. Perhaps there had been meaning in that roar . . .

There had been. "OUCH!" the machine exclaimed.

III

The next few hours were complicated. Dillingham now had to speak to the Enens via the Gleep muckamuck (after the episode in the cavity, he regretted this nomenclature acutely), who had been summoned for a diagnostic conference. This was accomplished by setting up shop in the creature's communications department.

The compartment was actually an offshoot from the Gleep lung, deep inside the body. It was a huge, internal air space with sensitive tentacles bunching from the walls. This was the manner in which the dominant species of this landless planet had developed fast-moving appendages whose manipulation led eventually to tools and intelligence. An entire technology had developed — *inside* the great bodies.

"So you see," he said, "I have to have an anesthetic that will do the job, and canned air to breathe while I'm working, and a power drill that will handle up to an eighteen-inch depth of rock. Also a sledgehammer and a dozen wedges. And a derrick and the following quantities of — " He went on to make a startling list of supplies.

The transcoder sprouted half a dozen tentacles and waved them in a dizzying semaphore. After a moment a group of the wall tentacles waved back. "It shall be accomplished," the muckamuck reply came.

Dillingham wondered what visual signal had projected the "ouch!" back in the patient's mouth. Then it came to him: the tentacles that had absconded with his drill and other transcoder were extensions of the creature's tongue! Naturally they talked.

"One other thing: while you're procuring my equipment, I'd like to see a diagram of the internal structure of your molars."

"Structure?" The tentacles were agitated.

"The pattern of enamel, dentin, and pulp, or whatever passes for it in your system. A schematic drawing would do nicely. Or a sagittal section showing both the nerves and the bony socket. That tooth is still quite sensitive, which means the nerve is still alive. I wouldn't want to damage it unnecessarily."

"We have no diagrams."

Dillingham was shocked. "Don't you *know* the anatomy of your teeth? How have you repaired them before?"

"We have never had trouble with them before. We have no dentists. That is why we summoned you."

He paced the floor of the chamber, amazed. How was it possible for such intelligent and powerful creatures to remain so ignorant of matters vital to their well-being? Never had trouble before? That cavity had obviously been festering for many years.

Yet he had faced similar ignorance daily during his Earth practice. "I'll be working blind, in that case," he said at last. "You must understand that while I'll naturally do my best, I cannot guarantee to save the tooth."

"We understand," the Gleep muckamuck replied contritely.

Back on the tooth (after a stern warning to Junior to keep those jaws apart no matter how uncomfortable things got), equipped with a face mask, respirator, elbow-length gloves, and hip boots, Dillingham began the hardest labor of his life. It was not intellectually demanding or particularly intricate — just hard. He was vaporizing the festering walls of the cavity with a thirty-pound laser drill, and in half an hour his arms were dead tired.

There *was* lateral extension of the infection. He had to wedge himself into a rotting, diminishing cavern, wielding the beam at arm's length before him. He had to twist the generator sidewise to penetrate every branching side pocket, all the while frankly terrified lest the beam slip and accidently touch part of his own body. He was playing with fire — a fiery beam that could slice off his arm and puff it into vapor in less than a careless second.

At least, he thought sweatily, he wasn't going to have to use the sledgehammer here. When he ordered the drill, he had expected a mechanical one similar to those pistons used to break up pavement on Earth. To the Gleep, however, a drill was a laser beam. This was indeed far superior to what he had had in mind. Deadly, yes — but real serendipity.

Backbreaking hours later it was done. Sterile walls of dentin lined the cavity on every side. Yet this was only the beginning.

Dillingham, after a short nap right there in the now aseptic cavity, roused himself to make careful measurements. He had to be certain that every alley was widest at the opening and that none were too sharply twisted. Wherever the measurements were unsatisfactory, he drilled away healthy material until the desired configuration had been achieved. He also adjusted the beam for "polish" and wiped away the rough surfaces.

He signaled the Enen sub and indicated by gestures that it was time for the tank of supercolloid. And resolved that *next* time he went anywhere, he would bring a trunkful of spare transcoders. He had problems enough without translation difficulties. At least he had been able to make clear that they had to send a scout back to the home planet to pick up the bulk supplies.

Supercolloid was a substance developed by the ingenious Enens in response to his exorbitant specifications of several months before. He had once entertained the notion that if he were slightly unreasonable, they would ship him home. Instead they had met the specifications exactly and increased his assessed value, neatly adding years to his term of captivity. He became more careful after that — but the substance remained a prosthodontist's dream.

Supercolloid was a fluid, stored under pressure, that set rapidly when released. It held its shape indefinitely without measurable distortion, yet was as flexible as rubber. It was ideal for difficult impressions, since it could give way while being withdrawn and spring immediately back to the proper shape. This saved time and reduced error. At 1300° Fahrenheit it melted suddenly into the thin, transparent fluid from which it started. This was its most important property.

Dillingham was about to make a very large cast. To begin the complex procedure, he had to fill every crevice of the cavity with colloid. Since the volume of the cleaned cavity came to about forty cubic feet, and supercolloid weighed fifty pounds per cubic foot when set, he required a good two thousand pounds of it, at the very least.

A full ton — to fill a single cavity. "Think big," he told himself.

He set up the tank and hauled the long hose into the pit. Once more he crawled headfirst into the lateral expansion, no longer needing the face mask. He aimed the nozzle without fear and squirted the foamy green liquid into the farthest offshoot, making certain that no air spaces remained. He backed off a few feet and filled the other crevices, but left the main section open.

In half an hour the lateral branch had been simplified considerably. It was now a deep, flat crack without offshoots. Dillingham put away the nozzle and crawled in with selected knives and brushes. He cut away projecting colloid, leaving each filling flush with the main crevice wall, and painted purple fixative over each surface.

Satisfied at last, he trotted out the colloid hose again and started the pump. This time he opened the nozzle to full aperture and filled the main crevice, backing away as the foam threatened to engulf him. Soon all of the space was full. He smoothed the green wall facing the main cavity and painted it in the same manner as the offshoots.

Now he was ready for the big one. So far he had used up about eight cubic feet of colloid, but the gaping center pit would require over thirty feet. He removed the nozzle entirely and let the tank heave itself out. The cavity was rapidly being filled.

"Turn it off," he yelled to the Enen by the pump as green foam bulged gently over the rim. One ton of supercolloid filled the tooth, and he was ready to carve it down and insert the special plastic loop in the center.

The foam continued to pump. "I said TURN IT OFF!" he cried again. Then he remembered that he had no transcoder for Enen. They could neither hear him nor comprehend him.

He flipped the hose away from the filling and aimed it over the edge of the tooth. He had no way to cut it off himself, since he had removed the nozzle. There couldn't be much left in the tank.

A rivulet of green coursed over the pink tissues, traveling toward the squidlike tongue. The tentacles reached out, grasping the foam as it solidified. They soon became festooned in green.

Dillingham laughed — but not for long. There was a steamwhistle sigh followed by a violent tremor of the entire jaw. "I'm going to . . . sneeze," the Gleep transcoder said, sounding fuzzy.

The colloid was interfering with the articulation of the Gleep's tongue.

A sneeze! Suddenly he realized what that would mean to him and the Enen crew.

"Get under cover!" he shouted to the Enens, again forgetting that they couldn't perceive the warning. But they had already grasped the significance of the tremors and were piling into the sub frantically.

"Hey — wait for me!" But he was too late. The air howled by with the titanic intake of breath. There was a terrible pause.

Dillingham lunged for the mound of colloid and dug his fingers into the almost-solid substance. "Keep your jaws apart!" he yelled at the Gleep, praying it could still pick up the message. "KEEP THEM OPEN!"

The sound of a tornado raged out of its throat. He buried his face in green as the hurricane struck, wrenching mercilessly at his body. His arms were wrenched cruelly; his fingers tore through the infirm colloid, slipping . . .

IV

The wind died, leaving him gasping at the edge of the tooth. He had survived it. The jaws had not closed.

He looked up. The upper cuspids hung only ten feet above, visible in the light from the charmed lamp hooked somehow to his foot.

He was past the point of reaction. "Open, please," he called in his best operative manner, hoping the transcoder was still in the vicinity, and went to peer over the edge.

There was no sign of the sub. The tank, with its discharging hose, was also gone.

He took a walk across the neighboring teeth, looking for whatever there was to see. He was appalled at the amount of decalcification and outright decay in evidence. This Gleep child would shortly be in pain again, unless substantial restorative work was done immediately.

But in a shallow cavity — one barely a foot deep — he found the transcoder. "It's an ill decalcification that bodes nobody good," he murmured, retrieving it.

The sub reappeared and disgorged its somewhat shaken passengers. Dillingham marched back over the rutted highway and joined them. But the question still nagged his mind: how could the caries he had observed be reconciled with the muckamuck's undoubtedly sincere statement that there had never been dental trouble before? What had changed?

He carved the green surface into an appropriate pattern and carefully applied his fixative. He was ready for the next step.

Now the derrick was brought up and put in play. Dillingham guided its dangling hook into the eyelet set in the colloid and signalled the Enen operator to lift. The chain went taut; the mass of solidified foam eased grandly out of its socket and hung in the air, an oddly shaped boulder.

He turned his attention to the big crevice-filling. He screwed in a corkscrew eyelet and arranged a pulley so that the derrick could act on it effectively. The purple fixative had prevented the surface of the main impression from attaching to that of the subsidiary one — just as it was also protecting the several smaller branches within.

There was no real trouble. In due course every segment of the impression was marked and laid out in the makeshift laboratory he had set up near the waterlift of the Gleep's mouth. They were ready for one more step.

The tank of prepared investment arrived. This, too, was a special composition. It remained fluid until triggered by a particular electric jolt, whereupon it solidified instantly. Once solid, it could not be affected by anything short of demolition by a sledgehammer.

Dillingham pumped a quantity into a great temporary vat. He attached a plastic handle to the smallest impression, dipped it into the vat, withdrew it entirely covered by white batter and touched the electrode to it. He handed the abruptly solid object to the nearest Enen.

Restorative procedure on Gleep differed somewhat from established Earth technique. All it took was a little human imagination and Enen technology.

The octopus-tongue approached while he worked. It reached for him. "Get out of here or I'll cram you into the burnout furnace!" he snapped into the transcoder. The tongue retreated.

The major section was a problem. It barely fit into the vat, and a solid foot of it projected over the top. He finally had the derrick lower it until it bumped bottom, then raise it a few inches and hold it steady. He passed out brushes, and he and the Enen crew went to work slopping the goo over the top and around the suspending hook.

He touched the electrode to the white monster. The derrick lifted the mass, letting the empty vat fall free. Yet another stage was done.

Two ovens were employed for the burnout. Each was big enough for a man to stand in. They placed the ends of the plastic rods in special holders and managed to fit all of the smaller units into one oven, fastening them into place by means of a heat-resistant framework. The main chunk sat in the other oven, propped upside-down.

They sealed the ovens and set their thermostats for 2000°. Dillingham lay down in the empty vat and slept.

Three hours later burnout was over. Even supercolloid took time to melt completely when heated in a fifteen-hundred-pound mass. But now the green liquid had been drained into reservoirs and sealed away, while the smaller quantities of melted plastic were allowed to collect in a disposal vat. The white investments were hollow shells, open only where the plastic rods had projected.

The casting was the most spectacular stage. Dillingham had decided to use gold, though he worried that its high specific gravity would overbalance the Gleep jaw. It was impossible under present conditions to arrange for a gold-plated, matching-density filling, and he was not familiar enough with other metals to be sure they were adaptable to his purpose. The expansion coefficient of his investment matched that of gold exactly, for example; anything else would solidify into the wrong size.

Gold, at any rate, was nothing to the muckamuck; his people refined it through their gills, extracting it from the surrounding water on order in any quantity.

The crucible arrived: a self-propelled boilerlike affair. They piled hundred-pound ingots of precise gold alloy into the hopper, while the volcanic innards of the crucible rumbled and belched and melted everything to rich bright liquid.

A line of Enens carried the smaller investments, which were shaped inside exactly like the original impressions, to the spigot and held them with tongs while the fluid fortune poured in. These were carefully deposited in the vat, now filled with cold water.

The last cast, of course, was the colossal vat-shaped one. This was simply propped up under the spigot while the tired crew kept feeding in ingots.

By the time this cast had been poured, twenty-four tons of gold had been used in all.

While the largest chunk was being hauled to the ocean inside the front of the mouth, Dillingham broke open the smaller investments and laid out the casts according to his chart of the cavity. He gave each a minimum of finishing; on so gross a scale, it could hardly make much difference.

The finished casts weighed more than twenty times as much as the original colloid impressions had, and even the smallest ones were distinctly awkward to maneuver into place. He marked them, checked off their positions on his chart, and had the Enens ferry them up with the derrick. At the other end, he manhandled each into its proper place, verified its fit and position and withdrew it to paint it with cement. No part of this filling would come loose in action.

Once again the branching cavern lost its projections, this time permanently, as each segment was secured and severed from its projecting sprue. He kept the sprues — the handles of gold, the shape of the original plastic handles — on until the end, because otherwise there would have been no purchase on the weighty casts. He had to have some handle to adjust them.

The derrick lowered the crevice-piece into the cavity. Two Enens pried it in with power crowbars. Dillingham stood by and squirted cement over the mass as it slid reluctantly into the hole.

It was necessary to attach a heavy weight to the derrick-hook and swing it repeatedly against the four-ton cast in order to tamp it in all the way.

At last it was time for the major assembly. Nineteen tons of gold descended slowly into the hole while they dumped quarts of liquid cement into a pool below. The cast touched bottom and settled into place, while the cement bubbled up around the edges and overflowed.

They danced a little jig on top of the filling — just to tamp it in properly, Dillingham told himself, wishing that a fraction of its value in Earth terms could be credited to his purchase-price. The job was over.

V

"A commendable performance," the high muckamuck said. "My son is frisking about in his pen like a regular tadpole and eating well."

Dillingham remembered what he had seen during the walk along the occlusive surfaces. "I'm afraid he won't be frisking long. In another year or two he'll be feeling half a dozen other caries. Decay is rampant."

"You mean this will happen again?" The tentacles waved so violently that the transcoder stuttered.

Dillingham decided to take the fish by the tail. "Are you still trying to tell me that no member of your species has suffered dental caries before this time?"

"Never."

This still did not make sense. "Does your son's diet differ in any important respect from yours, or from that of other children?"

"My son is a prince!"

"Meaning he can eat whatever he wants, whether it is good for him or not?"

The Gleep paused. "He gets so upset if he doesn't have his way. He's only a baby — hardly three centuries old."

Dillingham was getting used to differing standards. "Do you feed him delicacies — refined foods?"

"Naturally. Nothing but the best."

He sighed. "Muckamuck, my people also had perfect teeth — until they began consuming sweets and overly refined foods. Then dental caries became the most common disease among them. You're going to have to curb your boy's appetite."

"I couldn't." He could almost read the agitation of the tentacles without benefit of translation. "He'd throw a terrible tantrum."

He had expected this reaction. He'd encountered it many times on Earth. "In that case, you'd better begin training a crew of dentists. Your son will require constant attention."

"But we can't do such work ourselves. We have no suitable appendages, externally."

"Import some dentists, then. You have no alternative."

The creature signaled a sigh. "You make a convincing case." The tentacles relaxed while it thought. Suddenly they came alive again. "Enen — it seems we need a permanent technician. Will you sell us this one?"

Dillingham gaped, horrified at the thought of all that garbage in the patient's jaw. Surely they couldn't —

"Sell him!" the Enen chief replied angrily. Dillingham wondered how he was able to understand the words, then realized that his transcoder was picking up the Gleep signals translated by the other machine. From Enen to Gleep to English, via paired machines. Why hadn't he thought of that before?

"This is a human being," the Enen continued indignantly. "A member of an intelligent species dwelling far across the galaxy. He is the only exodontist in this entire sector of space, and a fine upstanding fellow at that. How dare you make such a crass suggestion!"

Bless him! Dillingham had always suspected that his hosts were basically creatures of principle.

"We're prepared to offer a full ton of superlative-grade frumpstiggle . . ." the muckamuck said enticingly.

"A full *ton?*" The Enens were aghast. Then, recovering: "True, the Earthman *has* taught us practically all he knows. We could probably get along without him now . . ."

"Now wait a minute!" Dillingham shouted; but the bargaining continued unabated.

After all — what is the value of a man, compared to frumpstiggle?

o/cean/og/ra/phy — the study and exploration of the world's oceans. The depths of the seas may be the next frontier, since we know relatively little about the resources and opportunities that undoubtedly exist there. Science fiction writers have been exploring the oceans of other planets and our own for several generations in books like *The Godwhale,* by T. J. Bass (Ballantine Books, 1974), and Kenneth Bulmer's *City Under The Sea* (Ace Books, 1957; Avon Books, 1980).

In the Abyss

H. G. WELLS

The lieutenant stood in front of the steel sphere and gnawed a piece of pine splinter. "What do you think of it, Steevens?" he asked.

"It's an idea," said Steevens, in the tone of one who keeps an open mind.

"I believe it will smash — flat," said the lieutenant.

"He seems to have calculated it all out pretty well," said Steevens, still impartial.

"But think of the pressure," said the lieutenant. "At the surface of the water it's fourteen pounds to the inch, thirty feet down it's double that; sixty, treble; ninety, four times; nine hundred, forty times; five thousand three hundred — that's a mile — it's two hundred and forty times fourteen pounds; that's — let's see — thirty hundredweight — a ton and a half, Steevens; *a ton and a half* to the square inch. And the ocean where he's going is five miles deep. That's seven and a half — "

"Sounds a lot," said Steevens, "but it's jolly thick steel."

The lieutenant made no answer, but resumed his pine splinter. The object of their conversation was a huge globe of steel, having an exterior diameter of perhaps eight feet. It looked like the shot for some titanic piece of artillery. It was elaborately nested in a monstrous scaffolding built into the framework of the vessel, and the gigantic spars that were presently to sling it overboard gave the stern of the ship an appearance that had raised the curiosity of every decent sailor who had sighted it, from the pool of London to the Tropic of Capricorn. In two places, one above the other, the steel gave place to a couple of circular windows of enormously thick glass, and one of these, set in a steel frame of great solidity, was now partially unscrewed. Both the men had seen the interior of this globe for the first time that morning. It was elaborately padded with air cushions, with little studs sunk between bulging pillows to work the simple mechanism of the affair. Everything was elaborately padded, even the Myer's apparatus which was to absorb carbonic acid and replace the oxygen inspired by its tenant, when he had crept in by the glass manhole and had been screwed in. It was so elaborately padded that a man might have been fired from a gun in it with perfect safety. And it had need to be, for presently a man was to crawl in through that glass manhole, to be screwed up tightly, and to be flung overboard, and to sink down — down — down, for five miles, even as the lieutenant said. It had taken the strongest hold of his imagination; it made him a bore at mess; and he found Steevens, the new arrival aboard, a godsend to talk to about it, over and over again.

"It's my opinion," said the lieutenant, "that that glass will simply bend in and bulge and smash, under a pressure of that sort. Daubrée has made rocks run like water under big pressures — and, you mark my words — "

"If the glass did break in," said Steevens, "what then?"

"The water would shoot in like a jet of iron. Have you ever felt a straight jet of high pressure water? It would hit as hard as a bullet. It would simply smash him and flatten him. It would tear down his throat, and into his lungs; it would blow in his ears — "

"What a detailed imagination you have," protested Steevens, who saw things vividly.

"It's a simple statement of the inevitable," said the lieutenant.

"And the globe?"

"Would just give out a few little bubbles, and it would settle down comfortably against the Day of Judgment, among the oozes and the bottom clay — with poor Elstead spread over his own smashed cushions like butter over bread."

He repeated this sentence as though he liked it very much. "Like butter over bread," he said.

"Having a look at the jigger?" said a voice behind them, and Elstead stood behind them, spick and span in white, with a cigarette between his teeth and his eyes smiling out of the shadow of his ample hat-brim. "What's that about bread and butter, Weybridge? Grumbling as usual about the insufficient pay of naval officers? It won't be more than a day now before I start. We are to get the slings ready today. This clean sky and gentle swell is just the kind of thing for swinging off twenty tons of lead and iron; isn't it?"

"It won't affect you much," said Weybridge.

"No. Seventy or eighty feet down, and I shall be there in a dozen seconds, there's not a particle moving, though the wind shriek itself hoarse up above and the water lifts halfway to the clouds. No. Down there — " He moved to the side of the ship and the other two followed him. All three leant forward on their elbows and stared down into the yellow-green water.

"Peace," said Elstead, finishing his thought aloud.

"Are you dead certain that clockwork will act?" asked Weybridge, presently.

"It has worked thirty-five times," said Elstead. "It's bound to work."

"But if it doesn't?"

"Why shouldn't it?"

"I wouldn't go down in that confounded thing," said Weybridge, "for twenty thousand pounds."

"Cheerful chap you are," said Elstead, and spat sociably at a bubble below.

"I don't understand yet how you mean to work the thing," said Steevens.

"In the first place I'm screwed into the sphere," said Elstead, "and when I've turned the electric light off and on three times to show I'm cheerful, I'm swung out over the stern by that crane, with all those big lead sinkers slung below me. The top lead weight has a roller carrying a hundred fathoms of strong cord rolled up, and that's all that joins the sinkers to the sphere, except the slings that will be cut when the affair is dropped. We use cord rather than wire rope because it's easier to cut and more buoyant — necessary points as you will see.

"Through each of these lead weights you notice there is a hole, and an iron rod will be run through that and will project six feet on the lower side. If that rod is rammed up from below it knocks up a lever and sets the clockwork in motion at the side of the cylinder on which the cord winds.

"Very well. The whole affair is lowered gently into the water, and the slings are cut. The sphere floats — with the air in it, it's lighter than water; but the lead weights go down straight and the cord runs out. When the cord is all paid out, the sphere will go down too, pulled down by the cord."

"But why the cord?" asked Steevens. "Why not fasten the weights directly to the sphere?"

"Because of the smash down below. The whole affair will go rushing down, mile after mile, at a headlong pace at last. It would be knocked to pieces on the bottom if it wasn't for that cord. But the weights will hit the bottom, and directly they do the buoyancy of the sphere will come into play. It will go on sinking slower and slower; come to a stop at last and then begin to float upward again.

"That's where the clockwork comes in. Directly the weights smash against the sea bottom, the rod will be knocked through and will kick up the clockwork, and the cord will be rewound on the reel. I shall be lugged down to the sea bottom. There I shall stay for half an hour, with the electric light on, looking about me. Then the clockwork will release a spring knife, the cord will be cut, and up I shall rush again, like a soda water bubble. The cord itself will help the flotation."

"And if you should chance to hit a ship?" said Weybridge.

"Should I come up at such a pace, I would go clean through it," said Elstead, "like a cannon ball. You needn't worry about that."

"And suppose some nimble crustacean should wriggle into your clock-work — "

"It would be a pressing sort of invitation for me to stop," said Elstead, turning his back on the water and staring at the sphere.

They had swung Elstead overboard by eleven o'clock. The day was serenely bright and calm, with the horizon lost in haze. The electric glare in the little upper compartment beamed cheerfully three times. Then they let him down slowly to the surface of the water, and a sailor in the stern chains hung ready to cut the tackle that held the lead weights and the sphere together. The globe, which had looked so large on deck, looked the smallest thing conceivable under the stern of the ship. It rolled a little, and its two dark windows, which floated uppermost, seemed like eyes turned up in round wonderment at the people who crowded the rail. A voice wondered how Elstead liked the rolling. "Are you ready?" sang out the commander. "Aye, aye, sir!" "Then let her go!"

The rope of the tackle tightened against the blade and was cut, and an eddy rolled over the globe in a grotesquely helpless fashion. Someone waved a handkerchief, someone else tried an ineffectual cheer, a middy was counting slowly: "Eight, nine, ten!" Another roll, then with a jerk and a splash the thing righted itself.

It seemed to be stationary for a moment, to grow rapidly smaller, and then the water closed over it, and it became visible, enlarged by refraction and dimmer, below the surface. Before one could count three it had disappeared. There was a flicker of white light far down in the water that diminished to a speck and vanished. Then there was nothing but a depth of water going down into blackness, through which a shark was swimming.

Then suddenly the screw of the cruiser began to rotate, the water was roiled, the shark disappeared in a wrinkled confusion, and a torrent of foam rushed across the crystalline clearness that had swallowed up Elstead. "What's the idee?" said one seaman to another.

"We're going to lay off about a couple of miles, 'fear he should hit us when he comes up," said his mate.

The ship steamed slowly to her new position. Aboard her almost everyone who was unoccupied remained watching the breathing swell into which the sphere had sunk. It is doubtful if, for the next half-hour, a word was spoken that did not bear directly or indirectly on Elstead. The December sun was now high in the sky, and the heat very considerable.

"He'll be cold enough down there," said Weybridge. "They say that below a certain depth seawater's always just about freezing."

"Where'll he come up?" asked Steevens. "I've lost my bearings."

"That's the spot," said the commander, who prided himself on his omni-science. He extended a precise finger south-eastward. "And this, I reckon, is pretty nearly the moment," he said. "He's been thirty-five minutes."

"How long does it take to reach the bottom of the ocean?" asked Steevens.

"For a depth of five miles, and reckoning — as we did — an acceleration to two foot per second, both ways, is just about three-quarters of a minute."

"Then he's overdue," said Weybridge.

"Pretty nearly," said the commander. "I suppose it takes a few minutes for that cord of his to wind in."

"I forgot that," said Weybridge, evidently relieved.

And then began the suspense. A minute slowly dragged itself out, and no sphere shot out of the water. Another followed, and nothing broke the low oily swell. The sailors explained to one another that little point about the winding-in of the cord. The rigging was dotted with expectant faces. "Come up, Elstead!" called one hairy-chested salt, impatiently, and the others caught it up, and shouted as though they were waiting for the curtain of a theater to rise.

The commander glanced irritably at them.

"Of course, if the acceleration's less than two," he said, "he'll be all the longer. We aren't absolutely certain that was the proper figure. I'm no slavish believer in calculations."

Steevens agreed concisely. No one on the quarter-deck spoke for a couple of minutes. Then Steevens's watch-case clicked.

When, twenty-one minutes after, the sun reached the zenith, they were still waiting for the globe to reappear, and not a man aboard had dared to whisper that hope was dead. It was Weybridge who first gave expression to that realization. He spoke while the sound of eight bells still hung in the air. "I always distrusted that window," he said quite suddenly to Steevens.

"Good God!" said Steevens, "you don't think — "

"Well!" said Weybridge, and left the rest to his imagination.

"I'm no great believer in calculations myself," said the commander, dubi-ously, "so that I'm not altogether hopeless yet." And at midnight the gunboat was steaming slowly in a spiral around the spot where the globe had sunk, and the white beam of the electric light fled and halted and swept discontent-edly onward again over the waste of phosphorescent waters under the little stars.

"If his window hasn't burst and smashed him," said Weybridge, "then it's a cursed sight worse, for his clockwork has gone wrong and he's alive now, five miles under our feet, down there in the cold and dark, anchored in that little bubble of his, where never a ray of light has shone or a human being lived since the waters were gathered together. He's there without food, feeling hungry and thirsty and scared, wondering whether he'll starve or stifle.

Which will it be? The Myer's apparatus is running out, I suppose. How long do they last?

"Good Heavens!" he exclaimed, "what little things we are! What daring little devils! Down there, miles and miles of water — all water, and all this empty water about us and this sky. Gulfs!" He threw his hands out, and as he did so a little white streak swept noiselessly up the sky, traveling more slowly, stopped, became a motionless dot as though a new star had fallen up into the sky. Then it went sliding back again and lost itself amidst the reflections of the stars and the white haze of the sea's phosphorescence.

At the sight he stopped, arm extended and mouth open. He shut his mouth, opened it again, and waved his arms with an impatient gesture. Then he turned, shouted, "El-stead ahoy," to the first watch, and went at a run to Lindley and the search light. "I saw him," he said. "Starboard there! His light's on and he's just shot out of the water. Bring the light round. We ought to see him drifting, when he lifts on the swell."

But they never picked up the explorer until dawn. Then they almost ran him down. The crane was swung out and a boat's crew hooked the chain to the sphere. When they had shipped the sphere they unscrewed the manhole and peered into the darkness of the interior (for the electric light chamber was intended to illuminate the water about the sphere, and was shut off entirely from its general cavity).

The air was very hot within the cavity, and the India rubber at the lip of the manhole was soft. There was no answer to their eager questions and no sound of movement within. Elstead seemed to be lying motionless, crumpled up in the bottom of the globe. The ship's doctor crawled in and lifted him out to the men outside. For a moment or so they did not know whether Elstead was alive or dead. His face, in the yellow glow of the ship's lamps, glistened with perspiration. They carried him down to his own cabin.

He was not dead, they found, but in a state of absolute nervous collapse, and cruelly bruised besides. For some days he had to lie perfectly still. It was a week before he could tell his experiences.

Almost his first words were that he was going down again. The sphere would have to be altered, he said, in order to allow him to throw off the cord if need be, and that was all. He had had the most marvellous experience. "You thought I should find nothing but ooze," he said. "You laughed at my explorations, and I've discovered a new world!" He told his story in disconnected fragments, and chiefly from the wrong end, so that it is impossible to retell it in his words. But what follows is the narrative of his experience.

It began atrociously, he said. Before the cord ran out the thing kept rolling over. He felt like a frog in a football. He could see nothing but the crane and the sky overhead, with an occasional glimpse of the people at the ship's rail. He couldn't tell a bit which way the thing would roll next. Suddenly he would find his feet going up and try to step, and over he went rolling, head over heels and just anyhow on the padding. Any other shape would have been more comfortable, but no other shape was to be relied upon under the huge pressure of the nethermost abyss.

Suddenly the swaying ceased; the globe righted, and when he had picked himself up, he saw the water all about him greeny-blue with an attenuated light filtering down from above, and a shoal of little floating things went rushing up past him, as it seemed to him, towards the light. And even as he looked it grew darker and darker, until the water above was as dark as the midnight sky, albeit of a greener shade, and the water below black. And little transparent things in the water developed a faint glint of luminosity, and shot past him in faint greenish streaks.

And the feeling of falling! It was just like the start of a lift, he said, only it kept on. One has to imagine what that means, that keeping on. It was then of all times that Elstead repented of his adventure. He saw the chances against him in an altogether new light. He thought of the big cuttlefish people knew to exist in the middle waters, the kind of things they find half-digested in whales at times, or floating dead and rotten and half eaten by fish. Suppose one caught hold and wouldn't leave go. And had the clockwork really been sufficiently tested? But whether he wanted to go on or go back mattered not the slightest now.

In fifty seconds everything was as black as night outside, except where the beam from his light struck through the waters, and picked out every now and then some fish or scrap of sinking matter. They flashed by too fast for him to see what they were. Once he thought he passed a shark. And then the sphere began to get hot by friction against the water. They had underestimated this, it seems.

The first thing he noticed was that he was perspiring, and then he heard a hissing, growing louder, under his feet, and saw a lot of little bubbles — very little bubbles they were — rushing upward like a fan through the water outside. Steam! He felt the window and it was hot. He turned on the minute glow-lamp that lit his own cavity, looked at the padded watch by the studs, and saw he had been travelling now for two minutes. It came into his head that the window would crack through the conflict of temperatures, for he knew the bottom water was very near freezing.

Then suddenly the floor of the sphere seemed to press against his feet, the rush of bubbles outside grew slower and slower and the hissing diminished. The sphere rolled a little. The window had not cracked, nothing had given, and he knew that the dangers of sinking, at any rate, were over.

In another minute or so he would be on the floor of the abyss. He thought, he said, of Steevens and Weybridge and the rest of them five miles overhead, higher to him than the very highest clouds that ever floated over land are to us, steaming slowly and staring down and wondering what had happened to him.

He peered out of the window. There were no more bubbles now, and the hissing had stopped. Outside there was a heavy blackness — as black as black velvet — except where the electric light pierced the empty water and showed the color of it — a yellow-green. Then three things like shapes of fire swam into sight, following each other through the water. Whether they were little and near, or big and far off, he could not tell.

Each was outlined in a bluish light almost as bright as the lights of a fishing smack, a light which seemed to be smoking greatly, and all along the sides of them were specks of this, like the lighted portholes of a ship. Their phosphorescence seemed to go out as they came into the radiance of his lamp, and he saw then that they were indeed fish of some strange sort, with huge heads, vast eyes, and dwindling bodies and tails. Their eyes were turned towards him, and he judged they were following him down. He supposed they were attracted by his glare.

Presently others of the same sort joined them. As he went on down he noticed that the water became of a pallid color, and that little specks twinkled in his ray like motes in a sunbeam. This was probably due to the clouds of ooze and mud that the impact of his leaden sinkers had disturbed.

By the time he was drawn down to the lead weights he was in a dense fog of white that his electric light failed altogether to pierce for more than a few yards, and many minutes elapsed before the hanging sheets of sediment subsided to any extent. Then, lit by his light and by the transient phosphorescence of a distant shoal of fishes, he was able to see under the huge blackness of the superincumbent water an undulating expanse of grayish-white ooze, broken here and there by tangled thickets of a growth of sea lilies, waving hungry tentacles in the air.

Farther away were the graceful translucent outlines of a group of gigantic sponges. About this floor there were scattered a number of bristling flattish tufts of rich purple and black, which he decided must be some sort of sea urchin, and small, large-eyed or blind things, having a curious resemblance — some to woodlice and others to lobsters — crawled sluggishly across the track of the light and vanished into the obscurity again, leaving furrowed trails behind them.

Then suddenly the hovering swarm of little fishes veered about and came towards him as a flight of starlings might do. They passed over him like a phosphorescent snow, and then he saw behind them some larger creature advancing towards the sphere.

At first he could see it only dimly, a faintly moving figure remotely suggestive of a walking man, and then it came into the spray of light that the lamp shot out. As the glare struck it, it shut its eyes, dazzled. He stared in rigid astonishment.

It was a strange, vertebrate animal. Its dark purple head was dimly suggestive of a chameleon, but it had such a high forehead and such a braincase as no reptile ever displayed before; the vertical pitch of its face gave it a most extraordinary resemblance to a human being.

Two large and protruding eyes projected from sockets in chameleon fashion, and it had a broad reptilian mouth with horny lips beneath its little nostrils. In the position of the ears were two huge gill covers, and out of these floated a branching tree of coralline filaments, almost like the treelike gills that very young rays and sharks possess.

But the humanity of the face was not the most extraordinary thing about the creature. It was a biped: its almost globular body was poised on a tripod of two froglike legs and a long thick tail, and its fore limbs, which grotesquely caricatured the human hand much as a frog's do, carried a long shaft of bone tipped with copper. The color of the creature was variegated: its head, hands, and legs were purple; but its skin, which hung loosely upon it, even as clothes might do, was a phosphorescent gray. And it stood there, blinded by the light.

At last this unknown creature of the abyss blinked its eyes open, and, shading them with its disengaged hand, opened its mouth and gave vent to a shouting noise, articulate almost as speech might be, that penetrated even the steel case and padded jacket of the sphere. How shouting may be accomplished without lungs Elstead does not profess to explain. It then moved sideways out of the glare into the mystery of shadow that bordered it on either side, and Elstead felt rather than saw that it was coming towards him. Fancying the light had attracted it, he turned the switch that cut off the current. In another moment something soft dabbed upon the steel, and the globe swayed.

Then the shouting was repeated, and it seemed to him that a distant echo answered it. The dabbing recurred, and the globe swayed and ground against the spindle over which the wire was rolled. He stood in the blackness, and peered out into the everlasting night of the abyss. And presently he saw, very faint and remote, other phosphorescent quasi-human forms hurrying towards him.

Hardly knowing what he did, he felt about in his swaying prison for the stud of the exterior electric light, and came by accident against his own small glow lamp in its padded recess. The sphere twisted and then threw him down; he heard shouts like shouts of surprise, and when he rose to his feet he saw two pairs of stalked eyes peering into the lower window and reflecting his light.

In another moment hands were dabbing vigorously at his steel casing, and there was a sound, horrible enough in his position, of the metal protection of the clockwork being vigorously hammered. That, indeed, sent his heart into his mouth, for if these strange creatures succeeded in stopping that his release would never occur. Scarcely had he thought as much when he felt the sphere sway violently, and the floor of it press hard against his feet. He turned off the small glow lamp that lit the interior, and sent the ray of the large light in the separate compartment out into the water. The sea floor and the manlike creatures had disappeared, and a couple of fish chasing each other dropped suddenly by the window.

He thought at once that these strange denizens of the deep sea had broken the wire rope and that he had escaped. He drove up faster and faster, and then stopped with a jerk that sent him flying against the padded roof of his prison. For half a minute perhaps he was too astonished to think.

Then he felt that the sphere was spinning slowly, and rocking, and it seemed to him that it was also being drawn through the water. By crouching close to the window he managed to make his weight effective and roll that part of the sphere downward, but he could see nothing save the pale ray of his light striking down ineffectively into the darkness. It occurred to him that he would see more if he turned the lamp off and allowed his eyes to grow accustomed to the profound obscurity.

In this he was wise. After some minutes the velvety blackness became a translucent blackness, and then far away, and as faint as the zodiacal light of an English summer evening, he saw shapes moving below. He judged these creatures had detached his cable and were towing him along the sea bottom.

And then he saw something faint and remote across the undulations of the submarine plain, a broad horizon of pale luminosity that extended this way and that way as far as the range of his little window permitted him to see. To this he was being towed, as a balloon might be towed by men out of the open country into a town. He approached it very slowly, and very slowly the dim irradiation was gathered together into more definite shapes.

It was nearly five o'clock before he came over this luminous area, and by that time he could make out an arrangement suggestive of streets and houses grouped about a vast roofless erection that was grotesquely suggestive of a ruined abbey. It was spread out like a map below him. The houses were all roofless enclosures of walls, and their substance being, as he afterwards saw, of phosphorescent bones, gave the place an appearance as if it were built of drowned moonshine.

Among the inner caves of the place waving trees of crinoid stretched their tentacles, and tall, slender, glassy sponges shot like shining minarets and lilies of filmy light out of the general glow of the city. In the open spaces of the place he could see a stirring movement as of crowds of people, but he was too many fathoms above them to distinguish the individuals in those crowds.

Then slowly they pulled him down, and as they did so the details of the place crept slowly upon his apprehension. He saw that the courses of the cloudy buildings were marked out with beaded lines of round objects, and then he perceived that at several points below him in broad open spaces were forms like encrusted ships.

Slowly and surely he was drawn down, and the forms below him became brighter, clearer, more distinct. He was being pulled down, he perceived, towards the large building in the center of the town, and he could catch a glimpse ever and again of the multitudinous forms that were lugging at his cord. He was astonished to see that the rigging of one of the ships, which formed such a prominent feature of the place, was crowded with a host of gesticulating figures regarding him, and then the walls of the great building rose about him silently and hid the city from his eyes.

And such walls they were, of water-logged wood, and twisted wire rope and iron spars, and copper, and the bones and skulls of dead men.

The skulls ran in curious zigzag lines and spirals and fantastic curves over the building; and in and out of their eye-sockets, and over the whole surface of the place, lurked and played a multitude of silvery little fishes.

And now he was at such a level that he could see these strange people of the abyss plainly once more. To his astonishment, he perceived that they were prostrating themselves before him, all save one, dressed as it seemed in a robe of placoid scales and crowned with a luminous diadem, who stood with his reptilian mouth opening and shutting as though he led the chanting of the worshippers.

They continued worshiping him, without rest or intermission, for the space of three hours.

Most circumstantial was Elstead's account of this astounding city and its people, these people of perpetual night, who have never seen sun or moon or stars, green vegetation, or any living air-breathing creatures, who know nothing of fire or any light but the phosphorescent light of living things.

Startling as is his story, it is yet more startling to find that scientific men of such eminence as Adams and Jenkins find nothing incredible in it. They tell me they see no reason why intelligent, water-breathing, vertebrate creatures inured to a low temperature and enormous pressure, and of such a heavy structure that neither alive nor dead would they float, might not live upon the bottom of the deep sea quite unsuspected by us, descendants like ourselves of the great Theriomorpha of the New Red Sandstone age.

We should be known to them, however, as strange meteoric creatures wont to fall catastrophically dead out of the mysterious blackness of their watery sky. And not only we ourselves, but our ships, our metals, our appliances, would come raining down out of the night. Sometimes sinking things would smite down and crush them, as if it were the judgment of some unseen power above, and sometimes would come things of the utmost rarity or utility or shapes of inspiring suggestion. One can understand, perhaps, something of their behavior at the descent of a living man, if one thinks what a barbaric people might do, to whom an enhaloed shining creature came suddenly out of the sky.

At one time or another Elstead probably told the officers of the *Ptarmigan* every detail of his strange twelve hours in the abyss. That he also intended to write them down is certain, but he never did, and so unhappily we have to piece together the discrepant fragments of his story from the reminiscences of Commander Simmons, Weybridge, Steevens, Lindley, and the others.

We see the thing darkly in fragmentary glimpses — the huge ghostly building, the bowing, chanting people, with their dark, chameleonlike heads and faintly luminous forms, and Elstead, with his light turned on again, vainly trying to convey to their minds that the cord by which the sphere was held was to be severed. Minute after minute slipped away, and Elstead, looking at his watch, was horrified to find that he had oxygen only for four hours more. But the chant in his honor kept on as remorselessly as if it were the marching song of his approaching death.

The manner of his release he does not understand, but to judge by the end of cord that hung from the sphere, it had been cut through by rubbing against the edge of the altar. Abruptly the sphere rolled over, and he swept up out of their world, as an ethereal creature clothed in a vacuum would sweep through our own atmosphere back to its native ether again. He must have torn out of their sight as a hydrogen bubble hastens upwards from our air. A strange ascension it must have seemed to them.

The sphere rushed up with even greater velocity than, when weighed with the lead sinkers, it had rushed down. It became exceedingly hot. It drove up with the windows uppermost, and he remembers the torrent of bubbles frothing against the glass. Every moment he expected this to fly. Then suddenly something like a huge wheel seemed to be released in his head, the padded compartment began spinning about him, and he fainted. His next recollection was of his cabin, and of the doctor's voice.

But that is the substance of the extraordinary story that Elstead related in fragments to the officers of the *Ptarmigan*. He promised to write it all down at a later date. His mind was chiefly occupied with the improvement of his apparatus, which was effected at Rio.

It remains only to tell that on February 2, 1896, he made his second descent into the ocean abyss, with the improvements his first experience suggested. What happened we shall probably never know. He never returned. The *Ptarmigan* beat about over the point of his submersion, seeking him in vain for thirteen days. Then she returned to Rio, and the news was telegraphed to his friends. So the matter remains for the present. But it is hardly probable that any further attempt will be made to verify his strange story of these hitherto unsuspected cities of the deep sea.

Custer's Last Jump

STEVEN UTLEY AND HOWARD WALDROP

Smithsonian Annals of Flight 39: *The Air War in the West*
Chapter 27: "The Krupp Monoplane"

INTRODUCTION

Its wings still hold the tears from many bullets. The ailerons are still scorched black, and the exploded Henry machine rifle is bent awkwardly in its blast port.

The right landing skid is missing, and the frame has been restraightened. It stands in the left wing of the Air Museum today, next to the French Devre jet and the X-FU-5 Flying Flapjack, the world's fastest fighter aircraft.

On its rudder is the swastika, an ugly reminder of days of glory fifty years ago.

A simple plaque describes the aircraft. It reads:

CRAZY HORSE'S KRUPP MONOPLANE
(Captured at the raid on Fort Carson, January 5, 1882)

GENERAL

1. To study the history of this plane is to delve into one of the most glorious eras of aviation history. To begin: the aircraft was manufactured by the Krupp plant in Haavesborg, Netherlands. The airframe was completed August 3, 1862, as part of the third shipment of Krupp aircraft to the Confeder-

ate States of America under terms of the Agreement of Atlanta of 1861. It was originally equipped with power plant #311 Zed of 87¼ horsepower, manufactured by the Jumo plant at Nordmung, Duchy of Austria, on May 3 of the year 1862. Wingspan of the craft is twenty-three feet; its length is seventeen feet three inches. The aircraft arrived in the port of Charlotte on September 21, 1862, aboard the transport *Mendenhall,* which had suffered heavy bombardment from GAR picket ships. The aircraft was possibly sent by rail to Confederate Army Air Corps Center at Fort Andrew Mott, Alabama. Unfortunately, records of rail movements during this time were lost in the burning of the Confederate archives at Ittebeha in March 1867, two weeks after the Truce of Haldeman was signed.

2. The aircraft was damaged during a training flight in December 1862. Student pilot was Flight Subaltern (Cadet) Neldoo J. Smith, CSAAC; flight instructor during the ill-fated flight was Air Captain Winslow Homer Winslow, on interservice instructor-duty loan from the Confederate States Navy.

Accident forms and maintenance officer's reports indicate that the original motor was replaced with one of the new 93½ horsepower Jumo engines which had just arrived from Holland by way of Mexico.

3. The aircraft served routinely through the remainder of Flight Subaltern Smith's training. We have records[141] which indicate that the aircraft was one of the first to be equipped with the Henry repeating machine rifle of the chain-driven type. Until December 1862, all CSAAC aircraft were equipped with the Sharps repeating rifles of the motor-driven, low-voltage type on wing or turret mounts.

As was the custom, the aircraft was flown by Flight Subaltern Smith to his first duty station at Thimblerig Aerodrome in Augusta, Georgia. Flight Subaltern Smith was assigned to Flight Platoon 2, 1st Aeroscout Squadron.

4. The aircraft, with Flight Subaltern Smith at the wheel, participated in three of the aerial expeditions against the Union Army in the Second Battle of the Manassas. Smith distinguished himself in the first and third missions. (He was assigned aerial picket duty south of the actual battle during his second mission.) On the first, he is credited with one kill and one probable (both bi-wing Airsharks). During the third mission, he destroyed one aircraft and forced another down behind Confederate lines. He then escorted the craft of his immediate commander, Air Captain Dalton Trump, to a safe landing on a field controlled by the Confederates. According to Trump's sworn testimony, Smith successfully fought off two Union craft and ranged ahead of Trump's crippled plane to strafe a group of Union soldiers who were in their flight path, discouraging them from firing on Trump's smoking aircraft.

For heroism on these two missions, Smith was awarded the Silver Star and Bar with Air Cluster. Presentation was made on March 3, 1863, by the late General J.E.B. Stuart, Chief of Staff of the CSAAC.

5. Flight Subaltern Smith was promoted to flight captain on April 12, 1863,

after distinguishing himself with two kills and two probables during the first day of the Battle of the Three Roads, North Carolina. One of his kills was an airship of the Moby class, with a crew of fourteen. Smith shared with only one other aviator the feat of bringing down one of these dirigibles during the War of Secession.

This was the first action the 1st Aeroscout Squadron had seen since Second Manassas, and Captain Smith seems to have been chafing under inaction. Perhaps this led him to volunteer for duty with Major John S. Mosby, then forming what would later become Mosby's Raiders. This was actually sound military strategy: the CSAAC was to send a unit to southwestern Kansas to carry out harassment raids against the poorly defended forts of the Far West. These raids would force the Union to send men and materiel sorely needed at the southern front far to the west, where they would be ineffectual in the outcome of the war. That this action was taken is pointed to by some[142] as a sign that the Confederate States envisioned defeat and were resorting to desperate measures four years before the Treaty of Haldeman.

At any rate, Captain Smith and his aircraft joined a triple flight of six aircraft each, which, after stopping at El Dorado, Arkansas, to refuel, flew away on a westerly course. This is the last time they ever operated in Confederate states. The date was June 5, 1863.

6. The Union forts stretched from a medium-well-defended line in Illinois to poorly garrisoned stations as far west as the Wyoming Territory and south to the Kansas–Indian Territory border. Southwestern Kansas was both sparsely settled and garrisoned. It was from this area that Mosby's Raiders, with the official designation 1st Western Interdiction Wing, CSAAC, operated.

A supply wagon train had been sent ahead a month before from Fort Worth, carrying petrol, ammunition, and material for shelters. A crude landing field, hangars, and barracks awaited the eighteen craft.

After two months of reconnaissance (done by mounted scouts due to the need to maintain the element of surprise, and, more importantly, by the limited amount of fuel available) the 1st WIW took to the air. The citizens of Riley, Kansas, long remembered the day: their first inkling that Confederates were closer than Texas came when motors were heard overhead and the Union garrison was literally blown off the face of the map.

7. Following the first raid, word went to the War Department headquarters in New York, with pleas for aid and reinforcements for all Kansas garrisons. Thus the CSAAC achieved its goal in the very first raid. The effects snowballed; as soon as the populace learned of the raid, it demanded protection from nearby garrisons. Farmers' organizations threatened to stop shipments of needed produce to eastern depots. The garrison commanders, unable to promise adequate protection, appealed to higher military authorities.

Meanwhile, the 1st WIW made a second raid on Abilene, heavily damaging the railways and stockyards with twenty-five-pound fragmentation bombs. They then circled the city, strafed the Army Quartermaster depot, and disappeared into the west.

8. This second raid, and the ensuing clamor from both the public and the commanders of western forces, convinced the War Department to divert new recruits and supplies, with seasoned members of the 18th Aeropursuit Squadron, to the Kansas-Missouri border, near Lawrence.

9. Inclement weather in the fall kept both the 18th AS and the 1st WIW grounded for seventy-two of the ninety days of the season. Aircraft from each of these units met several times; the 1st is credited with one kill, while pilots of the 18th downed two Confederate aircraft on the afternoon of December 12, 1863.

Both aircraft units were heavily resupplied during this time. The Battle of the Canadian River was fought on December 18, when mounted reconnaissance units of the Union and Confederacy met in Indian territory. Losses were small on both sides, but the skirmish was the first of what would become known as the Far Western Campaign.

10. Civilians spotted the massed formation of the 1st WIW as early as 10 A.M. Thursday, December 16, 1863. They headed northeast, making a leg due north when eighteen miles south of Lawrence. Two planes sped ahead to destroy the telegraph station at Felton, nine miles south of Lawrence. Nevertheless, a message of some sort reached Lawrence; a Union messenger on horseback was on his way to the aerodrome when the first flight of Confederate aircraft passed overhead.

In the ensuing raid, seven of the nineteen Union aircraft were destroyed on the ground and two were destroyed in the air, while the remaining aircraft were severely damaged and the barracks and hangars demolished.

The 1st WIW suffered one loss: during the raid a Union clerk attached for duty with the 18th AS manned an Agar machine rifle position and destroyed one Confederate aircraft. He was killed by machine rifle fire from the second wave of planes. Private Alden Evans Gunn was awarded the Congressional Medal of Honor posthumously for his gallantry during the attack.

For the next two months, the 1st WIW ruled the skies as far north as Illinois and as far east as Trenton, Missouri.

THE FAR WESTERN CAMPAIGN

1. At this juncture, the two most prominent figures of the next nineteen years of frontier history enter the picture: the Oglala Sioux Crazy Horse, and Lieutenant Colonel (Brevet Major General) George Armstrong Custer. The clerical error giving Custer the rank of Brigadier General is well known. It is not common knowledge that Custer was considered by the General Staff as a candidate for Far Western Commander as early as the spring of 1864, a duty he would not take up until May 1869, when the Far Western Com-

mand was the only theater of war operations within the Americas.

The General Staff, it is believed, considered Major General Custer for the job for two reasons: they thought Custer possessed those qualities of spirit suited to the warfare necessary in the Western Command, and that the Far West was the ideal place for the twenty-three-year-old Boy General.

Crazy Horse, the Oglala Sioux warrior, was with a hunting party far from Oglala territory, checking the size of the few remaining buffalo herds before they started their spring migrations. Legend has it that Crazy Horse and the party were crossing the prairies in early February 1864 when two aircraft belonging to the 1st WIW passed nearby. Some of the Sioux jumped to the ground, believing that they were looking on the Thunderbird and its mate. Only Crazy Horse stayed on his pony and watched the aircraft disappear into the south.

He sent word back by the rest of the party that he and two of his young warrior friends had gone looking for the nest of the Thunderbird.

2. The story of the 1st WIW here becomes the story of the shaping of the Indian wars, rather than part of the history of the last four years of the War of Secession. It is well known that increased alarm over the Kansas raids had shifted War Department thinking: the defense of the Far West changed in importance from a minor matter in the larger scheme of war to a problem of vital concern. For one thing, the Confederacy was courting the emperor Maximilian of Mexico, and through him the French, to entering the war on the Confederate side. The South wanted arms, but most necessarily to break the Union submarine blockade. Only the French navy possessed the capability.

The Union therefore sent the massed 5th Cavalry to Kansas and attached to it the 12th Air Destroyer Squadron and the 2nd Airship Command.

The 2nd Airship Command, at the time of its deployment, was equipped with the small pursuit airships known in later days as the "torpedo ship," from its double-pointed ends. These ships were used for reconnaissance and light interdiction duties, and were almost always accompanied by aircraft from the 12th ADS. They immediately set to work patrolling the Kansas skies from the renewed base of operations at Lawrence.

3. The idea of using Indian personnel in some phase of airfield operations in the west had been proposed by Mosby as early as June 1863. The C of C, CSA, disapproved in the strongest possible terms. It was not a new idea, therefore, when Crazy Horse and his two companions rode into the airfield, accompanied by the sentries who had challenged them far from the perimeter. They were taken to Major Mosby for questioning.

Through an interpreter, Mosby learned they were Oglala, not Crows sent to spy for the Union. When asked why they had come so far, Crazy Horse replied, "To see the nest of the Thunderbird."

Mosby is said to have laughed[143] and then taken the three Sioux to see the aircraft. Crazy Horse was said to have been stricken with awe when he found that men controlled their flight.

Crazy Horse then offered Mosby ten ponies for one of the craft. Mosby explained that they were not his to give, but his Great Father's, and that they were used to fight the Yellowlegs from the Northeast.

At this time, fate took a hand: the 12th Air Destroyer Squadron had just begun operations. The same day Crazy Horse was having his initial interview with Mosby, a scout plane returned with the news that the 12th was being reinforced by an airship combat group; the dirigibles had been seen maneuvering near the Kansas–Missouri border.

Mosby learned from Crazy Horse that the warrior was respected, if not in his own tribe, then with other Nations of the North. Mosby, with an eye toward those reinforcements arriving in Lawrence, asked Crazy Horse if he could guarantee safe conduct through the northern tribes and land for an airfield should the present one have to be abandoned.

Crazy Horse answered, "I can talk the idea to the people; it will be for them to decide."

Mosby told Crazy Horse that if he could secure the promise, he would grant him anything within his power.

Crazy Horse looked out the window toward the hangars. "I ask that you teach me and ten of my brother-friends to fly the Thunderbirds. We will help you fight the Yellowlegs."

Mosby, expecting requests for beef, blankets, or firearms, was taken aback. Unlike the others who had dealt with the Indians, he was a man of his word. He told Crazy Horse he would ask his Great Father if this could be done. Crazy Horse left, returning to his village in the middle of March. He and several warriors traveled extensively that spring, smoking the pipe, securing permissions from the other Nations for safe conduct for the Gray white men through their hunting lands. His hardest task came in convincing the Oglala themselves that the airfield could be built in their southern hunting grounds.

Crazy Horse, his two wives, seven warriors, and their women, children, and belongings rode into the CSAAC airfield in June 1864.

4. Mosby had been granted permission from Stuart to go ahead with the training program. Derision first met the request within the southern General Staff when Mosby's proposal was circulated. Stuart, though not entirely sympathetic to the idea, became its champion. Others objected, warning that ignorant savages should not be given modern weapons. Stuart reminded them that some of the good Tennessee boys already flying airplanes could neither read nor write.

Stuart's approval arrived a month before Crazy Horse and his band made camp on the edge of the airfield.

5. It fell to Captain Smith to train Crazy Horse. The Indian became what Smith in his journal[144] describes as "the best natural pilot I have seen or it

has been my pleasure to fly with." Part of this seems to have come from Smith's own modesty; by all accounts, Smith was one of the finer pilots of the war.

The operations of the 12th ADS and the 2nd Airship Command ranged closer to the CSAAC airfield. The dogfights came frequently and the fighting grew less gentlemanly. One 1st WIW fighter was pounced by three aircraft of the 12th simultaneously: they did not stop firing even when the pilot signaled that he was hit and that his engine was dead. Nor did they break off their runs until both pilot and craft plunged into the Kansas prairie. It is thought that the Union pilots were under secret orders to kill all members of the 1st WIW. There is some evidence[145] that this rankled with the more gentlemanly of the 12th Air Destroyer Squadron. Nevertheless, fighting intensified.

A flight of six more aircraft joined the 1st WIW some weeks after the Oglala Sioux started their training: this was the first of the ferry flights from Mexico through Texas and Indian territory to reach the airfield. Before the summer was over, a dozen additional craft would join the Wing, this before shipments were curtailed by Juarez's revolution against the French and the ouster and execution of Maximilian and his family.

Smith records[146] that Crazy Horse's first solo took place on August 14, 1864, and that the warrior, though deft in the air, still needed practice on his landings. He had a tendency to come in overpowered and to stall his engine out too soon. Minor repairs were made on the skids of the craft after his flight.

All this time Crazy Horse had flown Smith's craft. Smith, after another week of hard practice with the Indian, pronounced him "more qualified than most pilots the CSAAC in Alabama turned out"[147] and signed over the aircraft to him. Crazy Horse begged off. Then, seeing that Smith was sincere, he gave the captain many buffalo hides. Smith reminded the Indian that the craft was not his: during their off hours, when not training, the Indians had been given enough instruction in military discipline as Mosby, never a stickler, thought necessary. The Indians had only a rudimentary idea of government property. Of the seven other Indian men, three were qualified as pilots; the other four were given gunner positions in the Krupp bi-wing light bombers assigned to the squadron.

Soon after Smith presented the aircraft to Crazy Horse, the captain took off in a borrowed monoplane on what was to be the daily weather flight into northern Kansas. There is evidence[148] that it was Smith who encountered a flight of light dirigibles from the 2nd Airship Command and attacked them single-handedly. He crippled one airship; the other was rescued when two escort planes of the 12th ADS came to its defense. They raked the attacker with withering fire. The attacker escaped into the clouds.

It was not until 1897, when a group of schoolchildren on an outing found the wreckage, that it was known that Captain Smith had brought his crippled monoplane within five miles of the airfield before crashing into the rolling hills.

When Smith did not return from his flight, Crazy Horse went on a vigil, neither sleeping nor eating for a week. On the seventh day, Crazy Horse vowed vengeance on the men who had killed his white friend.

6. The devastating Union raid of September 23, 1864, caught the airfield unawares. Though the Indians were averse to fighting at night, Crazy Horse and two other Sioux were manning three of the four craft which got off the ground during the raid. The attack had been carried out by the 2nd Airship Command, traveling at twelve thousand feet, dropping fifty-pound fragmentation bombs and shrapnel canisters. The shrapnel played havoc with the aircraft on the ground. It also destroyed the mess hall, enlisted barracks, and three teepees.

The dirigibles turned away and were running fast before a tail wind when Crazy Horse gained their altitude.

The gunners on the dirigibles filled the skies with tracers from their light .30–30 machine rifles. Crazy Horse's monoplane was equipped with a single Henry .41–40 machine rifle. Unable to get in close killing distance, Crazy Horse and his companions stood off beyond the range of the lighter Union guns and raked the dirigibles with heavy machine rifle fire. They did enough damage to force one airship down twenty miles from its base, and to ground two others for two days while repairs were made. The intensity of fire convinced the airship commanders that more than four planes had made it off the ground, causing them to continue their headlong retreat.

Crazy Horse and the others returned and brought off the second windfall of the night; a group of 5th Cavalry raiders were to have attacked the airfield in the confusion of the airship raid and burn everything still standing. On their return flight, the four craft encountered the cavalry unit as it began its charge across open ground.

In three strafing runs, the aircraft killed thirty-seven men and wounded fifty-three, while twenty-nine were taken prisoner by the airfield's defenders. Thus, in his first combat mission for the CSAAC, Crazy Horse was credited with saving the airfield against overwhelming odds.

7. Meanwhile, Major General George A. Custer had distinguished himself at the Battle of Gettysburg. A few weeks after the battle, he enrolled himself in the GAR jump school at Watauga, New York. Howls of outrage came from the General Staff. Custer quoted the standing order: "any man who volunteered and of whom the commanding officer approved" could be enrolled. Custer then asked, in a letter to C of S, GAR, "how any military leader could be expected to plan maneuvers involving parachute infantry when he himself had never experienced a drop, or found the true capabilities of the parachute infantryman?"[149] The Chief of Staff shouted down the protest. There were mutterings among the General Staff[150] to the effect that the

real reason Custer wanted to become jump-qualified was so that he would have a better chance of leading the invasion of Atlanta, part of whose contingency plans called for attacks by airborne units.

During the three-week parachute course, Custer became acquainted with another man who would play an important part in the Western Campaign, Captain (Brevet Colonel) Frederick W. Benteen. Upon graduation from the jump school, Brevet Colonel Benteen assumed command of the 505th Balloon Infantry, stationed at Chicago, Illinois, for training purposes. Colonel Benteen would remain commander of the 505th until his capture at the Battle of Montgomery in 1866. While he was prisoner of war, his command was given to another, later to figure in the Western Campaign, Lieutenant Colonel Myles W. Keogh.

Custer, upon his successful completion of jump school, returned to his command of the 6th Cavalry Division and participated throughout the remainder of the war in that capacity. It was he who led the successful charge at the Battle of the Cape Fear which smashed Lee's flank and allowed the 1st Infantry to overrun the Confederate position and capture that southern leader. Custer distinguished himself and his command up until the cessation of hostilities in 1867.

8. The 1st WIW, CSAAC, moved to a new airfield in Wyoming Territory three weeks after the raid of September 24. At the same time, the 2nd WIW was formed and moved to an outpost in Indian territory. The 2nd WIW raided the Union airfield, took it totally by surprise, and inflicted casualties on the 12th ADS and 2nd AC so devastating as to render them ineffectual. The 2nd WIW then moved to a second field in Wyoming Territory. It was here, following the move, that a number of Indians, including Black Man's Hand, were trained by Crazy Horse.

9. We leave the history of the 2nd WIW here. It was redeployed for the defense of Montgomery. The Indians and aircraft in which they trained were sent north to join the 1st WIW. The 1st WIW patrolled the skies of Indiana, Nebraska, and the Dakotas. After the defeat of the 12th ADS and the 2nd AC, the Union forestalled attempts to retaliate until the cessation of southern hostilities in 1867.

We may at this point add that Crazy Horse, Black Man's Hand, and the other Indians sometimes left the airfield during periods of long inactivity. They returned to their nations for as long as three months at a time. Each time Crazy Horse returned, he brought one or two pilot or gunner recruits with him. Before the winter of 1866, more than thirty percent of the 1st WIW were Oglala, Sansarc Sioux, or Cheyenne.

The South, losing the war of attrition, diverted all supplies to Alabama and Mississippi in the fall of 1866. None were forthcoming for the 1st WIW, though a messenger arrived with orders for Major Mosby to return to Texas for the defense of Fort Worth, where he would later direct the Battle of the

Trinity. That Mosby was not ordered to deploy the 1st WIW to that defense
has been considered by many military strategists as a "lost turning point" of
the battle for Texas. Command of the 1st WIW was turned over to Acting
Major (Flight Captain) Natchitoches Hooley.

10. The loss of Mosby signaled the end of the 1st WIW. Not only did the
nondeployment of the 1st to Texas cost the South that territory, it also left
the 1st in an untenable position, which the Union was quick to realize. The
airfield was captured in May 1867 by a force of five hundred cavalry and three
hundred infantry sent from the Battle of the Arkansas, and a like force, plus
aircraft, from Chicago. Crazy Horse, seven Indians, and at least five Confederates escaped in their monoplanes. The victorious Union troops were surprised to find Indians at the field. Crazy Horse's people were eventually freed;
the army thought them to have been hired by the Confederates to hunt and
cook for the airfield. Mosby had provided for this in contingency plans long
before; he had not wanted the Plains tribes to suffer for Confederate acts. The
army did not know, and no one volunteered the information, that it had been
Indians doing the most considerable amount of damage to the Union garrisons lately.

Crazy Horse and three of his Indians landed their craft near the Black
Hills. The Cheyenne helped them carry the craft, on travois, to caves in the
sacred mountains. Here they mothballed the planes with mixtures of pine tar
and resins and sealed up the caves.

11. The aircraft remained stored until February 1872. During this time,
Crazy Horse and his Oglala Sioux operated, like the other Plains Indians, as
light cavalry, skirmishing with the army and with settlers up and down the
Dakotas and Montana. George Armstrong Custer was appointed commander of the new 7th Cavalry in 1869. Stationed first at Chicago (Far Western
Command Headquarters), they later moved to Fort Abraham Lincoln, Nebraska.

A column of troops moved against Indians on the warpath in the winter
of 1869. They reported a large group of Indians encamped on the Washita
River. Custer obtained permission for the 505th Balloon Infantry to join the
7th Cavalry. From that day on, the unit was officially Company I (Separate
Troops), 7th US Cavalry, though it kept its numerical designation. Also
attached to the 7th was the 12th Airship Squadron, as Company J.

Lieutenant Colonel Keogh, acting commander of the 505th for the last
twenty-one months, but who had never been on jump status, was appointed
by Custer as commander of K Company, 7th Cavalry.

It is known that only the 505th Balloon Infantry and the 12th Airship
Squadron were used in the raid on Black Kettle's village. Black Kettle was
a treaty Indian, "walking the white man's road." Reports have become
garbled in transmission: Custer and the 505th believed they were jumping
into a village of hostiles.

The event remained a mystery until Kellogg, the Chicago newspaperman, wrote his account in 1872.[151] The 505th, with Custer in command, flew the three (then numbered, after 1872, named) dirigibles No. 31, No. 76, and No. 93, with seventy-two jumpers each. Custer was in the first "stick" on Airship 76. The three sailed silently to the sleeping village. Custer gave the order to hook up at 5:42 Chicago time, 4:42 local time, and the 505th jumped into the village. Black Kettle's people were awakened when some of the balloon infantry crashed through their teepees; others died in their sleep. One of the first duties of the infantry was to moor the dirigibles; this done, the gunners on the airships opened up on the startled villagers with their Gatling and Agar machine rifles. Black Kettle himself was killed while waving an American flag at Airship No. 93.

After the battle, the men of the 505th climbed back up to the moored dirigibles by rope ladder, and the airships departed for Fort Lincoln. The Indians camped downriver heard the shooting and found horses stampeded during the attack. When they came to the village, they found only slaughter. Custer had taken his dead (three, one of whom died during the jump by being drowned in the Washita) and wounded (twelve) away. They left 307 dead men, women, and children, and 500 slaughtered horses.

There were no tracks leading in and out of the village except those of the frightened horses. The other Indians left the area, thinking the white men had magicked it.

Crazy Horse is said[152] to have visited the area soon after the massacre. It was this action by the 7th which spelled their doom seven years later.

12. Black Man's Hand joined Crazy Horse; so did other former 1st WIW pilots soon after Crazy Horse's two-plane raid on the airship hangars at Bismarck, in 1872. For that mission, Crazy Horse dropped twenty-five-pound fragmentation bombs tied to petrol canisters. The shrapnel ripped the dirigibles, the escaping hydrogen was ignited by the burning petrol: all — hangars, balloons, and maintenance crews — were lost.

It was written up as an unreconstructed Confederate's sabotage; a somewhat ignominious former Southern major was eventually hanged on circumstantial evidence. Reports by sentries that they heard aircraft just before the explosions were discounted. At the time, it was believed the only aircraft were those belonging to the army, and the carefully licensed commercial craft.

13. In 1874, Custer circulated rumors that the Black Hills were full of gold. It has been speculated that this was used to draw miners to the area so the Indians would attack them; then the cavalry would have unlimited freedom to deal with the red man.[153] Also that year, those who had become agency Indians were being shorted in their supplies by members of the scandal-plagued Indian Affairs Bureau under President Grant. When these left the reservations in search of food, the cavalry was sent to "bring them back." Those who were caught were usually killed.

The Sioux ignored the miners at first, expecting the gods to deal with them. When this did not happen, Sitting Bull sent out a party of two hundred warriors, who killed every miner they encountered. Public outrage demanded reprisals; Sheridan wired Custer to find and punish those responsible.

14. Fearing what was to come, Crazy Horse sent Yellow Dog and Red Chief with a war party of five hundred to raid the rebuilt Fort Phil Kearny. This they did successfully, capturing twelve planes and fuel and ammunition for many more. They hid these in the caverns with the 1st WIW craft.

The army would not have acted as rashly as it did had it known the planes pronounced missing in the reports on the Kearny raid were being given into the hands of experienced pilots.

The reprisal consisted of airship patrols which strafed any living thing on the plains. Untold thousands of deer and the few remaining buffalo were killed. Unofficial counts list as killed a little more than eight hundred Indians who were caught in the open during the next eight months.

Indians who jumped the agencies and who had seen or heard of the slaughter streamed to Sitting Bull's hidden camp on the Little Big Horn. They were treated as guests, except for the Sansarcs, who camped a little way down the river. It is estimated there were no less than ten thousand Indians, including some four thousand warriors, camped along the river for the Sun Dance ceremony of June 1876.

A three-pronged-pincers movement for the final eradication of the Sioux and Cheyenne worked toward them. The 7th Cavalry, under Keogh and Major Marcus Reno, set out from Fort Lincoln during the last week of May. General George Crook's command was coming up the Rosebud. The gunboat *Far West,* with three hundred reserves and supplies, steamed to the mouth of the Big Horn River. General Terry's command was coming from the northwest. All Indians they encountered were to be killed.

Just before the Sun Dance, Crazy Horse and his pilots got word of the movement of Crook's men up the Rosebud, hurried to the caves, and prepared their craft for flight. Only six planes were put in working condition in time. The other pilots remained behind while Crazy Horse, Black Man's Hand, and four others took to the skies. They destroyed two dirigibles, soundly trounced Crook, and chased his command back down the Rosebud in a rout. The column had to abandon its light-armored vehicles and fight its way back, on foot for the most part, to safety.

15. Sitting Bull's vision during the Sun Dance is well known.[154] He told it to Crazy Horse, the warrior who would see that it came true, as soon as the aviators returned to camp.

Two hundred fifty miles away, "Chutes and Saddles" was sounded on the morning of June 23, and the men of the 505th Balloon Infantry climbed aboard the airships *Benjamin Franklin, Samuel Adams, John Hancock,* and *Ethan Allen.* Custer was first man on stick one of the *Franklin.* The *Ethan*

Allen carried a scout aircraft which could hook up or detach in flight; the bi-winger was to serve as liaison between the three armies and the airships.

When Custer bade good-bye to his wife Elizabeth that morning, both were in good spirits. If either had an inkling of the fate which awaited Custer and the 7th three days away on the bluffs above a small stream, they did not show it.

The four airships sailed from Fort Lincoln, their silver sides and shark-tooth mouths gleaming in the sun, the eyes painted on the noses looking west. On the sides were the crossed sabers of the cavalry; above, the numeral 7; below, the numerals 505. It is said that they looked magnificent as they sailed away for their rendezvous with destiny.[155]

16. It is sufficient to say that the Indians attained their greatest victory over the army, and almost totally destroyed the 7th Cavalry, on June 25–26, 1876, due in large part to the efforts of Crazy Horse and his aviators. Surprise, swiftness, and the skill of the Indians cannot be discounted, nor can the military blunders made by Custer that morning. The repercussions of that summer day rang down the years and the events are still debated. The only sure fact is that the US Army lost its prestige, part of its spirit, and more than four hundred of its finest soldiers in the battle.

17. While the demoralized commands were sorting themselves out, the Cheyenne and Sioux left for the Canadian border. They took their aircraft with them on travois. With Sitting Bull, Crazy Horse and his band settled just across the border. The aircraft were rarely used again until the attack on the camp by the combined Canadian–US Cavalry offensive in 1879. Crazy Horse and his aviators, as they had done so many times before, escaped with their aircraft, using one of the planes to carry their remaining fuel. Two of the nine craft were shot down by a Canadian battery.

Crazy Horse, sensing the end, fought his way, with men on horseback and the planes on travois, from Montana to Colorado. After learning of the deaths of Sitting Bull and Chief Joseph, he took his small band as close as he dared to Fort Carson, where the cavalry was massing to wipe out the remaining American Indians.

He assembled his men for the last time. He made his proposal; all concurred and joined him for a last raid on the army. The five remaining planes came in low, the morning of January 5, 1882, toward the army airfield. They destroyed twelve aircraft on the ground, shot up the hangars and barracks, and ignited one of the two ammunition dumps of the stockade. At this time, army gunners manned the William's machine cannon batteries (improved by Thomas Edison's contract scientists) and blew three of the craft to flinders. The war gods must have smiled on Crazy Horse: his aircraft was crippled, the machine rifle was blown askew, the motor slivered, but he managed to set down intact. Black Man's Hand turned away; he was captured two months later, eating cottonwood bark in the snows of Arizona.

Crazy Horse jumped from his aircraft as most of Fort Carson ran toward him; he pulled two Sharps repeating carbines from the cockpit and blazed away at the astonished troopers, wounding six and killing one. His back to the craft, he continued to fire until more than one hundrd infantrymen fired a volley into his body.

The airplane was displayed for seven months at Fort Carson before being sent to the Smithsonian in Pittsburgh, where it stands today. Thus passed an era of military aviation.

— Lt. Gen. Frank Luke, Jr.
USAF, Ret.

From the December 2, 1939, issue of *Collier's Magazine*
Custer's Last Jump?
A. R. Redmond

Few events in American history have captured the imagination so thoroughly as the Battle of the Little Big Horn. Lieutenant Colonel George Armstrong Custer's devastating defeat at the hands of Sioux and Cheyenne Indians in June 1876 has been rendered time and again by such celebrated artists as George Russell and Frederic Remington. Books, factual and otherwise, which have been written around or about the battle would fill an entire library wing. The motion-picture industry has on numerous occasions drawn upon "Custer's last jump" for inspiration; latest in a long line of movieland Custers is Erroll Flynn, who appears with Olivia de Havilland and newcomer Anthony Quinn in Warner Brothers' soon-to-be-released *They Died with Their Chutes On.*

The impetuous and flamboyant Custer was an almost legendary figure long before the Battle of Little Big Horn, however. Appointed to West Point in 1857, Custer was placed in command of Troop G, 2nd Cavalry, in June 1861, and participated in a series of skirmishes with Confederate cavalry throughout the rest of the year. It was during the First Battle of Manassas, or Bull Run, that he distinguished himself. He continued to do so in other engagements — at Williamsburg, Chancellorsville, Gettysburg — and rose rapidly through the ranks. He was twenty-six years old when he received a promotion to Brigadier General. He was, of course, immediately dubbed the Boy General. He had become an authentic war hero when the Northerners were in dire need of nothing less during those discouraging months between First Manassas and Gettysburg.

With the cessation of hostilities in the East when Bragg surrendered to Grant at Haldeman, the small hamlet about eight miles from Morehead, Kentucky, Custer requested a transfer of command. He and his young bride wound up at Chicago, which was manned by the new 7th US Cavalry.

The war in the West lasted another few months; the tattered remnants of the Confederate Army staged last desperate stands throughout Texas, Colorado, Kansas, and Missouri. The final struggle at the Trinity River in October 1867 marked the close of conflict between North and South. Those few Mexican military advisers left in Texas quietly withdrew across the Rio Grande. The French, driven from Mexico in 1867 when Maximilian was ousted, lost interest in the Americas when they became embroiled with the newly united Prussian states.

During his first year in Chicago, Custer familiarized himself with the airships and aeroplanes of the 7th. The only jump-qualified general officer of the war, Custer seemed to have felt no resentment at the ultimate fate of mounted troops boded by the extremely mobile flying machines. The Ohio-born Boy General eventually preferred traveling aboard the airship *Benjamin Franklin,* one of the eight craft assigned to the 505th Balloon Infantry (Troop I, 7th Cavalry, commanded by Brevet Colonel Frederick Benteen) while his horse soldiers rode behind the very capable Captain (Brevet Lt. Col.) Myles Keogh.

The War Department in Pittsburgh did not know that various members of the Plains Indian tribes had been equipped with aeroplanes by the Confederates, and that many had actually flown against the Union garrisons in the West. (Curiously enough, those tribes which held out the longest against the army — most notably the Apaches under Geronimo in the deep Southwest — were those that did not have aircraft.) The problems of transporting and hiding, to say nothing of maintaining planes, outweighed the advantages. A Cheyenne warrior named Brave Bear is said to have traded his band's aircraft in disgust to Sitting Bull for three horses. Also, many of the Plains Indians hated the aircraft outright, as they had been used by the white men to decimate the great buffalo herds in the early 1860s.

Even so, certain Oglalas, Minneconjous, and Cheyenne did reasonably well in the aircraft given them by CS Army Air Corps Major John S. Mosby, whom the Indians called the "Gray White Man" or "Many-Feathers-in-Hat." The Oglala war chief Crazy Horse led the raid on the Bismarck hangars (1872) four months after the 7th Cavalry was transferred to Fort Abraham Lincoln, Dakota Territory, and made his presence felt at the Rosebud and Little Big Horn in 1876. The Cheyenne Black Man's Hand, trained by Crazy Horse himself, shot down two army machines at the Rosebud and was in the flight of planes that accomplished the annihilation of the 505th Balloon Infantry during the first phase of the Little Big Horn fiasco.

After the leveling of Fort Phil Kearny in February 1869, Custer was ordered to enter the Indian territories and punish those who had sought sanctuary there after the raid. Taking with him 150 parachutists aboard three airships, Custer left on the trail of a large band of Cheyenne.

On the afternoon of February 25, Lieutenant William van W. Reily, dispatched for scouting purposes in a Studebaker bi-winger, returned to report that he had shot up a hunting party near the Washita River. The Cheyenne, he thought, were encamped on the banks of the river some twenty miles away. They appeared not to have seen the close approach of the 7th Cavalry as they had not broken camp.

Just before dawn the next morning, the 505th Balloon Infantry, led by Custer, jumped into the village, killing all inhabitants and their animals.

For the next five years, Custer and the 7th chased the hostiles of the plains back and forth between Colorado and the Canadian border. Relocated at Fort Lincoln, Custer and an expedition of horse soldiers, geologists, and engineers discovered gold in the Black Hills. Though the Black Hills still belonged to the Sioux according to several treaties, prospectors began to pour into the area. The 7th was ordered to protect them. The Blackfeet, Minneconjous, and Hunkpapa — Sioux who had left the warpath on the promise that the Black Hills, their sacred lands, were theirs to keep for all time — protested, and when protests brought no results, took matters into their own hands. Prospectors turned up in various stages of mutilation, or not at all.

Conditions worsened over the remainder of 1875, during which time the United States Government ordered the Sioux out of the Black Hills. To make sure the Indians complied, airships patrolled the skies of the Dakota Territory.

By the end of 1875, plagued by the likes of Crazy Horse's Oglala Sioux, it was decided that there was but one solution to the Plains Indian problem — total extermination.

At this point, General Phil Sheridan, Commander in Chief of the United States Army, began working on the practical angle of this new policy toward the red men.

In January 1876, delegates from the Democratic Party approached George Armstrong Custer at Fort Abraham Lincoln and offered him the party's presidential nomination on the condition that he pull off a flashy victory over the red men before the national convention in Chicago in July.

On February 19, 1876, the Boy General's brother Thomas, commander of Troop C of the 7th, climbed into the observer's cockpit behind Lieutenant James C. Sturgis and took off on a routine patrol. Their aeroplane, a Whitney pushertype, did not return. Ten days later its wreckage was found sixty miles west of Fort Lincoln. Apparently, Sturgis and Tom Custer had stumbled on a party of mounted hostiles and, swooping low to fire or drop a handbomb, suffered a lucky hit from one of the Indian's firearms. The mutilated remains of the two officers were found a quarter mile from the wreckage, indicating that they had escaped on foot after the crash but were caught.

The shock of his brother's death, combined with the Democrats' offer, was to lead Lieutenant Colonel G.A. Custer into the worst defeat suffered by an officer of the United States Army.

Throughout the first part of 1876, Indians drifted into the Wyoming Territory from the east and south, driven by mounting pressure from the army. Raids on small Indian villages had been stepped up. Waning herds of buffalo were being systematically strafed by the airships. General Phil Sheridan received reports of tribes gathering in the vicinity of the Wolf Mountains, in what is now southern Montana, and devised a strategy by which the hostiles would be crushed for all time.

Three columns were to converge upon the massed Indians from the north, south, and east, the west being blocked by the Wolf Mountains. General George Crook's dirigibles, light tanks, and infantry were to come up the Rosebud River. General Alfred Terry would push from the northeast with infantry, cavalry, and field artillery. The 7th Cavalry was to move from the east. The Indians could not escape.

Commanded by Captain Keogh, Troops A, C, D, E, F, G, and H of the 7th — about 580 men, not counting civilian teamsters, interpreters, Crow and Arikara scouts — set out from Fort Lincoln five weeks ahead of the July 1 rendezvous at the junction of the Big Horn and Little Big Horn rivers. A month later, Custer and 150 balloon infantrymen aboard the airships *Franklin, Adams, Hancock,* and *Allen* set out on Keogh's trail.

Everything went wrong from that point onward.

The early summer of 1876 had been particularly hot and dry in the Wyoming Territory. Crook, proceeding up the Rosebud, was slowed by the tanks, which theoretically traveled at five miles per hour but kept breaking down from the heat and from the alkaline dust which worked its way into the engines through chinks in the three-inch armor plate. The crews roasted. On June 13, as Crook's column halted beside the Rosebud to let the tanks cool off, six monoplanes dived out of the clouds to attack the escorting airships *Paul Revere* and *John Paul Jones.* Caught by surprise, the two dirigibles were blown up and fell about five miles from Crook's position. The infantrymen watched, astonished, as the Indian aeronauts turned their craft toward them. While the foot soldiers ran for cover, several hundred mounted Sioux warriors showed up. In the ensuing rout, Crook lost forty-seven men and all his armored vehicles. He was still in headlong retreat when the Indians broke off their chase at nightfall.

The 7th Cavalry and the 505th Balloon Infantry linked up by liaison craft carried by the *Ethan Allen* some miles southeast of the hostile camp on the Little Big Horn on the evening of June 24. Neither they, nor Terry's column, had received word of Crook's retreat, but Keogh's scouts had sighted a large village ahead.

Custer did not know that this village contained not the five or six hundred Indians expected, but between eight and ten *thousand,* of whom slightly less than half were warriors. Spurred by his desire for revenge for his brother Tom, and filled with glory at the thought of the Democratic presidential nomination, Custer decided to hit the Indians before either Crook's or

Terry's columns could reach the village. He settled on a scaled-down version of Sheridan's tri-pronged movement, and dispatched Keogh to the south and Reno to the east, with himself and the 505th attacking from the north. A small column was to wait downriver with the pack train. On the evening of June 24, George Armstrong Custer waited, secure in the knowledge that he, personally, would deal the Plains Indians their mortal blow within a mere twenty-four hours.

Unfortunately, the Indians amassed on the banks of the Little Big Horn — Oglalas, Minneconjous, Arapaho, Hunkpapas, Blackfeet, Cheyenne, and so forth — had the idea that white men were on the way. During the Sun Dance ceremony the week before, the Hunkpapa chief Sitting Bull had had a dream about soldiers falling into his camp. The hostiles, assured of victory, waited.

On the morning of June 25, the *Benjamin Franklin, Samuel Adams, John Hancock,* and *Ethan Allen* drifted quietly over the hills toward the village. They were looping south when the Indians attacked.

Struck by several spin-stabilized rockets, the *Samuel Adams* blew up with a flash that might have been seen by the officers and men riding behind Captain Keogh up the valley of the Little Big Horn. Eight or twelve Indians had, in the gray dawn, climbed for altitude above the ships.

Still several miles short of their intended drop zone, the balloon infantrymen piled out of the burning and exploding craft. Though each ship was armed with two Gatling rifles fore and aft, the airships were helpless against the aeroplanes' bullets and rockets. Approximately one hundred men, Custer included, cleared the ships. The Indian aviators made passes through them, no doubt killing several in the air. The *Franklin* and *Hancock* burned and fell to the earth across the river from the village. The *Allen,* dumping water ballast to gain altitude, turned for the Wolf Mountains. Though riddled by machine rifle fire, it did not explode and settled to earth about fifteen miles from where now raged a full-scale battle between increasingly demoralized soldiers and battle-maddened Sioux and Cheyenne.

Major Reno had charged the opposite side of the village as soon as he heard the commotion. Wrote one of his officers later:

> A solid wall of Indians came out of the haze which had hidden the village from our eyes. They must have outnumbered us ten to one, and they were ready for us . . . Fully a third of the column was down in three minutes.

Reno, fearing he would be swallowed up, pulled his men back across the river and took up a position in a stand of timber on the riverward slope of the knoll. The Indians left a few hundred braves to make certain Reno did not escape and moved off to Reno's right to descend on Keogh's flank.

The hundred-odd parachute infantrymen who made good their escape from the airship were scattered over three square miles. The ravines and gullies cutting up the hills around the village quickly filled with mounted Indians who rode through unimpeded by the random fire of disorganized balloon infantrymen. They swept them up, on the way to Keogh. Keogh, unaware of the number of Indians and the rout of Reno's command, got as far as the north bank of the river before he was ground to pieces between two masses of hostiles. Of Keogh's command, less than a dozen escaped the slaughter. The actual battle lasted about thirty minutes.

The hostiles left the area that night, exhausted after their greatest victory over the soldiers. Most of the Indians went north to Canada; some escaped the mass extermination of their race which was to take place in the American West during the next six years.

Terry found Reno entrenched on the ridge the morning of the twenty-seventh. The scouts sent to find Custer and Keogh could not believe their eyes when they found the bodies of the 7th Cavalry six miles away.

Some of the men were not found for another two days. Terry and his men scoured the ravines and valleys. Custer himself was about four miles from the sight of Keogh's annihilation; the Boy General appeared to have been hit by a piece of exploding rocket shrapnel and may have been dead before he reached the ground. His body escaped the mutilation that befell most of Keogh's command, possibly because of its distance from the camp.

Custer's miscalculation cost the army 430 men, four dirigibles (plus the Studebaker scout from the *Ethan Allen*), and its prestige. An attempt was made to make a scapegoat of Major Reno, blaming his alleged cowardice for the failure of the 7th. Though Reno was acquitted, grumblings continued until the turn of the century. It is hoped the matter will be settled for all time by the opening, for private research, of the papers of the late President Phil Sheridan. As Commander in Chief, he had access to a mountain of material which was kept from the public at the time of the court of inquiry of 1879.

Extract from *Huckleberry Among the Hostiles:*
A Journal
by Mark Twain, edited by Bernard Van Dyne
Hutton and Company, New York, 1932.

EDITOR'S NOTE: In November 1886 Clemens drafted a tentative outline for a sequel to *The Adventures of Huckleberry Finn,* which had received mixed reviews on its publication in January 1885, but which had nonetheless enjoyed a second printing within five months of its release. The proposed sequel was intended to deal with Huckleberry's adventures as a young man on the frontier. To gather research material firsthand, Mark Twain boarded the airship *Peyton* in Cincinnati, Ohio, in mid-December 1886, and set out across the Southwest, amassing copious notes and reams of interviews with soldiers, frontiersmen, law enforcement officers, exhostiles, at least two notorious outlaws, and a number of less readily categorized persons. Twain had intended to spend four months out west. Unfortunately, his wife, Livy, fell gravely ill in late February 1887; Twain returned to her as soon as he received word in Fort Hood, Texas. He lost interest in all writing for two years after her death in April 1887. The proposed novel about Huckleberry Finn as a man was never written: we are left with 110,000 words of interviews and observations and an incomplete journal of the author's second trek across the American West. — BvD.

February 2: A more desolate place than the Indian Territory of Oklahoma would be impossible to imagine. It is flat the year 'round, stingingly cold in winter, hot and dry, I am told, during the summer (when the land turns brown save for scattered patches of greenery which serve only to make the landscape all the drearier; Arizona and New Mexico are devoid of greenery, which is to their credit — when those territories elected to become barren wastelands they did not lose heart halfway, but followed their chosen course to the end).

It is easy to see why the United States Government swept the few Indians into Godforsaken Oklahoma and ordered them to remain there under threat of extermination. The word "Godforsaken" is the vital clue. The white men who "gave" this land to the few remaining tribes for as long as the wind shall blow — which it certainly does in February — and the grass shall grow (which it does, in Missouri, perhaps) were Christians who knew better than to let heathen savages run loose in parts of the country still smiled upon by our heavenly malefactor.

February 4: Whatever I may have observed about Oklahoma from the cabin of the *Peyton* has been reinforced by a view from the ground. The airship was running into stiff winds from the north, so we put in at Fort Sill yesterday evening and are awaiting calmer weather. I have gone on with my work.

Fort Sill is located seventeen miles from the Cheyenne Indian reservation. It has taken me all day to learn (mainly from one Sergeant Howard, a gap-toothed, unwashed Texan who is apparently my unofficial guardian angel for whatever length of time I am to be marooned here) that the Cheyenne do not care much for Oklahoma, which is still another reason why the government keeps them there. One or two exhostiles will leave the reservation every month, taking with them their wives and meager belongings, and Major Rickards will have to send out a detachment of soldiers to haul the erring ones back, either in chains or over the backs of horses. I am told the reservation becomes particularly annoying in the winter months, as the poor boys who are detailed to pursue the Indians suffer greatly from the cold. At this, I remarked to Sergeant Howard that the red man can be terribly inconsiderate, even ungrateful, in view of all the blessings the white man has heaped upon him — smallpox and that French disease, to name two. The good sergeant scratched his head and grinned, and said, "You're right, sir."

I'll have to make Howard a character in the book.

February 5: Today, I was taken by Major Rickards to meet a Cheyenne named Black Man's Hand, one of the participants of the alleged massacre of the 7th Cavalry at the Little Big Horn River in '76. The major had this one Cheyenne brought in after a recent departure from the reservation. Black Man's Hand had been shackled and left to dwell upon his past misdeeds in an unheated hut at the edge of the airport, while two cold-benumbed privates stood on guard before the door. It was evidently feared this one savage would, if left unchained, do to Fort Sill that which he (with a modicum of assistance from four or five thousand of his race) had done to Custer. I nevertheless mentioned to Rickards that I was interested in talking to Black Man's Hand, as the Battle of the Little Big Horn would perfectly climax Huckleberry's adventures in the new book. Rickards was reluctant to grant permission but gave in abruptly, perhaps fearing I would model a villain after him.

Upon entering the hut where the Cheyenne sat, I asked Major Rickards if it were possible to have the Indian's manacles removed, as it makes me nervous to talk to a man who can rattle his chains at me whenever he chooses. Major Rickards said no and troubled himself to explain to me the need for limiting the movement of this specimen of ferocity within the walls of Fort Sill.

With a sigh, I seated myself across from Black Man's Hand and offered him one of my cigars. He accepted it with a faint smile. He appeared to be in his forties, though his face was deeply lined.

He was dressed in ragged leather leggings, thick calf-length woolen pajamas, and a faded army jacket. His vest appeared to have been fashioned from an old parachute harness. He had no hat, no footgear, and no blanket.

"Major Rickards," I said, "this man is freezing to death. Even if he isn't, I am. Can you provide this hut with a little warmth?"

The fretting major summarily dispatched one of the sentries for firewood and kindling for the little stove sitting uselessly in the corner of the hut.

I would have been altogether comfortable after that could I have had a decanter of brandy with which to force out the inner chill. But Indians are notoriously incapable of holding liquor, and I did not wish to be the cause of this poor wretch's further downfall.

Black Man's Hand speaks surprisingly good English. I spent an hour and a half with him, recording his remarks with as much attention paid to accuracy as my advanced years and cold fingers permitted. With luck, I'll be able to fill some gaps in his story before the *Peyton* resumes its flight across this griddlecake countryside.

Extract from *The Testament of Black Man's Hand.*
[NOTE: For the sake of easier reading, I have substituted a number of English terms for those provided by the Cheyenne Black Man's Hand. — MT]

I was young when I first met the Oglala mystic Crazy Horse and was taught by him to fly the Thunderbirds which the one called the Gray White Man had given him. [The Gray White Man — John S. Mosby, Major, CSAAC — MT.] Some of the older men among the People [as the Cheyenne call themselves, Major Rickards explains; I assured him that such egocentricity is by no means restricted to savages — MT] did not think much of the flying machines and said, "How will we be able to remain brave men when this would enable us to fly over the heads of our enemies, without counting coup or taking trophies?"

But the Oglala said, "The Gray White Man has asked us to help him."

"Why should we help him?" asked Two Pines.

"Because he fights the blueshirts and those who persecute us. We have known for many years that the men who cheated us and lied to us and killed our women and the buffalo are men without honor, cowards who fight only because there is no other way for them to get what they want. They cannot understand why we fight with the Crows and Pawnees — to be brave, to win honor for ourselves. They fight because it is a means to an end, and they fight us only because we have what they want. The blueshirts want to kill us all. They fight to win. If we are to fight them, we must fight with their own weapons. We must fight to win."

The older warriors shook their heads sorrowfully and spoke of younger days when they fought the Pawnees bravely, honorably, man-to-man. But I and several other young men wanted to learn how to control the Thunderbirds. And we knew Crazy Horse spoke the truth, that our lives would never be happy as long as there were white men in the world. Finally, because they could not forbid us to go with the Oglala, only advise against it and say that the Great Mystery had not intended us to fly, Red Horse and I and some others went with Crazy Horse. I did not see my village again, not even at the big camp on the Greasy Grass [Little Big Horn — MT] where we rubbed out Yellow Hair. I think perhaps the blueshirts came after I was gone and told Two Pines that he had to leave his home and come to this flat dead place.

The Oglala Crazy Horse taught us to fly the Thunderbirds. We learned a great many things about the Gray White Man's machines. With them, we killed yellowleg flyers. Soon I tired of the waiting and the hunger. We were raided once. It was a good fight. In the dark, we chased the Big Fish [the Indian word for dirigibles — MT] and killed many men on the ground.

I do not remember all of what happened those seasons. When we were finally chased away from the landing place, Crazy Horse had us hide the Thunderbirds in the Black Hills. I have heard the yellowlegs did not know we had the Thunderbirds; that they thought they were run by the gray white men only. It did not matter; we thought we had used them for the last time.

Many seasons later, we heard what happened to Black Kettle's village. I went to the place some time after the battle. I heard that Crazy Horse had been there and seen the place. I looked for him but he had gone north again. Black Kettle had been a treaty man: we talked among ourselves that the yellowlegs had no honor.

It was the winter I was sick [1872. The Plains Indians and the US Army alike were plagued that winter by what we would call the influenza. It was probably brought by some itinerant French trapper — MT] that I heard of Crazy Horse's raid on the landing place of the Big Fish. It was news of this that told us we must prepare to fight the yellowlegs.

When I was well, my wives and I and Eagle Hawk's band went looking for Crazy Horse. We found him in the fall. Already the army had killed many Sioux and Cheyenne that summer. Crazy Horse said we must band together, we who knew how to fly the Thunderbirds. He said we would someday have to fight the yellowlegs among the clouds as in the old days. We only had five Thunderbirds which had not been flown many seasons. We spent the summer planning to get more. Red Chief and Yellow Dog gathered a large band. We raided the Fort Kearny and stole many Thunderbirds and canisters of powder. We hid them in the Black Hills. It had been a good fight.

It was at this time Yellow Hair sent out many soldiers to protect the miners he had brought in by speaking false. They destroyed the sacred lands of the Sioux. We killed some of them, and the yellowlegs burned many of our villages. That was not a good time. The Big Fish killed many of our people.

We wanted to get the Thunderbirds and kill the Big Fish. Crazy Horse had us wait. He had been talking to Sitting Bull, the Hunkpapa chief. Sitting Bull said we should not go against the yellowlegs yet, that we could only kill a few at a time. Later, he said, they would all come. That would be a good day to die.

The next year they came. We did not know until just before the Sun Dance [about June 10, 1876 — MT] that they were coming. Crazy Horse and I and all those who flew the Thunderbirds went to get ours. It took us two days to get them going again, and we had only six Thunderbirds flying when we flew to stop the blueshirts. Crazy Horse, Yellow Dog, American Gun, Little Wolf, Big Tall, and I flew that day. It was a good fight. We killed two Big Fish and many men and horses. We stopped the Turtles-which-kill [that would be the light armored cars Crook had with him on the Rosebud River — MT] so they could not come toward the Greasy Grass where we camped. The Sioux under Spotted Pony killed more on the ground. We flew back and hid the Thunderbirds near camp.

When we returned, we told Sitting Bull of our victory. He said it was good, but that a bigger victory was to come. He said he had had a vision during the Sun Dance. He saw many soldiers and enemy Indians fall out of the sky on their heads into the village. He said ours was not the victory he had seen.

It was some days later we heard that a yellowlegs Thunderbird had been shot down. We went to the place where it lay. There was a strange device above its wing. Crazy Horse studied it many moments. Then he said, "I have seen such a thing before. It carries Thunderbirds beneath one of the Big Fish. We must get our Thunderbirds. It will be a good day to die."

We hurried to our Thunderbirds. We had twelve of them fixed now, and we had on them, besides the quick rifles [Henry machine rifles of calibers .41–40 or .30–30 — MT], the roaring spears [Hale spin-stabilized rockets, of two-and-a-half-inch diameter — MT]. We took off before noonday.

We arrived at the Greasy Grass and climbed into the clouds, where we scouted. Soon, to the south, we saw the dust of many men moving. But Crazy Horse held us back. Soon we saw why; four Big Fish were coming. We came at them out of the sun. They did not see us till we were on them. We fired our roaring sticks, and the Big Fish caught fire and burned. All except one, which drifted away, though it lost all its fat. Wild Horse, in his Thunderbird, was shot but still fought on with us that morning. We began to kill the men on the Big Fish when a new thing happened. Men began to float down on blankets. We began to kill them with our quick rifles as they fell. Then we attacked those who reached the ground, until we saw Spotted Pony and his men were on them. We turned south and killed many horse soldiers there. Then we flew back to the Greasy Grass and hid the Thunderbirds. At camp, we learned that many pony soldiers had been killed. Word came that more soldiers were coming.

I saw, as the sun went down, the women moving among the dead Men-Who-Float-Down, taking their clothes and supplies. They covered the ground like leaves in the autumn. It had been a good fight.

Extract From *The Seventh Cavalry: A History*
Colonel E. R. Burroughs
USA, Ret.

So much has been written about that hot June day in 1876, so much guess-work applied where knowledge was missing. Was Custer dead in his harness before he reached the ground? Or did he stand and fire at the aircraft stafing his men? How many reached the ground alive? Did any escape the battle itself, only to be killed by Indian patrols later that afternoon or the next day? No one really knows, and all the Indians are gone now, so history stands a blank.

Only one thing is certain: for the men of the 7th Cavalry there was only the reality of the exploding dirigibles, the snap of their chutes deploying, the roar of the aircraft among them, the bullets, and those terrible last moments on the bluff. Whatever the verdict of their peers, whatever the future may reveal, it can be said that they did not die in vain.

SUGGESTED READING

Anonymous. *Remember Ft. Sumter!* Washington: War Department Recruiting Pamphlet, 1862.

———. *Leviathans of the Skies.* Goodyear Publications, 1923.

———. *The Dirigible in War and Peace.* Goodyear Publications, 1911.

———. *Sitting Bull, Killer of Custer.* G. E. Putnam's, 1903.

———. *Comanche of the Seventh.* Chicago: Military Press, 1879.

———. *Thomas Edison and the Indian Wars.* Menlo Park, N.J.: Edison Press, 1921.

———. "Fearful Slaughter at Big Horn." *New York Herald-Times,* July 8, 1876, *et passim.*

———. *Custer's Gold Hoax.* Boston: Barnum Press, 1892.

———. "Reno's Treachery: New Light on the Massacre at The Little Big Horn." *Chicago Daily News-Mirror,* June 12–19, 1878.

———. "Grant Scandals and the Plains Indian Wars." *Life,* May 3, 1921.

———. *The Hunkpapa Chief Sitting Bull,* Famous Indians Series #3. New York: 1937.

Arnold, Henry H. *The Air War in the East,* Smithsonian Annals of Flight, Vol. 38. Four books 1932–1937.
  1. *Sumter to Bull Run*
  2. *Williamsburg to Second Manassas*
  3. *Gettysburg to the Wilderness*
  4. *The Bombing of Atlanta to Haldeman*

Ballows, Edward. *The Indian Ace: Crazy Horse.* G. E. Putnam's, 1903.

Benteen, Capt. Frederick. *Major Benteen's Letters to his Wife.* University of Oklahoma Press, 1921.

Brininstool, A. E. *A Paratrooper with Custer.* n.p.g., 1891.

Burroughs, Col. E. R., Ret. *The Seventh Cavalry: A History.* Chicago: 1931.

Clair-Britner, Edoard. *Haldeman: Where the War Ended.* Frankfort University Press, 1911.

Crook, General George C. *Yellowhair: Custer as the Indians Knew Him.* Cincinnati Press, 1882.

Custer, George A. *My Life on the Plains and in the Clouds.* Chicago: 1874.

——— and Custer, Elizabeth. *'Chutes and Saddles.* Chicago: 1876.

Custer's Luck, n.a, n.p.g. [1891].

DeCamp, L. Sprague and Pratt, Fletcher. *Franklin's Engine: Mover of the World.* Hanover House, 1939.

De Voto, Bernard. *The Road from Sumter.* Scribner's, 1931.

Elsee, D. V. *The Last Raid of Crazy Horse.* Random House, 1921.

The 505th: History of the Skies. DA Pamphlet 870–10–3. GPO Pittsburgh, May 12, 1903.

FM 23–13–2 Machine Rifle M3121A1 and M3121A1E1 Cal. .41–40 Operator's Manual, DA FM, July 12, 1873.

Goddard, Robert H. *Rocketry: From 400 B.C. to 1933.* Smithsonian Annals of Flight 31. GPO Pittsburgh, 1934.

Guide to the Custer Battlefield National Monument. U.S. Parks Services, GPO Pittsburgh, 1937.

The Indian Wars. 3 vols. GPO Pittsburgh, 1898.

Kalin, David. *Hook Up! The Story of the Balloon Infantry.* New York: 1932.

Kellogg, Mark W. *The Drop at Washita.* Chicago: Times Press, 1872.

Lockridge, Sgt. Robert. *History of the Airborne: From Shiloh to Ft. Bragg.* Chicago: Military Press, 1936.

Lowe, Thaddeus C. *Aircraft of the Civil War.* 4 vols. 1891–1896.

McCoy, Col. Tim. *The Vanished American.* Phoenix Press, 1934.

McGovern, Maj. William. *Death in the Dakotas.* Sioux Press, 1889.

Morison, Samuel Eliot. *France in the New World 1627–1864.* 1931.

Myren, Gundal. *The Sun Dance Ritual and the Last Indian Wars.* 1901.

Patton, Gen. George C. *Custer's Last Campaigns.* Military House, 1937.

Paul, Winston. *We Were There at the Bombing of Ft. Sumter.* Landmark Books, 1929.

Payley, David. *Where Custer Fell.* New York Press, 1931.

Powell, Maj. John Wesley. *Report on the Arid Lands.* GPO, 1881.

Proceedings, Reno Court of Inquiry. GPO Pittsburgh, 1881.

Report on the U.S.-Canadian Offensive Against Sitting Bull, 1879. GPO Pittsburgh, War Department, 1880.

Sandburg, Carl. *Mr. Lincoln's Airmen.* Chicago: Driftwind Press, 1921.

Settle, Sgt. Maj. Winslow. *Under the Crossed Sabers.* Military Press, 1898.

Sheridan, Gen. Phillip. *The Only Good Indian . . . .* Military House, 1889.

Singleton, William Warren. *J.E.B. Stuart, Attila of the Skies.* Boston, 1871.

Smith, Gregory. *The Gray White Man: Mosby's Expedition to the Northwest 1863–1866.* University of Oklahoma Press, 1921.

Smith, Neldoo. *He Gave Them Wings: Captain Smith's Journal 1861–1864.* Urbana: University of Illinois Press, 1927.

Steen, Nelson. *Opening of the West.* Jim Bridger Press, 1902.

Tapscott, Richard D. *He Came with the Comet.* University of Illinois Press, 1927.

Twain, Mark. *Huckleberry Among the Hostiles: A Journal.* Hutton Books, 1932.

P

post-hol/o/caust — the aftermath of a catastrophe, usually, but not necessarily, explained as nuclear war. While stories in such settings initially appear pessimistic, most can also be construed as beliefs in mankind's ability to triumph over great obstacles. Works set in the immediate aftermath stress survival and adaptation, those set in the intermediate aftermath stress reorganization and rebuilding, and those set in the distant aftermath stress rediscovery and investigation. A categorization of disasters can be found in *Catastrophes!* (Fawcett Books, 1981). An anthology about such aftermaths is *After the Fall* (Ace Books, 1981).

Game Preserve

ROG PHILLIPS

"Hi-hi-hi!" Big One shouted, and heaved erect with the front end of It.

"Hi-hi-hi," Fat One and the dozen others echoed more mildly, lifting wherever they could get a hold on It.

It was lifted and borne forward in a half-crouching trot.

"Hi-hi hi-hi-hihihi," Elf chanted, running and skipping alongside the panting men and their massive burden.

It was carried forward through the lush grass for perhaps fifty feet.

"Ah-ah-ah," Big One sighed loudly, slowly letting the front end of It down until it dug into the soft black soil.

"Ahhh," Fat One and the others sighed, letting go and standing up, stretching aching back muscles, rubbing cramped hands.

"Ah-ah-ah-ah-ah-ah," Elf sang, running around and in between the resting men. He came too close to Big One and was sent sprawling by a quick, good-humored push.

Everyone laughed, Big One laughing the loudest. Then Big One lifted Elf to his feet and patted him on the back affectionately, a broad grin forming a toothy gap at the top of his bushy black beard.

Elf answered the grin with one of his own, and at that moment his ever present yearning to grow up to be the biggest and the strongest like Big One flowed through him with new strength.

Abruptly Big One leaped to the front end of It, shouting "Hi-hi-HI!"

"Hi-hi-hi," the others echoed, scrambling to their places. Once again It was borne forward for fifty feet — and again and again, across the broad meadowland.

A vast matting of blackberry brambles came in to view off to one side. Big One veered his course toward it. The going was uphill now, so the forward surges shortened to forty feet, then thirty. By the time they reached the blackberries they were wet and glossy with sweat.

It was a healthy patch, loaded with large ripe berries. The men ate hungrily at first, then more leisurely, pointing to one another's stained beards and laughing. As they denuded one area they leaped to It, carried it another ten feet and started stripping another section, never getting more than a few feet from It.

Elf picked his blackberries with first one then another of the men. When his hunger was satisfied he became mischievous, picking a handful of berries and squashing them against the back or the chest of the nearest man and running away, laughing. It was dangerous sport, he knew, because if one of them caught him he would be tossed into the brambles.

Eventually they all had their fill, and thanks to Elf looked as though they were oozing blackberry juice from every pore. The sun was in its mid-afternoon position. In the distance a line of white-barked trees could be seen — evidence of a stream.

"Hi-hi-hi!" Big One shouted.

The journey toward the trees began. It was mostly downhill, so the forward spurts were often as much as a hundred feet.

Before they could hear the water they could smell it. They grunted their delight at the smell, a rich fish odor betokening plenty of food. Intermingled with this odor was the spicy scent of eucalyptus.

They pushed forward with renewed zeal so that the sweat ran down their skins, dissolving the berry juices and making rivulets that looked like purple blood.

When less than a hundred yards from the stream, which was still hidden beyond the tall grasses and the trees lining its bank, they heard the sound of high-pitched voices — women's voices. They became uneasy and nervous. Their surges forward shortened to ten feet, their rest periods became longer, they searched worriedly for signs of motion through the trees.

They changed their course to arrive a hundred yards downstream from the source of the women's voices. Soon they reached the edge of the tree belt. It was more difficult to carry It through the scatterings of bushes. Too, they would get part way through the trees and run into trees too close together to get It past them, and have to back out and try another place. It took almost two hours to work through the trees to the bank of the stream.

Only Elf recognized the place they finally broke through as the place they had left more than two days before. In that respect he knew he was different, not only from Big One and other grownups, but also all other Elfs except one, a girl Elf. He had known it as long as he could remember. He had learned it from many little things. For example, he had recognized the place when they reached it. Big One and the others never remembered anything for long. In getting It through the trees they blundered as they always had, and got through by trial and error with no memory of past blunderings.

Elf was different in another way, too. He could make more sounds than the others. Sometimes he would keep a little It with him until it gave him a feeling of security almost as strong as the big It, then wander off alone with It and play with making sounds, "Bz-bz. Walla-walla-walla-rue-rue-la-lo-hi. Da!" and all kinds of sounds. It excited him to be able to make different sounds and put them together so that they pleased his hearing, but such sounds made the others avoid him and look at him from a safe distance with worried expressions, so he had learned not to make *different* sounds within earshot of the others.

The women and Elfs were upstream a hundred yards, where they always remained. From the way they were milling around and acting alarmed it was evident to Elf they could no more remember the men having been here a few days before than the men could remember it themselves. It would be two or three days before they slowly lost their fear of one another. It would be the women and their Elfs who would cautiously approach, holding their portable Its clutched for security, until, finally losing all fear, they would join into one big group for a while.

Big One and the others carried It right to the water's edge so they could get into the water without ever being far from It. They shivered and shouted excitedly as they bathed. Fat One screamed with delight as he held a squirming fish up for the others to see. He bit into it with strong white teeth, water dripping from his heavy brown beard. Renewed hunger possessed him. He gobbled the fish and began searching for another. He always caught two fish for any other man's one, which was why he was fat.

Elf himself caught a fish. After eating it he lay on the grassy bank looking up at the white billowing clouds in the blue sky. The sun was now near the horizon, half hidden behind a cloud, sending divergent ramps of light downward. The clouds on the western horizon were slowly taking on color until red, orange, and green separated into definite areas. The soft murmur of the stream formed a lazy background to the excited voices of the men. From upstream, faintly, drifted the woman and Elf sounds.

Here, close to the ground, the rich earthy smell was stronger than that of the stream. After a time a slight breeze sprang up, bringing with it other odors, that of distant pines, the pungent eucalyptus, a musky animal scent.

Big One and the others were out of the water finally. Half-asleep, Elf watched them move It up to dry ground. As though that were what the sun had been waiting for, it sank rapidly below the horizon.

The clouds where the sun had been seemed now to blaze for a time with a smoldering redness that cooled to black. The stars came out, one by one.

A multitude of snorings erupted into the night. Elf crept among the sleeping forms until he found Big One, and settled down for the night, his head against Big One's chest, his right hand resting against the cool smooth metal of It.

Elf awoke with the bright morning sun directly in his eyes. Big One was gone, already wading in the stream after fish. Some of the others were with him. A few were still sleeping.

Elf leaped to his feet, paused to stretch elaborately, then splashed into the stream. As soon as he caught a fish he climbed out onto the bank and ate it. Then he turned to his search for a little It. There were many lying around, all exactly alike. He studied several, not touching some, touching and even nudging others. Since they all looked alike it was more a matter of *feel* than any real difference that he looked for. One and only one seemed to be the It. Elf returned his attention to it several times.

Finally he picked it up and carried it over to the big It, and hid it underneath. Big One, with shouts of sheer exuberance, climbed up onto the bank dripping water. He grinned at Elf.

Elf looked in the direction of the women and other Elfs. Some of them were wandering in his direction, each carrying an It of some sort, many of them similar to the one he had chosen.

In sudden alarm at the thought that someone might steal his new It, Elf rescued it from its hiding place. He tried to hide it behind him when any of the men looked his way. They scorned an individual It and, as men, preferred an It too heavy for one person.

As the day advanced, women and Elfs approached nearer, pretending to be unaware at times that the men were here, at other times openly fleeing back, overcome by panic.

The men never went farther than twenty feet from the big It. But as the women came closer the men grew surly toward one another. By noon two of them were trying to pick a fight with anyone who would stand up to them.

Elf clutched his little It closely and moved cautiously downstream until he was twenty feet from the big It. Tentatively he went another few feet — farther than any of the men dared go from the big It. At first he felt secure, then panic overcame him and he ran back, dropping the little It. He touched the big It until the panic was gone. After a while he went to the little It and picked it up. He walked around, carrying it, until he felt secure with it again. Finally he went downstream again, twenty feet, twenty-five feet, thirty . . . He felt panic finally, but not overwhelmingly. When it became almost unendurable he calmly turned around and walked back.

Confidence came to him. An hour later he went downstream until he was out of sight of the big It and the men. Security seemed to flow warmly from the little It.

Excitement possessed Elf. He ran here and there, clutching It closely so as not to drop it and lose it. He felt *free*.

"Bdlboo," he said aloud, experimentally. He liked the sounds. "Bdlboo-bdlboo-bdlboo." He saw a berry bush ahead and ran to it to munch on the delicious fruit. "Riddle piddle biddle," he said. It sounded nice.

He ran on, and after a time he found a soft, grassy spot and stretched out on his back, holding It carelessly in one hand. He looked up and up, at a layer of clouds going in one direction and another layer above it going in another direction.

Suddenly he heard voices.

At first he thought the wind must have changed so that it was carrying the voices of the men to him. He lay there listening. Slowly he realized these voices were different. They were putting sounds together like those he made himself.

A sense of wonder possessed him. How could there be anyone besides himself who could do that?

Unafraid, yet filled with caution, he clutched It closely to his chest and stole in the direction of the sounds.

After going a hundred yards he saw signs of movement through the trees. He dropped to the ground and lay still for a moment, then gained courage to rise cautiously, ready to run. Stooping low, he stole forward until he could see several moving figures. Darting from tree to tree he moved closer to them, listening with greater excitement than he had ever known to the smoothly flowing variety of beautiful sounds they were making.

This was something new, a sort of game they must be playing. One voice would make a string of sounds then stop, another would make a string of different sounds and stop, a third would take it up. They were good at it, too.

But the closer he got to them the more puzzled he became. They were shaped somewhat like people, they carried Its, they had hands and faces like people. That's as far as the similarity went. Their feet were solid, their arms, legs, and body were not skin at all but strangely colored and unliving in appearance. Their faces were smooth like women's, their hair short like babies', their voices deep like men's.

And the Its they carried were unlike any Elf had ever seen. Not only that, each of them carried more than one.

That was an *idea!* Elf became so excited he almost forgot to keep hidden. If you had more than one It, then if something happened to one you would still feel secure!

He resisted the urge to return to the stream and search for another little It to give him extra security. If he did that he might never again find these creatures that were so like men and yet so different. So instead, he filed the idea away to use at the earliest opportunity and followed the strange creatures, keeping well hidden from them.

Soon Elf could hear the shouts of the men in the distance. From the behavior of the creatures ahead, they had heard those shouts too. They changed their direction so as to reach the stream a hundred yards or more downstream at about the spot where Elf had left. They made no voice sounds now that Elf could hear. They clutched their strangely shaped, long Its before them tensely as though feeling greater security that way, their heads turning this way and that as they searched for any movement ahead.

They moved purposefully. An overwhelming sense of kinship brought tears to Elf's eyes. These creatures were *his kind.* Their differences from him were physical and therefore superficial, and even if those differences were greater it wouldn't have mattered.

He wanted, suddenly, to run to them. But the thought of it sent fear through him. Also they might run in panic from him if he suddenly revealed himself.

It would have to be a mutual approach, he felt. He was used to seeing them now. In due time he would reveal himself for a brief moment to them. Later he would stay in the open and watch them, making no move to approach until they got used to his being around. It might take days, but eventually, he felt sure, he could join them without causing them to panic.

After all, there had been the time when he absented himself from the men for three whole days and when he returned they had forgotten him, and his sudden appearance in their midst had sent even Big One into spasms of fear. Unable to flee from the security of the big It, and unable to bear his presence among them without being used to him, they had all fallen on the ground in a fit. He had had to retreat and wait until they recovered. Then, slowly, he had let them get used to his being in sight before approaching again. It had taken two full days to get to the point where they would accept him once more.

That experience, Elf felt, would be valuable to remember now. He wouldn't want to plunge these creatures into fits or see them scatter and run away.

Also, he was too afraid right now to reveal himself even though every atom of his being called for their companionship.

Suddenly he made another important discovery. Some of the Its these creatures carried had something like pliable vines attached to them so they could be hung about the neck! The thought was so staggering that Elf stopped and examined his It to see if that could be done to it. It was twice as long as his hand and round one way, tapering to a small end that opened to the hollow inside. It was too smooth to hold with a pliable vine unless — He visualized pliable vines woven together to hold It. He wasn't sure how it could be done, but maybe it could.

He set the idea aside for the future and caught up with the creatures again, looking at them with a new emotion, awe. The ideas he got just from watching them were so staggering he was getting dizzy!

Another new thought hit him. He rejected it at once as being too fantastic. It returned. Leaves are thin and pliable and can be wrapped around small objects like pebbles. Could it be that these creatures were really men of some sort, with bodies like men, covered with something thin like leaves are thin? It was a new and dizzy height in portable securities, and hardly likely. No. He rejected the idea with finality and turned his mind to other things.

He knew now where they could reach the stream. He decided to circle them and get ahead of them. For the next few minutes this occupied his full attention, leaving no room for crazy thoughts.

He reached the stream and hid behind some bushes where he would have a quick line of retreat if necessary. He clutched It tightly and waited. In a few moments he saw the first of the creatures emerge a hundred feet away. The others soon joined the first. Elf stole forward from concealment to concealment until he was only fifteen feet from them. His heart was pounding with a mixture of fear and excitement. His knuckles were white from clutching It.

The creatures were still carrying on their game of making sounds, but now in an amazing new way that made them barely audible. Elf listened to the incredibly varied sounds, enraptured.

"This colony seems to have remained pure."

"You never can tell."

"No, you never can tell. Get out the binoculars and look, Joe."

"Not just yet, Harold. I'm looking to see if I can spot one whose behavior shows intelligence."

Elf ached to imitate some of the beautiful combinations of sounds. He wanted to experiment and see if he could make the softly muted voices. He had an idea how it might be done, not make a noise in your throat but breathe out and form the sounds with your mouth just like you were uttering them aloud.

One of the creatures fumbled at an It hanging around his neck. The top of it hinged back. He reached in and brought out a gleaming It and held it so that it covered his eyes. He was facing toward the men upstream and stood up slowly.

"See something, Joe?"

Suddenly Elf was afraid. Was this some kind of magic? He had often puzzled over the problem of whether things were there when he didn't look at them. He had experimented, closing his eyes and then opening them suddenly to see if things were still there, and they always were; but maybe this was magic to make the men not be there. Elf waited, watching upstream, but Big One and the others did not vanish.

The one called Joe chuckled. "The toy the adult males have would be a museum piece if it were intact. A 1960 Ford, I think. Only one wheel on it, right front."

Elf's attention jerked back. One of the creatures was reaching over his shoulder, lifting on the large It fastened there. The top of the It pulled back. He reached inside, bringing out something that made Elf almost exclaim aloud. It was shaped exactly like the little It Elf was carrying, but it glistened in the sunlight and its interior was filled with a rich brown fluid.

"Anyone else want a Coke?"

"This used to be a picnic area," the one called Joe said, not taking his eyes from the binoculars. "I can see a lot of pop bottles lying around in the general area of that wreck of a Ford."

While Elf watched, breathless, the creature reached inside the skin of his hip and brought out a very small It and did something to the small end of the hollow It. Putting the very small It back under the skin of his hip, he put the hollow It to his lips and tilted it. Elf watched the brown liquid drain out. Here was magic. Such an It — the very one he carried — could be filled with water from the stream and carried around to drink any time!

When the It held no more liquid the creature dropped it to the ground. Elf could not take his eyes from it. He wanted it more than he had ever wanted anything. They might forget it. Sometimes the women dropped their Its and forgot them, picking up another one instead, and these creatures had beardless faces like women. Besides, each of them carried so many Its that they would feel just as secure without this one.

So many Its! One of the creatures held a flat white It in one hand and a very slim It shaped like a straight section of a bush stem, pointed at one end, with which he scratched on the white It at times, leaving black designs.

"There're fourteen males," the one called Joe whispered. The other wrote it down.

The way these creatures did things, Elf decided, was very similar to the way Big One and the other men went at moving the big It. They were very much like men in their actions, these creatures.

"Eighty-five or -six females."

"See any signs of intelligent action yet?"

"No. A couple of the males are fighting. Probably going to be a mating free-for-all tomorrow or next day. There's one! Just a minute, I want to make sure. It's a little girl, maybe eight or nine years old. Good forehead. Her eyes definitely lack that large marble-like quality of the submoron parent species. She's intelligent, all right. She's drawing something in the sand with a stick. Give me your rifle, Bill, it's got a better telescope sight on it than mine, and I don't want her to suffer."

That little It, abandoned on the ground. Elf wanted it. One of the creatures would be sure to pick it up. Elf worried. He would never get it then. If only the creatures would go, or not notice him. If only —

The creature with the thing over his eyes put it back where he had gotten it out of the thing hanging from his shoulder. He had taken one of the long slim things from another of the creatures and placed the thick end against his shoulder, the small end pointed upstream. The others were standing, their backs to Elf, all of them looking upstream. If they would remain that way, maybe he could dart out and get the little It. In another moment they might lose interest in whatever they were watching.

Elf darted out from his concealment and grabbed the It off the ground, and in the same instant an ear-shattering sound erupted from the long slim thing against the creature's shoulder.

"Got her!" the creature said.

Paralyzed with fright, Elf stood motionless. One of the creatures started to turn his way. At the last instant Elf darted back to his place of concealment. His heart was pounding so loudly he felt sure they would hear it.

"You sure, Joe?"

"Right through the head. She never knew what happened."

Elf held the new It close to him, ready to run if he were discovered. He didn't dare look at it yet. It wouldn't notice if he just held it and felt it without looking at it. It was cold at first, colder than the water in the stream. Slowly it warmed. He dared to steal a quick glance at it. It gleamed at him as though possessed of inner life. A new feeling of security grew within him, greater than he had ever known. The other It, the one half-filled with dried mud and deeply scratched from the violent rush of water over it when the stream went over its banks, lay forgotten at his feet.

"Well, that finishes the survey trip for this time."

Elf paid little attention to the voice whispers now, too wrapped up in his new feelings.

"Yes, and quite a haul. Twenty-two colonies — three more than ten years ago. Fourteen of them uncontaminated, seven with only one or two intelligent offspring to kill, only one colony so contaminated we had to wipe it out altogether. And one renegade."

"The renegades are growing scarcer every time. Another ten or twenty years and they'll be extinct."

"Then there won't be any more intelligent offspring in these colonies."

"Let's get going. It'll be dark in another hour or so."

The creatures were hiding some of their Its under their skin, in their carrying cases. There was a feeling about them of departure. Elf waited until they were on the move, back the way they had come, then he followed at a safe distance.

He debated whether to show himself now or wait. The sun was going down in the sky now. It wouldn't be long until it went down for the night. Should he wait until the morning to let them get their first glimpse of him?

He smiled to himself. He had plenty of time. Tomorrow and tomorrow. He would never return to Big One and the other men. Men or creatures, he would join with these new and wonderful creatures. They were *his kind*.

He thought of the girl Elf. They were her kind, too. If he could only get her to come with him.

On sudden impulse he decided to try. These creatures were going back the same way they had come. If he ran, and if she came right with him, they could catch up with the creatures before they went so far they would lose them.

He turned back, going carefully until he could no longer see the creatures, then he ran. He headed directly toward the place where the women and Elfs stayed. They would not be so easily alarmed as the men because there were so many of them they couldn't remember one another, and one more or less of the Elfs went unnoticed.

When he reached the clearing he slowed to a walk, looking for her. Ordinarily he didn't have to look much. She would see him and come to him, smiling in recognition of the fact that he was the only one like her.

He became a little angry. Was she hiding? Then he saw her. He went to her. She was on her stomach, motionless as though asleep, but something was different. There was a hole in one side of her head, and on the opposite side it was torn open, red and grayish white, with — He knelt down and touched her. She had the same inert feel to her that others had had who never again moved.

He studied her head curiously. He had never seen anything like this. He shook her. She remained limp. He sighed. He knew what would happen now. It was already happening. The odor was very faint yet, but she would not move again, and day after day the odor would get stronger. No one liked it.

He would have to hurry or he would lose the creatures. He turned and ran, never looking back. Once he started to cry, then stopped in surprise. Why had he been crying, he wondered. He hadn't hurt himself.

He caught up with the creatures. They were hurrying now, their long slender Its balanced on one shoulder, the big end resting in the palm of the hand. They no longer moved cautiously. Shortly it was new country. Elf had never been this far from the stream. Big One more or less led the men, and always more or less followed the same route in cross-country trips.

The creatures didn't spend hours stumbling along impossible paths. They looked ahead of them and selected a way, and took it. Also they didn't have a heavy It to transport, fifty feet at a time. Elf began to sense they had a destination in mind. Probably the place they lived.

Just ahead was a steep bank, higher than a man, running in a long line. The creatures climbed the bank and vanished on the other side. Cautiously Elf followed them, heading toward a large stone with It qualities at the top of the bank from whose concealment he could see where they had gone without being seen. He reached it and cautiously peeked around it. Just below him were the creatures, but what amazed Elf was the sight of the big It.

It was very much like the big It the men had, except that there were differences in shape, and instead of one round thing at one corner, it had one at each corner and rested on them so that it was held off the ground. It glistened instead of being dull. It had a strange odor that was quite strong.

The creatures were putting some of their Its into it; two of them had actually climbed into it — something neither Elf nor the men had ever dared to do with their own big It.

Elf took his eyes off of it for a moment to marvel at the ground. It seemed made of stone, but such stone as he had never before seen. It was an even width with edges going in straight lines that paralleled the long narrow hill on which he stood, and on the other side was a similar hill, extending as far as the eye could see.

He returned his attention to the creatures and their big It. The creatures had all climbed into it now. Possibly they were settling down for the night, though it was still early for that . . .

No matter. There was plenty of time. Tomorrow and tomorrow. Elf would show himself in the morning, then run away. He would come back again after a while and show himself a little longer, giving them time to get used to him so they wouldn't panic.

They were playing their game of making voice sounds to one another again. It seemed their major preoccupation. Elf thought how much fun it would be to be one of them, making voice sounds to his heart's content.

"I don't see why the government doesn't wipe out the whole lot," one of them was saying. "It's hopeless to keep them alive. Feeble-mindedness is dominant in them. They can't be absorbed into the race again, and any intelligent offspring they get from mating with a renegade would start a long line of descendants, at least one fourth of whom would be mindless idiots."

"Well," another of them said, "it's one of those things where there is no answer. Wipe them out, and next year it would be all the blond-haired people to be wiped out to keep the race of dark-haired people pure, or something. Probably in another hundred years nature will take care of the problem by wiping them out for us. Meanwhile we game wardens must make the rounds every two years and weed out any of them we can find that have intelligence." He looked up the embankment but did not notice Elf's head, concealed partially by the grass around the concrete marker. "It's an easy job. Any of them we missed seeing this time, we'll probably get next time. In the six or eight visits we make before the intelligent ones can become adults and mate we always find them."

"What I hate is when they see us, those intelligent ones," a third voice said. "When they walk right up to us and want to be friends with us it's too much like plain murder, except that they can't talk, and only make moronic sounds like 'Bdl-bdl-bdl.' Even so, it gets me when we kill them." The others laughed.

Suddenly Elf heard a new sound from the big It. It was not a voice sound, or if it was it was one that Elf felt he could not possibly match exactly. It was a growling, "RRrrRRrrRRrr." Suddenly it was replaced by still a different sound, a "p-p-p-p-p" going very rapidly. Perhaps it was the way these creatures snored. It was not unpleasant. Elf cocked his head to one side, listening to the sound, smiling. How exciting it would be when he could join with these creatures! He wanted to so much.

The big It began to move. In the first brief second Elf could not believe his senses. How could it move without being carried? But it was moving, and the creatures didn't seem to be aware of it! Or perhaps they were too overcome by fear to leap out!

Already the big It was moving faster than a walk, and was moving faster with every heartbeat. How could they remain unaware of it and not leap to safety?

Belatedly Elf abandoned caution and leaped down the embankment to the flat ribbon of rock, shouting. But already the big It was over a hundred yards away, and moving faster now than birds in flight!

He shouted, but the creatures didn't hear him — or perhaps they were so overcome with fright that they were frozen. Yes, that must be it.

Elf ran after the big It. If he could only catch up with it he would gladly join the creatures in their fate. Better to die with them than to lose them!

He ran and ran, refusing to believe he could never overtake the big It, even when it disappeared from view, going faster than the wind. He ran and ran until his legs could lift no more.

Blinded by tears, he tripped and sprawled full length on the wide ribbon of stone. His nose bled from hitting the hard surface. His knees were scraped and bleeding. He was unaware of this.

He was aware only that the creatures were gone, to what unimaginable fate he could not guess, but lost to him, perhaps forever.

Sobs welled up within him, spilled out, shaking his small naked body. He cried as he hadn't cried since he was a baby.

And the empty Coca-Cola bottle, clutched forgotten in his hand, glistened with the rays of the setting sun . . .

Life Hutch

HARLAN ELLISON

Terrence slid his right hand, the one out of sight of the robot, up his side. The razoring pain of the three broken ribs caused his eyes to widen momentarily in pain. Then he recovered himself and closed them till he was studying the machine through narrow slits.

If the eyeballs click, I'm dead, thought Terrence.

The intricate murmurings of the life hutch around him brought back the immediacy of his situation. His eyes again fastened on the medicine cabinet clamped to the wall next to the robot's duty-niche.

Cliché. So near yet so far. It could be all the way back on Antares-Base for all the good it's doing me, he thought, and a crazy laugh rang through his head. He caught himself just in time. *Easy! Three days is a nightmare, but cracking up will only make it end sooner.* That was the last thing he wanted. But it couldn't go on much longer.

He flexed the fingers of his right hand. It was all he *could* move. Silently he damned the technician who had passed the robot through. Or the politician who had let inferior robots get placed in the life hutches so he could get a rake-off from the government contract. Or the repairman who hadn't bothered checking closely his last time around. All of them; he damned them all.

They deserved it.

He was dying.

His death had started before he had reached the life hutch. Terrence had begun to die when he had gone into the battle.

He let his eyes close completely, let the sounds of the life hutch fade from around him. Slowly, the sound of the coolants hush-hushing through the wall-pipes, the relay machines feeding their messages without pause from all over the galaxy, the whirr of the antenna's standard turning in its socket atop the bubble, slowly they melted into silence. He had resorted to blocking himself off from reality many times during the past three days. It was either that or existing with the robot watching, and eventually he would have had to move. To move was to die. It was that simple.

He closed his ears to the whisperings of the life hutch; he listened to the whisperings within himself.

"Good God! There must be a million of them!"

It was the voice of the squadron leader, Resnick, ringing in his suit intercom.

"What kind of battle formation is *that* supposed to be?" came another voice. Terrence looked at the radar screen, at the flickering dots signifying Kyben ships.

"Who can tell with those toadstool-shaped ships of theirs," Resnick answered. "But remember, the whole front umbrella part is studded with cannon, and it has a helluva range of fire. Okay, watch yourselves, good luck — and give 'em Hell!"

The fleet dove straight for the Kyben armada.

To his mind came the sounds of war, across the gulf of space. It was all imagination; in that tomb there was no sound. Yet he could clearly detect the hiss of his scout's blaster as it poured beam after beam into the lead ship of the Kyben fleet.

His sniper-class scout had been near the point of that deadly Terran phalanx, driving like a wedge at the alien ships, converging on them in loose battle-formation. It was then it had happened.

One moment he had been heading into the middle of the battle, the left flank of the giant Kyben dreadnaught turning crimson under the impact of his firepower.

The next moment, he had skittered out of the formation which had slowed to let the Kyben craft overshoot, while the Earthmen decelerated to pick up maneuverability.

He had gone on at the old level and velocity, directly into the forward guns of a toadstool-shaped Kyben destroyer.

The first beam had burned the gun-mounts and directional equipment off the front of the ship, scorching down the aft side in a smear like oxidized chrome plate. He had managed to avoid the second beam.

His radio contact had been brief; he was going to make it back to Antares-Base if he could. If not, the formation would be listening for his homing-beam from a life hutch on whatever planetoid he might find for a crash-landing.

Which was what he had done. The charts had said the pebble spinning there was technically 1–333, 2–A, M & S, 3–804.39#, which would have meant nothing but three-dimensional coordinates had not the small # after the data indicated a life hutch somewhere on its surface.

His distaste for being knocked out of the fighting, being forced onto one of the life hutch planetoids, had been offset only by his fear of running out of fuel before he could locate himself. Of eventually drifting off into space somewhere, to finally wind up as an artificial satellite around some minor sun.

The ship pancaked in under minimal reverse drive, bounced high twice and caromed ten times, tearing out chunks of the rear section, but had come to rest a scant two miles from the life hutch, jammed into the rocks.

Terrence had high-leaped the two miles across the empty, airless planetoid to the hermetically sealed bubble in the rocks. His primary wish was to set the hutch's beacon signal so his returning fleet could track him.

He had let himself into the decompression chamber, palmed the switch through his thick spacesuit glove, and finally removed his helmet as he heard the air whistle into the chamber.

He had pulled off his gloves, opened the inner door, and entered the life hutch itself.

God bless you, little life hutch, Terrence had thought as he dropped the helmet and gloves. He had glanced around, noting the relay machines picking up messages from outside, sorting them, vectoring them off in other directions. He had seen the medicine chest clamped onto the wall, the refrigerator he knew would be well stocked if a previous tenant hadn't been there before the stockman could refill it. He had seen the all-purpose robot, immobile in its duty-niche. And the wall-chronometer, its face smashed. All of it in a second's glance.

God bless, too, the gentlemen who thought up the idea of these little rescue stations, stuck all over the place for just such emergencies as this, he thought thankfully. He had started to walk across the room.

It was at this point that the service robot, which kept the place in repair between tenants and unloaded supplies from the ships, had moved clankingly across the floor, and with one fearful smash of a steel arm thrown Terrence across the room.

The spaceman had been brought up short against the steel bulkhead, pain blossoming in his back, his side, his arms and legs. The machine's blow had instantly broken three of his ribs. He lay there for a moment, unable to move. For a few seconds he was too stunned to breathe, and it had been that, certainly, that had saved his life. His pain had immobilized him, and in that short space of time the robot had retreated with a muted internal clash of gears.

He had attempted to sit up straight, and the robot had hummed oddly and begun to move. He had stopped the movement. The robot had settled back.

Twice more had convinced him his position was as bad as he had thought.

The robot had worn down somewhere in its printed circuits. Its commands to lift had been erased or distorted so that now it was conditioned to smash, to hit, anything that moved.

He had seen the clock. He realized he should have suspected something was wrong when he saw its smashed face. Of course! The digital dials had moved, the robot had smashed the clock. Terrence had moved, the robot had smashed him.

And would again, if he moved again.

But for the unnoticeable movement of his eyelids, he had not moved in three days.

He had tried moving toward the decompression lock, stopping when the robot advanced and letting it settle back, then moving again, a little nearer. But the idea died with his first movement. His ribs were too painful. The pain was terrible. He was locked in one position, an uncomfortable, twisted position, and he would be there till the stalemate ended, one way or the other.

He was suddenly alert again. The reliving of his last three days brought back reality sharply.

He was twelve feet away from the communications panel, twelve feet away from the beacon that would guide his rescuers to him. Before he died of his wounds, before he starved to death, before the robot crushed him. It could have been twelve light-years, for all the nearer he could get to it.

What had gone wrong with the robot? Time to think was cheap. The robot could detect movement, but thinking was still possible. Not that it could help, but it was possible.

The companies that supplied the life hutch's needs were all government contracted. Somewhere along the line someone had thrown in impure steel or calibrated the circuit-cutting machines for a less expensive job. Somewhere along the line someone had not run the robot through its paces correctly. Somewhere along the line someone had committed murder.

He opened his eyes again. Only the barest fraction of opening. Any more and the robot would sense the movement of his eyelids. That would be fatal.

He looked at the machine.

It was not, strictly speaking, a robot. It was merely a remote-controlled hunk of jointed steel, invaluable for making beds, stacking steel plating, watching culture dishes, unloading spaceships, and sucking dirt from rugs. The robot body, roughly humanoid, but without what would have been a head on a human, was merely an appendage.

The real brain, a complex maze of plastic screens and printed circuits, was behind the wall. It would have been too dangerous to install those delicate parts in a heavy-duty mechanism. It was all too easy for the robot to drop itself from a loading shaft, or be hit by a meteorite, or get caught under a wrecked spaceship. So there were sensitive units in the robot appendage that "saw" and "heard" what was going on, and relayed them to the brain — behind the wall.

And somewhere along the line that brain had worn grooves too deeply into its circuits. It was now mad. Not mad in any way a human being might go mad, for there were an infinite number of ways a machine could go insane. Just mad enough to kill Terrence.

Even if I could *hit the robot with something, it wouldn't stop the thing.* He could perhaps throw something at the machine before it could get to him, but it would do no good. The robot brain would still be intact, and the appendage would continue to function. It was hopeless.

He stared at the massive, blocky hands of the robot. It seemed he could see his own blood on the jointed work-tool fingers of one hand. He knew it must be his imagination, but the idea persisted. He flexed the fingers of his hidden hand.

Three days had left him weak and dizzy from hunger. His head was light and his eyes burned steadily. He had been lying in his own filth till he no longer noticed the discomfort. His side ached and throbbed, and the pain of a blast furnace roared through him every time he breathed.

He thanked God his spacesuit was still on, lest the movement of his breathing bring the robot down on him. There was only one solution, and that solution was his death. He was almost delirious.

Several times during the past day — as well as he could gauge night and day without a clock or a sunrise — he had heard the roar of the fleet landing outside. Then he had realized there was no sound in dead space. Then he had realized they were all inside the relay machines, coming through subspace right into the life hutch. Then he had realized that such a thing was not possible. Then he had come to his senses and realized all that had gone before was hallucination.

Then he had awakened and known it *was* real. He *was* trapped, and there was no way out. Death had come to live with him. He was going to die.

Terrence had never been a coward, nor had he been a hero. He was one of the men who fight wars because they are always fought by *someone*. He was the kind of man who would allow himself to be torn from wife and home and flung into an abyss they called Space to defend what he had been told needed defense. But it was in moments like this that a man like Terrence began to think.

Why here? Why like this? What have I done that I should finish in a filthy spacesuit on a lost rock — and not gloriously like they said in the papers back home, but starving or bleeding to death alone with a crazy robot? Why me? Why me? Why alone?

He knew there could be no answers. He expected no answers.

He was not disappointed.

When he awoke, he instinctively looked at the clock. Its shattered face looked back at him, jarring him, forcing his eyes open in after-sleep terror. The robot hummed and emitted a spark. He kept his eyes open. The humming ceased. His eyes began to burn. He knew he couldn't keep them open too long.

The burning worked its way to the front of his eyes, from the top and bottom, bringing with it tears. It felt as though someone was shoving needles into the corners. The tears ran down over his cheeks.

His eyes snapped shut. The roaring grew in his ears. The robot didn't make a sound.

Could it be inoperative? Could it have worn down to immobility? Could he take the chance of experimenting?

He slid down to a more comfortable position. The robot charged forward the instant he moved. He froze in mid-movement, his heart a chunk of ice. The robot stopped, confused, a scant ten inches from his outstretched foot. The machine hummed to itself, the noise of it coming both from the machine before him and from somewhere behind the wall.

He was suddenly alert.

If it had been working correctly, there would have been little or no sound from the appendage, and none whatsoever from the brain. But it was *not* working properly, and the sound of its thinking was distinct.

The robot rolled backward, its "eyes" still toward Terrence. The sense orbs of the machine were in the torso, giving the machine the look of a squat metal gargoyle, squared and deadly.

The humming was growing louder, every now and then a sharp *pfffft!* of sparks mixed with it. Terrence had a moment's horror at the thought of a short circuit, a fire in the life hutch, and no service robot to put it out.

He listened carefully to pinpoint the location of the robot's brain built into the wall.

Then he thought he had it. Or was it there? It was either in the wall behind a bulkhead next to the refrigerator, or behind a bulkhead near the relay machines. The two possible housings were within a few feet of each other, but they might make a great deal of difference.

The distortion created by the steel plate in front of the brain, and the distracting background noise of the robot broadcasting it made it difficult to tell exactly which was the correct location.

He drew a deep breath.

The ribs slid a fraction of an inch together, their broken ends grinding. He moaned.

A high-pitched tortured moan that died quickly but throbbed back and forth inside his head, echoing and building itself into a paean of sheer agony! It forced his tongue out of his mouth, limp in a corner of his lips, moving slightly. The robot rolled forward. He drew his tongue in, clamped his mouth shut, cut off the scream inside his head at its high point!

The robot stopped, rolled back to its duty-niche.

Oh, God! The pain! The God God where are you pain!

Beads of sweat broke out on his body. He could feel their tickle inside his spacesuit, inside his jumper, inside the bodyshirt, on his skin. The pain of the ribs was suddenly heightened by an irresistible itching of his skin.

He moved infinitesimally within the suit, his outer appearance giving no indication of the movement. The itching did not subside. The more he tried to make it stop, the more he thought about not thinking about it, the worse it became. His armpits, the crooks of his arms, his thighs where the tight service-pants clung — suddenly too tightly — were madness. He had to scratch!

He almost started to make the movement. He stopped before he started. He knew he would never live to enjoy any relief. A laugh bubbled into his head. *God Almighty, and I always laughed at the slobs who suffered with the seven-year itch, the ones who always did a little dance when they were at attention during inspection, the ones who could scratch and sigh contentedly. God, how I envy them.* His thoughts were taking on a wild sound, even to him.

The prickling did not stop. He twisted faintly. It got worse. He took another deep breath.

The ribs sandpapered again.

This time, blessedly, he fainted from the pain.

"Well, Terrence, how do you like your first look at a Kyben?"

Ernie Terrence wrinkled his forehead and ran a finger up the side of his face. He looked at his Commander and shrugged. "Fantastic things, aren't they?"

"Why fantastic?" asked Commander Foley.

"Because they're just like us. Except of course the bright yellow pigmentation and the tentacle fingers. Other than that they're identical to a human being."

The Commander opaqued the examination-casket and drew a cigarette from a silver case, offering the Lieutenant one. He puffed it alight, staring with one eye closed against the smoke. "More than that, I'm afraid. Their insides look like someone had taken them out, liberally mixed them with spare parts from several other species, and jammed them back in any way that fitted conveniently. For the next twenty years we'll be knocking our heads together trying to figure out their metabolic *raison d'être.*"

Terrence grunted, rolling his unlit cigarette absently between two fingers. "That's the least of it."

"You're right," agreed the Commander. "For the next *thousand* years we'll be trying to figure out how they think, why they fight, what it takes to get along with them, what motivates them."

If they let us live that long, thought Terrence.

"Why are we at war with the Kyben?" he asked the older man. "I mean *really.*"

"Because the Kyben want to kill every human being they can recognize as a human being."

"What have they got against us?"

"Does it matter? Maybe it's because our skin isn't bright yellow; maybe it's because our fingers aren't silken and flexible; maybe it's because our cities are too noisy for them. Maybe a lot of maybes. But it doesn't matter. Survival never matters until you have to survive."

Terrence nodded. He understood. So did the Kyben. It grinned at him and drew its blaster. It fired point-blank, crimsoning the hull of the Kyben ship.

He swerved to avoid running into his gun's own backlash. The movement of the bucket seat sliding in its tracks, keeping his vision steady while maneuvering, made him dizzy. He closed his eyes for a moment.

When he opened them, the abyss was nearer, and he teetered, his lips whitening as they pressed together under his effort to steady himself. With a headlong gasp he fell sighing into the stomach. His long, silken fingers jointed steely humming clankingly toward the medicine chest ever over the plate behind the bulkhead.

The robot advanced on him grindingly. Small fine bits of metal rubbed together, ashing away into a breeze that came from nowhere as the machine raised lead boots toward his face.

Onward and onward till he had no room to move and then

The light came on, bright, brighter than any star Terrence had ever seen, glowing, broiling, flickering, shining, bobbing a ball of light on the chest of the robot, who staggered, stumbled, stepped.

The robot hissed, hummed and exploded into a million flying, racing fragments, shooting beams of light all over the abyss over which Terrence again teetered, teetering. He flailed his arms wildly trying to escape but at the last moment, before the fall

He awoke with a start!

He saved himself only by his unconscious. Even in the hell of a nightmare he was aware of the situation. He had not moaned and writhed in his delirium. He had kept motionless and silent.

He knew it was true, because he was still alive.

Only his surprised jerking, as he came back to consciousness, started the monster rolling from its niche. He came fully awake and sat silent, slumped against the wall. The robot retreated.

Thin breath came through his nostrils. Another moment and he would have put an end to the past three days — three days or more now? how long had he been asleep? — days of torture.

He was hungry. Lord how hungry he was. The pain in his side was worse now, a steady throbbing that made even shallow breathing torturous. He itched maddeningly. He was uncomfortably slouched against a cold steel bulkhead, every rivet having made a burrow for itself in his skin. He wished he was dead.

He didn't wish he was dead. It was all too easy to get his wish.

If he could only disable that robot brain. A total impossibility. If he could only wear Phobos and Deimos for watchfobs. If he could only shack up with a silicon-deb from Penares. If he could only use his large colon for a lasso.

It would take a thorough destruction of the brain to do it enough damage to stop the appendage before it could roll over and smash Terrence again.

With a steel bulkhead between him and the brain, his chances of success totaled minus zero every time.

He considered which part of his body the robot would smash first. One blow of that tool-hand would kill him if it was used a second time. With the state of his present wounds, even a strong breath might finish him.

Perhaps he could make a break and get through the lock into the decompression chamber . . .

Worthless. (A) The robot would catch him before he had gotten to his feet, in his present condition. (B) Even allowing a miracle, even if he did get through the lock, the robot would smash the lock port, letting in air, ruining the mechanism. (C) Even allowing a double miracle and it didn't, what the hell good would it do him? His helmet and gloves were in the hutch itself, and there was no place to go on the planetoid. The ship was ruined, so no signal could be sent from there.

Doom suddenly compounded itself.

The more he thought about it, the more certain he was that soon the light would flicker out for him.

The light would flicker out.

The light would flicker . . .

The light . . .

. . . light . . . ?

Oh God, is it possible? Can it be? Have I found an answer? He marveled at the simplicity of it. It had been there for more than three days waiting for him to use it. It was *so* simple it was magnificent. He could hardly restrain himself from moving, just out of sheer joy.

I'm not brilliant, I'm not a genius, why did this occur to me? For a few minutes the brilliance of the solution staggered him. Would a less intelligent man have solved the problem this easily? Would a *more* intelligent man have done it? Then he remembered the dream. The light in the dream. *He* hadn't solved the problem, his unconscious had. The answer had been there all the time, but he was too close to see it. His mind had been forced to devise a way to tell him. Luckily, it had.

And finally, he didn't care *how* he had uncovered it. His God, if he had
had anything to do with it, had heard him. Terrence was by no means a
religious man, but this was miracle enough to make him a believer. It wasn't
over yet, but the answer was there — and it *was* an answer.

He began to save himself.

Slowly, achingly slowly, he moved his right hand, the hand away from the
robot's sight, to his belt. On the belt hung the assorted implements a spaceman needs at any moment in his ship. A wrench. A packet of sleep-stavers.
A compass. A geiger counter. A flashlight.

The last was the miracle. Miracle in a tube.

He fingered it almost reverently, then unclipped it in a moment's frenzy,
still immobile to the robot's "eyes."

He held it at his side, away from his body by a fraction of an inch, pointing
up over the bulge of his spacesuited leg.

If the robot looked at him, all it would see would be the motionless bulk
of his leg, blocking off any movement on his part. To the machine, he was
inert. Motionless.

Now, he thought wildly, *where is the brain?*

If it is behind the relay machines, I'm still dead. If it is near the refrigerator,
I'm saved. He could afford to take no chances. He would have to move.

He lifted one leg.

The robot moved toward him. The humming and sparking were more
distinct this time. He dropped the leg.

Behind the plates above the refrigerator!

The robot stopped nearly at his side. Seconds had decided. The robot
hummed, sparked, and returned to its niche.

Now he knew!

He pressed the button. The invisible beam of the flashlight leaped out,
speared the bulkhead above the refrigerator. He pressed the button again and
again, the flat circle of light appearing, disappearing, appearing, disappearing
on the faceless metal of the life hutch's wall.

The robot sparked and rolled from its niche. It looked once at Terrence.
Its rollers changed direction in an instant and the machine ground toward
the refrigerator.

The steeled fist swung in a vicious arc, smashing with a deafening clang!
at the spot where the light bubble flickered on and off.

It swung again and again. Again and again till the bulkhead had been
gouged and crushed and opened, and the delicate coils and plates and circuits
and memorex modules behind it were refuse and rubble. Until the robot
froze, with arm half-ready to strike again. Dead. Immobile. Brain and appendage.

Even then Terrence did not stop pressing the flashlight button. Wildly he
thumbed it again and again and again.

Then he realized it was all over.

The robot was dead. He was alive. He would be saved. He had no doubts about that. *Now* he could cry.

The medicine chest grew large through the shimmering in his eyes. The relay machines smiled at him.

God bless you, little life hutch, he thought, before he fainted.

Q

quest — a search for someone or something that means a great deal to the person doing the searching. Quest stories are central to all literature, including science fiction. The search can be for an individual, a treasure, or simply love or power. An outstanding science fiction quest novel is *Lord Valentine's Castle,* by Robert Silverberg (Harper & Row, 1980).

The Silk and the Song

CHARLES L. FONTENAY

Alan first saw the Star Tower when he was twelve years old. His young master, Blik, rode him into the city of Falklyn that day.

Blik had to argue hard before he got permission to ride Alan, his favorite boy. Blik's father, Wiln, wanted Blik to ride a man, because Wiln thought the long trip to the city might be too much for a boy as young as Alan.

Blik had his way, though. Blik was rather spoiled, and when he began to whistle his father gave in.

"All right, the human is rather big for its age," surrendered Wiln. "You may ride it if you promise not to run it. I don't want you breaking the wind of any of my prize stock."

So Blik strapped the bridle-helmet with the handgrips on Alan's head and threw the saddle-chair on Alan's shoulders. Wiln saddled up Robb, a husky man he often rode on long trips, and they were off to the city at an easy trot.

The Star Tower was visible before they reached Falklyn. Alan could see its spire above the tops of the ttornot trees as soon as they emerged from the Blue Forest. Blik saw it at the same time. Holding onto the bridle-helmet with one four-fingered hand, Blik poked Alan and pointed.

"Look, Alan, the Star Tower!" cried Blik. "They say humans once lived in the Star Tower."

"Blik, when will you grow up and stop talking to the humans?" chided his father. "I'm going to punish you severely one of these days."

Alan did not answer Blik, for it was forbidden for humans to talk in the Hussir language except in reply to direct questions. But he kept his eager eyes on the Star Tower and watched it loom taller and taller ahead of them, striking into the sky far above the buildings of the city. He quickened his pace, so that he began to pull ahead of Robb, and Robb had to caution him.

Between the Blue Forest and Falklyn, they were still in wild country where the land was eroded and there were no farms and fields. Little clumps of ttornot trees huddled here and there among the gullies and low hills, thickening back toward the Blue Forest behind them, thinning toward the northwest plain, beyond which lay the distant mountains.

They rounded a curve in the dusty road, and Blik whistled in excitement from Alan's shoulders. A figure stood on a little promontory overhanging the road ahead of them.

At first Alan thought it was a tall, slender Hussir, for a short jacket partly concealed its nakedness. Then he saw it was a young human girl. No Hussir ever boasted that mop of tawny hair, that tailless posterior curve.

"A Wild Human!" growled Wiln in astonishment. Alan shivered. It was rumored the Wild Humans killed Hussirs and ate other humans.

The girl was looking away toward Falklyn. Wiln unslung his short bow and loosed an arrow at her.

The bolt exploded the dust near her feet. With a toss of bright hair, she turned her head and saw them. Then she was gone like a deer.

When they came up to where she had stood, there was a brightness in the bushes beside the road. It was a pair of the colorful trousers such as Hussirs wore, only trimmer, tangled inextricably in a thorny bush. Evidently the girl had been caught as she climbed up from the road, and had had to crawl out of them.

"They're getting too bold," said Wiln angrily. "This close to civilization, in broad daylight!"

Alan was astonished when they entered Falklyn. The streets and buildings were of stone. There was little stone on the other side of the Blue Forest, and Wiln Castle was built of polished wooden blocks. The smooth stone of Falklyn's streets was hot under the double sun. It burned Alan's feet, so that he hobbled a little and shook Blik up. Blik clouted him on the side of the head for it.

There were so many strange new things to see in the city that they made Alan dizzy. Some of the buildings were as much as three stories high, and the windows of a few of the biggest were covered, not with wooden shutters, but with a bright, transparent stuff that Wiln told Blik was called "glaz." Robb told Alan in the human language, which the Hussirs did not understand, that it was rumored humans themselves had invented this glaz and given it to their masters. Alan wondered how a human could invent anything, penned in open fields.

But it appeared that humans in the city lived closer to their masters. Several times Alan saw them coming out of houses, and a few that he saw were not entirely naked, but wore bright bits of cloth at various places on their bodies. Wiln expressed strong disapproval of this practice to Blik.

"Start putting clothing on these humans and they might get the idea they're Hussirs," he said. "If you ask me, that's why city people have more trouble controlling their humans than we do. Spoil the human and you make him savage, I say."

They had several places to go in Falklyn, and for a while Alan feared they would not see the Star Tower at close range. But Blik had never seen it before, and he begged and whistled until Wiln agreed to ride a few streets out of the way to look at it.

Alan forgot all the other wonders of Falklyn as the great monument towered bigger and bigger, dwarfing the buildings around it, dwarfing the whole city of Falklyn. There was a legend that humans had not only lived in the Star Tower once, but that they had built it and Falklyn had grown up around it when the humans abandoned it. Alan had heard this whispered, but he had been warned not to repeat it, for some Hussirs understood human language and repeating such tales was a good way to get whipped.

The Star Tower was in the center of a big circular park, and the houses around the park looked like dollhouses beneath it. It stretched up into the sky like a pointing finger, its strange dark walls reflecting the dual sunlight dully. Even the flying buttresses at its base curved up above the big trees in the park around it.

There was a railing around the park, and quite a few humans were chained or standing loose about it while their riders were looking at the Star Tower, for humans were not allowed inside the park. Blik was all for dismounting and looking at the inside of the tower, but Wiln would not hear of it.

"There'll be plenty of time for that when you're older and can understand some of the things you see," said Wiln.

They moved slowly around the street, outside the rail. In the park, the Hussirs moved in groups, some of them going up or coming down the long ramp that led into the Star Tower. The Hussirs were only about half the size of humans, with big heads and large pointed ears sticking straight out on each side, with thin legs and thick tails that helped to balance them. They wore loose jackets and baggy, colored trousers.

As they passed one group of humans standing outside the rail, Alan heard a familiar bit of verse, sung in an undertone:

Twinkle, twinkle, golden star,
I can reach you, though you're far.
Shut my mouth and find my head,
Find a worm —

Wiln swung Robb around quickly and laid his keen whip viciously across the singer's shoulders. Slash, slash, and red welts sprang out on the man's back. With a muffled shriek, the man ducked his head and threw up his arms to protect his face.

"Where is your master, human?" demanded Wiln savagely, the whip trembling in his four-fingered hand.

"My master lives in Northwesttown, your greatness," whimpered the human. "I belong to the merchant Senk."

"Where is Northwesttown?"

"It is a section of Falklyn, sir."

"And you are here at the Star Tower without your master?"

"Yes, sir. I am on free time."

Wiln gave him another lash with the whip.

"You should know humans are not allowed to run loose near the Star Tower," Wiln snapped. "Now go back to your master and tell him to whip you."

The human ran off. Wiln and Blik turned their mounts homeward. When they were beyond the streets and houses of the town and the dust of the roads provided welcome relief to the burning feet of the humans, Blik asked: "What did you think of the Star Tower, Alan?"

"Why has it no windows?" Alan asked, voicing the thought uppermost in his mind.

It was not, strictly speaking, an answer to Blik's question, and Alan risked punishment by speaking thus in Hussir. But Wiln had recovered his good humor with the prospect of getting home in time for supper.

"The windows are in the very top, little human," said Wiln indulgently. "You couldn't see them, because they're inside."

Alan puzzled over this all the way to Wiln Castle. How could windows be inside and none outside? If windows were windows, didn't they always go through both sides of a wall?

When the two suns had set and Alan was bedded down with the other children in a corner of the meadow, the exciting events of the day repeated themselves in his mind like a series of colored pictures. He would have liked to question Robb, but the grown men and older boys were kept in a field well separated from the women and children.

A little distance away the women were singing their babies to sleep with the traditional songs of the humans. Their voices drifted to him on the faint breeze, with the perfume of the fragrant grasses.

> Rock-a-bye, baby, in mother's arm,
> Nothing's nearby to do baby harm.
> Sleep and sweet dreams, till both suns arise,
> Then will be time to open your eyes.

That was a real baby song, the first he ever remembered. They sang others, and one was the song Wiln had interrupted at the Star Tower.

> Twinkle, twinkle, golden star,
> I can reach you, though you're far.
> Shut my mouth and find my head,
> Find a worm that's striped with red,
> Feed it to the turtle shell,
> Then go to sleep, for all is well.

Half asleep, Alan listened. That song was one of the children's favorites. They called it "The Star Tower Song," though he had never been able to find out why.

It must be a riddle, he thought drowsily. "Shut my mouth and find my head . . . " Shouldn't it be the other way around — "Find my head (first) and shut my mouth . . . "? Why wasn't it? And those other lines. Alan knew worms, for he had seen many of the creepy, crawly creatures, long things in many bright colors. But what was a turtle?

The refrain of another song reached his ears, and it seemed to the sleepy boy that they were singing it to him.

> Alan saw a little zird,
> Its wings were all aglow.
> He followed it away one night.
> It filled his heart with woe.

Only that wasn't the last line the children themselves sang. Optimistically, they always ended that song " . . . to where he liked to go."

Maybe he was asleep and dreamed it, or maybe he suddenly woke up with the distant music in his ears. Whichever it was, he was lying there, and a zird flew over the high fence and lit in the grass near him. Its luminous scales pulsed in the darkness, faintly lighting the faces of the children huddled asleep around him. It opened its beak and spoke to him in a raucous voice.

"Come with me to freedom, human," said the zird. "Come with me to freedom, human."

That was all it could say, and it repeated the invitation at least half a dozen times, until it grated on Alan's ears. But Alan knew that, despite the way the children sang the song, it brought only sorrow to a human to heed the call of a zird.

"Go away, zird," he said crossly, and the zird flew over the fence and faded into the darkness.

Sighing, Alan went back to sleep to dream of the Star Tower.

II

Blik died three years later. The young Hussir's death brought sorrow to Alan's heart, for Blik had been kind to him and their relationship was the close one of well-loved pet and master. The deprivation always would be associated to him with another emotional change in his life, for Blik's death came the day after Wiln caught Alan with the blonde girl down by the stream and transferred him to the field with the older boys and men.

"Switch it, I hope the boy hasn't gotten her with child," grumbled Wiln to his oldest son, Snuk, as they drove Alan to the new meadow. "I hadn't planned to add that girl to the milking herd for another year yet."

"That comes of letting Blik make a pet out of the human," said Snuk, who was nearly grown now and was being trained in the art of managing Wiln Castle to succeed his father. "It should have been worked while Blik has been sick, instead of allowed to roam idly around among the women and children."

Through the welter of new emotions that confused him, Alan recognized the justice of that remark. It had been pure boredom with the play of the younger children that had turned his interest to more mature experimentation. At that, he realized that only the aloofness he had developed as a result of being Blik's pet had prevented his being taken to the other field at least two years earlier.

He looked back over his shoulder. The tearful girl stood forlornly, watching him go. She waved and called after him.

"Maybe we'll see each other again at mating time."

He waved back at her, drawing a sharp cut across the shoulders from Snuk's whip. They would not turn him in with the women at mating time for at least another three years, but the girl was almost of mating age. By the time she saw him again, she probably would have forgotten him.

His transfer into adulthood was an immediate ordeal. Wiln and Snuk remained just outside the fence and whistled delightedly at the hazing Alan was given by the men and older boys. The ritual would have been more difficult for him had it not been so long delayed, but he found a place in the scheme of things somewhat high for a newcomer because he was older than most of them and big for his age. Scratched and battered, he gained the necessary initial respect from his new associates by trouncing several boys his own size.

That night, lonely and unhappy, Alan heard the keening of the Hussirs rise from Wiln Castle. The night songs of the men, deeper and lustier than those of the women and children, faded and stopped as the sound of mourning drifted to them on the wind. Alan knew it meant that Blik's long illness was over, that his young master was dead.

He found a secluded corner of the field and cried himself to sleep under the stars. He had loved Blik.

After Blik's death, Alan thought he might be put with the laboring men, to pull the plows and work the crops. He knew he did not have the training for work in and around the castle itself, and he did not think he would be retained with the riding stock.

But Snuk had different ideas.

"I saw your good qualities as a riding human before Blik ever picked you out for a pet," Snuk told him, laying his pointed ears back viciously. Snuk used the human language, for it was Snuk's theory that one could control humans better when one could listen in on their conversations among themselves. "Blik spoiled all the temper out of you, but I'll change that. I may be able to salvage you yet."

It was only a week since Blik's death, and Alan was still sad. Dispiritedly, he cooperated when Snuk put the bridle-helmet and saddle-chair on him, and knelt for Snuk to climb on his back.

When Alan stood up, Snuk jammed spurs savagely into his sides.

Alan leaped three feet into the air with an agonized yell.

"Silence, human!" shouted Snuk, beating him over the head with the whip. "I shall teach you to obey. Spurs mean go, like so!"

And he dug the spurs into Alan's ribs again.

Alan twisted and turned momentarily, but his common sense saved him. Had he fallen to the ground and rolled, or tried to rub Snuk off against a ttornot tree, it would have meant death for him. There was no appeal from his new master's cruelty.

A third time Snuk applied the spurs and Alan spurted down the tree-lined lane away from the castle at a dead run. Snuk gave him his head and raked his sides brutally. It was only when he slowed to a walk, panting and perspiring, that Snuk pulled on the reins and turned him back toward the castle. Then the Hussir forced him to trot back.

Wiln was waiting at the corral when they returned.

"Aren't you treating it a little rough, Snuk?" asked the older Hussir, looking the exhausted Alan up and down critically. Blood streamed from Alan's gashed sides.

"Just teaching it right at the outset who is master," replied Snuk casually. With an unnecessarily sharp rap on the head, he sent Alan to his knees and dismounted. "I think this one will make a valuable addition to my stable of riders, but I don't intend to pamper it like Blik."

Wiln flicked his ears.

"Well, you've proved you know how to handle humans by now, and you'll be master of them all in a few years," he said mildly. "Just take your father's advice, and don't break this one's wind."

The next few months were misery to Alan. He had the physical qualities Snuk liked in a mount, and Snuk rode him more frequently than any of his other saddle men.

Snuk liked to ride fast, and he ran Alan unmercifully. They would return at the end of a hot afternoon, Alan bathed in sweat and so tired his limbs trembled uncontrollably.

Besides, Snuk was an uncompromising master with more than a touch of cruelty in his make-up. He would whip Alan savagely for minor inattention, for failure to respond promptly to the reins, for speaking at all in his presence. Alan's back was soon covered with spur scars, and one eye often was half-closed from a whiplash across the face.

In desperation, Alan sought the counsel of his old friend, Robb, whom he saw often now that he was in the men's field.

"There's nothing you can do," Robb said. "I just thank the Golden Star that Wiln rides me and I'll be too old for Snuk to ride when Wiln dies. But then Snuk will be master of us all, and I dread that day."

"Couldn't one of us kill Snuk against a tree?" asked Alan. He had thought of doing it himself.

"Never think such a thought," warned Robb quickly. "If that happened, all the riding men would be butchered for meat. The Wiln family has enough money to buy new riding stables in Falklyn if they wish, and no Hussir will put up with a rebellious human."

That night Alan nursed his freshest wounds beside the fence closest to the women's and children's field and gave himself up to nostalgia. He longed for the happy days of his childhood and Blik's kind mastery.

Across the intervening fields, faintly, he heard the soft voices of the women. He could not make out the words, but he remembered them from the tune:

> Star light, star bright,
> Star that sheds a golden light,
> I wish I may, I wish I might,
> Reach you, star that shines at night.

From behind him came the voices of the men, nearer and louder:

> Human, see the little zird,
> Its wings are all aglow.
> Don't follow it away at night,
> For fear of grief and woe.

The children had sung it differently. And there had been a dream . . .
"Come with me to freedom, human," said the zird.

Alan had seen many zirds at night — they appeared only at night —
and had heard their call. It was the only thing they said, always in the human
language: "Come with me to freedom, human."

As he had before, he wondered. A zird was only a scaly-winged little night
creature. How could it speak human words? Where did zirds come from, and
where did they go in the daytime? For the first time in his life, he asked the
zird a question.

"What and where is freedom, zird?" Alan asked.

"Come with me to freedom, human," repeated the zird. It flapped
its wings, rising a few inches above the fence, and settled back on its
perch.

"Is that all you can say, zird?" asked Alan irritably. "How can I go with
you when I can't fly?"

"Come with me to freedom, human," said the zird.

A great boldness surged in Alan's heart, spurred by the dreary prospect
of having to endure Snuk's sadism again on the morrow. He looked at the
fence.

Alan had never paid much attention to a fence before. Humans did not try
to get out of the fenced enclosures, because the story parents told to children
who tried it was that strayed humans were always recaptured and butchered
for meat.

It was the strangest coincidence. It reminded him of that night long ago,
the night after he had gone into Falklyn with Blik and first seen the Star
Tower. Even as the words of the song died away in the night air, he saw the
glow of the zird approaching. It lit on top of the fence and squawked down
at him.

The links of the fence were close together, but he could get his fingers and
toes through them. Tentatively, he tried it. A mounting excitement taking
possession of him, he climbed.

It was ridiculously easy. He was in the next field. There were other fences,
of course, but they could be climbed. He could go into the field with the
women — his heart beat faster at the thought of the blonde girl — or he
could even climb his way to the open road to Falklyn.

It was the road he chose, after all. The zird flew ahead of him across each
field, lighting to wait for him to climb each fence. He crept along the fence

past the crooning women with a muffled sigh, through the field of ripening akko grain, through the waist-high sento plants. At last he climbed the last fence of all.

He was off the Wiln estate. The dust of the road to Falklyn was beneath his feet.

What now? If he went into Falklyn, he would be captured and returned to Wiln Castle. If he went the other way the same thing would happen. Stray humans were spotted easily. Should he turn back now? It would be easy to climb his way back to the men's field — and there would be innumerable nights ahead of him when the women's field would be easily accessible to him.

But there was Snuk to consider.

For the first time since he had climbed out of the men's field, the zird spoke.

"Come with me to freedom, human," it said.

It flew down the road, away from Falklyn, and lit in the dust, as though waiting. After a moment's hesitation, Alan followed.

The lights of Wiln Castle loomed up to his left, up the lane of ttornot trees. They fell behind and disappeared over a hill. The zird flew, matching its pace to his slow trot.

Alan's resolution began to weaken.

Then a figure loomed up beside him in the gloom, a human hand was laid on his arm and a female voice said: "I thought we'd never get another from Wiln Castle. Step it up a little, fellow. We've a long way to travel before dawn."

III

They traveled at a fast trot all that night, the zird leading the way like a giant firefly. By the time dawn grayed the eastern sky they were in the mountains west of Falklyn, and climbing.

When Alan was first able to make out details of his nocturnal guide, he thought for a minute she was a huge Hussir. She wore the Hussir loose jacket, open at the front, and the baggy trousers. But there was no tail, and there were no pointed ears. She was a girl his own age.

She was the first human Alan had ever seen fully clothed. Alan thought she looked rather ridiculous and, at the same time, he was slightly shocked, as by sacrilege.

They entered a high valley through a narrow pass and slowed to a walk. For the first time since they left the vicinity of Wiln Castle, they were able to talk in other than short, disconnected phrases.

"Who are you, and where are you taking me?" asked Alan. In the cold light of dawn he was beginning to doubt his impetuousness in fleeing the castle.

"My name is Mara," said the girl. "You've heard of the Wild Humans? I'm one of them, and we live in these mountains."

The hair prickled on the back of Alan's neck. He stopped in his tracks, and half turned to flee. Mara caught his arm.

"Why do all you slaves believe those fairy tales about cannibalism?" she asked scornfully. The word *cannibalism* was unfamiliar to Alan. "We aren't going to eat you, boy, we're going to make you free. What's your name?"

"Alan," he answered in a shaky voice, allowing himself to be led onward. "What is this freedom the zird was talking about?"

"You'll find out," she promised. "But the zird doesn't know. Zirds are just flying animals. We train them to say that one sentence and lead slaves to us."

"Why don't you just come in the fields yourselves?" he asked curiously, his fear dissipating. "You could climb the fences easily."

"That's been tried. The silly slaves just raise a clamor when they recognize a stranger. The Hussirs have caught several of us that way."

The two suns rose, first the blue one, the white one only a few minutes later. The mountains around them awoke with light.

In the dawn, he had thought Mara was dark, but her hair was tawny gold in the pearly morning. Her eyes were deep brown, like the fruit of the ttornot tree.

They stopped by a spring that gushed from between huge rocks, and Mara took the opportunity to appraise his slender, well-knit frame.

"You'll do," she said. "I wish all of them we get were as healthy."

In three weeks, Alan could not have been distinguished from the other Wild Humans — outwardly. He was getting used to wearing clothing and, somewhat awkwardly, carried the bow and arrows with which he was armed. He and Mara were ranging several miles from the caves in which the Wild Humans lived.

They were hunting animals for food, and Alan licked his lips in anticipation. He liked cooked meat. The Hussirs fed their human herds bean meal and scraps from the kitchens. The only meat he had ever eaten was raw meat from small animals he had been swift enough to catch in the fields.

They came up on a ridge and Mara, ahead of him, stopped. He came up beside her.

Not far below them, a Hussir moved, afoot, carrying a short, heavy bow and a quiver of arrows. The Hussir looked from side to side, as if hunting, but did not catch sight of them.

A quiver of fear ran through Alan. In that instant, he was a disobedient member of the herd, and death awaited him for his escape from the fields.

There was a sharp twang beside him, and the Hussir stumbled and fell, transfixed through the chest with an arrow. Mara calmly lowered her bow and smiled at the fright in his eyes.

"There's one that won't find Haafin," she said. "Haafin" was what the Wild Humans called their community.

"The — there are Hussirs in the mountains?" he quavered.

"A few. Hunters. If we get them before they run across the valley, we're all right. Some have seen us and gotten away, though. Haafin has been moved a dozen times in the last century, and we've always lost a lot of people fighting our way out. Those little devils attack in force."

"But what's the good of all this, then?" he asked hopelessly. "There aren't more than four or five hundred humans in Haafin. What good is hiding, and running somewhere else when the Hussirs find you, when sooner or later there'll come a time when they'll wipe you out?"

Mara sat down on a rock.

"You learn fast," she remarked. "You'll probably be surprised to learn that this community has managed to hang on in these mountains for more than a thousand years, but you've still put your finger right on the problem that has faced us for generations."

She hesitated and traced a pattern thoughtfully in the dust with a moccasined foot.

"It's a little early for you to be told, but you might as well start keeping your ears open," she said. "When you've been here a year, you'll be accepted as a member of the community. The way that's done is for you to have an interview with the Refugee, the leader of our people, and he always asks newcomers for their ideas on the solution of that very problem."

"But what will I listen for?" asked Alan anxiously.

"There are two major ideas on how to solve the problem, and I'll let you hear them from the people who believe in them," she said. "Just remember what the problem is: to save ourselves from death and the hundreds of thousands of other humans in the world from slavery, we have to find a way to force the Hussirs to accept humans as equals, not as animals."

Many things about Alan's new life in Haafin were not too different from the existence he had known. He had to do his share of work in the little fields that clung to the edges of the small river in the middle of the valley. He had to help hunt animals for meat, he had to help make tools such as the Hussirs used. He had to fight with his fists, on occasion, to protect his rights.

But this thing the Wild Humans called "freedom" was a strange element that touched everything they were and did. The word, Alan found, meant basically that the Wild Humans did not belong to the Hussirs, but were their own masters. When orders were given, they usually had to be obeyed, but they came from humans, not Hussirs.

There were other differences. There were no formal family relationships, for there were no social traditions behind people who for generations had been nothing more than domestic animals. But the pressure and deprivations of rigidly enforced mating seasons were missing, and some of the older couples were mated permanently.

"Freedom," Alan decided, meant a dignity which made a human the equal of a Hussir.

The anniversary of that night when Alan followed the zird came, and Mara led him early in the morning to the extreme end of the valley. She left him at the mouth of a small cave, from which presently emerged the man of whom Alan had heard much but whom he saw now for the first time.

The Refugee's hair and beard were gray and his face was lined with years.

"You are Alan, who came to us from Wiln Castle," said the old man.

"That is true, your greatness," replied Alan respectfully.

"Don't call me 'your greatness.' That's slave talk. I am Roand, the Refugee."

"Yes, sir."

"When you leave me today, you will be a member of the community of Haafin, the only free human community in the world," said Roand. "You will have a member's rights. No man may take a woman from you without her consent. No one may take from you the food you hunt or grow without your consent. If you are first in an empty cave, no one may move into it with you unless you give permission. That is freedom.

"But, as you were no doubt told long ago, you must offer your best idea on how to make all humans free."

"Sir — " began Alan.

"Before you express yourself," interrupted Roand, "I'm going to give you some help. Come into the cave."

Alan followed him inside. By the light of a torch, Roand showed him a series of diagrams drawn on one wall with soft stone, as one would draw things in the dust with a stick.

"These are maps, Alan," said Roand, and he explained to the boy what a map was. At last Alan nodded in comprehension.

"You know by now that there are two ways of thinking about what to do to set all humans free, but you do not entirely understand either of them," said Roand. "These maps show you the first one, which was conceived a hundred and fifty years ago but which our people have not been able to agree to try.

"This map shows how, by a surprise attack, we could take Falklyn, the central city of all this Hussir region, although the Hussirs in Falklyn number almost ten thousand. Holding Falklyn, we could free the nearly forty thousand humans in the city and we would have enough strength then to take the surrounding area and strike at the cities around it, gradually, as these other maps show."

Alan nodded.

"But I like the other way better," Alan said. "There must be a reason why they won't let humans enter the Star Tower."

Roand's toothless smile did not mar the innate dignity of his face. "You are a mystic, as I am, young Alan," he said. "But the tradition says that for a human to enter the Star Tower is not enough. Let me tell you of the tradition.

"The tradition says that the Star Tower was once the home of all humans. There were only a dozen or so humans then, but they had powers that were great and strange. But when they came out of the Star Tower, the Hussirs were able to enslave them through mere force of numbers.

"Three of those first humans escaped to these mountains and became the first Wild Humans. From them has come the tradition that has passed to their descendants and to the humans who have been rescued from Hussir slavery.

"The tradition says that a human who enters the Star Tower can free all the humans in the world — if he takes with him the Silk and the Song."

Roand reached into a crevice.

"This is the Silk," he said, drawing forth a peach-colored scarf on which something had been painted. Alan recognized it as writing, such as the Hussirs used and were rumored to have been taught by humans. Roand read it to him, reverently.

" 'REG. B-XII. CULTURE V. SOS.' "

"What does it mean?" asked Alan.

"No one knows," said Roand. "It is a great mystery. It may be a magical incantation."

He put the Silk back into the crevice.

"This is the only other writing we have handed down by our forebears," said Roand, and pulled out a fragment of very thin, brittle, yellowish material. To Alan it looked something like thin cloth that had hardened with age, yet it had a different texture. Roand handled it very carefully.

"This was torn and the rest of it lost centuries ago," said Roand, and he read. " 'October 3, 2 . . . ours to be the last . . . three lost expeditions . . . too far to keep trying . . . how we can get . . .' "

Alan could make no more sense of this than he could of the words of the Silk.

"What is the Song?" asked Alan.

"Every human knows it from childhood," said Roand. "It is the best known of all human songs."

" 'Twinkle, twinkle, golden star,' " quoted Alan at once, " 'I can reach you, though you're far . . . ' "

"That's right, but there is a second verse that only the Wild Humans know. You must learn it. It goes like this:

Twinkle, twinkle, little bug,
Long and round, of shiny hue.

In a room marked by a cross,
Sting my arm when I've found you.
Lay me down, in bed so deep,
And then there's naught to do but sleep.

"It doesn't make sense," said Alan. "No more than the first verse — though Mara showed me what a turtle looks like."

"They aren't supposed to make sense until you sing them in the Star Tower," said Roand, "and then only if you have the Silk with you."

Alan cogitated a while. Roand was silent, waiting.

"Some of the people want one human to try to reach the Star Tower and think that will make all humans miraculously free," said Alan at last. "The others think that is but a child's tale and we must conquer the Hussirs with bows and spears. It seems to me, sir, that one or the other must be tried. I'm sorry that I don't know enough to suggest another course."

Roand's face fell.

"So you will join one side or the other and argue about it for the rest of your life," he said sadly. "And nothing will ever be done, because the people can't agree."

"I don't see why that has to be, sir."

Roand looked at him with sudden hope.

"What do you mean?"

"Can't you or someone else order them to take one course or another?"

Roand shook his head.

"Here there are rules, but no man tells another what to do," he said. "We are free here."

"Sir, when I was a small child, we played a game called Two Herds," said Alan slowly. "The sides would be divided evenly, each with a tree for a haven. When two of opposite sides met in the field, the one last from his haven captured the other and took him back to join his side."

"I've played that game, many years ago," said Roand. "I don't see your point, boy."

"Well, sir, to win, one side had to capture all the people on the other side. But, with so many captures back and forth, sometimes night fell and the game was not ended. So we always played that, then, the side with the most children when the game ended was the winning side."

"Why couldn't it be done that way?"

Comprehension dawned slowly in Roand's face. There was something there, too, of the awe-inspiring revelation that he was present at the birth of a major advance in the science of human government.

"Let them count those for each proposal, eh, and agree to abide by the proposal having the greatest support?"

"Yes, sir."

Roand grinned his toothless grin.

"You have indeed brought us a new idea, my boy, but you and I will have to surrender our own viewpoint by it, I'm afraid. I keep close count. There are a few more people in Haafin who think we should attack the Hussirs with weapons than believe in the old tradition."

IV

When the armed mob of Wild Humans approached Falklyn in the dusk, Alan wore the Silk around his neck. Roand, one of the oldsters who stayed behind at Haafin, had given it to him.

"When Falklyn is taken, my boy, take the Silk with you into the Star Tower and sing the Song," were Roand's parting words. "There may be something to the old traditions after all."

After much argument among those Wild Humans who had given it thought for years, a military plan had emerged blessed with all the simplicity of a nonmilitary race. They would just march into the city, killing all Hussirs they saw, and stay there, still killing all Hussirs they saw. Their own strength would increase gradually as they freed the city's enslaved humans. No one could put a definite finger on anything wrong with the idea.

Falklyn was built like a wheel. Around the park in which stood the Star Tower the streets ran in concentric circles. Like spokes of the wheel, other streets struck from the park out to the edge of the city.

Without any sort of formation, the humans entered one of these spoke streets and moved inward, a few adventurous souls breaking away from the main body at each cross street. It was suppertime in Falklyn, and few Hussirs were abroad. The humans were jubilant as those who escaped their arrows fled, whistling in fright.

They were about a third of the way to the center of Falklyn when the bells began ringing, first near at hand and then all over the city. Hussirs popped out of doors and on to balconies, and arrows began to sail in among the humans to match their own. The motley army began to break up as its soldiers sought cover. Its progress was slowed, and there was some hand-to-hand fighting.

Alan found himself with Mara, crouching in a doorway. Ahead of them and behind them, Wild Humans scurried from house to house, still moving forward. An occasional Hussir hopped hastily across the street, sometimes making it, sometimes falling from a human arrow.

"This doesn't look so good," said Alan. "Nobody seemed to think of the Hussirs being prepared for an attack, but those bells must have been an alarm system."

"We're still moving ahead," replied Mara confidently.

Alan shook his head.

"That may just mean we'll have more trouble getting out of the city," he said. "The Hussirs outnumber us twenty to one, and they're killing more of us than we're killing of them."

The door beside them opened and a Hussir leaped all the way out before seeing them. Alan dispatched him with a blow from his spear. Mara at his heels, he ran forward to the next doorway. Shouts of humans and whistles and cries of Hussirs echoed back and forth down the street.

The fighting humans were perhaps halfway to the Star Tower when from ahead of them came the sound of shouting and chanting. From the dimness it seemed that a solid river of white was pouring toward them, filling the street from wall to wall.

A Wild Human across the street from Alan and Mara shouted in triumph. "They're humans! The slaves are coming to help us!"

A ragged shout went up from the embattled Wild Humans. But as it died down, they were able to distinguish the words of the chanting and the shouting from that naked mass of humanity.

"Kill the Wild Humans! Kill the Wild Humans! Kill the Wild Humans!"

Remembering his own childhood fear of Wild Humans, Alan suddenly understood. With a confidence fully justified, the Hussirs had turned the humans' own people against themselves.

The invaders looked at each other in alarm and drew closer together beneath the protection of overhanging balconies. Hussir arrows whistled near them unheeded.

They could not kill their enslaved brothers, and there was no chance of breaking through that oncoming avalanche of humanity. First by ones and twos, and then in groups, they turned to retreat from the city.

But the way was blocked. Up the street from the direction in which they had come moved orderly ranks of armed Hussirs. Some of the Wild Humans, among them Alan and Mara, ran for the nearest cross streets. Along them, too, approached companies of Hussirs.

The Wild Humans were trapped in the middle of Falklyn.

Terrified, the men and women of Haafin converged and swirled in a helpless knot in the center of the street. Hussir arrows from nearby windows picked them off one by one. The advancing Hussirs in the street were almost within bowshot, and the yelling, unarmed slave humans were even closer.

"Your clothes!" shouted Alan, on an inspiration. "Throw away your clothes and weapons! Try to get back to the mountains!"

In almost a single swift shrug, he divested himself of the open jacket and baggy trousers and threw his bow, arrows and spear from him. Only the Silk still fluttered from his neck.

As Mara stood openmouthed beside him, he jerked at her jacket impatiently. Suddenly getting his idea, she stripped quickly. The other Wild Humans began to follow suit.

The arrows of the Hussir squads were beginning to fall among them. Grabbing Mara's hand, Alan plunged headlong toward the avalanche of slave humans.

Slowed as he was by Mara, a dozen other Wild Humans raced ahead of him to break into the wall of humanity. Angry hands clutched at them as they tried to lose themselves among the slaves, and Alan and Mara, clinging to each other, were engulfed in a sudden swirl of shouting confusion.

There were naked, sweating bodies moving on all sides of them. They were buffeted back and forth like chips in the surf. Desperately they gripped hands and stayed close together.

They were crowded to one side of the street, against the wall. The human tide scraped them along the rough stone and battered them roughly into a doorway. The door yielded to the tremendous pressure and flew inward. Somehow, only the two of them lost their balance and sprawled on the carpeted floor inside.

A Hussir appeared from an inside door, a barbed spear upraised.

"Mercy, your greatness!" cried Alan in the Hussir tongue, groveling.

The Hussir lowered the spear.

"Who is your master, human?" he demanded.

A distant memory thrust itself into Alan's mind, haltingly.

"My master lives in Northwesttown, your greatness."

The spear moved in the Hussir's hand.

"This is Northwesttown, human," he said ominously.

"Yes, your greatness," whimpered Alan, and prayed for no more coincidences. "I belong to the merchant Senk."

The spear point dropped to the floor again.

"I felt sure you were a town human," said the Hussir, his eyes on the scarf around Alan's neck. "I know Senk well. And you, woman, who is your master?"

Alan did not wait to find out whether Mara spoke Hussir.

"She also belongs to my lord Senk, your greatness." Another recollection came to his aid, and he added, "It's mating season, your greatness."

The Hussir gave the peculiar whistle that served for a laugh among his race. He beckoned to them to rise.

"Go out the back door and return to your pen," he said kindly. "You're lucky you weren't separated from each other in that herd."

Gratefully, Alan and Mara slipped out the back door and made their way up a dark alley to a street. He led her to the left.

"We'll have to find a cross street to get out of Falklyn," he said. "This is one of the circular streets."

"I hope most of the others escape," she said fervently. "There's no one left in Haafin but the old people and the small children."

"We'll have to be careful," he said. "They may have guards at the edge of the city. We outtalked that Hussir, but you'd better go ahead of me till we get to the outskirts. It'll look less suspicious if we're not together."

At the cross street they turned right. Mara moved ahead about thirty feet, and he followed. He watched her slim white figure swaying under the flickering gaslights of Falklyn and suddenly he laughed quietly. The memory of the blonde girl at Wiln Castle had returned to him, and it occurred to him, too, that he had never missed her.

The streets were nearly empty. Once or twice a human crossed ahead of them at a trot, and several times Hussirs passed them. For a while Alan heard shouting and whistling not far away, then these sounds faded.

They had not been walking long when Mara stopped. Alan came up beside her.

"We must have reached the outskirts," she said, waving her hand at the open space ahead of them.

They walked quickly.

But there was something wrong. The cross street just ahead curved too much, and there was the glimmer of lights some distance beyond it.

"We took the wrong turn when we left the alley," said Alan miserably. "Look — straight ahead!"

Dimly against the stars loomed the dark bulk of the Star Tower.

V

The great metal building stretched up into the night sky, losing itself in the blackness. The park around it was unlighted, but they could see the glow of the lamps at the Star Tower's entrance, where the Hussir guards remained on duty.

"We'll have to turn back," said Alan dully.

She stood close to him and looked up at him with large eyes.

"All the way back through the city?" There was a tremor in her voice.

"I'm afraid so." He put his arm around her shoulders and they turned away from the Star Tower. He fumbled at his scarf as they walked slowly back down the street.

His scarf! He stopped, halting her with a jerk. The Silk!

He grasped her shoulders with both hands and looked down into her face.

"Mara," he said soberly, "we aren't going back to the mountains. We aren't going back out of the city. We're going into the Star Tower!"

They retraced their steps to the end of the spoke street. They raced across the last and smallest of the circular streets, vaulted the rail, slipped like wraiths into the shadows of the park.

They moved from bush to bush and from tree to tree with the quiet facility of creatures born to nights in the open air. Little knots of guards were scattered all over the park. Probably the guard had been strengthened because of the Wild Humans' invasion of Falklyn. But the guards all had small, shaded lights, and Hussirs could not see well in the dark. The two humans were able to avoid them easily.

They came up behind the Star Tower and circled it cautiously. At its base, the entrance ramp was twice Alan's height. There were two guards, talking in low tones under the lamps that hung on each side of the dark, open door to the tower.

"If we could only have brought a bow!" exclaimed Alan in a whisper. "I could handle one of them without a weapon, but not two."

"Couldn't both of us?" she whispered back.

"No! They're little, but they're strong. Much stronger than a woman."

Against the glow of the light something projected a few inches over the edge of the ramp above them.

"Maybe it's a spear," whispered Alan. "I'll lift you up."

In a moment she was down again, the object in her hands.

"Just an arrow," she muttered in disgust. "What good is it without a bow?"

"It may be enough," he said. "You stay here, and when I get to the foot of the ramp, make a noise to distract them. Then run for it — "

He crept on his stomach to the point where the ramp angled to the ground. He looked back. Mara was a lightness against the blackness of the corner.

Mara began banging against the side of the ramp with her fists and chanting in a low tone. Grabbing their bows, both Hussir guards moved quickly to the edge. Alan stood up and ran as fast as he could up the ramp, the arrow in his hand.

Their bows were drawn to shoot down where Mara was, when they felt the vibration of the ramp. They turned quickly.

Their arrows, hurriedly loosed, missed him. He plunged his own arrow through the throat of one and grappled with the other. In a savage burst of strength, he hurled the Hussir over the side to the ground below.

Mara cried out. A patrol of three Hussirs had been too close. She had nearly reached the foot of the ramp when one of them plunged from the darkness and locked his arms around her hips from behind. The other two were hopping up the ramp toward Alan, spears in hand.

Alan snatched up the bow and quiver of the Hussir he had slain. His first arrow took one of the approaching Hussirs, halfway down the ramp. The Hussir that had seized Mara hurled her away from him to the ground and raised his spear for the kill.

Alan's arrow only grazed the creature, but it dropped the spear, and Mara fled up the ramp.

The third Hussir lurched at Alan behind its spear. Alan dodged. The blade missed him but the haft burned his side, almost knocking him from the ramp. The Hussir recovered like lightning, poised the spear again. It was too close for Alan to use the bow, and he had no time to pick up a spear.

Mara leaped on the Hussir's back, locking her legs around its body and grappling its spear arm with both her hands. Before it could shake her off, Alan wrested the spear from the Hussir's hand and dispatched it.

The other guards were coming up from all directions. Arrows rang against the sides of the Star Tower as the two humans ducked inside.

There was a light inside the Star Tower, a softer light than the gas lamps but more effective. They were inside a small chamber, from which another door led to the interior of the tower.

The door, swung back against the wall on its hinges, was two feet thick and its diameter was greater than the height of a man. Both of them together were unable to move it.

Arrows were coming through the door. Alan had left the guards' weapons outside. In a moment the Hussirs would gain courage to rush the ramp.

Alan looked around in desperation for a weapon. The metal walls were bare except for some handrails and a panel from which projected three metal sticks. Alan wrenched at one, trying to pull it loose for a club. It pulled down and there was a hissing sound in the room, but it would not come loose. He tried a second, and again it swung down but stayed fast to the wall.

Mara shrieked behind him, and he whirled.

The big door was closing, by itself, slowly, and outside the ramp was raising itself from the ground and sliding into the wall of the Star Tower below them. The few Hussirs who had ventured onto the end of the ramp were falling from it to the ground, like ants.

The door closed with a clang of finality. The hissing in the room went on for a moment, then stopped. It was as still as death in the Star Tower.

They went through the inner door, timidly, holding hands. They were in a curved corridor. The other side of the corridor was a blank wall. They followed the corridor all the way around the Star Tower, back to the door, without finding an entrance through that inner wall.

But there was a ladder that went upward. They climbed it, Alan first, then Mara. They were in another corridor, and another ladder went upward.

Up and up they climbed, past level after level, and the blank inner wall gave way to spacious rooms in which was strange furniture. Some were compartmented, and on the compartment doors for three levels, red crosses were painted.

Both of them were bathed with perspiration when they reached the room with the windows. And here there were no more ladders.

"Mara, we're at the top of the Star Tower!" exclaimed Alan.

The room was domed, and from head level all the dome was windows. But, though the windows faced upward, those around the lower periphery showed the lighted city of Falklyn spread below them. There was even one of them that showed a section of the park, and the park was right under them, but they knew it was the park because they could see the Hussirs scurrying about in the light of the two gas lamps that still burned beside the closed door of the Star Tower.

All the windows in the upper part of the dome opened on the stars.

The lower part of the walls was covered with strange wheels and metal sticks and diagrams and little shining circles of colored lights.

"We're in the top of the Star Tower!" shouted Alan in a triumphant frenzy. "I have the Silk and I shall sing the Song!"

VI

Alan raised his voice and the words reverberated at them from the walls of the domed chamber.

> Twinkle, twinkle, golden star,
> I can reach you, though you're far.
> Shut my mouth and find my head,
> Find a worm that's striped with red,
> Feed it to the turtle shell,
> Then go to sleep, for all is well.

Nothing happened.

Alan sang the second verse, and still nothing happened.

"Do you suppose that if we went back out now the Hussirs would let all humans go free?" asked Mara doubtfully.

"That's silly," he said, staring at the window where an increasing number of Hussirs was crowding into the park. "It's a riddle. We have to do what it says."

"But how can we? What does it mean?"

"It has something to do with the Star Tower," he said thoughtfully. "Maybe the 'golden star' means the Star Tower, though I always thought it meant the Golden Star in the southern sky. Anyway, we've reached the Star Tower, and it's silly to think about reaching a real star.

"Let's take the next line. 'Shut my mouth and find my head.' How can you shut anyone's mouth before you find their head?"

"We had to shut the door to the Star Tower before we could climb to the top," she ventured.

"That's it!" he exclaimed. "Now, let's 'find a worm that's striped with red'!"

They looked all over the big room, in and under the strange crooked beds that would tilt forward to make chairs, behind the big, queer-looking objects that stood all over the floor. The bottom part of the walls had drawers and they pulled these out, one by one.

At last Mara dropped a little disc of metal and it popped in half on the floor. A flat spool fell out, and white tape unrolled from it in a tangle.

"Worm!" shouted Alan. "Find one striped with red!"

They popped open disc after metal disc — and there it was: a tape crossed diagonally with red stripes. There was lettering on the metal discs and Mara spelled out the letters on this one.

"EMERGENCY. TERRA. AUTOMATIC BLASTDOWN."

Neither of them could figure out what that meant. So they looked for the "turtle shell," and of course that would be the transparent dome-shaped object that sat on a pedestal between two of the chair-beds.

It was an awkward job trying to feed the striped worm to the turtle shell, for the only opening in the turtle shell was under it and to one side. But with Alan lying in one cushioned chair-bed and Mara lying in the other, and the two of them working together, they got the end of the worm into the turtle shell's mouth.

Immediately the turtle shell began eating the striped worm with a clicking chatter that lasted only a moment before it was drowned in a great rumbling roar from far down in the bowels of the Star Tower.

Then the windows that looked down on the park blossomed into flame that was almost too bright for human eyes to bear, and the lights of Falklyn began to fall away in the other windows around the rim of the dome. There was a great pressure that pushed them mightily down into the cushions on which they lay, and forced their senses from them.

Many months later, they would remember the second verse of the song. They would go into one of the chambers marked with a cross, they would sting themselves with the bugs that were hypodermic needles and sink down in the sleep of suspended animation.

But now they lay, naked and unconscious, in the control room of the accelerating starship. In the breeze from the air conditioners the silken message to Earth fluttered pink against Alan's throat.

R

rites of pas/sage — times or events in people's lives that are of particular importance, such as puberty and marriage. These events vary from one culture to another and in science fiction often involve alien anthropology. The transition from adolescence to adulthood is particularly important, as in the Hugo Award-winning novel *Rite of Passage,* by Alexei Panshin (Ace Books, 1968; Gregg Press, 1976).

Down to the Worlds of Men

ALEXEI PANSHIN

The horses and packs were loaded before we went aboard the scout ship. The scout bay is no more than a great oversized airlock with a dozen small ships squatting over their tubes, but it was the last of the Ship that I might ever see, so I took a long final look from the top of the ramp.

There were sixteen of us girls and thirteen boys. We took our places in the seats in the center of the scout. Riggy Allen made a joke that nobody bothered to laugh at, and then we were all silent. I was feeling lost and just beginning to enjoy it when Jimmy Dentremont came over to me. He's redheaded and has a face that makes him look about ten. An intelligent runt like me.

He said what I expected. "Mia, do you want to go partners if we can get together when we get down?"

I guess he thought that because we were always matched on study I liked him. Well, I did when I wasn't mad at him, but now I had that crack he'd made about being a snob in mind, so I said, "Not likely. I want to come back alive." It wasn't fair, but it was a good crack and he went back to his place without saying anything.

My name is Mia Havero. I'm fourteen, of course, or I wouldn't be telling this. I'm short, dark, and scrawny, though I don't expect that scrawniness to last much longer. Mother is very good looking. In the meantime, I've got brains as a consolation.

After we were all settled, George Fuhonin, the pilot, raised the ramps. We sat there for five minutes while they bled air out of our tube and then we just . . . dropped. My stomach turned flips. We didn't have to leave that way, but George thinks it's fun to be a hot pilot.

Thinking it over, I was almost sorry I'd been stinking to Jimmy D. He's the only competition I have my own age. The trouble is, you don't go partners with the competition, do you? Besides, there was still that crack about being a snob.

The planet chosen for our Trial was called Tintera. The last contact the Ship had had with it — and we were the ones who dropped them — was almost 150 years ago. No contact since. That had made the council debate a little before they dropped us there, but they decided it was all right in the end. It didn't make any practical difference to us kids because they never tell you anything about the place they're going to drop you. All I knew was the name. I wouldn't have known that much if Daddy weren't chairman of the council.

I felt like crawling in a corner of the ship and crying, but nobody else was breaking down, so I didn't. I did feel miserable. I cried when I said good-bye to Mother and Daddy — a real emotional scene — but that wasn't in public.

It wasn't the chance of not coming back that bothered me really, because I never believed that I wouldn't. The thought that made me unhappy was that I would have to be on a planet for a whole month. Planets make me feel wretched.

The gravity is always wrong, for one thing. Either your arches and calves ache or every time you step you think you're going to trip on a piece of fluff and break your neck. There are vegetables everywhere and little grubby things just looking for *you* to crawl on. If you can think of anything creepier than that, you've got a real nasty imagination. Worst of all, planets stink. Every single one smells — I've been on enough to know that. A planet is all right for a mud-eater, but not for me.

We have a place in the Ship like that — the Third Level — but it's only a thousand square miles and any time it gets on your nerves you can go up a level or down a level and be back in civilization.

When we reached Tintera, they started dropping us. We swung over the sea from the morning side and then dropped low over gray-green forested hills. Finally George spotted a clear area and dropped into it. They don't care what order you go in, so Jimmy D. jumped up, grabbed his gear and then led his horse down the ramp. I think he was still smarting from the slap I'd given him.

In a minute we were airborne again. I wondered if I would ever see Jimmy — if he would get back alive.

It's no game we play. When we turn fourteen, they drop us on the nearest colonized planet and come back one month later. That may sound like fun to you, but a lot of us never come back alive.

Don't think I was helpless. I'm hell on wheels. They don't let us grow for fourteen years and then kick us out to die. They prepare us. They do figure, though, that if you can't keep yourself alive by the time you're fourteen, you're too stupid, foolish, or unlucky to be any use to the Ship. There's sense behind it. It means that everybody on the Ship is a person who can take care of himself if he has to. Daddy says that something has to be done in a closed society to keep the population from decaying mentally and physically, and this is it. And it helps to keep the population steady.

I began to check my gear out — sonic pistol, pickup signal so I could be found at the end of the month, saddle and cinches, food and clothes. Venie Morlock has got a crush on Jimmy D., and when she saw me start getting ready to go, she began to check her gear, too. At our next landing, I grabbed Ninc's reins and cut Venie out smoothly. It didn't have anything to do with Jimmy. I just couldn't stand to put off the bad moment any longer.

The ship lifted impersonally away from Ninc and me like a rising bird, and in just a moment it was gone. Its gray-blue color was almost the color of the half-overcast sky, so I was never sure when I saw it last.

II

The first night was hell, I guess because I'm not used to having the lights out. That's when you really start to feel lonely, being alone in the dark. When the sun disappears, somehow you wonder in your stomach if it's really going to come back. But I lived through it — one day in thirty gone.

I rode in a spiral search pattern during the next two days. I had three things in mind — stay alive, find people, and find some of the others. The first was automatic. The second was to find out if there was a slot I could fit into for a month. If not, I would have to find a place to camp out, as nasty as that would be. The third was to join forces, though not with that meatball Jimmy D.

No, he isn't really a meatball. The trouble is that I don't take nothing from nobody, especially him, and he doesn't take nothing from nobody, especially me. So we do a lot of fighting.

I had a good month for Trial. My birthday is in November — too close to Year End Holiday for my taste, but this year it was all right. It was spring on Tintera, but it was December in the Ship, and after we got back we had five days of Holiday to celebrate. It gave me something to look forward to.

In two days of riding, I ran onto nothing but a few odd-looking animals. I shot one small one and ate it. It turned out to taste pretty good, though not as good as a slice from Hambone No. 4, to my mind the best meat vat on the Ship. I've eaten things so gruey-looking that I wondered that anybody had the guts to try them in the first place and they've turned out to taste good. And I've seen things that looked good that I couldn't keep on my stomach. So I guess I was lucky.

On the third day, I found the road. I brought Ninc down off the hillside, losing sight of the road in the trees, and then reaching it in the level below. It was narrow and made of sand spread over a hard base. Out of the marks in the sand, I could pick out the tracks of horses and both narrow and wide wheels. Other tracks I couldn't identify.

One of the smartest moves in history was to include horses when they dropped the colonies. I say "they" because, while we did the actual dropping, the idea originated with the whole evac plan back on Earth. Considering how short a time it was in which the colonies were established, there was no time to set up industry, so they had to have draft animals.

The first of the Great Ships was finished in 2025. One of the eight, as well as the two that were being built then, went up with everything else in the solar system in 2041. In that sixteen years 112 colonies were planted. I don't know how many of those planets had animals that *could* have been substituted but, even if they had, they would have had to be domesticated from scratch. That would have been stupid. I'll bet that half the colonies would have failed if they hadn't had horses.

We'd come in from the west over the ocean, so I traveled east on the road. That much water makes me nervous, and roads have to go somewhere.

I came on my first travelers three hours later. I rounded a tree-lined bend, ducking an overhanging branch, and pulled Ninc to a stop. There were five men on horseback herding a bunch of the ugliest creatures alive.

They were green and grotesque. They had squat bodies, long limbs, and knobby bulges at their joints. They had square, flat animal masks for faces. But they walked on their hind legs and they had paws that were almost hands, and that was enough to make them seem almost human. They made a wordless, chilling, lowing sound as they milled and plodded along.

I started Ninc up again and moved slowly to catch up with them. All the men on horseback had guns in saddle boots. They looked as nervous as cats with kittens. One of them had a string of packhorses on a line, and he saw me and called to another who seemed to be the leader. That one wheeled his black horse and rode back toward me.

He was a middle-aged man, maybe as old as my daddy. He was large and he had a hard face. Normal enough, but hard. He pulled to a halt when we reached each other, but I kept going. He had to come around and follow me. I believe in judging a person by his face. A man can't help the face he owns, but he can help the expression he wears on it. If a man looks mean, I generally believe that he is. This one looked mean. That was why I kept riding.

He said, "What be you doing out here, boy? Be you out of your head? There be escaped Losels in these woods."

I told you I hadn't finished filling out yet, but I hadn't thought it was that bad. I wasn't ready to make a fight over the point, though. Generally, I can't keep my bloody mouth shut, but now I didn't say anything. It seemed smart.

"Where be you from?" he asked.

I pointed to the road behind us.

"And where be you going?"

I pointed ahead. No other way to go.

He seemed exasperated. I have that effect sometimes. Even on Mother and Daddy, who should know better.

We were coming up on the others now, and the man said, "Maybe you'd better ride on from here with us. For protection."

He had an odd way of twisting his sounds, almost as though he had a mouthful of mush. I wondered whether he was just an oddball or whether everybody here spoke the same way. I'd never heard International English spoken any way but one, even on the planet Daddy made me visit with him.

One of the other outriders came easing by then. I suppose they'd been watching us all the while. He called to the hard man.

"He be awfully small, Horst. I doubt me a Losel'd even notice him at all. We mought as well throw him back again."

The rider looked at me. When I didn't dissolve in terror as he expected, he shrugged and one of the other men laughed.

The hard man said to the others, "This boy will be riding along with us to Forton for protection."

I looked down at the plodding, unhappy creatures they were driving along and one looked back at me with dull, expressionless, golden eyes. I felt uncomfortable.

I said, "I don't think so."

What the man did then surprised me. He said, "I do think so," and reached for the rifle in his saddle boot.

I whipped my sonic pistol out so fast that he was caught leaning over with the rifle half out. His jaw dropped. He knew what I held and he didn't want to be fried.

I said, "Ease your rifles out and drop them gently to the ground."

They did, watching me all the while with wary expressions.

When all the rifles were on the ground, I said, "All right, let's go."

They didn't want to move. They didn't want to leave the rifles. I could see that. Horst didn't say anything. He just watched me with narrowed eyes. But one of the others held up a hand and in wheedling tones said, "Look here, kid . . . "

"Shut up," I said, in as mean a voice as I could muster, and he did. It surprised me. I didn't think I sounded *that* mean. I decided he just didn't trust the crazy kid not to shoot.

After twenty minutes of easy riding for us and hard walking for the creatures, I said, "If you want your rifles, you can go back and get them now." I dug my heels into Ninc's sides and rode on. At the next bend I looked back and saw four of them holding their packhorses and the creatures still while one beat a dust-raising retreat down the road.

I put this episode in the "file and hold for analysis" section in my mind and rode on, feeling good. I think I even giggled once. Sometimes I even convince myself that I'm hell on wheels.

III

When I was nine, my Daddy gave me a painted wooden doll that my great-grandmother brought from Earth. The thing is that inside it, nestled one in another, are eleven more dolls, each one smaller than the last. I like to watch people when they open it for the first time.

My face must have been like that as I rode along the road.

The country leveled into a great rolling valley and the trees gave way to great farms and fields. In the fields, working, were some of the green creatures, which surprised me since the ones I'd seen before hadn't seemed smart enough to count to one, let alone do any work.

But it relieved me. I thought they might have been eating them or something.

I passed two crossroads and started to meet more people, but nobody questioned me. I met people on horseback, and twice I met trucks moving silently past. And I overtook a wagon driven by the oldest man I've seen in my life. He waved to me, and I waved back.

Near the end of the afternoon I came to the town, and there I received a jolt that sickened me.

By the time I came out on the other side, I was sick. My hands were cold and sweaty and my head was spinning, and I wanted to kick Ninc to a gallop.

I rode slowly in, looking all around, missing nothing. The town was all stone, wood, and brick. Out of date. Out of time, really. There were no machines more complicated than the trucks I'd seen earlier. At the edge of town, I passed a newspaper office with a headline pasted in the window — INVASION! I remember that. I wondered about it.

But I looked most closely at the people. In all that town, I didn't see one girl over ten years old and no grown-up women at all. There were little kids, there were boys and there were men, but no girls. All the boys and men wore pants, and so did I, which must have been why Horst and his buddies assumed I was a boy. It wasn't flattering, but I decided I'd not tell anybody different until I found what made the clocks tick on this planet.

But that wasn't what bothered me. It was the kids. My God! They swarmed. I saw a family come out of a house — a father and *four* children. It was the most foul thing I've ever seen. It struck me then — these people were Free Birthers! I felt a wave of nausea and I closed my eyes until it passed.

The first thing you learn in school is that if it weren't for idiot and criminal people like these, Earth would never have been destroyed. The evacuation would never have had to take place, and eight billion people wouldn't have died. There wouldn't have *been* eight billion people. But, no. They bred and they spread and they devoured everything in their path like a cancer. They gobbled up all the resources that Earth had and crowded and shoved one another until the final war came.

I am lucky. My great-great-grandparents were among those who had enough foresight to see what was coming. If it hadn't been for them and some others like them, there wouldn't be any humans left anywhere. And I wouldn't be here. That may not scare you, but it scares me.

What happened before, when people didn't use their heads and wound up blowing the solar system apart, is something nobody should forget. The older people don't let *us* forget. But these people had, and that the council should know.

For the first time since I landed on Tintera, I felt *really* frightened. There was too much going on that I didn't understand. I felt a blind urge to get away, and when I reached the edge of town, I whomped Ninc a good one and gave him his head.

I let him run for almost a mile before I pulled him down to a walk again. I couldn't help wishing for Jimmy D. Whatever else he is, he's smart and brains I needed.

How do you find out what's going on? Eavesdrop? That's a lousy method. For one thing, people can't be depended on to talk about the things you want to hear. For another, you're likely to get caught. Ask somebody? Who? Make the mistake of bracing a fellow like Horst and you might wind up with a sore head and an empty pocket. The best thing I could think of was to find a library, but that might be a job.

I'd had two bad shocks on this day, but they weren't the last. In the late afternoon, when the sun was starting to sink and a cool wind was starting to ripple the tree leaves, I saw the scout ship high in the sky. The dying sun colored it a deep red. Back again? I wondered what had gone wrong.

I reached down into my saddlebag and brought out my contact signal. The scout ship swung up in the sky in a familiar movement calculated to drop the stomach out of everybody aboard. George Fuhonin's style. I triggered the signal, my heart turning flips all the while. I didn't know why he was back, but I wasn't really sorry.

The ship swung around until it was coming back on a path almost over my head, going in the same direction. Then it went into a slip and started bucking so hard that I knew this wasn't hot piloting at all, just plain idiot stutter-fingered stupidity at the controls. As it skidded by me overhead, I got a good look at it and knew that it wasn't one of ours. Not too different, but not ours.

One more enigma. Where was it from? Not here. Even if you know how, and we wouldn't tell these mud-eaters how, a scout ship is something that takes an advanced technology to build.

I felt defeated and tired. Not much farther along the road I came to a campsite with two wagons pulled in for the night, and I couldn't help but pull in myself. The campsite was large and had two permanent buildings on it. One was a well enclosure and the other was little more than a high-walled pen. It didn't even have a roof.

I set up camp and ate my dinner. In the wagon closest to me were a man, his wife, and their three children. The kids were running around and playing, and one of them ran close to the high-walled pen. His father came and pulled him away.

The kids weren't to blame for their parents, but when one of them said hello to me, I didn't even answer. I know how lousy I would feel if I had two or three brothers and sisters, but it didn't strike me until that moment that it wouldn't even seem out of the ordinary to these kids. Isn't that horrible?

About the time I finished eating, and before it grew dark, the old man I had seen earlier in the day drove his wagon in. He fascinated me. He had white hair, something I had read about in stories but had never seen before.

When nightfall came, they started a large fire. Everybody gathered around. There was singing for a while, and then the father of the children tried to pack them off to bed. But they weren't ready to go, so the old man started telling them a story. In the old man's odd accent, and sitting there in the campfire light surrounded by darkness, it seemed just right.

It was about an old witch named Baba Yaga who lived in the forest in a house that stood on chicken legs. She was the nasty stepmother of a nice little girl, and to get rid of the kid she sent her on a phony errand into the deep dark woods at nightfall. I could appreciate the poor girl's position. All the little girl had to help her were the handkerchief, the comb, and the pearl that she had inherited from her dear dead mother. But, as it turned out, they were just enough to defeat nasty old Baba Yaga and bring the girl safely home.

I wished for the same for myself.

The old man had just finished and they were starting to drag the kids off to bed when there was a commotion on the road at the edge of the camp. I looked but my eyes were adjusted to the light of the fire and I couldn't see far into the dark.

A voice there said, "I'll be damned if I'll take another day like this one, Horst. We should have been here hours ago. It be your fault we're not."

Horst growled a retort. I decided that it was time for me to leave the campfire. I got up and eased away as Horst and his men came up to the fire, and cut back to where Ninc was parked. I grabbed up my blankets and mattress and started to roll them up. I had a pretty good idea now what they used the high-walled pen for.

I should have known that they would have to pen the animals up for the night. I should have used my head. I hadn't, and now it was time to take leave.

I never got the chance.

I was just heaving the saddle up on Ninc when I felt a hand on my shoulder and I was swung around.

"Well, well. Horst, look who we have here," he called. It was the one who'd made the joke about me being beneath the notice of a Losel. He was alone with me now, but with that call the others would be up fast.

I brought the saddle around as hard as I could and then up, and he went down. He started to get up again, so I dropped the saddle on him and reached inside my jacket for my gun. Somebody grabbed me then from behind and pinned my arms to my side.

I opened my mouth to scream — I have a good scream — but a rough smelly hand clamped down over it before I had a chance to get more than a lungful of air. I bit down hard — 5000 pounds psi, I'm told — but he didn't let me go. I started to kick, but Horst jerked me off my feet and dragged me off.

When we were behind the pen and out of earshot of the fire, he stopped dragging me and dropped me in a heap. "Make any noise," he said, "and I'll hurt you."

That was a silly way to put it, but somehow it said more than if he'd threatened to break my arm or my head. It left him a latitude of things to do if he pleased. He examined his hand. There was enough moonlight for that. "I ought to club you anyway," he said.

The one I'd dropped the saddle on came up then. The others were putting the animals in the pen. He started to kick me, but Horst stopped him.

"No," he said. "Look through the kid's gear, bring the horse and what we can use."

The other one didn't move. "Get going, Jack," Horst said in a menacing tone and they stood toe to toe for a long moment before Jack finally backed down. It seemed to me that Horst wasn't so much objecting to me being kicked, but rather was establishing who did the kicking in his bunch.

But I wasn't done yet. I was scared, but I still had the pistol under my jacket.

Horst turned back to me and I said, "You can't do this and get away with it."

He said, "Look, boy. You may not know it, but you be in a lot of trouble. So don't give me a hard time."

He still thought I was a boy. It was not time to correct him, but I didn't like to see the point go unchallenged. It was unflattering.

"The courts won't let you get away with this," I said. I'd passed a courthouse in the town with a carved motto over the doors: EQUAL JUSTICE UNDER THE LAW or TRUTH OUR SHIELD AND JUSTICE OUR SWORD or something stuffy like that.

He laughed, not a phony, villian-type laugh, but a real laugh, so I knew I'd goofed.

"Boy, boy. Don't talk about the courts. I be doing you a favor. I be taking what I can use of your gear, but I be letting you go. You go to court and they'll take everything and lock you up besides. I be leaving you your freedom."

"Why would they be doing that?" I asked. I slipped my hand under my jacket.

"Every time you open your mouth you shout that you be off one of the Ships," Horst said. "That be enough. They already have one of you brats in jail in Forton."

I was about to bring my gun out when up came Jack leading Ninc, with all my stuff loaded on. I mentally thanked him.

He said, "The kid's got some good equipment. But I can't make out what this be for." He held out my pickup signal.

Horst looked at it, then handed it back. "Throw it away," he said.

I leveled my gun at them — Hell on Wheels strikes again! I said, "Hand that over to me."

Horst made a disgusted sound.

"Don't make any noise," I said, "or you'll fry. Now hand it over."

I stowed it away, then paused with one hand on the leather horn of the saddle. "What's the name of the kid in jail in Forton?"

"I can't remember," he said. "But it be coming to me. Hold on."

I waited. Then suddenly my arm was hit a numbing blow from behind and the gun went flying. Jack pounced after it and Horst said, "Good enough," to the others who'd come up behind me.

I felt like a fool.

Horst stalked over and got the signal. He dropped it on the ground and said in a voice far colder than mine could ever be, because it was natural and mine wasn't, "The piece be yours." Then he tromped on it until it cracked and fell apart.

Then he said, "Pull a gun on me twice. Twice." He slapped me so hard that my ears rang. "You dirty little punk."

I said calmly, "You big louse."

It was a time I would have done better to keep my mouth shut. All I can remember is a flash of pain as his fist crunched against the side of my face and then nothing.

Brains are no good if you don't use them.

IV

I remember pain and sickness, and motion, but my next clear memory is waking in a bed in a house. I had a feeling that time had passed, but how much I didn't know. I looked around and found the old man who had told the story was sitting by my bed.

"How be you feeling this morning, young lady?" he asked. He had white hair and a seamed face and his hands were gnarled and old. His face was red, and the red and the white of his hair made a sharp contrast with the bright blue of his deep-set eyes. It was a good face.

"Not very healthy," I said. "How long has it been?"

"Two days," he said. "You'll get over it soon enough. I be Daniel Kutsov. And you?"

"I'm Mia Havero."

"I found you dumped in a ditch after Horst Fanger and his boys had left you," he said. "A very unpleasant man . . . as I suppose he be bound to be, herding Losels."

"Those green things were Losels? Why are they afraid of them?"

"The ones you saw beed drugged. They wouldn't obey otherwise. Once in a while a few be stronger than the drug and they escape to the woods. The drug cannot be so strong that they cannot work. So the strongest escape. They be some danger to most people, and a great danger to men like Horst Fanger who buy them from the ships. Every so often, hunters go out to thin them down."

"That seems like slavery," I said, yawning.

It was a stupid thing to say, like some comment about the idiocy of a Free Birth policy. Not the sentiment, but the timing.

Mr. Kutsov treated the comment with more respect than it deserved. "Only God can decide a question like that," he said gently. "Be it slavery to use my horses to work for me? I don't know anyone who would say so. A man be a different matter, though. The question be whether a Losel be like a horse or like a man, and that I can't answer. Now go to sleep again and in a while I will bring you some food."

He left then, but I didn't go to sleep. I was in trouble. I had no way to contact the scout ship. There was only one way out, and that was to find somebody else who did have his signal. That wasn't going to be easy.

Mr. Kutsov brought me some food later in the day, and I asked him then, "Why are you doing all this for me?"

He said, "I don't like to see children hurt, by people like Horst Fanger or by anyone."

"But I'm from one of the Ships," I said. "You know that, don't you?"

Mr. Kutsov nodded. "Yes, I know that."

"I understand that is pretty bad around here."

"With some people, true. But all the people who hate the Ships don't realize that if it beedn't for the Ships they wouldn't be here at all. They hold their grudge too close to their hearts. There be some of us who disagree with the government though it has lost us our families or years from our lives, and we would not destroy what we cannot agree with. When such an one as Horst Fanger uses this as an excuse to rob and injure a child, I will not agree. He has taken all that you have and there be no way to reclaim it, but what I can give of my house be yours."

I thanked him as best I could and then I asked him what the grudge was that they held against the Ships.

"It ben't a simple thing," he said. "You have seen how poor and backward we be. We realize it. Now and again, when you decide to stop, we see you people from the Ships. And you ben't poor or backward. You could call what we feel jealousy, if you wanted, but it be more than that and different. When we beed dropped here, there been no scientists or technicians among us. I can understand. Why should they leave the last places where they had a chance to use and develop their knowledge for a backward planet where there is no equipment, no opportunity? What be felt here be that all the men who survived the end of Earth and the solar system be the equal heirs of man's knowledge and accomplishment. But by bad luck, things didn't work out that way. So ideas urged by the Ships be ignored, and the Ships be despised, and people from the Ships be treated as shamefully as you have beed or worse."

I could think of a good example of an idea that the Ships had emphasized that had been ignored elsewhere. Only it was more than an idea or an opinion. It was a cold and deadly lesson taught by history. It was: Man is an organism that ultimately destroys itself unless he regulates his own size and growth. That was what I was taught.

I said, "I can understand how they might feel that way, but it's not fair. We pretty much support ourselves. As much as we can, we reuse things and salvage things, but we still need raw materials. The only thing we have to trade is knowledge. If we didn't have anything to trade for raw materials, that would be the end of us. Do we have a choice?"

"I don't hold you to blame," Mr. Kutsov said slowly, "but I can't help but to feel that you have made a mistake and that it will hurt you in the end."

I didn't say it, but I thought — when you lay blame, whom do you put it on? People who are obviously sick like these mud-eaters, or people who are normal like us?

After I got better, I had the run of Mr. Kutsov's house. It was a small place near the edge of Forton, surrounded by trees and with a small garden. Mr. Kutsov made a regular shipping run through the towns to the coast and back every second week. It was not a profitable business, but he said that at his age, profit was no longer very important. He was very good to me, but I didn't understand him.

He gave me lessons before he let me go outside into the town. Women were second-class citizens around here, but prejudice of that sort wasn't in Mr. Kutsov. Dressed as I was, as scrawny as I am, when people saw me here, they saw a boy. People see what they expect to see. I could get away with my sex, but not my accent. I might sound right on seven Ships and on III other planets, but here I was wrong. And I had two choices — sound right or shut up. One of these choices was impossible for me, so I set out to learn to sound like a Tinteran born and bred, with Mr. Kutsov's aid.

It was a long time before he was willing to give me a barely passing grade. He said, "All right. You should keep listening to people and correcting yourself, but I be satisfied. You talk as though you have a rag in your mouth, but I think you can get by."

Before I went out into town, I found out one more important thing. It was the answer to a question that I didn't ask Mr. Kutsov. I'd been searching for it in old newspapers, and at last I found the story I was looking for. The last sentence read: "After sentencing, Dentermount was sent to the territorial jail in Forton to serve his three-month term."

I thought, they misspelled his name. And then I thought, trust it to be Jimmy D. He gets in almost as much trouble as I do.

Though you may think it strange, my first stop was the library.

I've found that it helps to be well researched. I got what I could from Mr. Kutsov's books during the first days while he was outdoors working in his garden. In his library, I found a novel that he had written himself called *The White Way*.

He said, "It took me forty years to write it, and I have spent forty-two years since living with the political repercussions. It has beed an interesting forty-two years, but I am not sure that I would do it again. Read the book if you be interested."

I did read it, though I couldn't understand what the fuss was about. It seemed reasonable to me. But these mud-eaters were crazy anyway. I couldn't help but think that he and Daddy would have found a lot in common. They were both fine, tough-minded people, and though you would never know it to look at them, they were the same age. Except that at the age of eighty Mr. Kutsov was old, and at the age of eighty Daddy was not.

It cost me an effort to walk through the streets of Forton, but after my third trip, the pain was less, though the number of children still made me sick.

In the library, I spent four days getting a line on Tintera. I read their history. I studied their geography and, as sneakily as I could, I tore out the best local maps I could find.

On my trips through town, I took the time to look up Horst Fanger's place of business. It was a house, a shed and pen for the Losels, a stable, a truck garage (one truck — broken down) and a sale block, all housed in one rambling, shanty building. Mr. Horst Fanger was apparently a big man. Big deal.

When I was ready, I scouted out the jail. It was a raw unpleasant day, the sort that makes me hate planets, and rain was threatening when I reached the jailpen. It was a solid three-story building of great stone blocks, shaped like a fortress and protected by bars, an iron-spike fence, and two nasty-looking dogs. On my second trip around, the rain began. I beat it to the front and dodged in the entrance.

I was standing there shaking the rain off when a man in a green uniform came stalking out of one of the offices that lined the first-floor hallway. My heart stopped for a moment, but he went right by without giving me a second look and went upstairs. That gave me some confidence and so I started poking around.

I had covered the bulletin boards and the offices on one side of the hall when another man in green came into the hall and made straight for me. I didn't wait, I walked toward him, too. I said, as wide-eyed and innocent as I could, "Can you help me, sir?"

"Well, that depends. What sort of help do you need?" He was a big, rather slow man with one angled cloth bar on his shirt front over one pocket and a plate that said ROBARDS pinned over the pocket on the other side. He seemed good-natured.

I said, "Jerry had to write about the capital, and Jimmy got the governor, and I got *you.*"

"Hold on there. First, what be your name?"

"Billy Davidow," I said. "I don't know what to write, sir, and I thought you could show me around and tell me things."

"I be sorry, son," he said. "We be pretty caught up today. Could you make it some other afternoon or maybe some evening?"

I said slowly, "I have to hand the paper in this week."

After a minute, he said, "All right. I'll take you around. But I can't spare much time. It'll have to be a quick tour."

The offices were on the first floor. Storage rooms, an arms room, and a target range were in the basement. Most of the cells were on the second floor, with the very rough cases celled on the third.

"If the judge says maximum security, they go on the third, everybody else on the second unless we have an overflow. Have a boy upstairs now."

My heart sank.

"A real bad actor. Killed a man."

Well, that wasn't Jimmy. Not with a three-month sentence.

Maximum security had three sets of barred doors plus an armed guard. Sgt. Robards pointed it all out to me. "By this time next week, it will all be full in here," he said sadly. "The governor has ordered a roundup of all political agitators. The Anti-Redemptionists be getting out of hand and he be going to cool them off. Uh, don't put that in your paper."

"Oh, I won't," I said, crossing off on my notes.

The ordinary cells on the second floor weren't behind barred doors and I got a guided tour. I stared Jimmy D. right in the face, but he had the brains to keep his mouth shut.

When we had finished, I thanked Sgt. Robards enthusiastically. "It sure has been swell, sir."

"Not at all, son," he said. "I enjoyed it myself. If you have time some evening, drop by when I have the duty. My schedule bees on the bulletin board."

"Thank you, sir," I said. "Maybe I will."

v

Before I scouted the jail I had only vague notions of what I was going to do to spring Jimmy D. I had spent an hour or so, for instance, toying with the idea of forcing the territorial governor to release Jimmy at the point of a gun. I spent that much time with it because the idea was fun to think about, but I dropped it because it was stupid.

I finally decided on a very simple course of action, one that could easily go wrong. It was my choice because it was the only thing I could pull off by myself that had a chance of working.

Before I left the jail building, I copied down Sgt. Robards's duty schedule from the bulletin board. Then I went home.

I spent the next few days shoplifting. Mr. Kutsov was laying in supplies, too, loading his wagon for his regular trip. I helped him load up, saving my shopping for my spare time. Mr. Kutsov wanted me to go along with him, but I couldn't, of course, and I couldn't tell him why. He didn't want to argue and he couldn't *make* me do anything I didn't want to do, so I had an unfair advantage. I just dug in my heels.

Finally he agreed it was all right for me to stay alone in the house while he was gone. It was what I wanted, but I didn't enjoy the process of getting my own way as much as I did at home. There it is a more even battle.

The day he picked to leave was perfect for my purposes. Mr. Kutsov said, "I'll be back in six days. Be you sure that you will be all right?"

I said, "Yes. I'll be careful. You be careful, too."

"I don't think it matters much any more at my age," he smiled. "Stay out of trouble."

"I'll try," I said, and waved good-bye. That was what I meant to do, stay out of trouble.

Back in the house I wrote a note of explanation for Mr. Kutsov and thanked him for all he had done. Then I dug my two small packs out of hiding and I was ready.

I set out just after dark. It was sprinkling lightly, but I didn't mind it. It surprised me, but I enjoyed the feel of the spray on my face. In one pocket I had pencil and paper for protective coverage. In another pocket I had a single sock and a roll of tape.

Just before I got to the jail, I filled the sock with wet sand.

Inside there were lights on in only two first-floor offices. Sgt. Robards was in one of them.

"Hello, Sgt. Robards," I said, going in. "How be you tonight?"

"Well enough," he said. "It be pretty slow down here tonight. They be busy up on the third floor tonight, though."

"Oh?"

"They be picking up those Anti-Redemptionists tonight. How did your paper go?"

"I handed it in," I said. "I should get a good grade with your help."

"Oh, you found out everything you needed to know."

"Oh, yes. I just came by to visit tonight. I wondered if you'd show me the target range again. That was keen."

"Sure," he said. "Would you like to see me pop some targets? I be the local champion, you know."

"Gee, would you?"

We went downstairs, Sgt. Robards leading the way. This was the place I'd picked to drop him. He was about to slip the key in the door to the range when I slugged him across the back of the neck with my sock full of sand. I grabbed him and eased him down.

I tried the keys on either side of the target door key and opened the arsenal on the second try. I dragged him in there and got out my roll of tape. I took three quick turns about his ankles, then did the same with his wrists. I finished by putting a bar and two crosspieces over the mouth.

I picked out two weapons then. They had no sonics, of course, so I picked out two of the smallest and lightest pistols in the room. I figured out what cartridges fit them, and then dropped guns and cartridge clips into my pocket.

I swung the door shut and locked it again, leaving Sgt. Robards inside. I stood for a moment in the corridor with the keys in my hand. There were only ten keys, not enough to cover each individual cell. Yet Sgt. Robards had clinked these keys and said that he could unlock the cells.

Maybe I would have done better to stick up the territorial governor.

Well, here goes.

I eased up to the first floor. Nobody came out of the second office to check on the noise made by my pounding heart, which surprised me. Then up to the second floor. It was dark here, but light from the first and third floors leaking up and down the stairs made things bright enough for me to see what I was doing. There were voices on the third floor and somebody laughed up there. I held my breath and moved quietly to Jimmy's cell.

I whispered, "Jimmy!" and he came alert and moved to the door.

"Am I glad to see you," he whispered back.

I held up the keys. "Do any of these fit?"

"Yes, the D key. The D key. It fits the four cells in this corner."

I fumbled through until I had the key tagged D. I opened the cell with as few clinking noises as possible. "Come on," I said. "We've got to get out of here in a hurry."

He slipped out and pushed the door shut behind him. We headed for the stairs and were almost there when I heard somebody coming up. Jimmy must have heard it, too, because he grabbed my arm and pulled me back. We flattened out as best we could.

Talk about walking right into it! The policeman looked over at us and said, "What are you doing up here, Robards? Hey, you're not . . . "

I stepped out and brought out one of the pistols. I said, "Easy now. If things go wrong for us, I have nothing to lose by shooting you. If you want to live, play it straight."

He apparently believed me, because he put his hands where I could see them and shut up.

I herded him into Jimmy's cell and let Jimmy do the honors with the loaded sock. We taped him up and while Jimmy was locking him in, I heard somebody in one of the cells behind me say, "Shut up, there," to somebody else. I turned and said, "Do you want to get shot?"

The voice was collected. "No. No trouble here."

"Do you want to be let out?"

The voice was amused. "I don't think so. Thank you just the same."

Jimmy finished and I asked, "Where is your signal? We have to have that."

"In the basement with the rest of my gear."

The signal was all we took. When we were three blocks away and on a dark side street, I handed Jimmy his gun and ammunition. As he took them, he said, "Tell me something, Mia. Would you really have shot him?"

I said, "I couldn't have. I hadn't loaded my gun yet."

I led him through town following the back ways I'd worked out before. Somebody once said that good luck is no more nor less than careful preparation, and this time I meant to have good luck. I led Jimmy toward the Losel-selling district.

Jimmy is short and red-headed with a face that makes him look about four years younger than he is. That's a handicap any time. When you stand out anyway, it's likely to make you a little bit tart. But Jimmy's all right most of the time.

He said, "We're in trouble."

"That's brilliant."

"No," Jimmy said. "They have a scout ship from one of the other Ships. This is going to sound wild, but they intend to use the scout to take over a Ship and then use that to destroy the rest of the Ships. They're going to try. The police are rounding up everybody who is opposed who has any influence and are putting them in jail."

"So what?"

"Mia, are you mad at me for something?"

"What makes you think so?"

"You're being bitter about something."

"If you must know, it's that crack you made about me being a snob."

"That was a month ago."

"I still resent it."

"Why?" Jimmy asked. "It's true. You think that because you're from a Ship that you're automatically better than any mud-eater. That makes you a snob."

"Well, you're no better," I said.

"Maybe not, but I don't pretend. Hey, look, we can't get anywhere if we fight and we've got to stick together. I'll tell you what. I'll apologize. I'm sorry I said it, even if it is true. Make up?"

"Okay," I said. But that was a typical trick of his. Get the last blow in and then call the whole thing off.

When we got to Horst Fanger's place, I said, "I've got our packs all set up. This is where we get our horses." I'd left this until last, not wanting people running around looking for stolen horses while I was trying to break somebody out of the police jailpen. Besides, for this I wanted somebody along as lookout.

There was a fetid, unwashed odor that hung about the pens that the misting rain did nothing to dispel. We slipped by the pens, the Losels watching us but making no noise, and came to the stables, which smelled better. Jimmy stood guard while I broke the lock and slipped inside.

Ninc was there, good old Nincompoop, and a quick search turned up his saddle as well. I saddled him up and then stood watch while Jimmy picked himself out a horse and gear. I did one last thing before I left. I took out the pencil and paper in my pocket and wrote in *correct* Inter E, in great big letters: I'M A *GIRL,* YOU STINKER. I hung it on a nail. It may have been childish, but it felt good.

We rode from there to Mr. Kutsov's house, still following back alleys. As we rode, I told Jimmy about Mr. Kutsov and what he'd done for me.

When we got there we rode around to the back.

"Hold the horses," I said. "I'll slip in and get the packs. They're just inside."

We both dismounted and Jimmy took Ninc's reins. I bounded up the steps.

Mr. Kutsov was waiting in the dark inside. He said, "I read your note."

"Why did you come back?" I asked.

He smiled. "It didn't seem right to leave you here by yourself. I be sorry. I think I underestimated you. Be that Jimmy Dentremont outside?"

"You're not mad?"

"No. I ben't angry. I understand why you couldn't tell me."

For some reason, I started crying and couldn't stop. The tears ran down my face. "I'm sorry," I said. "I'm sorry."

The front door signal sounded then and Mr. Kutsov answered the door. A green-uniformed policeman stood in the doorway. "Daniel Kutsov?" he asked.

Instinctively, I shrank back out of sight of the doorway. I swiped at my face with my sleeve.

Mr. Kutsov said, "Yes. What can I do for you?"

The policeman moved one step inside the house where I could see him again. He said in a flat voice, "I have a warrant for your arrest."

There was only one light on in the house, in the front room. From the shadows at the rear I watched them both. The policeman had a hard mask for a face, no more human than a Losel. Mr. Kutsov was determined and I had the feeling that he had forgotten my presence.

"To jail again? For my book?" He shook his head. "No."

"It be nothing to do with any book I know of, Kutsov. It be known that you be an Anti-Redemptionist. So come along." He grasped Mr. Kutsov's arm.

Mr. Kutsov shook loose. "No. I won't go to jail again. It be no crime to be against stupidity. I won't go."

The policeman said,"You be coming whether you want to or not. You be under arrest."

Mr. Kutsov's voice had never shown his age before, but it shook now. "Get out of my house!"

A sense of coming destruction grew on me as I saw the policeman lift his gun from its holster and say, "You be coming if I have to shoot."

Mr. Kutsov swung his fist at the policeman and missed and, as though the man could afford to let nothing pass without retaliation, he swung the barrel of his pistol dully against the side of Mr. Kutsov's head. It rocked Mr. Kutsov, but he didn't fall. He raised his fist again. The policeman struck once more and waited but Mr. Kutsov still didn't fall. Instead, he swung again, and for the first time he landed, a blow that bounced weakly off the man's shoulder. Almost inevitably, it seemed, the policeman raised his pistol and fired directly at Mr. Kutsov, and then again, and as the second report rang Mr. Kutsov slid to the floor.

The silence was loud and gaunt. The policeman stood looking down at him and said, "Old fool!" under his breath. Then he came to himself and looked around. Then he picked a candlestick off the table and dropped it with a thud by Mr. Kutsov's empty outstretched hand.

The noise was a release for me and I moved for the first time. The policeman grunted and looked up and we stared at each other. Then again, slowly, he raised his gun and pointed it at me.

I heard a snickering sound and the three reports rang out, one following another. The policeman stood for a moment, balanced himself and then, like a crumpled sheet of paper, he fell to the floor. I didn't even look at Jimmy behind me. I started to cry and I went to Mr. Kutsov, passing by the policeman without even looking at him. As I bent down beside him, his eyes opened and he looked at me.

I couldn't stop crying. I held his head and cried. "I'm sorry," I said. "I'm sorry."

He smiled and said faintly, but clearly, "It be all right." After a minute he closed his eyes, and then he died.

After another minute, Jimmy touched my arm and said, "There's nothing we can do. Let's leave now, Mia, while we still can."

Outside, it was still raining. Standing in the rain I felt deserted.

VI

The final morning on Tintera was a fine day. We and the horses were in a rock-enclosed aerie where we had dodged the day before for shelter. In the aerie were grass and a small rock spring, and this day, the final day, was bright with blue and piled clouds riding high.

From where we sat, looking from the top of the rock wall, we could see over miles of expanse. Lower hills and curving valleys all covered with a rolling carpet of trees, a carpet of varying shades of gray and green. There were some natural upland meadows, and clearings in the valleys, and far away a line drawn in the trees that might be the path of a river. Down there, under that carpet, were all sorts of things — wild Losels, men hunting us, and — perhaps — some of the others from the Ship. We had seen the Losels and they had seen us; they had gone their way and we had gone ours. The men hunting us for blowing up their scout ship we hadn't seen for four days, and even then they hadn't seen us. As for the others, we hadn't seen them at all. But they might be there, under the anonymous carpet.

Jimmy got up from the ground and brushed himself off. He brought the signal over to me and said, "Should I, or do you want to?"

"Go ahead," I said.

He triggered it.

George Fuhonin was piloting and we were the sixth and seventh aboard. The other five crowded around and helped us put our gear away. Jimmy went on inside and I went upstairs to talk to George.

I was up there by the time we were airborne. "Hello, Halfpint," George said.

"Hi, Georgie-Worgie," I said, dealing blow for blow. "Have you had any trouble picking us up?"

"No trouble yet. You trying to wish me problems?"

"No," I said. "This is a real nasty planet. They had Jimmy D. locked up in jail. They hate everybody from the Ships."

"Oh." George raised his eyebrows. "Well, that might explain the board." He pointed to the board of lights above and to his left. Twenty-nine were marked for the twenty-nine of us. Of the twenty-nine, only twelve were lit. "The last light came on two hours ago. If there aren't any more, this will be the most fatal Trial Group I've ever picked up."

I stayed upstairs through two more pickups. Joe Fernandez-Fragoso, and then another double of which Venie Morlock was one-half. I went downstairs to say hello to her.

We were just settling down when George set off the alarm. He was speaking in the elder brother tone that I can't stand.

"All right, kids — shut up and listen. One of our people is down there. I didn't get close enough to see who. Whoever it is is surrounded by some of the local peasantry and we've got to bust him out. I'm going to buzz down and try to land on some of them. Then I want all of you outside and laying down a covering fire. Got that? I'm starting on down now."

Some of the kids had their weapons with them, but Jimmy and I didn't. We hopped for the gear racks and got out our pistols. There were ten of us and four ramps to the outside. Jimmy and I had No. 3 to ourselves. George is a hotrodder, as I've said, and after he gave us a long moment to get in place, he started down, a stomach-heaving swoop. Then he touched down light as a feather and dropped the ramps.

Jimmy and I dived down the ramp and I went left and he went right. We were on a slight slope facing down and my momentum and the slant put me right where I wanted to be — flat on my face. I rolled behind a tree and looked over to see Jimmy almost hidden in a bush.

Here, hundreds of miles from where we had been picked up, it was misting under a familiar rolled gray sky. In my ears was the sound of gunfire from the other side of the ship and from below us. Our boy was pinned fifty yards down the slope behind some rocks that barely protected him. He was fighting back. I could see the sighting beam of his sonic pistol slapping out. About thirty feet away from him toward us was the body of his horse. I recognized him then — a meatball named Riggy Allen.

I took all this in in seconds, and then I raised my pistol and fired, aiming at his attackers. They were dug in behind trees and rocks, at least partly hidden from Riggy as he was hidden from them. From where we were, though, above and looking down, they could be picked out. The distance was too great for my shot and it plowed up earth ten feet short, but the man I aimed at ducked back behind cover.

There was a certain satisfaction in one of these guns. Where a sonic pistol is silent, these made enough noise that you knew you were doing something. And when you missed with a sonic pistol, all you could expect at most was a shriveled branch or a sere and yellow leaf, but a miss with this gun could send up a gout of earth or drive a hole in a tree big enough to scare the steadiest man you can find.

I aimed higher and started to loft my shots in. Jimmy was doing the same thing, and the net effect was to keep their heads down. Riggy finally got the idea after a long moment. He stood up and started racing up the hill. Then my gun clicked empty, and a second later the firing to my right stopped. I started to fumble for another clip.

As our fire stopped, those heads popped back up again and took in the situation. They began to fire again and our boy Riggy took a long step and then dived over the body of his horse and went flat.

In a moment I was firing again, and then Jimmy was, too, and Riggy was up and running again. Then I started thinking clearly and held my fire while Jimmy emptied his clip. The instant he stopped, I started again, a regular squeeze, squeeze, squeeze. As I finished, Jimmy opened with his new clip and then Riggy was past us and up the ramp. He went flat in the doorway there and started firing his sonic pistol; its range was greater than our peashooters and he hosed the whole area down while Jimmy and I sprinted for the ramp.

As we hit the inside of the ship, I yelled, "Raise No. 3!" George had either been watching or listening, because it lifted smoothly up and locked in place.

Shots were still coming from the other sides of the ship, so I yelled at Jimmy to go left. Riggy just stood there for a moment fuzzy-headed, but Jimmy gave him a shove to the right and he finally got the idea. I cut through the middle. In the doorway of No. 1, I skidded flat on my face again and looked for targets. I dropped all my clips in front of me and began to fire. When the clip was empty, in two quick motions I pulled out the old one and slapped in the new and fired again. The three I was covering for used their heads and slipped in one at a time.

As the second one came aboard, I heard Jimmy's voice call from my left to raise No. 2. My third was Venie Morlock and as she ran aboard, I couldn't resist tripping her flat. I yelled to George to raise No. 1.

Venie glared at me and demanded, "What was that for?" as the ramp swung up.

"Just making sure you didn't get shot," I said, lying.

A second later, Riggy yelled that his side was okay and the last ramp was raised. My last view of Tintera was of a rain-soaked hillside and men doing their best to kill us, which all seems appropriate somehow. As the last ramp locked in place, George lifted the ship again and headed for the next pickup.

I went over to say hello to Riggy. He'd been completely unhurt by the barrage, but he had a great gash on his arm that was just starting to heal. He *said* that he was minding his own business in the woods one day when a Losel jumped out from behind a bush and slashed him. That may sound reasonable to you, but you don't know Riggy. I do. My opinion is that it was probably the other way around — the Losel was walking along in the woods one day, minding his own business, when *Riggy* jumped out from a bush and scared him. That is the sort of thing Riggy is inclined to do.

Riggy had been sneaking a look at my gun, and now he said, "Where did you get that neat pistol? Let me see it."

I handed it over.

After a minute of inspection, Riggy asked, "You wouldn't want to trade, would you?"

"For your sonic pistol?"

"Yes. You want to?"

I considered it for a minute, and then I said, "All right," and we traded. There is a certain amount of satisfaction in shooting an antique like that, but I know which is the more effective weapon. Besides, I only had one full clip of ammunition left.

There is a certain amount of prestige in coming back alive from Survival. It's your key to adulthood. There were no brass bands waiting for us when we got back, but our families were there, and that was enough.

The fifteen of us went down the lowered ramp, and when I stood again on solid rock, I looked around that ugly, bare scout bay and just drank it in. Home.

I turned to Jimmy then and I said, "Jimmy, it's a relief to be back, isn't it? And that isn't snobbery. It might have been before, but I don't think I am now."

And Jimmy nodded.

The waiting room wasn't bare. They had the decorations up for Year End, colored mobiles with lights that ranged through the spectrum, and more decorations on the walls. In the crowd of people waiting for us, I saw Jimmy's mother and her present husband, and Jimmy's father and *his* wife. When they saw Jimmy, they started waving and shouting.

Just as I said, "I'll see you tonight," I saw Mother and Daddy standing off to one side, and I waved. It was as though I had left the real world entirely for a month, and now at last I was back where things were going on and I wasn't missing a thing. I ran to them and I kissed Mother and hugged Daddy. Mother was crying.

I leaned back in Daddy's arms and looked up at him. He put a measuring hand over my head and said, "Mia, I believe you've grown some."

It might be so. I felt taller.

ro/bots — mobile *computers* (see that heading) that have varying degrees of capability. Robots in human form are called "androids" in science fiction. Quite common in science fiction, they used to serve as substitutes for oppressed peoples like blacks and Jews. They are generally depicted as friendly (as in "Star Wars" and "The Empire Strikes Back"), as opposed to computers, which are frequently given a menacing image. There have been many robot anthologies; three of the best are *The Pseudo People: Androids in Science Fiction* (Sherbourne Press, 1965); *Souls in Metal* (St. Martin's Press, 1977); and *The Robot and The Man* (Gnome Press, 1953).

Robbie

ISAAC ASIMOV

"Ninety-eight — ninety-nine — *one hundred.*" Gloria withdrew her chubby little forearm from before her eyes and stood for a moment, wrinkling her nose and blinking in the sunlight. Then, trying to watch in all directions at once, she withdrew a few cautious steps from the tree against which she had been leaning.

She craned her neck to investigate the possibilities of a clump of bushes to the right and then withdrew farther to obtain a better angle for viewing its dark recesses. The quiet was profound except for the incessant buzzing of insects and the occasional chirrup of some hardy bird, braving the midday sun.

Gloria pouted, "I bet he went inside the house, and I've told him a million times that that's not fair."

With tiny lips pressed together tightly and a severe frown crinkling her forehead, she moved determinedly up past the driveway toward the two-story building.

Too late she heard the rustling sound behind her, followed by the distinctive and rhythmic clump-clump of Robbie's metal feet. She whirled about to see her triumphing companion emerge from hiding and make for the home-tree at full speed.

Gloria shrieked in dismay. "Wait, Robbie! That wasn't fair. Robbie! You promised you wouldn't run until I found you." Her little feet could make no headway at all against Robbie's giant strides. Then, within ten feet of the goal, Robbie's pace slowed suddenly to the merest of crawls, and Gloria, with one final burst of wild speed, dashed pantingly past him to touch the welcome bark of home-tree first.

Gleefully she turned on the faithful Robbie, and with the basest of ingratitude rewarded him for his sacrifice by taunting him cruelly for a lack of running ability.

"Robbie can't run," she shouted at the top of her eight-year-old voice. "I can beat him any day. I can beat him any day." She chanted the words in a shrill rhythm.

Robbie didn't answer, of course — not in words. He pantomimed running, instead, inching away until Gloria found herself running after him as he dodged her narrowly, forcing her to veer in helpless circles, little arms outstretched and fanning at the air.

"Robbie," she squealed, "stand still!" — and the laughter was forced out of her in breathless jerks.

Until he turned suddenly and caught her up, whirling her round so that for her the world fell away for a moment, with a blue emptiness beneath and green trees stretching hungrily downward toward the void. Then she was down in the grass again, leaning against Robbie's leg and still holding a hard, metal finger.

After a while her breath returned. She pushed uselessly at her disheveled hair in vague imitation of one of her mother's gestures and twisted to see if her dress were torn.

She slapped her hand against Robbie's torso, "Bad boy! I'll spank you!"

And Robbie cowered, holding his hands over his face so that she had to add, "No, I won't, Robbie. I won't spank you. But anyway, it's my turn to hide now because you've got longer legs and you promised not to run till I found you."

Robbie nodded his head — a small parallelepiped with rounded edges and corners attached to a similar but much larger parallelepiped that served as torso, by means of a short, flexible stalk — and obediently faced the tree. A thin metal film descended over his glowing eyes, and from within his body came a steady, resonant ticking.

"Don't peek now — and don't skip any numbers," warned Gloria, and scurried for cover.

With unvarying regularity seconds were ticked off, and at the hundredth, up went the eyelids and the glowing red of Robbie's eyes swept the prospect. They rested for a moment on a bit of colorful gingham that protruded from behind a boulder. He advanced a few steps and convinced himself that it was Gloria who squatted behind it.

Slowly, remaining always between Gloria and home-tree, he advanced on the hiding place, and when Gloria was plainly in sight and could no longer even theorize to herself that she was not seen, he extended one arm toward her, slapping the other against his leg so that it rang out. Gloria emerged sulkily.

"You peeked!" she exclaimed with gross unfairness. "Besides, I'm tired of playing hide-and-seek. I want a ride."

But Robbie was hurt at the unjust accusation, so he seated himself carefully and shook his head ponderously from side to side.

Gloria changed her tone to one of gentle coaxing immediately. "Come on, Robbie. I didn't mean it about the peeking. Give me a ride."

Robbie was not to be won over so easily, though. He gazed stubbornly at the sky and shook his head even more emphatically.

"Please, Robbie, please give me a ride." She encircled his neck with rosy arms and hugged tightly. Then, changing moods in a moment, she moved away. "If you don't I'm going to cry," and her face twisted appallingly in preparation.

Hardhearted Robbie paid scant attention to this dreadful possibility, and shook his head a third time. Gloria found it necessary to play her trump card.

"If you don't," she exclaimed warmly, "I won't tell you any more stories, that's all. Not one!"

Robbie gave in immediately and unconditionally before this ultimatum, nodding his head vigorously until the metal of his neck hummed. Carefully he raised the little girl and placed her on his broad, flat shoulders.

Gloria's threatened tears vanished immediately and she crowed with delight. Robbie's metal skin, kept at a constant temperature of seventy by the high-resistance coils within, felt nice and comfortable, while the beautifully loud sound her heels made as they bumped rhythmically against his chest was enchanting.

"You're an air-coaster, Robbie, you're a big silver air-coaster. Hold out your arms straight. — You *got* to, Robbie, if you're going to be an air-coaster."

The logic was irrefutable. Robbie's arms were wings catching the air currents and he was a silver coaster.

Gloria twisted the robot's head and leaned to the right. He banked sharply. Gloria equipped the coaster with a motor that went "br-r-r" and then with weapons that went "powie" and "sh-sh-shshsh." Pirates were giving chase, and the ship's blasters were coming into play. The pirates dropped in a steady rain.

"Got another one. — Two more," she cried.

Then: "Faster, men," Gloria said pompously; "we're running out of ammunition." She aimed over her shoulder with undaunted courage, and Robbie was a blunt-nosed spaceship zooming through the void at maximum acceleration.

Clear across the field he sped, to the patch of tall grass on the other side, where he stopped with a suddenness that evoked a shriek from his flushed rider and then tumbled her onto the soft green carpet.

Gloria gasped and panted and gave voice to intermittent whispered exclamations of "that was *nice!*"

Robbie waited until she had caught her breath and then pulled gently at a lock of hair.

"You want something?" said Gloria, eyes wide in an apparently artless complexity that fooled her huge nursemaid not at all. He pulled the curl harder.

"Oh, I know. You want a story."

Robbie nodded rapidly.

"Which one?"

Robbie made a semicircle in the air with one finger.

The little girl protested, *"Again?* I've told you Cinderella a million times. Aren't you tired of it? It's for babies."

Another semicircle.

"Oh, well . . ." Gloria composed herself, ran over the details of the tale in her mind (together with her own elaborations, of which she had several), and began.

"Are you ready? Well — once upon a time there was a beautiful little girl whose name was Ella. And she had a terribly cruel stepmother and two very ugly and *very* cruel stepsisters and — "

Gloria was reaching the very climax of the tale — midnight was striking and everything was changing back to the shabby originals lickety-split, while Robbie listened tensely with burning eyes — when the interruption came.

"Gloria!"

It was the high-pitched sound of a woman who has been calling not once but several times, and had the nervous tone of one in whom anxiety was beginning to overcome impatience.

"Mama's calling me," said Gloria, not quite happily. "You'd better carry me back to the house, Robbie."

Robbie obeyed with alacrity, for somehow there was that in him which judged it best to obey Mrs. Weston without as much as a scrap of hesitation. Gloria's father was rarely home in the daytime except on Sunday — today, for instance — and when he was, he proved a genial and understanding person. Gloria's mother, however, was a source of uneasiness to Robbie, and there was always the impulse to sneak away from her sight.

Mrs. Weston caught sight of them the minute they rose above the masking tufts of long grass and retired inside the house to wait.

"I've shouted myself hoarse, Gloria," she said severely. "Where were you?"

"I was with Robbie," quavered Gloria. "I was telling him Cinderella, and I forgot it was dinnertime."

"Well, it's a pity Robbie forgot too." Then, as if that reminded her of the robot's presence, she whirled upon him. "You may go, Robbie. She doesn't need you now." Then, brutally, "And don't come back till I call you."

Robbie turned to go but hesitated as Gloria cried out in his defense, "Wait, Mama, you got to let him stay. I didn't finish Cinderella for him. I said I would tell him Cinderella and I'm not finished."

"Gloria!"

"Honest and truly, Mama, he'll stay so quiet you won't even know he's here. He can sit on the chair in the corner, and he won't say a word — I mean he won't *do* anything. Will you, Robbie?"

Robbie, appealed to, nodded his massive head up and down once.

"Gloria, if you don't stop this at once, you shan't see Robbie for a whole week."

The girl's eyes fell. "All right! But Cinderella is his favorite story and I didn't finish it. — And he likes it so much."

The robot left with a disconsolate step and Gloria choked back a sob.

George Weston was comfortable. It was a habit of his to be comfortable on Sunday afternoons. A good, hearty dinner below hatches; a nice, soft, dilapidated couch on which to sprawl; a copy of the *Times;* slippered feet and shirtless chest — how could anyone *help* but be comfortable?

He wasn't pleased, therefore, when his wife walked in. After ten years of married life he still was so unutterably foolish as to love her, and there was no question that he was always glad to see her — still, Sunday afternoons just after dinner were sacred to him, and his idea of solid comfort was to be left in utter solitude for two or three hours. Consequently he fixed his eyes firmly upon the latest reports of the Lefebre-Yoshida expedition to Mars (this one was to take off from Lunar Base and might actually succeed) and pretended she wasn't there.

Mrs. Weston waited patiently for two minutes, then impatiently for two more, and finally broke the silence.

"George!"

"Hmpph?"

"George, I say! *Will* you put down that paper and look at me?"

The paper rustled to the floor and Weston turned a weary face toward his wife. "What is it, dear?"

"You know what it is, George. It's Gloria and that terrible machine."

"What terrible machine?"

"Now don't pretend you don't know what I'm talking about. It's that robot Gloria calls Robbie. He doesn't leave her for a moment."

"Well, why should he? He's not supposed to. And he certainly isn't a terrible machine. He's the best darn robot money can buy, and I'm damned sure he set me back half a year's income. He's worth it, though — darn sight cleverer than half my office staff."

He made a move to pick up the paper again, but his wife was quicker and snatched it away.

"You listen to *me*, George. I won't have my daughter entrusted to a machine — and I don't care how clever it is. It has no soul, and no one knows what it may be thinking. A child just isn't *made* to be guarded by a thing of metal."

Weston frowned. "When did you decide this? He's been with Gloria two years now, and I haven't seen you worry till now."

"It was different at first. It was a novelty; it took a load off me, and — and it was a fashionable thing to do. But now I don't know. The neighbors — "

"Well, what have the neighbors to do with it? Now, look. A robot is infinitely more to be trusted than a human nursemaid. Robbie was constructed for only one purpose, really — to be the companion of a little child. His entire 'mentality' has been created for the purpose. He just can't help being faithful and loving and kind. He's a machine — *made so*. That's more than you can say for humans."

"But something might go wrong. Some — some — ". Mrs. Weston was a bit hazy about the insides of a robot — "some little jigger will come loose and the awful thing will go berserk and — and — " She couldn't bring herself to complete the quite obvious thought.

"Nonsense," Weston denied, with an involuntary nervous shiver. "That's completely ridiculous. We had a long discussion at the time we bought Robbie about the First Law of Robotics. You *know* that it is impossible for a robot to harm a human being; that long before enough can go wrong to alter that First Law, a robot would be completely inoperable. It's a mathematical impossibility. Besides, I have an engineer from US Robots here twice a year to give the poor gadget a complete overhaul. Why, there's no more chance of anything at all going wrong with Robbie than there is of you or I suddenly going loony — considerably less, in fact. Besides, how are you going to take him away from Gloria?"

He made another futile stab at the paper and his wife tossed it angrily into the next room.

"That's just it, George! She won't play with anyone else. There are dozens of little boys and girls that she should make friends with, but she won't. She won't go *near* them unless I make her. That's no way for a little girl to grow up. You want her to be normal, don't you? You want her to be able to take her part in society."

"You're jumping at shadows, Grace. Pretend Robbie's a dog. I've seen hundreds of children who would rather have their dog than their father."

"A dog is different, George. We *must* get rid of that horrible thing. You can sell it back to the company. I've asked, and you can."

"You've *asked?* Now look here, Grace, let's not go off the deep end. We're keeping the robot until Gloria is older, and I don't want the subject brought up again." And with that he walked out of the room in a huff.

Mrs. Weston met her husband at the door two evenings later. "You'll have to listen to this, George. There's bad feeling in the village."

"About what?" asked Weston. He stepped into the washroom and drowned out any possible answer by the splash of water.

Mrs. Weston waited. She said, "About Robbie."

Weston stepped out, towel in hand, face red and angry. "What are you talking about?"

"Oh, it's been building up and building up. I've tried to close my eyes to it, but I'm not going to any more. Most of the villagers consider Robbie dangerous. Children aren't allowed to go near our place in the evenings."

"We trust *our* child with the thing."

"Well, people aren't reasonable about these things."

"Then to hell with them."

"Saying that doesn't solve the problem. I've got to do my shopping down there. I've got to meet them every day. And it's even worse in the city, these days, when it comes to robots. New York has just passed an ordinance keeping robots off the streets between sunset and sunrise."

"All right, but they can't stop us from keeping a robot in our home — Grace, this is one of your campaigns. I recognize it. But it's no use. The answer is still no! We're keeping Robbie!"

And yet he loved his wife — and what was worse, his wife knew it. George Weston, after all, was only a man — poor thing — and his wife made full use of every device which a clumsier and more scrupulous sex had learned, with reason and futility, to fear.

Ten times in the ensuing week he cried, "Robbie stays — and that's *final!*" and each time it was weaker and accompanied by a louder and more agonized groan.

Came the day, at last, when Weston approached his daughter guiltily and suggested a "beautiful" visivox show in the village.

Gloria clapped her hands happily. "Can Robbie go?"

"No, dear," he said, and winced at the sound of his voice, "they won't allow robots at the visivox — but you can tell him all about it when you get home." He stumbled all over the last few words and looked away.

Gloria came back from town bubbling over with enthusiasm, for the visivox had been a gorgeous spectacle indeed.

She waited for her father to maneuver the jet car into the sunken garage. "Wait till I tell Robbie, Daddy. He would have liked it like anything. Especially when Francis Fran was backing away so-o-o quietly and backed right into one of the Leopard Men and had to run." She laughed again. "Daddy, are there really Leopard Men on the moon?"

"Probably not," said Weston absently. "It's just funny make-believe." He couldn't take much longer with the car. He'd have to face it.

Gloria ran across the lawn. "Robbie. — Robbie!"

Then she stopped suddenly at the sight of a beautiful collie which regarded her out of serious brown eyes as it wagged its tail on the porch.

"Oh, what a nice dog!" Gloria climbed the steps, approached cautiously, and patted it. "Is it for me, Daddy?"

Her mother had joined them. "Yes, it is, Gloria. Isn't it nice — soft and furry. It's very gentle. It *likes* little girls."

"Can he play games?"

"Surely. He can do any number of tricks. Would you like to see some?"

"Right away. I want Robbie to see him, too. — *Robbie!*" She stopped uncertainly and frowned. "I'll bet he's just staying in his room because he's mad at me for not taking him to the visivox. You'll have to explain to him, Daddy. He might not believe me, but he knows if you say it, it's so."

Weston's lips grew tighter. He looked toward his wife but could not catch her eye.

Gloria turned precipitously and ran down the basement steps, shouting as she went, "Robbie — come and see what Daddy and Mama brought me. They brought me a dog, Robbie."

In a minute she had returned, a frightened little girl. "Mama, Robbie isn't in his room. Where is he?" There was no answer, and George Weston coughed and was suddenly extremely interested in an aimlessly drifting cloud. Gloria's voice quavered on the verge of tears. "Where's Robbie, Mama?"

Mrs. Weston sat down and drew her daughter gently to her. "Don't feel bad, Gloria. Robbie has gone away, I think."

"Gone *away?* Where? Where's he gone away, Mama?"

"No one knows, darling. He just walked away. We've looked and we've looked and we've looked for him, but we can't find him."

"You mean he'll never come back again?" Her eyes were round with horror.

"We may find him soon. We'll keep looking for him. And meanwhile you can play with your nice new doggie. Look at him! His name is Lightning and he can — "

But Gloria's eyelids had overflowed. "I don't want the nasty dog — I want Robbie. I want you to find me Robbie." Her feelings became too deep for words and she spluttered into a shrill wail.

Mrs. Weston glanced at her husband for help, but he merely shuffled his feet morosely and did not withdraw his ardent stare from the heavens, so she bent to the task of consolation. "Why do you cry, Gloria? Robbie was only a machine, just a nasty old machine. He wasn't alive at all."

"He was *not* no machine!" screamed Gloria fiercely and ungrammatically. "He was a *person* like you and me and he was my *friend*. I want him back. Oh, Mama, I want him back."

Her mother groaned in defeat and left Gloria to her sorrow.

"Let her have her cry out," she told her husband. "Childish griefs are never lasting. In a few days she'll forget that awful robot ever existed."

But time proved Mrs. Weston a bit too optimistic. To be sure, Gloria ceased crying, but she ceased smiling, too, and the passing days found her ever more silent and shadowy. Gradually her attitude of passive unhappiness wore Mrs. Weston down, and all that kept her from yielding was the impossibility of admitting defeat to her husband.

Then one evening she flounced into the living room, sat down, folded her arms, and looked boiling mad.

Her husband stretched his neck in order to see her over his newspaper. "What now, Grace?"

"It's that child, George. I've had to send back the dog today. Gloria positively couldn't stand the sight of him, she said. She's driving me into a nervous breakdown."

Weston laid down the paper and a hopeful gleam entered his eye. "Maybe — Maybe we ought to get Robbie back. It might be done, you know. I can get in touch with — "

"No!" she replied grimly. "I won't hear of it. We're not giving up that easily. My child shall *not* be brought up by a robot if it takes years to break her of it."

Weston picked up his paper again with a disappointed air. "A year of this will have me prematurely gray."

"You're a big help, George," was the frigid answer. "What Gloria needs is a change of environment. Of course she can't forget Robbie here. How can she, when every tree and rock reminds her of him? It is really the *silliest* situation I have ever heard of. Imagine a child pining away for the loss of a robot."

"Well, stick to the point. What's the change in environment you're planning?"

"We're going to take her to New York."

"The city! In August! Say, do you know what New York is like in August? It's unbearable."

"Millions do bear it."

"They don't have a place like this to go to. If they didn't have to stay in New York, they wouldn't."

"Well, *we* have to. I say we're leaving now — or as soon as we can make the arrangements. In the city Gloria will find sufficient interests and sufficient friends to perk her up and make her forget that machine."

"Oh, Lord," groaned the lesser half, "those frying pavements!"

"We have to," was the unshaken response. "Gloria has lost five pounds in the last month, and my little girl's health is more important to me than your comfort."

"It's a pity you didn't think of your little girl's health before you deprived her of her pet robot," he muttered — but to himself.

Gloria displayed immediate signs of improvement when told of the impending trip to the city. She spoke little of it, but when she did it was always with lively anticipation. Again she began to smile and to eat with something of her former appetite.

Mrs. Weston hugged herself for joy and lost no opportunity to triumph over her still skeptical husband.

"You see, George, she helps with the packing like a little angel and chatters away as if she hadn't a care in the world. It's just as I told you — all we need do is substitute other interests."

"Hmpph," was the skeptical response. "I hope so."

Preliminaries were gone through quickly. Arrangements were made for the preparation of their city home and a couple were engaged as housekeepers for the country home. When the day of the trip finally did come, Gloria was all but her old self again, and no mention of Robbie passed her lips at all.

In high good humor the family took a taxi-gyro to the airport (Weston would have preferred using his own private gyro, but it was only a two-seater with no room for baggage) and entered the waiting liner.

"Come, Gloria," called Mrs. Weston. "I've saved you a seat near the window so you can watch the scenery."

Gloria trotted down the aisle cheerily, flattened her nose into a white oval against the thick, clear glass, and watched with an intentness that increased as the sudden coughing of the motor drifted backward into the interior. She was too young to be frightened when the ground dropped away as if let through a trap door and she herself suddenly became twice her usual weight, but not too young to be mightily interested. It wasn't until the ground had changed into a tiny patchwork quilt that she withdrew her nose and faced her mother again.

"Will we soon be in the city, Mama?" she asked, rubbing her chilled nose and watching with interest as the patch of moisture which her breath had formed on the pane shrank slowly and vanished.

"In about half an hour, dear." Then, with just the faintest trace of anxiety, "Aren't you glad we're going? Don't you think you'll be very happy in the city with all the buildings and people and things to see? We'll go to the visivox every day and see shows and go to the circus and the beach and — "

"Yes, Mama," was Gloria's unenthusiastic rejoinder. The liner passed over a bank of clouds at the moment, and Gloria was instantly absorbed in the unusual spectacle of clouds underneath one. Then they were over clear sky again, and she turned to her mother with a sudden mysterious air of secret knowledge.

"*I* know why we're going to the city, Mama."

"Do you?" Mrs. Weston was puzzled. "Why, dear?"

"You didn't tell me because you wanted it to be a surprise, but *I* know." For a moment she was lost in admiration at her own acute penetration, and then she laughed gaily. "We're going to New York so we can find Robbie, aren't we? — With detectives."

The statement caught George Weston in the middle of a drink of water, with disastrous results. There was a sort of strangled gasp, a geyser of water, and then a bout of choking coughs. When all was over he stood there, a red-faced, water-drenched, and very, very annoyed person.

Mrs. Weston maintained her composure, but when Gloria repeated her question in a more anxious tone of voice, she found her temper rather bent.

"Maybe," she retorted tartly. "Now sit and be still, for heaven's sake."

New York City, 1998 A.D., was a paradise for the sightseer more than ever in its history. Gloria's parents realized this and made the most of it.

On direct orders from his wife, George Weston arranged to have his business take care of itself for a month or so, in order to be free to spend the time in what he termed "dissipating Gloria to the verge of ruin." Like everything else Weston did, this was gone about in an efficient, thorough, and businesslike way. Before the month had passed nothing that could be done had not been done.

She was taken to the top of the half-mile-tall Roosevelt Building to gaze down in awe upon the jagged panorama of rooftops that blended far off into the fields of Long Island and the flatlands of New Jersey. They visited the zoo, where Gloria stared in delicious fright at the "real live lion" (rather disappointed that the keepers fed him raw steaks instead of human beings, as she had expected), and asked insistently and peremptorily to see "the whale."

The various museums came in for their share of attention, together with the parks and the beaches and the aquarium.

She was taken halfway up the Hudson in an excursion steamer fitted out in the archaism of the mad twenties. She traveled into the stratosphere on an exhibition trip, where the sky turned deep purple and the stars came out and the misty earth below looked like a huge concave bowl. Down under the waters of the Long Island Sound she was taken in a glass-walled subsea vessel, where in a green and wavering world quaint and curious sea things ogled her and wiggled suddenly away.

On a more prosaic level, Mrs. Weston took her to the department stores, where she could revel in another type of fairyland.

In fact, when the month had nearly sped by, the Westons were convinced that everything conceivable had been done to take Gloria's mind once and for all off the departed Robbie — but they were not quite sure they had succeeded.

The fact remained that wherever Gloria went, she displayed the most absorbed and concentrated interest in such robots as happened to be present. No matter how exciting the spectacle before her or how novel to her girlish eyes, she turned instantly if the corner of her eye caught a glimpse of metallic movement.

Mrs. Weston went out of her way to keep Gloria away from all robots.

And the matter was finally climaxed in the episode at the Museum of Science and Industry. The museum had announced a special "children's program" in which exhibits of scientific witchery scaled down to the child mind were to be shown. The Westons, of course, placed it upon their list of "absolutelies."

It was while the Westons were standing totally absorbed in the exploits of a powerful electromagnet that Mrs. Weston suddenly became aware of the fact that Gloria was no longer with her. Initial panic gave way to calm decision, and, enlisting the aid of three attendants, a careful search was begun.

Gloria, of course, was not one to wander aimlessly, however. For her age she was an unusually determined and purposeful girl, quite full of the maternal genes in that respect. She had seen a huge sign on the third floor which had said, "This Way to the Talking Robot." Having spelled it out to herself and having noticed that her parents did not seem to wish to move in the proper direction, she did the obvious thing. Waiting for an opportune moment of parental distraction, she calmly disengaged herself and followed the sign.

The Talking Robot was a *tour de force,* a thoroughly impractical device possessing publicity value only. Once an hour an escorted group stood before it and in careful whispers asked questions of the robot engineer in charge. Those the engineer decided were suitable for the robot's circuits were transmitted to the Talking Robot.

It was rather dull. It may be nice to know that the square of 14 is 196, that the temperature at the moment is 72° Fahrenheit and the air pressure 30.02 inches of mercury, that the atomic weight of sodium is 23, but one doesn't really need a robot for that. One especially does not need an unwieldy, totally immobile mass of wires and coils spreading over twenty-five square yards.

When Gloria entered the room her whole attention was directed to this large thing with the wheels. For a moment she hesitated in dismay. It didn't look like any robot she had ever seen. Cautiously and doubtfully she raised her treble voice. "Please, Mr. Robot, sir, are you the Talking Robot, sir?" She wasn't sure, but it seemed to her that a robot that actually talked was worth a great deal of politeness.

There was an oily whir of gears and a mechanically timbred voice boomed out in words that lacked accent and intonation, "I — am — the — robot — that — talks."

Gloria stared at it ruefully. It *did* talk, but the sound came from inside somewhere. There was no *face* to talk to. She said, "Can you help me, Mr. Robot, sir?"

The Talking Robot was designed to answer questions, and only such questions as it could answer had ever been put to it. It was quite confident of its ability, therefore. "I — can — help — you."

"Thank you, Mr. Robot, sir. Have you seen Robbie?"

"Who — is — Robbie?"

"He's a robot, Mr. Robot, sir." She stretched to tiptoes. "He's about so high, Mr. Robot, sir, only higher, and he's very nice. He's got a head, you know. I mean, you haven't, but he has, Mr. Robot, sir."

The Talking Robot had been left behind. "A — robot?"

"Yes, Mr. Robot, sir. A robot just like you, except he can't talk, of course, and — and looks like a real person."

"A — robot — like — me?"

"Yes, Mr. Robot, sir."

To which the Talking Robot's only response was an erratic splutter and an occasional incoherent sound. The radical generalization offered it, i.e., its existence not as a particular object but as a member of a general group, was too much for it. Loyally, it tried to encompass the concept, and half a dozen coils burned out. Little warning signals were buzzing.

Gloria stood waiting with carefully concealed impatience for the machine's answer, when she heard behind her the cry of "There she is," and recognized that cry as her mother's.

"What are you doing here, you bad girl?" cried Mrs. Weston, anxiety dissolving at once into anger. "Do you know you frightened your mama and daddy almost to death? Why did you run away?"

The robot engineer had also dashed in, tearing his hair and demanding who of the gathering crowd had tampered with the machine. "Can't anybody read signs?" he yelled. "You're not allowed in here without an attendant."

Gloria raised her grieved voice over the din. "I only came to see the Talking Robot, Mama. I thought he might know where Robbie was because they're both robots." And then, as the thought of Robbie was suddenly brought forcefully home to her, she burst into a sudden storm of tears. "And I *got* to find Robbie, Mama. I *got* to."

Mrs. Weston strangled a cry and said, "Oh, good heavens! Come home, George. This is more than I can stand."

That evening George Weston left for several hours, and the next morning he approached his wife with something that looked suspiciously like smug complacence.

"I've got an idea, Grace."

"About what?" was the gloomy, uninterested query.

"About Gloria."

"You're not going to suggest buying back that robot?"

"No, of course not."

"Then go ahead. I might as well listen to you. Nothing *I've* done seems to have done any good."

"All right. Here's what I've been thinking. The whole trouble with Gloria is that she thinks of Robbie as a *person* and not as a *machine*. Naturally, she can't forget him. Now if we managed to convince her that Robbie was nothing more than a mess of steel and copper in the form of sheets and wires, with electricity its juice of life, how long would her longings last? It's the psychological attack, if you see my point."

"How do you plan to do it?"

"Simple. Where do you suppose I went last night? I persuaded Robertson of US Robots and Mechanical Men, Inc., to arrange for a complete tour of his premises tomorrow. The three of us will go, and by the time we're through Gloria will have it drilled into her that a robot is *not* alive."

Mrs. Weston's eyes widened gradually, and something glinted in her eyes that was quite like sudden admiration. "Why George, that's a *good* idea."

And George Weston's vest buttons strained. "Only kind I have," he said.

Mr. Struthers was a conscientious general manager and naturally inclined to be a bit talkative. The combination, therefore, resulted in a tour that was fully explained, perhaps even overabundantly explained, at every step. However, Mrs. Weston was not bored. Indeed, she stopped him several times and begged him to repeat his statements in simpler language so that Gloria might understand. Under the influence of this appreciation of his narrative powers, Mr. Struthers expanded genially and became even more communicative, if possible.

George Weston, himself, showed a gathering impatience.

"Pardon me, Struthers," he said, breaking into the middle of a lecture on the photoelectric cell, "haven't you a section of the factory where only robot labor is employed?"

"Eh? Oh, yes! Yes, indeed!" He smiled at Mrs. Weston. "A vicious circle in a way, robots creating more robots. Of course, we are not making a general practice out of it. For one thing, the unions would never let us. But we can turn out a very few robots using robot labor exclusively, merely as a sort of scientific experiment. You see" — he tapped his pince-nez into one palm argumentatively — "what the labor unions don't realize — and I say this as a man who has always been very sympathetic with the labor movement in general — is that the advent of the robot, while involving some dislocation to begin with, will inevitably — "

"Yes, Struthers," said Weston, "but about that section of the factory you speak of — may we see it? It would be very interesting, I'm sure."

"Yes! Yes, of course!" Mr. Struthers replaced his pince-nez in one convulsive movement and gave vent to a soft cough of discomfiture. "Follow me, please."

He was comparatively quiet while leading the three through a long corridor and down a flight of stairs. Then, when they had entered a large well-lit room that buzzed with metallic activity, the sluices opened and the flood of explanation poured forth again.

"There you are!" he said with pride in his voice. "Robots only! Five men act as overseers and they don't even stay in this room. In five years, that is, since we began this project, not a single accident has occurred. Of course, the robots here assembled are comparatively simple, but . . ."

The general manager's voice had long since died to a rather soothing murmur in Gloria's ears. The whole trip seemed rather dull and pointless to her, though there *were* many robots in sight. None were even remotely like Robbie, though, and she surveyed them with open contempt.

In this room there weren't any people at all, she noticed. Then her eyes fell upon six or seven robots busily engaged at a round table halfway across the room. They widened in incredulous surprise. It was a big room. She couldn't see for sure, but one of the robots looked like — looked like — *it was!*

"Robbie!" Her shriek pierced the air, and one of the robots about the table faltered and dropped the tool he was holding. Gloria went almost mad with joy. Squeezing through the railing before either parent could stop her, she dropped lightly to the floor a few feet below and ran toward her Robbie, arms waving and hair flying.

And the three horrified adults, as they stood frozen in their tracks, saw what the excited little girl did not see — a huge, lumbering tractor bearing blindly down upon its appointed track.

It took split seconds for Weston to come to his senses, and those split seconds meant everything, for Gloria could not be overtaken. Although Weston vaulted the railing in a wild attempt, it was obviously hopeless. Mr. Struthers signaled wildly to the overseers to stop the tractor, but the overseers were only human, and it took time to act.

It was only Robbie that acted immediately and with precision.

With metal legs eating up the space between himself and his little mistress he charged down from the opposite direction. Everything then happened at once. With one sweep of an arm Robbie snatched up Gloria, slackening his speed not one iota, and consequently knocking every breath of air out of her. Weston, not quite comprehending all that was happening, felt, rather than saw, Robbie brush past him, and came to a sudden, bewildered halt. The tractor intersected Gloria's path half a second after Robbie had, rolled on ten feet farther, and came to a grinding, long-drawn-out stop.

Gloria regained her breath, submitted to a series of passionate hugs on the part of both her parents, and turned eagerly toward Robbie. As far as she was concerned, nothing had happened except that she had found her friend.

But Mrs. Weston's expression had changed from one of relief to one of dark suspicion. She turned to her husband, and despite her disheveled and undignified appearance managed to look quite formidable. *"You* engineered this, *didn't* you?"

George Weston swabbed at a hot forehead with his handkerchief. His hand was unsteady, and his lips could curve only into a tremulous and exceedingly weak smile.

Mrs. Weston pursued the thought. "Robbie wasn't designed for engineering or construction work. He couldn't be of any use to them. You had him placed there deliberately so that Gloria would find him. You know you did."

"Well, I did," said Weston. "But, Grace, how was I to know the reunion would be so violent? And Robbie has saved her life; you'll have to admit that. You *can't* send him away again."

Grace Weston considered. She turned toward Gloria and Robbie and watched them abstractedly for a moment. Gloria had a grip about the robot's neck that would have asphyxiated any creature but one of metal, and was prattling nonsense in half-hysterical frenzy. Robbie's chrome-steel arms (capable of bending a bar of steel two inches in diameter into a pretzel) wound about the little girl gently and lovingly, and his eyes glowed a deep, deep red.

"Well," said Mrs. Weston at last, "I guess he can stay with us until he rusts."

S

sen/ses — smell, touch, sight, hearing, and taste. In science fiction, mutants and aliens usually have enhanced senses of one kind or another. Sometimes, as in the following story, the senses are mixed, with funny or tragic results.

The Man with English

H. L. GOLD

Lying in the hospital, Edgar Stone added up his misfortunes as another might count blessings. There were enough to infuriate the most temperate man, which Stone notoriously was not. He smashed his fist down, accidentally hitting the metal side of the bed, and was astonished by the pleasant feeling. It enraged him even more. The really maddening thing was how simply he had goaded himself into the hospital.

He'd locked up his drygoods store and driven home for lunch. Nothing unusual about that; he did it every day. With his miserable digestion, he couldn't stand the restaurant food in town. He pulled into the driveway, rode over a collection of metal shapes his son Arnold had left lying around, and punctured a tire.

"Rita!" he yelled. "This is going too damned far! Where is that brat?"

"In here," she called truculently from the kitchen.

He kicked open the screen door. His foot went through the mesh.

"A ripped tire and a torn screen!" he shouted at Arnold, who was sprawled in angular adolescence over a blueprint on the kitchen table. "You'll pay for them, by God! They're coming out of your allowance!"

"I'm sorry, Pop," the boy said.

"Sorry, my left foot," Mrs. Stone shrieked. She whirled on her husband. "You could have watched where you were going. He promised to clean up his things from the driveway right after lunch. And it's about time you stopped kicking open the door every time you're mad."

"Mad? Who wouldn't be mad? Me hoping he'd get out of school and come into the store, and he wants to be an engineer. An engineer — and he can't even make change when he — hah! — helps me out in the store!"

"He'll be whatever he wants to be," she screamed in the conversational tone of the Stone household.

"Please," said Arnold. "I can't concentrate on this plan."

Edgar Stone was never one to restrain an angry impulse. He tore up the blueprint and flung the pieces down on the table.

"Aw, Pop!" Arnold protested.

"Don't say 'Aw, Pop' to me. You're not going to waste a summer vacation on junk like this. You'll eat your lunch and come down to the store. And you'll do it every day for the rest of the summer!"

"Oh, he will, will he?" demanded Mrs. Stone. "He'll catch up on his studies. And as for you, you can go back and eat in a restaurant."

"You know I can't stand that slop!"

"You'll eat it because you're not having lunch here any more. I've got enough to do without making three meals a day."

"But I can't drive back with that tire — "

He did, though not with the tire — he took a cab. It cost a dollar plus tip, lunch was a dollar and a half plus tip, and bicarb at Rite Drug Store a few doors away and in a great hurry came to another fifteen cents — only it didn't work.

And then Miss Ellis came in for some material. Miss Ellis could round out any miserable day. She was fifty, tall, skinny, and had thin, disapproving lips. She had a sliver of cloth, clipped very meagerly off a hem, which she intended to use as a sample.

"The arms of the slipcover on my reading chair wore through," she informed him. "I bought the material here, if you remember."

Stone didn't have to look at the fragmentary swatch. "That was about seven years ago — "

"Six and a half," she corrected. "I paid enough for it. You'd expect anything that expensive to last."

"The style was discontinued. I have something here that — "

"I do not want to make an entire slipcover, Mr. Stone. All I want is enough to make new panels for the arms. Two yards should do very nicely."

Stone smothered a bilious hiccup. "Two yards, Miss Ellis?"

"At the most."

"I sold the last of that material years ago." He pulled a bolt off a shelf and partly unrolled it for her. "Why not use a different pattern as a kind of contrast?"

"I want this same pattern," she said, her thin lips getting even thinner and more obstinate.

"Then I'll have to order it and hope one of my wholesalers still has some of it in stock."

"Not without looking for it first right here, you won't order it for me. You can't know *all* these materials you have on these shelves."

Stone felt all the familiar symptoms of fury — the sudden pulsing of the temples, the lurch and bump of his heart as adrenalin came surging in like the tide at the Firth of Forth, the quivering of his hands, the angry shout pulsing at his vocal cords from below.

"I'll take a look, Miss Ellis," he said.

She was president of the Ladies' Cultural Society and dominated it so thoroughly that the members would go clear to the next town for their dry goods, rather than deal with him, if he offended this sour stick of stubbornness.

If Stone's life insurance salesman had been there, he would have tried to keep Stone from climbing the ladder that ran around the three walls of the store. He probably wouldn't have been in time. Stone stamped up the ladder to reach the highest shelves, where there were scraps of bolts. One of them might have been the remnant of the material Miss Ellis had bought six and a half years ago. But Stone never found out.

He snatched one, glaring down meanwhile at the top of Miss Ellis's head, and the ladder skidded out from under him. He felt his skull collide with the counter. He didn't feel it hit the floor.

"God damn it!" Stone yelled. "You could at least turn on the lights."

"There, there, Edgar. Everything's fine, just fine."

It was his wife's voice and the tone was so uncommonly soft and soothing that it scared him into a panic.

"What's wrong with me?" he asked piteously. "Am I blind?"

"How many fingers am I holding up?" a man wanted to know.

Stone was peering into the blackness. All he could see before his eyes was a vague blot against a darker blot.

"None," he bleated. "Who are you?"

"Dr. Rankin. That was a nasty fall you had, Mr. Stone — concussion of course, and a splinter of bone driven into the brain. I had to operate to remove it."

"Then you cut out a nerve!" Stone said. "You did something to my eyes!"

The doctor's voice sounded puzzled. "There doesn't seem to be anything wrong with them. I'll take a look, though, and see."

"You'll be all right, dear," Mrs. Stone said reassuringly, but she didn't sound as if she believed it.

"Sure you will, Pop," said Arnold.

"Is that young stinker here?" Stone demanded. "He's the cause of all this!"

"Temper, temper," the doctor said. "Accidents happen."

Stone heard him lower the venetian blinds. As if they had been a switch, light sprang up and everything in the hospital became brightly visible.

"Well!" said Stone. "That's more like it. It's night and you're trying to save electricity, hey?"

"It's broad daylight, Edgar dear," his wife protested. "All Dr. Rankin did was lower the blinds and — "

"Please," the doctor said. "If you don't mind, I'd rather take care of any explanations that have to be made."

He came at Stone with an ophthalmoscope. When he flashed it into Stone's eyes, everything went black and Stone let him know it vociferously.

"Black?" Dr. Rankin repeated blankly. "Are you positive? Not a sudden glare?"

"Black," insisted Stone. "And what's the idea of putting me in a bed filled with bread crumbs?"

"It was freshly made — "

"Crumbs. You heard me. And the pillow has rocks in it."

"What else is bothering you?" asked the doctor worriedly.

"It's freezing in here." Stone felt the terror rise in him again. "It was summer when I fell off the ladder. Don't tell me I've been unconscious clear through till winter!"

"No, Pop," said Arnold. "That was yesterday — "

"I'll take care of this," Dr. Rankin said firmly. "I'm afraid you and your son will have to leave, Mrs. Stone. I have to do a few tests on your husband."

"Will he be all right?" she appealed.

"Of course, of course," he said inattentively, peering with a frown at the shivering patient. "Shock, you know," he added vaguely.

"Gosh, Pop," said Arnold. "I'm sorry this happened. I got the driveway all cleaned up."

"And we'll take care of the store till you're better," Mrs. Stone promised.

"Don't you dare!" yelled Stone. "You'll put me out of business!"

The doctor hastily shut the door on them and came back to the bed. Stone was clutching the light summer blanket around himself. He felt colder than he'd ever been in his life.

"Can't you get me more blankets?" he begged. "You don't want me to die of pneumonia, do you?"

Dr. Rankin opened the blinds and asked, "What's this like?"

"Night," chattered Stone. "A new idea to save electricity — hooking up the blinds to the light switch?"

The doctor closed the blinds and sat down beside the bed. He was sweating as he reached for the signal button and pressed it. A nurse came in, blinking in their direction.

"Why don't you turn on the light?" she asked.

"Huh?" said Stone. "They are."

"Nurse, I'm Dr. Rankin. Get me a piece of sandpaper, some cotton swabs, an ice cube, and Mr. Stone's lunch."

"Is there anything he shouldn't eat?"

"That's what I want to find out. Hurry, please."

"And some blankets," Stone put in, shaking with the chill.

"Blankets, Doctor?" she asked, startled.

"Half a dozen will do," he said. "I think."

It took her ten minutes to return with all the items. Stone wanted them to keep adding blankets until all seven were on him. He still felt cold.

"Maybe some hot coffee?" he suggested.

The doctor nodded and the nurse poured a cup, added the spoon and a half of sugar he requested, and he took a mouthful. He sprayed it out violently.

"Ice cold!" he yelped. "And who put salt in it?"

"Salt?" She fumbled around on the tray. "It's so dark here — "

"I'll attend to it," Dr. Rankin said hurriedly. "Thank you."

She walked cautiously to the door and went out.

"Try this," said the doctor, after filling another cup.

"Well, that's better!" Stone exclaimed. "Damned practical joker. They shouldn't be allowed to work in hospitals."

"And now, if you don't mind," said the doctor, "I'd like to try several tests."

Stone was still angry at the trick played on him, but he cooperated willingly.

Dr. Rankin finally sagged back in the chair. The sweat ran down his face and into his collar, and his expression was so dazed that Stone was alarmed.

"What's wrong, Doctor? Am I going to — going to — "

"No, no. It's not that. No danger. At least, I don't believe there is. But I can't even be sure of that any more."

"You can't be sure if I'll live or die?"

"Look." Dr. Rankin grimly pulled the chair closer. "It's broad daylight and yet you can't see until I darken the room. The coffee was hot and sweet, but it was cold and salty to you, so I added an ice cube and a spoonful of salt and it tasted fine, you said. This is one of the hottest days on record and you're freezing. You told me the sandpaper felt smooth and satiny, then yelled that somebody had put pins in the cotton swabs, when there weren't any, of course. I've tried you out with different colors around the room and you saw violet when you should have seen yellow, green for red, orange for blue, and so on. Now do you understand?"

"No," said Stone frightenedly. "What's wrong?"

"All I can do is guess. I had to remove that sliver of bone from your brain. It apparently shorted your sensory nerves."

"And what happened?"

"Every one of your senses has been reversed. You feel cold for heat, heat for cold, smooth for rough, rough for smooth, sour for sweet, sweet for sour, and so forth. And you see colors backward."

Stone sat up. "Murderer! Thief! You've ruined me!"

The doctor sprang for a hypodermic and sedative. Just in time, he changed his mind and took a bottle of stimulant instead. It worked fine, though injecting it into his screaming, thrashing patient took more strength than he'd known he owned. Stone fell asleep immediately.

There were nine blankets on Stone and he had a bag of cement for a pillow when he had his lawyer, Manny Lubin, in to hear the charges he wanted brought against Dr. Rankin. The doctor was there to defend himself. Mrs. Stone was present in spite of her husband's objections — "She always takes everybody's side against me," he explained in a roar.

"I'll be honest with you, Mr. Lubin," the doctor said, after Stone had finished on a note of shrill frustration. "I've hunted for cases like this in medical history and this is the first one ever to be reported. Except," he amended quickly, "that I haven't reported it yet. I'm hoping it reverses itself. That sometimes happens, you know."

"And what am I supposed to do in the meantime?" raged Stone. "I'll have to go out wearing an overcoat in the summer and shorts in the winter — people will think I'm a maniac. And they'll be sure of it because I'll have to keep the store closed during the day and open at night — I can't see except in the dark. And matching materials! I can't stand the feel of smooth cloth and I see colors backward!" He glared at the doctor before turning back to Lubin. "How would you like to have to put sugar on your food and salt in your coffee?"

"But we'll work it out, Edgar dear," his wife soothed. "Arnold and I can take care of the store. You always wanted him to come into the business, so that ought to please you — "

"As long as I'm there to watch him!"

"And Dr. Rankin said maybe things will straighten out."

"What about that, Doctor?" asked Lubin. "What are the chances?"

Dr. Rankin looked uncomfortable. "I don't know. This has never happened before. All we can do is hope."

"Hope, nothing!" Stone stormed. "I want to sue him. He had no right to go meddling around and turn me upside down. Any jury would give me a quarter of a million!"

"I'm no millionaire, Mr. Stone," said the doctor.

"But the hospital has money. We'll sue him and the trustees."

There was a pause while the attorney thought. "I'm afraid we wouldn't have a case, Mr. Stone." He went on more rapidly as Stone sat up, shivering, to argue loudly. "It was an emergency operation. Any surgeon would have had to operate. Am I right, Dr. Rankin?"

The doctor explained what would have happened if he had not removed the pressure on the brain, resulting from the concussion, and the danger that the bone splinter, if not extracted, might have gone on traveling and caused possible paralysis or death.

"That would be better than this," said Stone.

"But medical ethics couldn't allow him to let you die," Lubin objected. "He was doing his duty. That's point one."

"Mr. Lubin is absolutely right, Edgar," said Mrs. Stone.

"There, you see?" screamed her husband. "Everybody's right but me! Will you get her out of here before I have a stroke?"

"Her interests are also involved," Lubin pointed out. "Point two is that the emergency came first; the after-effects couldn't be known or considered."

Dr. Rankin brightened. "Any operation involves risk, even the excising of a corn. I had to take those risks."

"*You* had to take them?" Stone scoffed. "All right, what are you leading up to, Lubin?"

"We'd lose," said the attorney.

Stone subsided, but only for a moment. "So we'll lose. But if we sue, the publicity would ruin him. I want to sue!"

"For what, Edgar dear?" his wife persisted. "We'll have a hard enough time managing. Why throw good money after bad?"

"Why didn't I marry a woman who'd take my side, even when I'm wrong?" moaned Stone. "Revenge, that's what. And he won't be able to practice, so he'll have time to find out if there's a cure . . . and at no charge, either! I won't pay him another cent!"

The doctor stood up eagerly. "But I'm willing to see what can be done right now. And it wouldn't cost you anything, naturally."

"What do you mean?" Stone challenged suspiciously.

"If I were to perform another operation, I'll be able to see which nerves were involved. There's no need to go into the technical side right now, but it is possible to connect nerves. Of course, there are a good many, which complicates matters, especially since the splinter went through several layers — "

Lubin pointed a lawyer's impaling finger at him. "Are you offering to attempt to correct the injury — gratis?"

"Certainly. I mean to say, I'll do my absolute best. But keep in mind, please, that there is no medical precedent."

The attorney, however, was already questioning Stone and his wife. "In view of the fact that we have no legal grounds whatever for suit, does this offer of settlement satisfy your claim against him?"

"Oh, yes!" Mrs. Stone cried.

Her husband hesitated for a while, clearly tempted to take the opposite position out of habit. "I guess so," he reluctantly agreed.

"Well, then it's in your hands, Doctor," said Lubin.

Dr. Rankin buzzed excitedly for the nurse. "I'll have him prepared for surgery right away."

"It better work this time," warned Stone, clutching a handful of ice cubes to warm his fingers.

Stone came to foggily. He didn't know it, but he had given the anesthetist a bewildering problem, which finally had been solved by using fumes of aromatic spirits of ammonia. The four blurred figures around the bed seemed to be leaning precariously toward him.

"Pop!" said Arnold. "Look, he's coming out of it! Pop!"

"Speak to me, Edgar dear," Mrs. Stone beseeched.

Lubin said, "See how he is, Doctor."

"He's fine," the doctor insisted heartily, his usual bedside manner evidently having returned. "He must be — the blinds are open and he's not complaining that it's dark or that he's cold." He leaned over the bed. "How are we feeling, Mr. Stone?"

It took a minute or two for Stone to move his swollen tongue enough to answer. He wrinkled his nose in disgust.

"What smells purple?" he demanded.

space op/er/a — a science fiction term for adventure stories off of the planet Earth. The name comes from the term "horse opera," used to describe Western stories and films. In the space opera, the blaster replaces the six-shooter, the spaceship the horse, and the astronaut the cowboy. Good tales in this genre capture the sense of wonder that is the hallmark of science fiction. One of the most famous space opera series is the Lensmen novels of E. E. Smith (BJ Publishing Group, 1973–).

Transsar

RAYMOND E. BANKS

The small group of Earth colonists stood on a hill, tense and expectant, as their leader advanced. He walked slowly away from the huddled mob, holding up his gun. You could hear the mother weep.

I stood at ease to one side, as was proper. I knew what would happen, because I was from Transstar. We have been taught to understand the inevitable.

The child came running out of the woods. I noted that they were not the woods of Earth, though they were brown. Nor was the grass the grass of Earth, though it was green.

The child cried, "Mother!" The leader raised his gun and shot it.

Even though I understood that the child was no longer a "him" and had become an "it" since falling into the hands of the aliens, I felt a tremor underneath my conditioning. In Transstar you are taught that the conditioning is a sheath, pliable but breakable; you do not put all faith in it.

Now the important thing was the reaction of the small group of Earth colonists.

They had seen the heartbreaking inevitable. They knew with the logic of their minds that the boy had to die. On this planet there were two races, two kinds of life: the eaber and the Earthmen. The eaber would lure a child away if they could and see to its infection, returning it to the Earth colony.

It was a good trick the first time or two, and for the love of their children three thousand lives had been lost, two starting colonies wiped out. This third colony had to succeed. I suspected that was why Transstar sent me here.

The leader turned sadly towards his colonists. A man advanced: "A burial! It is safe to bury!"

"It is not safe to bury," said the leader.

The man raised his arm. The leader hesitated and lost both his leadership and his life, because the half-maddened parent shot him in the chest . . .

Rackrill came to my Transstar ship. "You stood there," he said, eyes accusing. "You sit here now. You let the eaber do these things to us — yet you're from Transstar, representing the incredible power of the Sol system. Why?"

"Transstar was formed to handle star-sized situations," I replied. "So far this colony is meeting only the problems of a local situation."

"Local situation!" He laughed bitterly. "I'm the third mayor in three weeks."

"There'll be no more children lost to the eaber," I said.

"That's for certain sure," he said, "but Transstar might lose one of its representatives if it doesn't help us in our fight against the eaber. Our colony is sickened to watch you with your magnificent starship and your empire of power, standing by while we suffer."

"I am sorry."

He raised his hands and stepped towards me, but an orange light hummed from the walls. He looked surprised. He dropped his hands.

"Now that you've properly cursed me, tell me the real reason for your visit, Mr. Mayor," I said, flicking the protective button off.

He eased into his chair wearily. It was a great planet to take the starch out of the leaders.

"We had a visit from the eaber." He went on talking eagerly. The eaber had picked this planet, Point Everready, as an advance planet-city for their own culture. They would kill the Earth colony if it didn't leave. Rackrill had told them about Transstar, about me. That I represented the total war capacity of the solar system. That I was in instantaneous touch with Transstar Prime, near Mars, and that behind me stood a million space ships and countless prime fighting men with weapons of power and vigor that could pulverize the eaber to dust. That I was there to see that the Earth colony survived.

"This is only partly true," I said. "I am here to see *whether* an Earth colony can survive."

Anyway, Rackrill had gotten the eaber stirred up. They were coming to see me. Okay?

"I am Transstar," I said. "I can only observe, not interfere."

He got mad again, but there was really no more to say. He left, going from the marvelous machinery of my ship back to the crudeness of the village. I felt sorry for him and his people and wished I could reassure him.

I could not.

Yet somewhere back at Transstar Prime there was more than ordinary interest in Point Everready. I wondered, as every Transstar agent must, how far Transstar would go on this project. Few Transstar men have ordered Condition Prime Total Red. Condition Prime Total Red is the complete amassing and release of our total war-making capacity directed at one enemy in one place at one time. You don't get a CPTR more than once in decades; men in Transstar have served a lifetime and never directed one.

This is good, because CPTR is devastating in cost, machines, and men. It is the most jealously guarded prerogative of the Transstar system, which is in itself merely a check-and-report to keep track of all Earth colonies spread out among the stars.

I looked at my condition panel. It glowed an off-white on the neat starship wall. Condition white, nothing unusual; the same color I had stared at for five years as a full agent and fifteen years before that as both associate and assistant, learning the Transstar operation.

I thought about the dead boy, sleeping now on the grasses of Everready, as I made my daily report, pricking a card with three simple marks, feeding it to the transmitter which reported back to Prime. It seemed unfair, even with all my years of Transstar conditioning, that a boy would only deserve three pinpricks in a daily report. The human race had not been standing behind him.

It probably would not stand behind this colony.

For that matter, though I had the safety of this rather expensive starship, the human race would probably not stand behind *me,* if the eaber turned out to be tough aliens. Many an agent has died in local or regional situations.

I drank a cup of tea, but the warm drink didn't help. Somehow these last years I had become more emotional. It was hard to be a Transstar agent — for, by the time you learned how, you were too knowing in the ways of space to keep that prep school enthusiasm. I remembered the men who had lived and the men who had died as I drank my tea and felt sad.

Towards midnight the colonists sent scout ships up, as ordered by Rackrill. They were met by an equal number of eaber scout ships.

The patrol fight was dull, with drones being chopped off by both sides. Nothing decisive. The eaber were good. I wondered if they also had a Transstar somewhere back at their home planet, a totality of force that might match Condition Prime Total Red, and result in a stand-off fight. This had never happened in history. Someday we might even find somebody better than CPTR.

At that instant expansion to the stars would stop, I knew.

Whatever I thought about the eaber at long distance, I'd have a chance to learn more. A couple of them were now approaching my ship.

They were sentient life. They were neither monsters nor particularly Earth-like. It was this balance of like-unlike that gave me the beginnings of a shudder under my conditioning.

The reddish one advanced into my cabin. "Euben," he said. He made a motion of turning with his hands, tapered fingers spread. A surge of sickness tickled in me, rushed up to a nerve agony. I just had time to relax and let the raping power of his ray, or whatever it was, knock me out into a welcome darkness. A nonconditioned man would have screamed and writhed on the floor, fighting the overpowering darkness. I rushed with it, gave in to it.

Presently there was a gentle bird-twitter. I sat up; Euben's power turned off. He laughed down at me.

"Some Earth-power, some potency," he said, gesturing at my control panel. I had, indeed, pushed my orange safety button, which should have frozen him immobile as it had Rackrill. It had no effect on him or his friend.

I tried to get up but was as weak and shaking as an old man. So I sat there.

"You are the protector to the Earthians," he said.

"No, Euben. I am merely here to observe."

"You'll observe them made extinct, Watcher," he said. "This is the perimeter of eaber. We want this planet ourselves."

"That remains to be seen," I said, finally rising stiffly and plopping into my chair. I turned off the useless orange button.

Euben roamed his eyes around the ship. "Better than your colony has. You are special."

"I am special," I said.

"They say you represent great power," he said.

"That is true."

"We have waited a long time to see this power," said Euben. "We have exterminated two of your colonies, and have not seen it."

"If this is all of eaber, it isn't very large," I said. "This planet could hardly hold a hundred thousand."

"I said we were perimeter. Behind us, thousands of planets. Trillions of eaber. There is nothing like us in the universe."

"We've heard that before."

This time he brought up two hands, to begin his twirling. I reacted with a hypnosis block, which shunted off all my natural functions for a micro-second (with the help of the plate I was standing on). The pain was much less. He merely brought me to my knees.

"Ah, you are not totally feeble," he said. "Still I make you bow to me with the twisting of my bare hands in the air."

"Yes. But Earthmen do not greet new races with tricks and talk like two small boys bragging about how tough their older brothers are," I said. "I am not here to brag tough. I am here to observe."

"If you don't like what you observe?"

"Perhaps we will do something about it. Perhaps not."

He threw back his head and laughed. "You will die, die, die," he said. "Watch this." He nudged the other eaber who stepped forward and brought something out of his robe.

It was a boned, dehydrated human.

The thing — evidently a human survivor of an earlier colony — had the floppy, mindless manner of a puppy dog, mewling and whimpering on its long chain. Euben snapped his fingers. The former human ki-yied and scampered back under its owner's robe.

"Cute," said Euben. "De-skeletoned Earthmen bring a good price in the pet-shops of eaber, so you are not a total loss in the universe."

There came a sudden scream and convulsion from the eaber's robe. The eaber jumped back. The tragic, deboned human fell to the floor dead, spending a thin, too-bright red ebb of blood.

"Eh — how did you do that?" asked Euben, stepping back a little.

"I am Transstar," I said. "Certain things we do not permit with our life-form. I urge you not to continue this practice."

"So — " said Euben toeing at the dead man. "And he was so cute, too. Ah, well. There are more out there."

I controlled my voice and did not look down. "Can you establish your need for this planet?" I asked.

"Yes. We are eaber; that is enough anywhere in space."

I stepped to a wall chart and made a gesture. "This planet also falls along our perimeter. We occupy this space — so. We have well utilized the solar and alpha planet systems, and it is time that we move out once more. This planet is but one of a thousand Earth colonies moving out to new space."

Euben shook his head. "What a ridiculous civilization! All space in this arc is eaber. We close the door, so — "

He made a fast gesture with his hand that tore inside of me, like a hot knife, scraping the bottom of my lungs. I was pretty much riding on my conditioning now. I was sickened, angry with Euben and his race. But it was slightly different from dealing with an Earth neighbor you dislike. Bravery and caution! Always bravery — and caution.

"So you block us here," I said. "Perhaps we will go elsewhere for a hundred or a thousand years. It's no use to fight over space. There are millions of planets."

"Do you truly believe so?" smiled Euben. "Naive! The eaber do not like unknown life-forms prowling the universe. We will come to solar and alpha, as you call them, and put you on a chain like that one dead on the floor."

"We might resist that," I said.

"How?" said Euben, bringing a black box out from under his robe.

I have had my share of black boxes in my Transstar years. Before it was barely in sight, I had retreated to my all-purpose closet. He laughed, peering at me through the observation window and trying the various rays and whatnot in his weapon. Nothing much happened for a while — heat, radiation, gas, sonic vibrations, the standard stuff. Pretty soon I knew he could take me; but it would take him about three days. Fair enough.

The eaber were tough, but not unbeatable — at least on what he had shown me.

He put away his black box. I stepped through the door. Decontamination worked all right, but the heat-reducer was wheezing like an asthma victim in a grain field.

"So. You are junior good," said Euben. He turned and left the ship, whistling in a very Earthian way, not bothering to look back.

The other eaber remained. I offered him a cup of tea, which he drank greedily. He had something that looked a little like a serpent's tongue which he ran quickly over the control board panels. He sniff-tasted the instruments, the furnishings, the modest weapons and communications equipment I had. Then he stepped back.

"You will not survive eaber," he said. He left, not bothering to step over the deboned Earthman.

I picked up the soft, cooling mass and set it on the TV cradle. I didn't call through channels. I slapped the Transstar Central button and let them have a look at the creature on the plate.

Hennessy was on the monitor at Transstar Prime, near Mars. He gasped. "That's not good," he said. "Just a minute."

I sank into the chair and made more tea with shaking hands. The screen above me lighted and I was staring at Twelve. Thirteen is as high as you get in Transstar. "You've bought it," he said. "In your arc you have the only mind-contact with the eaber. Elsewhere they've only made patrol war."

"Anybody solved them?" I asked.

"Yes and no," said Twelve Jackson slowly. "They can hit us with a freeze-burn system they've got. Explodes you. We can reach them with most of our conventionals, but they don't die easily. Range and depth of their civilization, unknown."

I told him about their trillion — according to Euben. Then I asked, "What's my condition?"

Jackson hesitated and I saw his hands twiddle over his buttons. "Condition orange," he said, taking me off white. Power reached through space. In seventy-five seconds I could feel the sudden, subtle shift in the ship's power fields, as they built up.

"Don't get excited," he said. "I've got a dozen oranges on the board."

"What about the colony here?" I said.

"A colony is a local situation," said Jackson. "Unfortunately, if we squandered our life-power every time a few colonists died, we'd still be confined to the moon. They colonize of their own free will."

I touched the dead Earthman.

"Yeah," he said. "Nobody knew about that. It'll get your planet plenty of free space in the TV casts. We'll get a little blubbering from the League for Space Safety."

"It makes me want to blubber a little myself," I said.

Twelve Jackson gave me a long, hard look. "Stay Transstar or get out," he said.

I gave him the rest of my report-interview on the tape and tried to get some sleep. The eaber came over the colony about midnight and bombed it a little, and I groaned awake.

It must have been a half hour later that I heard a scratching on the ship's window. It was Rackrill, peering in at me.

When I joined him in the soft spring night he was excited.

"I've got something to show your high-falutin boys back at Mars," he said. "A real something."

We went in silence to his headquarters through the sweet night grasses of Everready. It was truly a planet of richness and beauty in a natural sense, and I thought again of the contrast of the poisoned boy and the monstrosities of human pets that the eaber had created under this moon, in their eaber cities, on this fine world.

My mood was shattered the instant we stepped into Rackrill's combination mayor's home and administration center. The Colony Correspondent had arrived.

There are simply too many Earth colonies for the space news services to cover them all. So they assign a Colony correspondent to cover the whole arc, and you always find them where the most trouble is.

This one was a woman. She was of the young, peppy breed of females that start out life as a tomboy and remain in trouble all of their lives because they like to take chances. I was doubly disturbed. First, because it meant that wildly distorted stories would soon be muddying things back in solar and alpha; second, because this cute lady reminded me of my own Alicia, who had been a Transstar agent along with me, back a seeming thousand years ago when I was merely a Four. She had the same snapping black eyes, the same statuesque figure, the same light-humored air.

"Well, so Transstar is really here!" she said. "Hey, Chief, how about a Transstar quote?"

"Young lady, I am not Chief," I said drily. "My name is Webster, and I hold the Transstar rank of Seven, and you well know that all Transstar quotes must come from Transstar Prime."

"Those fossilized, dehumanized old men on Mars," she said. "Never mind. I'll find my own stories."

"Not here you won't," said Rackrill, with authority's natural fear of the tapes. "It's past midnight. Go to bed. Tomorrow my tape man will give you a tour."

She stuck out her tongue. "I've had the tour. They're all alike, full of lies and grease, signifying nothing. Only thing I ever learned on an official tour was how to defend myself against the passes of the tape men."

But she allowed herself to be pushed out. I guess it was the near-tragic urgency of our manner.

Rackrill led me into an inner room. On the bed rested a woman, but there was a strangeness to her. She was ancient in her skin, yet something about her bones told you she was hardly thirty. Her flesh was blue-splotched, the eyes animal-bright. Rackrill gestured at her; she whimpered and squirmed in her bed.

I laid a hand on his arm. "The eaber can hypnotize and make a hand gesture that tears you apart inside," I said. "Don't hold up your hands in front of her."

"We got her story," said Rackrill, low-voiced. "She's been a prisoner of the eaber for over a year. From Colony Two, I guess. The eaber used her for — breeding."

He led me to a smaller cot, where a blanket covered a figure. For a fleeting second I didn't want him to pull back the blanket. He pulled it back.

The creature on the bed was dead, shot with a Colony bullet. You could tell that it was a boy about three feet long. There was Earthman in him and eaber. The head and arms were Earthian, the rest eaber. It was shocking to see the hard-muscled, dwarf body under that placid, almost handsome head.

"Barely five months," whispered the hag on the bed. "Forced insemination. Always the hands twisting — always the pain."

"A friendly scientific experiment," said Rackrill. "They want drones for the slag jobs in their cities. Jobs eaber won't do. They've produced a hundred or so of those idiots from captive women colonists. Force-fed and raised — this one is barely five months old, yet look at his size!"

I said nothing, busy with taking my tape, holding on to my objectivity through a force of will and my conditioning.

Rackrill opened the dead mouth. It was an exaggerated eaber tongue, black and reptile shaped. "No speech, therefore no intellect. Nor does it have mind speech like true eaber. It begs for food and does crude tasks to get it. I showed it to the men. One of them shot it. Nobody blamed him. Tomorrow we're going out and take these rats, and rescue those poor women that are still over there. Does your highness condescend to ask for a little Transstar help?"

"Transstar won't like this life-form meddling," I said. "This is the second time."

Rackrill slumped into a chair, looking at the woman who whispered some private incantation against the evils she had come to know.

"I've got two thousand colonists, five hundred ships," he said. "With or without your help, we're going out tomorrow and take them."

"They've got a few more ships, Rackrill."

He appeared not to hear. He sat there staring at the woman while I gathered up the eaber drone's body to take back to my ship.

"For God's sake, get Transstar," he said, as I left, and it was a prayer.

Shortly before noon next day, Rackrill was back at my ship. He pointed to the sky over the colony, where his small fighting ships were rising. "What did your bosses say?" he asked.

"They said," I replied, "that Transstar has to look after the safety of the whole human race, and cannot match colonists man for man. There are safe places in alpha and solar to live — men are not obligated to seek danger. However, they are disturbed about the drone. I am to give an official protest and warning to Euben the eaber, which I have done."

"Is that *all!*"

I closed my eyes. "They also demoted me one rank, from a Seven to a Six, for having left my ship unattended in the middle of last night. During the time we examined the drone, a bumptious Colony correspondent sneaked in to my ship and taped an eaber monstrosity I had on the TV plate. She flung her sensationalism to the planets and nations of alpha and solar. To put it mildly, this has rocked the galaxy, which is fine with our Colony Correspondent. She gets paid according to the number of TV stations that play her tape."

"The universe should know!" cried Rackrill.

"The universe has always known," I said. "Every history book tells of worse things in almost every Middlesex village and town. Transstar is not in show business or in policy making. It observes and objectively attends to the broad general welfare of the Earthian universe."

Rackrill's voice was hoarse. "I have one empty ship," he said bitterly. "I lack a pilot. Will Transstar at least do me the favor of helping to fill that?"

"It will," I said, reaching for my combat slacks.

This was a wild, foolish mission, and I knew it. But I wanted to get as close as I could to eaber-land, which I had only observed at a distance. And I wanted to do something about the affronts to my system.

Sometimes it's good to fire a killing ray, even if it doesn't mean much.

We passed over three middle-sized eaber cities, the queerest cities I'd ever seen.

"Practically all landing fields," said a feminine voice in my ear. I looked to my left. The Colony Correspondent was riding a patrol ship on my right. I thanked her for achieving my embarrassment.

"Oh, that's all right, Doc," she said. "You're officialdom. Natural enemy. You'll get in your licks."

"I'd rather take mine in kicks. And I know where I'd like to plant my foot," I said.

I got a brash laugh. Foolish girl! Women do not have to be aggressive. There's the kind that makes a fetish of rushing in where brave men hesitate. On their maimed and dead persons the news tapes fatten and flourish.

Rackrill's group thought they were fighting the battle of the eon. They were trying to land at the most advanced city, where the captive Earthwomen were thought to be. The action was good. I was gloriously bashed around and managed to shoot down my eaber ship. It wasn't a difficult action for a Transstar-trained man. I was more interested in observing that the eaber had out an equal patrol of five hundred to oppose us. But, with all the noise and banging that a thousand-ship fight makes, I could observe that there were easily ten or fifteen thousand more eaber military ships on the ground we ranged over.

So the cities were not colonies. They were military bases for a large operation.

More interesting than the ships at hand were the extremely large areas being cleared and laid out for additional ship concentrations. I estimated that they could eventually base over a hundred thousand ships.

That would interest Transstar immensely.

Rackrill broke off the action when he had a mere hundred ships left. We limped back to the colony without being able to land in eaber territory. In fact, I doubted if the eaber chiefs regarded this as more than a quiet afternoon's patrol action. With their layout I couldn't blame them.

We almost missed the colony and had to sweep back once more. Yes, there was my Transstar ship, glowing orangely on the ground. But what a changed ground! It was brown and bare, a desert as far as the horizon.

During Rackrill's attack a secret eaber counterattack had swept the colony's transport ships, its buildings, and Rackrill's fifteen hundred colonists into oblivion.

In times of shock men do drastic — or foolish — things. Rackrill's group of survivors began to bring down the cooking equipment and bedding from their ships, preparing a camp for the night on the blighted cemetery of their colony, dazed and tearful.

"Ada, Ada," Rackrill moaned softly, his thick fingers picking at a gleaming aluminum pot. "Ada gone, Johnny gone — "

I noticed that Martha Stoner, the tape girl, had at last lost some of her high gloss. She stared at the scene, stunned. I could almost calibrate the change in her, from a high-spirited girl to a shocked and understanding woman.

I couldn't hold back comment. "Now you see the frontier," I said to her. "Now you've got a real tape that all the stations can use." She shook her head dumbly. "Go home, Rackrill," I advised the benumbed leader. "Take your men and go home."

He turned on me with teeth bared and lip trembling. "You — and that Transstar fraud. You let this happen! Tell your piddling button-pushers we will never go home!"

The words rang bravely on the scorched ground, while an eaber patrol, high up, gently wafted over us on an observation mission.

I shook my head. "At least go off in the forest where you have some protection — and some wood for your fires!"

I turned to go. A clod of soil struck my back, then a small stone.

"Go, Transstar filth, go!" They were all picking up the chant now.

"I'll file a tape all right!" cried Martha. "I can still get through to the world. The people will act, even if Transstar won't."

I didn't want to run.

I swear, this was my worst moment, because I had seen this distress many times. I understood their monumental shock. But if I did not run I could be seriously disabled by their attack. At any moment one might pull a gun. My job was to remain in good health so I could observe.

So I ran towards my ship.

They followed in a ragged company, shouting, cursing, and at last pulling guns. I barely escaped into the orange-hued safety of the Transstar ship before the rays flew. The colonists danced and pranced around the ship, shooting at it and beating on it, like nothing so much as forest natives attacking an interloper. I understood and discreetly closed the portholes.

"Order them home," I begged Twelve Jackson. "They are doomed here."

"We don't have the power," said Jackson. "We can only help them home if they want to go."

I rang up Euben on the eaber channel which I used for official communications — so far, mostly for protests. Euben made his innocent, bird-twitter laugh. "Thank you for your protest about the colony extinction," he said. "This keeps my clerks busy. Your colony may leave at any time. In fact, I recommend this. We will need all the space on this planet very soon."

Three days passed.

I found the remnant of Rackrill's tattered colony in a sort of forest stockade. They were stiff with me, embarrassed about the stoning incident. They were ghost men, and a few women, going through the motions of building crude houses and planting their food.

Martha was an exception.

"They will stay," she said proudly, her eyes glowing. "They will be buttressed by the great crusade our space tapes have started. First the story of the miserable pet-human, then the eaber drone thing, then the mass attack on the unguarded colony. Back home men are leaving their jobs, pouring their savings into fighting ships. Institutions are subscribing money. Governments are amassing new fighters. We've got the backing of all the thinking men in solar and alpha!"

"It is too late in civilization for an emotion-powered, unorganized mass movement to succeed," I said. "Only Transstar is properly equipped for space war."

"Even Transstar men are quitting to join us!" she cried.

"Possibly a few at the lower levels. Not the agents."

"No — not the dehumanized agents! Nor the feeble old men of Transstar Prime who stole their power from the governments of men, who drool over buttons they never dare push!"

"The eaber do this to provoke us," I said, "to show our power at their command, at their site of battle, at a time they control. That's why Transstar Prime won't be sucked into the trap."

"They want to fight us. The time is now!" she said.

"The time is not yet," I said.

I went back to my lonely ship, haunted by the faces of Rackrill and his men as they glowed on my report tapes. I hunted the news broadcasts of solar and alpha and watched the revulsion and convulsion of men back home — the enormous waste of the emotional jag. I saw ships starting from Earth to reach us, ill-prepared even to reach the Moon, hurling across space vastnesses to become derelicts. I saw men throwing their pocket money at passing paraders of the anti-eaber crusade, normal shipping woefully hampered by the ridiculous items being sent to Rackrill's defenders. Government leaders, sensing the temper of the voters, threw their weight at Transstar Prime, calling for action. They got nowhere. Transstar resists temporary popular politics just as it does local situations.

"You certainly can't call this a local situation!" I told Twelve Jackson.

He sighed. "No, not any more. But the principle is missing. Everybody's mad, but the eaber haven't yet posed a major threat to the human race."

"They've got a couple hundred thousand fighting ships at our perimeter," I said.

"They haven't invaded territory we call our own. All the fighting is in no man's land. We're trained to determine a real danger from a false one, and so far they don't seem to be a real danger."

"It can get late fast," I said.

"Are you ready to ask for Condition Prime Total Red?"

There was a silence while I tried to separate my sympathetic feelings from the intelligence of the military situation. "No, sir," I said.

"Thirteen Mayberry agrees with you," said Twelve, looking over his shoulder, and then I saw the shadow of a sleeve of the top man. Transstar's Prime Prime, as the agents half-jokingly called him.

At least the desiccated old men near Mars were getting more interested.

On the day the first Earth-crusade task force arrived, both Martha and Rackrill came to the ship.

"You know it's the end of Transstar," Martha told me. She was more subdued and serious, but she still had the high-school glow of mysticism in her eyes. "The people have been sold out for the last time."

"No one's been sold out," I said. "We are in a painful contact with a race that is both powerful and primitive. They can't be reasoned with, yet we can't blow them up until, at least, they give evidence that they intend to blow us up. So far it's only a border incident, as they used to be called in one-world days."

"We aren't waiting," said Martha. "Five thousand ships! The first wave of the anti-eaber crusade will attack soon."

Martha put me so much in mind of Alicia — the way she held her head, the way she moved her hands. Once both Alicia and I had been at a point of resigning from Transstar and leading normal lives. But something in the blood and bone had made our marriage to Transstar stronger — until she was killed on a mission, and it was forever too late for me to quit. I was aware that I was too loyal to the organization, which was, after all, merely another society of men.

Yet, right now, I found myself questioning Prime's judgment.

Certainly they could have given me power to negotiate for the colony with Euben. Certainly there were some potent weapons, short of total war, which we could have used on these vain primitives as easily as the ones they used on us. Nor need I have been brought to my knees in front of Euben.

Yet my orders were to observe — report — take no action.

We went aloft to watch the Earthmen's attack. Both Martha and Rackrill were set for an initial penetration to the first eaber city. As the massive fleet from Earth wheeled in from space and went directly to the attack, they cheered like students in a rooting section. I cautioned them that five thousand ships, strained from a long flight from alpha, could hardly upset the eaber.

"It's only the first group!" cried Martha. "This is only the glorious beginning!"

The eaber took no chances. They lofted fifteen thousand ships and pulled the Earthmen into a box.

It took them about four hours to defeat the Earth attack. When the four hours passed, only about three hundred of the Earth fleet remained to sink to the oblivion of Rackrill's colony and lick their wounds.

"No matter," said Martha as we landed. "There will be more tomorrow and the day after that and after that. We'll blacken the skies with ships."

But she went quickly, avoiding my eyes.

"You'll always have sanctuary on my ship," I told Rackrill as he went.

"Your ship!" he snorted. "After today I'd rather trust my own stockade when Euben comes around. Incidentally, he has been kidnaping my work parties. Tell him we don't like that. Tell him we've been able to catch a few eaber, and when we do we cut them into four equal parts while they're still alive."

"Please don't," I said.

Euben came along as I was having my evening tea. "Ah, my scholarly friend with the glasses and the tea-drinking, the big words and the scoldings. I must thank you for keeping at least a part of our fleet in practice. A rather nice patrol action today, Webster. Is that your Transstar?"

"No. I ask you now what your intentions are as to this planet and our future relations," I said, aware that Transstar Prime, through this ship, had been watching the long day's affairs.

Euben had brought his friend with him. They both lolled at their ease in my cabin.

"It has been hard to determine," said Euben. "We have finally decided that, rather than waste rays killing off all Earthmen, we shall simply turn them into eaber. An inferior eaber, but still eaber. We have taken a few samples from Rackrill's post as prototypes."

"This is forbidden!" I snapped.

"You will declare war?" asked Euben eagerly. I thought his eagerness had grown.

"We don't know whom we deal with," I said. "You may be only a patrol captain, with a small command."

"I could also be commander-in-chief of all the eaber in space," said Euben. "Which I happen to be."

He said it too offhandedly for it to be a lie, although I suspected he was really deputy commander to the silent eaber who stood behind him.

"Then I formally demand that you cease and desist all harassments, mutilations, and hostilities against humans," I said.

Euben looked at me a long time. Then he held out what could reasonably be called an arm, which his companion grasped.

My ship seemed to whirl about me. It was no such thing. Instead I was suspended upside down in the air over my desk, and Euben and the other left the ship. "Farewell, brave-foolish," called Euben mockingly. "Next time I come it is to collect you for eaberization!"

His laugh was proud and full of confidence.

When I finally managed to right myself and get back behind my desk, I called Transstar Prime and got Twelve Jackson. I feared I saw a flick of amusement in his eyes. "They are determined now for war," I said. "How do we stand?"

"You continue to observe," said Jackson. "Point Everready is not necessary to Earth. And you have not convinced us that a battle needs to be fought."

I had not convinced them. But what did *I* — a mere agent — have to do with it?

I rang off and closed the ship, in sorrow and anger. I had been aloof from the situation, to the point where Euben had stood me on my head and threatened to capture me bodily.

I put on my combat slacks and broke out my weapons. Transstar could remain uninvolved, but I wasn't going to sit at my desk, be stood on my ear, and blithely be turned into an eaber all for the glory of the organization.

I rode over to Rackrill's stockade full of cold purpose.

I was no rugged primitive colonist. I was a trained agent, with quite a few good weapons and considerable experience in hostilities, especially against alien life-forms. Euben would have no easy time taking me.

I found Rackrill in more trouble. "Look," he fumed, pointing to a dead eaber at the wall of the stockade. "We shot this fellow. Look closely."

It was easy to see that it was one of his own colonists, upon whom extensive biology had been used to turn him into something eaberlike.

"It's going to happen to us all," shuddered Martha. "The crusade has collapsed. There'll be no more Earth ships. Distances are too great — governments are too busy with their home affairs. We have been outlawed in all major planets."

I stared at the white-faced colonial leaders in distaste.

"For God's sake, quite sniveling and feeling sorry for yourselves," I said. "We're going to fight these beasts and do it right. First, I want an antenna. I can draw power from my ship that the eaber can't crack. Second, I want to fight an eaber-type war. Get your colonists together for indoctrination. These eaber have primitive mind-reading abilities; I want to start training our men to set up mind guards against that. Last, we're going to dig some tunnels in this ground and blow the eaber into orbit. They don't like things underground. They have no defense for it. So let's get organized!"

"Thank God!" cried Martha. "Transstar is coming in at last."

"No," I said. "Just Charles Webster."

We fought the eaber for twenty days.

They couldn't penetrate the power wall I set up with the help of the ship, using Transstar power. They couldn't waylay our work parties in the woods after I taught them how to use mind-blocks which were meaningless to the eaber.

We got our tunnel through and blew up one third of an eaber city with one of my strontium 90 pills. We were also able to capture a few eaber patrol ships and send them right back, with fair-sized atomic blasts. The rest we manned and used against the eaber. They were totally confused with being attacked by their own ships. It wasn't enough to destroy a twentieth of their operation. But it kept them busy.

I was never once outside my combat slacks.

I got little sleep. I lived for the present moment, working hand and shoulder with Rackrill's men. When disaster came, it came all at once.

I led a night patrol to place the next strontium 90 pill overland — tunneling was too slow. I caught an eaber freeze-ray that shattered my leg. In the confusion we lost Martha to the eaber, which I only learned when I'd been carried back to the stockade.

When dawn broke, Rackrill shook me out of a dazed sleep.

"Look," he said.

"Ten thousand ships to destroy two dozen men," I laughed. "It's all right, Alicia."

Rackrill slapped my face. "Better come out of it, Webster. Can we stand an attack like that?"

I gulped a wake-up pill and brought myself alert. "No, we cannot. This is our day for extinction. Our only decision now is to pick the time and place of our going. Let's get over to the Transstar ship as fast as possible."

"I'm not leaving Point Everready," growled Rackrill.

"Nor am I," I said. "Let's move, man."

It was a sticky hour getting back to my ship. By that time our stockade, power block and all, had been pulverized to dust behind us by the attacking weight of the eaber ships.

"Take me up, Rackrill," I said as we reached the bottom of the ship. "I can't climb any more."

He pointed up dumbly. The fox faces of Euben and his eternal companion grinned down at us. I shifted out a gun and took off the safety. "Take me up, Rackrill."

It was almost ceremonial as Rackrill and the bare half-dozen who had made it through gathered about me in the cabin. I eased painfully into my chair. Euben saw my leg and grinned. "Looks like an amputation before we can make you a useful eaber," he said.

My bullet skipped across his shoulder. "Stand over by that wall, you," I said. "You, Euben! I'm talking to you."

"You cannot order me," he said, but he moved back sprightly enough. "I humor you, you see," he said. "Your stockade is gone. You have nothing but this ship. I have decided to have it gently blasted into space as worthless junk."

He gestured out of the window, where his ships were making passes now.

My Transstar ship shuddered. "We can bounce it off the planet like a harmless rubber ball," he said. He gestured in back of me. "I have also returned your woman, of whom you think so much. She is worthless to become an eaber."

I turned and saw the thin shape of what had once been Martha, huddled on my navigator's bench. It was obvious that they had treated her roughly. From the trickle of blood at her mouth, she was badly hemorrhaged. She could not live.

I stared down at her. It was hard to tell if she still recognized me. She opened her mouth slightly, and I saw the black familiar shape of the eaber reptile tongue.

I turned away, light-headed with sorrow and anger.

I jabbed a button and looked up at the tall TV. It wasn't Twelve Jackson. It was Thirteen Mayberry, Mr. Prime himself.

"What are you staring at, you old goat?" I cried, a little hysterically. "Sore because I took action to save my own hide?"

"No, you young fool. I was just wondering how long you'd permit this minor outrage to go on."

"It ends now!" I said. "Listen, Prime, I have Earth people here who demand sanctuary of Transstar."

"You have it," he said. "We will up that ship, son. No power in the universe will keep it on the ground."

"The eaber are upping it quite nicely, thanks," I said. "But we don't want it upped!"

I had to stop talking while the thudding blows of the gentle eaber rays buffeted the ship.

"Not upped?" asked Mayberry.

"No, sir, not upped. We're staying! We hold the ground that this Transstar ship rests on, in the name of Earth. It isn't much, only about fifty feet long and twenty-five wide, but it's Earth territory. No race or force may deprive us of our real estate."

"You tell him!" cried Rackrill.

I turned to Euben. "Now, friend," I said, "just ease this ship back to our ground. It's Earth ground. We intend to hold it!"

"Your leg wound has made you mad," said Euben, with a shrug. "We have decided that you are not even worthy to be eaber pets."

"Last warning, Euben! You've got yourself a Transstar situation."

Euben didn't hesitate.

He turned his hands in the air. I rolled in pain, but I kept seated. When I could see again from the pain, I looked up. Mayberry and Jackson and Hennessy and the forty-one division commanders of Transstar were blazing from the wall. The TV looked like a Christmas tree.

"Transstar orders this ship down and that ground preserved in the name of Earth-alpha!" said Mayberry shortly to Euben.

Euben looked at the old man and shook his head. "Madmen," he said. "I spit on you." He spit on the screen at Mayberry. He had learned Earth insults well.

"My condition is Prime Total Red," I told Mayberry.

He leaned forward and closed the seldom-closed circuit at Transstar Prime.

"Your condition is Prime Total Red, and your ship is now command post for all Earth-alpha star power."

I leaned over and tapped a button. We left Point Everready in the beautiful swoop that only a Transstar ship could perform. I held us high in the atmosphere over the planet and looked sadly down. It had been a beautiful planet.

I hit another button and looked up at the forty-one division commanders of Transstar. "Your orders are to destroy the eaber," I said.

I sat back. For a few seconds it was deathly silent, while Euben sputtered and fussed about his quick ride up over the planet. Then there was the faintest whisper of — something — back and out and behind us.

"Brace yourselves, folks," I told the Earthmen. "It's going to be loud and crowded around here!"

Euben jabbered at some kind of communicator he held in his hands. His partner likewise gabbled.

"We have a hundred and fifty thousand ships," he told me. "We'll tear you to shreds!"

I kicked a chair over at him. "Sit down. You're going to want to sit in a minute."

"Something's wrong with the ship!" cried Rackrill. "It's heavy and dead!"

"We're drawing most of the broadcast power this side of Mars," I said. "In a minute you'll be glad we have that protection!"

Transstar came then. The fast patrols whisked out of black space and leaped into our atmosphere like gleaming fish, fired a rocking blast of weaponry, and were gone to rendezvous, reform, and pass again. They were like nothing the eaber had ever seen. They were made for a star-go like this, a burst of light, a dazzle, and a thunder that came and came and came. Behind them came the light patrols and then the medium patrols and then the heavy patrols and then the fast light shock ships and then the medium shock ships and then the heavy shocks, wave upon wave upon wave.

Even wrapped in our thick blanket of power we were stunned.

The planet came alight like a pearl below us. The air was jammed with sound shocks, the dazzle was like a spreading, thickening bomb of light that transfixed the eyeballs even through the dark screens I had set up.

"This is early stuff," I told Euben conversationally. "They just do a little holding till the important ships arrive. Patrols and first shocks — the usual things, you know."

Euben's mouth was open. He took time to swallow before he screamed orders to his ships below.

The patrols and shocks were suddenly past firing range. For a moment you could see the planet through the haze. Its shore lines and rivers had sickened and wavered. The eaber ships, which had been a blanket, were a tattered rag.

Hennessy, the headquarters jokester, couldn't resist a comment that probably earned him a fine. "Here comes the cavalry," he said over the TV.

And they came.

It was good professional stuff, geared to star action. Now we had the regulars. They came in waves of ten thousand, which was a wee bit impressive, I thought. There were the ground regulars, the medium regulars, and the high regulars, each division with thirty categories, each category with its subdivisions of missiles, rockets, and drones. The atmosphere screamed at us. The density of the light assumed sun proportions, and our poor little ship was like a chip on an angry ocean. Rackrill had his mouth wide open. He was yelling to relieve his tension at the awesome sight; the others were lost in the overwhelming cataclysm of it. I had seen it in movies.

I poured myself a cup of tea.

"These are just the on-call regulars," I told Euben. "Of course, you realize that in a Prime Red we're getting total mobilization. We'll get slightly less than a million ships in the first hour. The rest will come later."

Euben had stopped shouting orders. He stared at me. He said something that I couldn't hear. The pounding went on for fifteen minutes; then the planet cleared. There weren't any shore lines or rivers any more. There weren't very many eaber ships.

"Stop it," he said.

I shook my head. "Sorry. A Prime Red can't be stopped easily. Once the momentum starts it has to run its course. Get set now. Here come your specials."

As the specials started to arrive, I taunted the division commanders. "Transstar is getting rusty. You've hardly nicked the planet. Can't your boys shoot properly any more?"

They came in fat and sleek. Far off they waddled and wallowed, like a bunch of old ladies hitting a bargain counter. But suddenly they were serious, close up, and I had to close the portholes against the awesome roar and light of their work. You name the ray, bullet, bomb, gas — it was there.

A half hour later the din eased off and we looked. A large fragment of seared rock floated in space. The entire eaber fleet had long ago disappeared. So had everything else except that radioactive rock.

The last wave was the massive attack unit, very slow and lumbering compared to the others, but packed with power. The first five thousand took eager bites of the rock — and there was nothing left for the other twenty-five thousand. There was nothing left at all of Point Everready except some haze hanging below us in space. But it was too late to stop the attack.

To one side of us the returning waves began to streak by — the patrols, fast, light, medium, and heavy, the shocks, first, second, and third, the regulars in their streaming divisions and then the specials. Meanwhile, closer by, the second wave was coming in, first patrols and first shocks, darting a few shots to keep their hand in, at the floating dust patches.

Euben looked out and saw ships to his left and to his right and behind him and below him and above him and in all positions in between. It was such a heavy concentration that the stars were blocked out and, though no atmosphere existed for a nonexistent planet, we were a planet of moving ships, ourselves creating a gravity and a stinking jet-flame atmosphere. It was a moving dream of hell, enough to make your mind crack open with the motion of it. It was the phantom action of a near-million starships — and another million on the way.

This was the total war capacity delivered to order.

What it cost in disruption and money and waste was incredible to contemplate. But that was Prime Total Red — everything we had. And it wasn't at all pointless.

"The eaber surrender," said Euben.

He stood respectfully now, his commander behind him. I guess he was thinking of the remaining eaber colonies on other planets, as there was nothing left to surrender here.

I handed him a rag. "You may now wipe the spit off my TV plate receiver," I said. He did it with alacrity.

"We will go elsewhere," said Euben's companion. "After all, space is big. There is plenty of room for two great races."

"One great race," I said.

"Of course," he said affably. "May we have our lives spared?"

"We want you to have them — so you can take the word home."

The action outside had stilled. I opened the ports and began to move slowly towards another planet where the eaber had dwellings, as requested by the shaken Euben. Rackrill patted my shoulder. "Boy, that Transstar!" he exulted.

"It's quite a lot," I admitted. I painfully inched over to the stricken Martha and squeezed her hand. I thought she squeezed back. I thought I saw a flicker of joy at our success — but there was so much eaber and so much death in her eyes it was hard to know. I had to leave her then, for the medics came aboard for her.

I began to glide down on the new planet to discharge Euben and the other eaber. "Look," I said gesturing over my shoulder. Behind us the Transstar fleet followed docilely, the mass and weight of them, guns racked and quiet, the great beast behind my tiny patrol dot.

"We'll stay around a few days in case you want to argue some more," I told Euben.

He shook his head. "That will not be necessary, my good friend. We are not stupid. In the future you'll see very little of the eaber."

The ship settled. I opened the door and put down the ladder and Euben's companion descended, then Euben. "I am sorry — " he began.

But I thought of Martha and the dead boy who had died on Everready and the pet human and the drone eaber and the others who had suffered and died to make this creature sorry. So I planted my good foot on his rear. He crashed into his master and they both fell in the mud at the bottom of the ladder. They got up, mud-splattered, and ran like the wind towards eaberdom, capes flying out behind them.

Rackrill laughed. It was the first relaxed laugh I'd heard in all that assignment. It pulled things back to normal.

I turned back to my blazing board and hit a button. "Condition White," I said, "and don't kid me that you got up all these starships on seventy-five seconds' notice. They left Earth-alpha weeks ago. You knew from the first we were in for a Condition Prime Total Red with the eaber."

The old man grinned. "It's the agents who louse us up. We were afraid you'd observe so long that you'd start the action on an orange and build a whole new tradition — Ten."

Ten! I remembered then that anybody who ordered a CPTR was automatically up for Ten rank and sent to a nice, soft job at Prime.

"Save me a wide, plump chair at the TV console at Prime," I said. "Get me a desk-sized teapot, and a soft cushion for a bum leg."

I turned the ship around and started to lead the massive fleet home.

I stared at the far-flung stars of space as I drank my tea, eyes blurred a little with tears. I was an organization man. The organization was all I had, or would ever have. It didn't seem enough. Even the playing of the Transstar victory song left me depressed.

Then suddenly the light broke.

A Transstar agent is both the most and the least important of men. He is a fireman who puts out fires — a hero, but a shadow. A master sometimes, but mostly a servant. I winked at Mayberry on the screen. They saw I knew and winked back. They had finally lost a pompous, Transstar-impressed agent and gained a useful career man.

They were satisfied.

So was I.

sports — vigorous activity that is often organized competitively. There are individual sports, like jogging, and team sports, like basketball. Participating in and watching sports are some of the most popular activities in all cultures. Science fiction sports generally are extrapolations from existing ones, although new ones are sometimes invented by science fiction writers. Future sports of all kinds can be found in the stories in *Run to Starlight: Sports Through Science Fiction* (Delacorte Press, 1975); *Arena: Sports SF* (Doubleday, 1976); and *The Infinite Arena* (Thomas Nelson, 1977).

Open Warfare

JAMES E. GUNN

The tournament hadn't been conceded, exactly, but everybody agreed that Jim was the man to beat. Everybody — the professionals, the fans, the sportswriters . . .

Slim Jim Pearson, the hard-luck boy with the velvet swing, is finally going to cop that US Open crown. Look up these words five days from now.

He's no longer the Jim Pearson who swung eight times at a ball buried in a sand trap in 1957, or the Jim Pearson who four-putted a green and picked up in disgust in 1960 when he could have parred in to win. He's the Jim Pearson who has won ten major tournaments on the winter circuit, the last five straight, and collected $25,000 with a sparkling performance of cool, steady golf . . .

The Open didn't pay off anything close to $25,000, of course. The extras made up the difference. Fame was negotiable — testimonials, articles, books, sporting goods contracts.

Fifty thousand dollars . . .

And the money didn't mean a thing. It was just the price tag on a girl named Alice Hatcher, who was no different from any other attractive young girl except that Jim Pearson happened to love her, and her father happened to have uncountable millions of dollars. Like the marching Chinese, while you were counting them, more millions were born.

*

Pudgy Sam Hatcher, who would never break ninety, concealed his steely mind behind a soft face. Only after Jim was trapped had he recognized the inflexible purpose and the wily cleverness behind it.

"You're a good golfer, Jim," Hatcher said, easing off his spiked shoes with a sigh, "even if you can't teach me anything. We've been good to you at the country club. I want you to do something for me."

"Yes, sir?"

"Stay away from Alice!"

"But, Mr. Hatcher!"

"I won't have her marrying a man who has nothing but coordination and muscles. When I was only your age, I was making $50,000 a year. It takes brains to do that. Brains get more valuable. Muscles deteriorate. There's nothing muscles can't do that a machine can't do better."

"You don't think I could make $50,000?" Jim said angrily.

"I know damn well you couldn't," Hatcher said. "You haven't got the guts. If you ever got within sight of it, you'd blow up — like you did in St. Louis."

Before Jim had known it, he was wrapped up, sealed, addressed and — he feared — headed for the dead-letter office. If he could make $50,000 in a year, he could have Alice — if he could get her — with Hatcher's blessing. If he failed — well, he wouldn't see Alice again.

Jim had had a long time to think about it — the better part of a year — and to admire the way he had been outmaneuvered. Fifty thousand dollars — a shrewd figure. Right at the top of the possible. Not impossible, but so close to it as to be practically indistinguishable.

There had been side effects. Touring the tournament circuit had kept him away from Alice as effectively as walls and armed guards. And somehow — Jim had a good idea how — Alice had learned about the bet. A few days after Jim had won his first big tournament, he got a note.

I won't be bought and sold. Al.

That was that — or was it? For a few days Jim had been angry with a blind anger that cost him $5,000. And then he saw a picture over a caption that read:

Industrialist Samuel Hatcher bids bon voyage to his daughter, Alice, who will spend the next six months studying in England.

Jim studied Hatcher's expression of bland triumph. Suddenly, his anger became something else — something cold and determined. Nerves? Temperament? He didn't have any.

Each long, low, flat drive was a fist in Hatcher's face — each sure putt a dagger in his back. The prize money rolled in. The tournaments dropped behind, conquered, forgotten. And then it was Open time. The bet was almost won. And if Hatcher thought he couldn't lose, Jim had a surprise for him.

He would take the whole fifty thousand, Jim thought, and lay it in front of Alice and say, "I wasn't buying you, I was buying the right to tell you that I love you." And if that didn't work, he would set fire to the putting greens at night — all eighteen of them.

Maybe Hatcher knew finance — but he didn't know golf, and he didn't know the way of a man with a maiden.

All it took was the US Open. And nobody else could keep up the pace for four rounds. Jim grinned — it was going to be that easy.

And then Saul showed up.

The first hint of disaster came at the practice tee. Jim was methodically sharpening up his No. 1-wood when the spectators deserted him. The appreciative murmurs died away. Jim looked up. The mob had clotted around another tee several hundred feet away. Jim waved the caddy in and sauntered toward the attraction that had taken the crowd away from the man picked to win the Open. Not annoyed, not upset — just curious.

From a knoll behind the other tee, Jim got a good view of the big, tall golfer. The tanned, impassive features were unfamiliar. And then the driver came down in a glittering arc.

Jim pursed his lips in a soundless whistle. He knew all the professionals and most of the topnotch amateurs. No stranger should have a swing that good, that effortless, that grooved.

But the real shock came when Jim followed the smooth arc of the glistening ball. Jim's eyes were good, or he might have lost it as it dwindled in the distance. The caddy stood at least 280 yards down the fairway, with a ball bag in his hands. He didn't move — and the ball dropped right in the middle of the sack.

Accident, Jim thought shakily. But it happened a second time and a third, and so on until Jim lost count. Every club in the bag was used with the same incredible accuracy. The caddy had a snap job — he didn't have to stoop once.

Trick-shot artist, Jim told himself. Wait until he gets in competition. But there wasn't anybody that good. Not even old Joe Kirkwood.

"Quite a spectacle, eh, Jim?"

Jim knew that brisk, businesslike voice. He turned. "Hello, Hatcher." He tried to keep his voice friendly.

Hatcher was as fat as ever. "Must be unnerving to watch something like that."

"I can stand it."

"But will you be able to stand it when the going gets rough?" Hatcher asked solicitously. "Or will you blow up like you always do? It would be too bad, just when you're so close."

"You haven't forgotten our bet, then?"

"Of course not, Jim." He chuckled. "I never forget anything."

"You've kept close track," Jim said steadily. "What about Alice? Has she kept track, too?"

"I haven't the slightest idea. She's in England, you know. I suspect, however, that she has forgotten all about you."

"She'll remember. The next four days will remind her."

"I suppose so," Hatcher said thoughtfully. "Sadly, I'm afraid. Saul will see to that."

"Saul?"

Hatcher nodded toward the golfer on the tee. "Saul."

Jim's eyes narrowed. "You know him?"

Hatcher was enigmatic. "I brought him here — my own personal entry. His first tournament was the qualifying round, and he's going to beat you out of the Open."

Score up another one for Hatcher. "Then he's got something to learn," Jim said confidently.

Hatcher turned to watch Saul. The clean, crisp smack of club against ball came with clockwork regularity. "Just a dumb country boy," he said. "Never saw a golf club until a few months ago. But I think he might teach you something, Jim."

Jim's gaze drifted irresistibly to the golf balls soaring down the fairway into the canvas sack. That was what he would have to beat.

Jim's threesome teed off early in the morning. Jim felt good. A night's sound sleep had brought back his self-confidence. He was going to enjoy winning.

From the moment he drew his driver out of the leather bag he knew he was going to have a good day. The grip fitted snugly into his hand. His flat, thin muscles rippled without a twinge. His practice swings were loose and effortless.

The crowd was sympathetic. That always helped. They wanted to see him burn up the course. He had another rooter, too, and there was another thousand in the bank. An eager young man from a sporting goods company had talked him into using a new golf ball. The company had planned a big campaign to advertise it. *Guaranteed to add twenty yards to every drive.* They would like to add, *Used by Jim Pearson when he won the US Open.*

They'd have that chance, Jim thought firmly. He knelt to tee up his ball.

"Don't tighten up yet," said a voice he was coming to know too well. "Give the crowd a show for its money."

Jim turned. "You can't have much confidence in your champion, Hatcher, if you have to try psychological tricks like this."

"All the confidence in the world, Jim," Hatcher said breezily. "I just don't take chances. *You* take chances. That's why you always lose."

"Don't be too sure. I haven't lost yet."

Hatcher shrugged. "You haven't seen Alice, have you?"

Jim forced himself to take three deep breaths. When he stepped up to his ball, he was calm. He took a few experimental waggles. The crowd sighed as his deceptively easy swing sent his first drive soaring down the fairway. It was long and straight. The slightest hook would send the ball scooting down a slope to the left behind a clump of trees on the 530-yard par-five hole.

It wasn't too tough a birdie. The next four dropped in par. Cameras clicked and whirred. The crowd applauded, held its breath, or groaned in sympathy.

On the par-five sixth, Jim relaxed and lit a cigarette. It was a good day to be playing. The sky was an improbable blue — the fairway was green and springy. Jim took a deep breath and smiled at the crowd. They liked that. They applauded.

Jim got his second shock.

The white flash of a girl's face, the arch of a slim body in a cool summer dress . . . Jim started toward her.

"Al," he said, then stopped. He cursed silently. He was beginning to see things.

He tossed his cigarette away and ground it into the turf. The sixth fell, nevertheless, in birdie figures. Three more pars made him 34 for the first nine. Not brilliant golf, but the kind that won tournaments. And two putts might have dropped, but hadn't.

The second nine was even better. Jim played smoothly, confidently. The crowd, which had been tense and excited over his four birdies and three pars, began slipping away at the sixteenth. That didn't bother him. A roar of approval drifted faintly over the fairway from time to time. On the last two holes he got a birdie and a par.

He glanced quickly over the card. A 34 and a 32, for 66 on the eighteen. Six birdies — twelve pars. Three more like that should win easily.

The crowd around the eighteenth green opened in front of him as he walked toward the clubhouse. Strangers reached out to shake his hand and pound him on the back. Jim smiled for them.

"How was the golf ball, huh?" It was the eager young man.

"Fine," Jim said.

"I'll leave a couple of dozen with your caddy."

"Fine," Jim said.

Jim watched his score being posted on the big board. Most of the field was still out, but he was ahead of the closest competitor by three strokes. As he turned away, the crowd at the eighteenth green roared.

That usually meant a hot round. Jim waited. Maybe some joker had tied his 66.

A big, tall, bronzed golfer plodded silently through the crowd. Nobody shook his hand. Nobody pounded his back. But they looked at him with awe. Jim watched him for a moment and frowned.

He turned to watch Saul's score go down on the board, but two men were talking behind him. One of them was a syndicated sports writer.

"Wow!" the columnist said. "Clockwork precision! There's never been anything like it. Nerves? He never opened his mouth."

The other man mumbled something.

"Yes, I said it and I'll take it all back," the writer replied. "Saul's the man to beat, not Pearson."

Jim flushed, but the other man spoke up. "I'll still bet on Pearson."

"And I'll take all you can scrape together. This Saul's a machine — every shot just where he wants it. Let me put that down before I forget it — Silent Saul, the Mechanical Man."

Jim looked back to the scoreboard. His eyes flashed quickly across the row of precise figures.

    4 3 4 4 3 4 3 4 3 — 32
    3 3 4 4 4 3 3 4 4 32 — 64

That tied the course record and beat him by two. The procession of threes and fours was fantastic.

"What's the matter, Jim?" Hatcher said from behind him. "You don't look well."

Jim turned, smiling. It was an effort, but he made it. "One round isn't a tournament," he said casually.

Hatcher sighed. "Comfort yourself while you can. Saul's just getting warmed up. He's that mythical thing, the perfect golfer, but he's dumb. No brains, Jim — no brains at all."

Jim stared at the sports-page headline and lost all appetite for breakfast.

SILENT SAUL
THE MAN TO BEAT

Pearson's 66
Places Second
To Record-Tying 64

Jim Pearson, the fair-haired boy of the tournament circuit, rolled up a sparkling 66 for yesterday's first round of the US Open. But only a few minutes later, Silent Saul, mystery man of the tournament, blazed in . . .

Jim set his jaw firmly and forced down his bacon and eggs. The Open wasn't over yet. There was a lot of golf yet to be played. He glanced through his mail. An English stamp! *England.* He ripped open the letter.

> *A girl can change her mind.*
> *Win the Open — for me.*
>   *Al.*

Jim waited until his breathing slowed. He got up, stuffed the note in his pocket, sauntered to the practice tee.

So she *was* in England. But if she loved him, why did this one tournament matter? What difference did $50,000 make? He tried to see the situation from Alice's viewpoint and shook his head. Maybe Hatcher was right. Maybe he wasn't so smart. But there was one thing he *was* good at, one thing at which, when he was feeling his best, he was unbeatable.

An hour's practice went well. His hands felt good today, slim and strong. That was always a sign of readiness. He strolled over to the starting tee.

The crowd was small. When he stepped up to his ball, there was only a smattering of applause. His drive was as straight as the day before and longer by almost twenty yards.

Jim played grimly and accurately. From ahead, as regularly as a pulse, came roars of approval. That was Saul, he thought. His game became, if anything, crisper.

The crowd was larger as he teed off on number 10. The underdog, he thought — they always pull for the underdog if he's making a game fight. But if he appeared to be certain to lose — well, they were human. They liked to be on the winning side.

His second nine was a duplicate of the day before — another 32. But the applause, as he dropped the putt on the eighteenth, was perfunctory.

Jim puzzled over it as he handed the putter to his caddy. He had equalled Saul's record-tying score of yesterday. Surely Saul hadn't repeated. His luck had to run out.

It was worse than that. It was —

    4 2 3 4 3 4 3 4 4 — 31
    4 4 3 3 3 4 4 3 3   31 — 62

He had broken the record and beaten Jim by two strokes. Jim was four strokes down. He turned away, his face set and hard. He wasn't even surprised to find Hatcher behind him.

"What have you got to say, Jim?" Hatcher inquired.

What Jim wanted to say was unprintable. After a moment, however, he forced a smile.

"That's better," Hatcher said. "The good old American tradition. Good sportsmanship — that sort of thing. Bushwash! They pay off on winners."

"You haven't seen anything yet," Jim said.

"You know," Hatcher said, "I was just going to say the same thing."

Jim brushed past him and walked toward the clubhouse. There was something terribly wrong with the whole setup. In real life things didn't happen like this. People didn't pop out of nowhere and break all records to win the Open. Men didn't take up the game and become perfect golfers in a few months. Hatcher had said either too much or too little.

Saul had a weakness. There was no perfect golfer. But how could Jim find that weakness and take advantage of it!

"*Dave,*" Jim said. He caught the scurrying tournament manager by a sleeve.

"There's some dispute about a penalty," Dave said, trying to get away.

"When am I supposed to go out tomorrow?"

"Afternoon."

"And Saul?"

"A little later. What *is* this?" Dave scowled.

"Let me go out in the morning," Jim said.

"Well, I don't — "

"It means a lot," Jim said quickly. "I've got an appointment in the afternoon."

"Well," Dave said, "I don't see how it can hurt . . ."

"Thanks, Dave. You won't regret it." And, as the official broke into a trot Jim added under his breath, "But someone will."

Hatcher hadn't been content with a simple bet, not even with all the odds in his favor. He had played all angles and, when he was about to lose, had pulled a rabbit out of his hat. Any way to win. That was a two-sided game, also.

The out nine bowed for Jim in 32 again, as he missed his usual birdie on the first hole and got it back with a 2 on the second. On the back nine, he slipped a stroke to a 33. But he refused to blow up under the pressure of Saul's four-stroke lead.

His 195 total broke several fifty-four-hole records. And yet Saul could drop to a 69 to tie. Jim had a hunch Saul's game wasn't going to break. Not today.

He shook off the reporters, gobbled a sandwich, and returned to the starting tee almost unnoticed. He was lost in a crowd of thousands, gathered to see Silent Saul climb to new heights.

Saul's effortless swing belted the ball over 300 yards down the fairway, straight as the shortest distance between two points. Jim wasn't watching. His eyes were half-closed, studying the mental picture of that swing.

There was something wrong with it, something naggingly suspicious about it. Jim couldn't pin it down. It seemed — familiar — and yet Jim felt he'd never seen it before that first mad day.

Jim tramped the fairway with the rest of the spectators, drawing close enough to hear anything Saul might say to his caddy or Hatcher. There wasn't anything to hear. Saul was silent as a mute.

Saul sent one sweeping glance toward the green 240 yards distant, selected a club from the bag, took a few oddly familiar waggling gestures before he set his driver behind the ball, and swung. The ball lit on the front edge of the green and bit.

Saul's putt rolled straight for the hole until an unruly blade of grass deflected it an inch to the right of the cup. A birdie.

That was the pattern. The only luck Saul was playing in was bad. It rode his shoulders pickaback, spoiling the incredible accuracy of his shots. A gust of wind caught a lofting seven-iron pitch — a bad bounce called up a brilliant recovery — a spectator stopped the ball short of the green with his head.

Jim smiled ruefully. Against this combination of bad breaks, Saul had whipped the front nine in 32.

What would he do when he was lucky?

And still those familiarities of swing plagued Jim's memory. Wild ideas flitted through his mind — disguise — mass hallucination. He pushed them away. This was real. And there had never been anyone this good.

The only inconsistency about Saul were his unnecessary preparatory movements. The sports writer was right. Saul was a golfing machine, tuned to perfection for just one thing. And he did nothing else. He didn't even talk.

At the start of the eleventh hole, Hatcher caught sight of him. "Ah," he said, "come to take some lessons?"

"I hope to learn something," Jim said quietly.

"Watch Saul — you will." Hatcher smiled. "Of course, the papers will eat this up. 'Pearson watches Saul spike hopes for Open.' "

Jim didn't answer. He was watching Saul again. His drive cleared the trees to roll to a stop close to the green.

"Where did he learn to drive like that?" Jim mused.

"Saul?" Hatcher laughed. "Why, he's a natural-born golfer!"

Jim left him laughing and puffing far behind.

He got his first clue on the sixteenth green. Jim scowled as Saul drew back his putter in a smooth, wrist-powered arc. And Jim had part of the answer.

It might have been Tod Winters putting — Tod who was the most brilliant putter of the last ten years. Frowning, Jim's narrowed eyes obscured the physical difference, and the form leaped out at him. Saul had patterned his putting on that of Tod Winters.

No — that wasn't quite it. It was like a picture of Tod, every idiosyncrasy duplicated without reason, superimposed on Saul's massive frame.

The putt rimmed the cup and was dropped for a par. Jim walked dazedly with the crowd to the next tee. Watching Saul's drive, something sprang into his mind, then was gone before he could grasp it.

Jim shook his head and watched the long-iron shot arch beautifully to the green. That one was obvious. George Potter, who would have been a great champion if all his shots had been as well played as his long irons, was the model this time.

But again, the things that were duplicated were variations that added nothing to the success of the shots. No golfer in his right mind would have duplicated those. The waggles and twitches were Potter's way of preparing himself psychologically for the stroke.

Why had Saul duplicated everything? How had he done it so faithfully?

The crowd's roar brought Jim scurrying to the tree-embraced tee to watch Saul's last drive. This time the nagging thought leaped again — and stayed.

He might have been looking in a mirror. He should have realized it before. Of course, Saul would duplicate Jim's driving form. *He* was the boy with the velvet swing, the controlled drives that no one had outdistanced before Saul came along.

He didn't even have to watch the approach shot. Saul might be the golfer, but it would be Gordon Brown's technique. And then, as he watched Saul putt twice for a par, the answer came, the answer that was incredible but somehow — inescapably — true.

As Jim expected, Hatcher was at his elbow with a few well-chosen comments. "A 63 — you're six strokes behind with one round to go. Do you want to give up now?"

"I don't think I will," Jim said evenly. "You see, Hatcher, I did learn something — something I wasn't supposed to learn."

Hatcher was amused. "Yes? And what is that?"

"I think we'd better talk about it privately."

"Oh, that won't be necessary."

Jim shrugged. "It doesn't matter to me." He leaned closer to Hatcher and added softly, "But I know that Saul is a robot."

From the clubhouse dining room came sounds of carefree confusion — plates and silverware clinking, spiked shoes clomping across shredded floors, loud voices describing this one that rimmed or that one that dropped. Inside the little private room, where Hatcher stood looking out the window at the rolling, green fairway, there was silence.

A smile curled the corners of Hatcher's mouth. "So you think Saul is a robot."

"Isn't he?"

Hatcher chuckled. "Of course he is. How does it feel to be beaten at your own game by a mindless machine?"

"You haven't won yet," Jim said. "A golf ball takes some funny bounces."

"How did you find out — about Saul?"

"Saul is a lot of things," Jim said slowly, "but none of them is Saul. Saul is Tod Winters, George Potter, Gordon Brown, and me. Take us away and there's nothing left."

"Nothing human," Hatcher said. "Just a memory, a power source, a lot of wires, and a lot of motors."

Jim shook his head. "How did you do it?"

"Money can do anything. All it needs is a purpose. Someone has developed a colloidal memory bank. That's a brain — get it? The new miniature atomic power plant is ideal. Use it. Make thousands of tiny motors to serve as muscles. Throw in some sensory mechanisms, some relays, then feed in an analysis of a slow-motion pictorial study."

"And you have a golf machine."

"Exactly," Hatcher said.

"It must have cost hundreds of thousands of dollars," Jim said bitterly.

"Closer to a million." Hatcher was cheerful.

"A million dollars to keep me from winning twenty-five thousand," Jim said. "Don't you think that's unfair?"

"Unfair?" Hatcher echoed, smiling. *"There's* a machine response for you. That's what the loser always says. Be a little better, a little smarter, a little stronger than your competitor, and he runs to the government, yanks on its apron strings and screams, 'Unfair competition. Unfair competition!' Understand this, Jim — nothing's unfair that doesn't break the rules. And the only rule worth remembering is this — the best man always wins."

"You mean the best machine," Jim said sourly.

"A machine is only an extension of a man, like your driver. I don't happen to be endowed with golfing muscles and responses. You do. Those — and your golf clubs, Jim — let you hit a ball farther and straighter than anybody else. Saul lets me hit a ball farther and straighter than you do. It's as simple as that."

Jim said, "That wasn't the bet. The bet was that I couldn't make $50,000 in a year. Not that you couldn't spend twenty times that to keep me from making half as much. That was obvious from the start."

"Maybe that was *your* bet. It wasn't *mine.* I bet that I could beat you at your own game. I didn't think you were good enough for Alice, not smart enough, not man enough. Maybe you didn't have a chance anyway — *I* don't know. But she was spending too much time at the country club, and it wasn't just to improve her game. Should I let a few well-distributed, well-trained muscles blind her to what you really are?"

"And what's that?"

"Why, you're a quitter, Jim. You can't stand pressure. You're no competitor. You've proved that time after time. Maybe Alice couldn't see it. I had to keep her from a foolish mistake."

Jim frowned. Maybe it *had* been true. It wasn't true any more — if he could only prove it. "And yet I was going to win — until you threw your millions against me," he said.

Hatcher shook his head. His jowls wobbled. "Could I let luck give away what I value most? Of course not. Alice deserves the best, the smartest, the strongest. I knew you were a weakling. If you couldn't win at your own game, you couldn't win at anything else. At least I gave you that chance."

"Chance!" Jim's eyes studied the floor, moodily.

"Have you ever played poker, Jim?"

Jim looked up. "Sure."

"Then maybe you know that, over the long run, the smartest player always wins. *Over the long run.* You have to give luck time to even out. That means the winner is the man who can stay in the game the longest, the one with the most chips. There's a moral in that. Poor men should never play poker. Rich men should play nothing else."

"So you made sure I couldn't win," Jim said. "All because of a preconception that I'm a quitter. One ninety-five for 54 holes. I don't call that quitting."

Hatcher shrugged heavy shoulders. "What will you do tomorrow, Jim? Or next week? What will you do when it's more than just a game, when the going really gets rough? That's what it is now. This is for keeps. And it isn't enough just to come close. You've got to have the will to win. Everything is unacceptable but victory."

"According to my standards, Hatcher," Jim said grimly, "you haven't played fair. Suppose I should lose — through no fault of my own — and try to win Alice anyway?"

Hatcher's voice was just as grim. "Then I'd know that you are a welsher besides a quitter. And I'd act accordingly — without compunctions."

Jim knew what Hatcher could do if he wanted to. "And suppose I should win tomorrow?"

Hatcher's face relaxed. "Six strokes back? Playing against the perfect golfer?"

"Suppose!" Jim said firmly.

Hatcher sobered and studied Jim's face. "Then I'd have to admit I was wrong. You have my word on that. And you could have Alice — if she wants you."

There was a small sound from the doorway. Jim turned. She was standing there, cool, slim, desirable.

"Al . . ." he said, and knew that he loved her more than ever.

*

How long had she been there? Hatcher turned. *"Alice!* But I got a letter from you this morning — from England."

Her voice was low and musical, as Jim remembered it.

"I left them with a friend to mail for me." She walked forward slowly. "I wanted to keep myself out of this. I was afraid I might disturb something."

"But you should know," Hatcher said affectionately, "that you could never disturb me."

"I was thinking of Jim," she said slowly.

Jim straightened up. He looked intently into the face he loved.

Alice's red lips twisted ironically. "That's funny, isn't it? And it's funny to stand here like this and talk coldly about something that was never put into words before. And the funniest part is that I wasn't really in love with Jim — not then, not really."

"Al . . ." Jim began, and stopped. There was nothing he could say. Alice's blue eyes turned toward him, and Jim told himself that they held a warm promise.

"It probably wouldn't ever have come to anything, Dad," Alice said quietly. "But then you let me find out about the bet. I was mad at first, but then I started to think. The bet told me something. It told me Jim was in love with me, enough to make a crazy bet like that on the wild chance that he might win. That was something I had never been sure of before, with any man. And then you kept us apart. That was more. It's worked for thousands of years. It worked this time. I fell in love."

Jim swallowed hard. In a moment he would break out singing.

"You don't know how I prayed and fought every one of his tournaments with him. And, when he got so close, I had to be here. I had to be near him, even if I couldn't let him know, for fear that it would upset his game."

Hatcher nodded. "I can see why you'd be afraid of that."

"You're wrong, Dad," Alice said earnestly. "He's not a quitter. He's proved that. Anybody but you would admit it. Sure he's human. He's not a machine and I love him."

"Love?" Hatcher shrugged his shoulders. "It comes and goes. The only thing that doesn't change is character."

"You can't prove that with a machine," Alice said firmly.

"It's his own game. Remember that. If a machine can play it better than he can, he should lose. Take away his one ability and what have you got? Nothing!" He turned to Jim. "The bet still stands." He smiled gently at Alice. "I won't let you throw yourself away on a childish whim."

And he stalked out of the room with all the delicacy and refinement of a bull elephant.

Jim stared at Alice for a moment, then took two giant strides and gathered her in his arms. Eventually they drew apart.

"Did you mean that?" he asked. "About loving me."

She nodded, her eyes glistening with unshed tears.

"What can we do?" he continued.

"Nothing," she said hopelessly. "You heard what he said about not letting me throw myself away. He meant it. He could do it, too."

"Then I've got to beat Saul," Jim said bravely. But he knew, while he said it, that he was whistling in the dark. He wasn't playing against another golfer. He was playing against himself — *and* Tod Winters *and* George Potter *and* Gordon Brown, the best of each. Against perfection, he had only his own fallible, erratic skill. Against machine judgment and nerveless metal, he had to pit the illusioned human senses and nerves that could, he knew only too well, turn to quivering jelly.

"Somewhere," he said slowly, "Saul must have an Achilles heel. The prime fact about man is his adaptability. An imitation would have to have built-in limitations."

"That's *it!*" Alice said excitedly. "They had to build in at least one constant, if not more. If we can find it and alter the conditions . . ."

"Judgment?" Jim suggested. He tossed the idea away. "No — judgment has to be flexible. They couldn't know when he'd meet up with wind, rain, sunbaked courses, slow greens, fast ones, wormcasts . . ."

"He does it, too," Alice said. "I've watched him. Maybe we could find where he's kept. Tinker with him — smash him!"

"That wouldn't be fair. I could probably have him disqualified, of course. But that wouldn't be fair either."

"*Fair!*" Alice exploded. "Has *Dad* played fair? This isn't a game, Jim. We've got to win."

Jim smiled at the essential amorality of women and sobered. "That isn't what I meant. I mean your father wouldn't accept it. According to his lights, he's played fair with me. He could have had me crippled, poisoned, or taken out of action in lots of ways — and gotten away with it. But he's beating me on my own ground. And that's where we've got to beat him."

Alice shook her head. "All that skill and energy — wasted on something like this."

"And it could be such a wonderful thing," Jim said. "Profitable, too. Think of the things that machines could do, if they had memories and self-contained power! Not man-shapes, like Saul. That's useless. They could do all the jobs that man's too weak to do or that are too dangerous or too much drudgery."

"Mining," Alice said, "and manufacturing."

"Exploring — the cold places and the hot places. The deeps of the sea and space. Rebuilding — making uninhabitable places livable." Jim's eyes were distant. "The important thing is that they can't compete. Man won't stand for it. He'll destroy them first. And they can never conquer man, because he's too adaptable. Unless he lets them."

"That's wonderful," Alice said, her eyes glowing. "Tell Dad. He can recognize a good idea when he hears it. He won't think you're so dumb then."

"I could probably like him," Jim said, "except he won't give me the chance. Not unless we find the constant. I guess I'll just have to play my heart out tomorrow."

"You can't do it, darling. You'd have to shoot in the fifties!"

"A golf ball takes some funny bounces," Jim said. He turned to the window and stuck his hands moodily in his pockets. He started. It was as simple as that.

"There *is* a constant," he said exultantly, swinging around. "Look, Al. Here's the key to my locker. Get my caddy and Saul's. I think you'll have more luck with the boy than I would. Give him — oh, five or ten dollars. And here's what I want you to do . . ."

In the middle of the explanation, Alice caught fire, too. As he finished, she gave Jim a quick, proud kiss and hurried out. Jim's eyes followed her admiringly for a moment, and then he reluctantly turned toward the dining room.

Jim dragged Dave Simpson, the tournament official, protestingly away from a hearty meal. "I've just had a wonderful idea," he said. "Why don't you put Saul and me together for tomorrow's round?"

"*What!*" Dave exclaimed.

"Think of the crowds, Dave," Jim urged.

"But what about you? What chance will you have, playing with a man who has you down six strokes?"

"Oh, that's all right," Jim said bravely. "I don't mind. But if you're not interested . . ."

Jim moved to turn away. Dave caught him by an elbow.

"I didn't say I wasn't interested. If it's all right with you, I don't think anyone else will object."

Jim thought of Hatcher. "No," he said, "I don't think they will."

Jim walked away, whistling.

The reaction set in when he strode on to the tee next morning. The crowd was immense and noisy. It was all very well to plan something like this in the abstract. But, in the clutch, would his nerve fail him, as it had failed him before?

Alice was waiting for him, cool and lovely and infinitely desirable. She put her hand on his arm and warmed him with a smile.

On the other side of the broad tee, Hatcher's smile was mocking. Beside him, Saul, the robot, waited impassively. Jim knew then that it wasn't going to be as easy as he had thought.

It wouldn't be enough to hope that he had thrown a wrench into Saul's machinery. He would have to fight grimly, determinedly. He would have to play the greatest game of his life today, if he wanted to win.

The crowd was partisan. Like most Americans, they were pulling for the underdog. Jim knew that they wanted him to play brilliantly, if only to narrow the gap and make the match thrilling, and that if he failed to come through for them, they would swing to Saul.

Even realizing all this, it warmed him as they cheered him up to the tee — knowing that what they really wanted was to see golfing history made. God willing, that was what they would see.

Jim's drive took a tail-end hook. It dived into the rough behind a clump of trees. He stepped back, grimacing. He would have appreciated a happier start.

As Jim watched closely, Saul took a ball from his caddy, teed it up, settled himself, and swung. The ball sailed straight down the fairway, forty or fifty yards beyond the 300-yard marker. The crowd gasped. Jim smiled.

When he saw his lie, the smile was wiped away. Sensible golf would have been to play it safe, out onto the fairway, where he could hope to play his third shot straight enough for a par.

Sensible golf wouldn't win. Jim took out his two-iron, sighted through a small hole in the trees, and swung at the almost-hidden ball. It whipped through the opening and rolled to a stop just in front of the green.

Saul's easy four-iron shot was dead on the pin all the way, but the crowd moaned sympathetically as the ball hit the back edge of the green and hopped into the rough.

Hatcher looked puzzled as he stood beside the green. Jim's close approach set up an easy putt for a birdie. Saul's recovery was long, and two putts gave him a par.

Jim smiled grimly. That was one of the six strokes he needed.

Jim's game sparkled — Saul kept finding trouble. While Jim was getting down in two on the next hole, Saul was over the green again and back for a par three.

The third hole was shared in birdies, the fourth in pars, the fifth in birdies again. Then Jim eagled the par-five sixth, and Saul played back and forth across the green for a 5.

Four strokes, Jim thought, and cast a glance at Hatcher, whose face was worried and confused. Maybe now he was having doubts about his perfect machine.

But Saul matched pars with Jim on the next two, then got back a stroke on the ninth with a long putt while Jim was scrambling for a par.

Jim took a long breath as they walked to the tenth tee to begin the second nine, the crucial nine. He had come in with a scorching 30, while Saul had shot his worst nine of the tournament, a 33. If Jim hadn't been terrific, he wouldn't have picked up a stroke. It was going to be tough to keep up that pace.

When Alice lit his cigarette for him, her hand was shaking. He held the hand firmly and looked steadily into her eyes. In a moment the shaking stopped. "Thanks," she said.

"Nothing to it," Jim said, and hoped he sounded more confident than he felt.

Jim breathed a little easier when Saul's two-iron bounced far down the back edge of the tenth green. Jim played it carefully, landing on the front edge and sticking. Saul took a long recovery shot and two putts for his first bogey. Jim's two putts gave him a par. He was only two strokes behind.

They shared birdies on the eleventh and pars on twelfth. On the next, however, Jim got his second eagle, with a chip shot that dribbled to the lip, trembled, and finally dropped. Unperturbed, Saul holed his putt for a birdie.

One stroke behind? Jim muttered hoarsely to himself. The strain was beginning to tell. He had to steel himself before each shot to keep from trembling.

They each took pars on 14, birdie threes on 15. On the short sixteenth, Jim's seven-iron dropped ten feet in front of the pin, Saul's eleven feet behind. Saul's putt was straight in.

Jim's hand shook as he lined up the putt. If he missed this, he would be two strokes behind again with only two holes to go. He could never hope to catch up. He jabbed at the ball. It trickled off to the right, stopping a full foot from the hole. He steadied himself and dropped the next.

For a moment, he could feel the old, familiar sense of despair and rage creep through him. Then Alice put her arm confidently through his as they walked to the seventeenth tee. Fiercely, Jim drove his longest wood of the day. It still lacked thirty yards of Saul's.

Saul overshot the green by forty yards and ended with a par-five. Jim calmed himself to make a fifty-foot approach putt stop within three feet of the pin, but left himself a sharp downhill slope. He tapped the second one gingerly. The ball trickled to the lip and dropped with a cheerful thunk.

He was no Tod Winters, Jim told himself wryly, but he had his moments. Once more he was only one stroke behind. One stroke, and one hole to go. Pick up a stroke and tie, two strokes and win. Win Alice or lose her. It was like losing the world. A tie would be no good. There were excellent reasons why Saul's game wouldn't be off on the morrow. He had to get two strokes on this hole, somehow.

Jim's drive sliced behind a fringe of trees that divided the first and eighteenth fairways. Saul's drive, as usual, was long and straight. Jim wiped the sweat from his forehead. It was pain not to relax, not to quit, scream, and curse.

The green was hidden, 130 yards away. He had to shoot over the trees blind. He swung easily, smoothly. The ball cleared the trees and dropped from sight. He barely heard the smattering of applause.

Jim watched Saul's approach land over the crowd at the back of the green. Jim walked up slowly. When he had forced his way through the spectators, he saw that his ball had landed on the green — but twenty-five feet from the cup.

The crowd formed a lane for Saul's third shot. It hit the green and scooted, coming to rest on the front edge. His putt was straight for the hole all the way. The hush broke into a moan. The ball had rimmed.

Jim figured it up. That would give Saul a five. He could win with a three. He studied the green carefully, noting the slopes, the lay of the grass. After a minute he decided on his line. He took his stance. Once more, an unnatural silence settled over the crowd.

Jim stroked the ball. It ran swiftly at first, then slowing, trickling over the last slope, nearing the cup, gently turning. Eternities passed, and the ball hesitated on the lip, toppled, disappeared.

The scene was bedlam. Alice grabbed his arm with one hand, thrust the scorecard in front of his nose, and jumped up and down screaming happily. Jim steadied the card long enough to read the score. Another 30 — a 60 for the day. A 72-hole total of 255. A flock of broken records.

When the new US Open champion walked to Saul's caddy and removed the ball from the boy's fingers, Hatcher was at his side. He was frowning.

"How did you do it?" he shouted.

Hatcher had ceased to awe Jim. Hatcher was not infallible.

"Under certain extremely restricted sets of circumstances," Jim said, "a machine is better than a man. But, over the long run, over the gamut of situations, a machine doesn't have a chance. It just can't compete."

Hatcher was still frowning. "I still don't understand."

"Here," Jim said, handing him the golf ball Saul had been using.

Hatcher stared at it. "This isn't Saul's regular ball."

"That's right." Jim laughed. "It's a new one, guaranteed to add twenty yards to the average drive."

Slow understanding crossed Hatcher's face. "But that's unfair," he said. "That's . . ." He began to smile, and the smile broke into a chuckle. "I'll be damned!" he said.

"There are no perfect golfers," Jim said. "There are only good ones and better ones. I'll be around in a few days to talk about men and machines — and competition. I have $50,000 to invest in our new business — making robots — *useful* robots."

star trav/el — trips outside our solar system in spaceships normally equipped with "faster-than-light" drives. Sometimes such travel takes place over several centuries, with the crews placed in suspended animation; alternatively, the descendents of the original crews are the ones who reach the destination. Interstellar travel is described in stories in *Possible Worlds of Science Fiction* (Vanguard Press, 1951); *To the Stars* (Hawthorn Books, 1971); and *Faster Than Light: An Original Anthology About Interstellar Travel* (Harper & Row, 1976).

The Long Way Home

FRED SABERHAGEN

When Marty first saw the thing it was nearly dead ahead, eight hundred thousand kilometers away, a tiny green blip that repeated itself every five seconds on the screen of his distant search radar.

He was six and a half billion kilometers from Sol and heading out, working his way slowly through a small swarm of rock chunks that swung in a slow sun-orbit out here beyond Pluto, looking for valuable minerals in a concentration that would make mining profitable.

The thing on his radar screen looked quite small and therefore not too promising. But, as it was almost in his path, no great effort would be required to investigate. For all he knew, it might be solid germanium. And nothing better was in sight at the moment.

Marty leaned back in the control seat and said: "We've got one coming up, baby." He had no need to address himself any more exactly. Only one other human was aboard the *Clementine,* or, to his knowledge, anywhere within a couple of billion kilometers.

Laura's voice answered through a speaker, from the kitchen two decks below. "Oh, close? Have we got time for breakfast?"

Marty studied the radar. "About five hours if we maintain speed. Hope it won't be a waste of energy to decelerate and look the thing over." He gave *Clem*'s main computer the problem of finding the most economical engine use to approach his find and reach zero velocity relative to it.

"Come and eat!"

"All right." He and the computer studied the blip together for a few seconds. Then the man, not considering it anything of unusual importance, left the control room to have breakfast with his bride of three months. As he walked downstairs in the steadily maintained artificial gravity, he heard the engines starting.

A few hours later he examined his new find much more closely with a rapidly focusing alertness that balanced between an explorer's caution and a prospector's elation at a possibly huge strike.

The incredible shape of X, becoming apparent as *Clem* drew within a few hundred kilometers, was what had Marty on the edge of his chair. It was a needle fifty kilometers long, approximately, and about a hundred meters thick — dimensions that matched exactly nothing Marty could expect to find anywhere in space.

It was obviously no random chunk of rock. And it was no spaceship that he had ever seen or heard of. One end of it pointed in the direction of Sol, causing him to suggest to Laura the idea of a miniature comet, complete with tail. She took him seriously at first, then remembered some facts about comets and swatted him playfully. "Oh, you!" she said.

Another more real possibility quickly became obvious, with sobering effect. The ancient fear of the Alien that had haunted Earthmen through almost three thousand years of intermittent space exploration, but had never been realized, now peered into the snug control room through the green radar eye.

Aliens were always good for a joke when spacemen met and talked. But they turned out to be not particularly amusing when you were possibly confronting them, several billion kilometers from Earth. Especially, thought Marty, in a ship built for robot mining, ore refining, and hauling, not for diplomatic contacts or heroics. And with the only human assistance a girl on her first space trip, Marty hardly felt up to speaking for the human race in such a situation.

It took a minute to set the autopilot so that any sudden move by X would trigger alarms and such evasive tactics as *Clem* could manage. He then set a robot librarian to searching his microfilm files for any reference to a spaceship having X's incredible dimensions.

There was a chance — how good a chance he found hard to estimate, when any explanation looked somewhat wild — that X was a derelict, the wrecked hull of some ship dead for a decade, or a century, or a thousand years. By law of salvage, such a find would belong to him if he towed it into port. The value might be very high or very low. But the prospect was certainly intriguing.

Marty brought *Clem* to a stop relative to X, and noticed that his velocity to Sol now also hung at zero. "I wonder," he muttered. "Space anchor . . . ?"

The space anchor had been in use for thousands of years. It was a device that enabled a ship to fasten itself to a particular point in the gravitational field of a massive body such as the sun. If X was anchored, it did not prove that there was still life aboard her; once "dropped," an anchor could hold as long as a hull could last.

Laura brought sandwiches and a hot drink to him in the control room.

"If we call the navy and they bring it in we won't get anything out of it," he told her between bites. "That's assuming it's — not alien."

"Could there be someone alive on it?" She was staring into the screen. Her face was solemn, but, he thought, not frightened.

"If it's human, you mean? No. I *know* there hasn't been any ship remotely like that used in recent years. Way, way back the Old Empire built some that were even bigger, but none I ever heard of with this crazy shape . . ."

The robot librarian indicated that it had drawn a blank. "See?" said Marty. "And I've even got most of the ancient types in there."

There was silence for a little while. The evening's recorded music started somewhere in the background.

"What would you do if I weren't along?" Laura asked him.

He did not answer directly, but said something he had been considering. "I don't know the psychology of our hypothetical aliens. But it seems to me that if you set out exploring new solar systems, you do as Earthmen have always done — go with the best you have in the way of speed and weapons. Therefore if X is alien, I don't think *Clem* would stand a chance, trying to fight or run." He paused, frowning at the image of X. "That damned *shape* — it's just not right for anything."

"We could call the navy — not that I'm saying we should, darling," she added hastily. "You decide, and I'll never complain either way. I'm just trying to help you think it out."

He looked at her, believed it about there never being any complaints, and squeezed her hand. Anything more seemed superfluous. "If I were alone," he said, "I'd jump into a suit, go look that thing over, haul it back to Ganymede, and sell it for a unique whatever-it-is. Maybe I'd make enough money to marry you in real style, and trade in *Clem* for a first-rate ship — or maybe even terraform an asteroid and keep a couple of robot prospectors. I don't know, though. Maybe we'd better call the navy."

She laughed at him gently. "We're married enough already, and we had all the style I wanted. Besides, I don't think either of us would be very happy sitting on an asteroid. How long do you think it will take you to look it over?"

At the airlock door she had misgivings. "Oh, it *is* safe enough, isn't it? Marty, be careful and come back soon." She kissed him before he closed his helmet.

They had moved *Clem* to within a few kilometers of X. Marty mounted his spacebike and approached it slowly, from the side.

The vast length of X blotted out a thin strip of stars to his right and left, as if it were the distant shore of some vast island in a placid Terran sea, and the star clouds below him were the watery reflections of the ones above. But space was too black to permit such an illusion to endure.

The tiny FM radar on his bike showed him within three hundred meters of X. He killed his forward speed with a gentle application of retrojets and turned on a spotlight. Bright metal gleamed smoothly back at him as he swung the beam from side to side. Then he stopped it where a dark concavity showed up.

"Lifeboat berth . . . empty," he said aloud, looking through the bike's little telescope.

"Then it is a derelict? We're all right?" asked Laura's voice in his helmet.

"Looks that way, yeah, I guess there's no doubt of it. I'll go in for a closer look now." He eased his bike forward. X was evidently just some rare type of ship that neither he nor the compilers of the standard reference works in his library had ever heard of. Which sounded just a little foolish to him, but . . .

At ten meters' distance he killed the speed again, set the bike on automatic stay-clear, made sure a line from it was fast to his belt, and launched himself out of the saddle gently, headfirst toward X.

The armored hands of his suit touched down first, easily and expertly. In a moment he was standing upright on the hull, held in place by magnetic boots. He looked around. He detected no response to his arrival.

Marty turned toward Sol, sighting down the kilometers of dark cylinder that seemingly dwindled to a point in the starry distance, like a road on which a man might travel home toward a tiny sun.

Near at hand the hull was smooth, looking like that of any ordinary spaceship. In the direction away from Sol, quite distant, he could vaguely see some sort of projections at right angles to the hull. He mounted his bike again and set off in that direction. When he neared the nearest projection, a kilometer and a half down the hull, he saw it to be a sort of enormous clamp that encircled X — or rather, part of a clamp. It ended a few meters from the hull, in rounded globs of metal that had once been molten but were now too cold to affect the thermometer Marty held against them. His radiation counter showed nothing above the normal background.

"Ah," said Marty after a moment, looking at the half-clamp.

"Something?"

"I think I've got it figured out. Not quite as weird as we thought. Let me check for one thing more." He steered the bike slowly around the circumference of X.

A third of the way around he came upon what looked like a shallow trench, a little less than two meters wide and about half a meter deep, with a bottom that shone cloudy gray in his lights. It ran lengthwise on X as far as he could see in either direction.

A door-sized opening was cut in the clamp above the trench.

Marty nodded and smiled to himself, and gunned the bike around in an accelerating curve that aimed at the *Clementine.*

"It's not a spaceship at all, only a part of one," he told Laura a little later, digging in the microfilm file with his own hands, with the air of a man who knew what he was looking for. "That's why the librarian didn't turn it up. Now I remember reading about them. It's part of an Old Empire job of about two thousand years ago. They used a somewhat different drive than we do, one that made one enormous ship more economical to run than several normal-sized ones. They made these ships ready for a voyage by fastening together a number of long narrow sections side by side, how many depending on how much cargo they had to move. What we've found is obviously one of those sections."

Laura frowned. "It must have been a terrible job, putting those sections together and separating them, even in space."

"They used space anchors. That trench I mentioned? It has a force-field bottom, so an anchor could be sunk through it; then the whole section could be slid straight forward or back, in or out of the bunch . . . here, I've got it, I think. Put this strip in the viewer."

One picture, a photograph, showed what appeared to be one end of a bunch of long needles, in a glaring light, against a background of stars that looked unreal. The legend beneath gave a scanty description of the ship in flowing Old Empire script. Other pictures showed sections of the ship in some detail.

"This must be it, all right," said Marty thoughtfully. "Funny-looking old tub."

"I wonder what happened to wreck her."

"Drives sometimes exploded in those days, and that could have done it. And this one section got anchored to Sol somehow — it's funny."

"How long ago did it happen, do you suppose?" asked Laura. She had her arms folded as if she were a little cold, though it was not cold in the *Clementine.*

"Must be around two thousand years or more. These ships haven't been used for about that long." He picked up a stylus. "I better go over there with a big bag of tools tomorrow and take a look inside." He noted down a few things he thought he might need.

"Historians would probably pay a good price for the whole thing, untouched," she suggested, watching him draw doodles.

"That's a thought. But maybe there's something really valuable aboard — though I won't be able to give it anything like a thorough search, of course. The thing is anchored, remember. I'll probably have to break in anyway to release that."

She pointed to one of the diagrams. "Look, a section fifty kilometers long must be one of the passenger compartments. And according to this plan, it would have no drive at all of its own. We'll have to tow it."

He looked. "Right. Anyway, I don't think I'd care to try its drive if it had one."

He located airlocks on the plan and made himself generally familiar with it.

The next "morning" found Marty loading extra tools, gadgets, and explosives onto his bike. The trip to X (he still thought of it that way) was uneventful. This time he landed about a third of the way from one end, where he expected to find a handy airlock and have a choice of directions to explore once he got inside. He hoped to get the airlock open without letting out whatever atmosphere or gas was present in any of the main compartments, as a sudden drop in pressure might damage something in the unknown cargo.

He found a likely looking spot for entry where the plans had told him to expect one. It was a small auxiliary airlock, only a few meters from the space-anchor channel. The force-field bottom of that channel was, he knew, useless as a possible doorway. Though anchors could be raised and lowered through it, they remained partly imbedded in it at all times. Starting a new hole from scratch would cause the decompression he was trying to avoid, and possibly a dangerous explosion as well.

Marty began his attack on the airlock door cautiously, working with electronic sounding gear for a few minutes, trying to determine whether the inner door was closed as well. He had about decided that it was when something made him look up. He raised his head and sighted down the dark length of X toward Sol.

Something was moving toward him along the hull.

He was up in the bike saddle with his hand on a blaster before he realized what it was — that moving blur that distorted the stars seen through it, like heat waves in air. Without doubt, it was a space anchor. And it moved along the channel.

Marty rode the bike out a few meters and nudged it along slowly, following the anchor. It moved at about the pace of a fast walk. *Moved* . . . but it was sunk into space.

"Laura," he called. "Something odd here. Doppler this hull for me and see if it's moving."

Laura acknowledged in one businesslike word. Good girl, he thought. I won't have to worry about you. He coasted along the hull on the bike, staying even with the apparent movement of the anchor.

Laura's voice came: "It is moving now, toward Sol. About ten kilometers per hour. Maybe less — it's hard to read, so slow."

"Good, that's what I thought." He hoped he sounded reassuring. He pondered the situation. It was the hull moving then, the force-field channel sliding past the fixed anchor. Whatever was causing it, it did not seem to be directed against him or the *Clem.* "Look, baby," he went on. "Something peculiar is happening." He explained about the anchor. *"Clem* may be no battleship, but I guess she's a match for any piece of wreckage."

"But you're out *there!"*

"I have to see this. I never saw anything like it before. Don't worry, I'll pull back if it looks at all dangerous." Something in the back of his mind told him to go back to his ship and call the navy. He ignored the inner voice without much trouble. He had never thought much of calling the navy.

About four hours later the incomprehensible anchor neared the end of its track, within thirty meters of what seemed to be X's stern. It slowed down and came to a gradual stop a few meters from the end of the track. For a minute nothing else happened. Marty reported the facts to Laura. He sat straight in the bike saddle, regarding the universe, which offered him no enlightenment.

In the space between the anchor and the end of the track, a second patterned shimmer appeared. It must necessarily have been let "down" into space from inside X. Marty felt a creeping chill. After a little while the first anchor vanished, withdrawn through the force-field of the hull.

Marty sat watching for twenty minutes, but nothing further happened. He realized that he had a crushing grip on the bike controls and that he was quivering with fatigue.

Laura and Marty took turns sleeping and watching that night aboard the *Clementine.* About noon the next ship's day Laura was at the telescope when anchor number one reappeared, now at the "prow" of X. After a few moments the one at the stern vanished.

Marty looked at the communicator that he could use any time to call the navy. Faster-than-light travel not being practical so near a sun, it would take them at least several hours to arrive after he decided he needed them. Then he beat his fist against a table and swore. "It can only be that there's some kind of mechanism in her still operating." He went to the telescope and watched number one anchor begin its apparent slow journey sternward once more. "I don't know. I've got to settle this."

The doppler radar showed X was again creeping toward Sol at about ten kilometers an hour.

"Does it seem likely there'd be power left after two thousand years to operate such a mechanism?" Laura asked.

"I think so. Each passenger section had a hydrogen power lamp." He dug out the microfilm again. "Yeah, a small fusion lamp for electricity to light and heat the section, and to run the emergency equipment for . . ." His voice trailed off, then continued in a dazed tone: "For recycling food and water."

"Marty, what is it?"

He stood up, staring at the plan. "And the only radios were in the lifeboats, and the lifeboats are gone. I wonder . . . sure. The explosion could have torn them apart, blown them away so . . ."

"What are you talking about?"

He looked again at their communicator. "A transmitter that can get through the noise between here and Pluto wouldn't be easy to jury-rig, even now. In the Old Empire days . . ."

"*What?*"

"Now about air — " He seemed to wake up with a start and looked at her sheepishly. "Just an idea hit me." He grinned. "I'm making another trip."

An hour later he was landing on X for the third time, touching down near the "stern." He was riding the moving hull toward the anchor, but it was still many kilometers away.

The spot he had picked was near another small auxiliary airlock, upon which he began work immediately. After ascertaining that the inner door was closed, he drilled a hole in the outer door to relieve any inside pressure tending to hold it shut. The door-opening mechanism suffered from a cramp no doubt induced by twenty centuries of immobility, but a vibrator tool shook it loose enough to be operated by hand. The inside of the airlock looked like nothing more than the inside of an airlock.

He patched the hole he had made in the outer door so he would be able — he hoped — to open the inner one normally. He operated the outer door several times to make sure he could get out fast if he had to. After attaching a few extras from the bike to his suit, he said a quick and cheerful goodbye to Laura — not expecting his radio to work from inside the hull — and closed himself into the airlock. Using the vibrator again, he was able to work the control that should let whatever passed for hull atmosphere into the chamber. It came. His wrist gauge told him pressure was building up to approximately spaceship normal, and his suit mikes began to pick up a faint hollow humming from somewhere. He very definitely kept suit and helmet sealed.

The inner door worked perfectly, testifying to the skill of the Old Empire builders. Marty found himself nearly upside down as he went through, losing his footing and his sense of heroic adventure. In return he gained the knowledge that X's artificial gravity was still at least partially operational. Righting himself, he found that he was in a small anteroom banked with spacesuit lockers, now illuminated only by his suit lights but showing no signs of damage. There was a door in each wall.

He moved to try the one at his right. First drawing his blaster, he hesitated a moment, then slid it back into its holster. Swallowing, he eased the door open to find only another empty compartment, about the size of an average room and stripped of everything down to the bare deck and bulkheads.

Another door led him into a narrow passage where a few overhead lights burned dimly. Trying to watch over his shoulder and ahead at the same time, he followed the hall to a winding stair and began to climb, moving with all the silence possible in a spacesuit.

The stair brought him out onto a long gallery overlooking what could only be the main corridor of X, a passageway twenty meters wide and three decks high; it narrowed away to a point in the dim-lit distance.

A man came out of a doorway across the corridor, a deck below Marty.

He was an old man and may have been nearsighted, for he was unaware of the spacesuited figure gripping a railing and staring down at him. The old man wore a sort of tunic intricately embroidered with threads of different colors, and well tailored to his thin figure, leaving his legs and feet bare. He stood for a moment peering down the long corridor, while Marty stared down momentarily frozen in shock.

Recovering, Marty pulled back two slow steps from the railing, to where he stood mostly in shadow. Turning his head to follow the old man's gaze, he noticed that the force-field where the anchors traveled was visible running in a sunken strip down the center of the corridor. When the interstellar ship of which X was once a part had been in normal use, the strip might have been covered by a moving walkway of some kind.

The old man turned his attention to a tank where grew a mass of plants with flat, dark green leaves. He touched a leaf, then turned a valve that doled water into the tank from a thin pipe. Similar valves were clustered on the bulkhead behind the old man, and pipes ran from them to many other plant-filled tanks set at intervals down the corridor. "For oxygen," Marty said aloud in an almost calm voice, and was startled at the sound in his helmet. His helmet airspeaker was not turned on, so of course the old man did not hear him. The old man pulled a red berry from one of the plants and ate it absently.

Marty made a move with his chin toward the airspeaker switch inside his helmet, but did not complete the move. He half lifted an arm to wave, but awed fear held him, made him back up slowly into the shadows at the rear of the gallery. Turning his head to the right he could see the near end of the corridor, and an anchor there, not sunken in space but raised almost out of the force-field on a framework at the end of the strip.

Near the stair he had ascended was a half-open door, leading into darkness. Marty realized he had turned off his suit lights without being conscious of it. Moving carefully so the old man would not see, he lit one and probed the darkness beyond the door consciously. The room he entered was the first of a small suite that had once been a passenger cabin. The furniture was simple, but it was the first of any kind that he had seen aboard X. Garments hanging in one corner were similar to the old man's tunic, though no two were exactly alike in design. Marty fingered the fabric with one armored hand, holding it close to his faceplate. He nodded to himself; it seemed to be the kind of stuff produced by fiber-recycling machinery, and he doubted very much that it was anywhere near two thousand years old.

Marty emerged from the doorway of the little apartment, and stood in shadow with his suit lights out, looking around. The old man had disappeared. He remembered that the old man had gazed down the infinite-looking corridor as if expecting something. There was nothing new in sight that way. He turned up the gain of one of his suit mikes and focused it in that direction.

Many human voices were singing, somewhere down there, kilometers away. He started, and tried to interpret what he heard in some other way, but with an eerie thrill became convinced that his first interpretation was correct. While he contemplated going back to his bike and heading in that direction, he became aware that the singing was getting louder. And therefore no doubt closer.

He leaned back against the bulkhead in the shadow at the rear of the gallery. His dark suit would be practically invisible from the lighted corridor below, while he could see down with little difficulty. Part of his mind urged him to go back to Laura, to call the navy, that these unknown people could be dangerous to him. But he could not bring himself to leave without seeing more. He grinned wryly as he realized that he was not going to get any salvage out of X after all.

Sweating in spite of his suit's coolers, he listened to the singing grow rapidly louder. Male and female voices rose and fell in an intricate melody, sometimes blending, sometimes chanting separate parts. The language was unknown to him.

Suddenly the people were in sight, first only as a faint dot of color in the distance. As they drew nearer he could see that they walked in a long neat column eight abreast, four on each side of the central strip of force-field. Men and women, apparently teamed according to no fixed rule of age or sex or size — except that he saw no oldsters or young children.

The people sang and leaned forward as they walked, pulling their weight on heavy ropes that were intricately decorated, like their clothing and that of the old man who now stepped out of his doorway again to greet them. A few other oldsters of both sexes appeared near him to stand and wait. Through a briefly opened door Marty caught a glimpse of a well-lighted room holding machines he recognized as looms only because of the half-finished cloth they held. He shook his head wonderingly.

All at once the walkers were very near; hundreds of people pulling on ropes that led to a multiple whiffletree made of twisted metal pipes, that rode over the central trench. The whiffletree and the space anchor to which it was fastened were pulled past Marty — or rather the spot from which he watched was carried past the fixed anchor by the slow, human-powered thrust of X toward Sol.

Behind the anchor came a small group of children, from about the age of ten up to puberty. They pulled on ropes, drawing a cart that held what looked like containers for food and water. At the extreme rear of the procession marched a man in the prime of life, tall and athletic, wearing a magnificent headdress. About the time he drew even with Marty, this man stopped suddenly and uttered a sharp command. Instantly the pulling and singing ceased. Several men nearest the whiffletree moved in with quick precision and loosened it from the anchor. Others held the slackened ropes clear as the enormous inertia of X's mass carried the end of the force-field strip toward the anchor, which now jammed against the framework holding anchor number two, forcing the framework back where there had seemed to be no room.

A thick force-field pad now became visible to Marty behind the framework, expanding steadily as it absorbed the energy of the powerful stress between ship and anchor. Conduits of some kind, Marty saw, led away from the pad, possibly to where energy might be stored for use when it came time to start X creeping toward the sun again. A woman in a headdress now mounted the framework and released anchor number two, to drop into space "below" the hull and bind X fast to the place where it was now held by anchor number one. A crew of men came forward and began to raise anchor number one...

He found himself descending the stair, retracing his steps to the airlock. Behind him the voices of the people were raised in a steady recitation that might have been a prayer. Feeling somewhat as if he moved in a dream, he made no particular attempt at caution, but he met no one. He tried to think, to understand what he had witnessed. Vaguely, comprehension came.

Outside, he said: "I'm all right, Laura. I want to look at something at the other end and I'll come home." He scarcely heard what she said in reply, but realized that her answer had been almost instantaneous; she must have been listening steadily for his call all the time. He felt better.

The bike shot him fifty kilometers down the dreamlike length of X toward Sol in a few minutes. A lot faster than the people inside do their traveling, he thought . . . and Sol was dim ahead.

Almost recklessly he broke into X again, through an airlock near the prow. At this end of the force-field strip hung a gigantic block and tackle that would give a vast mechanical advantage to a few hundred people pulling against an anchor, when it came time for them to start the massive hull moving toward Sol once more.

He looked in almost unnoticed at a nursery, small children in the care of a few women. He thought one of the babies saw him and laughed at him as he watched through a hole in a bulkhead where a conduit had once passed.

"What is it?" asked Laura impatiently as he stepped exhausted out of the shower room aboard the *Clem,* wrapping a robe around himself. He could see his shock mirrored now in her face.

"People," he said, sitting down. "Alive over there. Earth people. Humans."

"You're all right?"

"Sure. It's just — God!" He told her about it briefly. "They must be descended from the survivors of the accident, whatever it was. Physically there's no reason why they couldn't live, when you come to think of it — even reproduce up to a limited number. Plants for oxygen — I bet their air's as good as ours. Recycling equipment for food and water, and the hydrogen power lamp still working to run it, and to give them light and gravity . . . they have about everything they need. Everything but a space-drive." He leaned back with a sigh and closed his eyes. It was hard for him to stop talking to her.

She was silent for a little, trying to assimilate it all. "But if they have hydrogen power couldn't they have rigged something?" she finally asked. "*Some* kind of drive, even if it was slow? Just one push and they'd keep moving."

Marty thought it over. "Moving a little faster won't help them." He sat up and opened his eyes again. "And they'd have a lot less work to do every day. I imagine too large a dose of leisure time could be fatal to all of them.

"Somehow they had the will to keep going, and the intelligence to find a way of life that worked for them, that kept them from going wild and killing each other. And their system evolved, and worked for their children and grandchildren, and after that . . ." Slowly he stood up. She followed him into the control room, where they stood watching the image of X that was still focused on the telescope screen.

"All those years," Laura whispered. "All that time."

"Do you realize what they're doing?" he asked softly. "They're not just surviving, turned inward on weaving and designing and music.

"In a few hours they're going to get up and start another day's work. They're going to pull anchor number one back to the front of their ship and lower it. That's their morning job. Then someone left in the rear will raise anchor number two. Then the main group will start pulling against number one, as I saw them doing a little while ago, and their ship will begin to move toward Sol. Every day they go through this they move about fifty kilometers closer to home.

"Honey, these people are walking home and pulling their ship with them. It must be a religion with them by now, or something very near it . . ." He put an arm around Laura.

"Marty — how long would it take them?"

"Space is big," he said in a flat voice, as if quoting something he had been required to memorize. After a few moments he continued: "I said just moving a little faster won't help them. Let's say they've traveled fifty kilometers a day for two thousand years. That's — somewhere near thirty-six million kilometers. Almost enough to get from Mars to Earth at their nearest approach. But they've got a long way to go to reach the neighborhood of Mars's orbit. We're well out beyond Pluto here. Practically speaking, they're just about where they started from." He smiled wanly. "Really they're not far from home, for an interstellar ship. They had their accident almost on the doorstep of their own solar system, and they've been walking toward the threshold ever since."

Laura went to the communicator and began to set it up for the call that would bring the navy. She paused. "How long would it take them now," she asked, "to get somewhere near Earth?"

"Hell would freeze over. But they can't know that anymore. Or maybe they still know it and it just doesn't bother them. They must just go on, tugging at that damned anchor day after day, year after year, with maybe a holiday now and then . . . I don't know how they do it. They work and sing and feel they're accomplishing something . . . and really they are, you know. They have a goal and they are moving toward it. I wonder what they say of Earth, how they think about it."

Slowly Laura continued to set up the communicator.

Marty watched her. "Are you sure?" he pleaded suddenly. "What are we doing to them?"

But she had already sent the call.

For better or worse, the long voyage was almost over.

T

time tra/vel — movement forward or backward in time. When backward, the result is often an "alternate world" story where the present is different because of alterations to the past. People from the future sometimes try to escape unpleasant lives by "hiding" in the present of the story. Time travel stories frequently involve complex and interesting paradoxes. Stories of time travel are found in *Voyagers in Time* (Hawthorn Books, 1967) and *Trips in Time* (Thomas Nelson, 1977).

Skirmish on a Summer Morning

BOB SHAW

A flash of silver on the trail about a mile ahead of him brought Gregg out of his reverie. He pulled back on the reins, easing the buckboard to a halt, and took a small leather-covered telescope from the jacket that was lying on the wooden seat beside him. Sliding its sections out with multiple clicks, he raised the telescope to his eye, frowning a little at the ragged, gritty pain flaring in his elbows. It was early in the morning and, in spite of the heat, his arms retained some of their nighttime stiffness.

The ground had already begun to bake, agitating the lower levels of air into trembling movement, and the telescope yielded only a swimmy, bleached-out image. It was of a young woman, possibly Mexican, in a silver dress. Gregg brought the instrument down, wiped sweat from his forehead, and tried to make sense of what he had just seen. A woman dressed in silver would have been a rare spectacle anywhere, even in the plushest saloons of Sacramento, but finding one alone on the trail three miles north of Copper Cross was an event for which he was totally unprepared. Another curious fact was that he had crossed a low ridge five minutes earlier, from which vantage point he had been able to see far ahead along the trail, and he would have sworn it was deserted.

He peered through the telescope again. The woman was standing still and seemed to be looking all around her, like a person who had lost her way, and this, too, puzzled Gregg. A stranger might easily go astray in this part of southern Arizona, but the realization that she was lost would have dawned long before she got near Copper Cross. She would hardly be scanning the monotonous landscape as though it were something new.

Gregg traversed the countryside with his telescope, searching for a carriage, a runaway or injured horse, anything that would account for the woman's presence. His attention was drawn by a smudge of dust centered on the distant specks of two riders on a branching trail that ran east to the Portfield ranch, and for an instant he thought he had solved the mystery. Josh Portfield sometimes brought a girl back from his expeditions across the border, and it would be in character for him — should one of his guests prove awkward — to dump her outside of town. But a further look at the riders showed they were approaching the main trail and possibly were not yet aware of the woman. Their appearance was, however, an extra factor which required Gregg's consideration, because their paths were likely to cross his.

He was not a cautious man by nature, and for his first forty-eight years had followed an almost deliberate policy of making life interesting by running headlong into every situation, trusting to good reflexes and a quick mind to get him out again if trouble developed. It was this philosophy that had led him to accept the post of unofficial town warden, and which — on the hottest afternoon of a cruel summer — had faced him with the impossible task of quieting down Josh Portfield and four of his cronies when they were inflamed with whisky. Gregg had emerged from the episode with crippled arms and a new habit of planning his every move with the thoughtfulness of a chess master.

The situation before him now did not seem dangerous, but it contained too many unknown factors for his liking. He took his shotgun from the floor of the buckboard, loaded it with two dully rattling shells, and snicked the hammers back. Swearing at the clumsy stiffness of his arms, he slipped the gun into the rawhide loops that were nailed to the underside of the buckboard's seat. It was a dangerous arrangement, not good firearms practice, but the hazard would be greatest for anyone who chose to ride alongside him, and he had the option of warning them off if they were friendly or not excessively hostile.

Gregg flicked the reins and his horse ambled forward, oily highlights stirring on its flanks. He kept his gaze fixed straight ahead and presently saw the two riders cut across the fork of the trail and halt at the fleck of silver fire, which was how the woman appeared to his naked eye. He hoped, for her sake, that they were two of the reasonably decent hands who kept the Portfield spread operating as a ranch, and not a couple of Josh's night-riding lieutenants. As he watched he saw that they were neither dismounting nor holding their horses in one place, but were riding in close slow circles around the woman. He deduced from that one observation that she had been unlucky in her encounter, and a fretful unease began to gnaw at his stomach. Before Gregg's arms had been ruined he would have lashed his horse into a gallop; now his impulse was to turn and go back the way he had come. He compromised by allowing himself to be carried toward the scene at an unhurried pace, hoping all the while that he could escape involvement.

As he drew near the woman, Gregg saw that she was not — as he had supposed — wearing a mantilla, but that her silver dress was an oddly styled garment, incorporating a hood which was drawn up over her head. She was turning this way and that as the riders moved around her. Gregg transferred his attention to the two men and, with a pang of unhappiness, recognized Wolf Caley and Siggy Sorenson. Caley's gray hair and white beard belied the fact that he possessed all the raw appetites and instincts of a young heathen, and as always he had an old fifty-four-bore Tranter shoved into his belt. Sorenson, a thick-set Swedish exminer of about thirty, was not wearing a gun, but that scarcely mattered because he had all the lethality of a firearm built into his massive limbs. Both men had been members of the group which, two years earlier, had punished Gregg for meddling in Portfield affairs. They pretended not to notice Gregg's approach, but continually circled the woman, occasionally leaning sideways in their saddles and trying to snatch the silver hood back from her face. Gregg pulled to a halt a few yards from them.

"What are you boys playing at?" he said in conversational tones. The woman turned toward him as soon as he spoke and he glimpsed the pale, haunted oval of her face. The sudden movement caused the unusual silver garment to tighten against her body, and Gregg was shocked to realize that she was in a late stage of pregnancy.

"Go away, Billy boy," Caley said carelessly, without turning his head.

"I think you should leave the lady alone."

"I think you must like the sound of your own bones a-breakin'," Caley replied. He made another grab for the woman's hood, and she ducked to avoid his hand.

"Now cut that out, Wolf." Gregg directed his gaze at the woman. "I'm sorry about this, ma'am. If you're going into town you can ride with me."

"Town? Ride?" Her voice was low and strangely accented. "You are English?"

Gregg had time to wonder why anybody should suspect him of being English rather than American merely because he spoke English. Then Caley moved into the intervening space.

"Stay out of this, Billy boy," he said. "We know how to deal with Mexicans who sneak over the line."

"She isn't Mexican."

"Who asked you?" Caley said irritably, his hand straying to the butt of the Tranter.

Sorenson wheeled his horse out of the circle, came alongside the buckboard, and looked in the back. His eyes widened as he saw the eight stone jars bedded in straw.

"Look here, Wolf," he called. "Mr. Gregg is takin' a whole parcel of his best *pulque* into town. We got us all the makin's of a good party here."

Caley turned to him at once, his bearded face looking almost benign. "Hand me one of those crocks."

Gregg slid his right hand under the buckboard's seat. "It'll cost you eight-fifty."

"I'm not payin' eight-fifty for no cactus juice." Caley shook his head as he urged his horse a little closer to the buckboard, coming almost into line with its transverse seat.

"That's what I get from Whalley's, but I tell you what I'll do," Gregg said reasonably. "I'll let you have a jar each on account and you can have yourselves a drink while I take the lady into town. It's obvious she's lost and . . ." Gregg stopped speaking as he saw that he had completely misjudged Caley's mood.

"Who do you think you are?" Caley demanded. "Talkin' to me like I was a kid! If I'd had my way I'd have finished you off a couple of years back, Gregg. In fact . . ." Caley's mouth compressed until it was visible only as a yellow stain on his white beard, and his china-blue eyes brightened with purpose. His hand was now full on the butt of the Tranter and, even though he had not drawn, his thumb was pulling the hammer back.

Gregg glanced around the shimmering, silent landscape, at the impersonal backdrop of the Sierra Madre, and he knew he had perhaps only one second left in which to make a decision and act on it. Caley had not come fully into line with the hidden shotgun, and as he was still on horseback he was far too high above the muzzle, but Gregg had no other resort. Forcing the calcified knot of his elbow to bend to his will, he managed to reach the shotgun's forward trigger and squeeze it hard. In the last instant Caley seemed to guess what was happening, and he tried to throw himself to one side. There was a thunderous blast and the tightly bunched swarm of pellets ripped through his riding boot, just above the ankle, before plowing a bloody furrow across' his horse's rear flank. The terrified animal reared up through a cloud of black gunsmoke, its eyes flaring whitely, and fell sideways with Caley still in the saddle. Gregg heard the sickening crack of a major bone breaking, then Caley began to scream.

"Don't!" Sorenson shouted from the back of his plunging mare. "Don't shoot!" He dug his spurs into the animal's side, rode about fifty yards, and stopped with his hands in the air.

Gregg stared at him blankly for a moment before realizing that — because of the noise, smoke, and confusion — the Swede had no idea of what had happened, nor of how vulnerable Gregg actually was. Caley's continued bellowing as the fallen horse struggled to get off him made it difficult for Gregg to think clearly. The enigmatic woman had drawn her shoulders up and was standing with her hands pressed over her face.

"Stay back there," Gregg shouted to Sorenson before turning to the woman. "Come on — we'd best get out of here."

She began to shiver violently, but made no move toward him. Gregg jumped down from his seat, pulled the shotgun out of his sling, went to the woman, and drew her toward the buckboard. She came submissively and allowed him to help her up into the seat. Gregg heard hoofbeats close behind him and spun around to see that Caley's horse had gotten free and was galloping away to the east, in the direction of the Portfield ranch. Caley was lying clutching a misshapen thigh. He had stopped screaming and seemed to be getting control of himself. Gregg went to him and, as a precaution, knelt and pulled the heavy five-shot pistol from the injured man's belt. It was still cocked.

"You're lucky this didn't go off," Gregg said, carefully lowering the hammer and tucking the gun into his own belt. "A busted leg isn't the worst thing that can happen to a man."

"You're a dead man, Gregg," Caley said faintly, peacefully, his eyes closed. "Josh is away right now . . . but he'll be back soon . . . and he'll bring you to me . . . alive . . . and I'll . . . ."

"Save your breath," Gregg advised, concealing his doubts about his own future. "Josh expects his men to be able to take care of their own affairs." He went back to the buckboard and climbed onto the seat beside the bowed, silver-clad figure of the woman.

"I'll take you into town now," he said to her, "but that's all I can do for you, ma'am. Where are you headed?"

"Headed?" She seemed to query the word, and he became certain that English was not her native tongue, although she still did not strike him as being Mexican or Spanish.

"Yes. Where are you going?"

"I cannot go to a town."

"Why not?"

"The prince would find me there. I cannot go to a town."

"Huh?" Gregg flicked the reins, and the buckboard began to roll forward. "Are you telling me you're wanted for something?"

She hesitated. "Yes."

"Well, it can't be all that serious, and they'd have to be lenient. I mean, in view of your . . ."

As Gregg was struggling for words, the woman pushed the hood back from her face with a hand that still trembled noticeably. She was in her mid-twenties, with fine golden hair and pale skin that suggested to Gregg that she was city-bred. He guessed that under normal circumstances she would have been lovely, but her features had been deadened by fear and shock, and perhaps exhaustion. Her gray eyes hunted over his face.

"I think you are a good man," she said slowly. "Where do you live?"

"Back along this trail about three miles."

"You live alone?"

"I do, but . . ." The directness of her questioning disturbed Gregg, and he sought inspiration. "Where's your husband, ma'am?"

"I have no husband."

Gregg looked away from her. "Oh. Well, we'd best get on into town."

"*No!*" The woman half rose, as though planning to jump from the buckboard while it was still in motion, then clutched at her swollen belly and slumped back onto the seat. Gregg felt the weight of her against his side, he looked all around for a possible source of assistance, but saw only Sorenson, who had returned to Caley and was kneeling beside him. Caley was sitting upright, and both men were watching the buckboard and its passengers with the bleak intensity of snakes.

Appalled at the suddenness with which his life had gotten out of control, Gregg swore softly to himself and turned the buckboard in a half circle for the drive back to his house.

The house was small, having begun its existence some ten years earlier as a line shack used by cowhands from a large but decaying ranch. Gregg had bought it and a section of land back in the days when it looked as though he might become a rancher in his own right, and had added two extra rooms, which gave it a patchy appearance from the outside. After his fateful brush with the Portfield men, which had left him unable to cope with more than a vegetable plot, he had been able to sell back most of the land and retain the house. The deal had not been a good one from the point of view of the original owner, but it was a token that some people in the area had appreciated his efforts to uphold the rule of law.

"Here we are," Gregg said. He helped the woman down from the buckboard, forced to support most of her weight and worried about the degree of personal contact involved. The woman was a complete mystery to him, but he knew she was not accustomed to being manhandled. He got her indoors and guided her into the most comfortable chair in the main room. She leaned back in it with her eyes closed, hands pressed to her abdomen.

"Ma'am?" Gregg said anxiously. "Is it time for . . . ? I mean, do you need a doctor?"

Her eyes opened wide. "No! No doctor!"

"But if you're . . ."

"That time is still above me," she said, her voice becoming firmer.

"Just as well — the nearest doctor's about fifty miles from here. Almost as far as the nearest sheriff." Gregg looked down at the woman and was surprised to note that her enveloping one-piece garment, which had shone like a newly minted silver dollar while outside in the sunlight, was now a rich blue-gray. He stared at the cloth and discovered he could detect no sign of seams or stitching. His puzzlement increased.

"I am thirsty," the woman said. "Have you a drink for me?"

"It was too hot for a fire so there's no coffee, but I've got some spring water."

"Water, please."

"There's plenty of whisky and *pulque*. I make it right here. It wouldn't harm you."

"The water, please."

"Right." Gregg went to the oaken bucket, uncovered it, and took out a dipper of cool water. When he turned he saw that the woman was surveying the room's bare pine walls and rough furniture with an expression of mingled revulsion and despair. He felt sorry for her.

"This place isn't much," he said, "but I live here alone, and I don't need much."

"You have no woman?"

Again Gregg was startled by the contrast between the woman's obvious gentility and the bluntness of her questioning. He thought briefly about Ruth Jefferson, who worked in the general store in Copper Cross and who might have been living in his house had things worked out differently, then shook his head. The woman accepted the enameled scoop from him and sipped some water.

"I want to stay here with you," she said.

"You're welcome to rest a while," Gregg replied uneasily, somehow aware of what was coming.

"I want to stay for six days." The woman gave him a direct calm stare. "Until after my son is born."

Gregg snorted his incredulity. "This is no hospital, and I'm no midwife."

"I'll pay you well." She reached inside her dress *cum* cloak and produced a strip of yellow metal that shone with the buttery luster of high-grade gold. It was about eight inches long by an inch wide, with rounded edges and corners. "One of these for each day. That will be six."

"This doesn't make any kind of sense," Gregg floundered. "I mean, you don't even know if six days will be enough."

"My son will be born on the day after tomorrow."

"You can't be sure of that."

"I can."

"Ma'am, I . . ." Gregg picked up the heavy metal tablet. "This would be worth a lot of money . . . to a bank."

"It isn't stolen, if that's what you mean."

He cleared his throat and, not wishing to contradict or quiz his visitor, examined the gold strip for markings. It had no indentations of any kind and had an almost oily feel, which suggested it might be twenty-four-carat pure.

"I didn't say it was stolen — but I don't often get monied ladies coming here to have their babies." He gave her a wry smile. "Fact is, you're the first."

"Delicately put," she said, mustering a smile in return. "I know how strange this must seem to you, but I'm not free to explain it. All I can tell you is that I have broken no laws."

"You must want to go into hiding for a spell."

"Please understand that there are other societies whose ways are not those of Mexico."

"Excuse me, ma'am," Gregg said, wondering, "this territory has been American since 1848."

"Excuse *me.*" She was contrite. "I never excelled at geography — and I'm very far from home."

Gregg suspected he was being manipulated and decided to resist. "How about the prince?"

Sunlight reflecting from the water in the dipper she was holding split into concentric rings. "It was wrong of me to think of involving you," she said. "I'll go as soon as I have rested."

"Go where?" Gregg, feeling himself becoming involved regardless of her wishes or his own, gave a scornful laugh. "Ma'am, you don't seem to realize how far you are from anywhere. How did you get out here, anyway?"

"I'll leave now." She stood up with some difficulty, her small face paler than ever. "Thank you for helping me as much as you did. I hope you will accept that piece of gold . . ."

"Sit down," Gregg said resignedly. "If you're crazy enough to want to stay here and have your baby, I guess I'm crazy enough to go along with it."

"Thank you." She sat down heavily, and he knew she had been close to fainting.

"There's no need to keep thanking me." Gregg spoke gruffly to disguise the fact that, in an obscure way, he was pleased that a young and beautiful woman was prepared to entrust herself to his care after such a brief acquaintanceship. *I think you are a good man* were almost the first words she had said to him, and in that moment he had abruptly become aware of how wearisome his life had been in the past two years. Semicrippled, dried out by fifty years of hard living, he should have been immune to romantic notions

— especially as the woman could well be a foreign aristocrat who would not even have glanced at him under normal circumstances. The fact remained, however, that he had acted as her protector, and on her behalf had been reintroduced to all the heady addictions of danger. Now the woman was dependent on him and prepared to live in his house. She was also young and beautiful and mysterious — a combination he found as irresistible now as he would have done a quarter of a century earlier.

"We'd best start being practical," he said, compensating for his private flight of fantasy. "You can have my bed for the week. It's clean, but we're going to need fresh linen. I'll go into town and pick up some supplies."

She looked alarmed. "Is that necessary?"

"Very necessary. Don't worry — I won't tell anybody you're here."

"Thank you," she said. "But what about the two men I met?"

"What about them?"

"They probably know I came here with you. Won't they talk about it?"

"Not where it matters. The Portfield men don't mix with the townsfolk or anybody else around here." Gregg took Caley's pistol from his belt and was putting it away in a cupboard when the woman held out her hand and asked if she could examine the weapon. Mildly surprised, he handed it to her and noticed the way in which her arm sank as it took the weight.

"It isn't a woman's gun," he commented.

"Obviously." She looked up at him. "What is the muzzle velocity of this weapon?"

Gregg snorted again, showing amusement. "You're not interested in things like that."

"That is a curious remark for you to make," she said, a hint of firmness returning to her voice, "when I have just expressed interest in it."

"Sorry, it's just that . . ." Gregg decided against referring to the terror she had shown earlier when he fired the shotgun. "I don't know the muzzle velocity, but it can't be very high. That's an old Tranter percussion five-shooter, and you don't see many of them about nowadays. It beats me why Caley took the trouble to lug it around."

"I see." She looked disappointed as she handed the pistol back. "It isn't any good."

Gregg hefted the weapon. "Don't get me wrong, ma'am. This sort of gun is troublesome to load, but it throws a fifty-four-bore slug that'll bowl over any man alive." He was looking at the woman as he spoke, and it seemed to him that, on his final words, an odd expression passed over her face.

"Were you thinking of bigger game?" he said. "Bear, perhaps?"

She ignored his questions. "Have you a pistol of your own?"

"Yes, but I don't carry it. That way I stay out of trouble." Gregg recalled the events of the past hour. "Usually I stay out of trouble."

"What is its muzzle velocity?"

"How would I know?" Gregg found it more and more difficult to reconcile the woman's general demeanor with her strange interest in the technicalities of firearms. "We don't think that way about guns around here. I've got a .44 Remington that always did what I wanted it to do, and that's all I ever needed to know about it."

Undeterred by the impatience in his voice, the woman looked around the room for a moment and pointed at the massive iron range on which he did his cooking. "What would happen if you fired it at that?"

"You'd get pieces of lead bouncing around the room."

"The shot wouldn't go through?"

Gregg chuckled. "There isn't a gun made that could do that. Would you mind telling me why you're so interested?"

She responded in a way he was learning to expect, by changing the subject. "Shall I call you Billy boy?"

"Billy is enough," he said. "If we're going to use our given names."

"My name is Morna, and of course we're going to use our Christian names." She gave him a twinkling glance. "There's no point in being formal . . . under the circumstances."

"I guess not." Gregg felt his cheeks grow warm, and he turned away.

"Have you ever delivered a baby before?"

"It isn't my line of work."

"Well, don't worry about it too much," she said. "I'll instruct you."

"Thanks," Gregg replied gruffly, wondering if he could have been wildly wrong in his guess that his visitor was a woman of high breeding. She had the looks and — now that she was no longer afraid — a certain imperious quality in her manner, but she appeared to have no idea that there were certain things a woman should only discuss with her intimates.

In the afternoon he drove into town, taking a longer route that kept him well clear of the Portfield ranch, and disposed of his eight gallons of *pulque* at Whalley's Saloon. The heat was intense, and perspiration had glued his shirt to his back, but he allowed himself one glass of beer before going to see Ruth Jefferson in her cousin's store. He found her alone at the rear of the store, struggling to lift a sack of beans onto a low shelf. She was a sturdy, attractive woman in her early forties, still straight-backed and narrow-waisted even though ten years of widowhood and self-sufficiency had scored deep lines at the sides of her mouth.

"Afternoon, Billy," she said on hearing his footsteps, then looked at him more closely. "What are you up to, Billy Gregg?"

Gregg felt his heart falter — this was precisely the sort of thing that made him wary of women. "What do you mean?"

"I mean why are you wearing a necktie on a day like that? And your good hat? And, if I'm not mistaken, your good boots?"

"Let me help you with that sack," he said, going forward.

"It's too much for those arms of yours."

"I can manage." Gregg stooped, put his chest close to the sack, and gripped it between his upper arms. He straightened up, holding the sack awkwardly but securely, and dropped it onto the shelf. "See? What did I tell you?"

"You've got dust all over yourself," she said severely, flicking at his clothing with her handkerchief.

"It doesn't matter. Don't fuss." In spite of his protests, Gregg stood obediently and allowed himself to be dusted off, enjoying the attention. "I need your help, Ruth," he said, making a decision.

She nodded. "I've been telling you that for years."

"This is for one special thing, and I can't even tell you about it unless you promise to keep it secret."

"I knew it! I knew you were up to something as soon as you walked in here."

Gregg extracted the promise he wanted, then went on to describe the events of the morning. As he talked, the lines at the sides of Ruth's mouth grew more pronounced, and her eyes developed a hard, uncompromising glitter. He was relieved when, just as he had finished speaking, two women came into the store and spent ten minutes buying a length of cloth. By the time Ruth had finished serving them the set look had gone from her face, but he could tell she was still angry with him.

"I don't understand you, Billy," she whispered. "I thought you had learned your lesson the last time you went up against the Portfield crowd."

"There was nothing else I could do," he said. "I had to help her."

"That's what I'm afraid of."

"What does that mean?"

"Billy Gregg, if I ever find out that you got some little saloon girl into trouble and then had the nerve to get me to help with the delivery . . ."

"Ruth!" Gregg was genuinely shocked by the new idea.

"It's a more likely story than the one you've just told me."

He sighed and took the slim gold bar from his pocket. "Would she be paying me? With this sort of thing?"

"I suppose not," Ruth said. "But it's all so . . . What kind of a name is Morna?"

"Don't ask me."

"Well, where is she from?"

"Don't ask me."

"You've had a shave, as well." She stared at him in perplexity for a moment. "I guess I'll just have to go out there and meet the woman who can make Billy Gregg start prettying himself up. I want to see what she's got that I haven't."

"Thanks, Ruth — I feel a lot easier in my mind now." Gregg looked around the big shady room with its loaded shelves and beams festooned with goods. "What sort of stuff should I be taking back with me?"

"I'll make up a bundle of everything that's needed and take it out to you before supper. I can borrow Sam's gig."

"That's great." Gregg smiled his gratitude. "Make sure you use the west road, though."

"Get out of here and let me get on with my chores," Ruth said briskly. "None of Portfield's saddle tramps are going to bother me."

"Right — see you later." Gregg was turning to leave when his attention was caught by the bolts of cloth stacked on the counter. He fingered a piece of silky material and frowned. "Ruth, did you ever hear of cloth that looks silver out of doors and turns blue indoors?"

"No, I never did."

"I thought not." Gregg walked to the door, hesitated, then went out into the heat and throbbing brilliance of Copper Cross's main street. He got onto his buckboard, flicked the reins, and drove slowly to the water trough, which was in an alley at the side of the livery stables. A young cowboy with a drooping, sandy mustache was already watering his horse. Gregg recognized him as Cal Masham, one of the passably honest hands who worked for Josh Portfield, and nodded a greeting.

"Billy." Masham nodded in return and took his pipe from his mouth. "Heard about your run-in with Wolf Caley this afternoon."

"News gets around fast."

Masham glanced up and down the alley. "I think you ought to know, Billy — Wolf's hurt real bad."

"Yeah, I heard his leg go when his horse came down on it. I owed him a broken bone or two." Gregg sniffed appreciatively. "Nice tobacco you've got in there."

"It wasn't a clean break, Billy. Last I heard his leg was all swole up and turned black. And he's got a fever."

In the heat of the afternoon Gregg suddenly felt cool. "Is he likely to die?"

"It looks that way, Billy." Masham looked around him again. "Don't tell anybody I told you, but Josh is due back in two or three days. If I was in your shoes I wouldn't hang around and wait for him to get here."

"Thanks for the tip, son." Gregg waited impassively until his horse had finished drinking, then he urged the animal forward. It lowered its head and drew him from the shadow of the stables into the searing arena of the street.

Gregg had left the woman, Morna, sleeping on his bed and still wrapped in the flowing outer garment whose properties were such a mystery to him. On his return he entered the house quietly, hoping to avoid disturbing her rest, and found Morna sitting at the table with a book spread out before her. She had removed her cloak to reveal a simple blue smock with half-length sleeves. The book was one of the dozen that Gregg owned, a well-worn school atlas, and it was open at a double-page map of North America.

Morna had tied her fair hair into a loose coil, and she looked more beautiful than Gregg had remembered, but his attention was drawn to the strange ornament on her wrist. It looked like a circular piece of dark red glass about the size of a dollar, rimmed with gold and held in place by a thin gold band. Its design was unusual enough, but the thing that held Gregg's gaze was that under the surface of the glass was a sliver of ruby light, equivalent in size and positioning to one hand of a watch, which blinked on and off at intervals of about two seconds.

She looked up at him and smiled. "I hope you don't mind." She indicated the atlas.

"Help yourself, ma'am."

"Morna."

"Help yourself . . . Morna." The familiarity did not sit easily with Gregg. "Are you feeling stronger?"

"I'm much better, thank you. I hadn't slept since . . . for quite a long time."

"I see." Gregg sat down at the other side of the table and allowed himself a closer look at the intriguing ornament. On its outer rim were faint markings like those of a compass, and the splinter of light continued its slow pulsing beneath the glass. "I don't mean to pry, ma'am — Morna," he said, "but in my whole life I've never seen anything like that thing on your wrist."

"It's nothing." Morna covered it with her hand. "It's just a trinket."

"But how can it keep sparking the way it does?"

"Oh, I don't understand these matters," she said airily. "I believe it works by electronics."

"Is that something to do with electricity?"

"Electricity is what I meant to say — my English is not very good."

"But what's it *for*?"

Morna laughed. "Do your women only wear what is useful?"

"I guess not," Gregg said doubtfully, aware he was being put off once again. After a few initial uncertainties, Morna's English had been very assured, and he suspected that the odd word she had used — electronics — had not been a mistake. He made up his mind to search for it in Ruth's dictionary, if he ever got the chance.

Morna looked down at the atlas, upon which she had placed a piece of straw running east to west, with one end at the approximate location of Copper Cross.

"According to this map we are about twelve hundred miles from New Orleans."

Gregg shook his head. "It's more than that to New Orleans."

"I've just measured it."

"That's the straight-line distance," he explained patiently. "It doesn't signify anything — 'less you can fly like a bird."

"But you agree that it is twelve hundred miles."

"That's about right — for a bird." Gregg jumped to his feet and, in his irritation, tried to do it in the normal way, with the assistance of his arms pushing against the table. His left elbow cracked loudly and gave way, bringing him down on that shoulder. Embarrassed, he stood up more slowly, trying not to show that he was hurt, and walked to the range. "We'll have to see about getting you some proper food."

"What's wrong with your arm?" Morna spoke softly, from close behind him.

"It's nothing for you to worry about," he said, surprised at her show of concern.

"Let me see it, Billy — I may be able to help."

"You're not a doctor, are you?" As he had expected, there was no reply to his question, but the possibility that the woman had had medical training prompted Gregg to roll up his sleeves and let her examine the misshapen elbow joints. Having unbent that far, he went on to tell her about how — in the absence of any law enforcement in the area — he had been foolish enough to let himself be talked into taking the job of unofficial town warden, and about how, even more foolishly, he had once interrupted Josh Portfield and four of his men in the middle of a drinking spree. He skimmed briefly over the details of how two men had held each of his wrists and whipped him bodily to and fro for over fifteen minutes until his elbows had snapped backward.

"Why is it always so?" she breathed.

"What was that, ma'am?"

Morna raised her eyes. "There's nothing I can do, Billy. The joints were fractured and now they have sclerosed over."

"Sclerosed, eh?" Gregg noted another word to be checked later.

"Do you get much pain?" She looked at the expression on his face. "That was a silly question, wasn't it?"

"It's a good thing I'm partial to whisky," he confessed. "Otherwise I wouldn't get much sleep some nights."

She smiled compassionately. "I think I can do something about the pain. It's in my own interest to get you as fit as possible by . . . What day is this?"

"Friday."

"By Sunday."

"Don't trouble yourself about Sunday," he said. "I've got a friend coming to help out. A woman friend," he added, as Morna stepped back from him, the hunted expression returning to her face.

"You promised not to tell anyone I was here."

"I know, but it's purely for your benefit. Ruth Jefferson is a fine lady, and

I know her as well as I know myself. She won't talk to a living soul."

Morna's face relaxed slightly. "Is she important to you?"

"We were supposed to get married."

"In that case I won't object," Morna said, her gray eyes unreadable. "But please remember it was your own decision to tell her about me."

Ruth Jefferson came into sight about an hour before sunset, driving her cousin's gig.

Gregg, who had been watching for her, went into the house and tapped the open door of the bedroom, where Morna had lain down to rest without undressing. She awoke instantly with a startled gasp, glancing at the gold bracelet on her wrist. From his viewpoint in the doorway, Gregg noted that the ornament's imprisoned splinter of light seemed always to point to the east, and he decided it could be a strange form of compass. It might have been his imagination, but he had an impression that the light's rate of pulsation had increased slightly since he had first observed it in the morning. More wonderful and strange, however, was the overall sight of the golden-haired young woman, heavy with new life, who had come to him from out of nowhere and whose presence seemed to shed a glow over the plain furniture of his bedroom. He found himself speculating anew about the circumstances that had stranded such a creature in the near wilderness of his part of the world.

"Ruth will be here in a minute," he said. "Would you like to come out and meet her?"

"Very much." Morna smiled as she stood up and walked to the door with him. Gregg was slightly taken aback that she did so without touching her hair or fussing about her dress — in his experience first meetings between women usually were edgy occasions. Then he noticed that her simple hairstyle was undisturbed, and that the material of the blue smock, in spite of having been lain on for several hours, was as sleek and as smooth as if it had just come off the hanger. It was yet another addition to the dossier of curious facts he was assembling about his guest.

"Hello, Ruth — glad you could come." Gregg went forward to steady the gig and help Ruth down from it.

"I'll bet you are," Ruth said. "Have you heard about Wolf Caley?"

Gregg lowered his voice. "I heard he was fixing to die."

"That's right. What are you going to do about it?"

"What *can* I do?"

"You could head north as soon as it gets dark and keep going. I'm crazy to suggest it, but I could stay here and look after your lady friend."

"That wouldn't be fair." Gregg shook his head slowly. "No, I'm staying on here, where I'm needed."

"Just what do you think you'll be able to do when Josh Portfield and his mob come for you?"

"Ruth," he whispered uneasily, "I wish you'd talk about something else — you're going to upset Morna. Now come and meet her."

Ruth gave him an exasperated look, but went quietly with him to the house, where he performed the introductions. The women shook hands in silence, and then — quite spontaneously — both began to smile, the roles of mother and daughter tacitly assigned and mutually accepted. Gregg knew that communication had taken place on a level he would never understand, and his ingrained awe of the female mind increased.

He was pleased to see that Ruth, who had obviously been prepared to have her worst suspicions confirmed, was impressed with Morna. It would make his own life a little easier. While the two women went indoors he unloaded the supplies Ruth had brought, gripping the wicker basket between his upper arms to avoid stressing his elbows. When he carried it into the house and set it on the table, Ruth and Morna were deep in conversation, and Ruth broke off long enough to point at the door, silently commanding him to leave again.

Even more gratified, Gregg lifted a pack of tailor-made cigarettes from a shelf and went out to the shack, where his *pulque* still was in operation. He preferred hand-rolled cigarettes, but was accustomed to doing without them now that his fingers were incapable of the fine control required in the rolling of tobacco. Making himself comfortable on a stool in the corner, he lit a cigarette and contentedly surveyed his little domain of copper cooling coils, retorts, and tubs of fermenting cactus pulp. The knowledge that there were two women in his house and that one of them was soon to have a child there gave him a warm sense of importance he had never known before. He spent some time indulging himself in dreams, projected on screens of aromatic smoke, in which Ruth was his wife, Morna was his daughter, and he was again fit enough to do a real day's work and provide for his family.

"I don't know how you can sit in this place." Ruth was standing in the doorway, with a shawl around her shoulders. "That smell can't be healthy."

"It never did anybody any harm," Gregg said, rising to his feet. "Fermentation is part of nature."

"So is cow dung." Ruth backed out of the shack and waited for him to join her. In the reddish, horizontal light of the setting sun she looked healthy and attractive, imbued with a mature competence. "I have to go back now," she said, "but I'll be here again tomorrow, in the morning, and I'm going to stay until that baby is safely delivered into this world."

"I thought Saturday was your busy day at the store."

"It is, but Sam will have to manage on his own. I can't leave that child to have the baby by herself. You'd be worse than useless to her."

"But what's Sam going to think?"

"It doesn't matter what Sam thinks — I'll tell him you're poorly." Ruth paused for a moment. "Where do you think she's from, Billy?"

"Couldn't rightly say. She talked some about New Orleans."

Ruth frowned in disagreement. "Her talk doesn't sound like Louisiana talk to me — and she's got some real foreign notions to go with it."

"I noticed," Gregg said emphatically.

"The way she only talks about having a son? Just won't entertain the idea that it's just as likely to be a girl."

"Mmm." Gregg had been thinking about muzzle velocities of revolvers. "I wish I knew what she's running away from."

Ruth's features softened unexpectedly. "I've read lots of stories about women from noble families . . . heiresses and such . . . not allowed to acknowledge their own babies because the fathers were commoners."

"Ruth Jefferson," Gregg said gleefully, "I didn't know you were going around that homely old store with your head stuffed full of romantic notions."

"I do nothing of the sort." Ruth's color deepened. "But it's as plain as the nose on your face that Morna comes from money — and it's probably her own folks she's in trouble with."

"Could be." Gregg remembered the abject terror he had seen in Morna's eyes. His instincts told him she had more on her mind than outraged parents, but he decided not to argue with Ruth. He stood and listened patiently while she explained that she had put Morna to bed, about his own sleeping arrangements in the other room, and about the type of breakfast he was to prepare in the morning.

"And you leave the whisky jar alone tonight," Ruth concluded. "I don't want you lying around in a drunken stupor if that child's pains start during the night. You hear me?"

"I hear you — I wasn't planning to do any drinking, anyway. Do you think the baby will arrive on Sunday, like Morna says?"

Ruth seated herself in the gig and gathered up the traces. "Somehow — I don't know why — I'm inclined to believe it will. See you, Billy."

"Thanks, Ruth." Gregg watched until the gig had passed out of sight beyond a rocky spur of the hillside upon which his house was built, then he turned and went indoors. The door of the bedroom was closed. He made up a bed on the floor with the blankets Ruth had left out for him, but knew he was unready for sleep. Chuckling a little with guilty pleasure, he poured himself a generous measure of corn whisky from the stone jar he kept in the cupboard and settled down with it in his most comfortable chair. The embers of the sunset filled the room with mellow light, and as he sipped the companionable liquor Gregg felt a sense of fulfillment in his role of watchdog.

He even allowed himself to hope that Morna would stay with him for longer than the six days she had planned.

Gregg awoke with a start at dawn to find himself still sitting in the chair, the empty cup clasped in his hand. He went to set the cup aside and almost groaned aloud as the flexing of his elbow produced a sensation akin to glass fragments crunching against a raw nerve. It must have been cool during the night, and his unprotected arms had stiffened up far more than usual. He stood up with difficulty, was dismayed to see that his shirt and pants were a mass of wrinkles, and it came to him that a man living alone should have clothes impervious to creases, clothes like those of . . .

Morna!

As recollections of the previous day fountained in his head, Gregg hurried to the range and began cleaning it out in preparation for lighting a fire. Ruth had left instructions that he was to heat milk and oatmeal for Morna's breakfast and provide her with a basin of warm water in her room. Partly because of his haste, and partly because of the difficulty of controlling his fingers, he dropped the fire irons several times and was hardly surprised to hear the bedroom door opening soon afterward. Morna appeared in the opening wearing a flowered dressing gown that Ruth must have brought for her. The familiar, feminine styling of the garment made her prettier in Gregg's eyes, and at the same time more approachable.

"Good morning," he said. "Sorry about all the noise. I hope I didn't . . . "

"I'd caught up on my sleep anyway." She came into the room, sat at the table, and placed on it a second of the slim gold bars. "This is for you, Billy."

He pushed it back toward her. "I don't want it. The one you gave me is worth more than anything I can do for you."

Morna gave him a calm, sad smile, and he was abruptly reminded that she was not a home-grown girl discussing payment for a domestic chore. "You risked your life for me — and I think you would do it again. Would you?"

Gregg looked away from her. "I didn't do much."

"But you did! I was watching you, Billy, and I saw that you were afraid — but I also saw that you were able to control the fear. It made you stronger instead of weaker, and that's something that even the finest of my people are unable . . . " Morna broke off and pressed the knuckles of one hand to her lips as though she had been on the verge of revealing a secret.

"We'll have something to eat soon." Gregg turned back toward the range. "As soon as I get a fire going."

"You haven't answered my question."

He shifted his feet. "What question?"

"If somebody came here to kill me — and to kill my son — would you defend us even if it meant placing your own life at risk?"

"This is just crazy," Gregg protested. "Why should anybody want to kill you?"

Her eyes locked fast on his. "Answer the question, Billy."

"I . . . " The words were as difficult for Gregg as a declaration of love. "Do I need to answer? Do you think I would run away?"

"No," she said gently. "That's all the answer I need."

"I'm pleased about that." Gregg's voice was gruffer than he had meant it to be, because Morna — who was half his age — kept straying in his mind from the role of foster daughter to that of lover wife, in spite of the facts that he scarcely knew her and that she was swollen with another man's child. He was oppressed by the sinfulness of his thinking and by fears of making a fool of himself, yet he was deeply gratified by Morna's trust. No man, he decided, no prince, not even the Prince of Darkness himself, was going to harm or distress her if there was anything he could do to prevent it. While he busied himself with getting a fire going, Gregg made up his mind to check the condition of his Remington as soon as he could do so without being seen by Morna or Ruth. In the unlikely event that he might need it, he would also inspect the percussion caps and loads in the old Tranter he had taken from Wolf Caley.

As though divining the turn of his thoughts, Morna said, "Billy, have you a long gun? A rifle?"

He puffed out his cheeks. "Never owned one."

"Why not? The longer barrel would allow the charge to impart more energy to the bullet and give you a more effective weapon."

Gregg hunched his shoulders and refused to turn round, somehow offended at hearing Morna's light, clear voice using the terminology of the armorer. "Never wanted one," he said.

"But *why* not?"

"I was never all that good with a rifle, even when my arms were all right, so it's safer for me not to carry one. There's no law to speak of in these parts, you see. If a man uses a revolver to kill another man he generally gets off with it, provided the man he shot was carrying a wheel gun too. Even if he didn't get a chance to draw it, it's classed as a fair fight. The same goes if they both have rifles, but I'm none too good with a rifle — so I'm not going to risk having somebody I crossed knock me over at two hundred yards and claim it was self-defense." The speech was the longest Gregg had made in months, and he expressed his displeasure at having had to make it by raking the ashes in the fire basket with unnecessary vigor.

"I see," Morna said thoughtfully behind him. "A simple duello variation. Are you accurate with a revolver?"

For a reply Gregg started slamming the range's cooking rings back into place.

Her voice assumed the imperious quality he had heard in it before. "Billy, are you accurate with a revolver?"

He wheeled on her, holding out his arms in such a way as to display the misshapen, knotted elbows. "I can point a six-shooter just like I always could, but it takes me so long to get it up there I wouldn't be a match for a ten-year-old boy. Is that what you wanted to know?"

"There is no room for anger between us." Morna stood up and took his outstretched hands in hers. She looked into his face with searching gray eyes. "You love me, don't you, Billy?"

"Yes." Gregg heard the word across a distance, knowing he could not have said it to a stranger.

"I'm proud that you do — now wait here." Morna went into the bedroom, took something from an inner part of her cloak, and returned with what at first seemed to be a small square of green glass. Gregg was surprised to see that it was as pliable as a piece of buckskin, and he watched with growing puzzlement as Morna pressed it to his left elbow. It was curiously warm against his skin, and a tingling sensation seemed to pass right through the joint.

"Bend your arm," Morna ordered, now as impersonal as an army surgeon.

Gregg did as he was told and was thrilled to find there was no pain, no grinding of arthritic glass needles. He was still flexing his left arm, speechless with disbelief, when Morna repeated the procedure with his right, achieving the same miraculous result. For the first time in two years, Gregg could bend his arms freely and without suffering in the process.

Morna smiled up at him. "How do they feel?"

"Like new — just like new."

"They'll never be as good or as strong as they were," Morna said, "but I can promise you there'll be no more pain." She went back into the bedroom and emerged a moment later without the transparent green square. "Now, I think you said something about food."

Gregg shook his head. "There's something going on here. You're not who you claim to be. Nobody can do the sort of . . . "

"I didn't claim to be anybody," Morna said quite sharply, with yet another of her swift changes of mood.

"Perhaps I should have said you're not *what* you claim to be."

"Don't spoil things, Billy . . . I have nobody but you." Morna sat down at the table and covered her face with her hands.

"I'm sorry." Gregg was reaching out to touch her when, for the first time that morning, he noticed the curious gold ornament on her wrist. The imprisoned splinter of light was pointing east as usual, but it was brighter than it had been yesterday and was definitely flashing at a higher rate. Gregg, becoming attuned to strangeness, was unable to avoid the impression that it was pulsing out some kind of warning.

True to her word, Ruth arrived early in the day.

She had brought extra supplies, including a jug of broth that was wrapped in a traveling rug to retain its warmth. Gregg was glad to see her and grateful for the womanly efficiency with which she took control of his household, yet he was discomfited at finding himself made redundant. He spent more and more time in the shack, tending to his stills, and that bright moment in which there had been talk of love between Morna and him began to seem like a figment of his imagination. He was not deluding himself that she had referred to husband-and-wife love, perhaps not father-and-daughter love either, but the mere use of the word had, for a brief span, made his life less sterile, and he treasured it.

Ruth, in contrast, spoke of commodity prices and scarcities, dress making and local affairs — and, in the aura of normalcy that surrounded her, Gregg decided against mentioning the fantastic cure that Morna had wrought on his arms. He had a feeling she would refuse to believe, and — by robbing him of his faith — neutralize the magic or unwork the miracle. Ruth came to visit him in the shack in the afternoon, covering her nose with her handkerchief, but it was only to tell him privately that Wolf Caley was not expected to last out the day, and that Josh Portfield and his men were reported to be riding north from Sonora.

Gregg thanked her for the information and gave no sign of being affected by it, but at the first opportunity he smuggled his Remington and Caley's Tranter out of the house and devoted some time to ensuring that they were in serviceable condition.

Portfield had always been an enigmatic figure in Gregg's life. The big spread he owned had been passed on to him by his father, and it was profitable; therefore there was no need for Josh to engage in unlawful activities. He had, however, acquired a taste for violence during the war, and the troubled territories of Mexico lying only a short distance to the south seemed to draw him like a magnet. Every now and then he would take a bunch of men and go on a kind of motiveless unofficial "raid" beyond the border. Portfield was far from being a mad dog, often leading a fairly normal existence for months on end, but he appeared to lack any conception of right and wrong.

For example, he genuinely believed he had been lenient with Gregg by merely ruining his arms, instead of killing him, for interrupting that fateful drinking spree. Afterward, on meeting Gregg on the trail or in Copper Cross, he had always hailed him in the friendliest manner possible, apparently under the impression he had earned Gregg's gratitude and respect. Each man, Gregg had discovered, lives in his own reality.

There was always the possibility that, when Portfield learned of Caley's misfortune, he would shrug and say that any man who worked for him ought to be able to cope with an aging cripple. Gregg had known Portfield to make equally unexpected judgments, but he had a suspicion that on this occasion the hammer of Portfield's anger was going to come down hard and that he was going to be squarely underneath it. In a way he could not understand, his apprehension was fed and magnified by Morna's own mysterious fears.

During the meals, while the three of them were seated at the rough wooden table, he was content to have Ruth carry the burden of conversation with Morna. The talk was mainly of domestic matters, on any of which Morna might have been drawn out to reveal something of her own background, but she skirted Ruth's various traps with easy diplomacy.

Late in the evening Morna began to experience the first contraction pains, and from that point Gregg found himself relegated by Ruth to the status of an inconvenient piece of furniture. He accepted the treatment without rancor, having been long familiar with the subdued hostility that women feel toward men during a confinement, and willingly performed every task given to him. Only an occasional brooding glance from Morna reminded him that between them was a covenant of which Ruth, for all her matronly competence, knew nothing.

The baby was born at noon on Sunday, and — as Morna had predicted — it was a boy.

"Don't let Morna do too much," Ruth said on Monday morning, as she seated herself in the gig. "She has no business being up and about so soon after a birth."

Gregg nodded. "Don't worry — I'll take care of all the chores."

"Do that." Ruth looked at him with sudden interest. "How are your arms these days?"

"Better. They feel a lot easier."

"That's good." Ruth picked up the reins but seemed reluctant to drive away. Her gaze strayed toward the house, where Morna was standing with the baby cradled in her arms. "I suppose you can't wait for me to go and leave you alone with your ready-made family."

"Now, you know that's not right, Ruth. You know how much I appreciate all you've done here. You're not jealous, are you?"

"Jealous?" Ruth shook her head, then gave him a level stare. "Morna is a strange girl. She's not like me, and she's not like you — but I've got a feeling there's something going on between you two."

Gregg's fear of Ruth's intuitive powers stirred anew. "You know, Ruth, you're starting to sound like one of those new phonographs."

"Oh, I don't mean hanky-panky," she said quickly, "but you're up to something. I know you."

"I'll be in to settle up my bill in a day or two," Gregg parried. "Soon as I can change one of those gold bars."

"Try to do it before Josh Portfield gets back." Ruth flicked the reins and drove down the hillside.

Gregg took a deep breath and surveyed the distant blue ramparts of the sierras before walking back to the house. Morna was still wearing the flowered dressing gown and, with the shawl-wrapped baby in her arms, she looked much like any other young mother. The single uncomformity in her appearance was the gold ornament on her wrist. Even in the brightness of the morning sunlight its needle of crimson light was harshly brilliant, and its pulsations had speeded up to several a second. Gregg had thought a lot about the ornament during his spells of solitude over the previous two days, and he had convinced himself he understood its function if not its nature. He felt that the time had come for some plain talking.

Morna went indoors with him. The birth had been straightforward and easy for her, but her face was pale and drawn, and there was a tentative quality about the smile she gave him as he closed the door.

"It feels strange for us to be alone again," Morna said quietly.

"Very strange." Gregg pointed at the flashing bracelet. "But it looks as though we won't be alone for very long."

She sat down abruptly and her baby raised one miniature pink hand in protest at the sudden movement. Morna drew the infant closer to her breast. She lowered her face to the baby, touching its forehead with hers, and her hair fell forward, screening it with strands of gold.

"I'm sorry," Gregg said, "but I need to know who it is that's coming out of the east. I need to know who I'm going up against."

"I can't tell you that, Billy."

"I see — I'm entitled to get killed, maybe, but not to know who does it, or why."

"Please don't." Her voice was muffled. "Please understand . . . that I can't tell you anything."

Gregg felt a pang of guilt. He went to Morna and knelt beside her. "Why don't we both — the three of us, I mean — get out of here right now? We could load up my buckboard and be gone in ten minutes."

Morna shook her head without looking up. "It wouldn't make any difference."

"It would make a difference to me."

At that, Morna raised her head and looked at him with anxious, brimming eyes. "This man, Portfield — will he try to kill you?"

"Did Ruth tell you about him?" Gregg clicked his tongue with annoyance. "She shouldn't have done that. You've got enough to . . . "

"Will he try to kill you?"

Gregg was compelled to tell the unvarnished truth. "It isn't so much a matter of him *trying* to kill me, Morna. He rides around in company with seven or eight hard cases, and if they decide to kill somebody they just go right ahead and do it."

"Oh!" Morna seemed to regain something of her former resolve. "My son can't travel yet, but I'll get him ready as soon as I can. I'll try hard, Billy."

"That's fine with me," Gregg said uncertainly. He had an uneasy feeling that the conversation had gotten beyond him in some way, but he had lost the initiative and was in no way equipped to deal with a woman's tears.

"That's all right, then." He got to his feet and looked down at the baby's absurdly tiny features. "Have you thought of a name for the little fellow yet?"

Morna relaxed momentarily, looking pleased. "It's too soon. The naming time is still above him."

"In English," Gregg gently corrected, "we say that the future is ahead of us, not above us."

"But that implies linear . . . " Morna checked her words. "You're right, of course — I should have said ahead."

"My mother was a schoolmarm," he said inconsequentially, once more with an odd sense that communications between them were failing. "I've got some work to do outside, but I'll be close by if you need me."

Gregg went to the door, and as he was closing it behind him he looked back into the room. He saw that, yet again, Morna was sitting with her forehead pressed to that of her son, something he had never seen other women doing. He dismissed it as the least puzzling of her idiosyncrasies. In fact, there was no pressing work to be done outside — but he had a gut feeling that the time had come for keeping an eye on all approaches to his house. He walked slowly to the top of the saddleback, threading his way among boulders that resembled grazing sheep, and settled down on the eastern crest. A careful scan with his telescope revealed no activity in the direction of the Portfield ranch or on the trail running south to Copper Cross. Gregg then pointed the little instrument due east toward where the Rio Grande flowed unseen between the northern extremities of the Sierra Madre and the Sacramento Mountains many miles away. Visibility was good, and his eye was dazzled with serried vistas of peaks and ranges on a scale too vast for comprehension.

You're letting yourself get spooked, he thought irritably. Nothing crosses country in a straight line like a bird — except another bird.

He contrived to spend most of the day on the vantage point, though he made frequent trips down to the house to check on Morna, to prepare two simple meals, and to boil water for washing the baby's diapers. It pleased him to note that the child slept almost continuously between feeds, thus giving Morna plenty of opportunity to rest. At times Ruth's phrase "ready-made family" came to his mind, and he realized how appropriate it had been. Even in the bizarre circumstances that prevailed, there was something deeply satisfying about having a woman and child under his roof, looking to him and to no other man for their welfare and safety. The relationship made him something more than he had been. Although he did his best to repress the thought, the possibility suggested itself that, were Morna and he to flee north together, she might never return to her former life. In that case, he might indeed acquire a ready-made family.

Gregg shied away from pursuing that line of thought too far.

Late in the evening, when the sun was dipping toward the lower ranges beyond far Mexicali, he saw a lone horseman approaching from the direction of the Portfield ranch. The rider was moving at a leisurely pace, and the fact that he was alone was an indication that there was no trouble afoot, but Gregg decided not to take any chances. He walked down the hill past the house, took the Remington from its hiding place in the shack, and went on down to take up his position on the spur of rock where the trail bent sharply. When the horseman came into view he was slumped casually in the saddle, obviously half asleep, and his hat was pulled down to screen his eyes from the low-slanted rays of the sun. Gregg recognized Cal Masham, the young cowboy he had spoken to in the town on Friday.

"What are you doing in these parts, Cal?" he shouted.

Masham jerked upright, his jaw sagging with shock. "Billy? You still here?"

"What does it look like?"

"Hell, I figured you'd be long gone by this time."

"And you wanted to see what I'd left behind — is that it?"

Masham grinned beneath the drooping mustache. "It seemed to me you'd leave those big heavy crocks of *pulque,* and it seemed to me I might as well have them as somebody else. After all . . . "

"You can have a drink on me any time," Gregg said firmly, "but not tonight. You'd best be on your way, Cal."

Masham looked displeased. "Seems to me you're wavin' that gun at the wrong people, Billy. Did you know that Wolf Caley's dead?"

"I hadn't heard."

"Well, he is. And Big Josh'll be home tomorrow. Max Tibbett rode in ahead this afternoon, and as soon as he heard about Wolf he took a fresh horse and rode south again to tell Josh. You just shouldn't *be* here, Billy." Masham's voice had taken on a rising note of complaint, and he seemed genuinely upset by Gregg's foolhardiness in remaining.

Gregg considered for a moment. "Come up and help yourself to a jar, but don't make any noise — I've got a guest and a newborn baby I don't want disturbed."

"Thanks, Billy." Masham dismounted and walked up the hill with Gregg. He accepted a heavy stone jar, glancing curiously toward the house, and rode off with his prize clasped to his chest.

Gregg watched him out of sight, put the Remington away, and decided that he was entitled to a shot of whisky to counter the effects of the news he had just received. He crossed the familiar ruts of the buckboard's turning circle and looked in through the front window of the house to see if Morna was in the main room. He had intended only to glance in quickly while passing the window, but the strange tableau within checked him in midstride.

Morna was dressed in her own maternity smock, which appeared to have been reshaped to her slimmer figure, although Gregg had not noticed her or Ruth doing any needlework. She had spread a white sheet over the table and her baby was lying in the center of it, naked except for the binder that crossed his navel. Morna was standing beside the table, with both hands clasping the baby's head. Her eyes were closed, lips moving silently, her face as cold and masklike as that of a high priestess performing an ancient ceremony.

Gregg desperately wanted to turn away, convinced he was guilty of an invasion of privacy, but a change was taking place in Morna's appearance and the slow progression of it induced a mesmeric paralysis of his limbs. As he watched, Morna's golden hair began to stir, as though it were some complex living creature in its own right. Her head was absolutely motionless, but gradually — over a period of about ten seconds — her hair fanned out, each strand becoming straight and seemingly rigid, to form a bright fearsome halo. Gregg felt his mouth go dry as he witnessed Morna's dreadful transformation from the normalcy of young motherhood to the semblance of a witch figure. She bent forward from the waist until her forehead was touching that of the baby.

There was a moment of utter stillness — and then her body became transparent.

Gregg felt icy ripples move upward from the back of his neck into his own hair as he realized that he could see right through Morna. She was indisputably present in the room, yet the lines of walls and furniture continued on through her body, as if she were an image superimposed on them by a magic lantern.

The baby made random pawing movements with his arms and legs, but otherwise appeared to be unaffected by what was happening. Morna remained in the same state, somewhere between matter and mirage, for several seconds, then quite abruptly she was as solid as before. She straightened up, and Gregg could see that her hair was beginning to subside into its previous helmet shape of loose waves. She smoothed it down with her hands and turned toward the window.

Gregg lunged to one side in terror and scampered, doubled over like a man dodging gunfire, for the cover of his buckboard, which he had left on the blind side of the house. He crouched there, breathing noisily, until he was sure Morna had not seen him, then made his way to his customary spot at the top of the saddleback, where he squatted down and lit a cigarette. Even with the same reassurance of tobacco it was some time before his heart slowed to a steady rhythm. He was not a superstitious man, but his limited reading had taught him that there was a special kind of woman — known from biblical En-dor to the Salem of more recent times — who could work magical cures, and who often had to flee from persecution. One part of his mind rebelled against applying that name to a child like Morna, but there was no denying what he had just seen, no getting away from all the other strange things about her.

He smoked four more cigarettes, taking perhaps an hour to do so, then went back to his house. Morna — looking as normal and sweet and whole-some as a freshly baked apple pie — had lit an oil lantern and was brewing coffee. Her baby was peacefully asleep in the basket Ruth had left for it. Morna had even removed her gold bracelet, as though deliberately setting out to make him forget that she was in any way out of the ordinary. When Gregg glanced into the darkness of the bedroom, however, he saw the ruby glow, flashing so quickly now that its warning was almost continuous.

And it was far into the night before he finally managed to sleep.

Gregg was awakened in the morning by the thin, lonely bleat of the baby crying. He listened to it for what seemed a long time, expecting to hear Morna respond, but no other sound reached him from beyond the closed door of the bedroom. No matter what else she might be, Morna had impressed Gregg as a conscientious mother, and her prolonged inactivity at first puzzled and then began to worry him. He got up out of his bedroll, pulled on his pants, and tapped on the door. There was no reply, apart from the baby's cries, which were as regular as breathing. He tapped again more loudly, and pushed the door open.

The baby was in its basket beside the bed — Gregg could see the movement of tiny fists — but Morna had gone.

Unable to accept the evidence of his eyes, Gregg walked all around the square room and even looked below the bed. Morna's clothes, including her cloak, were missing too, and the only conclusion Gregg could reach was that she had risen during the hours of darkness, dressed herself, and left the house. To do so she would have had to pass within a few feet of where he was sleeping on the floor of the main room without disturbing him, and he was positive that nobody, not the most practiced thief, not the most skillful Indian tracker, could have done that. But then — the slow stains of memory began to spread in his mind — he was thinking in terms of normal human beings, and he had proof that Morna was far from normal.

The baby went on crying, its eyes squeezed shut, protesting in the only way it knew how about the absence of food and maternal warmth. Gregg stared at it helplessly, and it occurred to him that Morna might have left for good, making the infant his permanent responsibility.

"Hold on there, little fellow," he said, recalling that he had not checked outside the house. He left the bedroom, went outside, and called Morna's name. His voice faded into the air, absorbed by the emptiness of the morning landscape, and his horse looked up in momentary surprise from its steady cropping of the grass near the water pump. Gregg made a hurried inspection of his two outbuildings — the distilling shack and the ramshackle sentry box that was his lavatory — then decided he would have to take the baby into town and hand it over to Ruth. He had no idea how long a child of that age could survive without food, and he did not want to take unnecessary risks.

Swearing under his breath, he turned back to the house and froze as he saw a flash of silver on the trail at the bottom of the hill.

Morna had just come around the spur of rock and was walking toward him. She was draped in her ubiquitous cloak, which had returned to its original color, and was carrying a small blue sack in one hand. Gregg's relief at seeing her pushed aside all his fears and reservations of the previous night, and he ran down the slope to meet her.

"Where have you been?" he called, while they were still some distance apart. "What was the idea of running off like that?"

"I didn't run off, Billy." She gave him a tired smile. "There were things I had to do."

"What sort of things? The baby's crying for a feed."

Morna's perfect young face was strangely hard. "What's a little hunger?"

"That's a funny way to talk," Gregg said, taken aback.

"The future simply doesn't exist for you, does it?" Morna looked at him with what seemed to be a mixture of pity and anger. "Don't you ever think ahead? Have you forgotten that we have . . . enemies?"

"I take things as they come. It's all a man can do."

Morna thrust the blue sack at him. "Take this as it comes."

"What is it?" Gregg accepted the bag and was immediately struck by the fact that it was not made of blue paper, as he had supposed. The material was thin, strong, smooth to the touch, more pliable than oilskin, and without oilskin's underlying texture. "What is this stuff?"

"It's a new waterproof material," Morna said impatiently. "The contents are more important."

Gregg opened the sack and took out a large black revolver. It was much lighter than he would have expected for its size, and it had something of the familiar lines of a Colt except that the grips were grooved for individual fingers and flared out at the top over his thumb. Gregg had never felt a gun settle itself in his hand so smoothly. He examined the weapon more closely and saw that it had a six-shot fluted cylinder that hinged out sideways for easy loading — a feature he had never seen on any other firearm. The gun lacked any kind of decoration, but was more perfectly machined and finished than he could have imagined possible. He read the engraving on the side of the long barrel.

"Colt .44 Magnum," he said slowly. "Never heard of it. Where did you get this gun, Morna?"

She hesitated. "I've been up for hours. I left this near the road where you first saw me, and I had time to go back for it."

The story did not ring true to Gregg, but his mind was fully occupied by the revolver itself. "I mean, where did you get it *before?* Where can you buy a gun like this?"

"That doesn't matter." Morna began walking toward the house. "The point is: Could you use it?"

"I guess so," Gregg said, glancing into the blue bag, which still contained a cardboard box of brass cartridges. The top of the box was missing, and many of the shells had fallen into the bottom of the bag. "It's a right handsome gun, but I doubt if it packs any more punch than my Remington."

"I would like you to try it out." Morna was walking so quickly that Gregg had difficulty in keeping up with her. "Please see if you can load it."

"You mean right now? Don't you want to see to the baby?" They had reached the flat area in front of the house, and the child's cries had become audible.

Morna glanced at her wrist, and he saw that the gold ornament was burning with a steady crimson light. "My son can wait a while longer," she said in a voice that was firm and yet edged with panic. "Please load the revolver."

"Whatever you say." Gregg walked to his buckboard and used it as a table. He cleared a space in the straw, set the gun down, and — under Morna's watchful gaze — carefully spilled the ammunition out of the blue bag. The center-fire shells were rather longer than he had ever seen for a handgun and, like the revolver itself, were finished with a degree of perfection he had never encountered previously. Their noses shone like polished steel.

"Everything's getting too fancy — adds to the price," Gregg muttered. He fumbled with the weapon until he saw how to swing the cylinder out, then slipped in six cartridges and closed it up. As he was doing so he noticed that the cardboard box had emerged from the bag upside down, and on its underside, stamped in pale blue ink, he saw a brief inscription: "OCT 1978." He picked it up and held it out to Morna.

"Wonder what that means."

Her eyes widened slightly, then she looked away without interest. "It's just a maker's code. A batch number."

"It looks like a date," Gregg commented, "except that they've made a mistake and put ... " He broke off, startled, as Morna knocked the box from his hands.

"Get on with it, you fool," she shouted, trampling the box underfoot. Her pale features were distorted with anger as she stared up at him with white-flaring eyes. They confronted each other for a moment, then her lips began to tremble. "I'm sorry, Billy. I'm so sorry ... It's just that there's almost no time above us ... and I'm afraid."

"It's all right," he said awkwardly. "I know I've got aggravating ways — Ruth's always telling me that — and I've been living alone for so long ... "

Morna stopped him by placing a hand on his wrist. "Don't, Billy. You're a good and kind man, but I want you — right now, please — to learn to handle that gun." Her quiet, controlled tones somehow gave Gregg a greater sense of urgency than anything said previously.

"Right." He turned away from the buckboard, looking for a suitable target, and began to ease the revolver's hammer back with his thumb.

"You don't need to do that," Morna said. "For rapid fire you just pull the trigger."

"I know — double action." Gregg cocked the gun regardless, to demonstrate his superior knowledge of firearms practice, and for a target selected a billet of wood that was leaning against the heavy stone water trough about twenty paces away. He was lining the gun's sights on it when Morna spoke again.

"You should hold it with both hands."

Gregg smiled indulgently. "Morna, you're a very well educated young lady, and I daresay you know all manner of things I never even heard of — but don't try to teach an old hand like me how to shoot a six-gun." He steadied the gun, held his breath, and squeezed off his first shot. There was an explosion like a clap of thunder, and something struck him a fierce blow on the forehead, blinding him with pain. His first confused thought was that the revolver had been faulty and had burst open, throwing a fragment into his face. Then he found it was intact in his hand, and it dawned on him that there had been a massive recoil, which had bent his weakened arm like a piece of straw, swinging the weapon all the way back to collide with his forehead. He wiped a warm trickle of blood away from his eyes and looked at the gun with awe and the beginning of a great respect.

"There isn't any smoke," he said. "There isn't even . . . "

His speech faltered as he looked beyond the gun in his hand and saw that the stone water trough, which had served as a backing for his target, had been utterly destroyed. Fragments of three-inch-thick earthenware were scattered over a triangular area running back about thirty yards. Without previous knowledge, Gregg would have guessed that the trough had been demolished by a cannon shot.

Morna took her hands away from her ears. "You've hurt yourself — I told you to hold it with both hands."

"I'm all right." He fended off her attempt to touch his forehead. "Morna, where did you get this . . . this *engine?*"

"Do you expect me to answer that?"

"I guess not, but I sure would like to know. This is something I could understand."

"Try it at longer range, and use both hands this time." Morna looked about her, apparently more composed now that Gregg was doing what she expected of him. She pointed at a whitish rock about three hundred yards off along the hillside. "That rock."

"That's getting beyond rifle range," Gregg explained. "Handguns don't . . . "

"Try it, Billy."

"All right — I'll try aiming way above it."

"Aim at it, near the top."

Gregg shrugged and did as he was told, suddenly aware that his right thumb was throbbing painfully where the big revolver had driven back against it. He squeezed off his second shot and experienced a deep pang of satisfaction, of a kind that only hunters understand, when he saw dust fountain into the air only about a yard to the right of the rock. Even with his two-handed grip the gun had kicked back until it was pointing almost vertically into the sky. Without waiting to be told, he fired again and saw rock fragments fly from his target.

Morna nodded her approval. "You appear to have a talent."

"This is the best gun I ever saw," he told her sincerely, "but I can't hold it down. These arms of mine can't handle the recoil."

"Then we'll bind your elbows."

"Too late for that," he said regretfully, pointing down the slope.

Several horsemen were coming into view, their presence in the formerly deserted landscape more shocking to Gregg than the discovery of a scorpion in a picnic hamper.

He began cursing his own carelessness in not having kept a lookout as more riders emerged from beyond the spur until there were eight of them fanning out across the bottom of the hill. They were a mixed bunch, slouching or riding high according to individual preference, on mounts that varied from quarter horses to tall stallions, and their dress ranged from greasy buckskin to gambler's black. Gregg knew, however, that they constituted a miniature army, disciplined and controlled by one man. He narrowed his eyes against the morning brilliance and picked out the distinctive figure of Josh Portfield on a chestnut stallion. As always, Portfield was wearing a white shirt and a suit of charcoal gray serge, which might have given him the look of a preacher had it not been for the pair of nickel-plated Smith & Wessons strapped to his waist.

"I was kind of hoping Big Josh would leave things as they were," Gregg said. "He must be in one of his righteous moods."

Morna took an involuntary step backward. "Can you defend yourself against so many?"

"Have to give it a try." Gregg began scooping up handfuls of cartridges and cramming them into his pockets. "You'd best get inside the house and bar the door."

Morna looked up at him, the hunted look returning to her face, then she stooped to pick up something from the ground and ran to the house. Glancing sideways, Gregg was unable to understand why she should have wasted time retrieving the flattened cartridge box, but he had more important things on his mind. He flipped the revolver's cylinder out, dropped the three empty cases, and replaced them with new shells. At last he turned toward the advancing riders. They had closed to within two hundred yards.

"Stay off my land, Josh," he shouted. "There's a law against trespassing."

Portfield stood up in his stirrups, and his powerful voice came clearly to Gregg in spite of his distance. "You're insolent, Billy. And you're ungrateful. And you've cost me a good man. I'm going to punish you for all those things, but most of all I'm going to punish you for your insolence and lack of respect." He sank down in the saddle and said something Gregg could not hear. A second later Siggy Sorenson urged his horse ahead of the pack and came riding up the hill with a pistol in his hand.

"This time I got a gun, too," Sorenson shouted. "This time we fight fair, eh?"

"If you come any farther I'll drop you," Gregg warned.

Sorenson began to laugh. "You're way out of range, you old fool. Can't you see any more?" He spurred his horse into a full gallop, and at the same time two other men went off to Gregg's left.

Gregg raised the big revolver and started to calculate bullet drop, then remembered it was practically nonexistent with the unholy weapon that fate had placed in his hands. This time the two-handed, knees-bent stance came to him naturally. He lined up on Sorenson, let him come on for another few seconds, and then squeezed the trigger. Sorenson's massive body, blasted right out of the saddle, turned over backward in midair and landed face down on the stony ground. His horse wheeled to one side and bolted. Realizing he would soon lose the advantage of surprise, Gregg turned on the two riders who were flanking him to the left. His second shot flicked the nearest man to the ground, and the third — fired too quickly — killed the other's horse. The animal dropped instantaneously, without a sound, and its rider threw himself into the shelter of its body, dragging a red-glinting leg.

Gregg looked back down the trail and in that moment discovered the quality of his opposition. He could see a knot of milling horses, but no men. In the brief respite given to them they had faded from sight behind rocks, no doubt with rifles taken from their saddle holsters. Suddenly becoming aware of how vulnerable he was in his exposed position at the top of the rise, Gregg bent low and ran for the cover of his shack. Crouching down behind it, he again dropped three expended cartridges and replaced them, appreciative of the speed with which the big gun could be loaded. He peered around a corner of the shack to make certain that nobody was working closer to him.

Shockingly, a pistol thundered and black smoke billowed only twenty yards away. Something gouged through his lower ribs. Gregg lurched back into cover and stared in disbelief at the ragged and bloody tear in his shirt. He had been within a handsbreadth of death.

"You're too slow, Mr. Gregg," a voice called, frighteningly close at hand. "That old buffalo gun you got yourself don't make no difference if you're too slow."

Gregg identified the speaker as Frenchy Martine, a young savage from the Canadian backwoods who had drifted into Copper Cross a year earlier. The near-fatal shot had come from the direction of the upright coffin that was Gregg's primitive lavatory. Gregg had no idea how Martine had gotten that close in the time available, and it came home to him that a man of fifty was out of his class when it came to standing off youngsters in their prime.

"Tell you something else, Mr. Gregg," Martine chuckled. "You're too old for that choice piece of woman flesh you got tucked away in your . . . "

Gregg took one step to the side and fired at the narrow structure, punching a hole through the one-inch timbers as if they had been paper. There was the sound of a body hitting the ground beyond it, and a pistol tumbled into view. Gregg stepped back into the lee of the shack just as a rifle cracked in the distance, and he heard the impact as the slug buried itself in the wood. He drew slight comfort from the knowledge that his opponents were armed with ordinary weapons — because the real battle was now about to begin.

Martine had assumed he was safe behind two thicknesses of timber, but there were at least four others who would not make the same fatal mistake. Their most likely tactic would be to surround Gregg, keeping in the shelter of rock all the way, and then nail him down with long-range rifle fire. Gregg failed to see how, even with the black engine of death in his hands, he was going to survive the next hour, especially as he was losing quantities of blood.

He knelt down, made a rectangular pad with his handkerchief, and tucked it into his shirt in an attempt to slow the bleeding. Nobody was firing at him for the minute, so he took advantage of the lull to discard the single empty shell and make up the full load again. A deceptive quietness had descended over the area.

He looked around him at the sunlit hillside, with its rocks like grazing sheep, and tried to guess where the next shot might come from. His view of his surroundings blurred slightly, and there followed the numb realization that he might know nothing about the next shot until it was plowing its way through his body. A throbbing hum began to fill his ears — familiar prelude to the loss of consciousness — and he looked across the open, dangerous space that separated him from the house, wondering if he could get that far without being hit again. The chances were not good, but if he could get inside the house he might have time to bind his chest properly.

Gregg stood up and then became aware of the curious fact that, although the humming sound had grown much louder, he was relatively clear-headed. It was dawning on him that the powerful sound, like the swarming of innumerable hornets, had an objective reality, when he heard a man's deep-chested bellow of fear, followed by a fusillade of shots. He flinched instinctively, but there were no sounds of bullet strikes close by. Gregg risked a look down the sloping trail, and what he saw caused an icy prickling on his forehead.

A tall, narrow-shouldered, black-cloaked figure, its face concealed by a black hood, was striding up the hill toward the house. It was surrounded by a strange aura of darkness, as though it had the ability to repel light itself, and it seemed to be the center from which emanated the ground-trembling, pulsating hum. Behind the awe-inspiring shape the horses belonging to the Portfield bunch were lying on their sides, apparently dead. As Gregg watched, Portfield himself and another man stood up from behind rocks and fired at the figure, using their rifles at point-blank range.

The only effect of their shots was to produce small purple flashes at the outer surface of its surrounding umbra. After perhaps a dozen shots had been absorbed harmlessly, the specter made a sweeping gesture with its left arm, and Portfield and his companion collapsed like puppets. The distance was too great for Gregg to be positive, but he received the ghastly impression that flesh had fallen away from their faces like tatters of cloth. Gregg's own horse whinnied in alarm and bolted away to his right.

Another Portfield man, Max Tibbett, driven by a desperate courage, emerged from cover on the other side of the trail and fired at the figure's back. There were more purple flashes on the edge of the aura of dimness. Without looking around, the being made the same careless gesture with its left arm — spreading the black cloak like a bat's wing — and Tibbett fell, withering and crumbling. If any of his companions were still alive they remained in concealment.

Its cloak flapping around it, the figure drew near the top of the rise, striding with inhuman speed on feet that seemed to be misshapen and disproportionately small. Without looking to left or right it went straight for the door of Gregg's house, and he knew that this was the hunter from whom Morna had been fleeing. The pervasive hum reached a mind-numbing intensity.

Gregg's previous fear of dying was as nothing compared to the dark dread that spurted and foamed through his soul. He was filled with an ancient and animalistic terror that swept away all reason, all courage, commanding him to cover his eyes and cringe in hiding until the shadow of evil had passed. He looked down at the black, gleaming gun in his hands and shook his head as a voice he had no wish to hear reminded him of a bargain sealed with gold, of a promise made by the man he had believed himself to be. There's nothing I can do, he thought. *I can't help you, Morna.*

In the same instant he was horrified to find that he was stepping out from the concealment of the shack. His hands steadied and aimed the gun without conscious guidance from his brain. He squeezed the trigger. There was a brilliant purple flash, which pierced the being's aura like a sword of lightning, and it staggered sideways with a raucous shriek which chilled Gregg's blood.

It turned toward him, left arm rising like the wing of a nightmarish bird.

Gregg saw the movement through the triangular arch of his own forearms, which had been driven back and upward by the gun's recoil. The weapon itself was pointing vertically, and uselessly, into the sky. An eternity passed as he fought to bring it down again to bear on an adversary who was gifted with demonic strength and speed. Gregg worked the trigger again, there was another flash, and the figure was hurled to the ground, shrilling and screaming. Gregg advanced on legs that tried to buckle with every step, blasting his enemy again and again with the gun's enormous power.

Incredibly, the dark being survived the massive blows. It rose to its feet, the space around it curiously distorted, like the image seen in a flawed lens, and began to back away. To Gregg's swimming senses, the figure seemed to cover an impossible distance with each step, as though it were treading an invisible surface that itself was retreating at great speed. The undulating hum of power faded to a whisper and was gone. He was alone in a bright, clean, slow-tilting world.

Gregg sank to his knees, grateful for the sunlight's warmth. He looked down at his chest and was astonished by the quantity of blood that had soaked through his clothing; then he was falling forward and unable to do anything about it.

It is forbidden for me to tell you anything . . . my poor, brave Billy . . . but you have been through so much on my behalf. The words will probably hold no meaning for you, anyway — assuming you can even hear them.

I tricked you, and you allowed yourself to be tricked, into taking part in a war . . . a war that has been fought for twenty thousand years and that may last forever . . .

There were long periods during which Gregg lay and stared at the knotted, grainy wood of the ceiling and tried to decide if it really was a ceiling, or if he was in some way suspended high above a floor. All he knew for certain was that he was being tended by a young woman, who came and went with soundless steps, and who spoke to him in a voice whose cadences were as measured and restful as the ocean tides.

We are evenly matched — my people and the Others — but our strengths are as different as our basic natures. They have superior mastery of space; our true domain is time . . .

There are standing waves in time . . . all presents are not equal . . . the "now" that you experience is known as the Prime Present, and has greater potential than any other. You are bound to it, just as the Others are bound to it . . . but the mental disciplines of my people enabled us to break free and migrate to another crest in the distant past . . . to safety . . .

Occasionally, Gregg was aware of the dressings on his chest being changed, and of his lips and brow being moistened with cool water. A beautiful young face hovered above his own, the gray eyes watchful and concerned, and he tried to remember the name he associated with it. Martha? Mary?

> To a woman of my race, the time of greatest danger is the last week of pregnancy . . . especially if the child is male and destined to have a certain cast of mind . . . In those circumstances the child can be drawn to your "now," the home time of all humanity, and the mother is drawn with it . . . Usually she can assert control soon after the child is born and return with it to the time of refuge . . . but there have been rare examples in which the male child resisted all attempts to influence its mental processes, and lived out its life in the Prime Present . . .
>
> Happily for me, my son is almost ready to travel . . . for the prince has grown clever and would soon return . . .

His enjoyment of the taste of the soup was Gregg's first indication that his body was making up its losses of blood, that his strength was returning, that he was not going to die. As the nourishing liquid was spooned into his mouth, he filled his eyes with the fresh young beauty of his daughter-wife, and was thankful for her kindness and grace. He forced into the deepest caverns of his mind all thoughts of the dreadful dark hunter who had menaced her.

> I'm sorry . . . my poor, brave Billy . . . my son and I must travel now. The longer we remain, the more strongly he will be linked to the Prime Present . . . and my people will be anxious until they learn that we are safe . . .
>
> I have been schooled to survive in your "now," though in less hazardous parts of it . . . which is why I am able to speak to you in English . . . but my ship came down in the wrong part of the world, all these thousands of years ago, and they will fear I have been lost . . .

A moment of lucidity. Gregg turned his head and looked through the open door of the bedroom into the house's main living space. Morna was standing at the table, her head surrounded by a vibrant golden halo of hair. She stooped to rest her forehead against that of her child.

They both became hazy, then transparent; then they were gone.

Gregg pushed himself upright in the bed, shaking his head, reaching for them with his free hand. The pain of the reopening wound burned across his chest and he fell back onto the pillows, gasping for breath as the darkness closed in on him again. An indeterminate time later he felt the coolness of a moist cloth being pressed against his forehead, and his crushing sense of loss abated.

He smiled and said, "I was afraid you had left."

"How could I leave you like this?" Ruth Jefferson replied. "What in God's name has been going on out here, Billy Gregg? I find you lying in bed with a bullet hole in you, and the place outside looking like a battleground. Sam and some of his friends are out there cleaning up the mess the buzzards left, and they say they haven't seen anything like it since the war."

Gregg opened his eyes and chose to give the sort of answer she would expect of him. "You missed a good fight, Ruth."

"Good fight!" Ruth clucked with exasperation. "You're more of an old fool than I took you for, Billy Gregg. What happened? Did the Portfield mob fall out with each other?"

"Something like that."

"Lucky for you," Ruth scolded. "And where were Morna and the baby when all this was going on? Where are they now?"

Gregg sorted through his memories, trying to separate dream and reality. "I don't know, Ruth. They . . . left."

"How?"

"They went with friends."

Ruth looked at him suspiciously, then gave a deep sigh. "I still think you've been up to something, but I've got a feeling I'll never find out what it was."

Gregg remained in bed for a further three days, being nursed to fitness by Ruth, and it seemed to him a perfectly natural outcome that they should revive their plans to be married. During that time there was a fairly steady stream of callers, men who were pleased that he was alive and that Josh Portfield was dead. All of them were curious about the details of the gun battle, which was fast becoming legendary, but he said nothing to dispel the notion that Portfield and his men had annihilated themselves in a sudden quarrel.

As soon as he had the house to himself, he searched it from one end to the other and found, tucked in behind his whisky jar, six slim gold bars neatly wrapped in a scrap of cloth. In keeping with his expectations, however, the big revolver — the black engine of death — was missing. He knew that Morna had decided he should not have it, and for a while he thought he might understand her reasons. There were words, half remembered from his delirium, that seemed as though they might explain all that had happened. It was only necessary to recall them properly, to get them into sharp focus in his mind. And at first the task appeared simple — the main requirement being a breathing space, time in which to think.

Gregg got his breathing space, but it was a long time before he could accept that, like the heat of summer, dreams can only fade.

trains — railroad cars that are pulled or pushed along rails by locomotives. Once the most important form of transportation in the world, trains have been making a comeback due to the energy crisis. A surprising number of science fiction stories are set on trains; some of them, in addition to excellent non-sf stories, can be found in *Midnight Specials* (Bobbs-Merrill, 1978).

Gantlet

RICHARD E. PECK

Jack Brens thumbed the ID sensor and waited for the sealed car doors to open. He had stayed too long in his office, hoping to avoid any conversation with the other commuters, and had been forced to trot through the fetid station. The doors split open; he put his head in and sucked gratefully at the cool air inside, then scrubbed his moist palms along his thighs and stepped quickly into the car. Rivulets of sweat ran down the small of his back. He stretched his lips into the parody of a confident smile.

Most of the passengers sat strapped in, a few feigning sleep, others trying to concentrate on the stiff, dried facsheets which rattled in their hands. Lances of light fell diagonally through the gloom; some of the boiler plate welded over the windows had apparently cracked under the twice-daily barrage.

Brens bit the tip of his tongue to remind himself to call Co-op Maintenance when he got home. Today the train was his responsibility — one day out of one hundred; one day out of twenty work weeks. If he didn't correct the flaws he noticed, he might suffer because of them tomorrow, though the responsibility would by then have shifted to someone else. To whom? Karras. Tomorrow Karras had window seat.

Brens nodded to several of the gray-haired passengers who greeted him.
"Hey, Brens. How's it going?"
"Hello, Mr. Brens."
"Go get 'em, Jack."
He strode down the aisle through the aura of acrid fear rising from the ninety-odd men huddled in their seats. A few of the commuters had already

pulled their individual smoking bells down from the overhead rack. Although the rules forbade smoking till the train got underway, Brens understood their feelings too well to make a point of it.

Only Karras sat at the front. The seats beside and behind him were empty. "Thought you weren't coming and I might have to take her out myself," Karras said. "But my turn tomorrow."

Brens nodded and slipped into the engineer's seat. While he familiarized himself with the instrument console, he felt Karras peering avidly past him at the window. Lights in the station tunnel faded and the darkness outside made the window a temporary mirror. Brens glanced at it once to see the split image of Karras reflected in the inner and outer layers of the bulletproof glass: four bulging eyes, a pair of glistening bald scalps wobbling in and out of focus.

The start buzzer sounded.

He checked the interior mirror. Only two empty seats, at the front of course. He'd heard of no resignations from the Co-op and therefore assumed that the men who should have occupied those seats were ill; it took something serious to make a man miss his scheduled car and incur the fine of a full day's salary.

The train thrummed to life. Lights flared, the fans whined toward full thrust, and the car danced unsteadily forward as it climbed onto its cushion of air. Brens concentrated on keeping his hovering hands near the throttle override.

"You really sweat this thing, don't you?" Karras said. "Relax. You've got nothing to do but enjoy the view, unless you think you're really playing engineer."

Brens tried to ignore him. It was true that the train was almost totally automatic. Yet the man who drew window seat did have certain responsibilities, functions to perform, and no time to waste. No time until the train was safely beyond the third circle — past Cityend, past Opensky, past Workring. And after that, an easy thirty miles home.

Brens pictured the city above them as the train bored its way through the subterranean darkness, pushing it back with a fan of brilliant light. City stretched for thirty blocks from center in this direction and then met the wall of defenses separating it from Opensky. The whole area of City was unified now, finally — buildings joined and sealed against the filth of the air outside that massive, nearly self-sufficient hive. Escalators up and down, beltways back and forth, interior temperature and pollution kept at an acceptable level — it was all rather pleasant.

It was heaven, compared to Opensky. Surrounding and continually threatening City lay the ring of Opensky and its incredible masses of people. Brens hadn't been there for years, not since driving through on his way to work had become impossibly time-consuming and dangerous. Twenty years ago he had been one of the last lucky ones, picked out by Welfare Control as "salvage-able"; these days, no one left Opensky. For that matter, no one with any common sense entered.

He could vaguely recall seeing single-family dwellings there, whether his wife Hazel believed that claim or not, and more vividly the single-family room he had shared with his parents and grandfather. He could even remember the first O-peddlers to appear on Sheridan Street. Huge, brawny men with green O-tanks strapped to their backs, they joked with the clamoring children who tugged at their sleeves and tried to beg a lungful of straight O for the high it was rumored to induce. But the peddlers dealt at first only with asthmatics and early-stage emphysemics who gathered on muggy afternoons to suck their metered dollar's worth from the grimy rubber mask looped over the peddler's arm. All that was before each family had a private bubble hooked directly to the City metering system.

He had no idea what life in Opensky was like now, except what he could gather from the statistics that crossed his desk in Welfare Control. Those figures meant little enough: so many schools to maintain, dole centers to keep stocked and guarded, restraint aides needed for various playgrounds — he merely converted City budget figures to percentages corresponding to the requests of fieldmen in Opensky. And he hadn't spoken to a fieldman in nearly a year. But he assumed it couldn't be pleasant there. Welfare Control had recently disbanded and reassigned to wall duty all riot suppression teams; the object now was not to suppress, but to contain. What went on in Opensky was the skyers' own business, so long as they didn't try to enter City.

So. Six miles through Opensky to Workring, three miles of Workring itself, where the skyers kept the furnaces bellowing and City industry alive. But that part of the trip wouldn't be too bad. Only responsible skyers were allowed to enter Workring, and most stuck to their jobs for fear of having their thumbprints erased from the sensors at each Opensky exit gate. Such strict control had seemed harsh, at first, but Brens now knew it to be necessary. Rampant sabotage in Workring had made it so. The skyers who chose to work had nearly free access to and from Workring. And those who chose not to work — well, that was their choice. They could occupy themselves somehow. Each year Welfare Control authorized more and more playgrounds in Opensky, and the public schools were open to anyone under fifty with no worse than a moderate arrest record.

Beyond Workring lay the commuter residential area. A few miles of high-rise suburbs, for secretaries and apprentice managerial staff, merging suddenly with the sprawling redevelopment apartment blocks, and then real country. To Brens the commuter line seemed a barometer of social responsibility: the greater one's worth to City, the farther away he could afford to live. Brens and his wife had moved for the last time only a year ago, to the end of the trainpad, thirty miles out. They had a small square of yellowed grass and two dwarf apple trees that would not bear. It was . . .

He shook off his daydreaming and tried to focus on the darkness rushing toward them. As their speed increased, he paradoxically lost the sense of motion conveyed by the lurching start and lumbering underground passage. Greater speed increased the amount of compression below as air entered the train's howling scoops and whooshed through the ducts down the car sides. Cityend lay moments ahead.

Brens concentrated on one of the few tasks not yet automated: at Cityend, and on the train's emergence from the tunnel, his real duty would begin. Three times in the past month skyers had sought to breach City defenses through the tunnel itself.

"Hey! You didn't check defense systems," Karras said.

"Thanks," Brens muttered through clenched teeth. "But they're okay." Then, because he knew Karras was right, he flipped the arming switch for the roof-mounted fifties and checked diverted-power availability for the nose lasers. The dials read in the green, as always.

Only Karras, who now sat hunched forward in anticipation, would have noticed the omission. Because Karras was sick. The man actually seemed to look forward to his turn in the window seat, not only for the sights all the other commuters in the Co-op tried to avoid, but also for the possible opportunity of turning loose the train's newly installed firepower.

"One of these days they're going to make a big try. They'd all give an arm to break into City, just to camp in the corridors. Now, if it was me out there, I'd be figuring a way to get out into Suburbs. But them? All they know is destroy. Besides, you think they'll take it lying down that we raised the O-tax? Forget it! They're out there waiting, and we both know it. That's why you ought to check all the gear we've got. Never know when . . . "

"Later, Karras! There it is." Brens felt his chest tighten as the distant circle of light swept toward them — tunnel exit, Cityend. His forearms tensed and he glared at the instruments, waiting for the possibility that he might have to override the controls and slam the train to a stop. But a green light flashed; ahead, the circle of sky brightened as the approaching train tripped the switch that cut off the spray of mist at the tunnel exit. And with that mist fading, the barrier of twenty thousand volts which ordinarily crackled between the exit uprights faded also. For the next few moments, while the train snaked its way into Opensky, City was potentially vulnerable.

Brens stared even harder at the opening, but saw nothing. The car flashed out into gray twilight, and he relaxed. But instinct, or a random impulse, drew his eyes to the train's exterior mirrors. And then he saw them: a shapeless huddle of bodies pouring into the tunnel back toward City. He hit a series of studs on the console and braced himself for the jolt.

There it was.

A murmur swept the crowded car behind him, but he ignored it and stared straight ahead.

"What the hell was it?" Karras asked. "I didn't see a thing."

"Skyers. They were waiting, I guess till the first car passed. They must have figured no one would see them that way."

"I don't mean who. I mean, what did you use? I didn't hear the fifties."

"For a man who's taking the run tomorrow, you don't keep up very well. Nothing fancy, none of the noise and flash some people get their kicks from. I just popped speed-breaks on the last three cars."

"In the tunnel? My God! Must have wiped them all the way out of the tunnel walls, like a squeegee. Who figured that one?"

"This morning's Co-op bulletin suggested it, remember?"

Karras sulked. "I've got better things to do than pay attention to every word those guys put out. They must spend all day dictating memos. We got a real bunch of clods running things this quarter."

"Why don't you volunteer?"

"I give them my four days' pay a month. Who needs that mishmash?"

Brens silently agreed. No one enjoyed keeping the Co-op alive. No one really knew how. And that was one of the major problems associated with having amateurs in charge: it's a hell of a way to run a railroad. But the only way, since the line itself had declared bankruptcy, and both city and state governments refused to take over. If it hadn't been for the Co-op, City would have died, a festering ulcer in the midst of the cancer of Opensky.

Opensky whirled past them now. Along the embankment on both sides, legs dangled a decorative fringe. People sat atop the pilings and hurled debris at the speeding stainless steel cars. Their accuracy had always amazed Brens. Even as he willed himself rigid, he flinched at the eggs, rocks, bottles, and assorted garbage that clattered and smeared across the window.

"Look at those sonsabitches throw, would you? You ever try and figure what kind of lead time you need to hit something moving as fast as we are?"

Brens shook his head. "I guess they're used to it."

"Why not? What else they got to do but practice?"

Behind them, gunfire crackled and bullets pattered along the boiler plate. Many of the commuters ducked at the opening burst.

"Look at them back there," Karras pointed down the aisle. "Scared blue, every one of them. I know this psychologist who's got a way to calm things down, he says. He had this idea to paint bull's-eyes on the sides of the cars, below the window. Did I tell you about it? He figures it'll work two or three ways. One, if the snipers hit the bull's-eyes, there's less chance of somebody getting tagged through a crack in the boiler plate. Two, maybe they'll quit firing at all, when they see we don't give a suck of sky about it. Or three, he says, even if they keep it up, it gives them something to do, sort of channels their aggression. If they take it out on the trains, maybe they'll ease up on City. What do you think?"

"Wouldn't it make more sense to put up shooting galleries in all the playgrounds? Or figure a way to get new cars for the trains? We can't keep patching and jury-rigging these old crates forever. The last thing we need right now is to make us more of a target than we already are."

"Okay. Have it your way. Only, I was thinking . . . "

Brens tuned him out and squinted at the last molten sliver of setting sun. Its rays smeared rainbows through the streaked eggs washing slowly across the window in the slipstream. The mess coagulated and darkened as airblown particles of ash settled in it and crusted over. When he could stand it no longer, Brens flipped on the wipers and watched the clotted slime smear across the glass, as he had known it would. But some of it scrubbed loose to flip back alongside the speeding train.

The people were still out there. If he looked carefully straight ahead, their presence became a mere shadow at the edges of the channel through which he watched the trainpad reeling toward him. Though he doubted any eye would catch his long enough to matter, he avoided the faces. There was always the slight chance that he might recognize one of them. Twenty years wasn't so long a time. Twenty years ago he had watched the trains from an embankment like these.

Now the train swooped upward to ride its cushion of air along the raised pad, level with second-story windows on each side. Blurred faces stared from those windows, here disembodied, there resting on a cupped hand and arm propped on a window ledge. The exterior mirrors showed him faces ducking away from the gust of wind fanning out behind the train and from the debris lifted whirling in the grimy evening air. He tried to picture the pattern left by the train's passage — dust settling out of the whirlwind like the lines of polarization around a magnet tip. A few of the faces wore respirators or simple, and relatively useless, cotton masks. Many didn't bother to draw back but hung exposed to the breeze that the train was stirring up. And now, as on each of his previous rare turns at the window seat, Brens had the impulse to slow the train, to let the wind die down and diminish behind them, out of what he himself considered misplaced and maudlin sympathy for the skyers, who seemed to enjoy the excitement of the train's glistening passage. It tempered the boredom of their day.

" . . . right about here the six-thirty had the explosion. Five months ago. Remember?"

"What?"

"Explosion. Some kids must have got hold of detonator caps and strung them on wires swinging from a tree. When the train hit them, they cracked the window all to hell. Nearly hurt somebody. But the crews came out and burned down all the trees along the right of way. Little bastards won't pull *that* one again."

Brens nodded. There was one of the armored repair vans ahead, on a siding under the protective stone lip of the embankment.

The train rose even higher to cross the river which marked the Opensky-Workring boundary. They were riding securely in the concave shell of the bridge. On the river below, a cat, or dog — it was hard to tell at this distance — picked its cautious way across the crusted algae which nearly covered the stream. The center of the turgid river steamed a molten beige; and upriver a short way, brilliant patches of green marked the mouth of the main Workring spillway.

At the far end of the bridge, a group of children scrambled out of the trough of the trainbed to hang over the side.

"Hey! Hit the lasers. Singe their butts for them." Karras bounced in his seat.

"Shut up for a minute, can't you? They're out of the way."

"Now what's that for? Can't you take a joke? Besides, you know they're sneaking into Workring to steal something. You saying we ought to let them get away with it?"

"I'm just telling you to shut up. I'm tired, that's all. Leave it at that."

"Sure. Big deal. Tired! But tomorrow the window seat's mine. So don't come sucking around for a look then, understand?"

"It's a promise."

Sulfurous clouds hung in the air, and Brens checked the car's interior pollution level. It was a safe 18, as he might have guessed. But the sight of buildings tarnished green, of bricks flaking and molting on every factory wall, always depressed him. The ride home was worse than the trip into City. Permissive hours ran from five to eight, when pollution controls were lifted. He knew the theory: evening air was more susceptible to condensation because of the temperature drop, and dumping pollutants into the night sky might actually bring on a cleansing rain. He also knew the practical considerations involved: twenty-four-hour control would almost certainly drive industry away. Compromise was essential, if City was to survive.

It would be good to get home.

The train swung into its gently curving descent toward Workring exit, and Brens instinctively clasped the seat arms as the seat pivoted on its gimbals. At the foot of the curve he saw the barricade. Something piled on the pad.

Not for an instant did he doubt what he saw. He lunged at the power override, but stopped himself in time. Dropping to the pad now, in midcurve, might tip the train or let it slide off the pad onto the potholed and eroded right of way where the uneven terrain offered no stable lift base for getting underway again.

"Ahead of you! On the tracks!" Karras reached for the controls, but Brens caught him with a straight-arm and slammed him to the floor. He concentrated on the roadbed flashing toward them. At the last instant, as the curve modified and tilted toward level, he popped all speed breaks and snatched the main circuit breaker loose.

From the sides of the cars vertical panels hissed out on their hydraulic pushrods to form baffles against the slipstream, and the train slammed to the pad. Tractor gear whined in protest, the shriek nearly drowning out the dying whirr of compressor fans, and the train shuddered to a stop.

Inside, lights dimmed and flickered. Voices rose in the darkness amid the noise of men struggling to their feet.

Brens depressed the circuit breaker and hit the emergency call switch overhead. "Hold it!" he shouted. "Quiet down, please! There's something on the pad, and I had to stop. Just keep calm. I've signaled for the work crews, and they'll be here any minute."

Then he ignored the passengers and focused his attention on the windows. The barricade lay no more than twenty feet ahead, rusted castings and discarded mold shells heaped on the roadbed. The jumbled pile seemed ablaze in the flickering red light from the emergency beacons rotating atop the train cars. Behind the barricade and along the right of way, faceless huddled forms rose erect in the demonic light and stood motionless, simply staring at the train. The stroboscopic light sweeping over them made each face a swarm of moving, melting shadows. Brens fired a preliminary burst from the fifties atop the first car, then quickly switched them to automatic, but the watching forms stood like statues.

"They must know," Karras said. He stood beside Brens and massaged his bruised shoulder. "Look. None of them moving."

Then one of the watchers broke and charged toward the car, waving a club. He managed two strides before the fifties homed on his movement and opened up. A quick chatter from overhead and the man collapsed. He hurled the club as he dropped and the fifties efficiently followed its arc through the air with homing-fire that made it dance in a shower of flashing sparks. It splintered to shreds before it hit the ground.

The other watchers stood motionless.

Brens stared at them a long moment before he could define what puzzled him about their appearance: none of them wore respirators. Were they trying to commit suicide? And why this useless attack? His eyes had grown accustomed to the flickering light and he scanned the mob. Young faces and old, mostly men but a few women scattered among them, all shades of color, united in appearance only by their clothing. Workring skyers in leather aprons and thick-soled shoes, probably escapees from a nearby factory. He flinched as one of them nodded slightly — surely they couldn't see him through the window. The nod grew more violent, and then he realized that the man was coughing. Paroxysms seized the man as he threw his hands to his mouth and bent forward helplessly. It was enough. The fifties chattered once more, and he fell.

"But what do they get out of it?" He turned his bewilderment to Karras.

"Who can tell? They're nuts, all of them. Malcontents, or anarchists. Mainly stupid, I'd say. Like the way they try and break into City. Even if they threw us out, they wouldn't know what to do next. Picture one of them sitting in your office. At your desk."

"I don't mean that. If they stop us from getting through, who takes care of them? I mean, we feed them, run their schools, bury them. I don't understand what they think all this will accomplish."

"Listen! The crew's coming. They'll take care of them."

A siren keened its rise and fall from the dimming twilight ahead, but still the watchers stood frozen. When the siren changed to a blatting klaxon, Brens switched the fifties back on manual to safeguard the approaching repair car. The mob melted away at the same signal. They were there, and then they were gone. They dropped from sight along the pad edge and blended into the shadows.

The work crew's crane hoisted the castings off the pad and dropped them on the right of way. In a few minutes they had finished. Green lights flashed at Brens, and the repair van sped away again.

Passing the Workring exit guards, Brens made a mental note to warn the Co-op. If the skyers were growing bold enough to show open rebellion within the security of Workring, the exit guards had better be augmented. Even Suburbs might not be safe any longer. At thirty miles' distance, he wasn't really concerned for his own home, but some of the commuters lived dangerously close to Workring.

He watched in the exterior mirror. The rear car detached itself and swung out onto a siding where it dropped to a halt while the body of the train went on. Every two miles, the scene repeated itself. Cars dropped off singly to await morning reassembly. Brens had often felt a strange sort of envy for the commuters who lived closer in: they never had the lead window seat on the way out of City. Responsibility for the whole train devolved on them only for short stretches and only on the way in.

But that was fair, he reminded himself. He lived the farthest out. With privilege go obligations. And he was through for another twenty weeks, his obligations met.

At the station, he telexed his report to the Co-op office and trotted outside to meet Hazel. The other wives had driven away. Only his carryall sat idling at the platform edge. He knew he ought to look forward to relaxing at home, but the trip itself still preyed on his mind unaccountably. He felt irritation at his inability to put the skyers out of his thoughts. His whole day was spent working for their benefit; his evenings ought to be his own.

He looked back toward City, but saw nothing in the smog-covered bowl at the foot of the hills that stretched away to the east. If it rained tonight, it might clear the air.

Hazel smiled and waved.

He grinned in answer. He could predict her reaction when she heard what he'd been through: a touch of wifely fear and concern for him, and that always made her more affectionate. Almost a hero's welcome. After all, he had acquitted himself rather well. A safe arrival, only a few minutes late, no injuries or major problems. And he wouldn't draw window seat for another several months. It was good to be home.

U

UFOs — the abbreviation for unidentified flying objects, a term used to describe claimed sightings of extraterrestial vehicles. Great controversy surrounds these claims, and hard evidence of UFOs' existence is lacking. Popularly known as "flying saucers," they occur in science fiction, although the great majority of writers and fans do not believe that Earth has been visited by them. "Close Encounters of the Third Kind" has renewed interest in the phenomenon. SF stories about UFOs are in *Flying Saucers in Fact and Fiction* (Lancer Books, 1968) and *Flying Saucers* (Fawcett Books, 1982).

Saucer of Loneliness

THEODORE STURGEON

If she's dead, I thought, I'll never find her in this white flood of moonlight on the white sea, with the surf seething in and over the pale, pale sand like a great shampoo. Almost always, suicides who stab themselves or shoot themselves in the heart carefully bare their chests; the same strange impulse generally makes the sea-suicide go naked.

A little earlier, I thought, or later, and there would be shadows for the dunes and the breathing toss of the foam. Now the only real shadow was mine, a tiny thing just under me, but black enough to feed the blackness of the shadow of a blimp.

A little earlier, I thought, and I might have seen her plodding up the silver shore, seeking a place lonely enough to die in. A little later and my legs would rebel against this shuffling trot through sand, the maddening sand that could not hold and would not help a hurrying man.

My legs did give way then and I knelt suddenly, sobbing — not for her, not yet; just for air. There was such a rush about me: wind, and tangled spray, and colors upon colors and shades of colors that were not colors at all but shifts of white and silver. If light like that were sound, it would sound like the sea on sand, and if my ears were eyes, they would see such a light.

I crouched there, gasping in the swirl of it, and a flood struck me, shallow and swift, turning up and outward like flower petals where it touched my knees, then soaking me to the waist in its bubble and crash. I pressed my knuckles to my eyes so they would open again. The sea was on my lips with the taste of tears and the whole white night shouted and wept aloud.

And there she was.

Her white shoulders were a taller curve in the sloping foam. She must have sensed me — perhaps I yelled — for she turned and saw me kneeling there. She put her fists to her temples and her face twisted, and she uttered a piercing wail of despair and fury, and then plunged seaward and sank.

I kicked off my shoes and ran into the breakers, shouting, hunting, grasping at flashes of white that turned to sea-salt and coldness in my fingers. I plunged right past her, and her body struck my side as a wave whipped my face and tumbled both of us. I gasped in solid water, opened my eyes beneath the surface and saw a greenish-white distorted moon hurtle as I spun. Then there was sucking sand under my feet again and my left hand was tangled in her hair.

The receding wave towed her away and for a moment she streamed out from my hand like steam from a whistle. In that moment I was sure she was dead, but as she settled to the sand, she fought and scrambled to her feet.

She hit my ear, wet, hard, and a huge pointed pain lanced into my head. She pulled, she lunged away from me, and all the while my hand was caught in her hair. I couldn't have freed her if I had wanted to. She spun to me with the next wave, battered and clawed at me, and we went into deeper water.

"Don't . . . don't . . . I can't swim!" I shouted, so she clawed me again.

"Leave me alone," she shrieked. "Oh, dear God, why can't you *leave*" (said her fingernails) "me . . . " (said her snapping teeth) *"alone!"* (said her small hard fist).

So by her hair I pulled her head down tight to her white shoulder; and with the edge of my free hand I hit her neck twice. She floated again, and I brought her ashore.

I carried her to where a dune was between us and the sea's broad noisy tongue, and the wind was above us somewhere. But the light was as bright. I rubbed her wrists and stroked her face and said, "It's all right," and, "There!" and some names I used to have for a dream I had long, long before I ever heard of her.

She lay still on her back with her breath hissing between her teeth, with her lips in a smile which her twisted-tight, wrinkle-sealed eyes made not a smile but a torture. She was well and conscious for many moments and still her breath hissed and her closed eyes twisted.

"Why couldn't you leave me alone?" she asked at last. She opened her eyes and looked at me. She had so much misery that there was no room for fear. She shut her eyes again and said, "You know who I am."

"I know," I said.

She began to cry.

I waited, and when she stopped crying, there were shadows among the dunes. A long time.

She said, "You don't know who I am. Nobody knows who I am."

I said, "It was in all the papers."

"That!" She opened her eyes slowly and her gaze traveled over my face, my shoulders, stopped at my mouth, touched my eyes for the briefest second. She curled her lips and turned away her head. "Nobody knows who I am."

I waited for her to move or speak, and finally I said, "Tell *me.*"

"Who are you?" she asked, with her head still turned away.

"Someone who . . . "

"Well?"

"Not now," I said. "Later, maybe."

She sat up suddenly and tried to hide herself. "Where are my clothes?"

"I didn't see them."

"Oh," she said. "I remember. I put them down and kicked sand over them, just where a dune would come and smooth them over, hide them as if they never were . . . I hate sand. I wanted to drown in the sand, but it wouldn't let me . . . You mustn't look at me!" she shouted. "I hate to have you looking at me!" She threw her head from side to side, seeking. "I can't stay here like this! What can I do? Where can I go?"

"Here," I said.

She let me help her up and then snatched her hand away, half turned from me. "Don't touch me. Get away from me."

"Here," I said again, and walked down the dune where it curved in the moonlight, tipped back into the wind and down and became not dune but beach. "Here." I pointed behind the dune.

At last she followed me. She peered over the dune where it was chest-high, and again where it was knee-high. "Back there?"

I nodded.

"I didn't see them."

"So dark . . . " She stepped over the low dune and into the aching black of those moon-shadows. She moved away cautiously, feeling tenderly with her feet, back to where the dune was higher. She sank down into the blackness and disappeared there. I sat on the sand in the light. "Stay away from me," she spat.

I rose and stepped back. Invisible in the shadows, she breathed, "Don't go away." I waited, then saw her hand press out of the clean-cut shadows. "There," she said, "over there. In the dark. Just be a . . . Stay away from me now . . . Be a — voice."

I did as she asked, and sat in the shadows perhaps six feet from her.

She told me about it. Not the way it was in the papers.

She was perhaps seventeen when it happened. She was in Central Park, in New York. It was too warm for such an early spring day, and the hammered brown slopes had a dusting of green of precisely the consistency of that morning's hoar frost on the rocks. But the frost was gone and the grass was brave and tempted some hundreds of pairs of feet from the asphalt and concrete to tread on it.

Hers were among them. The sprouting soil was a surprise to her feet, as the air was to her lungs. Her feet ceased to be shoes as she walked, her body was consciously more than clothes. It was the only kind of day which in itself can make a city-bred person raise his eyes. She did.

For a moment she felt separated from the life she lived, in which there was no fragrance, no silence, in which nothing ever quite fit or was quite filled. In that moment the ordered disapproval of the buildings around the pallid park could not reach her; for two, three clean breaths it no longer mattered that the whole wide world really belonged to images projected on a screen; to gently groomed goddesses in these steel and glass towers; that it belonged, in short, always, always to someone else.

So she raised her eyes, and there above her was the saucer.

It was beautiful. It was golden, with a dusty finish like that of an unripe Concord grape. It made a faint sound, a chord composed of two tones and a blunted hiss like the wind in tall wheat. It was darting about like a swallow, soaring and dropping. It circled and dropped and hovered like a fish, shimmering. It was like all these living things, but with that beauty it had all the loveliness of things turned and burnished, measured, machined, and metrical.

At first she felt no astonishment, for this was so different from anything she had ever seen before that it had to be a trick of the eye, a false evaluation of size and speed and distance that in a moment would resolve itself into a sun-flash on an airplane or the lingering glare of a welding arc.

She looked away from it and abruptly realized that many other people saw it — saw *something* — too. People all around her had stopped moving and speaking and were craning upward. Around her was a globe of silent astonishment, and outside it she was aware of the life-noise of the city, the hard-breathing giant who never inhales.

She looked up again, and at last began to realize how large and how far away the saucer was. No: rather, how small and how very near it was. It was just the size of the largest circle she might make with her two hands, and it floated not quite eighteen inches over her head.

Fear came then. She drew back and raised a forearm, but the saucer simply hung there. She bent far sideways, twisted away, leaped forward, looked back and upward to see if she had escaped it. At first she couldn't see it; then as she looked up and up, there it was, close and gleaming, quivering and crooning, right over her head.

She bit her tongue.

From the corner of her eye, she saw a man cross himself. She thought: He did that because he saw me standing here with a halo over my head. And that was the greatest single thing that had ever happened to her. No one had ever looked at her and made a respectful gesture before, not once, not ever. Through terror, through panic and wonderment, the comfort of that thought nestled into her, to wait to be taken out and looked at again in lonely times.

The terror was uppermost now, however. She backed away, staring upward, stepping a ludicrous cakewalk. She should have collided with people. There were plenty of people there, gaping and craning, but she reached none. She spun around and discovered to her horror that she was the center of a pointing, pressing crowd. Its mosaic of eyes all bulged and its inner circle braced its many legs to press back and away from her.

The saucer's gentle note deepened. It tilted, dropped an inch or so. Someone screamed, and the crowd broke away from her in all directions, milled about, and settled again in a new dynamic balance, a much larger ring, as more and more people raced to thicken it against the efforts of the inner circle to escape.

The saucer hummed and tilted, tilted . . .

She opened her mouth to scream, fell to her knees, and the saucer struck.

It dropped against her forehead and clung there. It seemed almost to lift her. She came erect on her knees, made one effort to raise her hands against it, and then her arms stiffened down and back, her hands not reaching the ground. For perhaps a second and a half the saucer held her rigid, and then it passed a single ecstatic quiver to her body and dropped it. She plumped to the ground, the backs of her thighs heavy and painful on her heels and ankles.

The saucer dropped beside her, rolled once in a small circle, once just around its edge, and lay still. It lay still and dull and metallic, different and dead.

Hazily, she lay and gazed at the gray-shrouded blue of the good spring sky, and hazily she heard whistles.

And some tardy screams.

And a great stupid voice bellowing "Give her air!" which made everyone press closer.

Then there wasn't so much sky because of the blue-clad bulk with its metal buttons and its leatherette notebook.

"Okay, okay, what's happened here stand back figods sake."

And the widening ripples of observation, interpretation, and comment: "It knocked her down." "Some guy knocked her down." "He knocked her down." "Some guy knocked her down and — " "Right in broad daylight this guy . . . " "The park's gettin' to be . . . " onward and outward, the adulteration of fact until it was lost altogether because excitement is so much more important.

Somebody with a harder shoulder than the rest bulling close, a notebook here, too, a witnessing eye over it, ready to change " . . . a beautiful brunette . . . " to "an attractive brunette" for the afternoon editions, because "attractive" is as dowdy as any woman is allowed to get if she is a victim in the news.

The glittering shield and the florid face bending close: "You hurt bad, sister?" And the echoes, back and back through the crowd, "Hurt bad, hurt bad, badly injured, he beat the hell out of her, broad daylight . . . "

And still another man, slim and purposeful, tan gabardine, cleft chin and beard-shadow: "Flyin' saucer, hm? Okay, Officer, I'll take over here."

"And who the hell might you be, takin' over?"

The flash of a brown leather wallet, a face so close behind that its chin was pressed into the gabardine shoulder. The face said, awed: "FBI." and that rippled outward, too. The policeman nodded — the entire policeman nodded in one single bobbing genuflection.

"Get some help and clear this area," said the gabardine.

"Yes, *sir!*" said the policeman.

"FBI, FBI," the crowd murmured, and there was more sky to look at above her.

She sat up and there was a glory in her face. "The saucer talked to me," she sang.

"You shut up," said the gabardine. "You'll have lots of chance to talk later."

"Yeah, sister," said the policeman. "My God, this mob could be full of Communists."

"You shut up, too," said the gabardine.

Someone in the crowd told someone else a Communist beat up this girl, while someone else was saying she got beat up because she was a Communist.

She started to rise, but solicitous hands forced her down again. There were thirty police there by that time.

"I can walk," she said.

"Now you just take it easy," they told her.

They put a stretcher down beside her and lifted her onto it and covered her with a big blanket.

"I can walk," she said as they carried her through the crowd.

A woman went white and turned away moaning, "Oh, my God, how awful!"

A small man with round eyes stared and stared at her and licked and licked his lips.

The ambulance. They slid her in. The gabardine was already there.

A white-coated man with very clean hands: "How did it happen, miss?"

"No questions," said the gabardine. "Security."

The hospital.

She said, "I got to get back to work."

"Take your clothes off," they told her.

She had a bedroom to herself then for the first time in her life. Whenever the door opened, she could see a policeman outside. It opened very often to admit the kind of civilians who were very polite to military people, and the kind of military people who were even more polite to certain civilians. She did not know what they all did or what they wanted. Every single day they asked her four million five hundred thousand questions. Apparently they never talked to each other because each of them asked her the same questions over and over.

"What is your name?"

"How old are you?"

"What year were you born?"

"What is your name?"

Sometimes they would push her down strange paths with their questions.

"Now your uncle. Married a woman from Middle Europe, did he? Where in Middle Europe?"

"What clubs or fraternal organizations do you belong to? Ah! Now about that Rinkeydinks gang on Sixty-third Street. Who was *really* behind it?"

But over and over again, "What did you mean when you said the saucer talked to you?"

And she would say, "It talked to me."

And they would say, "And it said — "

And she would shake her head.

There would be a lot of shouting ones, and then a lot of kind ones. No one had ever been so kind to her before, but she soon learned that no one was being kind to *her.* They were just getting her to relax, to think of other things, so they could suddenly shoot that question at her: "What do you mean it talked to you?"

Pretty soon it was just like Mom's or school or anyplace, and she used to sit with her mouth closed and let them yell. Once they sat her on a hard chair for hours and hours with a light in her eyes and let her get thirsty. Home, there was a transom over the bedroom door and Mom used to leave the kitchen light glaring through it all night, every night, so she wouldn't get the horrors. So the light didn't bother her at all.

They took her out of the hospital and put her in jail. Some ways it was good. The food. The bed was all right, too. Through the window she could see lots of women exercising in the yard. It was explained to her that they all had much harder beds.

"You are a very important young lady, you know."

That was nice at first, but as usual it turned out they didn't mean her at all. They kept working on her. Once they brought the saucer in to her. It was inside a big wooden crate with a padlock, and a steel box inside that with a Yale lock. It only weighed a couple of pounds, the saucer, but by the time they got it packed, it took two men to carry it and four men with guns to watch them.

They made her act out the whole thing just the way it happened, with some soldiers holding the saucer over her head. It wasn't the same. They'd cut a lot of chips and pieces out of the saucer and, besides, it was that dead gray color. They asked her if she knew anything about that and for once she told them.

"It's empty now," she said.

The only one she would ever talk to was a little man with a fat belly who said to her the first time he was alone with her, "Listen, I think the way they've been treating you stinks. Now get this: I have a job to do. My job is to find out *why* you won't tell what the saucer said. I don't want to know what it said and I'll never ask you. I don't even want you to tell me. Let's just find out why you're keeping it a secret."

Finding out why turned out to be hours of just talking about having pneumonia and the flower pot she made in second grade that Mom threw down the fire escape and getting left back in school and the dream about holding a wine glass in both hands and peeping over it at some man.

And one day she told him why she wouldn't say about the saucer, just the way it came to her: "Because it was talking to *me,* and it's just nobody else's business."

She even told him about the man crossing himself that day. It was the only other thing she had of her own.

He was nice. He was the one who warned her about the trial. "I have no business saying this, but they're going to give you the full treatment. Judge and jury and all. You just say what you want to say, no less and no more, hear? And don't let 'em get your goat. You have a right to own something."

He got up and swore and left.

First a man came and talked to her for a long time about how maybe this Earth would be attacked from outer space by beings much stronger and cleverer than we are, and maybe she had the key to a defense. So she owed it to the whole world. And then even if the Earth wasn't attacked, just think of what an advantage she might give this country over its enemies. Then he shook his finger in her face and said that what she was doing amounted to working *for* the enemies of her country. And he turned out to be the man who was defending her at the trial.

The jury found her guilty of contempt of court and the judge recited a long list of penalties he could give her. He gave her one of them and suspended it. They put her back in jail for a few more days, and one fine day they turned her loose.

That was wonderful at first. She got a job in a restaurant and rented a furnished room. She had been in the papers so much that Mom didn't want her back home. Mom was drunk most of the time and sometimes used to tear up the whole neighborhood, but all the same she had very special ideas about being respectable, and being in the papers all the time for spying was not her idea of being decent. So she put her maiden name on the mailbox downstairs and told her daughter not to live there any more.

At the restaurant she met a man who asked her for a date. The first time. She spent every cent she had on a red handbag to go with her red shoes. They weren't the same shade, but anyway they were both red. They went to the movies and afterward he didn't try to kiss her or anything, he just tried to find out what the flying saucer told her. She didn't say anything. She went home and cried all night.

Then some men sat in a booth talking and they shut up and glared at her every time she came past. They spoke to the boss, and he came and told her that they were electronics engineers working for the government and they were afraid to talk shop while she was around — wasn't she some sort of spy or something? So she got fired.

Once she saw her name on a juke box. She put in a nickel and punched that number, and the record was all about "the flyin' saucer came down one day / and taught her a brand new way to play / and what it was I will not say / but she took me out of this world." And while she was listening to it, someone in the juke joint recognized her and called her by name. Four of them followed her home and she had to block the door shut.

Sometimes she'd be all right for months on end, and then someone would ask for a date. Three times out of five, she and the date were followed. Once the man she was with arrested the man who was tailing them. Twice the man who was tailing them arrested the man she was with. Five times out of five, the date would try to find out about the saucer. Sometimes she would go out with someone and pretend that it was a real date, but she wasn't very good at it.

So she moved to the shore and got a job cleaning at night in offices and stores. There weren't many to clean, but that just meant there weren't many people to remember her face from the papers. Like clockwork, every eighteen months, some feature writer would drag it all out again in a magazine or a Sunday supplement; and every time anyone saw a headlight on a mountain or a light on a weather balloon it had to be a flying saucer, and there had to be some tired quip about the saucer wanting to tell secrets. Then for two or three weeks she'd stay off the streets in the daytime.

Once she thought she had it whipped. People didn't want her, so she began reading. The novels were all right for a while until she found out that most of them were like the movies — all about the pretty ones who really own the world. So she learned things — animals, trees. A lousy little chipmunk caught in a wire fence bit her. The animals didn't want her. The trees didn't care.

Then she hit on the idea of the bottles. She got all the bottles she could and wrote on papers which she corked into the bottles. She'd tramp miles up and down the beaches and throw the bottles out as far as she could. She knew that if the right person found one, it would give that person the only thing in the world that would help. Those bottles kept her going for three solid years. Everyone's got to have a secret little something they do.

And at last the time came when it was no use any more. You can go on trying to help someone who *maybe* exists; but soon you can't pretend there is such a person any more. And that's it. The end.

"Are you cold?" I asked when she was through telling me.

The surf was quieter and the shadows longer.

"No," she answered from the shadows. Suddenly she said, "Did you think I was mad at you because you saw me without my clothes?"

"Why shouldn't you be?"

"You know, I don't care? I wouldn't have wanted . . . wanted you to see me even in a ball gown or overalls. You can't cover up my carcass. It shows; it's there whatever. I just didn't want you to see me. At all."

"Me, or anyone?"

She hesitated. "You."

I got up and stretched and walked a little, thinking. "Didn't the FBI try to stop you throwing those bottles?"

"Oh, sure. They spent I don't know how much taxpayers' money gathering 'em up. They still make a spot check every once in a while. They're getting tired of it, though. All the writing in the bottles is the same." She laughed. I didn't know she could.

"What's funny?"

"All of 'em — judges, jailers, juke boxes — people. Do you know it wouldn't have saved me a minute's trouble if I'd told 'em the whole thing at the very beginning?"

"No?"

"No. They wouldn't have believed me. What they wanted was a new weapon. Superscience from a superrace, to slap hell out of the superrace if they ever got a chance, or out of our own if they don't. All those brains," she breathed, with more wonder than scorn, "all that brass. They think 'superrace' and it comes out 'superscience.' Don't they ever imagine a superrace has superfeelings, too — superlaughter, maybe, or super-hunger?" She paused. "Isn't it time you asked me what the saucer said?"

"I'll tell you," I blurted.

> There is in certain living souls
> A quality of loneliness unspeakable,
> So great it must be shared
> As company is shared by lesser beings.
> Such a loneliness is mine; so know by this
> That in immensity
> There is one lonelier than you.

"Dear Jesus," she said devoutly, and began to weep. "And how is it addressed?"

"To the loneliest one . . . "

"How did you know?" she whispered.

"It's what you put in the bottles, isn't it?"

"Yes," she said. "Whenever it gets to be too much, that no one cares, that no one ever did . . . you throw a bottle into the sea, and out goes a part of your own loneliness. You sit and think of someone somewhere finding it . . . learning for the first time that the worst there is can be understood."

The moon was setting and the surf was hushed. We looked up and out to the stars. She said, "We don't know what loneliness is like. People thought the saucer was a saucer, but it wasn't. It was a bottle with a message inside. It had a bigger ocean to cross — all of space — and not much chance of finding anybody. Loneliness? We don't know loneliness."

When I could, I asked her why she had tried to kill herself.

"I've had it good," she said, "with what the saucer told me. I wanted to . . . pay back. I was bad enough to be helped; I had to know I was good enough to help. No one wants me? Fine. But don't tell me no one, anywhere, wants my help. I can't stand that."

I took a deep breath. "I found one of your bottles two years ago. I've been looking for you ever since. Tide charts, current tables, maps, and . . . wandering. I heard some talk about you and the bottles hereabouts. Someone told me you'd quit doing it, you'd taken to wandering the dunes at night. I knew why. I ran all the way."

I needed another breath now. "I got a club foot. I think right, but the words don't come out of my mouth the way they're inside my head. I have this nose. I never had a woman. Nobody ever wanted to hire me to work where they'd have to look at me. You're beautiful," I said. "You're beautiful."

She said nothing, but it was as if a light came from her, more light and far less shadow than ever the practiced moon could cast. Among the many things it meant was that even to loneliness there is an end, for those who are lonely enough, long enough.

u/to/pi/as — situations of social perfection. Early science fiction featured many utopias like Edward Bellamy's *Looking Backward, 2000–1887* (1888), but they declined in number because the twentieth century became grimmer and because a true utopia lacks the dramatic tension necessary for entertaining fiction. Utopian short stories can be found in *The New Improved Sun: An Anthology of Utopian Science Fiction* (Harper & Row, 1975).

The Mother of Necessity

CHAD OLIVER

It isn't the easiest stunt in the world (the fairly young man said to the historian over a glass of beer) to be the son of a really famous man.

Now, Dad and I always got along okay; he was good to me and I like the old boy fine. But you can maybe imagine how it was after they kicked George Washington upstairs to be Grandfather, and stuck my dad in his exalted shoes.

George Sage, Father of His Country!

People are always tracking me down and asking about George. You'd think he's some kind of a saint or something. Don't get me wrong — I think Dad is swell. But what can I say to all these weirdies who want to know about their hero? If I give them the real scoop, they think I'm insulting my own father just because I make him human, like you or me.

I've pretty well given up trying to tell the truth; nowadays I usually just mumble something about a dedicated life and let it go at that.

But you're interested in history. You want the facts.

Okay. I'm with you.

But remember: my dad was just like a lot of other guys. He didn't go for all this saint stuff, and neither do I. I'll give him to you just the way he was; take him or leave him.

They call it Peace Monday now, that day when it all started. I was just a kid, but I remember like it was yesterday. It was a wet year, 2062 was, and that Monday was typical. It was gray and rainy outside, and you could hear the wind blowing, and you were glad you were in the apartment, where it was warm . . .

George Sage was stumped.

His ample body — not fat, but with a detectable paunch — was absolutely motionless in the hammock. His graying hair hadn't been combed all day. Distantly, he listened to the wind. His slightly glazed eyes examined nothing.

A slogan on the wall read: IT'S ALWAYS TIME FOR A CHANGE.

Lois, his wife, knew the signs. She was his only wife; she had to be sensitive to nuances. She tiptoed around the apartment as if the floor were liberally sprinkled with eggshells. She was glad that Bobby was staying in his room.

The silence thickened.

"Zero," George muttered cryptically, shifting in the hammock.

"What, dear?"

"There's nothing new under the sun," George amplified.

"Now, George," Lois said, trying to make a neutral noise.

"Don't nag, dammit! I'm plotting."

"I know you are, George."

"Sure," George said.

The silence flowed in again and congealed.

George breathed irritably.

Lois worked on her nails.

"Do you *have* to do that?" George asked finally.

Lois looked up innocently.

"Your nails," George explained. "You're scraping them."

"Oh." She put her equipment down and tried to sit very still. Outside, the rain was getting heavier; she hoped that it would let up soon so Bobby could go out and play. She was a little worried about George; he wasn't a young man any more, and he hadn't been as successful as Lloyd or Brigham. He was losing his confidence in himself, and of course that made it hard for him to come up with anything really *sharp*.

They had always hoped that Bobby might grow up and live in one of George's systems; that would have been nice. But there was only Westville left now, and even George found Westville a bit on the stale side.

She crossed over to his hammock and gently ruffled his uncombed hair. It was curious, she thought, how his hair had turned; about one strand in three was white as snow, and all the rest as brown as it had been twenty years before when they had met in college.

"Troubles?" she asked gently.

"You might put it that way, as the man said when he walked the plank."

"Try not to worry about it, dear."

George muttered something impolite, and then looked at her frankly. "We've tried everything, Lo," he said, his eyes very tired. "You know that.

The people out there have seen it all now, and you can't impress them these days just by tossing in a clan instead of a bilateral descent system. It all seemed kind of new and exciting once, but now — hell, I sometimes think there's nothing as dull as constant, everlasting change."

"Maybe that's the answer," she said, trying to help. "Maybe if you drew up one that was long on tradition — play on the let's-put-our-roots-in-the-soil routine — "

"Please. I may be an old man, but I've still got *some* pride. Anyhow, Lloyd tried a back-to-the-good-old-days gimmick in Miami just last year, and even he couldn't put it through. The devil of it is, there's just plain nothing new under the sun, to coin an inspired phrase."

"There never was, George."

"What?"

"You *always* used to say that, way back even before we were married. You said it was a little like writing — only ten and three-quarters basic plots, or whatever it was, but the trick was to string 'em together differently."

"Well," George admitted, "it's a long damned way from Homer to Joyce, but I guess the old boy's still Ulysses, no matter how you stick him together."

Lois waited patiently.

"Ummmmm," George said, and sat up in his hammock. "Maybe if we just filched an item here and there from different systems — even made a random assortment — and functioned them — "

Lois smiled and resumed work on her nails.

George walked over to the library line, dialed a stack of books, and proceeded to his desk. He sat down and began making rapid notes on his scratch pad.

Bobby stuck his blond head into the room and yawned. "Mom," he asked, "can I play in here?"

"Not now, Bobby," Lois said. "Your father's working."

Bobby eyed the ample figure of George at the desk, shrugged, and went back to his room, monumentally unimpressed.

Three weeks later, it was another Monday and the rain had showed up on schedule. It was a weary drizzle this time, and it exactly suited George Sage's mood.

Will Nolan, his promotions officer, slouched back behind his big desk, extracted the lenses from his eyes, and studied the ceiling without interest.

"It's great, George," he said flatly. "A great, great pattern."

George began to sweat. That was the mildest comment he had ever got from Nolan in fifteen years — ever since his nomadic-reindeer-herder program. It wouldn't have been so bad, but George had his own misgivings, even more so than usual.

"Really swell," Nolan continued. "Of course, there may be some small difficulty with the patent office."

"In other words, you don't think it's original enough to get a patent on. And if we can't get a patent, we can't put it on the market. That right?"

"Well, George," Nolan said, shifting uncomfortably. There was a pause of singular length. "Well, George," he repeated.

"Will, you've got to push this through. I don't care how you do it, but it's got to be done."

"Nothing to worry about," Nolan said insincerely.

George eyed his promotions officer, more in sympathy than in anger. George had few illusions about himself; he knew that his career as an inventor had been on the mediocre side. Naturally since he wasn't one of the big boys, he couldn't expect the top agencies to handle his promotions. He and Will Nolan were in the same boat, and it was not the sturdiest craft ever built.

"Let's look on the bright side," George said, trying to sell himself as much as Nolan. "It's not subversive, is it? It doesn't violate any of the American Ways of Life, does it?"

"It's clean, George. Real clean."

"Okay. It's got good things in it, right? It's got a small town deal with country stores and neighborliness and a slow pace; that gives tradition. Security. You know. It's got a cosmopolitan nucleus, right in the center, that only operates on market days and holidays. When the people Go To The City, they know they're supposed to act like an urban population; that takes the tedium out of it, get me? It's a kind of alternating social organization, and it requires enough service personnel in the urban nucleus to handle anyone who doesn't go for rural life no matter how he's brought up. The big city gives 'em direction, expansion. Now look, Will, the sex angle is good, you've got to admit that. The teen clubs give the kids a healthy outlet, and the merit badges give them status while they're adolescents. Not only that, but the chaperons give the older adults something to do with their time — their valuable experience isn't wasted at all. When the kids get ready to settle down and get married, they'll go into it with their eyes open."

"Sex is always good," Nolan admitted.

"That isn't all," George went on, warming to his topic. "Look at the way I've got the small businesses distributed: kids start right in manufacturing and selling equipment for the high school and the football team. Farm children supply the lunch wagons, city kids handle accounts at the banks."

"Free enterprise is always good," Nolan agreed.

"Sure, and I haven't neglected the spiritual side, either. Look at all the Sunday schools, and how about that Pilgrim Society? I tell you, Will, this system has got *everything.*"

"Has it got a name?"

"Not yet, no."

"Got to have a name, George. You know that. Can't sell a system without a name. We'll need some slogans, too."

"Okay, okay. What are your writers for?"

Will Nolan inserted the lenses in his eyes and made a few notations. "It's great, George," he said. "If we can just get it by the boys in Patents."

"They *can't* turn it down. It'd be against the Constitution. What grounds would they have?"

"They wouldn't have a leg to stand on, of course, not with a great, great idea like this one. It's just that there isn't anything in it that's — well — *new*. You know."

George waved his hand with a confidence he was far from feeling. "Hell, there's nothing new about pyramids, the Roman circus, the Empire State Building, wigwams — not all by their lonesomes. But all in one society, that's different, different in *kind.* "

"I'll push it, George," Nolan said. "Try not to worry."

George Sage was getting decidedly tired of having people tell him not to worry, but he realized that this was no time to blow up about it. He took a cue from Lois and made a neutral noise.

"I'll call you," Nolan said.

George left the promotions building and wandered aimlessly down past the Washington Monument. It was still raining: a bored, gray drizzle with all the character of a clam.

He walked on, hands in his pockets, beginning the long wait that always had emptiness at the end of it, emptiness that was neither success nor failure, but only existence.

"Damn the rain," he said. "Damn it anyway."

Election Day.

Perhaps it was of some significance — it had *better* be of some significance, George thought — that the weather could not have been more pleasant. A balmy sun coated the fields outside Natchezville with melted gold, and summer breezes whispered lazily through the sweet gum trees.

"Sit still, Bobby," Lois said. "Your father has to be careful not to fly our copter inside the city limits while voting is going on."

"Aaaaahh," Bobby commented, and continued to twitch around.

Not without some disgust at himself, George noticed that the fingers on his left hand were firmly crossed. Well, the election *was* important to him; if Natchezville didn't give it a tumble, he might as well turn himself out to pasture. Nolan had just barely snaked it through the patent office, and Mr. George Sage was not precisely the fair-haired boy around Washington these days.

More like a bald-headed mummy, in fact.

The copter loafed along in the sunshine, and George swerved a few degrees to make certain he did not get too close to an ancient blimp that Nolan had dredged up somewhere. The blimp hovered over Natchezville, trailing a long airsign: LET'S GIVE OUR KIDS A BETTER SOCIAL ORGANIZA-TION THAN WE HAD — FULL CIRCLE MEANS A FULLER LIFE!

Not bad, George thought. Not bad at all.

Natchezville spread out like a toy town below them, and to their left was a pretty little village with its white houses gleaming in the sun. It was surrounded by large cotton plantations, for Natchezville was currently pat-terned after the Old South. If you looked closely, you could see belles in crinolines sipping tall drinks on pillared porches, and gray robots dancing in the slave quarters.

The court house was a hive of activity as the voting picked up in tempo.

George switched on the TV. Yes, it was still there on Channel 7: a white circle flashing on and off, alternating with a bass voice that kept chanting: "Full Circle — a design for living designed for living — Full Circle — a design for living — "

George noticed that his hands were sweating, and wiped them on his handkerchief.

"We're lucky," he said for the tenth time, "that the competition isn't too hot this time around. Neither Lloyd nor Brigham has a system in the race — Natchezville would be pretty small potatoes for them. Really, we've got only three challengers going down there. Krause's Urbania routine is all right — but we've got that *plus* the rural appeal. Old Gingerton's Greenwich Village deal is strictly from senility, and the Mammoth Cave entry is just a dark horse."

Lois laughed dutifully.

George took the copter down almost to road level, where wagon and horses were plodding along toward Natchezville. He smiled and waved, but he was primarily intent on checking his roadsigns. Yes, there was one now, starting just ahead:

> WHEN YOU MAKE YOUR TURN
> ON YOUR ROAD AND MINE
> DON'T BE SCARED
> TO BE PREPARED
> TO GO TO THE END OF THE LINE
> *FULL CIRCLE*

"I like that, Dad," Bobby said. "That's good."

There was a conventional billboard not far ahead, but it was too close to the city limits for him to risk a close look at it. Basically, it seemed to show two stupendously healthy and starry-eyed children gazing worshipfully into a future filled with circles.

George waved again, and took the copter up.

"Damn this waiting," he said.

"Try not to worry, dear," Lois advised.

George thought of a cutting retort, but had been married long enough not to make it.

The copter hummed through the air like an insect, as the sunlight faded and night shadows darkened the land below. A cool breeze sprang up in the north, and Bobby was getting emphatic about his hunger.

It was close to midnight when the copter's private-line TV blinked into life. It was Will Nolan, and George knew the result by the glow on his face.

"We're in!" Nolan said. "Not a landslide, George boy, but a great, great victory. Congratulations!"

George grinned his thanks, put his arm around Lois, and headed the copter for home. Bobby made gentle boy-snores behind them. Stars sprinkled the sky and the moon was close and warm.

"I'm so proud of you, dear," Lois said.

"It wasn't really anything," George said. "But wait until the Concordburg elections next year! I've got an idea cooking that'll set them on their ears."

The copter hummed on through the friendly night.

Of course, as you might suppose (the historian said to young Robert Sage over a second glass of beer) what happened to your father and to Fullcircle is hardly understandable except in terms of the social and historical context of the phenomena. If I may interrupt you for a moment, I think I can show you what I mean.

Looking at the whole thing now, it all takes on a sort of spurious inevitability, as though it couldn't have happened any other way. That's the crudest sort of teleological thinking, to be sure, and we must be careful of it.

Still, if we consider certain tendencies in American culture during the last seventy-five years of the century just past — say from 1925 until the year 2000 — it helps us to explain your father and what happened to him.

Take two key ideas: individualism and progress. You are doubtless familiar enough with the notion of individuation, and the value American culture placed on the individual. You may not have realized that the idea of progress is a relatively recent one in history. A great many peoples failed to see that constant change necessarily meant improvement — how do you know that what you're getting is better than what you had, and what do you mean by *better?* But Americans believed in progress; it was part of their value system. If you weren't "making progress" you were as good as dead, in an individual as well as a national sense.

It was possible to demonstrate progress in some areas, such as technology. If by progress you mean efficiency, it could be shown that some tools were more efficient than other tools. Progress in terms of other spheres of culture was harder to define, but Americans believed in that kind of progress too. If you should ever go back and read some of the historical documents of that period, Robert, I'm sure you will be struck by the constant references to spiritual growth and social betterment.

Now, cultures are funny things. All of them change, but all of them are inherently conservative; they have to be. You can't have a culture — which is an integrated system — charging off in ten different directions at once. In America, the slogan might well have been this: the same, with a difference. In other words, you must preserve the traditions of your forefathers, but be more up-to-date than they were.

You probably know that our industry was not always robotized and controlled by cybernetic systems, but it is hard to imagine today that it was ever anything else. This was a fundamental change in our way of life. As long ago as the middle of the last century, a man named Riesman was already pointing out that our culture was becoming attuned to the *consumers;* he called it "other-direction," I believe, and he noticed the increasing dominance of peer groups and the growing discriminations of taste. People were becoming sophisticated in what they consumed, you might say.

Atomic power, as you have read in your elementary history books, meant the end of old-style warfare. War was no longer an efficient instrument of national policy. It became necessary to win men's minds. At the same time, the physical sciences went into a bit of a decline. Most of the work went into the making of bigger and better superweapons, which were never employed in warfare but were simply set off first in isolated areas, and later on the Moon — in order to keep the other side too scared to fight. The social sciences, meanwhile, had got far enough along to know what made sociocultural systems tick.

It was rather neat, really. Americans had always loved gadgets, and as they became more sophisticated they turned to really fundamental gadgets: social systems. It was all phrased in terms of healthy variety and showing the world what we could do with free enterprise and respect for the individual; but what it was, in fact, was social gadgeteering.

Inventors had always been highly regarded in America, but now the focus of their inventions changed. It was all very well for Edison to have thought up an electric light, of course, but how much more rewarding it was to invent a way of life for a whole generation!

What came out of it all was a series of flexible, delimited social groups — about the size of the old counties — with variant social systems competing for prestige. Every village and town had always thought of itself as different from and better than its neighbor down the road — perhaps you have heard of Boston or of some cities in Texas — and now they could really put on the dog. Of course, they weren't *completely* different; that would have been chaos. They were all American, but with the parts put together differently.

And there was a national service culture — a government — that was centered in Washington and had colonies in each area.

I hope you'll excuse me for talking so long, Robert, but I think all this has a bearing on what your father did. The defects — if that is the right word — of this way of running things were not apparent until after the Natchezville elections, where Fullcircle began. That's why I'm particularly anxious to hear about the next decade or so, when you were growing up. I recall that George lost the Concordburg elections the next year, but after that I'm a little hazy.

I have always wondered just how long it was before your father knew what had happened to him . . .

"Look," George Sage said, with a moderately successful imitation of long-suffering patience, "do you have to shoot marbles right under my hammock?"

"It's raining outside, Pop," Bob answered laconically, chalking another circle on the living-room carpet.

"It's always raining," George muttered, half to himself. "It's been raining for a million years."

"Don't be depressed, dear," Lois said.

"Now *you're* turning on me! How the hell am I supposed to get any work done?"

"Don't swear in front of Bobby, George."

"Aaaahh." George stared grimly at his son. "You know plenty of words worse than that, don't you, Bobby?"

"Sure," the boy said solemnly. "And my name is *Bob,* not Bobby."

"Hell," George said again.

"Come on, Bob," Lois said. "You run get in the copter and go to the store with Mother."

"Can I pilot?"

"Of course," Lois said, hiding a shiver of anticipation.

They hurried up to the roof.

George was alone.

It was ten years since he had won the Natchezville elections with his Full Circle. Not one of his ideas had panned out since. To make matters worse, he was in competition with himself.

And losing.

He swung out of his hammock, made some half-hearted notes on the pad on his desk, and called Will Nolan. The promotions officer faded into the screen like a reluctant spirit.

"Great to see you, George boy," he said with an appalling lack of sincerity. "What's new?"

"That's what *I* want to know. Any new figures on that Frankenstein of ours?"

"It wasn't Frankenstein," Nolan corrected, removing the lenses from his eyes. "It was Frankenstein's monster."

"Monster, shmonster. What's the box score?"

Nolan sighed, fixing his gaze on the ceiling. "Your little creation — it's written as one word now, 'Fullcircle,' you know — has spread to six more communities in the last two weeks. It's winning every blasted election. A great, great system!"

"Great," George agreed, in utter despair. "Still the same routine?"

"Yeah. Nobody put it on the ballot, since nobody can get any royalties on it after the first time around, but the thing keeps winning as a *write-in* candidate. No advertising, no promotion, no nothing!"

"The best advertisement," George repeated wearily, "is a satisfied customer."

"Great." Nolan paused, at a loss for words. "Great."

"Will, what have I done? I'm just an average kind of guy, just trying to make a living; I'm no revolutionary, dammit!"

"Well, George — "

"That monstrosity — that Full Circle — I mean Fullcircle — is too good, that's what's wrong. It's got *everything!* All the joys of rural living, all the joys of the city — how can you beat it? *I* can't beat it, and I thought it up! Where will the damned thing end, Will? *Where will it end?*"

"I strongly suspect," Will Nolan said in complete seriousness, "that it's going to take over the world."

"Oh my God."

"Too late to invoke the Deity, my friend. We're headed for technological unemployment. A great, great situation."

"Maybe I'll get a pension," George said.

"I'll work on that angle. I should get one too; I sold it in the first place. Don't call me, I'll call you."

"So long, Will."

George cut the screen off and walked unsteadily back to his hammock. He closed his eyes but he could not relax.

"Survival of the fittest," he remarked to the wall.

He was no fool. He saw what was happening, saw it with hideous clarity. There was a fight for survival among social systems as well as in the animal kingdom; there were no primitive hunters left in London. The set-up in the United States, with its emphasis on local variations, would work fine, until a social organization came along that was markedly superior to all the rest. And then —

And then it spread.

Everybody wanted one.

It was the end of an era.

"I am Achilles' heel," George said.

The empty rooms began to get on his nerves. He slipped into his rainsuit and went down and out the little-used street entrance. The rain was a gray drizzle in the air, and Washington was hushed and colorless.

George walked, aimlessly.

His feet squished wetly on the old cement.

He didn't even feel like smoking.

It was two hours before he saw another human being. At first, the figure was just a dark shadow, coming toward him. Then, as it walked nearer, it took on substance and features.

It was Henry Lloyd. A few short years ago he had been the most successful social inventory in the country.

Lloyd was looking very old.

"Hank!" George called out. "It's good to see you."

Lloyd stared at him icily.

"Monopolist," he said, and made a small detour to get around him. He said nothing more, and vanished up the wet street.

George Sage put his head down.

He walked slowly through the gray rain-haze, walked until night had come to the city. Then he headed back toward home, because he knew that Lois would be worried.

That wasn't the only reason, he supposed.

There just wasn't anywhere else for him to go.

So you see (Robert Sage said to the historian as they finished their third glass of beer) that it wasn't all milk and honey after Dad invented our way of life. There was a tough transition time, when Fullcircle was just catching on and a lot of people hated Dad's guts.

I'll tell you, getting that pension wasn't the easiest stunt in the world; there was a time when I thought we were all going to starve to death. People get sore when I mention that; they figure I'm just some spoiled brat who likes to tell lies, but it's the truth.

All that Father of His Country stuff came later — much later.

Well, that's the way it was. I could tell you wanted the facts, so I've given 'em to you straight. It's been a pleasure talking to you.

What's that? Sure, if you insist. I'll get 'em next time — that a deal?

Tell you what. Old George doesn't live far from here. Mother's dead, you know, so Dad is all alone. He still won't admit to himself that it's all over; that's the way artists are, I guess. Like as not, he'll be sitting at that old desk of his, making notes and cussing the weather. He'll look busy, Dad will, but don't let that fool you.

He's lonesome, and likes to be able to talk to people.

I'm going over there now. Won't you come along?

V

vi/sions — perceptions that come to people through "abnormal" processes. Visions play an important role in supernatural stories, but are less frequently encountered in science fiction. Occasionally, visions are received from alien forces (as in "Close Encounters of the Third Kind") and thus qualify as sf.

The Great Secret

GEORGE H. SMITH

"We can't seem to put a finger on this guy at all, sir," Detective Lieutenant Bolasky said to the district attorney. "We know that he's blackmailing these people, but we can't figure how or what about."

District Attorney Waters ran a neatly manicured hand through his silvery hair and frowned at the report on his desk. "These are big people, Bolasky. We can't let this phony crystal-gazer get away with this. What can he have on them anyway? What can they possibly have in their pasts that they're willing to pay him to keep quiet about?"

"That's the strangest part of the whole thing, sir. We've checked into the past of every one of the people Maraat has been working on and so far we haven't been able to find a thing they could be blackmailed for."

"I see. Then why . . . ?"

"We don't know. All we do know is that nearly all of the people he has approached have paid him off."

"Nearly all? You mean some of them haven't?"

"Approximately twenty-five of them have kicked in with very large sums of money. Doctors, lawyers, politicians, and prominent business executives. Maraat is so sure of himself that he even takes checks, and we can't touch him because no one will make a complaint. They won't tell how he's doing it; in fact, they won't even admit they are being blackmailed. Whatever it is, they're scared to death of him."

"But what about the ones who don't pay off?"

"There were five of them. They had Maraat kicked out of their offices, but within a week of his visit they all committed suicide."

"I don't get it," the D.A. said angrily. "There must be something you and your men are missing."

"I just wish that were true," Bolasky said sadly. "Well, I guess we'll have to turn him loose."

"If you people can't get any evidence against him, we have no other choice."

"I hate like hell to do it, but we can't hold him on suspicion any longer."

"Tell you what," the D.A. said as the other man turned to leave. "Before you do that, bring him up here. I'd like to see him and maybe *I* can get something out of him."

The detective looked worried. "He's awfully funny, Mr. Waters. Are you sure you want to do this? Most of the men at headquarters prefer to stay as far away from him as possible."

"Well, no wonder you've been unable to get anything on him. Bring him up here and I'll question him myself. I guarantee I'll find out how he's blackmailing these people."

A short time later, two police officers escorted a small, dark man into the district attorney's office. He seemed insignificant enough except for his eyes, which glowed and sparkled strangely. These seemingly bottomless pools of mystery made the D.A. uneasy as Maraat took a seat opposite him. To hide his disquiet, Waters spoke loudly and brusquely.

"I'll come straight to the point with you, Maraat. We *know* you've been practicing blackmail, but we don't know how you're doing it. We'll find out sooner or later, of course, and you'll make it easier on yourself if you tell us all about it now."

The man's thin lips curved in a smile. "I'll be glad to tell you all about it, Mr. Waters."

"What? You mean you'll confess?"

"I'll tell *you* about it, Mr. Waters. We won't need your stenographer."

"What is all this? If you're so willing to confess, why didn't you tell them down at headquarters?" Determined not to let the man see how nervous he was becoming, Waters nodded to the stenographer to leave. He wished suddenly that he had never sent for Maraat.

"It would hardly have been worth my while, Mr. District Attorney, to confess to those nonentities. I knew that if I waited long enough you would send for me."

"How could you possibly know that?"

"I knew, Mr. Waters, I knew."

The man must be lying, but his eyes said he wasn't. Those eyes! They were enough to drive a man mad. "Then suppose you tell me what it was you knew about the pasts of those persons who paid you such huge sums of money."

"I know nothing of their pasts, nothing. What I know about them, Edmond Waters, is in the future."

"What?" Waters felt suffocated, as though he were about to choke. It was those eyes, those unblinking, unwavering, somehow truthful eyes. Could they see into the future? Into his future?

Maraat leaned back in his chair with a smile of satisfaction and dropped his eyes from the D.A.'s face.

"So you see, Mr. Waters, it was really very simple. I just went to these persons and told them that I could see into the future and that I wanted money."

"You mean that they paid you for keeping something secret that they were going to do in the future? For not telling others?"

"No, not secret from others, Mr. Waters. For keeping it a secret from *them*. You see, I know when you are going to die. The year, the day, and the hour. But for a rather large sum of money *and* your protection . . . I won't tell you."

The district attorney's hand had already reached for his checkbook. "How much?" he asked.

W

West/erns — novels, television shows, and motion pictures about the American frontier, particularly the period from roughly 1850 to 1910. Westerns are very popular, not just in the United States but also in countries like Spain, Germany, Italy, and Japan. A number of science fiction and fantasy stories have been set in the Old West, including *Six-Gun Planet,* by John Jakes (Warner Books, 1970); *A Planet for Texans,* by H. Beam Piper and J. J. McGuire (Ace Books, 1958); and the "Gunslinger" stories of Stephen King.

The Draw

JEROME BIXBY

Joe Doolin's my name, cowhand — work for old Farrel over at Lazy F beyond the pass. Never had much of anything exciting happen to me — just punched cows and lit up on payday — until the day I happened to ride through the pass on my way to town and saw young Buck Tarrant's draw.

Now, Buck'd always been a damn good shot. Once he got his gun in his hand, he could put a bullet right where he wanted it up to twenty paces, and within an inch of his aim up to a hundred feet. But Lord God, he couldn't draw to save his life — I'd seen him a couple of times before in the pass, trying to. He'd face a tree and go into a crouch, and I'd know he was pretending the tree was Billy the Kid or somebody, and then he'd slap leather — and his clumsy hand would wallop his gunbutt, he'd yank like hell, his old Peacemaker would come staggering out of its holster like a bear in heat, and finally he'd line on his target and plug it dead center. But the whole business took about a second and a half, and by the time he'd ever finished his fumbling in a real fight, Billy the Kid or Sheriff Ben Randolph over in town or even me, Joe Doolin, could have cut him in half.

So this time, when I was riding along through the pass and saw Buck upslope from me under the trees, I just grinned and didn't pay too much attention.

He stood facing an old elm tree, and I could see he'd tacked a playing card about four feet up the trunk, about where a man's heart would be.

Out of the corner of my eye I saw him go into his gunman's crouch. He was about sixty feet away from me, and, like I said, I wasn't paying much mind to him.

I heard the shot flat down the rocky slope that separated us. I grinned again, picturing that fumbly draw of his, the wild slap at leather, the gun coming out drunklike, maybe even him dropping it — I'd seen him do that once or twice.

It got me to thinking about him, as I rode closer.

He was a bad one. Nobody said any different than that. Just bad. He was a bony runt of about eighteen, with bulging eyes and a wide mouth that was always turned down at the corners. He got this nickname Buck because he had buck teeth, not because he was heap man. He was some handy with his fists, and he liked to pick ruckuses with kids he was sure he could lick. But the tipoff on Buck is that he'd blat like a two-day calf to get out of mixing with somebody he was scared of — which meant somebody his own size or bigger. He'd jaw his way out of it, or just turn and slink away with his tail along his belly. His dad had died a couple years before, and he lived with his ma on a small ranch out near the pass. The place was falling to pieces because Buck wouldn't lift a hand to do any work around — his ma just couldn't handle him at all. Fences were down, and the yard was all weedgrown, and the house needed some repairs — but all Buck ever did was hang around town, trying to rub up against some of the tough customers who drank in the Once Again Saloon, or else he'd ride up and lie around under the trees along the top of the pass and just think — or, like he was today, he'd practice drawing and throwing down on trees and rocks.

Guess he always wanted to be tough. Really tough. He tried to walk with tough men, and, as we found out later, just about all he ever thought about while he was lying around was how he could be tougher than the next two guys. Maybe you've known characters like that — for some damfool reason they just got to be able to whup anybody who comes along, and they feel low and mean when they can't, as if the size of a man's fist was the size of the man.

So that was Buck Tarrant — a half-sized, poisonous, no-good kid who wanted to be a hardcase.

But he'd never be, not in a million years. That's what made it funny —
and kind of pitiful too. There wasn't no real strength in him, only a scared
hate. It takes guts as well as speed to be tough with a gun, and Buck was just
a nasty little rat of a kid who'd probably always counterpunch his way
through life when he punched at all. He'd kite for cover if you lifted a lip.

I heard another shot and looked up the slope. I was near enough now to
see that the card he was shooting at was a ten of diamonds — and that he
was plugging the pips one by one. Always could shoot, like I said.

Then he heard me coming, and whirled away from the tree, his gun
holstered, his hand held out in front of him like he must have imagined
Hickock or somebody held it when he was ready to draw.

I stopped my horse about ten feet away and just stared at him. He looked
real funny in his baggy old Levi's and dirty checkered shirt and that big gun
low on his hip, and me knowing he couldn't handle it worth a damn.

"Who you trying to scare, Buck?" I said. I looked him up and down and
snickered. "You look about as dangerous as a sheepherder's wife."

"And you're a son of a bitch," he said.

I stiffened and shoved out my jaw. "Watch that, runt, or I'll get off and
put my foot in your mouth and pull you on like a boot!"

"Will you now," he said nastily, "you son of a bitch!"

And he drew on me . . . and I goddam near fell backwards off my saddle!

I swear, I hadn't even seen his hand move, he'd drawn so fast! That gun
just practically *appeared* in his hand!

"Will you now?" he said again, and the bore of his gun looked like a
greased gate to Hell.

I sat in my saddle scared — spitless, wondering if this was when I was
going to die. I moved my hands out away from my body, and tried to look
friendly-like — actually, I'd never tangled with Buck, just razzed him a little
now and then like everybody did; and I couldn't see much reason why he'd
want to kill me.

But the expression on his face was full of gloating, full of wildness, full of
damn-you recklessness — exactly the expression you'd look to find on a kid
like Buck who suddenly found out he was the deadliest gunman alive.

And that's just what he was, believe me.

Once I saw Bat Masterson draw — and he was right up there with the very
best. Could draw and shoot accurately in maybe half a second or so —
you could hardly see his hand move; you just heard the slap of hand on
gunbutt and a split-second later the shot. It takes a lot of practice to be able
to get a gun out and on target in that space of time, and that's what makes
gunmen. Practice, and a knack to begin with. And, I guess, the yen to be a
gunman, like Buck Tarrant'd always had.

When I saw Masterson draw against Jeff Steward in Abilene, it was that
way — slap, crash, and Steward was three-eyed. Just a blur of motion.

But when Buck Tarrant drew on me, right now in the pass, I didn't see any motion *at all.* He just crouched, and then his gun was on me. Must have done it in a millionth of a second, if a second has millionths.

It was the fastest draw I'd ever seen. It was, I reckoned, the fastest draw anybody'd ever seen. It was an impossibly fast draw — a man's hand just couldn't move to his holster that fast, and grab and drag a heavy Peacemaker up in a two-foot arc that fast.

It was plain damn impossible — but there it was.

And there I was.

I didn't say a word. I just sat and thought about things, and my horse wandered a little farther up the slope and then stopped to chomp grass. All the time, Buck Tarrant was standing there, poised, that wild gloating look in his eyes, knowing he could kill me any time and knowing I knew it.

When he spoke, his voice was shaky — it sounded like he wanted to bust out laughing, and not a nice laugh either.

"Nothing to say, Doolin?" he said. "Pretty fast, huh?"

I said, "Yeah, Buck. Pretty fast." And my voice was shaky too, but not because I felt like laughing any.

He spat, eyeing me arrogantly. The ground rose to where he stood, and our heads were about on a level. But I felt he was looking down.

"Pretty fast!" he sneered. "Faster'n anybody!"

"I reckon it is, at that," I said.

"Know how I do it?"

"No."

"I *think,* Doolin. I *think* my gun into my hand. How d'you like that?"

"It's awful fast, Buck."

"I just *think,* and my gun is there in my hand. Some draw, huh!"

"Sure is."

"You're damn right it is, Doolin. Faster'n anybody!"

I didn't know what his gabbling about "thinking his gun into his hand" meant — at least not then, I didn't — but I sure wasn't minded to question him on it. He looked wild-eyed enough right now to start taking bites out of the nearest tree.

He spat again and looked me up and down. "You know, you can go to hell, Joe Doolin. You're a lousy, goddamn, white-livered son of a bitch." He grinned coldly.

Not an insult, I knew now, but a deliberate taunt. I'd broken jaws for a lot less — I'm no runt; and I'm quick enough to hand back crap if some lands on me. But now I wasn't interested.

He saw I was mad, though, and stood waiting.

"You're fast enough, Buck," I said, "so I got no idea of trying you. You want to murder me; I guess I can't stop you — but I ain't drawing. No, sir, that's for sure."

"And a coward to boot," he jeered.

"Maybe," I said. "Put yourself in my place, and ask yourself why in hell I should kill myself?"

"Yellow!" he snarled, looking at me with his bulging eyes full of meanness and confidence.

My shoulders got tight, and it ran down along my gun arm. I never took that from a man before.

"I won't draw," I said. "Reckon I'll move on instead, if you'll let me."

And I picked up my reins, moving my hands real careful-like, and turned my horse around and started down the slope. I could feel his eyes on me, and I was half waiting for a bullet in the back. But it didn't come. Instead Buck Tarrant called, "Doolin!"

I turned my head. "Yeah?"

He was standing there in the same position. Somehow he reminded me of a crazy runt wolf — his eyes were almost yellowish, and when he talked he moved his lips too much, mouthing his words, and his big crooked teeth flashed in the sun. I guess all the hankering for toughness in him was coming out — he was acting now like he'd always wanted to — cocky, unafraid, mean — because now he wore a bigger gun than anybody. It showed all over him, like poison coming out of his skin.

"Doolin," he called. "I'll be in town around three this afternoon. Tell Ben Randolph for me that he's a son of a bitch. Tell him he's a dunghead sheriff. Tell him he'd better look me up when I get there or else get outa town and stay out. You got that?"

"I got it, Buck."

"Call me Mr. Tarrant, you Irish bastard."

"Okay . . . Mr. Tarrant," I said, and reached the bottom of the slope and turned my horse along the road through the pass. About a hundred yards farther on, I hipped around in the saddle and looked back. He was practicing again — the crouch, the fantastic draw, the shot.

I rode on toward town, to tell Ben Randolph he'd either have to run or die.

Ben was a lanky, slab-sided Texan who'd come up north on a drive ten years before and liked the Arizona climate and stayed. He was a good sheriff — tough enough to handle most men, and smart enough to handle the rest. Fourteen years of it had kept him lean and fast.

When I told him about Buck, I could see he didn't know whether he was tough or smart or fast enough to get out of this one.

He leaned back in his chair and started to light his pipe, and then stared at the match until it burned his fingers without touching it to the tobacco.

"You sure, Joe?" he said.

"Ben, I saw it two times. At first I just couldn't believe my eyes — but I tell you, he's fast. He's faster'n you or me or Hickock or anybody. God knows where he got it, but he's got the speed."

"But," Ben Randolph said, lighting another match, "it just don't happen that way." His voice was almost mildly complaining. "Not overnight. Gun speed's something you work on — it comes slow, mighty slow. You know that. How in hell could Buck Tarrant turn into a fire-eating gunfighter in a few days?" He paused and puffed. "You sure, Joe?" he asked again, through a cloud of smoke.

"Yes."

"And he wants me."

"That's what he said."

Ben Randolph sighed. "He's a bad kid, Joe — just a bad kid. If his father hadn't died, I reckon he might have turned out better. But his mother ain't big enough to wallop his butt the way it needs."

"You took his gun away from him a couple times, didn't you, Ben?"

"Yeah. And ran him outa town too, when he got too pestiferous. Told him to get the hell home and help his ma."

"Guess that's why he wants you."

"That. And because I'm sheriff. I'm the biggest gun around here, and he don't want to start at the bottom, not him. He's gonna show the world right away."

"He can do it, Ben."

He sighed again. "I know. If what you say's true, he can sure show *me,* anyhow. Still, I got to take him up on it. You know that. I can't leave town."

I looked at his hand lying on his leg — the fingers were trembling. He curled them into a fist, and the fist trembled.

"You ought to, Ben," I said.

"Of course I ought to," he said, a little savagely. "But I can't. Why, what'd happen to this town if I was to cut and run? Is there anyone else who could handle him? Hell, no."

"A crazy galoot like that," I said slowly, "if he gets too damn nasty, is bound to get kilt." I hesitated. "Even in the back, if he's too good to take from the front."

"Sure," Ben Randolph said. "Sooner or later. But what about meantime? . . . how many people will he have to kill before somebody gets angry or nervy enough to kill *him?* That's my job, Joe — to take care of this kind of thing. Those people he'd kill are depending on me to get between him and them. Don't you see?"

I got up. "Sure, Ben, I see. I just wish *you* didn't."

He let out another mouthful of smoke. "You got any idea what he meant about thinking his gun into his hand?"

"Not the slightest. Some crazy explanation he made up to account for his sudden speed, I reckon."

Another puff. "You figure I'm a dead man, Joe, huh?"

"It looks kind of that way."

"Yeah, it kind of does, don't it?"

At four that afternoon Buck Tarrant came riding into town like he owned it. He sat his battered old saddle like a rajah on an elephant, and he held his right hand low beside his hip in an exaggerated gunman's stance. With his floppy hat over at a cocky angle, and his big eyes and scrawny frame, he'd have looked funny as hell trying to look like a tough hombre — except that he *was* tough now, and everybody in town knew it because I'd warned them. Otherwise somebody might have jibed him, and the way things were now, that could lead to a sudden grave.

Nobody said a word all along the street as he rode to the hitchrail in front of the Once Again and dismounted. There wasn't many people around *to* say anything — most everybody was inside, and all you could see of them was a shadow of movement behind a window here, the flutter of a curtain there.

Only a few men sat in chairs along the boardwalks under the porches, or leaned against the porch posts, and they just sort of stared around, looking at Buck for a second and then looking off again if he turned toward them.

I was standing near to where Buck hitched up. He swaggered up the steps of the saloon, his right hand poised, his bulging eyes full of hell.

"You tell him?" he asked.

I nodded. "He'll look you up, like you said."

Buck laughed shortly. "I'll be waiting. I don't like that lanky bastard. I reckon I got some scores to settle with him." He looked at me, and his face twisted into what he thought was a tough snarl. Funny — you could see he really wasn't tough down inside. There wasn't any hard core of confidence and strength. His toughness was in his holster, and all the rest of him was acting to match up to it.

"You know," he said, "I don't like you either, Irish. Maybe I oughta kill you. Hell, why not?"

Now, the only reason I'd stayed out of doors that afternoon was I figured Buck had already had one chance to kill me and had nothing against me, so I was safe. And I had an idea that maybe, when the showdown came, I might be able to help out Ben Randolph somehow.

Now, though, I wished to hell I hadn't stayed outside. I wished I was behind one of them windows, looking out at somebody else getting told by Buck Tarrant that maybe he oughta kill him.

"But I won't," Buck said, grinning nastily. "Because you done me a favor. You run off and told the sheriff just like I told you — just like the goddam white-livered Irish sheepherder you are. Ain't that so?"

I nodded, my jaw set so hard with anger that the flesh felt stretched.

He waited for me to move against him. When I didn't, he laughed and swaggered to the door of the saloon. "Come on, Irish," he said over his shoulder. "I'll buy you a drink of the best."

I followed him in and he went over to the bar, walking heavy, and looked old Menner right in the eye and said, "Give me a bottle of the best stuff you got in the house."

Menner looked at the kid he'd kicked out of his place a dozen times, and his face was white. He reached behind him and got a bottle and put it on the bar.

"Two glasses," said Buck Tarrant.

Menner carefully put two glasses on the bar.

"*Clean* glasses."

Menner polished two other glasses on his apron and set them down.

"You don't want no money for this likker, do you, Menner?" Buck asked.

"No, sir."

"You'd just take it home and spend it on that fat heifer of a wife you got, and on them two little half-wit brats, wouldn't you?"

Menner nodded.

"Hell, they really ain't worth the trouble, are they?"

"No, sir."

Buck snickered and poured two shots and handed me one. He looked around the saloon and saw that it was almost empty — just Menner behind the bar, and a drunk asleep with his head on his arms at a table near the back, and a little gent in fancy town clothes fingering his drink at a table near the front window and not even looking at us.

"Where is everybody?" he asked Menner.

"Why, sir, I reckon they're home, most of them," Menner said. "It being a hot day and all — "

"Bet it'll get hotter," Buck said, hard.

"Yes, sir."

"I guess they didn't want to really feel the heat, huh?"

"Yes, sir."

"Well, it's going to get so hot, you old bastard, that everybody'll feel it. You know that?"

"If you say so, sir."

"It might even get hot for you. Right now even. What do you think of that, huh?"

"I — I — "

"You thrown me outa here a couple times, remember?"

"Y-yes . . . but I — "

"Look at this!" Buck said — and his gun was in his hand, and he didn't seem to have moved at all, not an inch. I was looking right at him when he did it — his hand was on the bar, resting beside his shotglass, and then suddenly his gun was in it and pointing right at old Menner's belly.

"You know," Buck said, grinning at how Menner's fear was crawling all over his face, "I can put a bullet right where I want to. Wanta see me do it?"

His gun crashed, and flame leaped across the bar, and the mirror behind the bar had a spiderweb of cracks radiating from a round black hole.

Menner stood there, blood leaking down his neck from a split earlobe.

Buck's gun went off again, and the other earlobe was a red tatter.

And Buck's gun was back in its holster with the same speed it had come out — I just couldn't see his hand move.

"That's enough for now," he told Menner. "This is right good likker, and I guess I got to have somebody around to push it across the bar for me, and you're as good as anybody to do jackass jobs like that."

He didn't even look at Menner again. The old man leaned back against the shelf behind the bar, trembling, two trickles of red running down his neck and staining his shirt collar — I could see he wanted to touch the places where he'd been shot, to see how bad they were or just to rub at the pain, but he was afraid to raise a hand. He just stood there, looking sick.

Buck was staring at the little man in town clothes, over by the window. The little man had reared back at the shots, and now he was sitting up in his chair, his eyes straight on Buck. The table in front of him was wet where he'd spilled his drink when he'd jumped.

Buck looked at the little guy's fancy clothes and small mustache and grinned. "Come on," he said to me, and picked up his drink and started across the floor. "Find out who the dude is."

He pulled out a chair and sat down — and I saw he was careful to sit facing the front door, and also where he could see out the window.

I pulled out another chair and sat.

"Good shooting, huh?" Buck asked the little guy.

"Yes," said the little guy. "Very fine shooting. I confess, it quite startled me."

Buck laughed harshly. "Startled the old guy too . . . " He raised his voice. "Ain't that right, Menner? Wasn't you startled?"

"Yes, sir," came Menner's pain-filled voice from the bar.

Buck looked back at the little man — let his insolent gaze travel up and down the fancy waistcoat, the string tie, the sharp face with its mustache and narrow mouth and black eyes. He looked longest at the eyes, because they didn't seem to be scared.

He looked at the little guy, and the little guy looked at Buck, and finally Buck looked away. He tried to look wary as he did it, as if he was just fixing to make sure that nobody was around to sneak-shoot him — but you could see he'd been stared down.

When he looked back at the little guy, he was scowling. "Who're you, mister?" he said. "I never seen you before."

"My name is Jacob Pratt, sir. I'm traveling through to San Francisco. I'm waiting for the evening stage."

"Drummer?"

"Excuse me?"

For a second Buck's face got ugly. "You heard me, mister. You a drummer?"

"I heard you, young man, but I don't quite understand. Do you mean, am I a musician? A performer upon the drums?"

"No, you goddam fool — I mean, what're you selling? Snakebite medicine? Likker? Soap?"

"Why — I'm not selling anything. I'm a professor, sir."

"Well, I'll be damned." Buck looked at him a little more carefully. "A professor, huh? Of what?"

"Of psychology, sir."

"What's that?"

"It's the study of man's behavior — of the reasons why we act as we do."

Buck laughed again, and it was more of a snarl. "Well, professor, you just stick around here then, and I'll show you some *real* reasons for people acting like they do! From now on, I'm the big reason in this town . . . they'll jump when I yell frog, or else!"

His hand was flat on the table in front of him — and suddenly his Peacemaker was in it, pointing at the professor's fourth vest-button. "See what I mean, huh?"

The little man blinked. "Indeed I do," he said, and stared at the gun as if hypnotized. Funny, though — he still didn't seem scared — just a lot interested.

Sitting there and just listening, I thought about something else funny — how they were both just about of a size, Buck and the professor, and so strong in different ways. With the professor, you felt he was strong inside — a man who knew a lot, about things and about himself — while with Buck it was all on the outside, on the surface: he was just a milksop kid with a deadly sting.

Buck was still looking at the professor, as carefully as he had before. He seemed to hesitate for a second, his mouth twisting. Then he said, "You're an eddicated man, ain't you? I mean, you studied a lot. Ain't that right?"

"Yes, I suppose it is."

"Well . . . " Again Buck seemed to hesitate. The gun in his hand lowered until the end of the barrel rested on the table. "Look," he said slowly, "maybe you can tell me how in hell . . . "

When he didn't go on, the professor said, "Yes?"

"Nothing."

"You were going to say — ?"

"Nothing! I wasn't going to say nothing!"

"Of course you were," the little man said calmly.

Buck looked at him, his bulging eyes narrowed, the gunman's smirk on his lips again. "Are you telling me what's true and what ain't," he said softly, "with my gun on you?"

"Does the gun change anything?"

Buck tapped the heavy barrel on the table. "I say it changes a hell of a lot of things." *Tap* went the barrel. "You wanta argue?"

"Not with the gun," the professor said. "It always wins. I'll talk with you, however, if you'll talk with your mouth instead of with the gun."

By this time I was filled with admiration for the professor's guts, and fear that he'd get a bullet in them . . . I was all set to duck, in case Buck lost his temper and started throwing lead.

But suddenly Buck's gun was back in his holster. I saw the professor blink again in astonishment.

"You know," Buck said, grinning loosely, "you got a lotta nerve, professor. Maybe you *can* tell me what I wanta know."

He didn't look at the little man when he talked — he was glancing around, being "wary" again. And grinning that grin at the same time. You could see he was off balance — he was acting like everything was going just like he wanted it; but actually the professor had beaten him again, words against the gun, eyes against eyes.

The professor's dark eyes were level on Buck's right then. "What is it you want to know?"

"This — " Buck said, and his gun was in his hand again, and it was the first time when he did it that his face stayed sober and kind of stupid-looking, his normal expression, instead of getting wild and dangerous. "How — do you know how I *do* it?"

"Well," the professor said, "suppose you give me your answer first, if you have one. It might be the right one."

"I — " Buck shook his head — "Well, it's like I *think* the gun into my hand. It happened the first time this morning. I was standing out in the pass where I always practice drawing, and I was wishing I could draw faster'n anybody who ever lived — I was wishing I could just get my gun outa leather in no time at all. And — " the gun was back in his holster in the blink of an eye — "that's how it happened. My gun was in my hand. Just like that. I didn't even reach for it — I was just getting set to draw, and had my hand out in front of me . . . and my gun was in my hand before I knew what'd happened. God, I was so surprised I almost fell over!"

"I see," said the professor slowly. "You *think* it into your hand?"

"Yeah, kind of."

"Would you do it now, please?" And the professor leaned forward so he could see Buck's holster, eyes intent.

Buck's gun appeared in his hand.

The professor let out a long breath. "Now think it back into its holster."

It was there.

"You did not move your arm either time," said the professor.

"That's right," said Buck.

"The gun was just suddenly in your hand instead of in your holster. And then it was back in the holster."

"Right."

"Telekinesis," said the professor, almost reverently.

"Telewhat?"

"Telekinesis — the moving of material objects by mental force." The professor leaned back and studied the holstered gun. "It *must* be that. I hardly dared think it at first — the first time you did it. But the thought did occur to me. And now I'm virtually certain!"

"How do you say it?"

"Telekinesis."

"Well, how do I *do* it?"

"I can't answer that. Nobody knows. It's been the subject of many experiments, and there are many reported happenings — but I've never heard of any instance even remotely as impressive as this." The professor leaned across the table again. "Can you do it with other things, young man?"

"What other things?"

"That bottle on the bar, for example."

"Never tried."

"Try."

Buck stared at the bottle.

It wavered. Just a little. Rocked, and settled back.

Buck stared harder, eyes bulging.

The bottle shivered. That was all.

"Hell," Buck said. "I can't seem to — to get *ahold* of it with my mind, like I can with my gun."

"Try moving this glass on the table," the professor said. "It's smaller and closer."

Buck stared at the glass. It moved a fraction of an inch across the tabletop. No more.

Buck snarled like a dog and swatted the glass with his hand, knocking it halfway across the room.

"Possibly," the professor said, after a moment, "you can do it with your gun because you *want* to so very badly. The strength of your desire releases — or creates — whatever psychic forces are necessary to perform the act." He paused, looking thoughtful. "Young man, suppose you try to transport your gun to — say, to the top of the bar."

"Why?" Buck asked suspiciously.

"I want to see whether distance is a factor where the gun is concerned. Whether you can place the gun that far away from you, or whether the power operates only when you want your gun in your hand."

"No," Buck said in an ugly voice. "Damn if I will. I'd maybe get my gun over there and not be able to get it back, and then you'd jump me — the two of you. I ain't minded to experiment around too much, thank you."

"All right," the professor said, as if he didn't care. "The suggestion was purely in the scientific spirit — "

"Sure," said Buck. "Sure. Just don't get any more scientific, or I'll experiment on how many holes you can get in you before you die."

The professor sat back in his chair and looked Buck right in the eye. After a second, Buck looked away, scowling.

Me, I hadn't said a word the whole while, and I wasn't talking now.

"Wonder where that goddamn yellow-bellied sheriff is?" Buck said. He looked out the window, then glanced sharply at me. "He said he'd come, huh?"

"Yeah." When I was asked, I'd talk.

We sat in silence for a few moments.

The professor said, "Young man, you wouldn't care to come with me to San Francisco, would you? I and my colleagues would be very grateful for the opportunity to investigate this strange gift of yours — we would even be willing to pay you for your time and — "

Buck laughed. "Why, hell, I reckon I got bigger ideas'n that, mister! *Real* big ideas. There's no man alive I can't beat with a gun! I'm going to take Billy the Kid . . . Hickock . . . all of them! I'm going to get myself a rep bigger'n all theirs put together! Why, when I walk into a saloon they'll hand me likker. I walk into a bank, they'll give me the place. No lawman from Canada to Mexico will even stay in the same town with me! Hell, what could *you* give me, you goddam little dude?"

The professor shrugged. "Nothing that would satisfy you."

"That's right." Suddenly Buck stiffened, looking out the window. He got up, his bulging blue eyes staring down at us. "Randolph's coming down the street! You two just stay put, and maybe — just maybe — I'll let you live. Professor, I wanta talk to you some more about this telekinesis stuff. Maybe I can get even faster than I am, or control my bullets better at long range. So you *be* here, got that?"

He turned and walked out the door.

The professor said, "He's not sane."

"Nutty as a locoed steer," I said. "Been that way for a long time. An ugly shrimp who hates everything — and now he's in the saddle holding the reins, and some people are due to get rode down." I looked curiously at him. "Look, professor — this telekinesis stuff — is all that on the level?"

"Absolutely."

"He just *thinks* his gun into his hand?"

"Exactly."

"Faster than anyone could ever draw it?"

"Inconceivably faster. The time element is almost nonexistent."

I got up, feeling worse than I'd ever felt in my life. "Come on," I said. "Let's see what happens."

As if there was any doubt about what was bound to happen.

We stepped out onto the porch and over to the rail. I heard Menner come out behind us, too. I looked over my shoulder. He'd wrapped a towel around his head. Blood was leaking through it. He was looking at Buck, hating him clear through.

The street was deserted except for Buck standing about twenty feet away, and, at the far end, Sheriff Ben Randolph coming slowly toward him, putting one foot ahead of the other in the dust.

A few men were standing on porches, pressed back against the walls, mostly near doors. Nobody was sitting now — they were ready to groundhog if lead started flying wild.

"God damn it," I said in a low, savage voice. "Ben's too good a man to get kilt this way. By a punk kid with some crazy psychowhosis way of handling a gun."

I felt the professor's level eyes on me, and turned to look at him.

"Why," he said, "doesn't a group of you get together and face him down? Ten guns against his one. He'd have to surrender."

"No, he wouldn't," I said. "That ain't the way it works. He'd just dare any of us to be the first to try and stop him — and none of us would take him up on it. A group like that don't mean anything — it'd be each man against Buck Tarrant, and none of us good enough."

"I see," the professor said softly.

"God . . . " I clenched my fists so hard they hurt. "I wish we could think his gun right back into the holster or something!"

Ben and Buck were about forty feet apart now. Ben was coming on steadily, his hand over his gunbutt. He was a good man with a gun, Ben — nobody around these parts had dared tackle him for a long time. But he was outclassed now, and he knew it. I guess he was just hoping that Buck's first shot or two wouldn't kill him, and that he could place a good one himself before Buck let loose any more.

But Buck was a damn good shot. He just wouldn't miss.

The professor was staring at Buck with a strange look in his eyes.

"He should be stopped," he said.

"Stop him, then," I said sourly.

"After all," he mused, "if the ability to perform telekinesis lies dormant in all of us and is released by strong faith and desire to accomplish something that can be accomplished only by that means — then our desire to stop him might be able to counter his desire to — "

"Damn you and your big words," I said bitterly.

"It was your idea," the professor said, still looking at Buck. "What you said about thinking his gun back into its holster — after all, we *are* two to his one — "

I turned around and stared at him, really hearing him for the first time. "Yeah, that's right — I said that! My God . . . do you think we could *do* it?"

"We can try," he said. "We know it *can* be done, and evidently that is nine-tenths of the battle. He can do it, so we should be able to. We must want him *not* to more than he *wants* to."

"Lord," I said. "I wonder . . . "

Ben and Buck were about twenty feet apart now, and Ben stopped.

His voice was tired when he said, "Any time, Buck."

"You're a hell of a sheriff," Buck sneered. "You're a no-good bastard."

"Cuss me out," Ben said. "It don't hurt me none. I'll be ready when you start talking with guns."

"I'm ready now, beanpole," Buck grinned. "You draw first, huh?"

"Think of his gun!" the professor said in a fierce whisper. "Try to grab it with your mind — break his aim — pull it away from him — *you know it can be done! Think, think — "*

Ben Randolph had never in anyone's knowledge drawn first against a man. But now he did, and I guess nobody could blame him.

He slapped leather, his face already dead — and Buck's Peacemaker was in his hand —

And me and the professor were standing like statues on the porch of the Once Again, thinking at that gun, glaring at it, fists clenched, our breath rasping in our throats.

The gun appeared in Buck's hand, and wobbled just as he slipped hammer. The bullet sprayed dust at Ben's feet.

Ben's gun was halfway out.

Buck's gunbarrel pointed toward the ground, and he was trying so hard to lift it his hand got white. He drove a bullet into the dust at his own feet, and started to whine.

Ben's gun was up and aiming.

Buck shot himself in the foot.

Then Ben shot him once in the right elbow, once in the right shoulder. Buck screamed and dropped his gun and threw out his arms, and Ben, who was a thorough man, put a bullet through his right hand and another one on top of it.

Buck sat in the dust and flapped blood all around, and bawled when we came to get him.

The professor and I told Ben Randolph what had happened, and nobody else. I think he believed us.

Buck spent two weeks in the town jail, and then a year in the state pen for pulling on Randolph, and nobody's seen him now for six years. Don't know what happened to him, or care much. I reckon he's working as a cowhand someplace — anyway, he sends his mother money now and then, so he must have tamed down some and growed up some too.

While he was in the town jail, the professor talked to him a lot — the professor delayed his trip just to do it.

One night he told me, "Tarrant can't do anything like that again. Not at all, even with his left hand. The gunfight destroyed his faith in his ability to do it — or most of it, anyway. And I finished the job, I guess, asking all my questions. I guess you just can't think too much about that sort of thing."

The professor went on to San Francisco, where he's doing some interesting experiments. Or trying to. Because he has the memory of what happened that day — but, like Buck Tarrant, not the ability to do anything like that any more. He wrote me a couple times, and it seems that ever since that time he's been absolutely unable to do any telekinesis. He's tried a thousand times and can't even move a feather.

So he figures it was really me alone who saved Ben's life and stopped Buck in his tracks.

I wonder. Maybe the professor just knows too much not to be some skeptical, even with what he saw. Maybe the way he looks at things and tries to find reasons for them gets in the way of his faith.

Anyway, he wants me to come to San Francisco and get experimented on. Maybe some day I will. Might be fun, if I can find time off from my job.

I got a lot of faith, you see. What I see, I believe. And when Ben retired last year, I took over his job as sheriff — because I'm the fastest man with a gun in these parts. Or, actually, in the world. Probably if I wasn't the peaceable type, I'd be famous or something.

wom/en — female human beings. Long stereotyped as helpless damsels in distress or pretty scientists' daughters in science fiction, women in recent sf have finally been depicted as self-sufficient, talented individuals. There are many excellent women writers working in the science fiction field today. Anthologies of sf stories about women include *When Women Rule* (Walker, 1972); *Women of Wonder* (Vintage Books, 1975); and *The New Women of Wonder* (Vintage Books, 1978).

For the Sake of Grace

SUZETTE HADEN ELGIN

The Khadilh ban-harihn frowned at the disk he held in his hand, annoyed and apprehensive. There was always, of course, the chance of malfunction in the com-system. He reached forward and punched the transmit button again with one thumb, and the machine clicked to itself fitfully and delivered another disk in the message tray. He picked it up, looked at it, and swore a round assortment of colorful oaths, since no women were present.

There on the left was the matrix-mark that identified his family, the ban-harihn symbol quite clear; no possibility of error there. And from it curled the suitable number of small lines, yellow for the females, green for the males, one for each member of his household, all decorously in order. Except for one.

The yellow line that represented at all times the state of being of his wife, the Khadilha Althea, was definitely not as it should have been. It was interrupted at quarter-inch intervals by a small black dot, indicating that all was not well with the Khadilha. And the symbol at the end of the line was not the blue cross that would have classified the difficulty as purely physical; it was the indeterminate red star indicating only that the problem, whatever it was, could be looked upon as serious or about to become serious.

The Khadilh sighed. That could mean anything, from his wife's misuse of their credit cards through a security leak by one of her servants to an unsuitable love affair — although his own knowledge of the Khadilha's chilly nature made him consider the last highly unlikely. The only possible course for him was to ask for an immediate full report.

And just what, he wondered, would he do, if the report were to make it clear that he was needed at home at once? One did not simply pick up one's gear and tootle off home from the outposts of the Federation. It would take him at the very least nine months to arrive in his home city-cluster, even if he were able to command a priority flight with suspended-animation berths and warp facilities. Damn the woman anyway, what could she be up to?

He punched the button for voice transmittal, and the com-system began to hum at him, indicating readiness for dialing. He dialed, carefully selecting the planet code, since his last attempt to contact his home, on his wife's birthday, had resulted in a most embarrassing conversation with a squirmy-tentacled creature that he had gotten out of its (presumed) bed in the middle of its (presumed) sleep. And he'd had to pay in full for the call, too, all intergalactic communication being on a buyer-risk basis.

" . . . three-three-two-three-two . . . " he finished, very cautiously, and waited. The tiny screen lit up, and the words STAND BY appeared, to be replaced in a few seconds by SCRIBE (FEMALE) OF THE HOUSEHOLD BAN-HARIHN, which meant he had at least dialed correctly. The screen cleared and the words were replaced by the face of his household scribe, so distorted by distance as to be only by courtesy a face, but with the ban-harihn matrix-mark superimposed in green and yellow across the screen as security.

He spoke quickly, mindful of the com-rates at this distance.

"Scribe ban-harihn, this morning the state-of-being disk indicated some difficulty in the condition of the Khadilha Althea. Please advise if this condition could be described as an emergency."

After the usual brief lag for conversion to symbols, the reply was superimposed over the matrix-mark, and the Khadilh thought as usual that these tiny intergalactic screens became so cluttered before a conversation was terminated that one could hardly make out the messages involved.

The message in this case was "Negative," and the Khadilh smiled; the scribe was even more mindful than he of the cost of this transmittal.

He pushed the erase button and finished with, "Thank you, Scribe ban-harihn. You will then prepare at once a written report, in detail, and forward it to me by the fastest available means. Should the problem intensify to emergency point, I now authorize a com-system transmittal to that effect, to be initiated by any one of my sons. Terminate."

The screen went blank and the Khadilh, just for curiosity, punched one more time the state-of-being control. The machine delivered another disk, and sure enough, there it was again, black dots, red star and all. He threw it into the disposal, shrugged his shoulders helplessly and ordered coffee. There was nothing whatever that he could do until he received the scribe's report.

However, if it should turn out that he had wasted the cost of an intergalactic transmittal on some petty household dispute, there was going to be hell to pay, he promised himself, and a suitable punishment administered to the Khadilha by the nearest official of the Women's Discipline Unit. There certainly ought to be some way to make the state-of-being codes a bit more detailed so that everything from war to an argument with a serving woman didn't come across on the same symbol.

The report arrived by Tele-bounce in four days. Very wise choice, he thought approvingly, since the Bounce machinery was totally automatic and impersonal. It was somewhat difficult to read, since the scribe had specified that it was to be delivered to him without transcription other than into verbal symbols, and it was therefore necessary for him to scan a roll of yellow paper with a message eight symbols wide and seemingly miles long. He read only enough to convince him that no problem of discretion could possibly be involved, and then he ran the thing through the transcribe slot, receiving a standard letter on white paper in return.

"To the Khadilh ban-harihn," it read, "as requested, the following report from the scribe of his household:

"Three days ago, as the Khadilh is no doubt aware, the festival of the Spring Rains was celebrated here. The entire household, with the exception of the Khadilh himself, was present at a very large and elaborate procession held to mark the opening of the Alaharibahn-khalida Trance Hours. A suitable spot for watching the procession, entirely in accordance with decorum, had been chosen by the Khadilha Althea, and the women of the household were standing in the second row along the edge of the street set aside for the women.

"There had been a number of dancers, bands, and so on, followed by thirteen of the Poets of this city-cluster. The Poets had almost passed, along with the usual complement of exotic animals and mobile flowers and the like, and no untoward incident of any kind had occurred, when quite suddenly the Khadilh's daughter Jacinth was approached by (pardon my liberty of speech) the Poet Anna-Mary, who is, as the Khadilh knows, a female. The Poet leaned from her mount, indicating with her staff of bells that it was her wish to speak to the Khadilh's daughter, and halting the procession to do so. It was at this point that the incident occurred which has no doubt given rise to the variant marking in the state-of-being disk line for the Khadilha Althea. Quite unaccountably, the Khadilha, rather than sending the child forward to speak with the Poet (as would have been proper), grabbed the child Jacinth by the shoulders, whirling her around and covering her completely with her heavy robes so that she could neither speak nor see.

"The Poet Anna-Mary merely bowed from her horse and signaled for the procession to continue, but she was quite white and obviously offended. The family made a show of participating in the rest of the day's observances, but the Khadilh's sons took the entire household home by mid-afternoon, thereby preventing the Khadilha from participating in the Trance Hours. This was no doubt a wise course.

"What sequel there may have been to this, the scribe does not know, as no announcement has been made to the household. The scribe here indicates her respect and subservience to the Khadilh.

"Terminate with thanks."

"Well!" said the Khadilh. He laid the letter down on the top of his desk, thinking hard, rubbing his beard with one hand.

What could reasonably be expected in the way of repercussions from a public insult to an elderly — and touchy — Poet? It was hard to say.

As the only female Poet on the planet, the Poet Anna-Mary was much alone; as her duties were not arduous, she had much time to brood. And though she was a Poet, she remained only a female, with the female's inferior reasoning powers. She was accustomed to reverent homage, to women holding up their children to touch the hem of her robe. She could hardly be expected to react with pleasure to an insult in public, and from a female.

It was at his sons that she would be most likely to strike, through the university, he decided, and he could not chance that. He had worked too hard, and they had worked too hard, to allow a vindictive female, no matter how lofty her status, to destroy what they had built up. He had better go home and leave the orchards to take care of themselves; important as the lush peaches of Earth were to the economy of his home planet, his sons were of even greater importance.

It was not every family that could boast of five sons in the university, all five selected by competitive examination for the Major in Poetry. Sometimes a family might have two sons chosen, but the rest would be refused, as the Khadilh himself had been refused, and would then have to be satisfied with the selection of law or medicine or government or some other of the majors. He smiled proudly, remembering the respectful glances of his friends when each of his sons in turn had placed high in the examinations and been awarded the Poet Major, his oldest son entering at the Fourth Level. And when the youngest had been chosen, thus releasing the oldest from the customary vow of celibacy — since to impose it would have meant the end of the family line, an impossible situation — the Khadilh had had difficulty in maintaining even a pretense of modesty. The meaning, of course, was that he would have as grandson the direct offspring of a Poet, something that had not happened within his memory or his father's memory. He had been given to understand, in fact, that it had been more than three hundred years since all sons of any one family had entered the Poetry courses. (A family having only one son was prohibited by law from entering him in the Poetry Examinations, they told him.)

Yes, he must go home, and the hell with the peaches of Earth. Let them rot, if the garden-robots could not manage them.

He went to the com-system and punched through a curt transmittal of his intention, and then set to pulling the necessary strings to obtain a priority flight.

When the Khadilh arrived at his home, his sons were lined up in his study, waiting for him, each in the coarse brown student's tunic that was compulsory, but with the scarlet Poet's stripe around the hem to delight his eyes. He smiled at them, saying, "It is a pleasure to see you once more, my sons; you give rest to my eyes and joy to my heart."

Michael, the oldest, answered in kind.

"It is our pleasure to see you, Father."

"Let us all sit down," said the Khadilh, motioning them to their places about the study table that stood in the center of the room. When they were seated, he struck the table with his knuckles, in the old ritual, three times slowly.

"No doubt you know why I have chosen to abandon my orchards to the attention of the garden-robots and return home so suddenly," he said. "Unfortunately, it has taken me almost ten months to reach you. There was no more rapid way to get home to you, much as I wished for one."

"We understand, Father," said his oldest son.

"Then, Michael," went on the Khadilh, "would you please bring me up to date on the developments here since the incident at the procession of the Spring Rains."

His son seemed hesitant to speak, his black brows drawn together over his eyes, and the Khadilh smiled at him encouragingly.

"Come, Michael," he said, "surely it is not courteous to make your father wait in this fashion!"

"You will realize, Father," said the young man slowly, "that it has not been possible to communicate with you since the time of your last transmittal. You will also realize that this matter has not been one about which advice could easily be requested. I have had no choice but to make decisions as best I could."

"I realize that. Of course."

"Very well, then. I hope you will not be angry, Father."

"I shall indeed be angry if I am not told at once exactly what has occurred this past ten months. You make me uneasy, my son."

Michael took a deep breath and nodded. "All right, Father," he said. "I will be brief."

"And quick."

"Yes, Father. I took our household away from the festival as soon as I decently could without creating talk; when we arrived at home, I sent the Khadilha at once to her quarters, with orders to stay there until you should advise me to the contrary."

"Quite right," said the Khadilh. "Then what?"

"The Khadilha disobeyed me, Father."

"Disobeyed you? In what way?"

"The Khadilha Althea disregarded my orders entirely, and she took our sister into the Small Corridor, and there she allowed her to look into the cell where our aunt is kept, Father."

"My God!" shouted the Khadilh. "And you made no move to stop her?"

"Father," said Michael ban-harihn, "you must realize that no one could have anticipated the actions of the Khadilha Althea. We would certainly have stopped her had we known, but who would have thought that the Khadilha would disobey the order of an adult male? It was assumed that she would go to her quarters and remain there."

"I see."

"I did not contact the Women's Discipline Unit," Michael continued. "I preferred that such an order should come from you, Father. However, orders were given that the Khadilha should be restricted to her quarters, and no one has been allowed to see her except the serving women. The wires to her com-system were disconnected, and provision was made for suitable medication to be added to her diet. You will find her very docile, Father."

The Khadilh was trembling with indignation.

"Discipline will be provided at once, my son," he said. "I apologize for the disgusting behavior of the Khadilha. But please go on — what of my daughter?"

"That is perhaps the most distressing thing of all."

"In what way?"

Michael looked thoroughly miserable.

"Answer me at once," snapped the Khadilh, "and in full."

"Our sister Jacinth," said his second son, Nicolas, "was already twelve years of age at the time of the festival. When she returned from the Small Corridor, without notice to any one of us, she announced her intention by letter to the Poet Anna-Mary — her intention to compete in the examinations for the Major of Poetry."

"And the Poet Anna-Mary — "

"Turned the announcement immediately over to the authorities at the Poetry Unit," finished Michael. "Certainly she made no attempt to dissuade our sister."

"She is amply revenged then for the insult of the Khadilha," said the Khadilh bitterly. "Were there any other acts on the part of the Poet Anna-Mary?"

"None, Father. Our sister has been cloistered by government order since that time, of course, to prevent contamination of the other females."

"Oh, dear God," breathed the Khadilh, "how could such a thing have touched my household — for the second time?"

He thought a moment. "When are the examinations, then? I've lost all track of time."

"It has been ten months, Father."

"In about a month, then?"

"In three weeks."

"Will they let me see Jacinth?"

"No, Father," said Michael. "And, Father — "

"Yes, Michael?"

"It is my shame and my sorrow that this should have been the result of your leaving your household in my care."

The Khadilh reached over and grasped his hand firmly.

"You are very young, my son," he said, "and you have nothing to be ashamed of. When the females of a household take it upon themselves to upset the natural order of things and to violate the rules of decency, there is very little anyone can do."

"Thank you, Father."

"Now," said the Khadilh, turning to face them all, "I suggest that the next thing to do would be to initiate action by the Women's Discipline Unit. Do you wish me to have the Khadilha placed on permanent medication, my sons?"

He hoped they would not insist upon it, and was pleased to see that they did not.

"Let us wait, Father," said Michael, "until we know the outcome of the examinations."

"Surely the outcome is something about which there can be no question!"

"Could we wait, Father, all the same?"

It was the youngest of the boys. As was natural, he was still overly squeamish, still a bit tender. The Khadilh would not have had him be otherwise.

"A wise decision," he said. "In that case, once I have bathed and had my dinner, I will send for the Lawyer an-ahda. And you may go, my sons."

The boys filed out, led by the solemn Michael, leaving him with no company but the slow dance of a mobile flower from one of the tropical stars. It whirled gently in the middle of the corner hearth, humming to itself and giving off showers of silver sparks from time to time. He watched it suspiciously for a moment, and then pushed the com-system buttons for his housekeeper. When the face appeared on the screen he snapped at it.

"Housekeeper, are you familiar with the nature of the mobile plant that someone has put in my study?"

The housekeeper's voice, frightened, came back at once. "The Khadilh may have the plant removed — should I call the gardener?"

"All I wanted to know is the sex of the blasted thing," he bellowed at her. "Is it male or female?"

"Male, Khadilh, of the genus — "

He cut off the message while she was still telling him of the plant's pedigree. It was male; therefore it could stay. He would talk to it, while he ate his dinner, about the incredible behavior of his Khadilha.

The Lawyer an-ahda leaned back in the chair provided for him and smiled at his client.

"Yes, ban-harihn," he said amiably, having known the Khadilh since they were young men at the university, "what can I do to help the sun shine more brightly through your window?"

"This is a serious matter," said the Khadilh.

"Ah."

"You heard — never mind being polite and denying it — of my wife's behavior at the procession of the Spring Rains. I see that you did."

"Very impulsive," observed the Lawyer. "Most unwise. Undisciplined."

"Indeed it was. However, worse followed."

"Oh? The Poet Anna-Mary has tried for revenge, then?"

"Not in the sense that you mean, no. But worse has happened, my old friend, far worse."

"Tell me." The lawyer leaned forward attentively, listening, and when the Khadilh had finished, he cleared his throat.

"There isn't anything to be done, you know," he said. "You might as well know it at once."

"Nothing at all?"

"Nothing. The law provides that any woman may challenge and claim her right to compete in the Poetry Examinations, provided she is twelve years of age and a citizen of this planet. If she is not accepted, however, the penalty for having challenged and failed is solitary confinement for life, in the household of her family. And once she has announced to the faculty by signed communication that she intends to compete, she is cloistered until the day of the examinations, and she may not change her mind. The law is very clear on this point."

"She is very young."

"She is twelve. That is all the law requires."

"It's a cruel law."

"Not at all! Can you imagine, ban-harihn, the chaos that would result if every emotional young female, bored with awaiting marriage in the women's quarters, should decide that she had a vocation and claim her right to challenge? The purpose of the law is to discourage foolish young girls from creating difficulties for their households and for the state. Can you just imagine, if there were only a token penalty, and chaperons had to be provided by the faculty, and separate quarters provided, and — "

"Yes, I suppose I see! But why should women be allowed to compete at all? No such idiocy is allowed in the other professions."

"The law provides that since the Profession of Poetry is a religious office, there must be a channel provided for the rare occasion when the Creator might see fit to call a female to His service."

"What nonsense!"

"There is the Poet Anna-Mary, ban-harihn."

"And how many others?"

"She is the third."

"In nearly nine thousand years! Only three in so many centuries, and yet no exception can be made for one little twelve-year-old girl?"

"I am truly sorry, my friend," said the lawyer. "You could try a petition to the council, of course, but I am quite sure — *quite* sure — that it would be of no use. There is too much public reaction to a female's even attempting the examinations, because it seems blasphemous even to many very broad-minded people. The council would not dare to make an exception."

"I could make a galactic appeal."

"You could."

"There would be quite a scandal, you know, among the peoples of the galaxy, if they knew of this penalty being enforced on a child."

"My friend, my dear ban-harihn — think of what you are saying. You would create an international incident, an intergalactic international incident, with all that implies, bring down criticism upon our heads, most surely incur an investigation of our religious customs by the intergalactic police, which would in turn call for a protest from our government, which in its turn — "

"You know I would not do it."

"I hope not. It would parallel the Trojan War for folly, my friend — all that for the sake of one female child!"

"We are a barbaric people."

The lawyer nodded. "After ten thousand years, you know, if barbarism remains it becomes very firmly entrenched."

The lawyer rose to go, throwing his heavy blue cloak around him. "After all," he said, "it is only one female child."

It was all very well, thought the Khadilh when his friend was gone, all very well to say that. No doubt the lawyer had never had the opportunity to see the result of a lifetime of solitary confinement in total silence, or he would have been less willing to see a child condemned to such a fate.

The Khadilh's sister had been nearly thirty, and yet unmarried, when she had chosen to compete, and she was forty-six now. It had been an impulse of folly, born of thirty years of boredom, and the Khadilh blamed his parents.

Enough dowry should have been provided to make even Grace, ugly as she was, an acceptable bride for someone, somewhere.

The room in the Small Corridor, where she had been confined since her failure, had no window, no com-system, nothing. Her food was passed through a slot in one wall, as were the few books and papers which she was allowed — all these things being very rigidly regulated by the Women's Discipline Unit.

It was the duty of the Khadilha Althea to go each morning to the narrow grate that enclosed a one-way window into the cell and to observe the prisoner inside. On the two occasions when that observation had disclosed physical illness, a dart containing an anesthetic had been fired through the food slot, and Grace had been rendered unconscious for the amount of time necessary to let a doctor enter the cell and attend to her. She had had sixteen years of this, and it was the Khadilha who had had to watch her, through the first years when she alternately lay stuporous for days and then screamed and begged for release for days . . . and now she was quite mad. The Khadilh had observed her on two occasions when his wife had been too ill to go, and he had found it difficult to believe that the creature who crawled on all fours from one end of the room to the other, its matted hair thick with filth in spite of the servomechanisms that hurried from the walls to retrieve all waste and dirt, was his sister. It gibbered and whined and clawed at its flesh — it was hard to believe that it was human. And it had been only sixteen years. Jacinth was twelve!

The Khadilh called his wife's quarters and announced to her serving women that they were all to leave her. He went rapidly through the corridors of his house, over the delicate arched bridge that spanned the tea gardens around the women's quarters, and into the rooms where she stayed. He found her sitting in a small chair before her fireplace, watching the mobile plants that danced there to be near the warmth of the fire. As his sons had said, she was quite docile, and in very poor contact with reality.

He took a capsule from the pocket of his tunic and gave it to her to swallow, and when her eyes were clear of the mist of her drugged dreams, he spoke to her.

"You see that I have returned, Althea," he said. "I wish to know why my daughter has brought this ill fortune upon our household."

"It is her own idea," said the Khadilha in a bitter voice. "Since the last of her brothers was chosen, she has been thus determined, saying that it would be a great honor for our house should all of the children of ban-harihn be accepted for the faith."

It was as if a light had been turned on.

"This was not an impulse, then!" exclaimed the Khadilh.

"No. Since she was nine years old she has had this intention."

"But why was I not told? Why was I given no opportunity — " He stopped abruptly, knowing that he was being absurd. No woman would bother her husband with the problems of rearing a female child. But now he began to understand.

"She did not even know," his wife was saying, "that there was a living female Poet, although she had heard from someone that such a possibility existed. It was, she insisted, a matter of knowledge of the heart. When the Poet Anna-Mary singled her out at the procession . . . why, then she was sure. Then she knew, she said, that she had been chosen."

Of course. That in itself, being marked out for notice before the crowd, would have convinced the child that her selection was ordained by divine choice. He could see it all now. And the Khadilha had taken the child to see her aunt in her cell in a last desperate attempt to dissuade her.

"The child is strong-willed for a female," he mused, "if the sight of poor Grace did not shake her."

His wife did not answer, and he sat there, almost too tired to move. He was trying to place the child Jacinth in his mind's eye, but it was useless. It had been at least four years since he had seen her, dressed in a brief white shift that all little girls wore: he remembered a slender child, he remembered dark hair — but then all little girls among his people were slender and dark-haired.

"You don't even remember her," said his wife, and he jumped, irritated at her shrewdness.

"You are quite right," he said. "I don't. Is she pretty?"

"She is beautiful. Not that it matters now."

The Khadilh thought for a moment, watching his wife's stoic face, and then, choosing his words with care, he said, "It had been my intention to register a complaint with the Women's Discipline Unit for your behavior, Khadilha Althea."

"I expected you to do so."

"You have had a good deal of experience with the agents of the WDU — the prospect does not upset you?"

"I am indifferent to it."

He believed her. He remembered very well the behavior of his wife at her last impregnation, for it had required four agents from the unit to subdue her and fasten her to their marriage bed. And yet he knew that many women went willingly, even eagerly, to their appointments with their husbands. It was at times difficult for him to understand why he had not had Althea put on permanent medication from the very beginning; certainly, it would not have been difficult to secure permission to take a second, more womanly wife. Unfortunately he was softhearted, and she had been the mother of his eldest son, and so he had put up with her, relying upon his concubines for feminine softness and ardor. Certainly Althea had hardened with the years, not softened.

"I have decided," he finished abruptly, "that your behavior is not so scandalous as I had thought. I am not sure that I would not have reacted just as you did under the circumstances, if I had known the girl's plans. I will make no complaint, therefore."

"You are indulgent."

He scanned her face, still lovely for all her years, for signs of impertinence, but there were none, and he went on: "However, you understand that our eldest son must decide for himself if he wishes to forego his own complaint. Your disobedience to him was your first, you know. I have become accustomed to it."

He turned on his heel and left her, amused at his own weakness, but he canceled the medication order when he went past the entrance to her quarters. She was a woman, she had meant to keep her daughter from becoming what Grace had become; it was not so hard to understand, after all.

The family did not go to the university on the day of the examinations. They waited at home, prepared for the inevitable as well as they could prepare.

Another room near the room where Grace was kept had been made ready by the weeping serving women, and it stood open now, waiting.

The Khadilh had had his wife released from her quarters for the day, since she would have only the brief moment with her daughter, and thereafter would have only the duty of observing her each morning as she did her sister-in-law. She sat at his feet now in their common room, making no sound, her face bleached white, wondering, he supposed, what she would do now. She had no other daughter; there were no other sisters. She would be alone in the household except for her serving woman, until such a time as Michael should, perhaps, provide her with a granddaughter. His heart ached for her, alone in a household of men, and five of them, before very long, to be allowed to speak only in the rhymed couplets of the Poets.

"Father?"

The Khadilh looked up, surprised. It was his youngest son, the boy James.

"Father," said the boy, "could she pass? I mean, is it possible that she could pass?"

Michael answered for him. "James, she is only twelve, and a female. She has had no education; she can only just barely read. Don't ask foolish questions. Don't you remember the examinations?"

"I remember," said James firmly. "Still, I wondered. There is the Poet Anna-Mary."

"The third in who knows how many hundreds of years, James," Michael said. "I shouldn't count on it if I were you."

"But is it possible?" the boy insisted. "Is it possible, Father?"

"I don't think so, son," said the Khadilh gently. "It would be a very curious thing if an untrained twelve-year-old female could pass the examinations that I could not pass myself, when I was sixteen, don't you think?"

"And then," said the boy, "she may never see anyone again, so long as she lives, never speak to anyone, never look out a window, never leave that little room?"

"Never."

"That is a cruel law!" said the boy. "Why has it not been changed?"

"My son," said the Khadilh, "it is not something that happens often, and the council has many, many other things to do. It is an ancient law, and the knowledge that it exists offers to bored young females something exciting to think about. It is intended to frighten them, my son."

"One day, when I have power enough, I shall have it changed."

The Khadilh raised his hand to hush the laughter of the older boys. "Let him alone," he snapped. "He is young, and she is his sister. Let us have a spirit of compassion in this house, if we must have tragedy."

A thought occurred to him, then. "James," he said, "you take a great deal of interest in this matter. Is it possible that you were somehow involved in this idiocy of your sister's?"

At once he knew he had struck a sensitive spot; tears sprang to the boy's eyes and he bit his lip fiercely.

"James — in what way were you involved? What do you know of this affair?"

"You will be angry, my father," said James, "but that is not the worst. What is worse is that I will have condemned my sister to — "

"James," said the Khadilh, "I have no interest in your self-accusations. Explain at once, simply and without dramatics."

"Well, we used to practice, she and I," said the boy hastily, his eyes on the floor. "I did not think I would pass, you know. I could see it — all of the others would pass, and I would not, and there I would be, the only one. People would say, there he goes, the only one of the sons of the ban-harihn who could not pass the Poetry exam."

"And?"

"And so we practiced together, she and I," he said. "I would set the subject and the form and do the first stanza, and then she would write the reply."

"When did you do this? Where?"

"In the gardens, Father, ever since she was little. She's very good at it, she really is, Father."

"She can rhyme? She knows the forms?"

"Yes, Father! And she is good, she has a gift for it — Father, she's much better than I am. I am ashamed to say that of a female, but it would be a lie to say anything else."

The things that went on in one's household! The Khadilh was amazed and dismayed, and he was annoyed besides. Not that it was unusual for brothers and sisters, while still young, to spend time together, but surely one of the servants or one of the family ought to have noticed that the two little ones were playing at Poetry?

"What else goes on in my house beneath the blind eyes and deaf ears of those I entrust with its welfare?" he demanded furiously, and no one hazarded an answer. He made a sound of disgust and went to the window to look out over the gardens that stretched down to the narrow river behind the house. It had begun to rain, a soft green rain not much more than a mist, and the river was blurred velvet through the veil of water. Another time he would have enjoyed the view; indeed, he might well have sent for his pencils and his sketching pad to record its beauty. But this was not a day for pleasure.

Unless, of course, Jacinth did pass.

It was, on the face of it, an absurdity. The examinations for Poetry were far different than those for the other professions. In the others it was a straightforward matter: one went to the examining room, an examination was distributed, one spent perhaps six hours in such exams, and they were then scored by computer. Then, in a few days, there would come the little notice by com-system, stating that one had or had not passed the fitness exams for law or business or whatever.

Poetry was a different matter. There were many degrees of fitness, all the way from the First Level, which fitted a man for the lower offices of the faith, through five more subordinate levels, to the Seventh Level. Very rarely did anyone enter the Seventh Level. Since there was no question of being promoted from one level to another, a man being placed at his appropriate rank by the examinations at the very beginning, there were times when the Seventh Level remained vacant for as long as a year. Michael had been placed at the Fourth Level instead of the First, like the others of his sons, and the Khadilh had been awed at the implications.

For Poetry there was first an examination of the usual kind, marked by hand and scored by machine, just as in the other professions. But then, if that exam was passed, there was something unique to do. The Khadilh had not passed that exam and he had no knowledge of what came next, except that it involved the computers.

"Michael," he said, musing, "how does it go exactly, the Poetry exam by the computer?"

Michael came over to stand beside him. "You mean, should Jacinth pass the written examination, even if just by chance, then what happens?"

"Yes. Tell me."

"It's simple enough. You go into the booths where the computer panels are and push a READY button. Then the computer gives you your instructions."

"For example?"

"Let's see. For example, it might say — SUBJECT: LOVE OF COUNTRY . . . FORM: SONNET, UNRESTRICTED BUT RHYMED . . . STYLE: FORMAL,

SUITABLE FOR AN OFFICIAL BANQUET. And then you would begin."

"Are you allowed to use paper and pen, my son?"

"Oh, no, Father." Michael was smiling, no doubt, thought the Khadilh, at his father's innocence. "No paper or pencil. And you begin at once."

"No time to think."

"No, Father, none."

"Then what?"

"Then, sometimes, you are sent to another computer, one that gives more difficult subjects. I suppose it must be the same all the way to the Seventh Level, except that the subject would grow more difficult."

The Khadilh thought it over. For his own office of Khadilh, which meant little more than "Administrator of Large Estates and Households," he had had to take one oral examination, and that had been in ordinary straightforward prose, and the examiner had been a man, not a computer, and he still remembered the incredible stupidity of his answers. He had sat flabbergasted at the things that issued from his mouth, and he had been convinced that he could not possibly have passed the examination. And Jacinth was only twelve years old, with none of the training that boys received in prosody, none of the summer workshops in the different forms, scarcely even an acquaintance with the history of the classics. Surely she would be too terrified to speak? Why, the simple modesty of her femaleness ought to be enough to keep her mute, and then she would fail, even if she should somehow be lucky enough to pass the written exam. Damn the girl!

"Michael," he asked, "what is the level of the Poet Anna-Mary?"

"Second Level, Father."

"Thank you, my son. You have been very helpful — you may sit down now, if you like."

He stood a moment more, watching the rain, and then went back and sat down again by his wife. Her hands flew, busy with the little needles used to make the complicated hoods the Poets wore. She was determined that her sons should, in accordance with the ancient tradition, have every stitch of their installation garments made by her hands, although no one would have criticized her if she had had the work done by others, since she had so many sons needing the garments. He was pleased with her, for once, and he made a mental note to have a gift sent to her later.

The bells rang in the city, signaling the four o'clock Hour of Meditation, and the Khadilh's sons looked at one another, hesitating. By the rules of their Major that hour was to be spent in their rooms, but their father had specifically asked that they stay with him.

The Khadilh sighed, making another mental note, that he must sigh less. It was an unattractive habit.

"My sons," he said, "you must conform to the rules of your Major. Please consider that my first wish."

They thanked him and left the room, and there he sat, watching first the darting fingers of the Khadilha and then the dancing of the mobile flowers, until shadows began to streak across the tiled floor of the room. Six o'clock came, and then seven, and still no word. When his sons returned, he sent them away crossly, seeing no reason why they should share in his misery.

By the time the double suns had set over the river he had lost the compassion he had counseled for the others and become furious with Jacinth as well as the system. That one insignificant female child could create such havoc for him and for his household amazed him. He began to understand the significance of the rule; the law began to seem less harsh. He had missed his dinner and he had spent his day in unutterable tedium. His orchards were doubtless covered with insects and dying of thirst and neglect, his bank account was depleted by the expense of the trip home, the cost of extra garden-robots on Earth, the cost of the useless visit from the lawyer. And his nervous system was shattered, and the peace of his household destroyed. All this from the antics of one twelve-year-old female child! And when she had to be shut up, there would be the necessity of living with her mother as she watched the child deteriorate into a crawling mass of filth and madness as Grace had done. Was his family cursed, that its females should bring down the wrath of the universe at large in this manner?

He struck his fists together in rage and frustration, and the Khadilha jumped, startled.

"Shall I send for music, my husband?" she asked. "Or perhaps you would like to have your dinner served here? Perhaps you would like a good wine?"

"Perhaps a dozen dancing girls!" he shouted. "Perhaps a Venusian flame-tiger! Perhaps a parade of Earth elephants and a tentacle bird from the Extreme Moons! May all the suffering gods take pity upon me!"

"I beg your pardon," said the Khadilha. "I have angered you."

"It is not you who have angered me," he retorted; "it is that miserable female of a daughter that you bore me, who has caused me untold sorrow and expense, that has angered me!"

"Very soon now," pointed out the Khadilha softly, "she will be out of your sight and hearing forever; perhaps then she will anger you less."

The Khadilha's wit, sometimes put to uncomfortable uses, had been one of the reasons he had kept her all these years. At this moment, however, he wished her stupider and timider and a thousand light-years away.

"Must you be right, at a time like this?" he demanded. "It is unbecoming in a woman."

"Yes, my husband."

"It grows late."

"Yes, indeed."

"What could they be doing over there?"

He reached over to the com-system and instructed the housekeeper to send someone with a videocolor console. It was just possible that somewhere in the galaxy something was happening that would distract him from his misery.

He skimmed the videobands rapidly, muttering. There was a new drama by some unknown avant-garde playwright, depicting a liaison between the daughter of a council member and a servomechanism. There was a game of jidra, both teams apparently from the Extreme Moons, if their size could be taken as any indication. There were half a dozen variety programs, each worse than the last. Finally he found a newsband and leaned forward, his ear caught by the words of the improbably sleek young man reading the announcements.

Had he said — yes! He had. He was announcing the results of the examinations in Poetry. " — ended at four o'clock this afternoon, with only eighty-three candidates accepted out of almost three thousand who — "

"Of course!" he shouted. How stupid he had been not to have realized, sooner, that since all members of Poetry were bound by oath to observe the four o'clock Hour of Meditation, the examinations would have had to end by four o'clock! But why, then, had no one come to notify them or to return their daughter? It was very near nine o'clock.

The smallest whisper of hope touched him. It was possible, just possible, that the delay was because even the callous members of the Poetry Unit were finding it difficult to condemn a little girl to a life of solitary confinement. Perhaps they were meeting to discuss it, perhaps something was being arranged, some loophole in the law being found that could be used to prevent such a travesty of justice.

He switched off the video and punched the call numbers of the Poetry Unit on the com-system. At once the screen was filled by the embroidered hood and bearded face of a Poet, First Level, smiling helpfully through the superimposed matrix-mark of his household.

The Khadilh explained his problem, and the Poet smiled and nodded.

"Messengers are on their way to your household at this moment, Khadilh ban-harihn," he said. "We regret the delay, but it takes time, you know. All these things take time."

"What things?" demanded the Khadilh. "And why are you speaking to me in prose? Are you not a Poet?"

"The Khadilh seems upset," said the Poet in a soothing voice. "He should know that those Poets who serve the Poetry Unit as communicators are excused from the laws of verse-speaking while on duty."

"Someone is coming now?"

"Messengers are on their way."

"On foot? By Earth-style robot-mule? Why not a message by com-system?"

The Poet shook his head. "We are a very old profession, Khadilh ban-harihn. There are many traditions to be observed. Speed, I fear, is not among those traditions."

"What message are they bringing?"

"I am not at liberty to tell you that," said the Poet patiently.

Such control! thought the Khadilh. Such unending saintlike tolerance! It was maddening.

"Terminate with thanks," said the Khadilh, and turned off the bland face of the Poet. At his feet the Khadilha had set aside her work and sat trembling. He reached over and patted her hand, wishing there were some comfort he could offer.

Had they better go ahead and call for dinner? He wondered if either of them would be able to eat.

"Althea," he began, and at that moment the serving women showed in the messengers of the Poetry Unit, and the Khadilh rose to his feet.

"Well?" he demanded abruptly. He would be damned if he was going to engage in the usual interminable preliminaries. "Where is my daughter?"

"We have brought your daughter with us, Khadilh ban-harihn."

"Well, where is she?"

"If the Khadilh will only calm himself."

"I am calm! Now where is my daughter?"

The senior messenger raised one hand, formally, for silence, and in an irritating singsong he began to speak.

"The daughter of the Khadilh ban-harihn will be permitted to approach and to speak to her parents for one minute only, by the clock which I hold, giving to her parents whatever message of farewell she should choose. Once she has given her message, the daughter of the Khadilh will be taken away and it will not be possible for the Khadilh or his household to communicate with her again except by special petition from the council."

The Khadilh was dumbfounded. He could feel his wife shaking uncontrollably beside him — was she about to cause a second scandal?

"Leave the room if you cannot control your emotion, Khadilha," he ordered her softly, and she responded with an immediate and icy calm of bearing. Much better.

"What do you mean," he asked the messenger, "by stating that you are about to take my daughter away again? Surely it is not the desire of the council that she be punished outside the confines of my house!"

"Punished?" asked the messenger. "There is no punishment in question, Khadilh. It is merely that the course of study which she must follow henceforth cannot be provided for her except at the Temple of the University."

It was the Khadilh's turn to tremble now. She had passed!

"Please," he said hoarsely, "would you make yourself clear? Am I to understand that my daughter has passed the examination?"

"Certainly," said the messenger. "This is indeed a day of great honor for the household of the ban-harihn. You can be most proud, Khadilh, for your daughter has only just completed the final examination and has been placed in Seventh Level. A festival will be declared and an official announcement will be made. A day of holiday will be ordered for all citizens of the planet Abba, in all city-clusters and throughout the countryside. It is a time of great rejoicing!"

The man went on and on, his curiously contrived-sounding remarks unwinding amid punctuating sighs and nods from the other messengers, but the Khadilh did not hear any more. He sank back in his chair, deaf to the list of the multitude of honors and happenings that would come to pass as a result of this extraordinary thing. Seventh Level! How could such a thing be?

Dimly he was aware that the Khadilha was weeping quite openly, and he used one numb hand to draw her veils across her face.

"Only one minute, by the clock," the messenger was saying. "You do understand? You are not to touch the Poet Candidate, nor are you to interfere with her in any way. She is allowed one message of farewell, nothing more."

And then they let his daughter, this stranger who had performed a miracle, whom he would not even have recognized in a crowd, come forward into the room and approach him. She looked very young and tired, and he held his breath to hear what she would say to him.

However, it was no message of farewell that she had to give them. Said the Poet Candidate, Seventh Level, Jacinth ban-harihn: "You will send someone at once to inform my Aunt Grace that I have been appointed to the Seventh Level of the Profession of Poetry; permission has been granted by the council for the breaking of her solitary confinement for so long as it may take to make my aunt understand just what has happened."

And then she was gone, followed by the messengers, leaving only the muted tinkling showers of sparks from the dancing flowers and the soft drumming of the rain on the roof to punctuate the silence.

X

xen/o/bi/ol/o/gy — the study of the origin, structure, reproduction, growth, and development of extraterrestrial life forms. Now that we stand poised at the edge of interplanetary travel, xenobiology has become a legitimate science. However, as early as 1888, J.-H. Rosny aîné, a French science fiction writer, made a serious attempt to study the subject in "The Shapes," which appears in *Isaac Asimov Presents the Best Science Fiction of the 19th Century* (Beaufort Books, 1981).

A Death in the House

CLIFFORD D. SIMAK

Old Mose Abrams was out hunting cows when he found the alien. He didn't know it was an alien, but it was alive and it was in a lot of trouble and Old Mose, despite everything the neighbors said about him, was not the kind of man who could bear to leave a sick thing out there in the woods.

It was a horrid-looking thing, green and shiny, with some purple spots on it, and it was repulsive even twenty feet away. And it stank.

It had crawled, or tried to crawl, into a clump of hazel brush, but hadn't made it. The head part was in the brush and the rest lay out there naked in the open. Every now and then the parts that seemed to be arms and hands clawed feebly at the ground, trying to force itself deeper in the brush, but it was too weak; it never moved an inch.

It was groaning, too, but not too loud — just the kind of keening sound a lonesome wind might make around a wide, deep eave. But there was more in it than just the sound of winter wind; there was a frightened, desperate note that made the hair stand up on Old Mose's nape.

Old Mose stood there for quite a spell, making up his mind what he ought to do about it, and a while longer after that working up his courage, although most folks offhand would have said that he had plenty. But this was the sort of situation that took more than just ordinary screwed-up courage. It took a lot of foolhardiness.

But this was a wild, hurt thing and he couldn't leave it there, so he walked up to it and knelt down. It was pretty hard to look at, though there was a sort of fascination in its repulsiveness that was hard to figure out — as if it were so horrible that it dragged one to it. And it stank in a way that no one had ever smelled before.

Mose, however, was not finicky. In the neighborhood, he was not well known for fastidiousness. Ever since his wife had died almost ten years before, he had lived alone on his untidy farm, and the housekeeping that he did was the scandal of all the neighbor women. Once a year, if he got around to it, he sort of shoveled out the house, but the rest of the year he just let things accumulate.

So he wasn't as upset as some might have been with the way the creature smelled. But the sight of it upset him, and it took him quite a while before he could bring himself to touch it, and when he finally did, he was considerably surprised. He had been prepared for it to be either cold or slimy, or maybe even both. But it was neither. It was warm and hard and it had a clean feel to it, and he was reminded of the way a green cornstalk would feel.

He slid his hand beneath the hurt thing and pulled it gently from the clump of hazel brush and turned it over so he could see its face. It hadn't any face. It had an enlargement at the top of it, like a flower on top of a stalk, although its body wasn't any stalk, and there was a fringe around this enlargement that wiggled like a can of worms, and it was then that Mose almost turned around and ran.

But he stuck it out.

He squatted there, staring at the no-face with the fringe of worms, and he got cold all over and his stomach doubled up on him and he was stiff with fright — and the fright got worse when it seemed to him that the keening of the thing was coming from the worms.

Mose was a stubborn man. One had to be stubborn to run a runty farm like this. Stubborn and insensitive in a lot of ways. But not insensitive, of course, to a thing in pain.

Finally he was able to pick it up and hold it in his arms and there was nothing to it, for it didn't weigh much. Less than a half-grown shoat, he figured.

He went up the woods path with it, heading back for home, and it seemed to him the smell of it was less. He was hardly scared at all and he was warm again and not cold all over.

For the thing was quieter now and keening just a little. And although he could not be sure of it, there were times when it seemed as if the thing were snuggling up to him, the way a scared and hungry baby will snuggle to any grown person that comes and picks it up.

Old Mose reached the buildings and he stood out in the yard a minute, wondering whether he should take it to the barn or house. The barn, of course, was the natural place for it, for it wasn't human — it wasn't even as close to human as a dog or cat or sick lamb would be.

He didn't hesitate too long, however. He took it into the house and laid it on what he called a bed, next to the kitchen stove. He got it straightened out all neat and orderly, pulled a dirty blanket over it, and then went to the stove and stirred up the fire until there was some flame.

Then he pulled up a chair beside the bed and had a good, hard, wondering look at this thing he had brought home. It had quieted down a lot and seemed more comfortable than it had out in the woods. He tucked the blanket snug around it with a tenderness that surprised himself. He wondered what he had that it might eat, and even if he knew, how he'd manage feeding it, for it seemed to have no mouth.

"But you don't need to worry none," he told it. "Now that I got you under a roof, you'll be all right. I don't know too much about it, but I'll take care of you the best I can."

By now it was getting on toward evening, and he looked out the window and saw that the cows he had been hunting had come home by themselves.

"I got to go get the milking done and the other chores," he told the thing lying on the bed, "but it won't take me long. I'll be right back."

Old Mose loaded up the stove so the kitchen would stay warm and he tucked the thing in once again, then got his milk pails and went down to the barn.

He fed the sheep and pigs and horses and he milked the cows. He hunted eggs and shut the chicken house. He pumped a tank of water.

Then he went back to the house.

It was dark now and he lit the oil lamp on the table, for he was against electricity. He'd refused to sign up when REA had run out the line and a lot of the neighbors had gotten sore at him for being uncooperative. Not that he cared, of course.

He had a look at the thing upon the bed. It didn't seem to be any better, or any worse, for that matter. If it had been a sick lamb or an ailing calf, he would have known right off how it was getting on, but this thing was different. There was no way to tell.

He fixed himself some supper and ate it and wished he knew how to feed the thing. And he wished, too, that he knew how to help it. He'd got it under shelter and he had it warm, but was that right or wrong for something like this? He had no idea.

He wondered if he should try to get some help, then felt squeamish about asking help when he couldn't say exactly what had to be helped. But then he wondered how he would feel himself if he were in a far, strange country, all played out and sick, and no one to get him any help because they didn't know exactly what he was.

That made up his mind for him and he walked over to the phone. But should he call a doctor or a veterinarian? He decided to call the doctor because the thing was in the house. If it had been in the barn, he would have called the veterinarian.

He was on a rural line and the hearing wasn't good and he was halfway deaf, so he didn't use the phone too often. He had told himself at times it was nothing but another aggravation and there had been a dozen times he had threatened to have it taken out. But now he was glad he hadn't.

The operator got old Dr. Benson and they couldn't hear one another too well, but Mose finally made the doctor understand who was calling and that he needed him. The doctor said he'd come.

With some relief, Mose hung up the phone and was just standing there, not doing anything, when he was struck by the thought that there might be others of these things down there in the woods. He had no idea what they were or what they might be doing or where they might be going, but it was pretty evident that the one upon the bed was some sort of stranger from a very distant place. It stood to reason that there might be more than one of them, for far traveling was a lonely business and anyone — or anything — would like to have some company along.

He got the lantern down off the peg and lit it and went stumping out the door. The night was as black as a stack of cats and the lantern light was feeble, but that made not a bit of difference, for Mose knew this farm of his like the back of his hand.

He went down the path into the woods. It was a spooky place, but it took more than woods at night to spook Old Mose. At the place where he had found the thing, he looked around, pushing through the brush and holding the lantern high so he could see a bigger area, but he didn't find another one of them.

He did find something else, though — a sort of outsized birdcage made of metal latticework that had wrapped itself around an eight-inch hickory tree. He tried to pull it loose, but it was jammed so tight that he couldn't budge it.

He sighted back the way it must have come. He could see where it had plowed its way through the upper branches of the trees, and out beyond were stars, shining bleakly with the look of far away.

Mose had no doubt that the thing lying on his bed beside the kitchen stove had come in this birdcage contraption. He marveled some at that, but he didn't fret himself too much, for the whole thing was so unearthly that he knew he had little chance of figuring it out.

He walked back to the house. He scarcely had the lantern blown out and hung back on its peg when he heard a car drive up.

The doctor, when he came up to the door, became a little grumpy at seeing Old Mose standing there.

"You don't look sick to me," the doctor said. "Not sick enough to drag me clear out here at night."

"I ain't sick," said Mose.

"Well, then," said the doctor, more grumpily than ever, "what did you mean by phoning me?"

"I got someone who is sick," said Mose. "I hope you can help him. I would have tried myself, but I don't know how to go about it."

The doctor came inside and Mose shut the door behind him.

"You got something rotten in here?" asked the doctor.

"No, it's just the way he smells. It was pretty bad at first, but I'm getting used to it by now."

The doctor saw the thing lying on the bed and went over to it. Old Mose heard him sort of gasp and could see him standing there, very stiff and straight. Then he bent down and had a good look at the critter on the bed.

When he straightened up and turned around to Mose, the only thing that kept him from being downright angry was that he was so flabbergasted.

"Mose," he yelled, "what *is* this?"

"I don't know," said Mose. "I found it in the woods and it was hurt and wailing and I couldn't leave it there."

"You think it's sick?"

"I know it is," said Mose. "It needs help awful bad. I'm afraid it's dying."

The doctor turned back to the bed again and pulled the blanket down, then went and got the lamp so that he could see. He looked the critter up and down, and he prodded it with a skittish finger, and he made the kind of mysterious clucking sound that only doctors make.

Then he pulled the blanket back over it again and took the lamp back to the table.

"Mose," he said, "I can't do a thing for it."

"But you're a doctor!"

"A human doctor, Mose. I don't know what this thing is, but it isn't human. I couldn't even guess what is wrong with it, if anything. And I wouldn't know what could be safely done for it even if I could diagnose its illness. I'm not even sure it's an animal. There are a lot of things about it that argue it's a plant."

Then the doctor asked Mose straight out how he came to find it and Mose told him exactly how it happened. But he didn't tell him anything about the birdcage, for when he thought about it, it sounded so fantastic that he couldn't bring himself to tell it. Just finding the critter and having it here was bad enough, without throwing in the birdcage.

"I tell you what," the doctor said. "You got something here that's outside all human knowledge. I doubt there's ever been a thing like this seen on Earth before. I have no idea what it is and I wouldn't try to guess. If I were you, I'd get in touch with the university up at Madison. There might be someone there who could get it figured out. Even if they couldn't they'd be interested. They'd want to study it."

Mose went to the cupboard and got the cigar box almost full of silver dollars and paid the doctor. The doctor put the dollars in his pocket, joshing Mose about his eccentricity.

But Mose was stubborn about his silver dollars. "Paper money don't seem legal, somehow," he declared. "I like the feel of silver and the way it clinks. It's got authority."

The doctor left; he didn't seem as upset as Mose had been afraid he might be. As soon as he was gone, Mose pulled up a chair and sat down beside the bed.

It wasn't right, he thought, that the thing should be so sick and no one to help — no one who knew any way to help it.

He sat in the chair and listened to the ticking of the clock, loud in the kitchen silence, and the crackling of the wood burning in the stove.

Looking at the thing lying on the bed, he had an almost fierce hope that it could get well again and stay with him. Now that its birdcage was all banged up, maybe there'd be nothing it could do but stay. And he hoped it would, for already the house felt less lonely.

Sitting in the chair between the stove and bed, Mose realized how lonely it had been. It had not been quite so bad until Towser died. He had tried to bring himself to get another dog, but he never had been able to. For there was no dog that would take the place of Towser and it had seemed unfaithful even to try. He could have gotten a cat, of course, but that would remind him too much of Molly; she had been very fond of cats, and until the time she died, there had always been two or three of them underfoot around the place.

But now he was alone. Alone with his farm and his stubbornness and his silver dollars. The doctor thought, like all the rest of them, that the only silver Mose had was in the cigar box in the cupboard. There wasn't one of them who knew about the old iron kettle piled plumb full of them, hidden underneath the floor boards of the living room. He chuckled at the thought of how he had them fooled. He'd give a lot to see his neighbors' faces if they could only know. But he was not the one to tell them. If they were to find it out, they'd have to find it out themselves.

He nodded in the chair and finally he slept, sitting upright, with his chin resting on his chest and his crossed arms wrapped around himself as if to keep him warm.

When he woke, in the dark before the dawn, with the lamp flickering on the table and the fire in the stove burning low, the alien had died.

There was no doubt of death. The thing was cold and rigid and the husk that was its body was rough and drying out — as a corn stalk in the field dries out, whipping in the wind once the growing has been ended.

Mose pulled the blanket up to cover it, and although this was early to do the chores, he went out by lantern light and got them done.

After breakfast, he heated water and washed his face and shaved, and it was the first time in years he'd shaved any day but Sunday. Then he put on his one good suit and slicked down his hair and got the old jalopy out of the machine shed and drove into town.

He hunted up Eb Dennison, the town clerk, who also was the secretary of the cemetery association.

"Eb," he said, "I want to buy a lot."

"But you've got a lot," protested Eb.

"That plot," said Mose, "is a family plot. There's just room for me and Molly."

"Well, then," asked Eb, "why another one? You have no other members of the family."

"I found someone in the woods," said Mose. "I took him home and he died last night. I plan to bury him."

"If you found a dead man in the woods," Eb warned him, "you better notify the coroner and sheriff."

"In time I may," said Mose, not intending to. "Now how about that plot?"

Washing his hands of the affair entirely, Eb sold him the plot.

Having bought his plot, Mose went to the undertaking establishment run by Albert Jones.

"Al," he said, "there's been a death out at the house. A stranger I found out in the woods. He doesn't seem to have anyone and I aim to take care of it."

"You got a death certificate?" asked Al, who subscribed to none of the niceties affected by most funeral parlor operators.

"Well, no, I haven't."

"Was there a doctor in attendance?"

"Doc Benson came out last night."

"He should have made you out one. I'll give him a ring."

He phoned Dr. Benson and talked with him awhile and got red around the gills. He finally slammed down the phone and turned on Mose.

"I don't know what you're trying to pull off," he fumed, "but Doc tells me this thing of yours isn't even human. I don't take care of dogs or cats or — "

"This ain't no dog or cat."

"I don't care what it is. It's got to be human for me to handle it. And don't go trying to bury it in the cemetery, because it's against the law."

Considerably discouraged, Mose left the undertaking parlor and trudged slowly up the hill toward the town's one and only church.

He found the minister in his study working on a sermon. Mose sat down in a chair and fumbled his battered hat around and around in his work-scarred hands.

"Parson," he said, "I'll tell you the story from first to last," and he did. He added, "I don't know what it is. I guess no one else does, either. But it's dead and in need of decent burial and that's the least that I can do. I can't bury it in the cemetery, so I suppose I'll have to find a place for it on the farm. I wonder if you could bring yourself to come out and say a word or two."

The minister gave the matter some deep consideration.

"I'm sorry, Mose," he said at last. "I don't believe I can. I am not sure at all the church would approve of it."

"This thing may not be human," said Old Mose, "but it is one of God's critters."

The minister thought some more, and did some wondering out loud, but made up his mind finally that he couldn't do it.

So Mose went down the street to where his car was waiting and drove home, thinking about what heels some humans are.

Back at the farm again, he got a pick and shovel and went into the garden, and there, in one corner of it, he dug a grave. He went out to the machine shed to hunt up some boards to make the thing a casket, but it turned out that he had used the last of the lumber to patch up the hog pen.

Mose went to the house and dug around in a chest in one of the back rooms which had not been used for years, hunting for a sheet to use as a shroud, since there would be no casket. He couldn't find a sheet, but he did unearth an old white linen tablecloth. He figured that would do, so he took it to the kitchen.

He pulled back the blanket and looked at the critter lying there in death and a sort of lump came into his throat at the thought of it — how it had died so lonely and so far from home without a creature of its own to spend its final hours with. And naked, too, without a stitch of clothing and with no possessions, with not a thing to leave behind as a remembrance of itself.

He spread the tablecloth out on the floor beside the bed and lifted the thing and laid it on the cloth. As he laid it down, he saw the pocket in it — if it was a pocket — a sort of slitted flap in the center of what could be its chest. He ran his hand across the pocket area. There was a lump inside it. He crouched for a long moment beside the body, wondering what to do.

Finally he reached his fingers into the flap and took out the thing that bulged. It was a ball, a little bigger than a tennis ball, made of cloudy glass — or, at least, it looked like glass. He squatted there, staring at it, then took it to the window for a better look.

There was nothing strange at all about the ball. It was just a cloudy ball of glass and it had a rough, dead feel about it, just as the body had.

He shook his head, took the ball back and put it where he'd found it, and wrapped the body securely in the cloth. He carried it to the garden and put it in the grave. Standing solemnly at the head of the grave, he said a few short words and then shoveled in the dirt.

He had meant to make a mound above the grave and he had intended to put up a cross, but at the last he didn't do either one of these. There would be snoopers. The word would get around and they'd be coming out and hunting for the spot where he had buried this thing he had found out in the woods. So there must be no mound to mark the place and no cross as well. Perhaps it was for the best, he told himself, for what could he have carved or written on the cross?

By this time it was well past noon and he was getting hungry, but he didn't stop to eat, because there were other things to do. He went out into the pasture to catch Bess, and hitching her to the stoneboat, went down into the woods.

He hitched her to the birdcage that was wrapped around the tree and she pulled it loose as pretty as you please. Then he loaded it on the stoneboat, hauled it up the hill, and stowed it in the back of the machine shed, in the far corner by the forge.

After that, he hitched Bess to the garden plow and gave the garden a cultivating that it didn't need, so it would be fresh dirt all over and no one could locate where he'd dug the grave.

He was just finishing the plowing when Sheriff Doyle drove up and got out of the car. The sheriff was a soft-spoken man, but he was no dawdler. He got right to the point.

"I hear," he said, "you found something in the woods."

"That I did," said Mose.

"I hear it died on you."

"Sheriff, you heard right."

"I'd like to see it, Mose."

"Can't. I buried it. And I ain't telling where."

"Mose," the sheriff said, "I don't want to make you trouble, but you did an illegal thing. You can't go finding people in the woods and just bury them when they up and die on you."

"You talk to Doc Benson?"

The sheriff nodded. "He said it wasn't any kind of thing he'd ever seen before. He said it wasn't human."

"Well, then," said Mose, "I guess that lets you out. If it wasn't human, there could be no crime against a person. And if it wasn't owned, there ain't any crime against property. There's been no one around to claim they owned the thing, is there?"

The sheriff rubbed his chin. "No, there hasn't. Maybe you're right. Where did you study law?"

"I never studied law. I never studied nothing. I just use common sense."

"Doc said something about the folks up at the university might want a look at it."

"I tell you, Sheriff," said Mose. "This thing came here from somewhere and it died. I don't know where it came from and I don't know what it was and I don't hanker none to know. To me it was just a living thing that needed help real bad. It was alive and it had its dignity and in death it deserved some respect. When the rest of you refused it decent burial, I did the best I could. And that is all there is to it."

"All right, Mose," the sheriff said, "if that's how you want it."

He turned around and stalked back to the car. Mose stood beside old Bess hitched to her plow and watched him drive away. He drove fast and reckless as if he might be angry.

Mose put the plow away and turned the horse back to the pasture; by now it was time to do chores again.

He got the chores all finished, made himself some supper and after supper sat beside the stove, listening to the ticking of the clock, loud in the silent house, and the crackle of the fire.

All night long the house was lonely.

The next afternoon, as Mose was plowing corn, a reporter came and walked up the row with him and talked with him when he came to the end of the row. Mose didn't like this reporter much. He was too flip and he asked some funny questions, so Mose clammed up and didn't tell him much.

A few days later, a man showed up from the university and showed him the story the reporter had gone back and written. The story made fun of Mose.

"I'm sorry," the professor said. "These newspapermen are unaccountable. I wouldn't worry too much about anything they write."

"I don't," Mose told him.

The man from the university asked a lot of questions and made quite a point about how important it was that he should see the body.

But Mose only shook his head. "It's at peace," he said. "I aim to leave it that way."

The man went away disgusted, but still quite dignified.

For several days there were people driving by and dropping in, the idly curious, and there were some neighbors Mose hadn't seen for months. But he gave them all short shrift and in a little while they left him alone and he went on with his farming and the house stayed lonely.

He thought again that maybe he should get a dog, but he thought of Towser and he couldn't do it.

One day, working in the garden, he found the plant that grew out of the grave. It was a funny-looking plant and his first impulse was to root it out.

But he didn't do it, for the plant intrigued him. It was a kind he'd never seen before and he decided he would let it grow, for a while at least, to see what kind it was. It was a bulky, fleshy plant, with heavy, dark green, curling leaves, and it reminded him in some ways of the skunk cabbage that burgeoned in the woods come spring.

There was another visitor, the queerest of the lot. He was a dark and intense man who said he was the president of a flying saucer club. He wanted to know if Mose had talked with the thing he'd found out in the woods and seemed terribly disappointed when Mose told him he hadn't. He wanted to know if Mose had found a vehicle the creature might have traveled in and Mose lied to him about it. He was afraid, the wild way the man was acting, that he might demand to search the place, and if he had, he'd likely have found the birdcage hidden in the machine shed back in the corner by the forge. But the man got to lecturing Mose about withholding vital information.

Finally Mose had taken all he could of it, so he stepped into the house and picked up the shotgun from behind the door. The president of the flying saucer club said good-bye rather hastily and got out of there.

Farm life went on as usual, with the corn laid by and the haying started, and out in the garden the strange plant kept on growing and now was taking shape. Old Mose couldn't believe his eyes when he saw the sort of shape it took and he spent long evening hours just standing in the garden, watching it and wondering if his loneliness were playing tricks on him.

The morning came when he found the plant standing at the door and waiting for him. He should have been surprised, of course, but he really wasn't, for he had lived with it, watching it of eventide, and although he had not dared admit it even to himself, he had known what it was.

For here was the creature he'd found in the woods, no longer sick and keening, no longer close to death, but full of life and youth.

It was not entirely the same, though. He stood and looked at it and could see the differences — the little differences that might have been those between youth and age, or between a father and a son, or again the differences expressed in an evolutionary pattern.

"Good morning," said Mose, not feeling strange at all to be talking to the thing. "It's good to have you back."

The thing standing in the yard did not answer him. But that was not important; he had not expected that it would. The one important point was that he had something he could talk to.

"I'm going out to do the chores," said Mose. "You want to tag along?"

It tagged along with him and it watched him as he did the chores and he talked to it, which was a vast improvement over talking to himself.

At breakfast, he laid an extra plate for it and pulled up an extra chair, but it turned out the critter was not equipped to use a chair, for it wasn't hinged to sit.

Nor did it eat. That bothered Mose at first, for he was hospitable, but he told himself that a big, strong, strapping youngster like this one knew enough to take care of itself, and he probably didn't need to worry too much about how it got along.

After breakfast, he went out to the garden with the critter accompanying him, and sure enough, the plant was gone. There was a collapsed husk lying on the ground, the outer covering that had been the cradle of the creature now at his side.

Then he went to the machine shed. The creature saw the birdcage, rushed over to it, and looked it over minutely. Then it turned around to Mose and made a sort of pleading gesture.

Mose went over to it and laid his hands on one of the twisted bars and the critter stood beside him and laid its hands on, too, and they pulled together. It was no use. They could move the metal some, but not enough to pull it back in shape again.

They stood and looked at one another, although looking may not be the word, for the critter had no eyes to look with. It made some funny motions with its hands, but Mose couldn't understand. Then it lay down on the floor and showed him how the birdcage ribs were fastened to the base.

It took a while for Mose to understand how the fastening worked and he never did know exactly why it did. There wasn't actually any reason that it should work that way.

First you applied some pressure, just the right amount at the exact and correct angle, and the bar would move a little. Then you applied some more pressure, again the exact amount and at the proper angle, and the bar would move some more. You did this three times and the bar came loose, although there was, God knows, no reason why it should.

Mose started a fire in the forge and shoveled in some coal and worked the bellows while the critter watched. But when he picked up the bar to put it in the fire, the critter got between him and the forge and wouldn't let him near. Mose realized then he couldn't — or wasn't supposed to — heat the bar to straighten it and he never questioned the entire rightness of it. For, he told himself, this thing must surely know the proper way to do it.

So he took the bar over to the anvil and started hammering it back into shape again, cold, without the use of fire, while the critter tried to show him the shape that it should be. It took quite a while, but finally it was straightened out to the critter's satisfaction.

Mose figured they'd have themselves a time getting the bar back in place again, but it slipped on as slick as could be.

Then they took off another bar and this one went faster, now that Mose had the hang of it.

But it was hard and grueling labor. They worked all day and only straightened out five bars.

It took four solid days to get the bars on the birdcage hammered into shape and all the time the hay was waiting to be cut.

But it was all right with Mose. He had someone to talk to and the house had lost its loneliness.

When they got the bars back in place, the critter slipped into the cage and starting fooling with a dingus on the roof of it that looked like a complicated basket. Mose, watching, figured that the basket was some sort of control.

The critter was discouraged. It walked around the shed looking for something and seemed unable to find it. It came back to Mose and made its despairing, pleading gesture. Mose showed it iron and steel; he dug into a carton where he kept bolts and clamps and bushings and scraps of metal and other odds and ends, finding brass and copper and even some aluminum, but it wasn't any of these.

And Mose was glad — a bit ashamed for feeling glad, but glad all the same.

For it had been clear to him that when the birdcage was all ready, the critter would be leaving him. It had been impossible for Mose to stand in the way of the repair of the cage, or to refuse to help. But now that it apparently couldn't be, he found himself well pleased.

Now the critter would have to stay with him and he'd have someone to talk to and the house would not be lonely. It would be welcome, he told himself, to have folks again. The critter was almost as good a companion as Towser.

Next morning, while Mose was fixing breakfast, he reached up in the cupboard to get the box of oatmeal and his hand struck the cigar box. It came crashing to the floor. It fell over on its side and the lid came open; the dollars went free-wheeling all around the kitchen.

Out of the corner of his eye, Mose saw the critter leaping quickly in pursuit of one of them. It snatched it up and turned to Mose, with the coin held between its fingers, and a sort of thrumming noise was coming out of the nest of worms on top of it.

It bent and scooped up more of them and cuddled them and danced a sort of jig, and Mose knew, with a sinking heart, that it had been silver the critter had been hunting.

So Mose got down on his hands and knees and helped the critter gather up all the dollars. They put them back into the cigar box and Mose picked up the box and gave it to the critter.

The critter took it and hefted it and had a disappointed look. Taking the box over to the table, it took the dollars out and stacked them in neat piles, and Mose could see it was very disappointed.

Perhaps, after all, Mose thought, it had not been silver the thing had been hunting for. Maybe it had made a mistake in thinking that the silver was some other kind of metal.

Mose got down the oatmeal and poured it into some water and put it on the stove. When it was cooked and the coffee was ready, he carried his breakfast to the table and sat down to eat.

The critter still was standing across the table from him, stacking and restacking the piles of silver dollars. And now it showed him, with a hand held above the stacks, that it needed more of them. This many stacks, it showed him, and each stack so high.

Mose sat stricken, with a spoon full of oatmeal halfway to his mouth. He thought of all those other dollars, the iron kettle packed with them, underneath the floor boards in the living room. And he couldn't do it; they were the only thing he had — except the critter now. And he could not give them up so the critter could go and leave him too.

He ate his bowl of oatmeal without tasting it and drank two cups of coffee. And all the time the critter stood there and showed him how much more it needed.

"I can't do it for you," Old Mose said. "I've done all you can expect of any living being. I found you in the woods and I gave you warmth and shelter. I tried to help you, and when I couldn't, at least I gave you a place to die in. I buried you and protected you from all those other people and I didn't pull you up when you started growing once again. Surely you can't expect me to keep on giving endlessly."

But it was no good. The critter could not hear him and he did not convince himself.

He got up from the table and walked into the living room with the critter trailing him. He loosened the floor boards and took out the kettle, and the critter, when it saw what was in the kettle, put its arms around itself and hugged in happiness.

They lugged the money out to the machine shed and Mose built a fire in the forge and put the kettle in the fire and started melting down that hard-saved money.

There were times he thought he couldn't finish the job, but he did.

The critter got the basket out of the birdcage and put it down beside the forge and dipped out the molten silver with an iron ladle and poured it here and there into the basket, shaping it in place with careful hammer taps.

It took a long time, for it was exacting work, but finally it was done and the silver almost gone. The critter lugged the basket back into the birdcage and fastened it in place.

It was almost evening now and Mose had to go and do the chores. He half expected the thing might haul out the birdcage and be gone when he came back to the house. And he tried to be sore at it for its selfishness — it had taken from him and had not tried to pay him back — it had not, so far as he could tell, even tried to thank him. But he made a poor job of being sore at it.

It was waiting for him when he came from the barn carrying two pails full of milk. It followed him inside the house and stood around and he tried to talk to it. But he didn't have the heart to do much talking. He could not forget that it would be leaving, and the pleasure of its present company was lost in his terror of the loneliness to come.

For now he didn't even have his money to help ward off the loneliness.

As he lay in bed that night, strange thoughts came creeping in upon him — the thought of an even greater loneliness than he had ever known upon this runty farm, the terrible, devastating loneliness of the empty wastes that lay between the stars, a driven loneliness while one hunted for a place or person that remained a misty thought one could not define, but which it was most important that one should find.

It was a strange thing for him to be thinking, and quite suddenly he knew it was no thought of his, but of this other that was in the room with him.

He tried to raise himself, he fought to raise himself, but he couldn't do it. He held his head up a moment, then fell back upon the pillow and went sound asleep.

Next morning, after Mose had eaten breakfast, the two of them went to the machine shed and dragged the birdcage out. It stood there, a weird alien thing, in the chill brightness of the dawn.

The critter walked up to it and started to slide between two of the bars, but when it was halfway through, it stepped out again and moved over to confront Old Mose.

"Good-bye, friend," said Mose. "I'll miss you."

There was a strange stinging in his eyes.

The other held out its hand in farewell, and Mose took it and there was something in the hand he grasped, something round and smooth that was transferred from its hand to his.

The thing took its hand away and stepped quickly to the birdcage and slid between the bars. The hands reached for the basket, there was a sudden flicker, and the birdcage was no longer there.

Mose stood lonely in the barnyard, looking at the place where there was no birdcage and remembering what he had felt or thought — or been told? — the night before as he lay in bed.

Already the critter would be there, out between the stars, in that black and utter loneliness, hunting for a place or thing or person that no human mind could grasp.

Slowly Mose turned around to go back to the house, to get the pails and go down to the barn to get the milking done.

He remembered the object in his hand and lifted his still-clenched fist in front of him. He opened his fingers and the little crystal ball lay there in his palm — and it was exactly like the one he'd found in the slitted flap in the body he had buried in the garden. Except that one had been dead and cloudy and this one had the living glow of a distant-burning fire.

Looking at it, he had the strange feeling of a happiness and comfort such as he had seldom known before, as if there were many people with him and all of them were friends.

He closed his hand upon it and the happiness stayed on — and it was all wrong, for there was not a single reason that he should be happy. The critter finally had left him and his money was all gone and he had no friends, but still he kept on feeling good.

He put the ball into his pocket and stepped spryly for the house to get the milking pails. He pursed up his whiskered lips and began to whistle though it had been a long, long time since he had even thought to whistle.

Maybe he was happy, he told himself, because the critter had not left without stopping to take his hand and try to say good-bye.

And a gift, no matter how worthless it might be, how cheap a trinket, still had a basic value in simple sentiment. It had been many years since anyone had bothered to give him a gift.

It was dark and lonely and unending in the depths of space with no Companion. It might be long before another was obtainable.

It perhaps was a foolish thing to do, but the old creature had been such a kind savage, so fumbling and so pitiful and eager to help. And one who travels far and fast must likewise travel light. There had been nothing else to give.

Y

---

ye/ti — native name for the "abominable snowman" of the Himalayas, a
creature whose existence has yet to be proved, although several sightings have
been reported. The yeti has starred in only a few science fiction stories —
"Creature of the Snows" is one of the best.

Creature of the Snows

WILLIAM SAMBROT

Ed McKale straightened up under his load of cameras and equipment,
squinting against the blasting wind, peering, staring, sweeping the jagged,
unending expanse of snow and wind-scoured rock. Looking, searching, as
he'd been doing now for two months, cameras at the ready.

Nothing. Nothing but the towering Himalayas, thrusting miles high on all
sides, stretching in awesome grandeur from horizon to horizon, each pinnacle
tipped with immense banners of snow plumes, streaming out in the wind,
vivid against the darkly blue sky. The vista was one of surpassing beauty;
viewing it, Ed automatically thought of light settings, focal length, color
filters — then just as automatically rejected the thought. He was here, on top
of the world, to photograph something infinitely more newsworthy —
if only he could find it.

The expedition paused, strung out along a ridge of blue snow,
with shadows falling away to the right and left into terrifying abysses,
and Ed sucked for air. Twenty thousand feet is really quite high, although

many of the peaks beyond rose nearly ten thousand feet above him.

Up ahead, the Sherpa porters — each a marvelous shot, gap-toothed, ebullient grins, seamed faces, leathery brown — bowed under stupendous loads for this altitude, leaning on their coolie crutches, waiting for Dr. Schenk to make up his mind. Schenk, the expedition leader, was arguing with the guides again, his breath spurting little puffs of vapor, waving his arms, pointing — down.

Obviously Schenk was calling it quits. He was within his rights, Ed knew; two months was all Schenk had contracted for. Two months of probing snow and ice; scrambling over crevasses, up rotten rock cliffs, wind-ravaged, bleak, stretching endlessly toward Tibet and the never-never lands beyond. Two months of searching for footprints where none should be. Searching for odors, for droppings, anything to disclose the presence of creatures other than themselves. Without success.

Two months of nothing. Big, fat nothing.

The expedition was a bust. The goofiest assignment of this or any other century, as Ed felt it would be from the moment he'd sat across a desk from the big boss in the picture magazine's New York office, two months ago, looking at the blurred photograph, while the boss filled him in on the weird details.

The photograph, his boss had told him gravely, had been taken in the Himalayan mountains, at an altitude of twenty-one thousand feet, by a man soaring overhead in a motorless glider.

"A glider," Ed had said noncommittally, staring at the fuzzy, enlarged snapshot of a great expanse of snow and rocky ledges, full of harsh light and shadows, a sort of roughly bowl-shaped plateau, apparently, and in the middle of it a group of indistinct figures, tiny, lost against the immensity of great ice pinnacles. Ed looked closer. Were the figures people? If so — what had happened to their clothes?

"A glider," his boss reiterated firmly. The glider pilot, the boss said, was maneuvering in an updraft, attempting to do the incredible — soar over Mount Everest in a homemade glider. The wide-winged glider had been unable to achieve the flight over Everest, but, flitting silently about seeking updrafts, it cleared a jagged pinnacle and there, less than a thousand feet below, the pilot saw movement where none should have been. And dropping lower, startled, he'd seen, the boss said dryly, "creatures — creatures that looked exactly like a group of naked men and women and kids, playing in the snow, at an altitude of twenty thousand five hundred feet." He'd had the presence of mind to take a few hasty snapshots before the group disappeared. Only one of the pictures had developed.

Looking at the snapshot with professional scorn, Ed had said, "These things are indistinct. I think he's selling you a bill of goods."

"No," the boss said, "we checked on the guy. He really did make the glider flight. We've had experts go over that blowup. The picture's genuine. Those are naked biped, erect-walking creatures." He flipped the picture irritably. "I can't publish this thing; I want close-ups, action shots, the sort of thing our subscribers have come to expect of us."

He'd lighted a cigar slowly. "Bring me back some pictures I can publish, Ed, and you can write your own ticket."

"You're asking me to climb Mount Everest," Ed said, carefully keeping the sarcasm out of his voice. "To search for this plateau here," he tapped the shoddy photograph, "and take pix of — what are they, biped, erect-walking creatures, you say?"

The boss cleared his throat. "Not Mount Everest, Ed. It's Gauri Sankar, one of the peaks near Mount Everest. Roughly, it's only about twenty-three thousand feet or so high."

"That's pretty rough," Ed said.

The boss looked pained. "Actually, it's not Gauri Sankar either. Just one of the lesser peaks of the Gauri Sankar massif. Well under twenty-three thousand. Certainly nothing to bother a hot-shot exparatrooper like you, Ed."

Ed winced, and the boss continued, "This guy — this glider pilot — wasn't able to pin-point the spot, but he did come up with a pretty fair map of the terrain — for a pretty fair price. We've checked it out with the American Alpine Club; it conforms well with their own charts of the general area. Several expeditions have been in the vicinity, but not this exact spot, they tell me. It's not a piece of cake by any means, but it's far from being another Annapurna, or K2, for accessibility."

He sucked at his cigar thoughtfully. "The Alpine Club says we've got only about two months of good weather before the inevitable monsoons hit that area — so time, as they say, is of the essence, Ed. But two months for this kind of thing ought to be plenty. Everything will be first class; we're even including these new gas guns that shoot hypodermic needles, or something similar. We'll fly the essentials into Katmandu and air-drop everything possible along the route up to your base at" — he squinted at a map — "Namche Bazar. A Sherpa village which is twelve thousand feet high."

He smiled amiably at Ed. "That's a couple of weeks' march up from the nearest railroad, and ought to get you acclimatized nicely. Plenty of experienced porters at Namche, all Sherpas. We've lined up a couple of expert mountain climbers with Himalayan background. And the expedition leader will be Dr. Schenk — top man in his field."

"What is his field?" Ed asked gloomily.

"Zoology. Whatever these things are in this picture, they're animal, which is his field. Everyone will be sworn to secrecy; you'll be the only one permitted to use a camera, Ed. This could be the biggest thing you'll ever cover, if these things are what I think they are."

"What do you think they are?"

"An unknown species of man — or subman," his boss said, and prudently Ed remained silent. Two months would tell the tale.

But two months didn't tell. Oh, there were plenty of wild rumors by the Nepalese all along the upper route. Hushed stories of the two-legged creature that walked like a man. A monster the Sherpas called yeti. Legends. Strange encounters; drums sounding from snow-swept heights; wild snatches of song drifting down from peaks that were inaccessible to ordinary men. And one concrete fact: a ban, laid on by the Buddhist monks, against the taking of any life in the high Himalayas. What life? Ed wondered.

Stories, legends — but nothing else.

Two months of it. Starting from the tropical flatlands, up through the lush, exotic rain forest, where sun struggled through immense trees festooned with orchids. Two months, moving up into the arid foothills, where foliage abruptly ceased and the rocks and wind took over. Up and ever up, to where the first heavy snow pack lay. And higher still, following the trail laid out by the glider pilot — and what impelled a man, Ed wondered, to soar over Mount Everest in a homemade glider?

Two months, during which Ed had come to dislike Dr. Schenk intensely. Tall, saturnine, smelling strongly of formaldehyde, Schenk classified everything into terms of vertebrate and invertebrate.

So now, standing on this wind-scoured ridge with the shadows falling into the abysses on either side, Ed peered through ice-encrusted goggles, watching Schenk arguing with the guides. He motioned to the ledge above, and obediently the Sherpas moved toward it. Obviously that would be the final camping spot. The two months were over by several days; Schenk was within his rights to call it quits. It was only Ed's assurances that the plateau they were seeking lay just ahead that had kept Schenk from bowing out exactly on the appointed time; that and the burning desire to secure his niche in zoology forever with a new specimen: biped, erect-walking — what?

But the plateau just ahead, and the one after that, and all the rest beyond had proved just as empty as those behind.

A bust. Whatever the unknown creatures were that the glider pilot had photographed, they would remain just that — unknown.

And yet, as Ed slogged slowly up toward where the porters were setting up the bright blue-and-yellow nylon tents, he was nagged by a feeling that that odd-shaped pinnacle ahead looked awfully much like the one in the blurred photograph. With his unfailing memory for pictures, Ed remembered the tall, jagged cone that had cast a black shadow across a snowy plateau, pointing directly toward the little group that was in the center of the picture.

But Schenk wasn't having any more plateaus. He shook his head vehemently, white-daubed lips a grim line on his sun-blistered face. "Last camp, Ed," he said firmly. "We agreed this would be the final plateau. I'm already a week behind schedule. If the monsoons hit us, we could be in serious trouble below. We have to get started back. I know exactly how you feel, but — I'm afraid this is it."

Later that night, while the wind moved ceaselessly, sucking at the tent, they burrowed in sleeping bags, talking.

"There must be some basis of fact in those stories," Ed said to Dr. Schenk. "I've given them a lot of thought. Has it occurred to you that every one of the sightings, the few face-to-face meetings of the natives and these — these unknowns, has generally been just around dawn, and usually when the native was alone?"

Schenk smiled dubiously. "Whatever this creature may be — and I'm convinced that it's either a species of large bear or one of the great anthropoids — it certainly must keep off the well-traveled routes. There are very few passes through these peaks, of course, and it would be quite simple for them to avoid these locales."

"But we're not on any known trail," Ed said thoughtfully. "I believe our methods have been all wrong — stringing out a bunch of men, looking for trails in the snow. All we've done is announce our presence to anything with ears for miles around. That glider pilot made no sound; he came on them without warning."

Ed looked intently at Schenk. "I'd like to try that peak up ahead — and the plateau beyond." When Schenk uttered a protesting cry, Ed said, "Wait; this time I'll go alone — with just one Sherpa guide. We could leave several hours before daybreak. No equipment other than oxygen, food for one meal — and my cameras, of course. Maintain a strict silence. We could be back before noon. Will you wait long enough for this one last try?" Schenk hesitated. "Only a few hours more," Ed urged.

Schenk stared at him, then he nodded slowly. "Agreed. But aren't you forgetting the most important item of all?" When Ed looked blank, Schenk smiled. "The gas gun. If you should run across one, we'll need more proof than just your word for it."

There was very little wind and no moon, but cold, the cold approaching that of outer space, as Ed and one Sherpa porter started away from the sleeping camp, up the shattered floor of an ice river that swept down from the jagged peak ahead.

They moved up, hearing only the squeak of equipment, the peculiar gritty sound of crampons biting into packed snow, an occasional hollow crash of falling ice blocks. To the east already a faint line of gray was visible; daylight was hours away, but at this tremendous height sunrise came early. They moved slowly, the thin air cutting cruelly into their lungs, moving up, up.

They stopped once for hot chocolate from a vacuum bottle, and Ed slapped the Sherpa's shoulder, grinning, pointing ahead to where the jagged peak glowed pink and gold in the first slanting rays of the sun. The Sherpa looked at the peak and quickly shifted his glance to the sky. He gave a long, careful look at the gathering clouds in the east, then muttered something, shaking his head, pointing back, back down to where the camp was hidden in the inky shadows of enormous boulders.

When Ed resumed the climb, the Sherpa removed the long nylon line which had joined them. The route was now comparatively level, on a huge sweeping expanse of snow-covered glacier that flowed about at the base of the peak. The Sherpa, no longer in the lead, began dropping behind as Ed pressed eagerly forward.

The sun was up, and with it the wind began keening again, bitterly sharp, bringing with it a scent of coming snow. In the east, beyond the jagged peak just ahead, the immense escarpment of the Himalayas was lost in approaching cloud. Ed hurried as best he could; it would snow, and soon. He'd have to make better time.

But above, the sky was blue, infinitely blue, and behind, the sun was well up, although the camp was still lost in night below. The peak thrust up ahead, quite near, with what appeared to be a natural pass skirting its flank. Ed made for it. As he circled an upthrust ridge of reddish, rotten rock, he glanced ahead. The plateau spread out before him, gently sloping, a natural amphitheater full of deep, smooth snow, with peaks surrounding it, and the central peak thrusting a long black shadow directly across the center. He paused, glancing back. The Sherpa had stopped, well below him, his face a dark blur, looking up, gesticulating frantically, pointing to the clouds. Ed motioned, then moved around, leaning against the rock, peering ahead.

That great shadow against the snow was certainly similar to the one in the photo — only, of course, the shadow pointed west now, when, later, it would point northwest, as the sun swung to the south. And when it did, most certainly it was the precise — He sucked in a sharp, lung-piercing breath.

He stared, squinting against the rising wind that seemed to blow from earth's outermost reaches. Three figures stirred slightly, and suddenly leaped into focus, almost perfectly camouflaged against the snow and wind-blasted rock. Three figures, not more than a hundred feet below him. Two small, one larger.

He leaned forward, his heart thudding terribly at this twenty-thousand-foot height. A tremor of excitement shook him. My Lord — it was true. They existed. He was looking at what was undeniably a female and two smaller — what? Apes?

They were covered with downy hair, nearly white, resembling nothing so much as tight-fitting leotards. The female was exactly like any woman on earth — except for the hair. No larger than most women, with arms slightly longer, more muscular. Thighs heavier, legs out of proportion to the trunk — shorter. Breasts full and firm. Not apes.

Hardly breathing, Ed squinted, staring, motionless. Not apes. Not standing so erectly. Not with those broad, high brows. Not with the undeniable intelligence of the two young capering about their mother. Not — and seeing this, Ed trembled against the freezing rock — not with the sudden affectionate sweep of the female as she lifted the smaller and pressed it to her breast, smoothing back hair from its face with a motion common to every human mother on earth. A wonderfully tender gesture.

What were they? Less than human? Perhaps. He couldn't be certain, but he thought he heard a faint gurgle of laughter from the female, fondling the small one, and the sound stirred him strangely. Dr. Schenk had assured him that no animal was capable of genuine laughter; only man.

But they laughed, those three, and, hearing it, watching the mother tickling the younger one, watching its delighted squirming, Ed knew that in that marvelous little grouping below, perfectly lighted, perfectly staged, he was privileged to observe one of the earth's most guarded secrets.

He should get started, shooting his pictures; afterward he should stun the group into unconsciousness with the gas gun and then send the Sherpa back down for Dr. Schenk and the others. Clouds were massing, immensities of blue-black. Already the first few flakes of snow, huge and wet, drifted against his face.

But for a long moment more he remained motionless, oddly unwilling to do anything to destroy the harmony, the aching purity of the scene below, so vividly etched in brilliant light and shadow. The female, child slung casually on one hip, stood erect, hand shading her eyes, and Ed grinned. Artless, but perfectly posed. She was looking carefully about and above, scanning the great outcroppings of rock, obviously searching for something.

Then she paused. She was staring directly at him.

Ed froze, even though he knew he was perfectly concealed by the deep shadows of the high cliff behind him. She was still looking directly at him, and then, slowly her hand came up. She waved.

He shivered uncontrollably in the biting wind, trying to remain motionless. The two young ones suddenly began to jump up and down and show every evidence of joy. And suddenly Ed knew.

He turned slowly, very slowly, and with the sensation of a freezing knife plunging deeply into his chest, he saw the male less than five yards away.

He was huge, easily twice the size of the female below. And, crazily, Ed thought of Schenk's little lecture, given what seemed like eons ago, in the incredible tropical grove far below and six weeks before, where rhododendrons grew in wild profusion and enormous butterflies flitted about: "In primitive man," Schenk had said, "as in the great apes today, the male was far larger than the female."

The gas gun was hopelessly out of reach, securely strapped to his shoulder pack. Ed stared, knowing there was absolutely nothing he could do to protect himself before this creature, fully eight feet tall, with arms as big as Ed's own thighs, and eyes *(My Lord — blue eyes!)* boring into his. There was a light of savage intelligence there — and something else.

The creature made no move against him, and Ed stared at it, breathing rapidly, shallowly and with difficulty, noting with his photographer's eyes the immense chest span, the easy rise and fall of his breathing, the large, square, white teeth, the somber cast of his face. There was long, sandy fur on the shoulders, chest and back, shortening to off-white over the rest of the magnificent torso. Ears rather small and close to the head. Short, thick neck, rising up from the broad shoulders to the back of the head in a straight line. Toes long and definitely prehensile.

They looked intently at each other across the abyss of time and mystery. Man and — what? How long, Ed wondered, had it stood there, observing him? Why hadn't it attacked? Had it been waiting for Ed to make a single threatening gesture — such as pointing a gun or camera? Seeing the calm awareness in those long, slanting, blue eyes, Ed sped a silent prayer of thanks upward; most certainly if he had made a move for camera or gun, that move would have been his last.

They looked at each other through the falling snow, and suddenly there was a perfect instantaneous understanding between them. Ed made an awkward, half-frozen little bow, moving backward. The great creature stood motionless, merely watching, and then Ed did a strange thing: He held out his hands, palms up, gave a wry grin — and ducked quickly around the outcropping of rock and began a plunging, sliding return down the way he'd come. In spite of the harsh, snow-laden wind, bitterly cold, he was perspiring.

Ed glanced back once. Nothing. Only the thickening veil of swift-blowing snow, blanking out the pinnacle, erasing every trace — every proof that anyone, anything, had stood there moments before. Only the snow, only the rocks, only the unending wind-filled silence of the top of the world. Nothing else.

The Sherpa was struggling up to him from below, terribly anxious to get started back; the storm was rising. Without a word they hooked up and began the groping, stumbling descent back to the last camp. They found the camp already broken, Sherpas already moving out. Schenk paused only long enough to give Ed a questioning look.

What could Ed say? Schenk was a scientist, demanding material proof: If not a corpse, at the very least a photograph. The only photographs Ed had were etched in his mind — not on film. And even if he could persuade Schenk to wait, when the storm cleared, the forewarned giant would be gone. Some farther peak, some remoter plateau would echo to his young ones' laughter.

Feeling not a bit bad about it, Ed gave Schenk a barely perceptible negative nod. Instantly Schenk shrugged, turned and went plunging down, into the thickening snow, back into the world of littler men. Ed trailed behind.

On the arduous trek back, through that first great storm, through the snow line, through the rain forest hot and humid, Ed thought of the giant, back up there where the air was thin and pure.

Who, what was he, and his race? Castaways on this planet, forever marooned, yearning for a distant, never-to-be-reached home?

Or did they date in unbroken descent from the Pleistocene — man's first beginning — when all the races of not-quite-man were giants; unable or unwilling to take the fork in the road that led to smaller, cleverer man, forced to retreat higher and higher, to more remote areas, until finally there was only one corner of earth left to them — the high Himalayas?

Or were he and his kind earth's last reserves: not-yet-men, waiting for the opening of still another chapter in earth's unending mystery story?

Whatever the giant was, his secret was safe with him, Ed thought. For who would believe it — even if he chose to tell?

Z

---

ze/ro pop/u/la/tion growth — a movement to encourage nations and families to practice birth control so that total population stabilizes at its present level. The rationale behind such a position is that limited world resources may be unable to support, at least at a quality level, many more people. However, as one might imagine, even within the movement, there are radically different ideas about the best way to accomplish such a goal.

A Criminal Act

HARRY HARRISON

The first blow of the hammer shook the door in its frame, and the second blow made the thin wood boom like a drum. Benedict Vernall threw the door open before a third stroke could fall and pushed his gun into the stomach of the man with the hammer.

"Get going. Get out of here," Benedict said, in a much shriller voice than he had planned to use.

"Don't be foolish," the bailiff said quietly, stepping aside so that the two guards behind him in the hall were clearly visible. "I am the bailiff and I am doing my duty. If I am attacked these men have orders to shoot you and everyone else in your apartment. Be intelligent. Yours is not the first case like this. Such things are planned for."

One of the guards clicked off the safety catch on his submachine gun, smirking at Benedict as he did it. Benedict let the pistol fall slowly to his side.

"Much better," the bailiff told him and struck the nail once more with the hammer so that the notice was fixed firmly to the door.

"Take that filthy thing down," Benedict said, choking over the words.

"Benedict Vernall," the bailiff said, adjusting his glasses on his nose as he read from the proclamation he had just posted. "This is to inform you that pursuant to the Criminal Birth Act of 1993 you are guilty of the act of criminal birth and are hereby proscribed and no longer protected from bodily injury by the forces of this sovereign state . . . "

"You're going to let some madman kill me . . . what kind of a dirty law is that?"

The bailiff removed his glasses and gazed coldly along his nose at Benedict. "Mr. Vernall," he said, "have the decency to accept the results of your own actions. Did you or did you not have an illegal baby?"

"Illegal — never! A harmless infant . . . "

"Do you or do you not already have the legal maximum of two children?"

"We have two, but . . . "

"You refused advice or aid from your local birth-control clinic. You expelled, with force, the birth guidance officer who called on you. You rejected the offer of the abortion clinic . . . "

"Murderers!"

" . . . and the advice of the Family Planning Board. The statutory six months have elapsed without any action on your part. You have had the three advance warnings and have ignored them. Your family still contains one consumer more than is prescribed by law, therefore the proclamation has been posted. You alone are responsible, Mr. Vernall, you can blame no one else."

"I can blame this foul law."

"It is the law of the land," the bailiff said, drawing himself up sternly. "It is not for you or me to question." He took a whistle from his pocket and raised it to his mouth. "It is my legal duty to remind you that you still have one course open, even at this last moment, and may still avail yourself of the services of the Euthanasia Clinic."

"Go straight to hell!"

"Indeed. I've been told that before." The bailiff snapped the whistle to his lips and blew a shrill blast. He almost smiled as Benedict slammed shut the apartment door.

There was an animal-throated roar from the stairwell as the policemen who were blocking it stepped aside. A knot of fiercely tangled men burst out, running and fighting at the same time. One of them surged ahead of the pack but fell as a fist caught him on the side of the head; the others trampled him under foot. Shouting and cursing, the mob came on and it looked as though it would be a draw, but a few yards short of the door one of the leaders tripped and brought two others down. A short fat man in the second rank leaped their bodies and crashed headlong into Vernall's door with such force that the ballpoint pen he held extended pierced the paper of the notice and sank into the wood beneath.

"A volunteer has been selected," the bailiff shouted, and the waiting police and guards closed in on the wailing men and began to force them back towards the stairs. One of the men remained behind on the floor, saliva running down his cheeks as he chewed hysterically at a strip of the threadbare carpet. Two white-garbed hospital attendants were looking out for this sort of thing, and one of them jabbed the man expertly in the neck with a hypodermic needle while the other unrolled the stretcher.

Under the bailiff's watchful eye the volunteer painstakingly wrote his name in the correct space on the proclamation, then carefully put the pen back in his vest pocket.

"Very glad to accept you as a volunteer for this important public duty, Mr. . . . " the bailiff leaned forward to peer at the paper, "Mr. Mortimer," he said.

"Mortimer is my first name," the man said in a soft dry voice as he dabbed lightly at his forehead with his breast-pocket handkerchief.

"Understand, sir, that your anonymity will be respected as is the right of all volunteers. Might I presume that you are acquainted with the rest of the regulations?"

"You may. Paragraph 46 of the Criminal Birth Act of 1993, subsection 14, governing the selection of volunteers. Firstly, I have volunteered for the maximum period of twenty-four hours. Secondly, I will neither attempt nor commit violence of any form upon any other members of the public during this time, and if I do so I will be held responsible by law for my acts."

"Very good. But isn't there more?"

Mortimer folded the handkerchief precisely and tucked it back into his pocket. "Thirdly," he said, and patted it smooth, "I shall not be liable to prosecution by law if I take the life of the proscribed individual, one Benedict Vernall."

"Perfectly correct." The bailiff nodded and pointed to a large suitcase that a policeman had set down on the floor and was opening. The hall had been cleared. "If you would step over here and take your choice." They both gazed down into the suitcase that was filled to overflowing with instruments of death. "I hope you also understand that your own life will be in jeopardy during this period and if you are injured or killed you will not be protected by law?"

"Don't take me for a fool," Mortimer said curtly, then pointed into the suitcase. "I want one of those concussion grenades."

"You cannot have it," the bailiff told him in a cutting voice, injured by the other's manner. There was a correct way to do these things. "Those are only for use in open districts where the innocent cannot be injured. Not in an apartment building. You have your choice of all the short-range weapons, however."

Mortimer laced his fingers together and stood with his head bowed, almost in the attitude of prayer, as he examined the contents: machine pistols, grenades, automatics, knives, knuckle dusters, vials of acid, whips, straight razors, broken glass, poison darts, morning stars, maces, gas bombs and tear-gas pens.

"Is there any limit?" he asked.

"Take what you feel you will need. Just remember that it must all be accounted for and returned."

"I want the Reisling machine pistol with five of the twenty-cartridge magazines and the commando knife with the spikes on the handguard and fountain pen tear-gas gun."

The bailiff was making quick check marks on a mimeographed form attached to his clipboard while Mortimer spoke. "Is that all?" he asked.

Mortimer nodded, took the extended board, and scrawled his name on the bottom of the sheet without examining it, then began at once to fill his pockets with the weapons and ammunition.

"Twenty-four hours," the bailiff said, looking at his watch and filling in one more space in the form. "You have until 1745 hours tomorrow."

"Get away from the door, please, Ben," Maria begged.

"Quiet," Benedict whispered, his ear pressed to the panel. "I want to hear what they are saying." His face screwed up as he struggled to understand the muffled voices. "It's no good," he said, turning away, "I can't make it out. Not that it makes any difference. I know what's happening . . . "

"There's a man coming to kill you," Maria said in her delicate, little girl's voice. The baby started to whimper and she hugged him to her.

"Please, Maria, go back into the bathroom as we agreed. You have the bed in there, and the food, and there aren't any windows. As long as you stay along the wall away from the door nothing can possibly happen to you. Do that for me, darling — so I won't have to worry about either of you."

"Then you will be out here alone."

Benedict squared his narrow shoulders and clutched the pistol firmly. "That is where I belong, out in front, defending my family. That is as old as the history of man."

"Family," she said and looked around worriedly. "What about Matthew and Agnes?"

"They'll be all right with your mother. She promised to look after them until we got in touch with her again. You can still be there with them. I wish you were."

"No, I couldn't go. I couldn't bear being anywhere else now. And I couldn't leave the baby there, he would be so hungry." She looked down at the infant who was still whimpering, then began to unbutton the top of her dress.

"Please, darling," Benedict said, edging back from the door. "I want you to go into the bathroom with the baby and stay there. You must. He could be coming at any time now."

She reluctantly obeyed him, and he waited until the door had closed and he heard the lock being turned. Then he tried to force their presence from his mind because they were only a distraction that could interfere with what must be done. He had worked out the details of his plan of defense long before, and he went slowly around the apartment making sure that everything was as it should be. First the front door, the only door into the apartment. It was locked and bolted and the night chain was attached. All that remained was to push the big wardrobe up against it. The killer could not enter now without a noisy struggle, and if he tried, Benedict would be there waiting with his gun. That took care of the door.

There were no windows in either the kitchen or the bathroom, so he could forget about those rooms. The bedroom was a possibility since its window looked out onto the fire escape, but he had a plan for this, too. The window was locked and the only way it could be opened from the outside was by breaking the glass. He would hear that and would have time to push the couch in the hall up against the bedroom door. He didn't want to block it now in case he had to retreat into the bedroom himself.

Only one room remained, the living room, and this was where he was going to make his stand. There were two windows in the living room and the far one could be entered from the fire escape, as could the bedroom window. The killer might come this way. The other window could not be reached from the fire escape, though shots could still be fired through it from the windows across the court. But the corner was out of the line of fire, and this was where he would be. He had pushed the big armchair right up against the wall and, after checking once more that both windows were locked, he dropped into it.

His gun rested on his lap and pointed at the far window by the fire escape. He would shoot if anyone tried to come through it. The other window was close by, but no harm could come that way unless he stood in front of it. The thin fabric curtains were drawn, and once it was dark he could see through them without being seen himself. By shifting the gun barrel a few degrees he could cover the door into the hall. If there were a disturbance at the front door he could be there in a few steps. He had done everything he could. He settled back into the chair.

Once the daylight faded the room was quite dark, yet he could see well enough by the light of the city sky that filtered in through the drawn curtains. It was very quiet; whenever he shifted position he could hear the rusty chair springs twang beneath him. After only a few hours he realized one slight flaw in his plan. He was thirsty.

At first he could ignore it, but by nine o'clock his mouth was as dry as cotton wool. He knew he couldn't last the night like this, it was too distracting. He should have brought a jug of water in with him. The wisest thing would be to go and get it as soon as possible, yet he did not want to leave the protection of the corner. He had heard nothing of the killer and this only made him more concerned about his unseen presence.

Then he heard Maria calling to him. Very softly at first, then louder and louder. She was worried. Was he all right? He dared not answer her, not from here. The only thing to do was to go to her, whisper through the door that everything was fine and that she should be quiet. Perhaps then she would go to sleep. And he could get some water in the kitchen and bring it back.

As quietly as he could he rose and stretched his stiff legs, keeping his eyes on the gray square of the second window. Putting the toe of one foot against the heel of the other he pulled his shoes off, then went on silent tiptoe across the room. Maria was calling louder now, rattling at the bathroom door, and he had to silence her. Why couldn't she realize the danger she was putting him in?

As he passed through the door the hall light above him came on.

"What are you doing?" he screamed at Maria, who stood by the switch, blinking in the sudden glare.

"I was so worried . . . "

The crash of breaking glass from the living room was punctuated by the hammering boom of the machine pistol. Arrows of pain tore at Benedict and he hurled himself sprawling into the hall.

"Into the bathroom!" he screeched, and fired his own revolver back through the dark doorway.

He was only half aware of Maria's muffled squeal as she slammed the door and, for the moment, he forgot the pain of the wounds. There was the metallic smell of burnt gunpowder and a blue haze hung in the air. Something scraped in the living room and he fired again into the darkness. He winced as the answering fire crashed thunder and flame towards him and the bullets tore holes in the plaster of the hall opposite the door.

The firing stopped, but he kept his gun pointed as he realized that the killer's fire couldn't reach him where he lay against the wall away from the open doorway. The man would have to come into the hall to shoot him and if he did that Benedict would fire first and kill him. More shots slammed into the wall, but he did not bother to answer them. When the silence stretched out for more than a minute he took a chance and silently broke his revolver and pulled out the empty shells, putting live cartridges in their place. There was a pool of blood under his leg.

Keeping the gun pointed at the doorway he clumsily rolled up his pants leg with his left hand, then took a quick glimpse. There was more blood running down his ankle and sopping his sock. A bullet had torn through his calf muscle and made two round, dark holes from which the thick blood pumped. It made him dizzy to look at it, then he remembered and pointed the wavering pistol back at the doorway. The living room was silent. His side hurt too, but when he pulled his shirt out of his trousers and looked he realized that although this wound was painful, it was not as bad as the one in his leg. A second bullet had burned along his side, glancing off the ribs and leaving a shallow wound. It wasn't bleeding badly. Something would have to be done about his leg.

"You moved fast, Benedict, I must congratulate you — "

Benedict's finger contracted with shock and he pumped two bullets into the room, towards the sound of the man's voice. The man laughed.

"Nerves, Benedict, nerves. Just because I am here to kill you doesn't mean that we can't talk."

"You're a filthy beast, a foul, filthy beast!" Benedict splattered the words from his lips and followed them with a string of obscenities, expressions he hadn't used or even heard since his school days. He stopped suddenly as he realized that Maria could hear him. She had never heard him curse before.

"Nerves, Benedict?" The dry laugh sounded again. "Calling me insulting names won't alter this situation."

"Why don't you leave, I won't try to stop you," Benedict said as he slowly pulled his left arm out of his shirt. "I don't want to see you or know you. Why don't you go away?"

"I'm afraid that it is not that easy, Ben. You have created this situation: in one sense you have called me here. Like a sorcerer summoning some evil genie. That's a pleasant simile, isn't it? May I introduce myself. My name is Mortimer."

"I don't want to know your name, you . . . piece of filth." Benedict half mumbled, his attention concentrated on the silent removal of his shirt. It hung from his right wrist and he shifted the gun to his left hand for a moment while he slipped it off. His leg throbbed with pain when he draped it over the wound in his calf and he gasped, then spoke quickly to disguise the sound. "You came here because you wanted to — and I'm going to kill you for that."

"Very good, Benedict, that is much more the type of spirit I expected from you. After all you are the closest we can come to a dedicated lawbreaker these days, the antisocial individualist who stands alone, who will carry on the traditions of the Dillingers and the James brothers. Though they brought death and you brought life, and your weapon is far humbler than their guns and their . . . " The words ended with a dry chuckle.

"You have a warped mind, Mortimer, just what I would suspect of a man who accepts a free license to kill. You're sick."

*

Benedict wanted to keep the other man talking, at least for a few minutes more until he could bandage his leg. The shirt was sticky with blood and he couldn't knot it right with his left hand. "You must be sick to come here," he said. "What other reason could you possibly have?" He laid the gun down silently, then fumbled with haste to bandage the wound.

"Sickness is relative," the voice in the darkness said, "as is crime. Man invents societies and the rules of his invented societies determine the crimes. *O tempora! O mores!* Homosexuals in Periclean Greece were honored men, and respected for their love. Homosexuals in industrial England were shunned and prosecuted for a criminal act. Who commits the crime — society or the man? Which of them is the criminal? You may attempt to argue a higher authority than man, but that would be only an abstract predication and what we are discussing here are realities. The law states that you are a criminal. I am here to enforce that law." The thunder of his gun added punctuation to his words, and long splinters of wood flew from the door-frame. Benedict jerked the knot tight and grabbed up his pistol again.

"I do invoke a higher authority," he said. "Natural law, the sanctity of life, the inviolability of marriage. Under this authority I wed and I love, and my children are the blessings of this union."

"Your blessings — and the blessings of the rest of mankind — are consuming this world like locusts," Mortimer said. "But that is an observation. First, I must deal with your arguments.

"*Primus.* The only natural law is written in the sedimentary rocks and the spectra of suns. What you call natural law is manmade law and varies with the varieties of religion. Argument invalid.

"*Secundus.* Life is prolific and today's generations must die so that tomorrow's may live. All religions have the faces of Janus. They frown at killing and at the same time smile at war and capital punishment. Argument invalid.

"*Ultimus.* The forms of male and female union are as varied as the societies that harbor them. Argument invalid. Your higher authority does not apply to the world of facts and law. Believe in it if you wish, if it gives you satisfaction, but do not invoke it to condone your criminal acts."

"Criminal!" Benedict shouted, and fired two shots through the doorway, then cringed as an answering storm of bullets crackled by. Dimly, through the bathroom door, he heard the baby crying, awakened by the noise. He dropped out the empty shells and angrily pulled live cartridges from his pocket, jamming them into the cylinder. "You're the criminal who is trying to murder me," he said. "You are the tool of the criminals who invade my house with their unholy laws and tell me I can have no more children. You cannot give me orders about this."

"What a fool you are," Mortimer sighed. "You are a social animal and do not hesitate to accept the benefits of your society. You accept medicine, so your children live now though they would have died in the past, and you accept a ration of food to feed them, food you do not work for. This suits you, so you accept. But you do not accept planning for your family and you attempt to reject it. It is impossible. You must accept all or reject all. You must leave your society — or abide by its rules. You eat the food, you must pay the price."

"I don't ask for more food. The baby has its mother's milk, we will share our food ration . . ."

"Don't be fatuous. You and your irresponsible kind have filled this world to bursting with your get, and still you will not stop. You have been reasoned with, railed against, cajoled, bribed, and threatened, all to no avail. Now you must be stopped. You have refused all aid to prevent your bringing one more mouth into this hungry world and, since you have done so anyway, you are to be held responsible for closing another mouth and removing it from this same world. The law is a humane one, rising out of our history of individualism and the frontier spirit, and gives you a chance to defend your ideals with a gun. And your life."

"The law is not humane," Benedict said. "How can you possibly suggest that? It is harsh, cruel, and pointless."

"Quite the contrary, the system makes very good sense. Try and step outside yourself for a moment — forget your prejudices and look at the problem that faces our race. The universe is cruel — but it's not ruthless. The conservation of mass is one of the universe's most ruthlessly enforced laws. We have been insane to ignore it so long, and it is sanity that now forces us to limit the sheer mass of human flesh on this globe. Appeals to reason have never succeeded in slowing the population growth so, with great reluctance, laws have been passed. Love, marriage, and the family are not affected — up to a reasonable maximum of children. After that a man *voluntarily* forsakes the protection of society and must take the consequences of his own acts. If he is insanely selfish, his death will benefit society by ridding it of his presence. If he is not insane and has determination and enough guts to win — well then, he is the sort of man that society needs, and he represents a noble contribution to the gene pool. Good and law-abiding citizens are not menaced by these laws."

"How dare you!" Benedict shouted. "Is a poor, helpless mother of an illegitimate baby a criminal?"

"No, only if she refuses all aid. She is even allowed a single child without endangering herself. If she persists in her folly, she must pay for her acts. There are countless frustrated women willing to volunteer for battle to even the score. They, like myself, are on the side of the law and eager to enforce it. So close my mouth if you can, Benedict, because I look forward with pleasure to closing your incredibly selfish one."

"Madman!" Benedict hissed and felt his teeth grate together with the intensity of his passion. "Scum of society. This obscene law brings forth the insane dregs of humanity and arms them and gives them license to kill."

"It does that, and a useful device it is, too. The maladjusted expose themselves and can be watched. Better the insane killer coming publicly and boldly than trapping and butchering your child in the park. Now he risks his life and whoever is killed serves humanity with his death."

"You admit you are a madman — a licensed killer?" Benedict started to stand but the hall began to spin dizzily and grow dark; he dropped back heavily.

"Not I," Mortimer said tonelessly. "I am a man who wishes to aid the law and wipe out your vile, proliferating kind."

"You're an invert then, hating the love of man and woman."

The only answer was a cold laugh that infuriated Benedict.

"Sick!" he screamed, "or mad. Or sterile, incapable of fathering children of your own and hating those who can . . ."

"That's enough! I've talked enough to you, Benedict. Now I shall kill you."

Benedict could hear anger for the first time in the other's voice and knew that he had goaded the man with the prod of truth. He was silent, sick and weak, the blood still seeping through his rough bandage and widening in a pool on the floor. He had to save what little strength he had to aim and fire when the killer came through the doorway. Behind him he heard the almost silent opening of the bathroom door and the rustle of footsteps. He looked up helplessly into Maria's tearstained face.

"Who's there with you?" Mortimer shouted, from where he crouched behind the armchair. "I hear you whispering. If your wife is there with you, Benedict, send her away. I won't be responsible for the cow's safety. You've brought this upon yourself, Benedict, and the time has now come to pay the price of your errors, and I shall be the instrumentality of that payment."

He stood and emptied the remainder of the magazine of bullets through the doorway, then pressed the button to release the magazine and hurled it after the bullets, clicking a new one instantly into place. With a quick pull he worked the slide to shove a live cartridge into the chamber and crouched, ready to attack.

This was it. He wouldn't need the knife. Walk a few feet forward. Fire through the doorway, then throw in the tear-gas pen. It would either blind the man or spoil his aim. Then walk through, firing with the trigger jammed down and the bullets spraying like water and the man would be dead. Mortimer took a deep, shuddering breath — then stopped and gaped as Benedict's hand snaked through the doorway and felt its way up the wall.

It was so unexpected that for a moment he didn't fire, and when he did fire he missed. A hand is a difficult target for an automatic weapon. The hand jerked down over the light switch and vanished as the ceiling lights came on.

Mortimer cursed and fired after the hand and fired into the wall and through the doorway, hitting nothing except insensate plaster and feeling terribly exposed beneath the glare of light.

The first shot from the pistol went unheard in the roar of his gun, and he did not realize that he was under fire until the second bullet ripped into the floor close to his feet. He stopped shooting, spun round, and gaped.

On the fire escape outside the broken window stood the woman. Slight and wide-eyed and swaying as though a strong wind tore at her, she pointed the gun at him with both hands and jerked the trigger spasmodically. The bullets came close but did not hit him, and in panic he pulled the machine pistol up, spraying bullets in an arc towards the window. "Don't! I don't want to hurt you!" he shouted even as he did it.

The last of his bullets hit the wall and his gun clicked and locked out of battery as the magazine emptied. He hurled the barren metal magazine away and tried to jam a full one in. The pistol banged again, and the bullet hit him in the side and spun him about. When he fell the gun flew from his hand. Benedict, who had been crawling slowly and painfully across the floor, reached him at the same moment and clutched at his throat with hungry fingers.

"Don't . . ." Mortimer croaked and thrashed about. He had never learned to fight and did not know what else to do.

"Please, Benedict, don't," Maria said, climbing through the window and running to them. "You're killing him."

"No . . . I'm not," Benedict gasped. "No strength. My hands are too weak."

Looking up he saw the pistol near his head, so he reached and tore it from her.

"One less mouth now!" he shouted, and pressed the hot muzzle against Mortimer's chest and pulled the trigger. The muffled shot tore into the man, who kicked violently once and died.

"Darling, you're all right?" Maria wailed, kneeling and clutching him to her.

"Yes . . . all right. Weak, but that's from loss of blood, I imagine. The bleeding has stopped now. It's all over. We've won. We'll have the food ration now, and they won't bother us anymore and everyone will be satisfied."

"I'm so glad," she said, and actually managed to smile through her tears. "I really didn't want to tell you before, not bother you with all this other trouble going on. But there's going to be . . ." She dropped her eyes.

"What?" he asked incredulously. "You can't possibly mean . . ."

"But I do." She patted the rounded mound of her midriff. "Aren't we lucky?"

All he could do was look up at her, his mouth wide and gaping like some helpless fish cast up on the shore.

The Cage

A. BERTRAM CHANDLER

Imprisonment is always a humiliating experience, no matter how philosophical the prisoner. Imprisonment by one's own kind is bad enough — but one can, at least, talk to one's captors, one can make one's wants understood; one can, on occasion, appeal to them man to man.

Imprisonment is doubly humiliating when one's captors, in all honesty, treat one as a lower animal.

The party from the survey ship could, perhaps, be excused for failing to recognize the survivors from the interstellar liner *Lode Star* as rational beings. At least two hundred days had passed since their landing on the planet without a name — an unintentional landing made when *Lode Star's* Erenhaft generators, driven far in excess of their normal capacity by a breakdown of the electronic regulator, had flung her far from the regular shipping lanes to an unexplored region of space. *Lode Star* had landed safely enough, but shortly thereafter (troubles never come singly) her atomic pile had got out of control and her captain had ordered his first mate to evacuate the passengers and such crew members as were not needed to cope with the emergency, and to get them as far from the ship as possible.

Hawkins and his charges were well clear when there was a flare of released energy, a not very violent explosion. The survivors wanted to turn to watch, but Hawkins drove them on with curses and, at times, blows. Luckily they were upwind from the ship and so escaped the fallout.

When the fireworks seemed to be over, Hawkins, accompanied by Dr. Boyle, the ship's surgeon, returned to the scene of the disaster. The two men, wary of radioactivity, were cautious and stayed a safe distance from the shallow, still-smoking crater that marked where the ship had been. It was all too obvious to them that the captain, together with his officers and technicians, was now no more than an infinitesimal part of the incandescent cloud that had mushroomed up into the low overcast.

Thereafter the fifty-odd men and women, the survivors of *Lode Star,* had degenerated. It hadn't been a fast process — Hawkins and Boyle, aided by a committee of the more responsible passengers, had fought a stout rearguard action. But it had been a hopeless sort of fight. The climate was against them, for a start. Hot it was, always in the neighborhood of 85° Fahrenheit. And it was wet — a thin, warm drizzle falling all the time. The air seemed to abound with the spores of fungi — luckily these did not attack living skin but throve on dead organic matter, on clothing. They throve to only a slightly lesser degree on metals and on the synthetic fabrics that many of the castaways wore.

Danger, outside danger, would have helped to maintain morale. But there were no dangerous animals. There were only little smooth-skinned things, not unlike frogs, that hopped through the sodden undergrowth, and, in the numerous rivers, fishlike creatures ranging in size from the shark to the tadpole, and all of them possessing the bellicosity of the latter.

Food had been no problem after the first few hungry hours. Volunteers had tried a large, succulent fungus growing on the boles of the huge fernlike trees. They had pronounced it good. After a lapse of five hours they had neither died nor even complained of abdominal pains. That fungus was to become the staple diet of the castaways. In the weeks that followed other fungi had been found, and berries, and roots — all of them edible. They provided a welcome variety.

Fire — in spite of the all-pervading heat — was the blessing most missed by the castaways. With it they could have supplemented their diet by catching and cooking the little frog-things of the rain forest, the fishes of the streams. Some of the hardier spirits did eat these animals raw, but they were frowned upon by most of the other members of the community. Too, fire would have helped to drive back the darkness of the long nights and would, by its real warmth and light, have dispelled the illusion of cold produced by the ceaseless dripping of water from every leaf and frond.

When they fled from the ship most of the survivors had possessed pocket lighters — but the lighters had been lost when the pockets, together with the clothing surrounding them, had disintegrated. In any case, all attempts to start a fire in the days when there were still pocket lighters had failed — there was not, Hawkins swore, a single dry spot on the whole accursed planet. Now the making of fire was quite impossible: even if there had been present an expert on the rubbing together of two dry sticks he could have found no material with which to work.

They made their permanent settlement on the crest of a low hill. (There were, so far as they could discover, no mountains.) It was less thickly wooded there than the surrounding plains, and the ground was less marshy underfoot. They succeeded in wrenching fronds from the fern-like trees and built for themselves crude shelters — more for the sake of privacy than for any comfort that they afforded. They clung, with a certain desperation, to the governmental forms of the worlds that they had left, and elected themselves a council. Boyle, the ship's surgeon, was their chief. Hawkins, rather to his surprise, was returned as a council member by a majority of only two votes — on thinking it over he realized that many of the passengers must still have borne a grudge against the ship's executive staff for their present predicament.

The first council meeting was held in a hut — if so it could be called — especially constructed for the purpose. The council members squatted in a rough circle. Boyle, the president, got slowly to his feet. Hawkins grinned wryly as he compared the surgeon's nudity with the pomposity that he seemed to have assumed with his elected rank, as he compared the man's dignity with the unkempt appearance presented by his uncut, uncombed gray hair, his uncombed and straggling gray beard.

"Ladies and gentlemen," began Boyle.

Hawkins looked around him at the naked, pallid bodies, at the stringy, lusterless hair, the long, dirty fingernails of the men and the unpainted lips of the women. He thought, I don't suppose I look much like an officer and a gentleman myself.

"Ladies and gentlemen," said Boyle. "We have been, as you know, elected to represent the human community upon this planet. I suggest that at this, our first meeting, we discuss our chances of survival — not as individuals, but as a race — "

"I'd like to ask Mr. Hawkins what our chances are of being picked up," shouted one of the two women members, a dried-up, spinsterish creature with prominent ribs and vertebrae.

"Slim," said Hawkins. "As you know, no communication is possible with other ships or with planet stations when the Interstellar Drive is operating. When we snapped out of the drive and came in for our landing we sent out a distress call — but we couldn't say where we were. Furthermore, we don't know that the call was received — "

"Miss Taylor," said Boyle huffily. "Mr. Hawkins. I would remind you that I am the duly elected president of this council. There will be time for a general discussion later.

"As most of you may already have assumed, the age of this planet, biologically speaking, corresponds roughly with that of Earth during the Carboniferous era. As we already know, no species yet exists to challenge our supremacy. By the time such a species does emerge — something analogous to the giant lizards of Earth's Triassic era — we should be well established — "

"*We* shall be dead!" called one of the men.

"*We* shall be dead," agreed the doctor, "but our descendants will be very much alive. We have to decide how to give them as good a start as possible. Language we shall bequeath to them — "

"Never mind the language, Doc," called the other woman member. She was a small blonde, slim, with a hard face. "It's just this question of descendants that I'm here to look after. I represent the women of childbearing age — there are, as you must know, fifteen of us here. So far the girls have been very, very careful. We have reason to be. Can you, as a medical man, guarantee — bearing in mind that you have no drugs, no instruments — safe deliveries? Can you guarantee that our children will have a good chance of survival?"

Boyle dropped his pomposity like a worn-out garment.

"I'll be frank," he said. "I have not — as you, Miss Hart, have pointed out — either drugs or instruments. But I can assure you, Miss Hart, that your chances of a safe delivery are far better than they would have been on Earth during, say, the eighteenth century. And I'll tell you why. On this planet, so far as we know (and we have been here long enough now to find out the hard way), there exist no microorganisms harmful to Man. Did such organisms exist, the bodies of those of us still surviving would be, by this time, mere masses of suppuration. Most of us, of course, would have died of septicemia long ago. And that, I think, answers *both* your questions."

"I haven't finished yet," she said. "Here's another point. There are fifty-three of us here, men and women. There are ten married couples — so we'll count them out. That leaves thirty-three people, of whom twenty are men. Twenty men to thirteen (aren't we girls always unlucky?) women. All of us aren't young — but we're all of us women. What sort of marriage set-up do we have? Monogamy? Polyandry?"

"Monogamy, of course," said a tall, thin man sharply. He was the only one of those present who wore clothing — if so it could be called. The disintegrating fronds lashed around his waist with a strand of vine did little to serve any useful purpose.

"All right, then," said the girl. "Monogamy. I rather prefer it that way myself. But I warn you that if that's the way we play it there's going to be trouble. And in any murder involving passion and jealousy the woman is as liable to be a victim as either of the men — and I don't want *that.*"

"What do you propose, then, Miss Hart?" asked Boyle.

"Just this, Doc. When it comes to our matings we leave love out of it. If two men want to marry the same woman, then let them fight it out. The best man gets the girl — and keeps her."

"Natural selection . . ." murmured the surgeon. "I'm in favor — but we must put it to the vote."

At the crest of the low hill was a shallow depression, a natural arena. Round the rim sat the castaways — all but four of them. One of the four was Dr. Boyle — he had discovered that his duties as president embraced those of a referee; it had been held that he was best competent to judge when one of the contestants was liable to suffer permanent damage. Another of the four was the girl Mary Hart. She had found a serrated twig with which to comb her long hair, she had contrived a wreath of yellow flowers with which to crown the victor. Was it, wondered Hawkins as he sat with the other council members, a hankering after an Earthly wedding ceremony, or was it a harking back to something older and darker?

"A pity that these blasted molds got our watches," said the fat man on Hawkins's right. "If we had any means of telling the time we could have rounds, make a proper prize fight of it."

Hawkins nodded. He looked at the four in the center of the arena — at the strutting, barbaric woman, at the pompous old man, at the two dark-bearded young men with their glistening white bodies. He knew them both — Fennet had been a senior cadet of the ill-fated *Lode Star;* Clemens, at least seven years Fennet's senior, was a passenger and had been a prospector on the frontier worlds.

"If we had anything to bet with," said the fat man happily, "I'd lay it on Clemens. That cadet of yours hasn't a snowball's chance in hell. He's been brought up to fight clean — Clemens has been brought up to fight dirty."

"Fennet's in better condition," said Hawkins. "He's been taking exercise, while Clemens has just been lying around sleeping and eating. Look at the paunch on him!"

"There's nothing wrong with good, healthy flesh and muscle," said the fat man, patting his own paunch.

"No gouging, no biting!" called the doctor. "And may the best man win!"

He stepped smartly back away from the contestants and stood with the Hart woman.

There was an air of embarrassment about the pair of them as they stood there, each with his fists hanging at his sides. Each seemed to be regretting that matters had come to such a pass.

"Go *on!*" screamed Mary Hart at last. "Don't you want me? You'll live to a ripe old age here — and it'll be lonely with no woman!"

"They can always wait around until your daughters grow up, Mary!" shouted one of her friends.

"If I ever have any daughters!" she called. "I shan't at this rate!"

"Go on!" shouted the crowd. "Go on!"

Fennet made a start. He stepped forward almost diffidently, dabbed with his right fist at Clemens's unprotected face. It wasn't a hard blow, but it must have been painful. Clemens put his hand up to his nose, brought it away, and stared at the bright blood staining it. He growled, lumbered forward with arms open to hug and crush. The cadet danced back, scoring twice more with his right.

"Why doesn't he *hit* him?" demanded the fat man.

"And break every bone in his fist? They aren't wearing gloves, you know," said Hawkins.

Fennet decided to make a stand. He stood firm, his feet slightly apart, and brought his right into play once more. This time he left his opponent's face alone, went for his belly instead. Hawkins was surprised to see that the prospector was taking the blows with apparent equanimity — he must be, he decided, much tougher in actuality than in appearance.

The cadet sidestepped smartly . . . and slipped on the wet grass. Clemens fell heavily on his opponent; Hawkins could hear the *whoosh* as the air was forced from the lad's lungs. The prospector's thick arms encircled Fennet's body — and Fennet's knee came up viciously to Clemens's groin. The prospector squealed, but hung on grimly. One of his hands was around Fennet's throat now, and the other one, its fingers viciously hooked, was clawing for the cadet's eyes.

"No gouging!" Boyle was screaming. "No gouging!"

He dropped down to his knees, caught Clemens's thick wrist with both his hands.

Something made Hawkins look up then. It may have been a sound, although this is doubtful; the spectators were behaving like boxing fans at a prize fight. They could hardly be blamed — this was the first piece of real excitement that had come their way since the loss of the ship. It may have been a sound that made Hawkins look up, it may have been the sixth sense possessed by all good spacemen. What he saw made him cry out.

Hovering above the arena was a helicopter. There was something about the design of it, a subtle oddness, that told Hawkins that this was no Earth machine. Suddenly, from its smooth, shining belly, dropped a net, seemingly of dull metal. It enveloped the struggling figures on the ground, trapped the doctor and Mary Hart.

Hawkins shouted again — a wordless cry. He jumped to his feet, ran to the assistance of his ensnared companions. The net seemed to be alive. It twisted itself around his wrists, bound his ankles. Others of the castaways rushed to aid Hawkins.

"Keep away!" he shouted. "Scatter!"

The low drone of the helicopter's rotors rose in pitch. The machine lifted. In an incredibly short space of time the arena was to the first mate's eyes no more than a pale green saucer in which little white ants scurried aimlessly. Then the flying machine was above and through the base of the low clouds, and there was nothing to be seen but drifting whiteness.

When, at last, it made its descent Hawkins was not surprised to see the silvery tower of a great spaceship standing among the low trees on a level plateau.

The world to which they were taken would have been a marked improvement on the world they had left had it not been for the mistaken kindness of their captors. The cage in which the three men were housed duplicated, with remarkable fidelity, the climatic conditions of the planet upon which *Lode Star* had been lost. It was glassed in, and from sprinklers in its roof fell a steady drizzle of warm water. A couple of dispirited tree ferns provided little shelter from the depressing precipitation. Twice a day a hatch at the back of the cage, which was made of a sort of concrete, opened, and slabs of a fungus remarkably similar to that on which they had been subsisting were thrown in. There was a hole in the floor of the cage; this the prisoners rightly assumed was for sanitary purposes.

On either side of them were other cages. In one of them was Mary Hart — alone. She could gesture to them, wave to them, and that was all. The cage on the other side held a beast built on the same general lines as a lobster, but with a strong hint of squid. Across the broad roadway they could see other cages, but could not see what they housed.

Hawkins, Boyle, and Fennet sat on the damp floor and stared through the thick glass and the bars at the beings outside who stared at them.

"If only they were humanoid," sighed the doctor. "If only they were the same shape as we are we might make a start towards convincing them that we, too, are intelligent beings."

"They aren't the same shape," said Hawkins. "And we, were the situations reversed, would take some convincing that three six-legged beer barrels were men and brothers . . . Try the Pythagorean theorem again," he said to the cadet.

Without enthusiasm the youth broke fronds from the nearest tree fern. He broke them into smaller pieces, then on the mossy floor laid them out in the design of a right-angled triangle with squares constructed on all three sides. The natives — a large one, one slightly smaller, and a little one — regarded him incuriously with their flat, dull eyes. The large one put the tip of a tentacle into a pocket — the things wore clothing — and pulled out a brightly colored packet, handed it to the little one. The little one tore off the wrapping, started stuffing pieces of some bright blue confection into the slot on its upper side that, obviously, served it as a mouth.

"I wish they were allowed to feed the animals," sighed Hawkins. "I'm sick of that damned fungus."

"Let's recapitulate," said the doctor. "After all, we've nothing else to do.

We were taken from our camp by the helicopter — six of us. We were taken to the survey ship — a vessel that seemed in no way superior to our own interstellar ships. You assure us, Hawkins, that the ship used the Ehrenhaft drive or something so near to it as to be its twin . . ."

"Correct," agreed Hawkins.

"On the ship we're kept in separate cages. There's no ill treatment, we're fed and watered at frequent intervals. We land on this strange planet, but we see nothing of it. We're hustled out of cages, like so many cattle, into a covered van. We know that we're being driven *somewhere,* that's all. The van stops, the door opens, and a couple of these animated beer barrels poke in poles with smaller editions of those fancy nets on the end of them. They catch Clemens and Miss Taylor, drag them out. We never see them again. The rest of us spend the night and the following day and night in individual cages. The next day we're taken to this . . . zoo . . ."

"Do you think they were vivisected?" asked Fennet. "I never liked Clemens, but . . ."

"I'm afraid they were," said Boyle. "Our captors must have learned of the difference between the sexes by it. Unluckily there's no way of determining intelligence by vivisection — "

"The filthy brutes!" shouted the cadet.

"Easy, son," counseled Hawkins. "You can't blame them, you know. We've vivisected animals a lot more like us than we are to these things."

"The problem," the doctor went on, "is to convince these things — as you call them, Hawkins — that we are rational beings like themselves. How would they define a rational being? How would *we* define a rational being?"

"Somebody who knows the Pythagorean theorem," said the cadet sulkily.

"I read somewhere," said Hawkins, "that the history of man is the history of the fire-making, tool-making animal . . ."

"Then make fire," suggested the doctor. "Make us some tools, and use them."

"Don't be silly. You know that there's not an artifact among the bunch of us. No false teeth even — not even a metal filling. Even so . . ." He paused. "When I was a youngster there was, among the cadets in the interstellar ships, a revival of the old arts and crafts. We considered ourselves in a direct line of descent from the old windjammer sailormen, so we learned how to splice rope and wire, how to make sennit and fancy knots and all the rest of it. Then one of us hit on the idea of basketmaking. We were in a passenger ship, and we used to make our baskets secretly, daub them with violent colors, and then sell them to passengers as genuine souvenirs from the Lost Planet of Arcturus VI. There was a most distressing scene when the Old Man and the mate found out . . ."

"What are you driving at?" asked the doctor.

"Just this. We will demonstrate our manual dexterity by the weaving of baskets — I'll teach you how."

"It might work . . ." said Boyle slowly. "It might just work . . . On the other hand, don't forget that certain birds and animals do the same sort of thing. On Earth there's the beaver, who builds quite cunning dams. There's the bower bird, who makes a bower for his mate as part of the courtship ritual . . ."

The head keeper must have known of creatures whose courting habits resembled those of the Terran bower bird. After the men spent three days in feverish basketmaking, which consumed all the bedding and stripped the tree ferns, Mary Hart was taken from her cage and put in with the three men. After she had got over her hysterical pleasure at having somebody to talk to again she was rather indignant.

It was good, thought Hawkins drowsily, to have Mary with them. A few more days of solitary confinement must surely have driven the girl crazy. Even so, having Mary in the same cage had its drawbacks. He had to keep a watchful eye on young Fennet. He even had to keep a watchful eye on Boyle — the old goat!

Mary screamed.

Hawkins jerked into complete wakefulness. He could see the pale form of Mary — on this world it was never completely dark at night — and, on the other side of the cage, the forms of Fennet and Boyle. He got hastily to his feet, stumbled to the girl's side.

"What is it?" he asked.

"I . . . I don't know . . . Something small, with sharp claws . . . It ran over me . . ."

"Oh," said Hawkins, "that was only Joe."

"*Joe?*" she demanded.

"I don't know exactly what he — or she — is," said the man.

"I think he's definitely *he,*" said the doctor.

"What is Joe?" she asked again.

"He must be the local equivalent of a mouse," said the doctor, "although he looks nothing like one. He comes up through the floor somewhere to look for scraps of food. We're trying to tame him — "

"You encourage the brute?" she screamed. "I demand that you do something about him — at once! Poison him, or trap him. Now!"

"Tomorrow," said Hawkins.

"Now!" she screamed.

"Tomorrow," said Hawkins firmly.

*

The capture of Joe proved to be easy. Two flat baskets, hinged like the valves of an oyster shell, made the trap. There was bait inside — a large piece of the fungus. There was a cunningly arranged upright that would fall at the least tug at the bait. Hawkins, lying sleepless on his damp bed, heard the tiny click and thud that told him that the trap had been sprung. He heard Joe's indignant chitterings, heard the tiny claws scrabbling at the stout basket-work.

Mary Hart was asleep. He shook her.

"We've caught him," he said.

"Then kill him," she answered drowsily.

But Joe was not killed. The three men were rather attached to him. With the coming of daylight they transferred him to a cage that Hawkins had fashioned. Even the girl relented when she saw the harmless ball of multi-colored fur bouncing indignantly up and down in its prison. She insisted on feeding the little animal, exclaimed gleefully when the thin tentacles reached out and took the fragment of fungus from her fingers.

For three days they made much of their pet. On the fourth day beings whom they took to be keepers entered the cage with their nets, immobilized the occupants, and carried off Joe and Hawkins.

"I'm afraid it's hopeless," Boyle said. "He's gone the same way . . ."

"They'll have him stuffed and mounted in some museum," said Fennet glumly.

"No," said the girl. "They couldn't!"

"They could," said the doctor.

Abruptly the hatch at the back of the cage opened.

Before the three humans could retreat to the scant protection supplied by a corner a voice called, "It's all right, come on out!"

Hawkins walked into the cage. He was shaved, and the beginnings of a healthy tan had darkened the pallor of his skin. He was wearing a pair of trunks fashioned from some bright red material.

"Come on out," he said again. "Our hosts have apologized very sincerely, and they have more suitable accommodation prepared for us. Then, as soon as they have a ship ready, we're to go to pick up the other survivors."

"Not so fast," said Boyle. "Put us in the picture, will you? What made them realize that we were rational beings?"

Hawkins's face darkened.

"Only rational beings," he said, "put other beings in cages."